The Furthest Horizon

ALSO BY GARDNER DOZOIS

ANTHOLOGIES

FICTION

NONFICTION

The Furthest Horizon

SF ADVENTURES TO THE FAR FUTURE

Edited by Gardner Dozois

St. Martin's Griffin

New York

ISBN 0-312-263260

First Edition: May 2000

10 9 8 7 6 5 4 3 2 1

Contents

Preface

Most science fiction takes place in the future, but even within the genre, few writers have ever had the imagination, poetic skills, and visionary scope to write convincingly about the *really* far future, and stories of that sort, which usually take place at least thousands and often millions of years from now, are among the rarest in science fiction.

Of course, the very *idea* of the far future, of a time thousands or millions of years removed from our own present day, is itself comparatively recent. To postulate a future millions of years from now, you first have to have a sense of a *past* that stretches millions of years behind us, an intuition into what has been called "deep time," the kind of time, measured out in geological eras, in which mountains rise and fall, rock is laid down in patiently accumulating strata at the bottom of the sea before being thrust up into the air as naked new peaks, continents drift lazily around the globe, whole species of animals die, and new species evolve to replace them. When the officially sanctioned concept of the age of the Earth is that the Earth is no more than 6,000 years old (Creation having happened at 9:00 A.M. on October 26, 4004 B.C., according to the calculations of Bishop Ussher in the seventeenth century), and when it's intensely controversial, if not downright dangerous, to declare otherwise, little thinking about either the really distant past or the really far future gets done (or if it does, it doesn't get *talked* about much in public).

The idea of deep time, of a past that stretches back for millions and millions of years, rather than a few thousand, is a concept that really doesn't begin to crop up in public discourse and scientific debate until the late eighteenth and early nineteenth centuries, when people such as James Hutton, Charles Lyell, Jean Louis Agassiz (with his then-radical concept of an Ice Age, with the face of Europe covered by and reshaped by immense mile-thick glaciers instead of by Noah's Flood), and Charles Darwin (whose *On the Origin of Species* proposed not only that species could become extinct—itself a fiercely controversial, much-debated concept—but also that all species *evolved*, the incremental result of many small changes over a period of time that certainly must have been immensely longer than any span imagined by Bishop Ussher) launched the first serious challenges to the concept of the Earth as a place only six thousand years old, gradually beginning to replace it with a vision of an Earth that was countless millions of years old—a span of time so staggeringly huge, so dismayingly vast, that it is difficult for the human mind, used to measuring things on the mayfly scale of our own eye-blink lives, to even grasp it.

It's probable that you have to have an understanding of this concept of deep time, though, of time stretching endlessly back into the past, before it's even possible to conceive of the idea of the *far future*, to wrap your mind around the concept that time will continue on *past* the current day and keep on going for millions of years more . . . a concept that, through extrapolation, leads inevitably to the realization that changes as sweeping and dramatic as those that took place in remote geological ages past will *continue* to happen in the future—that the Earth of the future will be as radically different from the Earth of today as today's Earth is from the Earth of the Cretaceous or the Mesozoic.

That being so, it's not surprising that it isn't until 1895, after the concept of deep time had become part of the intellectual/scientific discourse of the day, that we get the first clear vision of the far future in fiction, from H. G. Wells's *The Time Machine*, as the Time Traveller presses ever onward through time:

. . . the dim outlines of a desolate beach grew visible.

I stopped very gently and sat upon the Time Machine, looking round. The sky was no longer blue. Northeastward it was inky black, and out of the blackness shone brightly and steadily the pale white stars. Overhead it was a deep Indian red and starless, and southeastward it grew brighter to a glowing scarlet where, cut by the horizon, lay the huge hull of the sun, red and motionless.

. . . I cannot convey the sense of abominable desolation that hung over the world. The red eastern sky, the northward blackness, the salt Dead Sea, the stony beach crawling with these foul, slow-stirring monsters [giant crab-like creatures], the uniform poisonous-looking green of the lichenous plants, the thin air that hurts one's lungs: all contributed to an appalling effect. I moved on a hundred years, and there was the same red sun—a little larger, a little duller—the same dying sea, the same chill air, and the same crowd of earthy crustacea creeping in and out among the green weed and the red rocks. . . .

So I traveled, stopping ever and again, in great strides of a thousand years or more, drawn on by the mystery of the earth's fate, watching with a strange fascination the sun grow larger and duller in the westward sky, and the life of the old earth ebb away . . .

He ends up at last in bitter cold and near-total "great darkness" on the same desolate beach, now empty even of crawling crab-things. He is nauseated and sick, and he can hardly breathe. He can't go on. He can penetrate no further into the future, having reached Earth's furthest horizon, the End of Time. Appalled by the "remote and awful twilight" of the distant future, he flees back toward the warmer and more hospitable past.

Although Wells himself was certainly influenced by thinkers such as

Lyell, Agassiz, and Darwin, it is this vision of the far future, concentrated and intensified through the lens of fiction, Wells's vision of a bleak and desolate landscape brooded over by the dull red ball of the dying sun, that would for the next hundred years be the dominant vision of what the far future would be like—and which, for the most part, is still the dominant vision even today. It's possible to trace that vision through early works such as William Hope Hodgson's *The Night Land* and *The House on the Borderland* to J. B. S. Haldane's "The Last Judgement" and Olaf Stapledon's monumental (and extravagantly imaginative) *Last and First Men*, and on to the point where it enters the hothouse of the genre SF market in the early thirties via stories such as John W. Campbell's classic "Twilight" (written under the pseudonym of Don A. Stuart) and, perhaps even more significant, the *Zothique* stories of Clark Ashton Smith (which would go on to influence directly the work of Jack Vance in the fifties, whose work would then go on to influence directly Gene Wolfe in the eighties, whose work . . . and so on). With startling rapidity after that, we quickly come to the first great "modern" far-future SF novel (and still one of the very best), Arthur C. Clarke's *Against the Fall of Night*, in 1948.

Which brings us down to the territory of this anthology, which covers the years 1950 to 1998, an arbitrary period, chosen mostly for symmetry, but one that is not wholly indefensible: By 1950, the SF world was beginning to get back into full swing again after the partial interregnum of World War II, and the Campbellian Revolution in science fiction—circa 1939, when the new editor of *Astounding* magazine, John W. Campbell, began downplaying the melodramatic pulp stuff in favor of more thoughtful material that actually made a stab at rigor and scientific accuracy—had already taken place, with its lessons in the process of being absorbed and applied. Although "literary" writers such as Wells had been able to play in the far future only a few decades before, from this point on the development of the far-future story would take place almost entirely within the boundaries of the SF genre; indeed, the really far future is literary territory almost totally ignored by "mainstream" writers to this very day, even here, nearly to the beginning of a new millennium.

Perhaps this is not surprising, since, as I said in opening, even within science fiction itself, even within a genre whose writers are trained to think about the future and the majority of stories are set at least some distance into it, stories dealing with the really far future are, if not quite as rare as hens' teeth, then at least *comparatively* rare. Perhaps this is because the special scope and sweep of vision called for to conjure up an evocative and poetically intense portrait of the far future calls for a degree—and a *kind*—of imagination rare even among SF writers. (Why so *many* Brits write far-future stories, and why so *few* women do, way out of proportion demographically in both cases, I'll leave for wiser critics than me to try to puzzle out.)

This anthology, then, gives you an overview of the evolution of the far-future story—and of the evolution of ideas about what the far future will be like—from the middle of the twentieth century almost to the beginning of the twenty-first. Not at all incidentally, it also brings you some of the most vivid, evocative, entertaining, and mind-stretchingly imaginative science fiction ever written, stories that will take you so far into the future that our familiar everyday world, everything that we see around us, all our history and culture, everything we *are*, is at best a fading distant memory, blurred almost to nothing by time—if, indeed, it is re-membered at all . . . if, indeed, our remote descendants in that future are even *human* at all, as we today would understand the term. . . .

And, far from having to pant and shiver on that desolate terminal beach, you won't even have to get up from your chair!

Enjoy.

The Furthest Horizon

Guyal of Sfere

JACK VANCE

Here's one of the classic visions of the far future, from Jack Vance's The Dying Earth, *taking us millions of years into the future, to the Earth at the end of time, when the sun is growing cold and the world is on the brink of being plunged into eternal Night, grues and deodands creep through the haunted forests, and technology has (as per Arthur C. Clarke's famous dictum) become indistinguishable from magic . . .*

Born in San Francisco in 1920, Jack Vance served throughout World War II in the U.S. Merchant Navy. Most of the individual stories that would later be melded into his first novel, The Dying Earth, *were written while Vance was at sea—he was unable to sell them, a problem he would also have with the book itself, the market for fantasy being almost nonexistent at the time.* The Dying Earth *was eventually published in an obscure edition in 1950 by a small semi-professional press, went out of print almost immediately, and remained out of print for more than a decade thereafter. Nevertheless, this slender little volume of stories became an underground cult classic, and was of immense evolutionary importance to the development of both modern fantasy and modern science fiction, as well as being one of the keystone works in the development of the hybrid form sometimes referred to as science-fantasy. Although it itself was clearly influenced by earlier work such as Clark Ashton Smith's* Zothique *and William Hope Hodgson's* The Night Land, *the effect of* The Dying Earth *on future generations of writers is incalculable: for one example, out of many,* The Dying Earth *is one of the most recognizable influences on Gene Wolfe's* The Book of the New Sun. *(Wolfe has said, for instance, that* The Book of Gold, *which is mentioned by Severian, is supposed to be* The Dying Earth.*) Vance returned to this milieu in 1965, with a series of stories that would be melded into* The Eyes of the Overworld, *and, in the early eighties, returned yet again with* Cugel's Saga *and* Rhialto the Marvellous—*taken together,* The Dying Earth *and the three volumes of* Cugel *stories represent one of the most impressive achievements in science-fantasy.*

*Vance is also a towering ancestral figure in science fiction proper, where he has produced some of the very best work of the last forty years. His most famous SF novels—*The Dragon Masters, The Last Castle, Big Planet, Emphyrio, *the five-volume* Demon Princes *series (the best known of which are* The Star King *and* The Killing Machine), Blue World, The Anome, The Languages of Pao, *among many others—as well as dazzling short works such as "The New Prime," "The Miracle Workers," "The Last Castle," and "The Moon Moth" have had such a widespread impact that writers describing distant worlds and alien societies with strange alien customs write inevitably in the shadow of Vance: no one in the history of the field has brought more intelligence, imagination, or inexhaustible fertility of invention to that theme than he has, a fertility that shows no sign of slackening even here at the end of the nineties, with recent books such as* Night

Lamp as richly and lushly imaginative as the stuff he was writing in the fifties; even ostensible potboilers such as his Planet of Adventure *series are full of vivid and richly portrayed alien societies and bizarre and often profoundly disturbing insights into the ways in which human psychology might be altered by immersion in alien values and cultural systems.*

Vance has won two Hugo Awards, a Nebula Award, two World Fantasy Awards (one the prestigious Life Achievement Award), a Grandmaster Nebula Award for Life Achievement, and the Edgar Award for best mystery novel. His other books include The Palace of Love, City of the Chasch, To Live Forever, The Dirdir, The Pnume, The Gray Prince, The Brave Free Men, Space Opera, Showboat World, Marune: Alastor 933, Wyst: Alastor 1716, Lyonesse, The Green Pearl, Madouc, Araminta Station, Ecce and Olde Earth, *and* Throy, *among many others. His short fiction has been collected in* Eight Fantasms and Magics, The Best of Jack Vance, Green Magic, Lost Moons, The Complete Magnus Ridolph, The World Between and Other Stories, The Dark Side of the Moon, *and* The Narrow Land. *His most recent books are an omnibus volume,* Alastor, *collecting three of his* Alastor *novels, and the new novels* Night Lamp *and* Ports of Call.

Guyal of Sfere had been born one apart from his fellows and early proved vexation for his sire. Normal in outward configuration, there existed within his mind a void which ached for nourishment. It was as if a spell had been cast upon his birth, a harassment visited on the child in a spirit of sardonic mockery, so that every occurrence, *no* matter how trifling, became a source of wonder. Even as young as four seasons he was expounding such inquiries as:

"Why do squares have more sides than triangles?"

"How will we see when the sun goes dark?"

"Do flowers grow under the ocean?"

"Do stars hiss and sizzle when rain comes by night?"

To which his impatient sire gave answers:

"So it was ordained by the Pragmatica; squares and triangles must obey the rote."

"We will be forced to grope and feel our way."

"I have not verified this matter; only the Curator would know."

"Never. The stars are above the rain, higher even than the highest clouds, and swim in a rarified air where rain can never breed."

As Guyal grew to youth, this void in his mind, instead of dwindling becoming sedimented with wax, throbbed with a more violent ache. And so he asked:

"Why do people die when they are killed?"

"Where does beauty vanish when it goes?"

"How long have men lived on Earth?"

"What is beyond the sky?"

To which his sire, biting acerbity back from his lips, would respond:

"Death is the heritage of life; a man's vitality is like air in a bladder. Poinct this bubble and away, away, away, flees life, like the color of fading dream."

"Beauty is a luster which love bestows to guile the eye. Therefore it may be said that only when the brain is without love will the eye look and see no beauty."

"Some say men germinated in the soil like grubs in a corpse; others aver that the first men desired residence and so created Earth by sorcery. The question is shrouded in technicality; only the Curator may answer with exactness."

"An endless waste."

Guyal pondered and postulated, proposed and expounded, until he found himself the subject of surreptitious humor. The demesne was visited by a rumor that a gleft, coming upon Guyal's mother in labor, had stolen part of Guyal's brain, which deficiency he now industriously sought to restore.

Guyal therefore drew himself apart and roamed the grassy hills of Sfere in solitude. But ever was his mind acquisitive, ever did he seek to exhaust the lore of all around him, until at last his father in vexation refused to hear further inquiries, declaring that all knowledge had been known, that the trivial and useless had been discarded, leaving only that residue necessary to a sound man.

At this time Guyal was in his first manhood, a slight but erect youth with wide clear eyes, a penchant for severely elegant dress, a firm somewhat compressed mouth.

Hearing his father's angry statement, Guyal said, "One more question, then I ask no more."

"Speak," declared his father. "One more question I grant you."

"You have often referred me to the Curator; who is he, and where may I find him?"

A moment the father scrutinized the son whom he now considered past the verge of madness. Then he responded in a quiet voice, "The Curator guards the Museum of Man, which antique legend places in the Land of the Falling Wall—beyond the mountains of Fer Aquila and north of Ascolais. It is not certain that either Curator or Museum still exist; still it would seem that if the Curator knows all things, as is the legend, then surely he would know the wizardly foil to death."

Guyal said, "I would seek the Curator and the Museum of Man, that I likewise may know all things."

The father said with patience, "I will bestow on you my fine white horse, my Expansible Egg for your shelter, my Scintillant Dagger to illuminate the night. In addition, I lay a blessing along the trail, and danger will slide you by so long as you never wander aside."

Guyal quelled the hundred new questions at his tongue, including an inquisition as to where his father had learned these manifestations of sorcery, and accepted the gifts: the horse, the magic shelter, the dagger with the luminous pommel, and the blessing to guard him from the disadvantageous circumstances which plagued those who travelled the dim trails of Ascolais.

He caparisoned the horse, honed the dagger, cast a last glance around the old manse at Sfere, and set forth to the north.

He ferried the River Scaum on an old barge. Aboard the barge, and so off the trail, the blessing lost its cogency and in fact seemed to stimulate a counterinfluence, so that the barge-tender, who coveted Guyal's rich accoutrements, struck out suddenly with his cudgel. Guyal fended off the blow and tripped the man into the murky deep.

Mounting the north bank of the Scaum he saw ahead the Porphiron Scar, the dark poplars and white columns of Kaiin, the dull gleam of Sanreale Bay.

Wandering the crumbled streets, he put the languid inhabitants such a spate of questions that one in wry jocularity commended him to a professional augur.

This, a lank hermetic with red-rimmed eyes and a stained white beard, dwelled in a booth painted with the Signs of the Aumoklopelastianic Cabal.

"What are your fees?" inquired Guyal cautiously.

"I respond to three questions," stated the augur. "For twenty terces I phrase the answer in clear and decisive language; for ten I use a professional cant, which occasionally admits of ambiguity; for five I speak a parable which you must interpret as you will; and for one terce I babble in an unknown tongue."

"First I must inquire, how profound is your knowledge?"

"I know all," responded the augur. "The secrets of red and the secrets of black, the lost spells of Grand Motholam, the way of the fish and the voice of the bird."

"And where have you learned all these things?"

"By pure induction," explained the augur. "I retire into my booth, I closet myself with never a glint of light and, so sequestered, I resolve the mysteries of the world."

"Controlling such efficacy," ventured Guyal, "why do you live so meagerly, with not an ounce of fat to your frame and miserable rags to your back?"

The augur stood back in fury. "Go along with you! Already I have wasted fifty terces of wisdom on you who have never a copper to your pouch. If you desire free enlightenment," and he cackled in mirth, "seek out the Curator." He sheltered himself in his booth.

Guyal took lodging for the night, and in the morning went on his way. The trail made a wide detour around the haunted ruins of Old Town, then took to the fabulous forest.

For many a day Guyal rode toward the north. By night he surrounded himself and his horse in the Expansible Egg, a membrane impermeable to thew, claw, pressure, sound, and chill, and rested at ease despite the avid creatures of the dark.

The dull sun fell behind; the days grew wan and the nights bitter, and at last the crags of Fer Aquila showed as a tracing on the north horizon. In this region the forest was a scattering of phalurge and daobado; these last, massive constructions of heavy bronze branches clumped with dark balls of foliage. Beside a giant of the species Guyal came upon a village of turf huts. A group of surly louts appeared and surrounded him with expressions of curiosity. Guyal, no less than the villagers, had questions to ask, but none would speak till the hetman strode up—a burly man in a shaggy fur hat, a cloak of brown fur, and a bristling beard, so that it was hard to see where one ended and the other began. He exuded a rancid odor which displeased Guyal, although from motives of courtesy, he took pains to keep his distaste concealed.

"Where go you?" asked the hetman.

"I wish to cross the mountains to the Museum of Man," said Guyal. "Which way does the trail lead?"

The hetman pointed out a notch on the silhouette of the mountains. "There is Omona Gap, which is the shortest and best route, though there is no trail. None comes and none goes, since when you pass the Gap, you walk an unknown land. And with no traffic there manifestly need be no trail."

The news did not cheer Guyal.

"How then is it known that Omona Gap is on the way to the Museum?"

The hetman shrugged. "Such is our tradition."

Guyal turned his head at a hoarse snuffling and saw a pen of woven wattles. In a litter of filth and matted straw stood a number of hulking men eight or nine feet tall. They were naked, with wax-colored faces, shocks of dirty yellow hair and watery blue eyes. As Guyal watched, one of them ambled to a trough and noisily began to gulp gray mash.

Guyal said, "What manner of things are these?"

The hetman guffawed at Guyal's ignorance. "They are oasts, naturally." He indicated Guyal's white horse. "Never have I seen a stranger oast than the one you bestride. Ours carry us more easily and appear to be less vicious; in addition, no flesh is more delicious than oast properly braised and kettled."

Standing close he fondled the metal of Guyal's saddle and the red and yellow embroidered quilt. "Your deckings however are rich and of superb quality. I will therefore bestow you my large and weighty oast in return for this creature with its accoutrements."

Guyal politely declared himself satisfied with his present mount, and the hetman shrugged his shoulders.

A horn sounded. The hetman looked about, then turned back to Guyal. "Food is prepared; will you eat?"

Guyal glanced toward the oast-pen. "I am not presently hungry, and I must hasten forward. However, I am grateful for your kindness."

He departed; as he passed under the arch of the great daobado he turned a glance back toward the village. There seemed an unwonted activity among the huts. Remembering the hetman's covetous touch at his saddle, and aware that no longer did he ride the trail, Guyal urged his horse forward and pounded fast under the trees.

As he neared the foothills the forest dwindled to a savanna, floored with a dull, jointed grass that creaked under the horse's hooves. Guyal glanced up and down the plain. The sun wallowed in the southwest; the light across the plain was dim and watery. Another hour, then the dark night of the latter-day Earth. Guyal twisted in the saddle, looked behind him. Four oasts, carrying men on their shoulders, came trotting from the forest. Sighting Guyal they broke into a lumbering run. With a crawling skin Guyal wheeled his horse and eased the reins; the white horse loped across the plain toward Omona Gap. Behind ran the oasts, bestraddled by the fur-cloaked villagers.

The sun touched the horizon. Guyal looked back to his pursuers, bounding now a mile behind, then turned his gaze to the forest ahead. An ill place to ride by night, but where was his choice?

The foliage loomed above him; he passed under the first gnarled dao-bados. He changed directions, turned once, twice, a third time, then stood his horse to listen. Far away a crashing in the brake reached his ears. Guyal dismounted, led the horse into a deep hollow where a bank of foliage made a screen. Presently the four men on their hulking oasts passed across the afterglow, black double-shapes in attitudes suggestive of ill-temper and disappointment.

The thud and pad of feet dwindled and died.

The horse moved restlessly; the foliage rustled.

A damp air passed down the hollow and chilled the back of Guyal's neck. Darkness stood in the hollow like ink in a basin.

Guyal urged his horse up to the height and sat listening. Far down the wind he heard a hoarse call. Turning in the opposite direction he let the horse choose its own path.

Branches and boughs knit patterns on the fading sky; the air smelt of moss and mold. The horse stopped short. Guyal, tensing in every muscle, leaned a little forward. The air was still, uncanny; his eyes could plumb not ten feet into the black. Somewhere near was death—grinding death, to come as a sudden shock.

Sweating cold, afraid to stir a muscle, he forced himself to dismount. Stiffly he slid from the saddle, brought forth the Expansible Egg and flung it around his horse and himself. Safety. Guyal released the pressure of his breath.

➤

Guyal of Sfere had lost his way in a land of wind and naked crags. As night came he slouched numbly in the saddle while his horse took him where it would. Somewhere the ancient way through Omona Gap led to the northern tundra, but now, under a chilly overcast, north, east, south, and west were alike.

The horse halted and Guyal found himself at the brink of a quiet valley. Guyal leaned forward, staring. Below spread a dark city. Mist blew along the streets; the afterglow fell dull on slate roofs.

The horse snorted and scraped the stony ground.

"A strange town," said Guyal, "with no lights, no sound, no smell of smoke. . . . Doubtless an abandoned ruin from ancient times. . . ."

He debated descending to the streets. At times the old ruins were haunted by peculiar distillations. On the other hand such a ruin might be joined to the tundra by a trail. With this thought in mind he started his horse down the slope.

He entered the town and the hooves rang loud and sharp on the cobbles. The buildings were stone and dark mortar and seemed in uncommonly good preservation. A few lintels had cracked and sagged, a few walls gaped open, but for the most part the stone houses had successfully met the gnaw of time. . . . Guyal scented smoke. Did people live here still? He would proceed with caution.

Before a building which seemed to be a hostelry flowers bloomed in an urn. Guyal reined his horse and reflected that flowers were rarely cherished by persons of hostile disposition.

"Hello!" he called—once, twice.

No heads peered from the doors, no orange flicker brightened the windows. Guyal slowly turned and rode on.

The street widened and twisted toward a large hall, where Guyal saw a light. The building had a high façade, broken by four large windows, each shielded by two blinds of corroded bronze filigree. A marble balustrade fronting the terrace shimmered bone-white behind, a portal of massive wood stood slightly ajar; from here came the beam of light and also a strain of music.

Guyal of Sfere, halting, gazed not at the house nor at the light through the door. He dismounted and bowed to the young woman who sat pensively along the course of the balustrade. Though it was very cold, she wore but a simple gown, yellow-orange, a daffodil's color. Topaz hair fell loose to her shoulders and gave her face a cast of gravity and thoughtfulness.

As Guyal straightened from his greeting, the woman nodded, smiled slightly, and absently fingered the hair by her cheek.

"A bitter night for travelers."

"A bitter night for musing on the stars," responded Guyal.

She smiled again. "I am not cold. I sit and dream. . . . I listen to the music."

"What place is this?" inquired Guyal, looking up the street, down the street, and once more to the girl. "Are there any here but yourself?"

"This is Carchasel," said the girl, "abandoned by all ten thousand years ago. Only I and my aged uncle live here, finding this place a refuge from the Saponids of the tundra." She rose to her feet. "But you are cold and weary," said the girl, "and I keep you standing in the street. Our hospitality is yours."

"Which I gladly accept," said Guyal, "First I must stable my horse."

"He will be content in the house yonder. We have no stable." She indicated a long stone building with a door opening into blackness.

Guyal took the white horse thither and removed the bridle and saddle; then, standing in the doorway, he listened to the music he had noted before, the piping of an ancient air.

"Strange," he muttered, stroking the horse's muzzle. "The uncle plays music, the girl stares alone at the stars of the night. . . ." He considered a moment. "I may be over-suspicious. If witch she be, there is naught to be gained from me. If they be simple refugees as she says, and lovers of music, they may enjoy the airs from Ascolais; it will repay, in some measure, their hospitality." He reached into his saddlebag, brought forth his flute, and tucked it into his boot.

He returned to where the girl awaited him.

"You have not told me your name," she reminded him, "that I may introduce you to my uncle."

"I am Guyal of Sfere, by the River Scaum in Ascolais. And you?"

She smiled, pushing the portal wider. Warm yellow light fell into the cobbled street.

"I have no name. I need none. There has never been any but my uncle; and when he speaks there is no one to answer but I."

Guyal stared in astonishment; then, deeming his wonder too apparent for courtesy he controlled his expression. Perhaps she suspected him of wizardry and feared to pronounce her name lest he make magic with it.

They entered a flagged hall and the sound of piping grew louder.

"I will call you Ameth, if I may," said Guyal. "That is a flower of the south, as golden and kind as you seem to be."

She nodded. "You may call me Ameth."

They entered a tapestry-hung chamber. A great fire glowed at one wall, and here stood a table bearing food. On a bench sat the musician—an old man, untidy, unkempt. White hair hung tangled down his back; his beard, in no better case, was dirty and yellow. He wore a ragged kirtle, by no means clean, and the leather of his sandals had broken into dry cracks. Strangely, he did not take the flute from his mouth but kept up his piping; and the girl in yellow, so Guyal noted, seemed to move in rhythm to the tones.

"Uncle Ludowik," she cried in a gay voice, "I bring you a guest, Sir Guyal of Sfere."

Guyal looked into the man's face and wondered. The eyes, though somewhat rheumy with age, were gray and intelligent and, so Guyal thought, bright with a strange joy, which further puzzled Guyal, for the lines of the face indicated nothing other than years of misery.

"Perhaps you play?" inquired Ameth. "My uncle is a great musician, and this is his time for music. He has kept the routine for many years. . . ." She turned and smiled at Ludowik the musician, who jerked his head and contrived an acquiescent grin, never taking the flute from his mouth.

Ameth motioned to the bounteous table. "Eat, Guyal, and I will pour you wine. Afterwards perhaps you will play the flute for us."

"Gladly," said Guyal, and he noticed how the joy on Ludowik's face grew more apparent, quivering around the corners of his mouth.

He ate and Ameth poured him golden wine until his head went to reeling. And never did Ludowik cease his piping—a tender melody of running water, then a grave tune that told of the lost ocean to the west, then a simple melody such as a child might sing at his games. Guyal noted with wonder how Ameth fitted her mood to the music—grave and gay as the music led her. Strange! thought Guyal. But then—people thus isolated were apt to develop peculiar mannerisms, and they seemed kindly withal.

He finished his meal and stood erect, steadying himself against the table. Ludowik was lilting a melody of glass birds swinging round and round in the sunlight. Ameth came dancing over to him and stood close, so that he smelled the perfume of her loose golden hair. Her face was happy and wild. . . . Peculiar how Ludowik watched so grimly, and yet without a word. Perhaps he misdoubted a stranger's intent. Still . . .

"Now," breathed Ameth, "perhaps you will play the flute; you are strong and young." Then she said, as she saw Guyal's eyes widen. "I mean you will play on the flute for old Uncle Ludowik, and he will be happy and go off to bed—and then we will sit and talk far into the night."

"Gladly will I play the flute," said Guyal. "I am accounted quite skillful at my home in Sfere." Glancing at Ludowik, he surprised an expression of crazy gladness. Marvelous that a man should be so fond of music!

"Then—play!" breathed Ameth, urging him a little toward Ludowik and the flute.

"Perhaps," suggested Guyal, "I had better wait till your uncle pauses. I would seem discourteous—"

"No, as soon as you indicate that you wish to play, he will let off. Merely take the flute. You see," she confided, "he is rather deaf."

"Very well," said Guyal, "except that I have my own flute." And he brought it out from his boot. "Why—what is the matter?" For a change had come over the girl and the old man. A quick light had risen in her eyes, and Ludowik's strange gladness had gone, and there was but dull hopelessness in his eyes, stupid resignation.

Guyal slowly stood back, bewildered. "Do you not wish me to play?"

There was a pause. "Of course," said Ameth, young and charming once more. "But I'm sure that Uncle Ludowik would enjoy hearing you play his flute. He is accustomed to the pitch; another scale might be unfamiliar. . . ."

Ludowik nodded, and hope again shone in the rheumy old eyes. It was indeed a fine flute, Guyal saw, a rich piece of white metal, chased and set with gold, and Ludowik clutched this flute as if he would never let go.

"Take the flute," suggested Ameth. "He will not mind in the least." Ludowik shook his head, to signify the absence of objection. But Guyal, noting with distaste the long, stained beard, also shook his head. "I can play any scale, any tone on my flute. There is no need for me to use that of your uncle and possibly distress him. Listen," and he raised his instrument. "Here is a song of Kaiin, called 'The Opal, the Pearl, and the Peacock.' "

He put the pipe to his lips and began to play, very skillfully indeed, and Ludowik followed him, filling in gaps, making chords. Ameth, forgetting her vexation, listened with eyes half closed, and moved her arm to the rhythm.

"Did you enjoy that?" asked Guyal when he had finished.

"Very much. Perhaps you would try it on Uncle Ludowik's flute? It is a fine flute to play, very soft and easy to the breath."

"No," said Guyal, with sudden obstinacy. "I am able to play only my own instrument." He blew again, and it was a dance of the festival, a quirking carnival air. Ludowik, playing with supernal skill, ran merry phrases as might fit, and Ameth, carried away by the rhythm, danced a dance of her own, a merry step in time to the music.

Guyal played a tarantella of the peasant folk, and Ameth danced wilder and faster, flung her arms, wheeled, jerked her head in a fine display. And Ludowik's flute played a brilliant obbligato, hurtling over, now under, chording, veering, warping little silver strings of sound around Guyal's melody, adding urgent little grace-phrases.

Ludowik's eyes now clung to the whirling figure of the dancing girl. And suddenly he struck up a theme of his own, a tune of wildest abandon, of a frenzied beating rhythm; and Guyal, carried away by the force of the music, blew as he never had blown before, invented trills and runs, gyrating arpeggios, blew high and shrill, loud and fast and clear.

It was as nothing to Ludowik's music. His eyes were starting; sweat streamed from his seamed old forehead; his flute tore the air into shreds.

Ameth danced frenzy; she was no longer beautiful, she appeared grotesque and unfamiliar. The music became something more than the senses could bear. Guyal's vision turned pink and gray; he saw Ameth fall in a faint, in a foaming fit; and Ludowik, fiery-eyed, staggered erect, hobbled to her body and began a terrible intense concord, slow measures of most solemn and frightening meaning.

Ludowik played death.

Guyal of Sfere turned and ran wide-eyed from the hall. Ludowik, never noticing, continued his terrible piping, played as if every note were a skewer through the twitching girl's shoulder blades.

Guyal ran through the night and cold air bit at him like sleet. He burst into the shed, and the white horse nickered. On with the saddle, on with the bridle, away down the streets of old Carchasel, along the starlit cobbles, past the gaping black windows, away from the music of death!

Guyal of Sfere galloped up the mountain with the stars in his face, and not until he came to the shoulder did he turn in the saddle to look back.

The verging of dawn trembled into the stony valley. Where was Carchasel? There was no city, only a crumble of ruins. . . .

Hark! A far sound?

No. All was silence.

And yet . . .

Only dark stones on the floor of the valley.

Guyal, fixed of eye, turned and went his way along the trail which stretched north before him.

⚬

The walls of the defile were gray granite, stained dull scarlet and black by lichen. The horse's hooves made a clop-clop-clop on the stone. After the sleepless night Guyal began to sag in the saddle. He resolved to round one more bend in the trail and then take rest.

The rock looming above hid the sky. The trail twisted around a shoulder of rock; ahead shone a patch of indigo. One more turning, Guyal told himself. The defile fell open, the mountains were at his back. He looked out across a hundred miles of steppe: a land shaded with subtle colors, fading and melting into the haze at the horizon. To the east he saw a lone eminence cloaked by a a dark company of trees, the glisten of a lake at its foot. To the west a ranked mass of gray-white ruins was barely discernible. The Museum of Man? . . . Guyal dismounted and sought sleep within the Expansible Egg.

The sun rolled in sad majesty behind the mountains; murk fell across the tundra. Guyal awoke and refreshed himself. He gave meal to his horse, ate dry fruit and bread; then he mounted and rode down the trail. Gloom deepened; the plain sank from sight like a drowned land. Guyal reined his horse. Better, he thought, to ride in the morning. If he lost the trail in the dark, who could tell what he might encounter?

A mournful sound. Guyal turned his face to the sky. A sigh? A moan? . . . Another sound, closer: the rustle of cloth. Guyal cringed into his saddle. Floating slowly across the darkness came a shape robed in white. Under the cowl and glowing with witch-light was a drawn face with eyes like the holes in a skull.

It breathed a sad sound and drifted away.

Guyal drew a shuddering breath and slumped against the pommel. Then he slipped to the ground and established the Egg about himself and his horse; presently, as he lay staring into the dark, sleep came on him and so the night passed.

He awoke before dawn and set forth. The trail was a ribbon of white sand between banks of gray furze; the miles passed swiftly.

As he neared the tree-shrouded hillock he saw roofs through the foliage and smoke rising into the sharp air. And presently to right and left spread fields of spikenard, callow, and mead-apple. Guyal continued with eyes watchful for men.

The trail passed beside a fence of stone and black timber enclosing a region of churned and scorched earth, which Guyal paused to examine. The horse started nervously; Guyal, turning, saw three men who had come quietly upon him: individuals tall and well-formed, somewhat solemn, with golden-ivory skin and jet-black hair. Their garments implied an ancient convention: tight suits of maroon leather trimmed with black lace and silver chain, maroon cloth hats crumpled in precise creases, with black leather flaps extended horizontally over each ear. Their attitudes expressed neither threat nor welcome. "Greetings, stranger," said one. "Whither bound?"

"I go as fate directs," replied Guyal cautiously. "You are Saponids?"

"That is our race, though now we are few. Before you is our final city, Issane." He inspected Guyal with frank curiosity. "And what of yourself?"

"I am Guyal of Sfere, which is in Ascolais, far to the south."

The Saponids regarded Guyal with respect. "You have come a long and perilous way."

Guyal looked back at the mountains. "Through the north forests and the wastes of Fer Aquila. At nightfall yesterday I passed through the mountains. In the dark a ghost hovered above till I thought the grave had marked me for its own."

He paused in surprise; his words seemed to have released a powerful emotion in the Saponids. Their features lengthened, their mouths grew white. The spokesman, his polite detachment a trifle diminished, searched the sky. "A ghost. . . . In a white garment, floating on high?"

"Yes; is it a known familiar of the region?"

There was a pause.

"In a certain sense," said the Saponid. "It is a signal of woe. . . . But I interrupt your tale."

"There is little to tell. I took shelter for the night, and this morning I fared down to the plain."

"Were you not molested further? By the Walking Serpent, who ranges the slopes like fate?"

"I saw neither walking serpent nor so much as a lizard; still, a blessing protects my trail and I come to no harm so long as I keep my course."

"Interesting, interesting."

"Now," said Guyal, "permit me to inquire of you, since there is much I would learn; what is this ghost, what event does he commemorate, and what are the portents?"

"You ask beyond my certain knowledge," replied the Saponid cautiously. "Of this ghost it is well not to speak lest our attention reinforce its malignity."

"As you will," replied Guyal. "Perhaps—" He caught his tongue. Before inquiring for the Museum of Man it would be wise to learn in what regard the Saponids held it, lest learning his interest they should seek to deny him knowledge.

"Yes?" inquired the Saponids. "What is your lack?"

Guyal indicated the seared area behind the fence of stone and timber. "What is the cause of this devastation?"

The Saponid looked across the area with a blank expression.

"It is one of the ancient places; so much is known, no more. You will desire to rest and refresh yourself at Issane. Come; we will guide you."

He turned down the trail; Guyal finding neither words nor reasons to reject the idea, urged his horse forward.

The Saponids walked in silence; Guyal, though he seethed with a thousand questions, likewise held his tongue. They skirted a placid lake. The surface mirrored the sky, shoals of reeds, boats in the shape of sickles, with bow and stern curving high from the water.

So they entered Issane: a town of no great pretense. The houses were hewn timber, golden brown, russet, weathered black. The construction was intricate and ornate, the walls rising three stories to steep gables. Pillars and piers were carved with complex designs: meshing ribbons, tendrils, leaves, lizards. The screens that guarded the windows were likewise carved, with foliage patterns, animal faces, radiant stars; rich textures in the mellow wood. Much effort, much expressiveness, had been expended on the carving.

They proceeded up a steep lane under the gloom cast by the trees, and the Saponids came forth to stare. They moved quietly and spoke in low voices, and their garments were of an elegance Guyal had not expected to see on the northern steppe.

One of the men turned to Guyal. "Will you oblige us by waiting until the First Elder is informed, so that he may prepare a suitable reception?"

The request was framed in candid words and with guileless eyes. Guyal thought to perceive ambiguity in the phrasing, but since the hooves of his horse were planted in the center of the road, and since he did not propose leaving the road, Guyal assented with an open face. The Saponids disappeared and Guyal sat musing on the pleasant town perched so high above the plain.

A group of girls came to look at Guyal with curious eyes. Guyal returned the inspection, and sensed a lack about their persons, a discrepancy which he could not instantly identify. They wore graceful garments of woven wool, striped and dyed various colors; they were supple and slender, and seemed not lacking in coquetry. And yet . . .

The Saponid returned. "Now, Sir Guyal, may we proceed?"

Guyal, endeavoring to remove any flavor of suspicion from his words, said, "You will understand that by the very nature of my father's blessing I dare not leave the delineated trail; for then, instantly, I would become liable to any curse placed on me along the way."

The Saponid made an understanding gesture. "Naturally; you follow a sound principle."

Guyal bowed in gratification, and they continued up the road.

A hundred paces and the road leveled, crossing a common planted with small, fluttering, heart-shaped leaves, colored in all shades of purple, red, and black.

The Saponid turned to Guyal. "As a stranger I must caution you never to set foot on the common. It is one of our sacred places, and tradition requires that a severe penalty be exacted for transgressions and sacrilege."

"I note your warning," said Guyal. "I will respectfully obey your law."

They passed a dense thicket; with hideous clamor a bestial shape sprang from concealment, a creature with tremendous fanged jaws. Guyal's horse shied, bolted, sprang out upon the sacred common and trampled the fluttering leaves.

A number of Saponid men rushed forth, grasped the horse, seized Guyal and dragged him from the saddle.

"Wait!" cried Guyal. "What means this? Release me!"

The Saponid who had been his guide advanced, shaking his head in reproach. "Indeed, and only had I just impressed upon you the gravity of such an offense!"

"But the monster frightened my horse!" said Guyal. "I am nowise responsible for this trespass; release me, let us proceed to the reception."

The Saponid said, "I fear that the penalties prescribed by tradition must first come into effect. Your protests, though of superficial plausibility, will not sustain examination. For instance, the creature you term a monster is in reality a harmless domesticated beast. Secondly, I observe the animal you bestride; he will not make a turn or twist without the twitch of the reins. Thirdly, even if your postulates were conceded, you thereby admit to guilt by virtue of negligence and omission. You should have secured a mount less apt to unpredictable action, or upon learning of the sanctitude of the common, you should have considered such a contingency as even now occurred, and therefore dismounted, leading your beast. Therefore, Sir Guyal, though loath, I am forced to believe you guilty of impertinence, impiety, disregard and impudicity. Therefore, as Castellan and Sergeant-Reader of the Litany, so responsible for the detention of law-breakers, I must order you secured, contained, pent, incarcerated and confined until such time as the penalties will be exacted."

"The entire episode is mockery!" raged Guyal. "Are you savages, then, thus to mistreat a lone wayfarer?"

"By no means," replied the Castellan. "We are a civilized people, with customs bequeathed us by the past. Since the past was more glorious than the present, we would show presumption by questioning these laws!"

Guyal fell quiet. "And what are the usual penalties for my act?"

The Castellan made a reassuring motion. "The rote prescribes three acts of penance, which in your case, I am sure will be nominal. But—the forms must be observed, and it is necessary that you be constrained in the Felon's Caseboard." He motioned to the men who held Guyal's arm. "Away with him, cross neither track nor trail, for then your grasp will be nerveless and he will be delivered from justice."

Guyal was pent in a well aired but poorly lighted cellar of stone. The floor he found dry, the ceiling free of crawling insects. He had not been searched, nor had his Scintillant Dagger been removed from his sash. With suspicions crowding his brain he lay on the rush bed and, after a period, slept.

Now ensued the passing of a day. He was given food and drink; and at last the Castellan came to visit him.

"You are indeed fortunate," said the Saponid, "in that, as a witness, I was able to suggest your delinquencies to be more the result of negligence than malice. The last penalties exacted for the crime were stringent; the felon was ordered to perform the following three acts: First, to cut off his toes and sew the severed members into the skin at his neck; second, to revile his forbears for three hours, commencing with a Common Bill of Anathema, including feigned madness and hereditary disease, and at last defiling the hearth of his clan; and third, walking a mile under the lake with leaded shoes in search of the Lost Book of Caraz." And the Castellan regarded Guyal with complacency.

"What deeds must I perform?" inquired Guyal drily.

The Castellan joined the tips of his fingers together. "As I say, the penances are nominal, by decree of the Elder. First, you must swear never again to repeat your crime."

"That I gladly do," said Guyal, and so bound himself.

"Second," said the Castellan with a slight smile, "you must adjudicate at a Grand Pageant of Pulchritude among the maids of the village and select her whom you consider the most beautiful."

"Scarcely an arduous task," commented Guyal. "Why does it fall to my lot?"

The Castellan looked vaguely to the ceiling. "There are a number of concomitants to victory in this contest. . . . Every person in the town would find relations among the participants—a daughter, a sister, a niece—and so would hardly be considered unprejudiced. The charge of favoritism could never be leveled against you; therefore you make an ideal selection for this important post."

Guyal seemed to hear the ring of sincerity in the Saponid's voice; still he wondered why the selection of the town's loveliest was a matter of such import.

"And third?" he inquired.

"That will be revealed after the contest, which occurs this afternoon."

The Saponid departed the cell.

Guyal, who was not without vanity, spent several hours restoring himself and his costume from the ravages of travel. He bathed, trimmed his hair, shaved his face, and, when the Castellan came to unlock the door, he felt that he made no discreditable picture.

He was led out upon the road and directed up the hill toward the summit of the terraced town of Saponce. Turning to the Castellan he said, "How is it that you permit me to walk the trail once more? You must know that now I am safe from molestation. . . ."

The Castellan shrugged. "True. But you would gain little by insisting upon your temporary immunity. Ahead the trail crosses a bridge which we could demolish; behind we need but breach the dam to Green Torrent; then, should you walk the trail you would be swept to the side and so rendered vulnerable. No, Sir Guyal of Sfere, once the secret of your immunity is abroad then you are liable to a variety of stratagems. For instance, a large wall might be placed athwart the way, before and behind you. No doubt the spell would preserve you from thirst and hunger but what then? So would you sit till the sun went out."

Guyal said no word. Across the lake he noticed a trio of the crescent boats approaching the docks, prows and sterns rocking and dipping into the shaded water with a graceful motion. The void in his mind made itself known. "Why are your boats constructed in such fashion?"

The Castellan looked blankly at him. "It is the only practicable method. Do not the oe-pods grow thusly to the south?"

"Never have I seen oe-pods."

"They are the fruit of a great vine, and grow in scimitar-shape. When sufficiently large we cut and clean them, slit the inner edge, grapple end to end with strong line, and constrict till the pod opens as is desirable. When cured, dried, varnished, carved, burnished and lacquered, fitted with deck, thwarts and gussets—then have we our boats."

They entered the plaza, a flat area at the summit surrounded on three sides by tall houses. To Guyal's surprise there seemed to be no preliminary ceremonies or formalities to the contest, and small spirit of festivity was manifest among the townspeople. Indeed they seemed beset by subdued despondency and eyed him without enthusiasm.

A hundred girls stood in a disconsolate group. It seemed to Guyal that they had gone to few pains to embellish themselves. To the contrary, they wore shapeless rags, their hair seemed deliberately misarranged, their faces were dirty and scowling.

Guyal turned to his guide. "The girls seem not to covet the garland of pulchritude."

The Castellan nodded wryly. "As you see, they are by no means jealous for distinction; modesty has always been a Saponid trait."

Guyal hesitated. "What is the form of procedure? I do not desire in my ignorance to violate another of your arcane regulations."

The Castellan said with a blank face, "There are no formalities. We conduct these pageants with expedition and the least possible ceremony. You need but pass among these maidens and point out her whom you deem the most attractive."

Guyal advanced to his task, feeling more than half foolish. Then he reflected: this is a penalty for contravening an absurd tradition; I will conduct myself with efficiency and so the quicker rid myself of the obligation.

He stood before the hundred girls who eyed him with hostility and anxiety, and Guyal saw that his task would not be simple, since, on the whole, they were of a comeliness which even the dirt, grimacing, and rags could not disguise.

"Range yourselves, if you please, into a line," said Guyal. "In this way, none will be at disadvantage."

Sullenly the girls formed a line.

Guyal surveyed the group. He saw at once that a number could be eliminated: the squat, the obese, the lean, the pocked and coarse-featured—perhaps a quarter of the group. He said suavely, "Never have I seen such unanimous loveliness; each of you might legitimately claim the cordon. My task is arduous; I must weigh fine imponderables; in the end my choice will undoubtedly be based on subjectivity and those of real charm will no doubt be the first discharged from the competition." He stepped forward. "Those whom I indicate may retire."

He walked down the line, pointing, and the ugliest, with expressions of unmistakable relief, hastened to the sidelines.

A second time Guyal made his inspection, and now, somewhat more familiar with those he judged, he was able to discharge those who, while suffering no whit from ugliness, were merely plain.

Roughly a third of the original group remained. These stared at Guyal with varying degrees of apprehension and truculence as he passed before them, studying each in turn.

. . . All at once his mind was determined, and his choice definite.

Guyal made one last survey down the line. No, he had been accurate in his choice. There were girls here as comely as the senses could desire, girls with opal-glowing eyes and hyacinth features, girls as lissome as reeds, with hair silky and fine despite the dust which they seemed to have rubbed upon themselves.

The girl whom Guyal had selected was slighter than the others and possessed of a beauty not at once obvious. She had a small triangular face, great wistful eyes, and thick black hair cut short at the ears. Her skin was of a transparent paleness, like the finest ivory; her form slender, graceful, and of a compelling magnetism. She seemed to have sensed his decision and her eyes widened.

Guyal took her hand, led her forward, and turned to the Elder—an old man sitting stolidly in a heavy chair.

"This is she whom I find the loveliest among your maidens."

There was silence through the square. Then there came a hoarse sound, a cry of sadness from the Castellan and Sergeant-Reader. He came forward, sagging of face, limp of body. "Guyal of Sfere, you have wrought a great revenge for my tricking you. This is my beloved daughter, Shierl, whom you have designated."

Guyal stammered, "I meant but complete impersonality. Your daughter Shierl I find the loveliest creature of my experience; I cannot understand where I have offended."

"No, Guyal," said the Castellan, "you have chosen fairly, for such indeed is my own thought."

"Well, then," said Guyal, "reveal to me now my third task that I may finish, and then continue my pilgrimage."

The Castellan said, "Three leagues to the north lies the ruin which tradition tells us to be the olden Museum of Man."

"Ah," said Guyal, "go on, I attend."

"You must, as your third charge, conduct my daughter Shierl to the Museum of Man. At the portal you will strike on a copper gong and announce to whoever responds: 'We are those summoned from Issane.' "

Guyal frowned. "How is this? 'We'?"

"Such is your charge," said the Castellan in a voice like thunder.

Guyal looked to left, right, forward, and behind. But he stood in the center of the plaza surrounded by the hardy men of Issane.

"When must this charge be executed?" he inquired in a controlled voice.

The Castellan said in a voice bitter as gall: "Even now Shierl goes to clothe herself in yellow. In one hour shall she appear; in one hour shall you set forth for the Museum of Man."

"And then?"

"And then—for good or for evil, it is not known. You fare as thirteen thousand have fared before you."

Down from the plaza, down the leafy lanes of Issane came Guyal, indignant and clamped of mouth, though the pit of his stomach felt heavy with trepidation. The ritual carried distasteful overtones. Guyal's step faltered.

The Castellan seized his elbow with a hard hand. "Forward."

The faces along the lane swam with morbid curiosity, inner excitement.

The eminence, with the tall trees and carved dark houses was at his back; he walked out into the claret sunlight of the tundra. Eighty women in white gowns with ceremonial buckets of woven straw over their heads surrounded a tall tent of yellow silk. Here the Castellan halted Guyal and beckoned to the Ritual Matron. She flung back the hangings at the door of the tent; Shierl came slowly forth, eyes dark with fright. She wore a stiff gown of yellow brocade, and the wand of her body seemed pent and constrained within. She stared at Guyal, at her father, as if she had never seen them before. The Ritual Matron put a hand on her waist, propelled her forward. Shierl stepped once, twice, irresolutely halted. The Castellan brought Guyal forward and placed him at the girl's side; now two children, a boy and a girl, came hastening up with cups which they proffered to Guyal and Shierl. Dully she accepted the cup. Guyal glanced suspiciously at the murky brew. He asked the Castellan: "What is the nature of this potion?"

"Drink," said the Castellan. "So will your way seem the shorter; you will march to the Museum with a steadier step."

"I will not drink," said Guyal. "My senses must be my own when I meet the Curator. I have come far for the privilege; I would not stultify the occasion stumbling and staggering."

Shierl stared dully at the cup she held. Said Guyal: "I advise you likewise to avoid the drug; so will we come to the Museum of Man with our dignity."

She returned the cup. The Castellan's brow clouded, but he made no protest.

An old man in a black costume brought forward a satin pillow on which rested a whip with a handle of carved steel. The Castellan now lifted this whip, and advancing, laid three light strokes across the shoulders of both Shierl and Guyal.

"Now," said the Castellan, "go from Issane outlawed forever. Seek succor at the Museum of Man. Never look back, leave all thoughts of past and future here. Go, I command; go, go, go!"

Shierl sunk her teeth into her lower lip; tears coursed her cheek though she made no sound. With hanging head she started across the tundra. Guyal, with a swift stride, joined her.

For a space the murmurs, the nervous sounds followed their ears; then they were alone. The north lay across the horizon; the tundra filled the foreground and background, an expanse dreary and dun. The Museum of Man rose before them; along the faint trail they walked.

Guyal said in a tentative tone, "There is much I would understand."

"Speak," said Shierl.

"Why are we forced to this mission?"

"It is thus because it has always been thus. Is this not reason enough?"

"Sufficient possibly for you," said Guyal, "but not for me. In fact, my thirst for knowledge drew me here, to find the Museum of Man."

She looked at him in wonder. "Are all to the south as scholarly as you?"

"In no degree," said Guyal. "The habitants perform the acts which fed them yesterday, last week, a year ago. 'Why strive for a pedant's accumulation?' I have been asked. 'Why seek and search? Earth grows cold; man gasps his last; why forgo merriment, music, and revelry for the abstract?' "

"Indeed," said Shierl. "Such is the consensus at Issane. But ask what you will; I will try to answer."

He studied the charming triangle of her face, the heavy black hair, the lustrous eyes, dark as sapphires. "In happier circumstances, there would be other yearnings for you to ease."

"Ask," said Shierl of Issane. "The Museum of Man is close; there is occasion for naught but words."

"Why are we thus sent to the Museum?"

"The immediate cause is the ghost you saw on the hill. When the ghost appears, then we of Issane know that the most beautiful maiden and the most handsome youth must be dispatched to the Museum. The basis of the custom I do not know. So it is; so it has been; so it will be till the sun gutters out like a coal in the rain."

"But what is our mission? Who greets us, what is our fate?"

"Such details are unknown."

Guyal mused, "The likelihood of pleasure seems small. . . . You are beyond doubt the loveliest creature of the Saponids, the loveliest creature of Earth—but I, a casual stranger, am hardly the most well-favored youth of the town."

She smiled. "You are not uncomely."

Guyal said somberly, "More cogent is the fact that I am a stranger and so bring little loss to Issane."

"That aspect has no doubt been considered."

Guyal searched the horizon. "Let us then avoid the Museum of Man, let us circumvent this unknown fate and take to the mountains."

She shook her head. "Do you suppose that we would gain by the ruse? The eyes of a hundred warriors will follow until we pass through the portals of the Museum. Should we attempt to avoid our duty we should be bound to stakes, stripped of our skins by the inch, and at last placed in bags with a thousand scorpions. Such is the traditional penalty; twelve times in history has it been invoked."

Guyal threw back his shoulders. He spoke in a nervous voice, "Ah, well—the Museum of Man has been my goal for many years. On this motive I set forth from Sfere, so now I would seek the Curator and satisfy my obsession for brain-filling."

"You are blessed with great fortune," said Shierl, "for you are being granted your heart's desire."

Guyal could find nothing to say, so for a space they walked in silence. Presently she touched his arm. "Guyal, I am greatly frightened."

Guyal gazed at the ground beneath his feet, and a blossom of hope sprang alive in his brain. "See the marking through the lichen?"

"Yes; what then?"

"Is it a trail?"

Dubiously she responded, "It is a way worn by the passage of many feet. So then—it is a trail."

"Here then is safety," declared Guyal. "But I must guard you; you must never leave my side, you must swim in the charm which protects me; perhaps then we will survive."

Shierl said sadly, "Let us not delude our reason, Guyal of Sfere."

But as they walked, the trail grew plainer, and Guyal became correspondingly sanguine. And ever larger bulked the crumble that marked the Museum of Man.

If a storehouse of knowledge had existed here, little sign remained. There was a great flat floor, flagged in white stone, now chalky, broken and grown over with weeds. The surrounding monoliths, pocked and worn, were toppled off at various heights. The rains had washed the marble, the dust from the mountains had been laid on and swept off, laid on and swept off, and those who had built the Museum were less than a mote of this dust, so far and forgotten were they.

"Think," said Guyal, "think of the vastness of knowledge which once was gathered here and which is now one with the soil—unless, of course, the Curator has salvaged and preserved."

Shierl looked about apprehensively. "I think rather of the portal, and that which awaits us. . . . Guyal," she whispered, "I fear, I fear greatly. . . . Suppose they tear us apart? Suppose there is torture and death? I fear a tremendous impingement."

Guyal's own throat was hot and full. He looked about with challenge. "While I still breathe and hold power in my arms to fight, there will be none to harm us."

Shierl groaned softly. "Guyal, Guyal, Guyal of Sfere—why did you choose me?"

"Because," said Guyal, "you were the loveliest and I thought nothing but good in store for you."

Shierl said, "I must be courageous; after all, if it were not I it would be some other maid equally fearful. . . . And there is the portal."

Guyal inhaled deeply, inclined his head, and strode forward. "Let us be to it, and know."

The portal opened into a wall supporting the first floor; a door of flat black metal. Guyal followed the trail to the door and rapped staunchly with his fist on the small copper gong to the side.

The door groaned wide on its hinges, and cool air, smelling of the under-earth, billowed forth.

"Hello within!" cried Guyal.

A soft voice, full of catches and quavers, as if just after weeping, said, "Come you, come you forward. You are desired and awaited."

Guyal leaned his head forward, straining to see. "Give us light, that we may not wander from the trail and bottom ourselves."

The breathless quaver of a voice said, "Light is not needed; anywhere you step, that will be your trail, by an arrangement so agreed with the Way-Maker."

"No," said Guyal, "we would see the visage of our host. We come at his invitation; the minimum of his courtesy is light; light there must be before we set foot inside the dungeon. Know we come as seekers after knowledge; we are visitors to be honored."

"Ah, knowledge, knowledge," came the sad breathlessness. "That shall be yours, in fullness; oh, you shall swim in a tide of knowledge——"

Guyal interrupted the sad, sighing voice. "Are you the Curator? Hundreds of leagues have I come to know the Curator and put him my inquiries. Are you he?"

"By no means. I revile the name of the Curator as a nonessential."

"Who then may you be?"

"I am no one, nothing. I am an abstraction, an emotion, the shake in the air when a scream has departed."

"You speak with the voice of man."

"Why not? Such things as I speak lie in the dearest center of the human brain."

Guyal said in a subdued voice, "You do not make your invitation as enticing as might be hoped."

"No matter, no matter; enter you must, into the dark and on the instant."

"If light there be, we enter."

"No light, no insolent scorch, is ever found in the Museum."

"In this case," said Guyal, drawing forth his Scintillant Dagger, "I innovate a welcome reform. For see, now there is light!"

From the under-pommel issued a searching glare; the ghost tall before them screeched and fell into twinkling ribbons like pulverized tinsel. There were a few vagrant motes in the air; he was gone.

Shierl, who had stood stark and stiff as one mesmerized, gasped a soft warm gasp and fell against Guyal. "How can you be so defiant?"

Guyal said in a voice, half-laugh, half-quaver, "In truth I do not know. ... Perhaps I find it incredible that I should come from Sfere, through forest and across crag, into the northern waste, merely to play the role of victim. I disbelieve; I am bold."

He moved the dagger to right and left, and they saw themselves to be at the portal of a keep, cut from concreted rock. At the back opened a black depth. Crossing the floor swiftly, Guyal kneeled and listened.

He heard no sound. Shierl, at his back, stared with eyes as black and deep as the pit itself.

Leaning with his glowing dagger, Guyal saw a crazy rack of stairs voyaging down into the dark, and his light showed them and their shadows in so confusing a guise that he blinked and drew back.

Shierl said, "What do you fear?"

Guyal rose. "We are momentarily untended here in the Museum of Man. If we stay here we shall be once more arranged in harmony with the hostile pattern. If we go forward boldly we may come to a position of advantage. I propose that we descend these stairs and seek the Curator."

"But does he exist?"

"The ghost spoke fervently against him."

"Let us go, then," said Shierl. "I am resigned."

"We go."

They started down the stairs.

Back, forth, back, forth, down flights at varying angles, stages of varying heights, treads at varying widths, so that each step was a matter for concentration. Back, forth, down, down, down, and the black barred shadows moved and jerked in bizarre modes on the wall.

The flight ended; they stood in a room similar to the entry above, facing another black door, polished at one spot by use. On the walls to either side brass plaques carried messages in unfamiliar characters.

Guyal opened the door against a pressure of cold air, which, blowing through the aperture, made a slight rush, ceasing when Guyal opened the door farther.

"Listen."

It was a far sound, an intermittent clacking, and it raised the hairs at Guyal's neck. He felt Shierl's hand gripping his with clammy pressure.

Dimming the dagger's glow to a glimmer, Guyal passed through the door, with Shierl coming after. From afar came the evil sound, and by the echoes they knew they stood in a great hall.

Guyal directed the light to the floor: it was of a black resilient material. Next the wall: polished stone. He permitted the light to glow in the direction opposite to the sound, and a few paces distant they saw a bulky black case, studded with copper bosses.

With the purpose of the black case not apparent, they followed the wall, and as they walked similar cases appeared, looming heavy and dull, at regular intervals. The clacking receded as they walked; then they came to a right angle, and turning the corner, they seemed to approach the sound. Black case after black case passed; slowly, tense as foxes, they walked, eyes groping for sight through the darkness.

The wall made another angle, and here there was a door. Guyal hesitated. To follow the new direction of the wall would mean approaching the source of the sound. Would it be better to discover the worst quickly or to reconnoiter as they went?

He propounded the dilemma to Shierl, who shrugged. "It is all one; sooner or later the ghosts will flit down to pluck at us; then we are lost."

"Not while I possess light to stare them away to wisps and shreds," said Guyal. "Now I would find the Curator. Possibly he is behind this door. We will so discover."

He laid his shoulder to the door; it eased ajar with a crack of golden light. Guyal peered through. He sighed, a muffled sound of wonder.

Now he opened the door farther; Shierl clutched at his arm.

"This is the Museum," said Guyal in rapt tone. "Here there is no danger." He flung wide the door.

The light came from an unknown source, from the air itself, as if leaking from the discrete atoms; every breath was luminous, the room floated full of invigorating glow. Beautiful works of human fashioning ranked the walls: panels of rich woods; scenes of olden times; formulas of color, designed to convey emotion rather than reality. Here were representations of three hundred marvelous flowers no longer extant on waning Earth; as many star-burst patterns; a multitude of other creations.

The door thudded softly behind them; the two from Earth's final time moved forward through the hall.

"Somewhere near must be the Curator," whispered Guyal. "There has been careful tending and great effort here."

"Look."

Opposite was a door which Guyal was unable to open, for it bore no latch, key, handle knob, or bar. He rapped with his knuckles and waited; no sound returned.

Shierl tugged at his arm. "These are private regions. It is best not to venture too rudely."

Guyal turned away and they continued down the gallery, past the real expression of man's brightest dreamings, until the concentration of so much fire and spirit put them into awe. "Great minds lie on the dust," said Guyal. "Gorgeous souls have vanished. Nevermore will there be the like."

The room turned a corner, widened. And now the clacking sound they had noticed in the dark outer hall returned, louder, more suggestive of unpleasantness. It seemed to enter the gallery through an arched doorway opposite.

Guyal moved quietly to this door, with Shierl at his heels, and so they peered into the next chamber.

A great face looked from the wall, a face taller than Guyal, as tall as Guyal might reach with hands on high. The chin rested on the floor, the scalp slanted back into the panel.

Guyal stared, taken aback. In this pageant of beautiful objects, the grotesque visage was the disparity and dissonance a lunatic might have created. Ugly and vile was the face. The skin shone a gun-metal sheen, the eyes gazed from slanting folds. The nose was a lump, the mouth a pulp.

Guyal turned to Shierl. "Does this not seem an odd work to be honored here in the Museum of Man?"

With hands jerking, she grabbed his arm, staggered back into the gallery.

"Guyal," she cried, "Guyal, come away!"

He faced her in surprise. "What are you saying?"

"That horrible thing in there——"

"The diseased effort of an elder artist."

"It lives."

"How is this?"

"It lives!" she babbled. "It looked at me, then looked at you."

Guyal shrugged off her hand; in disbelief he looked through the doorway.

The face had changed. The torpor had evaporated; the glaze had departed the eye. The mouth squirmed; a hiss of escaping gas sounded. The mouth opened; a gray tongue protruded, and from this tongue darted a tendril. It terminated in a grasping hand, which groped for Guyal's neck. He jumped aside; the hand missed its clutch, the tendril coiled.

Guyal sprang back into the gallery. The hand seized Shierl, grasped her ankle. The eyes glistened; and now the flabby tongue sprouted a new member. . . . Shierl stumbled, fell limp, her eyes staring, foam at her lips. Guyal shouting in a voice he could not hear, ran forward with his dagger. He cut at the gray wrist, but his knife sprang away as if the steel itself were horrified. He seized the tendril; with a mighty effort he broke it against his knee.

The face winced, the tendril jerked back. Guyal dragged Shierl into the gallery, back out of reach.

Through the doorway now, Guyal glared in hate and fear. The mouth had closed; it sneered disappointment. From the dank nostril oozed a wisp of white which swirled, writhed, formed a tall thing in a white robe—a thing with a drawn face and eyes like holes in a skull. Whimpering and mewing in distaste for the light, it wavered forward into the gallery, moving with curious little pauses and hesitancies.

Guyal stood still. Fear had exceeded its power; fear no longer persuaded. A brain could react only to the maximum of its intensity; how could this thing harm him now? He would smash it with his hands, beat it into sighing fog.

"Hold, hold, hold!" came a new voice. "Hold, hold, hold. My charms and tokens, an ill day for Thorsingol. . . . Be off with you, ghost, back to the orifice, back, I say! Go, else I loose the actinics; trespass is not allowed, by supreme command from the Lycurgat; aye, the Lycurgat of Thorsingol." This was the voice of the old man who had hobbled into the gallery.

Back to the snoring face wandered the ghost, and let itself be sucked up into the nostril.

The face rumbled and belched a white fiery lick, flapping at the old man who moved not an inch. From a rod high on the door frame came a whirling disk of golden sparks, which cut and dismembered the white sheet, destroyed it back to the mouth of the face, whence now issued a black bar. This bar edged into the whirling disk and absorbed the sparks. There was an instant of dead silence.

Then the old man crowed, "Ah, you evil episode; you seek to interrupt my tenure. My clever baton holds you in abeyance; you are as naught. Disengage! Retreat into Jeldred!"

The mouth opened to display a gray viscous cavern; the eyes glittered in titanic emotion. The mouth yelled, a wave of sound to buffet the head and drive shock like a nail into the mind.

The baton sprayed a mist; the sound was captured and consumed; it was never heard.

The old man said, "You are captious today! You would disturb poor old Kerlin in his duties? So ho. Baton!" He turned and peered at the rod. "You have tasted that sound? Spew out a penalty."

The fog balled, struck at the nose, buried itself in the pulp. An explosion; the face seethed; the nose was a clutter of shredded gray plasms. They waved like starfish arms and grew together once more, and now the nose was pointed like a cone.

Kerlin the Curator laughed, a shrill yammer on a single tone. He stopped short and the laugh vanished as if it had never begun. He turned to Guyal and Shierl, who stood pressed together in the door frame.

"How now? You are after the gong; the study hours are ended. Why do you linger?" He shook a stern finger. "The Museum is not the site for roguery; this I admonish. So now be off, home to Thorsingol; be more prompt the next time; you disturb the order. . . ." He paused and threw a fretful glance over his shoulder. "The day has gone ill; the Nocturnal Key-keeper is inexcusably late. . . . I have waited an hour on the sluggard; the Lycurgat shall be so informed. I would be home to couch and hearth; here is ill use for old Kerlin. And, further, the encroachment of you two laggards; away now, and be off; out into the twilight!" And he advanced, making directive motions with his hands.

Guyal said, "My lord Curator, I must speak with you."

The old man halted, peered. "Eh? What now? At the end of a long day's effort? No, no, you are out of order; regulation must be observed. Attend my audiarium at the fourth circuit tomorrow morning; then we shall hear you. So go now, go."

Guyal stood back, nonplussed. Shierl fell on her knees. "Sir Curator, we beg you for help; we have no place to go."

Kerlin the Curator looked at her blankly. "No place to go! What folly you utter! Go to your domicile, or to the Pubescentarium, or to the Temple, or to the Outward Inn. The Museum is no casual tavern."

"My lord," cried Guyal desperately, "will you hear me? We speak from emergency."

"Say on then."

"Some malignancy has bewitched your brain. Will you credit this?"

"Ah, indeed?" ruminated the Curator.

"There is no Thorsingol. There is naught but dark waste. Your city is an aeon gone."

The Curator smiled benevolently. "A sad case. So it is with these younger minds." He shook his head. "My duty is clear. Tired bones, you must wait your rest. Fatigue—begone; duty to humanity makes demands; here is madness to be countered and cleared. And in any event the Nocturnal Key-keeper is not here to relieve me of my tedium." He beckoned. "Come."

Hesitantly, Guyal and Shierl followed him. He opened one of his doors, passed through muttering and expostulating. Guyal and Shierl came after.

The room was cubical, floored with dull black stuff. A hooded chair occupied the center of the room and beside it was a chest-high lectern whose face displayed a number of toggles and knurled wheels.

"This is the Curator's own Chair of Clarity," explained Kerlin. "As such it will, upon proper adjustment, impose the Pattern of Hynomeneural Clarity." He manipulated the manuals. "Now, if you will compose yourself I will repair your hallucination. It is beyond my call of duty, but I would not be spoken of as mean or unwilling."

Guyal inquired anxiously, "Lord Curator, this Chair of Clarity, how will it affect me?"

Kerlin the Curator said grandly, "The fibers of your brain are snarled and frayed, and so make contact with unintentional areas. By the marvelous craft of our modern cerebrologists this hood will compose your synapses with the correct readings from the library—those of normality, you must understand—and so repair the skein, and make you once more a whole man."

"Once I sit in the chair," Guyal inquired, "What will you do?"

"Merely close this contact, engage this arm, throw in this toggle—then you daze. In thirty seconds, this bulb glows, signaling the success and completion of the treatment. Then I reverse the manipulation and you arise a creature of renewed sanity."

Guyal looked at Shierl. "Did you hear and comprehend?"

"Yes, Guyal."

"Remember." Then to the Curator: "Marvelous. But how must I sit?"

"Merely relax in the seat. Then I pull the hood slightly forward, to shield the eyes from distraction."

Guyal leaned forward, peered gingerly into the hood. "I fear I do not understand."

The Curator hopped forward impatiently. "It is an act of the utmost facility. Like this." He sat in the chair.

"And how will the hood be applied?"

"In this wise." Kerlin seized a handle, pulled the shield over his face.

"Quick," said Guyal to Shierl. She sprang to the lectern; Kerlin the Curator made a motion to release the hood; Guyal seized the spindly frame, held it. Shierl flung the switches; the Curator relaxed, sighed.

Shierl gazed at Guyal, dark eyes wide and liquid as the great water-flamerian of South Almery. "Is he . . . dead?"

"I hope not."

They gazed uncertainly at the relaxed form. Seconds passed.

A clanging noise sounded from afar—a crush, a wrench, an exultant bellow.

Guyal rushed to the door. Prancing, wavering, sidling into the gallery came a dozen ghosts; through the open door behind, Guyal could see the great head. It was shoving out, pushing into the room. Great ears appeared, part of a neck, wreathed with purple wattles. The wall cracked, sagged, crumbled. A great hand thrust through, a forearm. . . .

Shierl screamed. Guyal, pale and quivering, slammed the door in the face of the nearest ghost. It seeped around the jamb, wisp by wisp.

Guyal sprang to the lectern. The bulb showed dullness. Guyal's hands twitched along the controls. "Only Kerlin's awareness controls the magic of the baton," he panted. "So much is clear." he stared into the bulb with agonized urgency.

"Glow, bulb, glow. . . ."

The bulb glowed. With a sharp cry Guyal returned the switches to neutrality, jumped down, flung up the hood.

Kerlin the Curator sat looking at him.

Behind, the ghost formed itself—a tall white thing in white robes, and the dark eye-holes stared like outlets into nonimagination.

Kerlin the Curator sat looking.

The ghost moved under the robes. A hand like a bird's foot appeared, holding a clod of dingy matter. The ghost cast the matter to the floor; it exploded into a puff of black dust. The motes of the cloud grew, became a myriad of wriggling insects. With one accord they darted across the floor, growing as they spread, and became scuttling creatures with monkey-heads.

Kerlin the Curator moved. "Baton," he said. He held up his hand. It held the baton. The baton spat an orange gout—red-dust. It puffed before the rushing horde and each mote became a red scorpion. So ensued a ferocious battle, and little shrieks and chittering sounds rose from the floor.

The monkey-headed things were killed, routed. The ghost sighed, moved his claw-hand once more. But the baton spat forth a ray of purest light and the ghost sloughed into nothingness.

"Kerlin!" cried Guyal. "The demon is breaking into the gallery."

Kerlin flung open the door, stepped forth.

"Baton," said Kerlin, "perform thy utmost."

The demon said, "No, Kerlin, hold the magic; I thought you dazed. Now I retreat."

With a vast quaking and heaving he pulled back until once more only his face showed through the hole.

"Baton," said Kerlin, "rest on guard."

The baton disappeared from his hand.

Kerlin turned and faced Guyal and Shierl.

"There is need for many words, for now I die. I die, and the Museum shall lie alone. So let us speak quickly, quickly, quickly. . . ."

Kerlin moved with feeble steps to a portal which snapped aside as he approached. Guyal and Shierl stood hesitantly to the rear.

"Come, come," said Kerlin in sharp impatience. "My strength flags, I die. You have been my death."

Guyal moved slowly forward, with Shierl half a pace behind.

Kerlin surveyed them with a thin grin. "Halt your misgivings and hasten; I wane; my sight flickers. . . ."

He waved a despairing hand, then, turning, led them into the inner chamber where he slumped into a great chair. With many uneasy glances at the door Guyal and Shierl settled upon a padded couch.

Kerlin jeered in a feeble voice, "You fear the white phantasms? Poh, they are held from the gallery by the baton. Only when I am smitten out of mind—or dead—will the baton cease its function. You must know," he added with somewhat more vigor, "that the energies and dynamics do not channel from my brain but from the central potentium of the Museum, which is perpetual; I merely direct and order the rod."

"But this demon—who or what is he? Why does he come to look through the walls?"

"He is Blikdak, of the demon-world Jeldred. He wrenched the hole intent on taking the knowledge of the Museum into his mind, but I forestalled him; so he sits waiting in the hole till I die. Then he will glut himself with erudition to the great disadvantage of men."

"Why cannot this demon be exhorted hence and the hole abolished?"

Kerlin the Curator shook his head. "The furious powers I control are not valid in the air of the demon-world, where substance and form are of different entity. So far as you see him, he has brought his environment with him; so far he is safe. When he ventures farther the power of Earth dissolves the Jeldred mode; then may I strike him with fervor from the potentium. . . . But enough of Blikdak; tell me, what is the news of Thorsingol?"

Guyal said in a halting voice, "Thorsingol is passed beyond memory. There is naught above but arid tundra and the old town of the Saponids. This girl Shierl is of the Saponids; we came to the Museum at the behest of Blikdak's ghosts."

"Ah," breathed Kerlin, "have I been so aimless? These youthful shapes by which Blikdak relieved his tedium: they flit down my memory like May flies. . . . I put them aside as creatures of his own conception."

Shierl grimaced. "What use to him are human creatures?"

Kerlin said dully, "Blikdak is past your conceiving. These human creatures are his play, on whom he practices various junctures, nauseas, antics, and at last struggles to the death. Then he sends forth a ghost demanding further youth and beauty."

Guyal said in puzzlement, "Such acts would seem derangements of humanity. They are anthropoid by the very nature of the functioning organs. Since Blikdak is a demon—"

"Consider him!" spoke Kerlin. "His lineaments, his apparatus. He is nothing else but anthropoid, and such is his origin, together with all the demons, frits, and winged glowing-eyed creatures that infest latter-day Earth. Blikdak, like the others, derives from the mind of man. The condensation, the cloacal humors, the scatophiliac whims that have drained through humanity formed a vast tumor; so Blikdak assumed his being. But of Blikdak, enough. I die, I die!" He sank into the chair with heaving chest. "My eyes vary and waver. My breath is shallow as a bird's, my bones are the pith of an old vine. I have lived beyond knowledge; in my madness I knew no passage of time. Now I remember the years and centuries, the millennia, the epochs—they are like quick glimpses through a shutter. Curing my madness, you have killed me."

"But when you die," cried Shierl, "what then?"

Guyal asked, "In the Museum of Man are there no exorcisms to dissolve this demon?

"Blikdak must be eradicated," said Kerlin. "Then will I die in ease; then must you assume the care of the Museum." He licked his white lips. "An ancient principle specifies that, in order to destroy a substance the nature of the substance must be determined. In short, before Blikdak may be dissolved, we must discover his nature." And his eyes moved glassily to Guyal.

"Your pronouncement is sound beyond argument," admitted Guyal, "but how may this be accomplished? Blikdak will never submit to investigation."

"No; there must be subterfuge, some instrumentality. . . ."

"The ghosts are part of Blikdak's stuff?"

"Indeed."

"Can the ghosts be stayed and prevented?"

"Indeed; in a box of light, the which I can effect by a thought. Yes, a ghost we must have." Kerlin raised his head. "Baton! One ghost; admit a ghost!"

A moment passed; Kerlin held up his hand. There was a faint scratch at the door and a soft whine. "Open," said a voice, full of sobs and catches and quavers. "Open and let forth the youthful creatures."

Kerlin laboriously rose to his feet. "It is done."

From behind the door came a sad voice, "I am pent, I am snared in scorching brilliance!"

"Now we experiment," said Guyal. "What dissolves the ghost dissolves Blikdak."

"True indeed," assented Kerlin.

"Why not light?" inquired Shierl. "Light parts the fabric of the ghosts as wind tatters the fog."

"But merely for their fragility; Blikdak is harsh and solid." Kerlin mused. After a moment he gestured to the door. "We go to the image-expander; there we will explode the ghost to macroid dimension; so shall we find his basis. Guyal of Sfere, you must support my frailness; my limbs are weak as wax."

On Guyal's arm he tottered forward, and with Shierl close at their heels they gained the gallery. Here the ghost wept in its cage of light, and searched constantly for a dark aperture to seep his essence through.

Paying him no heed Kerlin hobbled and limped across the gallery. In their wake followed the box of light and perforce the ghost.

"Open the great door," cried Kerlin in a voice beset with cracking and hoarseness. "The great door into the Cognitive Repository!"

Shierl ran ahead and thrust her force against the door; it slid aside, and they looked into the great dark hall, and the golden light from the gallery dwindled into the shadows and was lost.

"Call for light," Kerlin said.

"Light!" cried Guyal.

Illumination came to the great hall, and it proved so tall that pilasters along the wall dwindled to threads, and so long and wide that perspective was distorted. Spaced in equal rows were the black cases with the copper bosses that Guyal and Shierl had noted on their entry. Above each hung five similar cases, precisely fixed, floating without support.

"What are these?" asked Guyal.

"Would my poor brain encompassed a hundredth part of what these banks know," panted Kerlin. "They are repositories crammed with all that has been experienced, achieved, or recorded by man. Here is the lost lore, early and late, the fabulous imaginings, the history of ten million cities, the beginnings of time and the presumed finalities; the reason for human existence and the reason for the reason. Daily I have labored and toiled in these banks; my achievement has been a synopsis of the most superficial sort: a panorama across a wide and multifarious country."

Said Shierl, "Would not the craft to destroy Blikdak be contained here?"

"Indeed, indeed; our task would be merely to find the information. Under which casting would we search? Consider these categories: Demon-lands; Killings and Mortefactions; Expositions and Dissolutions of Evil; History of Granvilunde (where such an entity was repelled); Attractive and Detractive Hyperordnets; Therapy for Hallucinants and Ghost-takers; Constructive Journal, item for regeneration of burst walls, subdivision for invasion by demons; Procedural Suggestions in Time of Risk. . . . Aye, these and a thousand more. Somewhere is knowledge. But where to look? There is no Index Major; none except the poor synopsis of my compilation. He who seeks specific knowledge must often go on an extended search. . . ." His voice trailed off. Then: "Forward! Forward through the banks to the Mechanismus."

So through the banks they went, like roaches in a maze, and behind drifted the cage of light with the wailing ghost. At last they entered a chamber smelling of metal; again Kerlin instructed Guyal and Guyal called for light.

At a tall booth Kerlin halted the cage of light. A pane dropped before the ghost. "Observe now," Kerlin said, and manipulated the activants.

They saw the ghost, depicted and projected: the flowing robe, the haggard visage. The face grew large, flattened; a segment under the vacant eye became a scabrous white place. It separated into pustules, and a single pustule swelled to fill the pane. The crater of the pustule was an intricate stippled surface, a mesh as of fabric, knit in a lacy pattern.

"Behold!" said Shierl. "He is a thing woven as if by thread."

Guyal turned eagerly to Kerlin; Kerlin raised a finger. "Indeed, indeed, a goodly thought, especially since here beside us is a rotor of extreme swiftness, used in reeling the cognitive filaments of the cases. . . . Now then observe: I reach to this panel, I select a mesh, I withdraw a thread, and note! The meshes ravel and loosen and part. And now to the bobbin on the rotor, and I wrap the thread, and now with a twist we have the cincture made. . . ."

Shierl said dubiously, "Does not the ghost observe and note your doing?"

"The pane shields our actions; he is too exercised to attend. And now I dissolve the cage and he is free."

The ghost wandered forth, cringing from the light.

"Go!" cried Kerlin. "Back to your genetrix, back, return and go!"

The ghost departed. Kerlin said to Guyal, "Follow; find when Blikdak snuffs him up."

At a cautious distance Guyal watched the ghost seep up into the black nostril, and returned to where Kerlin waited by the rotor. "The ghost has once more become part of Blikdak."

"Now then," said Kerlin, "we cause the rotor to twist, the bobbin to whirl, and we shall observe."

The rotor whirled to a blur; the bobbin (as long as Guyal's arm) be-

came spun with ghost-thread, at first glowing pastel polychrome, then
nacre, then fine milk-ivory.

The rotor spun, a million times a minute, and the thread drawn unseen
and unknown from Blikdak thickened on the bobbin.

The rotor spun; the bobbin was full—a cylinder shining with glossy
silken sheen. Kerlin slowed the rotor: Guyal snapped a new bobbin into
place, and the unraveling of Blikdak continued.

Three bobbins—four—four—five—and Guyal, observing Blikdak from
afar, found the giant face quiescent, the mouth working and sucking,
creating the clacking sound which had first caused them apprehension.

Eight bobbins. Blikdak opened his eyes, stared in puzzlement around
the chamber.

Twelve bobbins; a discolored spot appeared on the sagging cheek, and
Blikdak quivered in uneasiness.

Twenty bobbins: the spot spread across Blikdak's visage, across the
slanted fore-dome, and his mouth hung lax; he hissed and fretted.

Thirty bobbins: Blikdak's head seemed stale and putrid; the gunmetal
sheen had become an angry maroon, the eyes bulged, the mouth hung
open, the tongue lolled limp.

Fifty bobbins: Blikdak collapsed. His dome lowered against his mouth;
his eyes shone like feverish coals.

Sixty bobbins, seventy bobbins; Blikdak was no more. The breach in
the wall gave on barren rock, unbroken and rigid.

And in the Mechanismus seventy shining bobbins lay stacked.

Kerlin fell back against the wall. "My time has come. I have guarded
the Museum; together we have won it from Blikdak. . . . Attend me now.
Into your hands I pass the curacy; now the Museum is your charge to
guard and preserve."

"For what end?" asked Shierl. "Earth expires, almost as you. . . .
Wherefore knowledge?"

"More now than ever," gasped Kerlin. "Attend: the stars are bright,
the stars are fair; the banks know blessed magic to fleet you to youthful
climes. Now . . . I go. I die."

"Wait!" cried Guyal. "Wait, I beseech!"

"Why wait?" whispered Kerlin. "You call me back?"

"How do I extract from the banks?"

"The key to the index is in my chambers, the index of my life. . . ."
And Kerlin died.

❧

Guyal and Shierl climbed to the upper ways and stood outside the portal
on the ancient floor. It was night; the marble shone faintly underfoot, the
broken columns loomed on the sky.

Across the plain the yellow lights of Issane shone warm through the
trees; above in the sky shone the stars.

Guyal said to Shierl, "There is your home; do you wish to return?"

She shook her head. "We have looked through the eyes of knowledge.
We have seen old Thorsingol, and the Sherrit Empire before it, and

Golwan Andra before that, and the Forty Kades even before. We have seen the warlike green-men, and the knowledgeable Pharials and the Clambs who departed Earth for the stars, as did the Merioneth before them and the Gray Sorcerers still earlier. We have seen oceans rise and fall, the mountains crust up, peak and melt in the beat of rain; we have looked on the sun when it glowed hot and full and yellow. . . . No, Guyal, there is no place for me at Issane. . . ."

Guyal, leaning back on the weathered pillar, looked up to the stars. "Knowledge is ours, Shierl—all of knowing to our call. And what shall we do?"

Together they looked up to the white stars.

"What shall we do . . ."

Old Hundredth

BRIAN W. ALDISS

The far future seems to hold a special fascination and allure for Brian W. Aldiss, and in a field where such stories are relatively rare, he has almost made a specialty out of writing about it. The Long Afternoon of Earth *(also known as the* Hothouse *series, under which title it won a special Hugo Award in 1962) remains one of the classic visions of the distant future of Earth, as well as being a foundation stone of the subgenre of science-fantasy, but Aldiss has also handled the theme with grace and a wealth of poetic imagination in many other stories, including classics such as "The Worm That Flies" and "Full Sun," as well as the novels of the* Helliconia *trilogy (and handles a closely related theme with similar excellence in* The Malacia Tapestry *as well).*

Never has he envisioned the far future more vividly than in the story that follows, though, which takes us to a muted, autumnal future, full of echoes and old ghosts; an ancient and ruinous Earth from which humankind has forever departed; a strange world of involutes and Impures and musicolumns, with Venus for a moon and hogs as big as hippos; a world of stately, living music under dusty umbrella trees. . . .

One of the true giants of the field, Brian W. Aldiss has been publishing science fiction for nearly half a century and has more than two dozen books to his credit. "The Saliva Tree" *won a Nebula Award in 1965, and his novel* Starship *won the Prix Jules Verne in 1977. He took another Hugo Award in 1987 for his critical study of science fiction,* Trillion Year Spree, *written with David Wingrove.*

In many ways, Brian W. Aldiss was the enfant terrible of the late fifties, exploding into the SF world and shaking it up with the ferocious verve and pyrotechnic verbal brilliance of stories like "Poor Little Warrior!," "Outside," "The New Father Christmas," "Who Can Replace a Man?," and "A Kind of Artistry" and with the somber beauty and unsettling poetic vision—in the main, of a world where mankind signally has not *triumphantly conquered the universe, as the Campbellian dogma of the time insisted that he would—of his classic novels* Starship (Non-Stop *and* The Long Afternoon of Earth *in Britain). All this made him one of the most controversial writers of the day . . . and, some years later, he'd be one of the most controversial figures of the New Wave era as well, shaking up the SF world of the mid-sixties in an even more dramatic and drastic fashion with the ferociously Joycean "acidhead war" stories that would be melded into* Barefoot in the Head, *with the irreverent* Cryptozoic!, *and with his surrealistic antinovel* Report on Probability A.

*But Aldiss has never been willing to work any one patch of ground for very long. By 1976, he had worked his way through two controversial British mainstream best-sellers—*The Hand-Reared Boy *and* A Soldier Erect—*and the strange transmuted Gothic of* Frankenstein Unbound *and gone on to produce a lyrical* *masterpiece of science-fantasy,* The Malacia Tapestry, *one of his best books and certainly one of the best novels of the seventies. Ahead, in the decade of the eighties, was the monumental accomplishment of his* Helliconia trilogy— Helliconia Spring, Helliconia Summer, *and* Helliconia Winter—*and by the end of that decade only the grumpiest of reactionary critics could deny that Aldiss was one of the true giants of the field, a figure of artistic complexity and amazing vigor, as much on the cutting edge in the nineties as he had been in the fifties.*

Aldiss's other books include An Island Called Moreau, Graybeard, Dracula Unbound, Enemies of the System, A Rude Awakening, Life in the West, Forgotten Life, *and* Remembrance Day, *a memoir,* Bury My Heart at W. H. Smith's, *and a collection of poems,* Home Life with Cats. *His short fiction has been collected in* Space, Time, and Nathaniel; Who Can Replace a Man?, New Arrivals, Old Encounters; Galaxies like Grains of Sand; *and* Seasons in Flight. *His many anthologies include* The Penguin Science Fiction Omnibus *and, with Harry Harrison,* Decade: The 1940s, Decade: The 1950s, *and* Decade: The 1960s. *Aldiss's latest books include a collection,* Common Clay, *and an autobiography,* The Twinkling of an Eye. *His Utopia,* White Mars, *has just been published. He lives in Oxford.*

The road climbed dustily down between trees as symmetrical as umbrellas. Its length was punctuated at one point by a musicolumn standing on the verge. From a distance, the column was only a stain in the air. As sentient creatures neared it, their psyches activated it, it drew on their vitalities, and then it could be heard as well as seen. Their presence made it flower into pleasant sound, instrumental or chant.

All this region was called Ghinomon, for no one lived here now, not even the odd hermit Impure. It was given over to grass and the weight of time. Only a wild goat or two activated the musicolumn nowadays, or a scampering vole wrung a chord from it in passing.

When old Dandi Lashadusa came riding on her baluchitherium, the column began to intone. It was no more than an indigo trace in the air, hardly visible, for it represented only a bonded pattern of music locked into the fabric of that particular area of space. It was also a transubstantio-spatial shrine, the eternal part of a being that had dematerialized itself into music.

The baluchitherium whinnied, lowered its head, and sneezed onto the gritty road.

"Gently, Lass," Dandi told her mare, savoring the growth of the chords that increased in volume as she approached. Her long nose twitched with pleasure as if she could feel the melody along her olfactory nerves.

Obediently, the baluchitherium slowed, turning aside to crop fern, although it kept an eye on the indigo stain. It liked things to have being or not to have being; these half-and-half objects disturbed it, though they could not impair its immense appetite.

Dandi climbed down her ladder onto the ground, glad to feel the ancient dust under her feet. She smoothed her hair and stretched as she listened to the music.

She spoke aloud to her mentor, half a world away, but he was not listening. His mind closed to her thoughts, and he muttered an obscure exposition that darkened what it sought to clarify.

". . . useless to deny that it is well-nigh impossible to improve anything, however faulty, that has so much tradition behind it. And the origins of your bit of metricism are indeed embedded in such an antiquity that we must needs—"

"Tush, Mentor, come out of your black box and forget your hatred of my 'metricism' a moment," Dandi Lashadusa said, cutting her thought into his. "Listen to the bit of 'metricism' I've found here; look at where I have come to; let your argument rest."

She turned her eyes around, scanning the tawny rocks near at hand, the brown line of the road, the distant black-and-white magnificence of ancient Oldorajo's town, doing this all for him, tiresome old fellow. Her mentor was blind, never left his cell in Aeterbroe to go farther than the sandy courtyard, hadn't physically left that green cathedral pile for over a century. Womanlike, she thought he needed change. Soul, how he rambled on! Even now, he was managing to ignore her and refute her.

". . . for consider, Lashadusa woman, nobody can be found to father it. Nobody wrought or thought it, phrases of it merely *came* together. Even the old nations of men could not own it. None of them know who composed it. An element here from a Spanish pavan, an influence there of a French psalm tune, a flavor here of early English carol, a savor there of later German chorale. All primitive—ancient beyond ken. Nor are the faults of your bit of metricism confined to bastardy—"

"Stay in your black box then, if you won't see or listen," Dandi said. She could not get into his mind; it was the mentor's privilege to lodge in her mind, and in the minds of those few other wards he had, scattered around Earth. Only the mentors had the power to inhabit another's mind—which made them rather tiring on occasions like this, when they would not get out. For over seventy centuries, Dandi's mentor had been persuading her to die into a dirge of his choosing (and composing). Let her die, yes, let her transubstantio-spatialize herself a thousand times! His quarrel was not with her decision but with her taste, which he considered execrable.

Leaving the baluchitherium to crop, Dandi walked away from the musicolumn toward a hillock. Still fed by her steed's psyche, the column continued to play. Its music was of a simplicity, with a dominant-tonic recurrent bass part suggesting pessimism. To Dandi, a savant in musicolumnology, it yielded other data. She could tell to within a few years when its founder had died and also what sort of creature, generally speaking, he had been.

Climbing the hillock, Dandi looked about. To the south where the road led were low hills, lilac in the poor light. There lay her home. At last she was returning, after wanderings covering three hundred centuries and most of the globe.

Apart from the blind beauty of Oldorajo's town lying to the west, there

was only one landmark she recognized. That was the Involute. It seemed
to hang iridial above the ground a few leagues ahead; just to look on it
made her feel she must go nearer.

Before summoning the baluchitherium, Dandi listened once more to
the sounds of the musicolumn, making sure she had them fixed in her
head. The pity was that her old fool wise man would not share it. She
could still feel his sulks floating like sediment through her mind.

"Are you listening now, Mentor?"

"Eh? An interesting point is that back in 1556 Pre-Involutary, your
same little tune may be discovered lurking in Knox's Anglo-Genevan Psalter, where it espoused the cause of the third psalm—"

"You dreary old fish! Wake yourself! How can you criticize my intended way of dying when you have such a fustian way of living?"

This time he heard her words. So close did he seem that his peevish
pinching at the bridge of his snuffy old nose tickled hers, too.

"What are you doing *now*, Dandi?" he inquired.

"If you had been listening, you'd know. Here's where I am, on the last
Ghinomon plain before Crotheria and home." She swept the landscape
again and he took it in, drank it almost greedily. Many mentors went
blind early in life shut in their monastic underwater life; their most effective vision was conducted through the eyes of their wards.

His view of what she saw enriched hers. He knew the history, the myth
behind this forsaken land. He could stock the tired old landscape with
pageantry, delighting her and surprising her. Back and forward he went,
painting her pictures: the Youdicans, the Lombards, the Ex-Europa Emissary, the Grites, the Risorgimento, the Involuters—and catchwords, costumes, customs, courtesans, pelted briefly through Dandi Lashadusa's
mind. Ah, she thought admiringly, who could truly live without these
priestly, beastly, erudite, erratic mentors?

"Erratic?" he inquired, snatching at her lick of thought. "A thousand
years I live, for all that time to absent myself from the world, to eat
mashed fish here with my brothers, learning history, studying rapport,
sleeping with my bones on stones—a humble being, a being in a million,
a mentor in a myriad, and your standards of judgment are so mundane
you find no stronger label for me than erratic?! Fie, Lashadusa, bother
me no more for fifty years!"

The words squeaked in her head as if she spoke herself. She felt his
old chops work phantomlike in hers, and half in anger half in laughter
called aloud, "I'll be dead by then!"

He snicked back hot and holy to reply, "And another thing about your
footloose swan song—in Marot and Beza's Genevan Psalter of 1551, Old
Time, it was musical midwife to the one hundred and thirty-fourth psalm.
Like you, it never seemed to settle!" Then he was gone.

"Pooh!" Dandi said. She whistled. "Lass."

Obediently her great rhinolike creature, eighteen feet high at the
shoulder, ambled over. The musicolumn died as the mare left it, faded,
sank to a whisper, silenced: only the purple stain remained, noiseless, in

the lonely air. Lowering its great Oligocene head, Lass nuzzled its mistress's hand. She climbed the ladder onto the ridged plateau of its back.

They made toward the Involute, lulled by the simple and intricate feeling of being alive.

Night was settling in now. Hidden behind banks of mist, the sun prepared to set. But Venus was high, a gallant half-crescent four times as big as the moon had been before the moon, spiraling farther and farther from Earth, had shaken off its parent's clutch to go dance around the sun, a second Mercury. Even by that time Venus had been moved by gravitotraction into Earth's orbit, so that the two sister worlds circled each other as they circled the sun.

The stamp of that great event still lay everywhere, its tokens not only in the crescent in the sky. For Venus placed a strange spell on the hearts of man, and a more penetrating displacement in his genes. Even when its atmosphere was transformed into a muffled breathability, it remained an alien world; against logic, its opportunities, its possibilities, were its own. It shaped men, just as Earth had shaped them.

On Venus, men bred themselves anew.

And they bred the so-called Impures. They bred new plants, new fruits, new creatures—original ones, and duplications of creatures not seen on Earth for eons past. From one line of these familiar strangers Dandi's baluchitherium was descended. So, for that matter, was Dandi.

The huge creature came now to the Involute, or as near as it cared to get. Again it began to crop at thistles, thrusting its nose through dewy spiders' webs and ground mist.

"Like you, I'm a vegetarian," Dandi said, climbing down to the ground. A grove of low fruit trees grew nearby; she reached up into the branches, gathered, and ate, before turning to inspect the Involute. Already her spine tingled at the nearness of it; awe, loathing, and love made a part-pleasant sensation near her heart.

The Involute was not beautiful. True, its colors changed with the changing light, yet the colors were fish-cold, for they belonged to another dimension. Though they reacted to dusk and dawn, Earth had no stronger power over them. They pricked the eyes. Perhaps, too, they were painful because they were the last signs of materialist man. Even Lass moved uneasily before that ill-defined lattice, the upper limits of which were lost in thickening gloom.

"Don't fear," Dandi said. "There's an explanation for this, old girl." She added, "There's an explanation for everything, if we can find it."

She could feel all the personalities in the Involute. It was a frozen screen of personality. All over the old planet the structures stood, to shed their awe on those who were left behind. They were the essence of man. They were man—all that remained of him on Earth.

When the first flint, the first shell, was shaped into a weapon, that action shaped man. As he molded and complicated his tools, so they molded and complicated him. He became the first scientific animal. And at last, via information theory and great computers, he gained knowledge of all his parts. He formed the Laws of Integration, which reveal all beings as part of a pattern and show them their part in the pattern. There is only the pattern; the pattern is all the universe, creator and created. For the first time it became possible to duplicate that pattern artificially—the transubstantio-spatializers were built.

Men left their strange hobbies on Earth and Venus and projected themselves into the pattern. Their entire personalities were merged with the texture of space itself. Through science, they reached immortality.

It was a one-way passage.

They did not return. Each Involute carried thousands or even millions of people. There they were, not dead, not living. How they exulted or wept in their transubstantiation, no one left could say. Only this could be said: man had gone, and a great emptiness was fallen over Earth.

‹›

"Your thoughts are heavy, Dandi Lashadusa. Get you home." Her mentor was back in her mind. She caught the feeling of him moving around and around in his coral-formed cell.

"I must think of man," she said.

"Your thoughts mean nothing, do nothing."

"Man created us: I want to consider him in peace."

"He only shaped a stream of life that was always entirely out of his control. Forget him. Get onto your mare and ride home."

"Mentor—"

"Get home, woman. Moping does not become you, I want to hear no more of your swan song, for I've given you my final word on that. Use a theme of your own, not of man's. I've said it a million times, and I say it again."

"I wasn't going to mention my music. I was only going to tell you that—"

"What then?" His thought was querulous. She felt his powerful tail tremble, disturbing the quiet water of his cell.

"I don't know—"

"Get home then."

"I'm lonely."

He shot her a picture from another of his wards before leaving her. Dandi had seen this ward before in similar dreamlike glimpses. It was a huge mole creature, still boring underground as it had been for the last hundred years. Occasionally it crawled through vast caves; once it swam in a subterranean lake; most of the time it just bored through rock. Its motivations were obscure to Dandi, although her mentor referred to it as "a geologer." Doubtless if the mole was vouchsafed occasional glimpses of Dandi and her musicolumnology, it would find her as baffling. At least the mentor's point was made: loneliness was psychological, not statistical.

Why, a million personalities glittered almost before her eyes!

She mounted the great baluchitherium mare and headed for home. Time and old monuments made glum company.

Twilight now, with just one streak of antique gold left in the sky,

Venus sweetly bright, and stars peppering the purple. A fine evening in which to be alive, particularly with one's last bedtime close at hand.

And yes, for all her mentor said, she was going to turn into that old little piece derived from one of the tunes in the 1540 *Souter Liedekens*, that splendid source of Netherlands folk music. For a moment, Dandi Lashadusa chuckled almost as eruditely as her mentor. The sixteenth century, with the virtual death of plainsong and virtual birth of the violin, was most interesting to her. Ah, the richness of facts, the texture of man's brief history on Earth! Pure joy! Then she remembered herself.

After all, she was only a megatherium, a sloth as big as a small elephant, whose kind had been extinct for millions of years until man reconstituted a few of them in the Venusian experiments. Her modifications in the way of fingers and enlarged brain gave her no real qualification to think up to man's level.

Early next morning, they arrived at the ramparts of the town Crotheria, where Dandi lived. The ubiquitous goats thronged about them, some no bigger than hedgehogs, some almost as big as hippos—what madness in his last days had provoked man to so many variations on one undistinguished theme?—as Lass and her mistress moved up the last slope and under the archway.

It was good to be back, to push among the trails fringed with bracken, among the palms, oaks, and treeferns. Almost all the town was deeply green and private from the sun, curtained by swathes of Spanish moss. Here and there were houses—caves, pits, crude piles of boulders, or even genuine man-type buildings, grand in ruin. Dandi climbed down, walking ahead of her mount, her long hair curling in pleasure. The air was cool with the coo of doves or the occasional bleat of a merino.

As she explored familiar ways, though, disappointment overcame her. Her friends were all away, even the dreamy bison whose wallow lay at the corner of the street in which Dandi lived. Only pure animals were here, rooting happily and mindlessly in the lanes, beggars who owned the Earth. The Impures—descendants of the Venusian experimental stock— were all absent from Crotheria.

That was understandable. For obvious reasons man had increased the abilities of herbivores rather than carnivores. After the Involution, with man gone, these Impures had taken to his towns as they took to his ways, as far as this was possible to their natures. Both Dandi and Lass, and many of the others, consumed massive amounts of vegetable matter every day. Gradually a wider and wider circle of desolation grew about each town (the greenery in the town itself was sacrosanct), forcing a semi-nomadic life onto its vegetarian inhabitants.

This thinning in its turn led to a decline in the birthrate. The travelers grew fewer, the towns greener and emptier; in time they had become little oases of forest studding the grassless plains.

"Rest here, Lass," Dandi said at last, pausing by a bank of brightly flowering cycads. "I'm going into my house."

A giant beech grew before the stone façade of her home, so close that it was hard to determine whether it did not help support the ancient building. A crumbling balcony jutted from the first floor; reaching up, Dandi seized the balustrade and hauled herself onto it.

This was her normal way of entering her home, for the ground floor was taken over by goats and hogs, just as the third floor had been appropriated by doves and parakeets. Trampling over the greenery self-sown on the balcony, she moved into the front room. Dandi smiled. Here were her old things, the broken furniture on which she liked to sleep, the vision screens on which nothing could be seen, the heavy manuscript books in which, guided by her know-all mentor, she wrote down the outpourings of the musicolumns she had visited all over the world.

She ambled through to the next room.

She paused, her peace of mind suddenly broken.

A brown bear stood there. One of its heavy hands was clenched over the hilt of a knife.

"I am no vulgar thief," it said, curling its thick black lips over the syllables. "I am an archaeologer. If this is your place, you must grant me permission to remove the man things. Obviously you have no idea of the worth of some of the equipment here. We bears require it. We must have it."

It came toward her, panting doggy fashion, its jaws open. From under bristling eyebrows gleamed the lust to kill.

Dandi was frightened. Peaceful by nature, she feared the bears above all creatures for their fierceness and their ability to organize. The bears were few: they were the only creatures to show signs of wishing to emulate man's old aggressiveness.

She knew what the bears did. They hurled themselves through the Involutes to increase their power; by penetrating those patterns, they nourished their psychic drive, so the mentor said. It was forbidden. They were transgressors. They were killers.

"Mentor!" she screamed.

The bear hesitated. As far as he was concerned, the hulking creature before him was merely an obstacle in the way of progress, something to be thrust aside without hate. Killing would be pleasant but irrelevant; more important items remained to be done. Much of the equipment housed here could be used in the rebuilding of the world, the world of which bears had such high, haphazard dreams. Holding the knife threateningly, he moved forward.

The mentor was in Dandi's head, answering her cry, seeing through her eyes, though he had no sight of his own. He scanned the bear and took over her mind instantly, knifing himself into place like a guillotine.

No longer was he a blind old dolphin lurking in one cell of a cathedral pile of coral under tropical seas, a theologer, an inculcator of wisdom into feebler-minded beings. He was a killer more savage than the bear, keen to kill anything that might covet the vacant throne once held by men. The mere thought of men could send this mentor into sharklike fury at times.

Caught up in his fury, Dandi found herself advancing. For all the bear's strength, she could vanquish it. In the open, where she could have brought her heavy tail into action, it would have been an easy matter. Here her weighty forearms must come into play. She felt them lift to her mentor's command as he planned for her to clout the bear to death.

The bear stepped back, awed by an opponent twice its size, suddenly unsure.

She advanced.

"No! Stop!" Dandi cried.

Instead of fighting the bear, she fought her mentor, hating his hate. Her mind twisted, her dim mind full of that steely, fishy one, as she blocked his resolution.

"I'm for peace!" she cried.

"Then kill the bear!"

"I'm for peace, not killing!"

She rocked back and forth. When she staggered into a wall, it shook; dust spread in the old room. The mentor's fury was terrible to feel.

"Get out quickly!" Dandi called to the bear.

Hesitating, it stared at her. Then it turned and made for the window. For a moment it hung with its shaggy hind-quarters in the room. Momentarily she saw it for what it was, an old animal in an old world, without direction. It jumped. It was gone. Goats blared confusion on its retreat.

The mentor screamed. Insane with frustration, he hurled Dandi against the doorway with all the force of his mind.

Wood cracked and splintered. The lintel came crashing down. Brick and stone shifted, grumbled, fell. Powdered filth billowed up. With a great roar, one wall collapsed. Dandi struggled to get free. Her house was tumbling about her. It had never been intended to carry so much weight, so many centuries.

She reached the balcony and jumped clumsily to safety, just as the building avalanched in on itself, sending a cloud of plaster and powdered mortar into the overhanging trees.

For a horribly long while the world was full of dust, goat bleats, and panic-stricken parakeets.

⬤

Heavily astride her baluchitherium once more, Dandi Lashadusa headed back to the empty region called Ghinomon. She fought her bitterness, trying to urge herself toward resignation.

All she had was destroyed—not that she set store by possessions: that was a man trait. Much more terrible was the knowledge that her mentor had left her forever; she had transgressed too badly to be forgiven this time.

Suddenly she was lonely for his persnickety voice in her head, for the wisdom he fed her, for the scraps of dead knowledge he tossed her—yes, even for the love he gave her. She had never seen him, never could: yet no two beings could have been more intimate.

She also missed those other wards of his she would glimpse no more: the mole creature tunneling in Earth's depths, the seal family that barked with laughter on a desolate coast, a senile gorilla that endlessly collected and classified spiders, an aurochs—seen only once, but then unforgetta-bly—that lived with smaller creatures in an Arctic city it had helped build in the ice.

She was excommunicated.

Well, it was time for her to change, to disintegrate, to transubstantiate into a pattern not of flesh but music. That discipline at least the mentor had taught and could not take away.

"This will do, Lass," she said.

Her gigantic mount stopped obediently. Lovingly, she patted its neck. It was young; it would be free.

Following the dusty trail, she went ahead, alone. Somewhere afar a bird called. Coming to a mound of boulders, Dandi squatted among gorse, the points of which could not prick through her thick old coat. Already her selected music poured through her head, already it seemed to loosen the chemical bonds of her being.

Why should she not choose an old human tune? She was an antiquar-ian. Things that were gone solaced her for things that were to come. In her dim way, she had always stood out against her mentor's absolute hatred of men. The thing to hate was hatred. Men in their finer moments had risen above hate. Her death psalm was an instance of that—a multiple instance, for it had been fingered and changed over the ages, as the men-tor himself insisted, by men of a variety of races, all with their minds directed to worship rather than hate.

Locking herself into thought disciplines, Dandi began to dissolve. Man had needed machines to help him do it, to fit into the Involutes. She was a lesser animal: she could change herself into the humbler shape of a musicolumn. It was just a matter of *rearranging*—and without pain she formed into a pattern that was not a shaggy megatherium body, but an indigo column, hardly visible. . . .

For a long while Lass cropped thistle and cacti. Then she ambled forward to seek the hairy creature she fondly—and a little condescend-ingly—regarded as her equal. But of the sloth there was no sign.

Almost the only landmark was a violet-blue dye in the air. As the baluchitherium mare approached, a sweet old music grew in volume from the dye. It was a music almost as ancient as the landscape itself, and certainly as much traveled, a tune once known to men as Old Hundredth. And there were voices singing: "All creatures that on Earth do dwell. . . ."

Alpha Ralpha Boulevard

CORDWAINER SMITH

The late Cordwainer Smith—in "real" life Dr. Paul M. A. Linebarger, scholar, statesman, and author of the definitive text (still taught from today) on the art of psychological warfare—was a writer of enormous talents who, from 1948 until his untimely death in 1966, produced a double-handful of some of the best short fiction this genre has ever seen: "On the Storm Planet," "A Planet Named Shayol," "Mother Hitton's Littul Kittons," "The Ballad of Lost C'Mell," "The Dead Lady of Clown Town," "The Game of Rat and Dragon," "Drunkboat," "The Lady Who Sailed The Soul," *"Under Old Earth," and "Scanners Live in Vain," as well as a large number of lesser, but still fascinating, stories, all twisted and blended and woven into an interrelated tapestry of incredible lushness and intricacy. Smith created a baroque cosmology unrivaled even today for its scope and complexity: a millennia spanning Future History, logically outlandish and elegantly strange, set against a vivid, richly colored, mythically intense universe where animals assume the shape of men, vast planoform ships whisper through multidimensional space, immense sick sheep are the most valuable objects in the universe, immortality can be bought, and the mysterious Lords of the Instrumentality rule a hunted Earth too old for history. . . .*

It is a cosmology that looks as evocative and bizarre today in the 1990s as it did in the 1960s—certainly for sheer sweep and daring of conceptualization, in its vision of how different and strange the future will be, it rivals any contemporary vision conjured up by Young Turks such as Bruce Sterling and Greg Bear, and I suspect that it is timeless.

In the famous story that follows, Smith shows us a future so ultracivilized and overcontrolled and unshakably placid, so utterly safe and predictable in every possible way, that the only way that can be found to make the inhabitants really human again is to give up all that control and let Chaos and Old Night back into the world again—but, of course, once you do that, you then have to deal with the consequences, no matter where they lead you. . . .

Cordwainer Smith's books include the novel Norstrilia *and the collections* Space Lords—*one of the landmark collections of the genre*—The Best of Cordwainer Smith, Quest of the Three Worlds, Stardreamer, You Will Never Be the Same, *and* The Instrumentality of Mankind. *Under the name Felix C. Forrest he published two mainstream novels,* Ria *and* Carola, *and under the name Carmichael Smith, he published the thriller* Atomsk.

His most recent book is the posthumous collection The Rediscovery of Man: The Complete Short Science Fiction of Cordwainer Smith *(NESFA Press, P.O. Box 809, Framingham, MA 07101-0203, $24.95), a huge book that collects almost all of his short fiction and will certainly stand as one of the very best collections of the decade—a book that belongs in every complete SF collection.*

We were drunk with happiness in those early years. Everybody was, especially the young people. These were the first years of the Rediscovery of Man, when the Instrumentality dug deep in the treasury, reconstructing the old cultures, the old languages, and even the old troubles. The nightmare of perfection had taken our forefathers to the edge of suicide. Now under the leadership of the Lord Jestocost and the Lady Alice More, the ancient civilizations were rising like great land masses out of the sea of the past.

I myself was the first man to put a postage stamp on a letter, after fourteen thousand years. I took Virginia to hear the first piano recital. We watched at the eye-machine when cholera was released in Tasmania, and we saw the Tasmanians dancing in the streets, now that they did not have to be protected any more. Everywhere, things became exciting. Everywhere, men and women worked with a wild will to build a more imperfect world.

I myself went into a hospital and came out French. Of course I remembered my early life; I remembered *it*, but it did not matter. Viginia was French, too, and we had the years of our future lying ahead of us like ripe fruit hanging in an orchard of perpetual summers. We had no idea when we would die. Formerly, I would be able to go to bed and think, "The government has given me four hundred years. Three hundred and seventy-four years from now, they will stop the stroon injections and I will then die." Now I knew anything could happen. The safety devices had been turned off. The diseases ran free. With luck, and hope, and love, I might live a thousand years. Or I might die tomorrow. I was free.

We revelled in every moment of the day.

Virginia and I brought the first French newspaper to appear since the Most Ancient World fell. We found delight in the news, even in the advertisements. Some parts of the culture were hard to reconstruct. It was difficult to talk about foods of which only the names survived but the homunculi and the machines, working tirelessly in Downdeep-downdeep, kept the surface of the world filled with enough novelties to fill anyone's heart with hope. We knew that all of this was make-believe, and yet it was not. We knew that when the diseases had killed the statistically correct number of people, they would be turned off; when the accident rate rose too high, it would stop without our knowing why. We knew that over us all, the Instrumentality watched. We had confidence that the Lord Jestocost and the Lady Alice More would play with us as friends and not use us as victims of a game.

Take for example, Virginia. She had been called Menerima, which represented the coded sounds of her birth number. She was small, verging on chubby; she was compact; her head was covered with tight brown curls: her eyes were a brown so deep and so rich that it took sunlight, with her squinting against it, to bring forth the treasures of her irises. I had known her well, but never known her. I had seen her often, but never seen her with my heart, until we met just outside the hospital, after becoming French.

I was pleased to see an old friend and started to speak in the Old

Common Tongue, but the words jammed, and as I tried to speak it was not Menerima any longer, but someone of ancient beauty, rare and strange—someone who had wandered into these latter days from the treasure worlds of time past. All I could do was to stammer:

"What do you call yourself now?" And I said it in ancient French.

She answered in the same language, "Je m'appelle Virginie."

Looking at her and falling in love was a single process. There was something strong, something wild in her, wrapped and hidden by the tenderness and youth of her girlish body. It was as though destiny spoke to me out of the certain brown eyes, eyes which questioned me surely and wonderingly, just as we both questioned the fresh new world which lay about us.

"May I?" said I, offering her my arm, as I had learned in the hours of hypnopedia. She took my arm and we walked away from the hospital.

I hummed a tune which had come into my mind, along with the ancient French language.

She tugged gently on my arm, and smiled up at me.

"What is it," she asked, "or don't you know?"

The words came soft and unbidden to my lips and I sang it very quietly, muting my voice in her curly hair, half-singing half-whispering the popular song which had poured into my mind with all the other things which the Rediscovery of Man had given me:

> "She wasn't the woman I went to seek.
> I met her by the merest chance.
> She did not speak the French of France,
> But the surded French of Martinique.
>
> She wasn't rich. She wasn't chic.
> She had a most entrancing glance,
> And that was all . . . "

Suddenly I ran out of words, "I seem to have forgotten the rest of it. It's called 'Macouba' and it has something to do with a wonderful island which the ancient French called Martinique."

"I know where that is," she cried. She had been given the same memories that I had. "You can see it from Earthport!"

This was a sudden return to the world we had known. Earthport stood on its single pedestal, twelve miles high, at the eastern edge of the small continent. At the top of it, the lords worked amid machines which had no meaning any more. There the ships whispered their way in from the stars. I had seen pictures of it, but I had never been there. As a matter of fact, I had never known anyone who had actually been up Earthport. Why should we have gone? We might not have been welcome, and we could always see it just as well through the pictures on the eye-machine. For Menerima—familiar, dully pleasant, dear little Menerima—to have gone there was uncanny. It made me think that in the Old Perfect World things had not been as plain or forthright as they seemed.

Virginia, the new Menerima, tried to speak in the Old Common Tongue, but she gave up and used French instead:

"My aunt," she said, meaning a kindred lady, since no one had had aunts for thousands of years, "was a Believer. She took me to the Abba-dingo. To get holiness and luck."

The old me was a little shocked; the French me was disquieted by the fact that this girl had done something unusual even before mankind itself turned to the unusual. The Abba-dingo was a long-obsolete computer set partway up the column of Earthport. The homunculi treated it as a god, and occasionally people went to it. To do so was tedious and vulgar.

Or had been. Till all things became new again.

Keeping the annoyance out of my voice, I asked her:

"What was it like?"

She laughed lightly, yet there was a trill to her laughter which gave me a shiver. If the old Menerima had had secrets, what might the new Virginia do? I almost hated the fate which made me love her, which made me feel that the touch of her hand on my arm was a link between me and time-forever.

She smiled at me instead of answering my question. The surfaceway was under repair; we followed a ramp down to the level of the top underground, where it was legal for true persons and hominids and homunculi to walk.

I did not like the feeling; I had never gone more than twenty minutes' trip from my birthplace. This ramp looked safe enough. There were few hominids around these days, men from the stars who (though of true human stock) had been changed to fit the conditions of a thousand worlds. The homunculi were morally repulsive, though many of them looked like very handsome people; bred from animals into the shape of men, they took over the tedious chores of working with machines where no real man would wish to go. It was whispered that some of them had even bred with actual people, and I would not want my Virginia to be exposed to the presence of such a creature.

She had been holding my arm. When we walked down the ramp to the busy passage, I slipped my arm free and put it over her shoulders, drawing her closer to me. It was light enough, bright enough to be clearer than the daylight which we had left behind, but it was strange and full of danger. In the old days, I would have turned around and gone home rather than to expose myself to the presence of such dreadful beings. At this time, in this moment, I could not bear to part from my newfound love, and I was afraid that if I went back to my own apartment in the tower, she might go to hers. Anyhow, being French gave a spice to danger.

Actually, the people in the traffic looked commonplace enough. There were many busy machines, some in human form and some not. I did not see a single hominid. Other people, whom I knew to be homunculi because they yielded the right of way to us, looked no different from the real human beings on the surface. A brilliantly beautiful girl gave me a look which I did not like—saucy, intelligent, provocative beyond all limits

of flirtation. I suspected her of being a dog by origin. Among the homunculi, d'persons are the ones most apt to take liberties. They even have
a dog-man philosopher who once produced a tape arguing that since dogs
are the most ancient of men's allies, they have the right to be closer to
man than any other form of life. When I saw the tape, I thought it amusing that a dog should be bred into the form of a Socrates; here, in the
top underground, I was not so sure at all. What would I do if one of
them became insolent? Kill him? That meant a brush with the law and a
talk with the subcommissioners of the Instrumentality.

Virginia noticed none of this.

She had not answered my question, but was asking me questions about
the top underground instead. I had been there only once before, when I
was small, but it was flattering to have her wondering, husky voice murmuring in my ear.

Then it happened.

At first I thought he was a man, foreshortened by some trick of the
underground light. When he came closer, I saw that it was not. He must
have been five feet across the shoulders. Ugly red scars on his forehead
showed where the horns had been dug out of his skull. He was a hu-
munculus, obviously derived from cattle stock. Frankly, I had never
known that they left them that ill-formed.

And he was drunk.

As he came closer I could pick up the buzz of his mind. . . . *they're not
people, they're not hominids, and they're not Us—what are they doing here?
The words they think confuse me.* He had never telepathed French before.

This was bad. For him to talk was common enough, but only a few of
the homunculi were telepathic—those with special jobs, such as in the
Downdeep-downdeep, where only telepathy could relay instructions.

Virginia clung to me.

Thought I, in clear Common Tongue: *True men are we. You must let
us pass.*

There was no answer but a roar. I do not know where he got drunk,
or on what, but he did not get my message.

I could see his thoughts forming up into panic, helplessness, hate.
Then he charged, almost dancing toward us, as though he could crush
our bodies.

My mind focused and I threw the stop order at him.

It did not work.

Horror-stricken, I realized that I had thought French at him.

Virginia screamed.

The bull-man was upon us.

At the last moment he swerved, passed us blindly, and let out a roar
which filled the enormous passage. He had raced beyond us.

Still holding Virginia, I turned around to see what had made him
pass us.

What I beheld was odd in the extreme.

Our figures ran down the corridor away from us—my black-purple
cloak flying in the still air as my image ran, Virginia's golden dress swim-

ming out behind her as she ran with me. The images were perfect and the bull-man pursued them.

I stared around in bewilderment. We had been told that the safeguards no longer protected us.

A girl stood quietly next to the wall. I had almost mistaken her for a statue. Then she spoke,

"Come no closer. I am a cat. It was easy enough to fool him. You had better get back to the surface."

"Thank you," I said, "thank you. What is your name?"

"Does it matter?" said the girl. "I'm not a person."

A little offended, I insisted, "I just wanted to thank you." As I spoke to her I saw that she was as beautiful and as bright as a flame. Her skin was clear, the color of cream, and her hair—finer than any human hair could possibly be—was the wild golden orange of a Persian cat.

"I'm C'mell," said the girl, "and I work at Earthport."

That stopped both Virginia and me. Cat-people were below us, and should be shunned, but Earthport was above us, and had to be respected. Which was C'mell?

She smiled, and her smile was better suited for my eyes than for Virginia's. It spoke a whole world of voluptous knowledge. I knew she wasn't trying to do anything to me; the rest of her manner showed that. Perhaps it was the only smile she knew.

"Don't worry," she said, "about the formalities. You'd better take these steps here. I hear him coming back."

I spun around, looking for the drunken bull-man. He was not to be seen.

"Go up here," urged C'mell, "They are emergency steps and you will be back on the surface. I can keep him from following. Was that French you were speaking?"

"Yes," said I. "How did you—?"

"Get along," she said. "Sorry I asked. Hurry!"

I entered the small door. A spiral staircase went to the surface. It was below our dignity as true people to use steps, but with C'mell urging me, there was nothing else I could do. I nodded goodbye to C'mell and drew Virginia after me up the stairs.

At the surface we stopped.

Virginia gasped, "Wasn't it horrible?"

"We're safe now," said I.

"It's not safety," she said. "It's the dirtiness of it. Imagine having to talk to her!"

Virginia meant that C'mell was worse than the drunken bull-man. She sensed my reserve because she said,

"The sad thing is, you'll see her again . . ."

"What! How do you know that?"

"I don't know it," said Virginia. "I guess it. But I guess good, very good. After all, I went to the Abba-dingo."

"I asked you, darling, to tell me what happened there."

She shook her head mutely and began walking down the streetway. I had no choice but to follow her. It made me a little irritable.

I asked again, more crossly, "What was it like?"

With hurt girlish dignity she said, "Nothing, nothing. It was a long climb. The old woman made me go with her. It turned out that the machine was not talking that day, anyhow, so we got permission to drop down a shaft and to come back on the rolling road. It was just a wasted day."

She had been talking straight ahead, not to me, as though the memory were a little ugly.

Then she turned her face to me. The brown eyes looked into my eyes as though she were searching for my soul. (Soul. There's a word we have in French, and there is nothing quite like it in the Old Common Tongue.) She brightened and pleaded with me:

"Let's not be dull on the new day. Let's be good to the new us, Paul. Let's do something really French, if that's what we are to be."

"A café," I cried. "We need a café. And I know where one is."

"Where?"

"Two undergrounds over. Where the machines come out and where they permit the homunculi to peer in the window." The thought of homunculi peering at us struck the new me as amusing, though the old me had taken them as much for granted as windows or tables. The old me never met any, but knew that they weren't exactly people, since they were bred from animals, but they looked just about like people, and they could talk. It took a Frenchman like the new me to realize that they could be ugly, or beautiful, or picturesque. More than picturesque: romantic.

Evidently Virginia now thought the same, for she said, "But they're *nette*, just adorable. What is the café called?"

"The Greasy Cat," said I.

The Greasy Cat. How was I to know that this led to a nightmare between high waters, and to the winds which cried? How was I to suppose that this had anything to do with Alpha Ralpha Boulevard?

No force in the world could have taken me there, if I had known.

Other new-French people had gotten to the café before us.

A waiter with a big brown moustache took our order. I looked closely at him to see if he might be a licensed homunculus, allowed to work among people because his services were indispensable; but he was not. He was pure machine, though his voice rang out with old-Parisian heartiness, and the designers had even built into him the nervous habit of mopping the back of his hand against his big moustache, and had fixed him so that little beads of sweat showed high up on his brow, just below the hairline.

"Mamselle? M'sieu? Beer? Coffee? Red wine next month. The sun will shine in the quarter after the hour and after the half-hour. At twenty minutes to the hour it will rain for five minutes so that you can enjoy these umbrellas. I am a native of Alsace. You may speak French or German to me."

"Anything," said Virginia. "You decide, Paul."

"Beer, please," said I. "Blonde beer for both of us."

"But certainly, M'sieu," said the waiter.

He left, waving his cloth wildly over his arm.

Virginia puckered up her eyes against the sun and said, "I wish it would rain now. I've never seen real rain."

"Be patient, honey."

She turned earnestly to me. "What is 'German,' Paul?"

"Another language, another culture. I read they will bring it to life next year. But don't you like being French?"

"I like it fine," she said. "Much better than being a number. But Paul—" And then she stopped, her eyes blurred with perplexity.

"Yes, darling?"

"Paul," she said, and the statement of my name was a cry of hope from some depth of her mind beyond new me, beyond old me, beyond even the contrivances of the lords who moulded us. I reached for her hand.

Said I, "You can tell me, darling."

"Paul," she said, and it was almost weeping, "Paul, why does it all happen so fast? This is our first day, and we both feel that we may spend the rest of our lives together. There's something about marriage, whatever that is, and we're supposed to find a priest, and I don't understand that, either. Paul, Paul, Paul, why does it happen so fast? I want to love you. I do love you. But I don't want to be *made* to love you. I want it to be the real me," and as she spoke, tears poured from her eyes though her voice remained steady enough.

Then it was that I said the wrong thing.

"You don't have to worry, honey. I'm sure that the lords of the Instrumentality have programmed everything well."

At that, she burst into tears, loudly and uncontrollably. I had never seen an adult weep before. It was strange and frightening.

A man from the next table came over and stood beside me, but I did not so much as glance at him.

"Darling," said I, reasonably, "darling, we can work it out—"

"Paul, let me leave you, so that I may be yours. Let me go away for a few days or a few weeks or a few years. Then, if—if—if I *do* come back, you'll know it's me and not some program ordered by a machine. For God's sake. Paul—for God's sake!" In a different voice she said, "What is God, Paul? They gave us the words to speak, but I do not know what they mean."

The man beside me spoke. "I can take you to God," he said.

"Who are you?" said I. "And who asked you to interfere?" This was not the kind of language that we had ever used when speaking the Old Common Tongue—when they had given us a new language they had built in temperament as well.

The stranger kept his politeness—he was as French as we but he kept his temper well.

"My name," he said, "is Maximilien Macht, and I used to be a Believer."

Virginia's eyes lit up. She wiped her face absentmindedly while staring at the man. He was tall, lean, sunburned. (How could he have gotten sunburned so soon?) He had reddish hair and a moustache almost like that of the robot waiter.

"You asked about God, Mamselle," said the stranger. "God is where he has always been—around us, near us, in us."

This was strange talk from a man who looked worldly. I rose to my feet to bid him goodbye. Virginia guessed what I was doing and she said:

"That's nice of you, Paul. Give him a chair."

There was warmth in her voice.

The machine waiter came back with two conical beakers made of glass. They had a golden fluid in them with a cap of foam on top. I had never seen or heard of beer before, but I knew exactly how it would taste. I put imaginary money on the tray, received imaginary change, paid the waiter an imaginary tip. The Instrumentality had not yet figured out how to have separate kinds of money for all the new cultures, and of course you could not use real money to pay for food or drink. Food and drink are free.

The machine wiped his moustache, used his serviette (checked red and white) to dab the sweat off his brow, and then looked inquiringly at Monsieur Macht.

"M'sieu, you will sit here?"

"Indeed," said Macht.

"Shall I serve you here?"

"But why not?" said Macht. "If these good people permit."

"Very well," said the machine, wiping his moustache with the back of his hand. He fled to the dark recesses of the bar.

All this time Virginia had not taken her eyes off Macht.

"You are a Believer?" she asked. "You are still a Believer, when you have been made French like us? How do you know you're you? Why do I love Paul? Are the lords and their machines controlling everything in us? I want to be *me*. Do you know how to be *me*?"

"Not you, Mamselle," said Macht, "that would be too great an honor. But I am learning how to be myself. You see," he added, turning to me, "I have been French for two weeks now, and I know how much of me is myself, and how much has been added by this new process of giving us language and danger again."

The waiter came back with a small beaker. It stood on a stem, so that it looked like an evil little miniature of Earthport. The fluid it contained was milky white.

Macht lifted his glass to us. "Your health!"

Virginia stared at him as if she were going to cry again. When he and I sipped, she blew her nose and put her handkerchief away. It was the first time I had ever seen a person perform that act of blowing the nose, but it seemed to go well with our new culture.

Macht smiled at both of us, as if he were going to begin a speech. The sun came out, right on time. It gave him a halo, and made him look like a devil or a saint.

But it was Virginia who spoke first.

"You have been there?"

Macht raised his eyebrows a little, frowned, and said, "Yes," very quietly.

"Did you get a word?" she persisted.

"Yes." He looked glum, and a little troubled.

"What did it say?"

For answer, he shook his head at her, as if there were things which should never be mentioned in public.

I wanted to break in, to find out what this was all about.

Virginia went on, heeding me not at all: "But it did say something!"

"Yes," said Macht.

"Was it important?"

"Mamselle, let us not talk about it."

"We must," she cried. "It's life or death." Her hands were clenched so tightly together that her knuckles showed white. Her beer stood in front of her, untouched, growing warm in the sunlight.

"Very well," said Macht, "you may ask . . . I cannot guarantee to answer."

I controlled myself no longer. "What's all this about?"

Virginia looked at me with scorn, but even her scorn was the scorn of a lover, not the cold remoteness of the past. "Please, Paul, you wouldn't know. Wait a while. What did it say to you, M'sieu Macht?"

"That I, Maximilien Macht, would live or die with a brown-haired girl who was already betrothed." He smiled wrily, "And I do not even quite know what 'betrothed' means."

"We'll find out," said Virginia. "When did it say this?"

"Who is 'it'?" I shouted at them. "For God's sake, what is this all about?"

Macht looked at me and dropped his voice when he spoke: "The Abba-dingo." To her he said, "Last week."

Virginia turned white. "So it does work, it does, it does. Paul darling, it said nothing to me. But it said to my aunt something which I can't ever forget!"

I held her arm firmly and tenderly and tried to look into her eyes, but she looked away. Said I, "What did it say?"

"Paul and Virginia."

"So what?" said I.

I scarcely knew her. Her lips were tense and compressed. She was not angry. It was something different, worse. She was in the grip of tension. I suppose we had not seen that for thousands of years, either. "Paul, seize this simple fact, if you can grasp it. The machine gave that woman our names—but it gave them to her twelve years ago."

Macht stood up so suddenly that his chair fell over, and the waiter began running toward us.

"That settles it." he said. "We're all going back."

"Going where?" I said.

"To the Abba-dingo."

"But why now?" said I; and, "Will it work?" said Virginia, both at the same time.

"It always works," said Macht, "if you go on the northern side."

"How do you get there?" said Virginia.

Macht frowned sadly, "There's only one way. By Alpha Ralpha Boulevard." Virginia stood up. And so did I.

Then, as I rose, I remembered. Alpha Ralpha Boulevard. It was a ruined street hanging in the sky, faint as a vapor trail. It had been a processional highway once, where conquerors came down and tribute went up. But it was ruined, lost in the clouds, closed to mankind for a hundred centuries.

"I know it," said I. "It's ruined."

Macht said nothing, but he stared at me as if I were an outsider . . .

Virginia, very quiet and white of countenance, said, "Come along."

"But why?" said I. "Why?"

"You fool," she said, "if we don't have a God, at least we have a machine. This is the only thing left on or off the world which the Instrumentality doesn't understand. Maybe it tells the future. Maybe it's an un-machine. It certainly comes from a different time. Can't you use it, darling? If it says we're us, we're *us.*"

"And if it doesn't?"

"Then we're not." Her face was sullen with grief.

"What do you mean?"

"If we're not us," she said, "we're just toys, dolls, puppets that the lords have written on. You're not you and I'm not me. But if the Abba-dingo, which knew the names Paul and Virginia twelve years before it happened—if the Abba-dingo says that we are us, I don't care if it's a predicting machine or a god or a devil or a what. I don't care, but I'll have the truth."

What could I have answered to that? Macht led, she followed, and I walked third in single file. He left the sunlight of The Greasy Cat; just as we left, a light rain began to fall. The waiter, looking momentarily like the machine that he was, stared straight ahead. We crossed the lip of the underground and went down to the fast expressway.

When we came out, we were in a region of fine homes. All were in ruins. The trees had thrust their way into the buildings. Flowers rioted across the lawn, through the open doors, and blazed in the roofless rooms. Who needed a house in the open, when the population of Earth had dropped so that the cities were commodious and empty?

Once I thought I saw a family of homunculi, including little ones, peering at me as we trudged along the soft gravel road. Maybe the faces I had seen at the edge of the house were fantasies.

Macht said nothing.

Virginia and I held hands as we walked beside him. I could have been happy at this odd excursion, but her hand was tightly clenched in mine. She bit her lower lip from time to time. I knew it mattered to her—she was on a pilgrimage. (A pilgrimage was an ancient walk to some powerful place, very good for body and soul.) I didn't mind going along. In fact, they could not have kept me from coming, once she and Macht decided to leave the café. But I didn't have to take it seriously. Did I?

What did Macht want?

Who was Macht? What thoughts had that mind learned in two short weeks? How had he preceded us into a new world of danger and adventure? I did not trust him. For the first time in my life I felt alone. Always, always, up to now, I had only to think about the Instrumentality and some protector leaped fully armed into my mind. Telepathy guarded against all dangers; healed all hurts, carried each of us forward to the one hundred and forty-six thousand and ninety-seven days which had been allotted us. Now it was different. I did not know this man, and it was on him that I relied, not on the powers which had shielded and protected us.

We turned from the ruined road into an immense boulevard. The pavement was so smooth and unbroken that nothing grew on it, save where the wind and dust had deposited random little pockets of earth.

Macht stopped.

"This is it," he said. "Alpha Ralpha Boulevard."

We fell silent and looked at the causeway of forgotten empires.

To our left the boulevard disappeared in a gentle curve. It led far north of the city in which I had been reared. I knew that there was another city to the north, but I had forgotten its name. Why should I have remembered it? It was sure to be just like my own.

But to the right—

To the right the boulevard rose sharply, like a ramp. It disappeared into the clouds. Just at the edge of the cloud-line there was a hint of disaster. I could not see for sure, but it looked to me as though the whole boulevard had been sheared off by unimaginable forces. Somewhere beyond the clouds there stood the Abba-dingo, the place where all questions were answered . . .

Or so they thought.

Virginia cuddled close to me.

"Let's turn back," said I. "We are city people. We don't know anything about ruins."

"You can if you want to," said Macht. "I was just trying to do you a favor."

We both looked at Virginia.

She looked up at me with those brown eyes. From the eyes there came a plea older than woman or man, older than the human race. I knew what she was going to say before she said it. She was going to say that she *had* to know.

Macht was idly crushing some soft rocks near his foot.

At last Virginia spoke up: "Paul, I don't want danger for its own sake. But I meant what I said back there. Isn't there a chance that we were *told* to love each other? What sort of a life would it be if our happiness, our own selves, depended on a thread in a machine or on a mechanical voice which spoke to us when we were asleep and learning French? It may be fun to go back to the old world. I guess it is. I know that you give me a kind of happiness which I never even suspected before this day. If it's really us, we have something wonderful, and we ought to know it. But if it isn't—" She burst into sobs.

I wanted to say, "If it isn't, it will seem just the same," but the ominous sulky face of Macht looked at me over Virginia's shoulder as I drew her to me. There was nothing to say.

I held her close.

From beneath Macht's foot there flowed a trickle of blood. The dust drank it up.

"Macht," said I, "are you hurt?"

Virginia turned around, too.

Macht raised his eyebrows at me and said with unconcern, "No. Why?"

"The blood. At your feet."

He glanced down. "Oh, those," he said, "they're nothing. Just the eggs of some kind of an un-bird which does not even fly."

"Stop it!" I shouted telepathically, using the Old Common Tongue. I did not even try to think in our new-learned French.

He stepped back a pace in surprise.

Out of nothing there came to me a message: *thankyou thankyou good-great gohomeplease thankyou goodgreat goaway manbad manbad manbad . . .* Somewhere an animal or bird was warning me against Macht. I thought a casual *thanks* to it and turned my attention to Macht.

He and I stared at each other. Was this what *culture* was? Were we now men? Did freedom always include the freedom to mistrust, to fear, to hate?

I liked him not at all. The words of forgotten crimes came into my mind: *assassination, murder, abduction, insanity, rape, robbery . . .*

We had known none of these things and yet I felt them all.

He spoke evenly to me. We had both been careful to guard our minds against being read telepathically, so that our only means of communication were empathy and French. "It's your idea," he said, most untruthfully, "or at least your lady's . . ."

"Has lying already come into the world," said I, "so that we walk into the clouds for no reason at all?"

"There is a reason," said Macht.

I pushed Virginia gently aside and capped my mind so tightly that the anti-telepathy felt like a headache.

"Macht," said I, and I myself could hear the snarl of an animal in my own voice, "tell me why you have brought us here or I will kill you."

He did not retreat. He faced me, ready for a fight. He said, "Kill? You mean, to make me dead?" but his words did not carry conviction. Neither one of us knew how to fight, but he readied for defense and I for attack.

Underneath my thought shield an animal thought crept in: *goodman goodman take him by the neck no-air he-aaah no-air he-aaah like broken egg . . .*

I took the advice without worrying where it came from. It was simple. I walked over to Macht, reached my hands around his throat and squeezed. He tried to push my hands away. Then he tried to kick me. All I did was hang on to his throat. If I had been a lord or a Go-captain, I might have known about fighting. But I did not, and neither did he.

It ended when a sudden weight dragged at my hands.

Out of surprise, I let go.

Macht had become unconscious. Was that *dead?*

It could not have been, because he sat up. Virginia ran to him. He rubbed his throat and said with a rough voice:

"You should not have done that."

This gave me courage. "Tell me," I spat at him, "tell me why you wanted us to come, or I will do it again."

Macht grinned weakly. He leaned his head against Virginia's arm. "It's fear," he said. "Fear."

"Fear?" I knew the word—*peur*—but not the meaning. Was it some kind of disquiet or animal alarm?

I had been thinking with my mind open; he thought back *yes.*

"But why do you like it?" I asked.

It is delicious, he thought. *It makes me sick and thrilly and alive. It is like strong medicine, almost as good as stroon. I went there before. High up, I had much fear. It was wonderful and bad and good, all at the same time. I lived a thousand years in a single hour. I wanted more of it, but I thought it would be even more exciting with other people.*

"Now I will kill you," said I in French. "You are very—very . . ." I had to look for the word. "You are very evil."

"No," said Virginia, "let him talk."

He thought at me, not bothering with words. *This is what the lords of the Instrumentality never let us have. Fear. Reality. We were born in a stupor and we died in a dream. Even the underpeople, the animals, had more life than we did. The machines did not have fear. That's what we were. Machines who thought they were men. And now we are free.*

He saw the edge of raw, red anger in my mind, and he changed the subject. *I did not lie to you. This is the way to the Abba-dingo. I have been there. It works. On this side, it always works.*

"It works," cried Virginia. "You see he says so. It works! He is telling the truth. Oh, Paul, do let's go on!"

"All right," said I, "we'll go."

I helped him rise. He looked embarrassed, like a man who has shown something of which he is ashamed.

We walked onto the surface of the indestructible boulevard. It was comfortable to the feet.

At the bottom of my mind the little unseen bird or animal babbled its thoughts at me: *goodman goodman make him dead take water take water . . .*

I paid no attention as I walked forward with her and him, Virginia between us. I paid no attention.

I wish I had.

We walked for a long time.

The process was new to us. There was something exhilarating in knowing that no one guarded us, that the air was free air, moving without benefit of weather machines. We saw many birds, and when I thought at them I found their minds startled and opaque; they were natural birds, the like of which I had never seen before. Virginia asked me their names, and I outrageously applied all the bird-names which we had learned in French without knowing whether they were historically right or not.

Maximilien Macht cheered up, too, and he even sang us a song, rather off key, to the effect that we would take the high road and he the low one, but that he would be in Scotland before us. It did not make sense, but the lilt was pleasant. Whenever he got a certain distance ahead of Virginia and me, I made up variations on "Macouba" and sang-whispered the phrases into her pretty ear:

> *"She wasn't the woman I went to seek.*
> *I met her by the merest chance.*
> *She did not speak the French of France,*
> *But the surded French of Martinique."*

We were happy in adventure and freedom, until we became hungry. Then our troubles began.

Virginia stepped up to a lamp-post, struck it lightly with her fist and said, "Feed me." The post should either have opened, serving us a dinner, or else told us where, within the next few hundred yards, food was to be had. It did neither. It did nothing. It must have been broken.

With that, we began to make a game of hitting every single post.

Alpha Ralpha Boulevard had risen about half a kilometer above the surrounding countryside. The wild birds wheeled below us. There was less dust on the pavement, and fewer patches of weeds. The immense road, with no pylons below it, curved like an unsupported ribbon into the clouds.

We wearied of beating posts and there was neither food nor water.

Virginia became fretful: "It won't do any good to go back now. Food is even farther the other way. I do wish you'd brought something."

How should I have thought to carry food? Who ever carries food? Why would they carry it, when it is everywhere? My darling was unreasonable, but she was my darling and I loved her all the more for the sweet imperfections of her temper.

Macht kept tapping pillars, partly to keep out of our fight, and obtained an unexpected result.

At one moment I saw him leaning over to give the pillar of a large lamp the usual hearty but guarded *whop*—in the next instant he yelped like a dog and was sliding uphill at a high rate of speed. I heard him shout something, but could not make out the words, before he disappeared into the clouds ahead.

Virginia looked at me. "Do you want to go back now? Macht is gone. We can say that I got tired."

"Are you serious?"

"Of course, darling."

I laughed, a little angrily. She had insisted that we come, and now she was ready to turn around and give it up, just to please me.

"Never mind," said I. "It can't be far now. Let's go on."

"Paul . . ." She stood close to me. Her brown eyes were troubled, as though she were trying to see all the way into my mind through my eyes. I thought to her, *Do you want to talk this way?*

"No," said she, in French. "I want to say things one at a time. Paul, I do want to go to the Abba-dingo. I need to go. It's the biggest need in my life. But at the same time. I don't want to go. There is something wrong up there. I would rather have you on the wrong terms than not have you at all. Something could happen."

Edgily, I demanded, "Are you getting this 'fear' that Macht was talking about?"

"Oh, no, Paul, not at all. This feeling isn't exciting. It feels like something broken in a machine—"

"Listen!" I interrupted her.

From far ahead, from within the clouds, there came a sound like an animal wailing. There were words in it. It must have been Macht. I thought I heard "take care." When I sought him with my mind, the distance made circles and I got dizzy.

"Let's follow, darling," said I.

"Yes, Paul," said she, and in her voice there was an unfathomable mixture of happiness, resignation, and despair . . .

Before we moved on, I looked carefully at her. She *was* my girl. The sky had turned yellow and the lights were not yet on. In the yellow rich sky her brown curls were tinted with gold, her brown eyes approached the black in their irises, her young and fate-haunted face seemed more meaningful than any other human face I had ever seen.

"You *are* mine," I said.

"Yes, Paul," She answered me and then smiled brightly. "*You* said it! That is doubly nice."

A bird on the railing looked sharply at us and then left. Perhaps he did not approve of human nonsense, so flung himself downward into dark air. I saw him catch himself, far below, and ride lazily on his wings.

"We're not as free as birds, darling," I told Virginia, "but we are freer than people have been for a hundred centuries."

For her answer she hugged my arm and smiled at me.

"And now," I added, "to follow Macht. Put your arms around me and hold me tight. I'll try hitting that post. If we don't get dinner we may get a ride."

I felt her take hold tightly and then I struck the post.

Which post? An instant later the posts were sailing by us in a blur. The ground beneath our feet seemed steady, but we were moving at a fast rate. Even in the service underground I had never seen a roadway as fast as this. Virginia's dress was blowing so hard that it made snapping sounds like the snap of fingers. In no time at all we were in the cloud and out of it again.

A new world surrounded us. The clouds lay below and above. Here and there blue sky shone through. We were steady. The ancient engineers must have devised the walkway cleverly. We rode up, up, up without getting dizzy.

Another cloud.

Then things happened so fast that the telling of them takes longer than the event.

Something dark rushed at me from up ahead. A violent blow hit me in the chest. Only much later did I realize that this was Macht's arm trying to grab me before we went over the edge. Then we went into another cloud. Before I could even speak to Virginia a second blow struck me. The pain was terrible. I had never felt anything like that in all my life. For some reason, Virginia had fallen over me and beyond me. She was pulling at my hands.

I tried to tell her to stop pulling me, because it hurt, but I had no breath. Rather than argue, I tried to do what she wanted. I struggled toward her. Only then did I realize that there was nothing below my feet—no bridge, no jetway, nothing.

I was on the edge of the boulevard, the broken edge of the upper side. There was nothing below me except for some looped cables, and, far underneath them, a tiny ribbon which was either a river or a road.

We had jumped blindly across the great gap and I had fallen just far enough to catch the upper edge of the roadway on my chest.

It did not matter, the pain.

In a moment the doctor-robot would be there to repair me.

A look at Virginia's face reminded me there was no doctor-robot, no world, no Instrumentality, nothing but wind and pain. She was crying. It took a moment for me to hear what she was saying.

"I did it, I did it, darling, are you dead?"

Neither one of us was sure what "dead" meant, because people always went away at their appointed time, but we knew that it meant a cessation of life. I tried to tell her that I was living, but she fluttered over me and kept dragging me farther from the edge of the drop.

I used my hands to push myself into a sitting position.

She knelt beside me and covered my face with kisses.

At last I was able to gasp, "Where's Macht?"

She looked back. "I don't see him."

I tried to look too. Rather than have me struggle, she said, "You stay quiet. I'll look again."

Bravely she walked to the edge of the sheared-off boulevard. She looked over toward the lower side of the gap, peering through the clouds which drifted past us as rapidly as smoke sucked by a ventilator. Then she cried out:

"I see him. He looks so funny. Like an insect in the museum. He is crawling across on the cables."

Struggling to my hands and knees, I neared her and looked too. There he was, a dot moving along a thread, with the birds soaring by beneath him. It looked very unsafe. Perhaps he was getting all the "fear" that he needed to keep himself happy. I did not want that "fear," whatever it was. I wanted food, water, and a doctor-robot.

None of these were here.

I struggled to my feet. Virginia tried to help me but I was standing before she could do more than touch my sleeve.

"Let's go on."

"On?" she said.

"On to the Abba-dingo. There may be friendly machines up there. Here there is nothing but cold and wind, and the lights have not yet gone on."

She frowned. "But Macht . . . ?"

"It will be hours before he gets here. We can come back."

She obeyed.

Once again we went to the left of the boulevard. I told her to squeeze my waist while I struck the pillars, one by one. Surely there must have been a reactivating device for the passengers on the road.

The fourth time, it worked.

Once again the wind whipped our clothing as we raced upward on Alpha Ralpha Boulevard.

We almost fell as the road veered to the left. I caught my balance, only to have it veer the other way.

And then we stopped.

This was the Abba-dingo.

A walkway littered with white objects—knobs and rods and imperfectly formed balls about the size of my head.

Virginia stood beside me, silent.

About the size of my head? I kicked one of the objects aside and then knew, knew for sure, what it was. It was people. The inside parts. I had never seen such things before. And that, that on the ground, must once have been a hand. There were hundreds of such things along the walk.

"Come, Virginia," said I, keeping my voice even, and my thoughts hidden.

She followed without saying a word. She was curious about the things on the ground, but she did not seem to recognize them.

For my part, I was watching the wall.

At last I found them—the little doors of Abba-dingo.

One said METEOROLOGICAL. It was not Old Common Tongue, nor was it French, but it was so close that I knew it had something to do with the behavior of air. I put my hand against the panel of the door. The panel became translucent and ancient writing showed through. There were numbers which meant nothing, words which meant nothing, and then:

Typhoon coming.

My French had not taught me what a "coming" was, but "typhoon" was plainly *typhon*, a major air disturbance. Thought I, *let the weather machines take care of the matter*. It had nothing to do with us.

"That's no help," said I.

"What does it mean?" she said.

"The air will be disturbed."

"Oh," said she. "That couldn't matter to us, could it?"

"Of course not."

I tried the next panel, which said FOOD. When my hand touched the little door, there was an aching creak inside the wall, as though the whole tower retched. The door opened a little bit and a horrible odor came out of it. Then the door closed again.

The third door said HELP and when I touched it nothing happened. Perhaps it was some kind of tax-collecting device from the ancient days. It yielded nothing to my touch. The fourth door was larger and already partly open at the bottom. At the top, the name of the door was PREDICTIONS. Plain enough, that one was, to anyone who knew Old French. The name at the bottom was more mysterious: PUT PAPER HERE it said, and I could not guess what it meant.

I tried telepathy. Nothing happened. The wind whistled past us. Some of the calcium balls and knobs rolled on the pavement. I tried again, trying my utmost for the imprint of long-departed thoughts. A scream entered my mind, a thin long scream which did not sound much like people. That was all.

Perhaps it did upset me. I did not feel "fear," but I was worried about Virginia.

She was staring at the ground.

"Paul," she said, "isn't that a man's coat on the ground among those funny things?"

Once I had seen an ancient X-ray in the museum, so I knew that the coat still surrounded the material which had provided the inner structure of the man. There was no ball there, so that I was quite sure he was *dead*. How could that have happened in the old days? Why did the Instrumentality let it happen? But then, the Instrumentality had always forbidden this side of the tower. Perhaps the violators had met their own punishment in some way I could not fathom.

"Look, Paul," said Virginia. "I can put my hand in."

Before I could stop her, she had thrust her hand into the flat open slot which said PUT PAPER HERE.

She screamed.

Her hand was caught.

I tried to pull at her arm, but it did not move. She began gasping with pain. Suddenly her hand came free.

Clear words were cut into the living skin. I tore my cloak off and wrapped her hand.

As she sobbed beside me I unbandaged her hand. As I did so she saw the words on her skin.

The words said, in clear French: *You will love Paul all your life.*

Virginia let me bandage her hand with my cloak and then she lifted her face to be kissed. "It was worth it," she said; "it was worth all the trouble, Paul. Let's see if we can get down. Now I know."

I kissed her again and said, reassuringly, "You do know, don't you?"

"Of course," she smiled through her tears. "The Instrumentality could not have contrived this. What a clever old machine! Is it a god or a devil, Paul?"

I had not studied those words at that time, so I patted her instead of answering. We turned to leave.

At the last minute I realized that I had not tried PREDICTIONS myself. "Just a moment, darling. Let me tear a little piece off the bandage."

She waited patiently. I tore a piece the size of my hand, and then I picked up one of the ex-person units on the ground. It may have been the front of an arm. I returned to push the cloth into the slot, but when I turned to the door, an enormous bird was sitting there.

I used my hand to push the bird aside, and he cawed at me. He even seemed to threaten me with his cries and his sharp beak. I could not dislodge him.

Then I tried telepathy. *I am a true man. Go away!*

The bird's dim mind flashed back at me nothing but *no-no-no-no-no*!

With that I struck him so hard with my fist that he fluttered to the ground. He righted himself amid the white litter on the pavement and then, opening his wings, he let the wind carry him away.

I pushed in the scrap of cloth, counted to twenty in my mind, and pulled the scrap out.

The words were plain, but they meant nothing: *You will love Virginia twenty-one more minutes.*

Her happy voice, reassured by the prediction but still unsteady from the pain in her written-on hand, came to me as though it were far away. "What does it say, darling?"

Accidentally on purpose, I let the wind take the scrap. It fluttered away like a bird. Virginia saw it go.

"Oh," she cried disappointedly. "We've lost it! What did it say?"

"Just what yours did."

"But what words, Paul? How did it say it?"

With love and heartbreak and perhaps a little "fear," I lied to her and whispered gently.

"It said, 'Paul will always love Virginia.' "

She smiled at me radiantly. Her stocky, full figure stood firmly and happily against the wind. Once again she was the chubby, pretty Menerima whom I had noticed in our block when we both were children. And she was more than that. She was my new-found love in our new-found world. She was my mademoiselle from Martinique. The message was foolish. We had seen from the food-slot that the machine was broken.

"There's no food or water here," said I. Actually, there was a puddle of water near the railing, but it had been blown over the human structural elements on the ground, and I had no heart to drink it.

Virginia was so happy that, despite her wounded hand, her lack of water and her lack of food, she walked vigorously and cheerfully.

Thought I to myself, *Twenty-one minutes. About six hours have passed. If we stay here we face unknown dangers.*

Vigorously we walked downward, down Alpha Ralpha Boulevard. We had met the Abba-dingo and were still "alive." I did not think that I was "dead," but the words had been meaningless so long that it was hard to think them.

The ramp was so steep going down that we pranced like horses. The wind blew into our faces with incredible force. That's what it was, wind, but I looked up the word *vent* only after it was all over.

We never did see the whole tower—just the wall at which the ancient jetway had deposited us. The rest of the tower was hidden by clouds which fluttered like torn rags as they raced past the heavy material.

The sky was red on one side and a dirty yellow on the other.

Big drops of water began to strike at us.

"The weather machines are broken," I shouted to Virginia.

She tried to shout back to me but the wind carried her words away. I repeated what I had said about the weather machines. She nodded happily and warmly, though the wind was by now whipping her hair past her face and the pieces of water which fell from up above were spotting her flame-golden gown. It did not matter. She clung to my arm. Her happy face smiled at me as we stamped downward, bracing ourselves against the decline in the ramp. Her brown eyes were full of confidence and life. She saw me looking at her and she kissed me on the upper arm without losing step. She was my own girl forever, and she knew it.

The water-from-above, which I later knew was actual "rain," came in increasing volume. Suddenly it included birds. A large bird flapped his way vigorously against the whistling air and managed to stand still in front of my face, though his air speed was many leagues per hour. He cawed in my face and then was carried away by the wind. No sooner had that one gone than another bird struck me in the body. I looked down at it but it too was carried away by the racing current of air. All I got was a telepathic echo from its bright blank mind: *no-no-no-no!*

Now what? thought I. A bird's advice is not much to go upon.

Virginia grabbed my arm and stopped.

I too stopped.

The broken edge of Alpha Ralpha Boulevard was just ahead. Ugly yellow clouds swam through the break like poisonous fish hastening on an inexplicable errand.

Virginia was shouting.

I could not hear her, so I leaned down. That way her mouth could almost touch my ear.

"Where is Macht?" she shouted.

Carefully I took her to the left side of the road, where the railing gave us some protection against the heavy racing air, and against the water commingled with it. By now neither of us could see very far. I made her drop to her knees. I got down beside her. The falling water pelted our backs. The light around us had turned to a dark dirty yellow.

We could still see, but we could not see much.

I was willing to sit in the shelter of the railing, but she nudged me. She wanted us to do something about Macht. What anyone could do, that was beyond me. If he had found shelter, he was safe, but if he was out on those cables, the wild pushing air would soon carry him off and then there would be no more Maximilien Macht. He would be "dead" and his interior parts would bleach somewhere on the open ground.

Virginia insisted.

We crept to the edge.

A bird swept in, true as a bullet, aiming for my face. I flinched. A wing touched me. It stung against my cheek like fire. I did not know that feathers were so tough. The birds must all have damaged mental mechanisms, thought I, if they hit people on Alpha Ralpha. That is not the right way to behave toward true people.

At last we reached the edge, crawling on our bellies. I tried to dig the fingernails of my left hand into the stone-like material of the railing, but it was flat, and there was nothing much to hold to, save for the ornamental fluting. My right arm was around Virginia. It hurt me badly to crawl forward that way, because my body was still damaged from the blow against the edge of the road, on the way coming up. When I hesitated, Virginia thrust herself forward.

We saw nothing.

The gloom was around us.

The wind and the water beat at us like fists.

Her gown pulled at her like a dog worrying its master. I wanted to get her back into the shelter of the railing, where we could wait for the air-disturbance to end.

Abruptly, the light shone all around us. It was wild electricity, which the ancients called *lightning*. Later I found that it occurs quite frequently in the areas beyond the reach of the weather machines.

The bright quick light showed us a white face staring at us. He hung on the cables below us. His mouth was open, so he must have been shouting. I shall never know whether the expression on his face showed "fear" or great happiness. It was full of excitement. The bright light went out and I thought that I heard the echo of a call. I reached for his mind telepathically and there was nothing there. Just some dim, obstinate bird thinking at me, *no-no-no-no-no!*

Virginia tightened in my arms. She squirmed around. I shouted at her in French. She could not hear.

Then I called with my mind.

Someone else was there.

Virginia's mind blazed at me, full of revulsion, *The cat girl. She is going to touch me!*

She twisted. My right arm was suddenly empty. I saw the gleam of a golden gown flash over the edge, even in the dim light. I reached with my mind, and I caught her cry:

"Paul, Paul, I love you. Paul . . . help me!"

The thoughts faded as her body dropped.

The someone else was C'mell, whom we had first met in the corridor.

I came to get you both, she thought at me; *not that the birds cared about her.*

What have the birds got to do with it?

You saved them. You saved their young, when the red-topped man was killing them all. All of us have been worried about what you true people would do to us when you were free. We found out. Some of you are bad and kill other kinds of life. Others of you are good and protect life.

Thought I, is that all there is to *good* and *bad?*

Perhaps I should not have left myself off guard. People did not have to understand fighting, but the homunculi did. They were bred amidst battle and they served through troubles. C'mell, cat-girl that she was, caught me on the chin with a pistonlike fist. She had no anesthesia and the only way—cat or no cat—that she could carry me across the cables in the "typhoon" was to have me unconscious and relaxed.

I awakened in my own room. I felt very well indeed. The robot-doctor was there. Said he:

"You've had a shock. I've already reached the subcommissioner of the Instrumentality, and I can erase the memories of the last full day, if you want me to."

His expression was pleasant.

Where was the racing wind? The air falling like stone around us? The water driving where no weather machines controlled it? Where was the golden gown and the wild fear-hungry face of Maximilien Macht?

I thought these things, but the robot-doctor, not being telepathic, caught none of it. I stared hard at him.

"Where," I cried, "is my own true love?"

Robots cannot sneer, but this one attempted to do so. "The naked cat-girl with the blazing hair? She left to get some clothing."

I stared at him.

His fuddy-duddy little machine mind cooked up its own nasty little thoughts, "I must say, sir, you 'free people' change very fast indeed . . ."

Who argues with a machine? It wasn't worth answering him.

But that other machine? Twenty-one minutes. How could that work out? How could it have known? I did not want to argue with that other machine either. It must have been a very powerful left-over machine— perhaps something used in ancient wars. I had no intention of finding out. Some people might call it a god. I call it nothing. I do not need "fear" and I do not propose to go back to Alpha Ralpha Boulevard again.

But hear, oh heart of mine!—how can you ever visit the café again?

C'mell came in and the robot-doctor left.

Day Million

FREDERIK POHL

Here's an ingenious and razor-sharp little story that was decades ahead of its time when originally published and has had an impact on subsequent thinking about the nature of the far future way out of proportion to its length. Many far-future stories, although they may feature societies so many years removed from ours that almost all memory of our civilization may have been lost, show the inhabitants of that far-future society continuing to live much the same sort of day-to-day life, on a basic human level, that we do now—in fact, many far-future stories even have a retro tinge, so that people are shown as getting around on horseback, drinking in torch-lit taverns, staying on straw mats in half-timbered roadside inns, cooking their meals over open campfires, and so forth, much as they might have in the Middle Ages of our own society's past. But "Day Million" challenges all that, instead suggesting that the dweller in the far future might lead a life that's different from our own in every detail, different from anything that's come before in human history . . . that that future dweller, in fact, might be so different from us that we might hardly recognize him as human at all—an insight that will go ringing on down through the eighties and nineties in story after story about the far future, as this very anthology will demonstrate.

*Frederik Pohl broke into the professional SF world in 1939 as the nineteen-year-old editor of two SF magazines (*Astonishing Stories *and* Super Science Stories*) and ever since has been one of the genre's major shaping forces, as writer, editor, and anthologist.*

On the editorial side of the state, Pohl founded science fiction's first continuing original anthology series (the famous Star *series, which lasted from 1953 to 1960), was the editor of the* Galaxy *group of magazines from 1960 to 1969 (during which time he won three consecutive Best Professional Magazine Hugos for* Worlds of If, Galaxy's *sister magazine), and served throughout the mid-seventies as a consulting SF editor for Bantam, where he was responsible for the buying of such novels as Delany's* Dhalgren *and Russ's* The Female Man.

Pohl was science fiction's first important literary agent, and, as such, played a vital role in encouraging publishing houses such as Ballantine to develop the first category SF book lines in the early fifties.

As a writer, Pohl first came to prominence with a series of novels written in collaboration with the late C. M. Kornbluth, including The Space Merchants *(one of the most famous SF novels of the fifties,* Gladiator-at-Law *(a book that comes to seem less and less like a satire every time you turn on your television set),* Search the Sky, *and* Wolfbane *(perhaps the best of the Pohl/Kornbluth novels, and decades ahead of its time in its depiction of humans forced to function as plug-in component parts in an organic alien computer). Pohl was relatively quiet as a writer throughout the last half of the sixties but came strongly out his slump in the early seventies, producing work a quantum jump better than most of his previous solo work. The effect of the sudden appearance of such powerful Pohl stories as "The Gold at the Starbow's End," "The Merchants of Venus," Man Plus (for which he won a Nebula Award), and, most especially, Gateway (for which he won both the Nebula and the Hugo and which is widely regarded as one of the best novels of the seventies) was almost to make it appear as if a totally new writer had made a dramatic debut. Pohl, whose solo work had tended to be somewhat undervalued until then (he was widely—and unfairly—considered to be the junior partner in the Pohl/Kornbluth collaborations and had even been accused of riding on Kornbluth's coattails), was suddenly doing work that placed him at the very forefront of the SF writers of the day . . . and that's where he's stayed, ever since.*

In addition to his editing Hugos (he may be the only person ever to have won the Hugo both as writer and as editor), Frederik Pohl also won a Hugo for a story called "The Meeting" (completed by Pohl from an incomplete Kornbluth draft after Kornbluth's death), the American Book Award, and the French Prix Apollo and in 1993 was honored with the prestigious Grandmaster Nebula Award for Lifetime Achievement. His many other books include the novels A Plague of Pythons, Slave Ship, Jem, Beyond the Blue Event Horizon, Heechee Rendezvous, The Coming of the Quantum Cats, The World at the End of Time, The Gateway Trip, *and* Mining the Oort; *the collections* The Best of Frederik Pohl, The Gold at the Starbow's End, The Years of the City, Critical Mass (in collaboration with Kornbluth), In the Problem Pit, *and* Pohl stars; *a nonfiction book in collaboration with the late Isaac Asimov,* Our Angry Earth; *and an autobiography,* The Way the Future Was. *His most recent books are the novels* O Pioneer!, The Siege of Eternity, *and* The Far Shore of Time.

On this day I want to tell you about, which will be about ten thousand years from now, there were a boy, a girl and a love story.

Now, although I haven't said much so far, none of it is true. The boy was not what you and I would normally think of as a boy, because he was a hundred and eighty-seven years old. Nor was the girl a girl, for other reasons. And the love story did not entail that sublimation of the urge to rape, and concurrent postponement of the instinct to submit, which we at present understand in such matters. You won't care much for this story if you don't grasp these facts at once. If, however, you will make the effort you'll likely enough find it jampacked, chockful and tiptop-crammed with laughter, tears and poignant sentiment which may, or may not, be worthwhile. The reason the girl was not a girl was that she was a boy.

How angrily you recoil from the page! You say, who the hell wants to read about a pair of queers? Calm yourself. Here are no hot-breathing secrets of perversion for the coterie trade. In fact, if you were to see this girl you would not guess that she was in any sense a boy. Breasts, two; reproductive organs, female. Hips, callipygean; face hairless, supra-orbital lobes nonexistent. You would term her female on sight, although it is true that you might wonder just what species she was a female of, being confused by the tail, the silky pelt, and the gill slits behind each ear.

Now you recoil again. Cripes, man, take my word for it. This is a sweet kid, and if you, as a normal male, spent as much as an hour in a room with her you would bend heaven and Earth to get her in the sack. Dora—we will call her that; her "name" was omicron-Dibase seven-group-totter-oot S Doradus 5314, the last part of which is a color specification corresponding to a shade of green—Dora, I say, was feminine, charming and cute. I admit she doesn't sound that way. She was, as you might put it, a dancer. Her art involved qualities of intellection and expertise of a very high order, requiring both tremendous natural capacities and endless practice; it was performed in null-gravity and I can best describe it by saying that it was something like the performance of a contortionist and something like classical ballet, maybe resembling Danilova's dying swan. It was also pretty damned sexy. In a symbolic way, to be sure; but face it, most of the things we call "sexy" are symbolic, you know, except perhaps an exhibitionist's open clothing. On Day Million when Dora danced, the people who saw her panted, and you would too.

About this business of her being a boy. It didn't matter to her audiences that genetically she was a male. It wouldn't matter to you, if you were among them, because you wouldn't know it—not unless you took a biopsy cutting of her flesh and put it under an electron-microscope to find the XY chromosome—and it didn't matter to them because they didn't care. Through techniques which are not only complex but haven't yet been discovered, these people were able to determine a great deal about the aptitudes and easements of babies quite a long time before they were born—at about the second horizon of cell-division, to be exact, when the segmenting egg is becoming a free blastocyst—and then they naturally helped those aptitudes along. Wouldn't we? If we find a child with an aptitude for music we give him a scholarship to Juillard. If they found a child whose aptitudes were for being a woman, they made him one. As sex had long been dissociated from reproduction this was relatively easy to do and caused no trouble, and no, or at least very little, comment.

How much is "very little"? Oh, about as much as would be caused by our own tampering with Divine Will by filling a tooth. Less than would be caused by wearing a hearing aid. Does it still sound awful? Then look closely at the next busty babe you meet and reflect that she may be a Dora, for adults who are genetically male but somatically female are far from unknown even in our own time. An accident of environment in the womb overwhelms the blueprints of heredity. The difference is that with us it happens only by accident and we don't know about it except rarely, after close study; whereas the people of Day Million did it often, on purpose, because they wanted to.

Well, that's enough to tell you about Dora. It would only confuse you to add that she was seven feet tall and smelled of peanut butter. Let us begin our story.

On Day Million, Dora swam out of her house, entered a transportation tube, was sucked briskly to the surface in its flow of water and ejected in its plume of spray to an elastic platform in front of her—ah—call it her rehearsal hall. "Oh, hell!" she cried in pretty confusion, reaching out to catch her balance and finding herself tumbled against a total stranger, whom we will call Don.

They met cute. Don was on his way to have his legs renewed. Love was the farthest thing from his mind. But when, absentmindedly taking a shortcut across the landing platform for submarinites and finding himself drenched, he discovered his arms full of the loveliest girl he had ever seen, he knew at once they were meant for each other. "Will you marry me?" he asked. She said softly, "Wednesday," and the promise was like a caress.

➤

Don was tall, muscular, bronze and exciting. His name was no more Don than Dora's was Dora, but the personal part of it was Adonis in tribute to his vibrant maleness, and so we will call him Don for short. His personality color-code, in angstrom units, was 5290, or only a few degrees bluer than Dora's 5314—a measure of what they had intuitively discovered at first sight: that they possessed many affinities of taste and interest.

I despair of telling you exactly what it was that Don did for a living—I don't mean for the sake of making money, I mean for the sake of giving purpose and meaning to his life, to keep him from going off his nut with boredom—except to say that it involved a lot of traveling. He traveled in interstellar spaceships. In order to make a spaceship go really fast, about thirty-one male and seven genetically female human beings had to do certain things, and Don was one of the thirty-one. Actually, he contemplated options. This involved a lot of exposure to radiation flux—not so much from his own station in the propulsive system as in the spill-over from the next stage, where a genetic female preferred selections, and the sub-nuclear particles making the selections she preferred demolished themselves in a shower of quanta. Well, you don't give a rat's ass for that, but it meant that Don had to be clad at all times in a skin of light, resilient, extremely strong copper-colored metal. I have already mentioned this, but you probably thought I meant he was sunburned.

More than that, he was a cybernetic man. Most of his ruder parts had been long since replaced with mechanisms of vastly more permanence and use. A cadmium centrifuge, not a heart, pumped his blood. His lungs moved only when he wanted to speak out loud, for a cascade of osmotic filters rebreathed oxygen out of his own wastes. In a way, he probably would have looked peculiar to a man from the 20th century, with his glowing eyes and seven-fingered hands. But to himself, and of course to Dora, he looked mighty manly and grand. In the course of his voyages Don had circled Proxima Centauri, Procyon and the puzzling worlds of Mira Ceti; he had carried agricultural templates to the planets of Canopus and brought back warm, witty pets from the pale companion of Aldebaran. Blue-hot or red-cool, he had seen a thousand stars and their ten thousand planets. He had, in fact, been traveling the starlanes, with only brief leaves on Earth, for pushing two centuries. But you don't care about that, either. It is people who make stories, not the circumstances they find themselves in, and you want to hear about these two people. Well, they made it. The great thing they had for each other grew and flowered and burst into fruition on Wednesday, just as Dora had promised. They met at the encoding room, with a couple of well-wishing friends apiece to cheer them on, and while their identities were being taped and stored they smiled and whispered to each other and bore the jokes of their friends with blushing repartee. Then they exchanged their mathematical analogues and went away, Dora to her dwelling beneath the surface of the sea and Don to his ship.

It was an idyll, really. They lived happily ever after—or anyway, until they decided not to bother any more and died.

Of course, they never set eyes on each other again.

◆

Oh, I can see you now, you eaters of charcoal-broiled steak, scratching an incipient bunion with one hand and holding this story with the other, while the stereo plays d'Indy or Monk. You don't believe a word or it, do you? Not for one minute. People wouldn't live like that, you say with a grunt as you get up to put fresh ice in a drink.

And yet there's Dora, hurrying back through the flushing commuter pipes toward her underwater home (she prefers it there; has had herself somatically altered to breathe the stuff). If I tell you with what sweet fulfillment she fits the recorded analogue of Don into the symbol manipulator, hooks herself in and turns herself on . . . if I try to tell you any of that you will simply stare. Or glare; and grumble, what the hell kind of love-making is this? And yet I assure you, friend. I really do assure you that Dora's ecstasies are as creamy and passionate as any of James Bond's lady spies, and one hell of a lot more so than anything you are going to find in "real life." Go ahead, glare and grumble. Dora doesn't care. If she thinks of you at all, her thirty-times-great-great-grandfather, she thinks you're a pretty primordial sort of brute. You are. Why, Dora is farther removed from you than you are from the australopithecines of five thousand centuries ago. You could not swim a second in the strong currents of her life. You don't think progress goes in a straight line, do you? Do you recognize that it is an ascending, accelerating, maybe even exponential curve? It takes hell's own time to get started, but when it goes it goes like a bomb. And you, you Scotch-drinking steak-eater in your relaxacizing chair, you've just barely lighted the primacord of the fuse. What is it now, the six or seven hundred thousandth day after Christ? Dora lives in Day Million. Ten thousand years from now. Her body fats are polyunsaturated, like Crisco. Her wastes are hemodialyzed out of her bloodstream while she sleeps—that means she doesn't have to go to the bathroom. On whim, to pass a slow half-hour, she can command more energy than the entire nation of Portugal can spend today, and use it to launch a weekend satellite or remold a crater on the Moon. She loves Don very much. She keeps his every gesture, mannerism, nuance, touch of hand, thrill of intercourse, passion of kiss stored in symbolic-mathematical form. And when she wants him, all she has to do is turn the machine on and she has him.

And Don, of course, has Dora. Adrift on a sponson city a few hundred yards over her head, or orbiting Arcturus fifty light-years away, Don has only to command his own symbol-manipulator to rescue Dora from the ferrite files and bring her to life for him, and there she is; and rapturously, tirelessly they love all night. Not in the flesh, of course; but then his flesh has been extensively altered and it wouldn't really be much fun. He doesn't need the flesh for pleasure. Genital organs feel nothing. Neither do hands, nor breasts, nor lips; they are only receptors, accepting and transmitting impulses. It is the brain that feels; it is the interpretation of those impulses that make agony or orgasm, and Don's symbol-manipulator gives him the analogue of cuddling, the analogue of kissing, the analogue of wild, ardent hours with the eternal, exquisite and incorruptible analogue of Dora. Or Diane. Or sweet Rose, or laughing Alicia: for to be sure, they have each of them exchanged analogues before, and will again.

Rats, you say, it looks crazy to me. And you—with your aftershave lotion and your little red car, pushing papers across a desk all day and chasing tail all night—tell me, just how the hell do you think you would look to Tiglath-Pileser, say, or Attila the Hun?

Bumberboom

AVRAM DAVIDSON

For many years, the late Avram Davidson was one of the most eloquent and individual voices in science fiction and fantasy, and there were few writers in any
literary field who could match his wit, his erudition, or the stylish elegance of his
prose. Certainly he deserves to be ranked with, at the very least, Collier and Saki
and Thurber and to be included in the same kind of academic anthologies in
which they are taught—and no doubt would be if he had not spent his entire
forty-year career laboring in the obscurity of genre pulp magazines. The fact is
that, at his best, Davidson was simply one of the best short-story writers of modern
times, in any genre.

During his long career, Davidson won the Hugo Award (for that other mad little
classic "Or All the Seas with Oysters," which detailed the sex cycles of coat
hangers and safety pins), the Edgar Award, and the World Fantasy Award, including the prestigious Lifetime Achievement Award. Although all of his novels are
erudite and entertaining and a few are memorable (including one of the most
influential of modern fantasy novels, The Phoenix and the Mirror), Davidson's
talents found their purest expression in his short fiction. He sold his first story in
1954 and by only the next year had written the classic story "The Golem," which
appeared, as much of his output would over the following decades, in The Magazine of Fantasy & Science Fiction . . . a magazine that he edited for several years
in the early sixties. (In some ways, in fact, Davidson can be thought of as the
ideal or archetypical F&SF author, much as critics discussing H. L. Gold's reign
sometimes cite Damon Knight, Alfred Bester, or Theodore Sturgeon as quintes-
sential Galaxy writers, or as L. Sprague De Camp is sometimes cited as the quin-
tessential Unknown writer.) After a silence of several years in the midsixties,
Davidson returned to writing toward the end of that decade, and by the midsev-
enties he was engaged in turning out a long series of stories about the bizarre
exploits of Doctor Engelbert Eszterhazy (later gathered in one of the best fantasy
collections ever published, the marvelous The Adventures of Doctor Eszterhazy)
and another series detailing the strange adventures of Jack Limekiller (inexpli-
cably, as yet uncollected—alas), which represent Davidson at the height of his
considerable powers and must be counted as some of the very finest work produced in the final decades of the century, in any genre.

Davidson's short work has been assembled in landmark collections such as
The Best of Avram Davidson, Or All the Seas with Oysters, The Redward Edward
Papers, What Strange Stars and Shore, Collected Fantasies, and The Adventures
of Doctor Eszterhazy. His novels include Masters of the Maze, Rogue Dragon,
Peregrine: Primus, Rork!, Clash of Star Kings, Vergil in Averno, and a novel written
in collaboration with Grania Davis, Marco Polo and the Sleeping Beauty. Davidson's most recent books are a posthumously released collection of his erudite

and witty essays, Adventures in Unhistory, *and a mammoth retrospective collection,* The Avram Davidson Treasury, *which appeared on just about every critic's list as one of the best collections of 1998.*

Davidson rarely visited the far future, usually preferring little-known regions of our present-day world or obscure and long-forgotten corners of the past (both of which were transmuted in his hands into unique and magical realms all his own, full of ironies, marvels, and wonders no one else but he ever suspected were there), but he does so memorably in the mannered, elegant, lyrical, shrewdly observed, and wryly funny story that follows, a story that takes us into a bizarre future far beyond the Great Gene Shift, to introduce us to a varied and eccentric cast of characters, as well as to that most singular and puissant of objects— Bumberboom.

Along the narrow road, marked a few times with cairns of whitewashed stones, a young man came by with a careful look and a deliberate gait and a something in his budget which went drip-a-drip red. The land showed gardens and fenced fields and flowering fruit trees. The bleating of sheep sounded faintly. The young man's somewhat large mouth became somewhat smaller as he reflected how well such a land might yield . . . and as he wondered who might hold the yield of it.

Around the road's bend he came upon a small house of wood with an old man peering from the door with weepy eyes that gave a sudden start on seeing who it was whose feet-sounds on the road had brought him from his fusty bed. And his scrannel legs shook.

"Fortune favor you, senior," the young man said, showing his empty palms. "I do but seek a chance and place to build a fire to broil the pair of leverets which fortune has sent my way for breakfast."

The old man shook his head and stubble beard. "Leverets, my young, should not be seared on a naked fire. Leverets should be stewed gently in a proper pot with carrots, onions, and a leek and a leaf of laurel, to say the least."

With a sigh and a smile and a shrug, the young man said, "You speak as much to the wit as would my own father, who (I will conceal nothing) is High Man to the Hereditor of Land Qanaras, a land not totally without Fortune's favor, though not the puissant realm it was before the Great Gene Shift. Woe!—and my own name, it is Mallian, son Hazelip."

The old man nodded and bobbled his throat. "This place, to which I make you free, though poor in all but such mere things as pot and fire and garden herbs—this place, I say, is mine. Ronan, it is called, and I am by salutary custom called only 'Ronan's.' To be sure, I have another name, but in view of my age and ill health you will excuse my not pronouncing it, lest some ill-disposed person overhear and use the knowledge to work a malevolence upon me. . . . Yonder is the well at which you may fill the pot. So. So. And who can be ignorant—ahem-hum-hem—of the past and present fame of Land Qanaras, that diligent and canny country in which doubtless flourishes a mastery of medicine of geography, medicine of art and craft, and medicine of magic as well as other forms of healing; who? Enough, enough. Water, my young. The leverets are already dead and need not be drowned."

The stew of young hares was sweet and savory, and Ronan's put his crusts to soak in the juice, remarking that they would do him well for his noonmeal. "Ah ahah!" he said, with a pleasurable eructation. "How much better are hares in the pot with carrots than in the garden with them! And what brings you here, my young"—he sought for a fragment of flesh caught by a rotting tush—"to the small enclave which is this Section, not properly termable a Land, and under the beneficent protection of Themselves, the Kings of the Dwerfs; what? eh? um ahum. . . ." He rolled his rufous and watery eyes swiftly to his guest, then ostentatiously away.

Mallian gave a start, and his hand twitched towards his sling and pouch, none of which totally escaped rheumy old Ronan's, for all his silly miming. "I should have known!" Mallian growled, bringing his thick brown brows together in a scowl. "Those cairns of white stones. . . . It is a Bandy sign, isn't it?"

Now how the old senior rolled his watery eyes up and down and shook his head! "*We* make no use of that pejorative expression, my young! *We* do not call Them 'Bandies,' *No! We* call Them the Kings of the Dwerfs, so." He winked, pouching up one cheek, squeezing out a tear. "And we are grateful for Their benevolences, yes we are." He drew down the corners of his cavernous and hound-lip mouth in a mocking expression. "*Let* the Dwerfs humorously call us 'Stickpins'! But—'Bandy'? Hem! Hem! No sir, that word is not to be used." And he rambled on and on about the Dwerfymen and his loyalty, meanwhile drawing his face into all sorts of mimes and mows which mocked of his words, when there came in from the distance a confused noise, at which he felt silent and harkened, his mouth drooping open and nasty.

It was not until they were outside in the clear day that they could hear the noise resolve into a shouting or a howling and a continuous rumbling and rattling. Old Ronan's began to shake and mumble, keeping very close to his visitor, as though having observed again that this one had large hands and shoulders and was young and seemingly strong. "Fortune forfend that there should be foreign troops in the Section," he quavered. "An outrage not to be born—do I not pay my tax and levy, for all that I'm a Stickpin? Go up a bit, my young, on that hill where I point, and see what is the cause and source of all this unseemly riot—not exposing yourself unduly, but taking pains to spy out everything."

So up Mallian went, spiraling along the hill through the fragrant acacias and the stinking reptilian sumacs, and so to the top, where, through the coppice peering, he could see all these good fenced fat lands and the deep wide grasslands.

But more immediately below and along the road he saw a most unprecedented sight, stood open-mouthed and tugged the coarse bottoms of his bifurcated beard, grunting in astonishment. He turned and, through cupped hands, called once, "*Come up—!*" and turned again to watch further, paying no wit to the querulous pipings and pantings of the ancient.

Up from around the concealing curve of another hill and along what Mallian conceived must be the famed Broad Road which led to and through the whole length of the Erst Marshes came a procession in some ways reminiscent of pilgrim throngs or decimated tribes fleeing famine or pestilence or plunder—men and women and children clad in rags when clad at all, some few afree afoot, some fewer riding, but most of them attached in one way or other to the thing ridden: a thing, immense, of great length, tubular, rather like the most gigantic blow-gun the most inflamed imagination might conceive of, trundling and rumbling along on enormous and metal-shod wheels, the spokes and rims as thick as a man—some of them in harness to which they bent so low that they were horizontal, squatting as though for greater traction—some bowing as though at huge oars, some straining their arms against the rims of the wheels or against the body or butt of the monstrous engine—others pushing with their backs—

This tremendous contrivance rocked and rumbled and shook and rolled on, and all the while its attendance roared and shouted and howled, and the wind shifted and flung the stink of them into Mallian's face. "In Fortune's name, what is it?" he demanded of old Ronan's, extending an arm to pull him up. The senior looked and shrieked and moaned and pressed his cheeks with his palms.

"What is it?" cried Mallian, shaking him.

Ronan's threw out his arms. "Juggernaut!" he screamed. "Juggernaut! Bumberboom!"

All that frightened old Ronan's had to do—indeed, was able to do—was skitter back to his little house and release the pigeon whose arrival in the proper belled cage of its home dove-cote would not only inform the local confederate Dwerf King that something was wrong in his realm but would inform him a fairly close approximation of *where.* Yet the old man refused utterly to perform this small task by himself, would not unhand Mallian at all, and pulled along with him until they were back at the senior's place and the bird released.

"Remain, remain with me, my young," he pleaded, loose tears coursing down his twitching face. "At least until the Sectional Constabulary shall have arrived and set things aright."

But the last thing which Mallian wanted was an interview with a Bandy border-guardsman. He arose and shook his head.

"Stay, stay, do. I have smoked pullets and both black beer and white, strained comb-honey, dried fruits," he began to enumerate the attractions of abiding, but was interrupted in a way he had not fancied to be.

A smile full of teeth parted Mallian's light brown beard. "Good, good. Not bad for one of your priorly announced poverty; well may one envy the rich of this Section. Now—as a reward for my accompanying you back here, to say nothing of the work of topping that mountainous hill to obtain intelligence for you—let you replenish, and quickly! my budget here with as many such smokelings as will fit. Then you may fill the chinks and interstices with the aforesaid dried fruits. No, no, another word not. I am too modest to appreciate the compliments you would pay me by a continued solicitation of my presence. One jug of black beer I may be persuaded to take; the honey I must forego until another occasion. So.

"Fortune favor you, senior Ronan's. One further deed we may do each other. You will not need to inform your Dwerfymen of my presence or passage; I, in turn, will not need to inform them—unless I am stopped by them, of repetitions of the fell name of *Bandy*. Sun shine upon you, and forfend the shadow of the Juggernaut Bumberboom!"

Thus, laughing loudly, he left the ancient as he had first found him, weeping and alarmed, and went on his way. Indeed, he had fully retraced his way to the top of the hill before he realized that he had not asked *the* question. He scowled and fingered his long moustaches, deliberating a return, but finally decided against it. "Such an old queery man would know no medicine of any sort," he assured himself. "Let alone wit of this most vital matter. But I will keep in mind his words about the vaporous device which pumps and drains the Erst Marshes, for—if, indeed, it is not a mere vapor of the senior himself (and how he cozened me out of half a hare; shame!)—for such medicine may well imply the presence of more. Hem, hem, we will see."

The road was riddled and griddled with great ruts from the gigantic gunwheels. Amidst clots of filth lay a man who had unjudiciously interposed his neck between wheel and road, and a child who mewed and yippered at Mallian but made no attempt to walk. Man and child, quick and dead, looked as like as the spit of their mouths—blond hair so pale as to be almost as white as that of the People of the Moon—equally pale, but pale, pale blue of small, small eyes—a sort of squinting blankness of expression—and slack, silly mouths. Idiot father and idiot son, was Mallian's impression. And he wondered how they had come to be with the gun crew. And he went on.

Warm was the day and the beer soon went down swift. Mallian was about to hoist the jug for the last time when he heard a too-well-remembered thudding on the road and looked, quickly, from one to another side for cover. But the land was flat for many arms' lengths on either side of the road. "Curse!" he muttered, and reached with a sigh for sling and stones, when he bethought that he might hide—did he trot fast—behind a certain maple tree.

Mallian trotted, saw the ditch behind the tree, tumbled into it cod over cap, and had just time to right himself and peer out as the *thudthud-thudthud* of hooves came by, and he saw the mounts.

There two of them, fat and hairy barrel-bodied Bandy ponies—a description which would as well have fit the two squat Dwerfymen riders, whose short legs fit the curves of their mounts' sides as though steamed and bent thereto. Large heads, broad backs, beards which would reach to their protruding navels if not whipped away by wind, faces neither grim nor alarmed but intent and determined, the Bandies came at the gallop. The scabbards of their slashers were on their backs, within quick reach of their hands. They looked to neither side nor did they speak; in a moment more they were gone.

➥

But the crossroads, when he came to them, swarmed with people.

"They have taken everything, everything eatable in my house!" a woman wailed, gesturing to the empty shelves revealed by the open doors.

But another cried, " 'Take'? I did not wait for them to *take*—I *gave* them all there was to eat in mine!"

"Wisely done, wisely done!" a man agreed, wiping from his red face a sweat which came from agitation rather than heat. "Food can always be purchased, food is even now growing and grazing—food, in short can be replaced. But how can one replace that destroyed by the destruction sure to be caused if the Crew of Bumberboom were to fire even one shot from their enormous cannon? Surely it would shatter bodies and houses alike!"

And a fourth person, by his look and manner probably someone of some stature in the community, said in a sober tone of voice as he patted the middle front of his well-filled tunic, "All this is very true, but since the community and property of the Section as a whole is threatened, it is not a problem to be entirely dealt with by individuals. Fortunately, as we have seen, our protectors have been alerted. Two of their constables have already passed by and, by now, are doubtless making arrangements with the cannon's Crew. It is equally fortunate," he pointed out, looking around and gathering in the approval of the crowd, "that the demands of the Crew of Bumberboom are so modest . . . that it is only food they seek and not women or power or dominion. Eh ahem? For who could resist in the face of that tremendous and destructive engine!"

Someone else muttered that it might be better for the Crew if their needs were not limited to food alone but included water, soap, and a change of clothing. There were scattered laughs at this. The magnate, however, pursed his lips and drew his face into lines of disproval. "That is as it may be," he said, severely. "The educated person knows that customs differ among different people, and it is not for us to risk offending the Crew of Bumberboom by making gauche comments on such matters. For my part, so long as they withdraw satisfied from the Section, I care not if they ever or never bathe again, eh ahem?"

Clearly he spoke for the majority and the majority slowly began to disperse to go about their other business, confident that the Dwerf agents would deal with the matter which had so excited and upset them. Mallian approached the magnate and saluted him, the latter returning the gesture with an air of mildly surprised condescension. "Whence and whither, strange my young?" he inquired. "And for why?"

Mal sighed. "Ah, senior, your question not only sums up the matter, it places a finger upon the sore center of it. The whence is easily answered: Land Qanaras, a Land afflicted and perplexed. As to whither, I do not yet know, and can say only that I am wandering in search of a medicine which will supply an answer. Which last, I perceive you have already realized, comprises the why. But before I speak of that I would inquire of you concerning a current matter Sympathize with my ignorance and inform me as to what is Bumberboom, or Juggernaut, as I have heard it also denominated, and who its Crew may be."

The magnate's face had shown a conflict between flattery at Mal's compliments and unease at the prospect of being involved in his problems. But the gathering around of a few gaping loungers eager for free diversion decided his mind. "Important matters," he said, importantly, holding up his chin so that his jowls withdrew, "are not to be discussed where every lack-work may gawp and crane at an inoffensive visitor. Come along with me, my young, and I will not scruple to take time away from my many important affairs and inform you."

And, as they walked slowly through the crossroads hamlet, he related to him that Bumberboom was an engine or contrivance of both great size and potency, founded upon the principles of a medicine known only to its Crew. It had the capacity of casting great shots over great distances accompanied (so it was said) by hideous and deadly fires and deadly and hideous noises. Whence it had been derived, when and by whom made, only the Crew itself could say, and they—perhaps naturally enough— would not. "Suffice it that they have the secret of this medicine and that they use it to go whither they will, depending for sustenance upon the inevitable desire of those among whom they wander that they immediately wander elsewhere without giving an exhibition of their powers, which would prove painful in the extreme. Thus, my young, is your question answered.

"As for your problems, hem hem, I greatly regret that my civic and commercial duties do not permit me to indulge in hearing them. I must content myself reluctantly with saying that no Land under the beneficent protection of the Kings of the Dwerfs can be either afflicted or perplexed, and on this note I, alas, must take my leave. Fortune favor you!"

He waddled off briskly towards a showy dwelling-place from which came kitchen smells indicative that at least one household had left the supply of food to the Crew of Bumberboom for the governing powers to deal with.

"Sun shine upon you," Mal said, somewhat glumly, for he had learned very little from the man which he had not already been able to deduce by himself. But as he reflected on the possible uses of Bumberboom it occurred to him that therein it was conceivable lay an answer to his quest and question, though not in any way which he had previously considered.

The hamlet fell away behind him, and as he continued along the famed Broad Road he saw upon its dusty surface the hoofprints of the Dwerfish ponies, and the grooves made by the great wheels of Bumberboom. Slowly he began to smile, and then he quickened his steps and strode briskly along.

The situation at the border was perhaps brittle rather than tense; so occupied with their affairs were those gathered there that they did not observe Mallian approaching. He heard a hoarse babble of voices from farther away and saw the huge muzzle of Bumberboom lifted up from behind a rise of ground. The whitewashed stone cairns marking the dominion of the Dwerfs stood on each side of the road, and beyond them on each side of the road was another symbol consisting of two long wooden beams painted red. Their ends were planted in the ground and they inclined towards each other until for a short space they crisscrossed. The sight of the two Dwerfs brought him to pause a moment and to consider concealment . . . but they were on foot, and their mounts were tethered off at a distance, and moreover their territory clearly came to an end here, although he was not familiar with what new territory might be symbolized by the red beams.

Neither had he before ever seen men like those who stood conversing with the Bandies. They wore not the breeches, shirt, and tunic so common elsewhere, but close-fitting upper garments extending as a sort of hood or cap closely over the scalp and to which a sort of curious simulated ears were attached. And tights of cloth they wore about their loins. These garments had not the rough look of wool nor (it suddenly seemed) the dull look of linen, but they had a mightily attractive smoothness and sheen and glow, and they rippled when even a muscle was moved.

"Oh, we are so infinitely obliged to the Kings of the Dwerfs," one was saying, in a tone which seemed to indicate very little sense of true obligation. Rays of sunlight slanted through the bowering branches of the trees and picked out the emblematics embroidered upon the red tunics of the Dwerfymen. "We are so obliged to them—through their constables of course—" (he bowed and put more expression into the salute than was in his face) "for having sent us this number of greatly desirable guests. And such guests as they are, too!"

And a second said, with a dull and lowering look, "Our appreciation will be conveyed from our Masters to yours, very shortly, have no fears."

One of the Dwerfs said with a shrug, "They would away, as we have told you, and who can hold what will away? Furthermore, who can argue with Bumberboom?"

The other Dwerf, hearing or perhaps subtly feeling the approach of someone behind, glanced back and saw Mal coming. He took his comrade's arm and turned him around. "Hold, Raflin. Do you remember that report?"

Raflin puckered his caterpillar brows and nodded. "I do. And I do believe, Gorlin, that this is one with whom we would speak. Halt, fellow, in the names of the Kings!"

But Mal, skipping nimbly, said, "It is a false report to begin with, and a case of erroneous identification to continue with. Furthermore, the names of your Kings are as nothing to me for I was never their subject, and lastly—"

"Hold! Hold!"

"—lastly," Mal said, lining up beside the stranger-men, "I am not at the present moment any longer in your Section or your Land at all, and accordingly I defy you, Bandy rogues that you are!" And he spraddled his legs in contempt at them.

The Dwerfs grunted their rage and simultaneously began to reach for their slashers and to move forward upon their crook legs, but the guards from the other side of the border took several paces toward them and regarded them with extreme disfavor. They stopped.

"So be it, then," said Raflin, after a moment. "We will not invoke the doctrine of close pursuit. But be assured, Stickpin," he flung the term at unflinching Mallian, "and be assured, you other Stickpins, that we will complain upon you for harboring a malignant, an enemy, a ruffian, fugitive, and recusant, a rapiner and an otherwise offender against our Kings, their Crowns and Staves; and we will demand and, I do not doubt, will obtain his return."

Mallian bracked his tongue and again spraddled his legs.

Said one of the other guards, "Demand, then. It may be you will secure his return—and with him, too, the return of Bumberboom and all its Crew."

The Dwerfs made no reply to this but turned and proceeded to their ponies. One of them, however, whirled around and flung out his hand and forefinger at Mal. "As for you, fellow!" he declared roundly, "were you at all instructed in any wise of medicine of history, you would understand—you would *know*—that the bodily form of the Dwerfs is the original bodily form of all mankind. We have only pity for you who descend out of those misshapen sufferers from the Great Gene Shift." He swung himself about once more and neither of them spoke again. The two stout ponies went trot-a-trot down the road, dust motes rising to dance in the sunbeams.

Mallian turned his head to see the stranger-men regarding him without expression. He thrust his hand into his bosom and withdrew the letter of statements in its pouch. He handed it out . . . to the air, as it were, for none reached to take it. After a moment and in some perplexity he asked, "Does none desire to examine the well-phrased let-pass with which my natal territory—or, to be more precise, its governance—has supplied me?"

With a slight yawn one of them said, and he shook his head, "None of whom I know. . . . Such ceremonies are reserved for those arrived on official purposes, and not for mere proletaries or profugitives."

Stung by such belittling indifference, Mallian exclaimed to the effect that he was indeed on just such purposes arrived. The strangers smiled at him a trifle scornfully. "These pretensions are at the moment and under the circumstances amusing," they said, "but they will not do, barbado; a-no-no, they will not do at all. Those arrived on official purposes unto this Land of Elver State, of which we of the corps of guards are both the internal and the external defense, arrive with proper pomp. They, for one thing, are dressed in garments of serrycloth, as indeed are we, ahem hum. For another, they ride upon smooth-haired horses adorned with many trappings of broideries and burnishments, and so do all their party— which, by definition, is numerous. And for another and the last, though this by no means the least, they come provided with a multitude of rich donatives of which distribution is made to the members of the corps of guards."

Mallian cast down his eyes and gnawed upon his lips. "Nonetheless," he declared, "I have been issued with this letter of statements directing all to let me pass, and the fact of your having made no gesture to prevent my passage at all would not altogether seem to justify my failing to present it. And inasmuch as you desire not to trouble to read it, it would be a pretty courtesy on my part to read it to you. I have oftentimes been commended for my reading voice, and I doubt not but that you gallants of the Elver Guards will desire to do the same, and furthermore, the problem set down herein, which is the high purpose of my journeyings, may so move you as to search among your minds to see if peradventure you know of a medicine which may shed both light and hope thereon."

And he read them the let-pass, or letter of statements, as he had done to the pseudomorphs, and to the People of the Moon.

"Ah, well," said one with a sniffle of his nose, "interesting and absorbing as the beardy one's problem is, and while I doubt not that the medicines of our Masters contains an answer to it—it is no more than the speck of a fly compared to the problem lying over the rise there. Anent which, let us move and consider, for an action of some sort will assuredly be required of our hands."

They proceeded upward and then paused, considering, Mal with them. There had evidently been a house of some sort there below, but it had been unstrategically situated in terms of the attempts of the Crew of Bumberboom to pass with their weapon along the road above it. It had gone off the road, and the marks of its going were eaten into the berm, and before it had either been brought to rest or come to rest of its own accord, it had thoroughly crushed the house—the fragments of which were being now unskillfully transformed into cook-fires. The harnesses hung empty, the guideropes lay ignored upon the ground. The Crew was both at rest and at meat. And, it became at once apparent, at other occupations as well.

"Scandalous!" exclaimed Mallian. "Shocking!"

One of the Elver Guards shrugged. "As well be scandalized or shocked at cats and dogs," he said.

Mal protested. "But dogs and cats are not human—"

The upper lip of the Elver Guard went up further. "Are *those?*" he demanded.

Not overmuch regarding this remark, Mal allowed his mind to run still more over a notion which, in seedling form, had occurred to him before. Cautiously, tentatively, he began to broach the matter. "I have been in some measure too overwhelmed by your kindliness in offering me refuge," he explained, "from those hangmen Dwerfs to express my gratification fully. But—"

"No need, no need," the Elver murmured, scratching his armhole— then, as though only then becoming aware of what he was doing, he stepped back from the berm with a curse and a scowl. "A tetany upon those wittol Swine! They must have fleas as large as mice—if indeed no worse. I am for going away and constructing a steam-lodge and boiling self and habit."

"Do, Naccanath," murmured another Elver. "And when asked how you proceeded to rid the State of this lumbering menace, be prepared to answer, 'I bathed me.' But for praise or commendation, do not be prepared."

The guard Naccanath hesitated, muttered, scratched.

Mallian moved his mouth against the sudden fretful silence. "But now that I am able to take two consecutive breaths free from fear of Bandymen pursuit and am made aware not only of my safety and refuge but of the wisdom of those whose—"

A fight broke out among the Crew below, but was soon settled.

An Elver said, in a faintly dissatisfied tone, "Ah . . . he did but club him. I had thought he might well eat him; it would surprise me not a whit."

And another said, a peevish note in his voice, bruising a blossom under his nose to counteract the noisome taint now rising from below, "Why need they eat each other when all the world rushes to supply them with far less gamy food? In fact"—his face became a sight brighter—"may this not be a possible solution?—videlicet, simply to supply them with a steady ration of victual, thus depriving them of incentive to leave their present location. Denizened right here, they remain under supervision and do no further damage and post no further threat."

Musing a moment, the others then shook their heads. Another said, "They would breed. Durraneth, at a rate which would soon enough make their maintenance a cost not to be considered. Further, experience has shown that nomads do not easily take to denization."

They sighed and sucked their lips and their unhappy breaths caused their smooth garments to ripple and shimmer in a marvelous manner, for which Mallian, nevertheless, had but small eyes.

"—whose tolerance has undoubtedly saved my life," he continued resolutely—and a shade more loudly. The Elver Guards now turned to consider him and his words.

"What is the point of your narration, profugitive?" demanded the one called Durraneth, in his voice a coolness only to be expected in one whose own proposal had just now been considered and dismissed.

Barely had he finished asking his question when a head appeared above the berm, its countenance vacant and filthy, and looked at them openmouthed as they stepped backwards with fastidious precaution. "Cappin?" it inquired. "Cappin Mog?" A bellow from below diverted it so that it turned, released its hold, slid down and away and did not return.

"The point of my narration, gallant Guards Elver, is just this: that I would ask of you a consideration for which I offer to perform a service, thus and thus: inform me kindly where I may inquire of your Masters a medicine to solve the problems of my own Land Qanaras, and in return I will rid you and all the Land of Elver State forever of Bumberboom and its Crew."

The green shade flashed blue as a jay noisily chased another through the trees. Narrowly the guards regarded him. Then Naccanath said, "Seemingly such an agreement would be of benefit to all and of detriment to none. Still, I am moved to inquire—not from suspicion, fie upon such a thought, hem hem, but out of mere curiosity and interest—how do you propose to do this?"

Mallian's fingers stroked the left and then the right tip of his short beard, through which a slight smile peeped deprecatingly. "To reveal this before an agreement has been reached would perhaps be out of keeping with the traditions of negotiating. I point this out, not from suspicion, fie upon the thought, hem hem, but simply because I have been very traditionally reared and do not desire to cast reflection upon my upbringing by departing therefrom even in trifles."

After another silence. Durraneth said, with something like a frown. "Would it be untraditional for you to indicate by which route you intend for yourself and them to depart, and your destination as well?"

Mallian said it would not. Logic, he pointed out, would indicate a departure by the shortest route (other than the one back into the nearlying Section of the Dwerf Kings' dominions) out of Elver State, and to show his perfect good will and trust in the matter he would entreat the advice of the company as to a good route to achieve this purpose—accompanied, perhaps, by a map—and, as for his destination, well:

"I am a hill man by origin, and lonely therefore. Nevertheless there is nought of the hermit in my background or makeup; I admire also the proximity of fair lowlands and goodly towns to which one may conveniently descend to purchase merchandise with the modest yield of the hills. And therefore—"

Durraneth cleared his throat and cast a slant glance at his fellows. "And therefore—inform me if I understand you arightly, Mallian son Hazelip— and therefore you desire information about a place lying outside of Elver State and situated upon a hill overlooking fair lowlands and goodly towns, or perhaps at least one goodly town. Is it so?"

Mal frankly admitted that the conjecture was correct. "At least one goodly town," he murmured, "although two or even three would be better."

➤

The guard-lodge had a stark neatness about it which Mallian, familiar with the companionable disorder of Qanaras and the opulent show of the Dwerfs, found a bit chilling. There were, to be sure, many contrivances visible which seemed both curious and interesting, as well as an entire shelf bearing nought but books, which much impressed him. " 'Where are much books is much medicine,' " he quoted, reverently.

The Elver Guards gave but a nod or two at this and began to spread a table with maps and to converse in low tones among themselves, paying to Mal's thoughtfully-pointed-out observation that it was now high noon and mealtime, inattention which the very best of wills could only call coarse. He therefore did not feel a compunction at devoting himself forthwith to the smoked pullets and dried fruits with which his budget had thoughtfully been filled by old Ronan's. And when the guard Naccanath said, over his shoulder, "Attend hither, profugitive," he replied that he in no wise feared that Elver folk would work him a malignancy via use and medicine of his own and proper name, and therefore he would cheerfully respond to it, which was Mallian, son Hazelip High Man to the Hereditor of Land Qanaras. "But at the moment I eat," he pointed out. He raised his brows and bit and chewed.

➤

The Crewmen's supply had all been eaten to a faretheewell, and they sat or lay about snorting or scratching or simply staring about them as Mal approached. He had come quite near before it occurred to them to stare at him. He was already among them before any of them had made up their minds that he perhaps ought not to be. But it was not until he had begun to make a circuit of the ponderous engine that anything like concern began really to make itself evident. The sight of Bumberboom at close up proved interesting enough even to banish the train of thought caused by the sight of the crew close up. The same near-idiot face repeated over and over again in varying stages of grime, the same snaggle and snarl of pale hair and small, vacant, pale blue eyes—what did it mean?

It scarcely could mean that the same moron Crew which was now attached to Bumberboom had created it in the first place. They could never have fashioned those immense and massy wheels of stout wood reinforced with iron and rimmed with broad iron tires. Never could they have founded that gigantic tube whereon, in the casting, figures of beasts and monsters had been fixed, never have devised that ornate breech in the shape of a bearded face with lips puckered as though whistling, nor the even more ornate and in fact rather frightening face which terminated the great tube's other end, mouth distended into an enormous shout—mouth silent now, but threatening of anything but silence. . . .

Anything but silence now among the Crew, whose disturbance bore more resemblance to a poultry-yard than an anthill, running and squawking—thrice in succession people fell full-tilt against Mallian, but it was certain from their great alarm that it had not been their aim to do so.

And as they trotted about they set up a cry and howl which presently resolved itself in Mallian's ears into the same words, meaningless as yet, which he had heard before from one of them . . . now, however, not as a question, but as an appeal for aid. "Cappin Mog! Cappin Mog! *Cappin Mog!*"

And Mal meanwhile continued his perambulation and examination. The carriage was fitted with large boxes, but these were locked. He was about to make a closer inspection when someone bellowed close by, and at the same moment, something struck him between the shoulder blades. He took a quick step sideways before spinning around, and the sight of his face acted as instant deterrent to the one who had evidently flung the cold and was now doing a sort of angry dance with another cold in his hand. His arms were inordinately long and thickly thewed; chest and trunk were barrel-thick; neck there was none visible, and the broadnosed face was alive with fury.

"Gid 'way!" it shouted, though perhaps with a shade more caution than in its previous bellow. "Gid 'way! Gid oud! Don' touch-a! Killya! Cutcha-troat!"

And the others of the Crew, male and female, taking courage from this couthless champion, began to draw in behind him, shaking their fists.

"Cutcha-troat, tellya! Gid oud! Don't touch-a! Bumberboom! Bumberboom!"

The rabble, highly approving these sentiments, at once began to shout the word most familiar to them: "Bumberboom! Bumberboom! Bumberboom! *Bumberboom! Bumberboom!*"

Mallian stood where he was and let them howl, and by and by they began to tire of it. He had by now become a familiar object to them and, as he neither moved nor spoke nor did anything of further interest, they grew bored with him, and—one by one—he could see some emotion too faint to be wonder, perplexity of a low order, perhaps, begin to overtake them. They did not really know any more why they were there or why they were so loudly engaged. And so, first one by one, and then, as regarded those who were left, all of a sudden, they ceased their commotion and wandered off.

Not so the one who had thrown both turf and threats at Mal. Highly intelligent he was not, but neither was he an utter idiot. He knew that Mal had no business near the great weapon, and he was determined to get him away from it. Regardless of the defection of his Crew he now came a step nearer, hitched up his dissolving breeches, and menaced with his hands.

"Toll ya, gid oud!" he bellowed. "Trow ya down and kill-ya, ya don' gid oud!"

Mal asked, "Who are you?"

A look of astonishment came upon the man's face. He had evidently never been asked the question before, and it was not any doubt as to his identity but a shock that his identity was not universally known which made him go slack.

After a moment he said, "Who my? My Cappin Mog! Is who." And for emphasis shouted, "Mog! Mog! Cappin Mog! Cappin of Bumberboom and alla Crew! Is who—"

Mallian allowed his own face to register an extreme mixture of enlightenment, astonishment, impressment, and self-deprecation. "Oh, *you* are Captain Mog!"

The captain gave an emphatic nod and grunt, patted his stomach, clearly quite pleased with the effect. "My Cappin Mog," he affirmed. "Is who."

"Pardon, senior . . . pardon, Captain. . . ." He bowed and showed his palms. "I did not know, you see. . . ." The man nodded and came close to smirking and in fact emitted a pleased sound which came close enough to being a giggle to be identified as such, grotesque as the sound seemed coming from him. He gazed from side to side and wiped his loose mouth with the back of his bristly paw. And at that, Mallian gave a bound and a jump and sailed forward and upward and kicked him in the side of the head and felled him like a tree.

◕

Some of the Crew observed what happened and their hoots of astonishment brought others back from casual wandering about the vicinity. They formed a rough circle about the two, though it was without either intention of doing so or awareness of the utility thereof. Several of them growled and even shouted at Mallian and bared their dirty teeth and spat. One or two even went so far as to look about for a weapon—but what immediately came to view was an overlooked loaf of bread, and in a moment they were too concerned with an idiot quarrel about it to pursue the audacious gesture.

Mog lay a while on his side, his eyes opened, he frowned, he rolled over on his elbows and gazed at Mallian and at the Crewmen. He smacked his lips tentatively. "Cutcha-troat," he said, but without real passion. Then he raised his rump and so in stages got to his feet. "Gid oud," he repeated. "Killya. . . ." He looked around for some means of accomplishing this, saw nothing save his slack-mouthed followers and the great gun. Toward this he flung up his arms. *"Bumberboom!"* he cried, warningly. *"Bumberboom!"* Goddam sunamabitchen big noise! *Drop-down-dead!"*

His small pale eyes observed approvingly that Mal, apparently convinced by this fearsome threat, had begun to walk away, and he drew back a trifle to let him pass. Whereat Mal repeated his spring and his sally and knocked him down again. This time he remained down a much longer time, and when he next arose, it was not to address himself to Mal at all. He put his hands at his hips and threw back his head and shouted. The words meant nothing of themselves to Mal, but the effect was immediate. The Crewmen left their places in the circle and bent to their positions in the harness and elsewhere. Mog took a deep breath. He cried, "Forehead . . . *harsh!"* They bent, dug in their feet, groaned.

"Bumber*boom!"* they cried.

"Bumber*boom!"* The limber lifted.

"Bumber*boom!"* The trail lifted.

"Bum . . . ber . . . boom!" The ponderous equipage trembled, shifted. The great wheels shivered, dropped dirt and turf. Turned. Turned slowly. But turned.

Bumberboom began to move forward.

"You may stop her here, Captain Mog," Mal said, presently. The man looked at him. "Stop? *Here?"* Mog's face moved, uncertainly. Mal gestured, pointed. Then he gave a slight teeter or two, as though readying himself to jump. Mog crouched, cried out, covered his head with his arms. He shouted, walking backwards. And the cannon's wheels ceased to turn and the crew promptly slipped its harness and lay down in the road like dogs.

•

Elver Guard Naccanath asked, coming forward with his compeers, "You do not propose to leave them there, I trust?"

"Not for any longer than is required for us to settle our indentures. You have an information to give me—or, rather, two; likewise, a map."

Naccanath's thin lips parted in his thin, smooth-shaven face. He unrolled something in his hands. "Attend, then, pro—hem—Mallian son Hazelip High Man to the Hereditor of Land Qanaras. Here is a carto or map which is limned upon strong linen, and we have marked with red a few several places which bear upon this present business. Thus: this border station. This road. Follow my finger, now. . . . This road forks *here* and *here* and *here.* The right of this last one leads to our capital community, wherein our Masters of a surety can medicate your question—

but thither you go not now, for instead you are to follow via the left fork of this first furcation, and this leads, as is clearly delineated, to the Great Rift and all the Land Nor.

"And concerning this same, observe how we have reddled for you a choice of hills, few of which overlook less than a league of fine fat flatland nor fewer than two prosperous trading towns."

Mallian's pursed lips thrust out in concentration between his beard and his moustachioes, he nodded, traced the lines with his brown and furry fingers, so different from the thin pale digit of his present informer, who, asked what sundry of produce and people Land Nor afforded, replied that it was a good yielder of hogs and hides and horses, as well as grain and small timber, but that its people were of a sullen and willful disposition. "Though I do not doubt," he concluded, "that they will be willing enough to trade with you."

"Nor do I," Mallian said, well enough pleased. He reached his hand for the map, but it was not forthcoming. "Come, come, Elver senior," he said, reproachfully; "surely you do not think that even my own keen mind can have committed the carto to memory? Why, unless you relinquish it, neither I nor my newly-gained companions can be sure of finding our way out of Elver State as expeditiously as all of us might wish."

Naccanath rolled the map up and thrust it into a tube of worked leather. "You may be well sure of it," he said, "for guard Durraneth and I will accompany you as far as the Rift. We would think it but ill hospitality," he said, "to do other."

Mallian cleared his throat and avoided eyes. "I am like to be overwhelmed by such high courtesy. But so be it. . . . Captain Mog! *On!*"

He took his seat, with some sullenness, upon the cases fixed by the gun-carriage, and, the procession underway, diverted himself by picking the locks. He found in one nothing but some handfuls of a moldy-powdery substance, and in the other nothing but an ill-made book. With a shrug of his shoulders, he began to turn the dusty pages and to read. Presently he cast a glance, swiftly and suspiciously, at the Elver pair. But they, absorbed in moody thought, spared him no look but rode silently along on their lean horses. He grunted and turned a leaf.

The pothecary in the first town wherein they paused threw up his hands as Mallian entered. "I have no victualry at all to supply you with," he cried, in a trembling and petulant voice. "By reason of lacking either wife or servant-woman, I eat in the cookshops. Moreover, such treacles and comfits as my shelves afford are of a highly bitter and aperient sort, though a measured quantity may never harm you if you are of a costive disposition. . . . But what can these terms mean to him?" he added, in a lower tone, as though to himself. "Is it not known to me, if to none other, that all these cannoneers are as dull of wits as dogs, by virtue of having neither bred nor gendered outside their number for generations? Still, they have the medicine of the deadly noise, and it behooves me to speak dulcetly," he sighed. "What would you, senior?"

"Sixteen and one-half measures of crushed charcoal," said Mallian, "to begin with . . . large measures, the largest you have."

The pothecary's lower lip drooped. "Hem, hem, this would suffice to rid of wind the stomachs of a small army, though to be sure it is a small army which . . ." The apple of his throat bobbed in sudden perceptive terror. "Pay no heed to my previous comments, Master!" he pleaded. "I perceive with utter conviction the falsity of my conjectures. Charcoal— sixteen and one-half large measures. Immediately, Master! Immediately!"

He scurried about from keg to ladle to scales, darting looks of bewilderment at Mallian. Presently he inquired, "And what next is your design, lordling? You say fourteen and a half large measures of sulphur? It will be my delight—nonetheless, may I not point out that sulphur is not in current favor for fumations? Asafoedita is much preferred nowadays as an ingredient to banish the daemons and miasmas, as well—hem! Observe how I fawn contritely for having made the suggestion! Sulphur it shall be. . . ."

The third substance caused him no little concern; he nibbled his mouth and frowned and snuvvled. "Snowy nitrum, Master? Forgive both the poverty of my mind and shop alike, but—Hold! I adjure but myself, Master-Lord! Is not 'snowy nitrum' another name for what is also termed the saline stone, or saltpeter? In one moment I shall have looked into my lexicon. Thus, thus. And my conjecture was correct! Sixty-nine large measures of saltpeter, more correctly denominated 'snowy nitrum' . . . it may well exhaust my supply, but of that, nothing. The drysalters must wait their pickled meats upon a fresh supply, whenever.

"I know not the use nor preparation of this triune of charcoal, sulphur and saltpeter. Shall I triturate it for you with a mortar and pestle?"

"By no means," Mallian said, hastily. "That is . . . hem. Reflection seems demanded here." He pulled a bit on his beard and peeped from under his lashes at the pothecary, a small and bony-browed man of no particular age. There were things which this one was accustomed to doing which Mallian had never done himself; furthermore, he had said a thing which Mallian wished to hear be said again and at more length. The more he considered the more he favored the notion. At last he cleared his throat and spoke.

"Senior pothecary, is yours a trade which might be swiftly sold for a profit?"

The drugsman looked out the open door in a quick and fearful look. He put his dry lips up to Mallian's sun-browned ear. "There is no business to be sold for a profit in Elver State," he hissed. "The taxers lurk like beasts of prey. . . . Why do you ask? There is no business even to be *held* for a profit. Why, lordling mine, do you ask? What is stational commerce to you? You pass through, Master, with your giant thundermaker and you are supplied and you pass on and you pass on. Neither profits nor taxes nor stocks nor sales are matters you need review. . . . *Why do you ask?*"

Indeed, the shop did have a decidedly well-taxed look to it and its meager shelves. Mal was fortunate in having obtained the things he wanted. "The Free Company of Cannoneers—" He caught the open mouth, blank look. "Bumberboom, that is—"

"Oh, aye, Master. Bumberboom."

"—The Free Company of Cannoneers is in need of the services of a responsible and learned man, versed in such medicines as history and, for another example, pothecation. And it thus befalls me to wonder—"

The pothecary genuflected and kissed Mallian's hands and knees. He locked his shop and deposited the keys with the local chirurgeon. And that night whilst the Crew lay deep in snoring and the Elver Guards camped disdainfully apart with heads upon saddles, he and the pothecary spoke long and low together beside a guttering fire, and the coldly indifferent stars pulsed overhead.

"No," said the chymist, whose name was Zembac Pix. "No, Master-Lord, I have made no especial study of the matter. All of my life, Bumberboom—or, as some call it, Juggernaut—has been a byword. Bad mothers frighten bad children with it. One comes across references to it in chronicles. Whence it first came, neither do I nor anyone else know. Nor who first devised it. I was a younger man when first I saw it; most fled in terror or hasted to bring out food, but I tarried as near as I dared. So it was, or so it seemed, that none but I noticed that these fearsome fellows were little better, if better at all, than idiots. This one Mog was not then their captain. I know not what he was named—'twas long ago and my mind has been crammed overfull ever since of drug receipts and tax-demands. Well, hem a hum. But he was not quite an idiot; indeed, I think he was a wit wittier than this one. Let us say a moron, then. And off they trundled, I wondering as they went. Twice more before today have I seen them. And heard of them more than twice. It has been counted a cause for thanks that, unlike other wandering armsmen, they never ravished nor rapted away any women. They took no recruits, either.

"The reason for this gensual clannishness, I cannot say. But its results are plain: No fresh genes have come their way since, aye, hem, who knows when? And whatsoever flaws they had amongst them to start with, such have been multiplied and squared and cubed, to use the tongue of the medicine called mathematic. And thus only idiot habit keeps them going and coming and passing to and fro. And only equally idiot habit keeps the rest of the world afearing them and yielding to them. I cannot say how old this olden book you've found may be—a century at least, I venture. It is not by the gun alone, then, nor by medicine alone, then, that the great noise and destruction comes . . . No. . . . But by these three substances, mixed and moisted and dried and cracked and sieved. By my cod and cullions, this is no small thing you have discovered!"

Mallian spat into the fire. Then he reached out in the dimness and gently took Zembac Pix, the pothecary, by the throat. "You must remember that pronoun," he said softly. He felt the apple of the throat bob up and down. "*I*. Not you. *I*. Not we. *I*. . . . Fortunately Mallian son Hazelip is of a trusting nature." He released his grasp.

"*Fortunately.* . . ." said Pix, in a tremulous whisper.

"I have great plans. Great needs. I can offer great rewards. You, potionman, may become the councillor of the councillors of kings. Therefore be exceedingly virtuous. And exceedingly cautious."

He gazed into the other's eyes, glinted by a single dull-red spot of fire-glow in each. And watched them move as the other nodded.

☙

They stood upon the lip of the cliff. There down beyond lay the Rift, wide and uneven and hummocked here and there; and beyond on the other side the ruins huddled haggardly. Mallian spat stoutly. "It will be no easy crossing," he observed. "Still, I perceive there is a road of sorts, and cross we must. Nevertheless . . ."

He paused so long that Durraneth and Naccanath stirred somewhat restlessly, and the unease communicated itself to the other Elvers who had ridden out from their near-adjacent city to witness both arrival and departure.

"What mean you by *nevertheless?*" Naccanath asked—perhaps still recollecting his flea-bite, he reined his horse up a way apart from Bumberboom and its Crew. The way hither had followed no rigid schedule. The Crew waked to the day when it felt the day full upon it, was by no means immediately prepared for toil, and made up for its swiftness at eating by its almost pythonic requirements for post-digestive rests. Naccanath had urgently hinted for more speed; Mal had—rather less urgently—passed it on to Captain Mog, and Captain Mog had cursed and kicked and cudgeled . . . and gotten a short burst of increased pace . . . for a moment or so. At intervals.

"By *nevertheless,*" Mallian said, rather slowly, "I mean that there is something which we must do before we begin to cross." He issued a loud order to Mog, who issued a louder one. Mog knew nothing of Mallian's quest, nothing of the problem behind Mallian's question. All he knew to the point was that if Mal asked him to do something and he did not do it, he would be kicked in the head. He had tried a number of ways to avoid this, but the only one which ever worked was to obey orders. Quickly.

Slowly, therefore, erratically, Bumberboom began to move around until its great muzzle was pointing toward the Rift. Another order, and the massive gun was unlimbered. Its trail now rested on the ground. Naccanath cleared his throat, looked at Durraneth. Durraneth returned the look.

"What—and I point out the extreme civility with which the question is asked—what is it your intention to have done now, son Hazelip?"

Mal stroked the points of his beard. "It is my intention to fire the gun," he said.

The horsemen backed up a pace or two or three as though they had practiced the movement. "Fire—fire Bumberboom?"

"So some call it. Others, I understand, prefer the name of Juggernaut."

One of the Elvers said, "I have not heard that this has been done at all of late." He cleared his throat twice.

"So much the better for doing it now. The crew wants practice, and no one can object to whatever damage may be done the Rift."

Naccanath said, rather sharply, "The Rift! It is not the Rift which concerns us—we are still on Elver soil, and I consider the possible great damage which may be done thereto . . . including, and this is no small consideration, to us—It would be much better for you to wait until you are already in the Rift."

"No it would not. I desire to calculate a matter called range . . . a matter of arcane medicine which it will henceforth be important for me to know . . . and in particular the trajectory as calculated from an eminence of land, as it might be a cliff or hill."

The Elvers consulted hurriedly together and then requested that Mallian might delay his calculations until they were able to get well away from the site. He frowned, gave a short and slightly impatient nod, and they were off even faster than the two Dwerfymen had gone, the time Mallian had hidden in the ditch.

"They fear the fatal noise," he said to Zembac Pix, with a twisted grin. "It is as well. The less they see, the better so. Well. Down goes the large-grained powder as the book directs. Hold firm the ladle, Zembac Pix. So. So. Smoothly. So." Mallian took the ram and tried to follow the directions so that the powder was securely back where it should be but not so firmly packed that it would not properly ignite. Then, satisfied, he ordered the shot brought forward. Mog and his mates came up with the great round stone, hoisted it . . . dropped it. The man responsible howled for his toes and then howled for his ribs as Mog beat upon them. But it was done at last.

Next the fine powder was laid in a train along the groove to the touch-hole. "What next?" asked Mallian.

Pix looked into the book. "Next is fire," he said. "Captain Mog! A brand of fire!"

The Crewmen seemed unsure of how they should seem. What memories they might hold of actual gunfire must be at many removes and quite dim, muted not by time alone but by the thick membranes of their sluggish minds. They had been bred to the gun, lived by and for the gun, had nought but the great gun at all. Yet they had never fired it, had forgotten how to make its fuel, forgotten perhaps all save some dim glints of recollections of old mumblings and mutterings which served them for history. They were excited. They were uneasy. Something new had come into their brute lives. One of them, who had watched the loading, perhaps spoke for all. "Bumberboom . . . Bumberboom *eat*," he said.

Zembac Pix received the burning stick and said, before handing it to Mal, "Stand carefully as the handbook directs, lest the cannon crush you by its—" But Mallian, impatient, seized the fire and thrust it at the train of powder. It hissed, vanished. Then, with a roar like thunder waging war on thunder, the hideous muzzle-mouth spewed flame and smoke. The gun leaped as though wounded, fell back, subsided. Darkness, thick darkness, evil stench, surrounded them. Gradually, it cleared away. They looked at each other. ". . . recoil," Zembac Pix finished his sentence.

The Crew rose slowly from the ground, idiot faces round with awe and terror and joy. The occasion required words. They found them—or, at least, it. "Bumberboom! *Bum*berboom! *Bumberboom!*" They leaped and lurched and shouted and roared.

"Bumberboom!"

"*Bumberboom!*"
"*Bumberboom!*"

Zembac Pix pointed far out into the Rift. "The shot seems to have scored a trench along that hillock. Ha! Ahem hum-hum!"

"So I see . . . yes. Suppose that were a row of houses. Ha! Ha-ha!"

"Elver houses!"

"Bandy houses!"

"Ha *ha!*"

Something caught their eye. Something gleamed there in the trench now as clouds drifted away and the sun came through—a something which seemed to have slightly deflected the path of the stone shot. They discussed what it might be, agreed that whatever it might be could well go on waiting. "Captain Mog! On!"

"Forehead . . . *harsh!*"

It was a while later that they saw the Elvers descending by another road which allowed them to steer far clear of the great gun and its Crew—a line of Elver horsemen and behind each guard and riding on the crupper, a man with a spade. "Curious," said Mal. "Very curious, Master-Lord," agreed Zembac Pix. But by the time they themselves had gotten close enough to leave the toiling, chanting Crew and go and see, the sight was more than merely curious.

"Observe, Mallian son Hazelip," said Naccanath, in an odd tone and a gesture. "See what sight the monstrous voice of Bumberboom has uncovered."

It was a sight indeed. The hillock had been shoveled and the ground excavated a good way beneath the surface of the general ground-level. There lay revealed the immense figure of an image with upraised arm and with a crown or coronet upon its head from which radiated a series of great spikes at least twice the length of a man. As far as they could see, it was clad in a flowing garment of some strange sort. It was an unfamiliar shade of blue-green which was almost black.

"What is it?" asked Mallian, voice low with awe.

The Elvers shrugged. "Who can say? . . . it seems to be hollow." Thus Naccanath. Durraneth had something else to say.

"Do you recall, Prince of Qanaras," he began—Mallian noted his own promotion in rank but showed nothing on his face—"Do you recall what said the Dwerfy constable? . . . as say they all, of course . . . that before the Great Gene Shift all men were of their dwerfish size?"

Mallian said, "I do recall. What of it?"

Slowly Durraneth said, "This great image is hollow. There are passages within. But the spaces seem exceedingly small. Do you suppose—"

"Do I suppose that this evidences a possible truth to the absurd Bandy boast? Never! As well declare that the gigantic statue demonstrates that the original form of mankind was that of the race of the gigants!"

Durraneth nodded slowly. Then his eyes moved from gigantic statue to gigantic gun and back once more. "I wish . . ." he began. "I wish I knew what it had held in its hand . . ." he said. "Oh, I do not know, of course, that it had held anything in its hand. It has an arm, it must have had a hand. . . . No consequence; it was a mere sudden fancy, of no rational importance."

But Mallian had now a question of his own. He pointed down into the pit, past a fallen tree, to where four Elvers stood regarding the newly-found wonder and a fifth stood upon its face. On the brim stood a box of strange sort, from which wires led down to the body of the statue. "What is that?" he asked.

Durraneth shrugged. "An engine . . . a toy, really. It simulates a magnetical current. Really, it tells us nothing—save only that the entire figure seems to be made of metal. All of it! Incredible. No, I suppose you are correct. About the original stature of man. The matter, I must suppose, remains as before. . . ." For yet another moment he stood there, musing. Then he said, "When you are ready, Prince, to pose your question, we will be ready to serve you in seeking its answer. Do not tarry too long among the morose and barbarous folk of Nor. Fare you well. Fare you well."

◆

The morose and barbarous folk of Nor had for the most part, forewarned by the echoing roar of Bumberboom's sole shot and, further, by the sight of it being toiled across the Trans-Rift Road, fled into the raddled ruins where it was hardly practicable to follow them. They had taken much of their substance with them, but the Crew were experienced foragers; noses keen as dogs', they soon sniffed out food and even sooner devoured it.

Mallian had no desire to go groping about in the ruins after anyone. He consulted the map—Naccanath still held the leathern tube, but Mal held the map, whether Naccanath knew it or not—and consulted Zembac Pix as well. "I would that I had reflected to demand, hem a hum, to request horses of the Elvers. Doubtless they could be trained to pull the gun."

The pothecary's eyes narrowed beneath their bony brows, and he smiled a knowing smile. "Horses will come later," he said. "Horses . . . and many other things. . . ."

Getting Bumberboom up a hill had to come first. After that would come supplies—not hastily proffered or hastily seized to be hastily gobbled, but efficiently levied, to be efficiently distributed. And efficiently consumed? Not all of them. The key word was *surplus*. Surplus of commodity meant trade, which meant wealth and power. One area of farms and towns to start with. Power firmly established there meant a fulcrum firmly established there. And with a fulcrum once established, what might not leverage do?

But haste was not to be indulged in. Leaving Zembac Pix in charge of gun and crew, Mal set off to scout out the land, with a particular emphasis on hills. The first one he came to overlooked, to be sure, fine fat fields and no less than four towns, all of them prosperous, but the roads leading up the hill were too narrow by far to admit of Bumberboom's huge carriage being taken up. Widening would be a matter of months. Not to be thought of. The second hill was easy of access but looked down on one small town only, and that none too favorsome in its appearance. He sighed, pressed on. A third hill was well-located but culminated in a peak of rocky scarps such as could afford abiding-place only to birds. A fourth. . . . A fifth. . . .

Perhaps it was the seventh hill which seemed so ideal in every way but one. There was a slope of mountable angle, the top was both flat and wide, with enough trees to provide shade when desired and yet without interfering with the maneuverability of the great gun. From the summit Mal could see widespread and fruitful fields, and the rooftops of several towns. He had passed by two of them and observed with approbation the signs of good care and productivity, and a third appeared to be large enough to justify an assumption of the same. It was as tempting, as inviting from above as it had seemed from below; therefore, he had surmounted it despite a difficulty exemplified in the mud even now drying on his feet and shanks. There was definitely a current; one could not exactly say that a swamp lay at the foot of the hill athwart the only possible approach, but there was no gravel-bottomed shallow ford, though carefully he looked for one. Mud, sticky, catchy mud—and Bumberboom mired securely was as good as no Bumberboom at all. Mallian sighed and retraced his steps.

There was a man in the water when he came through it again, breeches slung around his shoulder and shirt tucked up shamelessly around his ribs, and he was spearing small fish with a trident. "Fortune favor you," said Mal.

The man said, "Mm."

"Fortune favor you," repeated Mal, a trifle louder, a trifle annoyed.

"We don't say 'Fortune favor you' in these parts."

"Oh? What do you say, then?"

"We say 'Mm.' "

"Oh. Well, then—Mm."

"Mm." And the man speared another small fish, and another, gutted them and strung them. He had set up a small makeshift smokehouse ashore, and now proceeded to deposit his catch therein before returning to securing more.

"You prefer smoked fish to fresh fish?"

"No, I don't," the man said decidedly. "But they keep and fresh ones don't. Be you purblind? Looksee that dried mud yonder side. And nigh side. I catch fish while there be water. Soon there'll be none till the rains."

Mallian wondered that he had not observed this before. "Senior, I thank you," he said sincerely. "Now indulgently inform me what you say in these parts for farewell."

The man peered into the water. "We say 'Mm,' " he answered.

Mal sighed. "Mm."

"Mm," said the fisherman. He scratched his navel and speared another fish.

"What governance have you in these parts?" he inquired of a man leading a pack-horse as he passed through the next town.

"None," said the man. "And wants none. The Land Nor is nongovernanced, by definition."

"I see. I thank you. Mm," said Mal.

"Mm," said the packman.

He accompanied the great gun all the way, but sent Zembac Pix ahead and aside to spread the word that other lands and their rulers—as it might be the Kings of the Dwerfs or the Masters of Elver State—envying the ungovernanced condition of Land Nor, had determined to send armies, troops, spies, and other means of assault thereto, with the intention of establishing a governance over it and over its people. But that the Free Company of Cannoneers, hearing of the daemonical plan, had come unsolicited to the defense of Land Nor with a weapon more utile than a thousand swords, videlicet, the great cannon BUMBERBOOM. Zembac Pix went forth and fro and by and by caught up with Mal and Mog and crew where they were encamped on a threshing-floor.

"Spread you the word?"

"Most diligently, Master-Lord."

"And with what countenance and comments did they receive it?"

The pothecary seemed to hesitate. "For the most part," he said, "without change of countenance and with no other comment than the labial consonant, Mm."

Mal pondered. Then he raised his eyes. "You say, 'For the most part'—"

"A true relation of my statement, Master-Lord. There was an exception, a tiresome and philosophizing man who keeps an hostelry for the distribution of liquor of malt"—here Zembac Pix wet his lips very slightly and made a small smile—"and his comment was to the effect that Land Nor is nongovernanced by definition and it thus follows that Land Nor cannot be governanced inasmuch as according to the laws of logic, a thing is not what it is not but is what it is, and to speak of the governancing of Land Nor is to speak of the moving of the immovable, which is to speak nonsense. And much other words he spoke, but only to recapitulate what he had already spoken."

Mal said nothing, but after a moment he shook his head. Then he rose from the threshing-floor. "Captain Mog! On!"

Captain Mog rose from the threshing-floor. "Forehead—*harsh!*"

The crew rose from the threshing-floor and fell to in its sundry posts and places. "Bumberboom! *Bum*berboom! Bumber*boom!*

"*Bumberboom!*"

The great wheels trembled.

"*Bumberboom!*"

The great wheels moved.

"*Bumberboom!*"

The great wheels turned.

Along the dusty roads it trundled and rumbled. Not in one day did it reach the base of the hill, nor in two, nor three. But by the time it reached it, most of the marshy stream had vanished away, leaving a foundation of good hard, sun-baked mud. Fallen trees were selected and trimmed to act as brakes and props. And when the now-dwindled stream had dwindled to a mere trickle, they began the ascent. They shouted, they chanted, they grunted rhythmically, they howled. They pushed, they pulled, they levered. Now and then they turned a rope around a stout tree; now and then they rested the gun upon the logs and panted and drew breath, then fell to once again. "Bumber*boom!* Bumber*boom!* Bumber*boom!*"

And at last they dragged it up upon the very crown and summit of the hill, wheeled it into the best place of vantage, and unlimbered it. "Now," said Mal, "to compose and distribute a proclamation." Zembac Pix assisted him in the wording of it, which was to the effect that the Free Company of Cannoneers had now commenced the arduous duty of defending Land Nor against alien and hostile forces intent upon establishing a governance over the Land aforesaid. And that in order to compensate the previously denominated Free Company and in order to sustain it subsequently and to guarantee its defensive postures, voluntary contributions according to the schedule subappended would be received. Each town was held responsible for collecting the donatives of its citizens and should any town fail to collect and transport the voluntaries assessed it, this would reveal that it was secretly supporting the tyrannical alien pro-governance plan. Whereat, it would be necessary for the Free Company to bombard the town aforesaid. And herein fail not.

"How shall we sign it?" asked Mal, mightily pleased by the several crisp turns of phrase.

"Might I suggest, Master-Lord, a succinct: *Mallian, General-Commandanting?*"

"Hem a hum. . . . Very good. But . . . do you not recollect how the Elver Guard referred to me as 'Prince'? I do not wish to appear highflown or much-given to elaborate titles. What think you, then, of a simple *Mallian, Prince;* what?"

Zembac Pix nibbled the end of his quill. "Beautifully suggested, Lordling. Subsequently. When they are ready. One must not seem overhumble to commence with."

A breeze wafted up from the terrain below and it conveyed in it a hint of hogs, hides, horses, and others of the rich usufructs of the land. A faint smile played upon Mallian's features. "I allow myself to be persuaded," he said. "So be it. Go now, have copies made, post them in the public places and proclaim it at the cross-roads. You may accompany the first train of tribute, a hum hum, of donative . . . if you wish."

Zembac Pix declared it would be his pleasure. He descended. He ascended. Time had elapsed. "Canting and poxy pothecary!" Mal cried, raging. "Where have you been? And why so long? Where are the voluntaries of food and drink and staples, of steeds and of trade-goods and manufactured articlery? From what Knacker's yard did you steal that wretched beast which mocks the name of horse? Answer! Reply! And give good account, else I will spread you to the off-wheel of Juggernaut and flog you with the traces!"

Zembac Pix descended delicately from the scrap of rug bound with a rope cinch which served him for saddle, and was momentarily seized with a spasmodic contraction of the glottis which impeded his speech and may possibly have been responsible as well for the slight instability of his gait.

And in his arms he tenderly cuddled a firkin containing some sort of liqueous matter.

"Master-Lord," he began, "with the utmost diligence have I carried out every word of your instructions, whether plainly expressed or merely implied. I purchased writing materials, I made clear copies in the most exquisite calligraphy, and I long retained in my possession a specimen the mere sight of which would instantly persuade you; alas, that on returning hither I was with infinite reluctance constrained to employ it for a usage too gross to be named between us—hem hem—though even kings must live by nature.

"Furthermore I posted them in the public places and I proclaimed their message at the cross-roads. Moreover I entered into all places of resort and refreshment in order the more thoroughly to disseminate the matter. Conceive, then, with what incredulous and tearful regret I must report that, far from hastening to contribute to the meritorious support of the Free Company, they merely hastened to confect pellets of wool and wax to stuff into their ears 'to save them,' as they said, 'from the horrid noise and torturesome sound' of Bumberboom. . . . The steed and this firkin of liquor of malt do not represent, Lordling, even one single poor contributor but only my success in a game of skill at which I was constrained to participate, they threatening me with many mischiefs and malignancies should I refuse."

There was a long, long, silence. Then Zembac Pix, sighing deeply, drew from the firkin of liquor a quantity in a leather cup and offered it to Mallian. And in truth it did not smell ill. The breeze played upon the hill; the crewmen dozed or picked for lice; the sun was warm. "To think of such ingratitude," Mal said, after a while. Zembac Pix wept afresh to think of it. They were mildly surprised to find themselves holding to the wheels of the cannon and gazing down upon the reprobate lands below.

"I owe it to my father not to disgrace his name and station by a breach of my word, would you not agree?"

"Utterly, Master-Lord."

"I said that contumacy would merit bombardment." He belched slightly upon the vowels of the last word. "And so it must be."

In this they were in perfect accord, but a slight difference of opinion now arose as to whether the town nearest below lay at a distance of two hundred lengths or at one nearer to three hundred lengths—and also whether the demonstrated distance of Bumberboom's range was as much as three hundred lengths or as little as two hundred lengths. They concluded that it was better to use more force than necessary rather than less than necessary, and they accordingly loaded a charge a third heavier than that used before. Furthermore, on the same principle, they rammed a double shot down the barrel.

"And now for to prime her," said Zembac Pix, giggling slightly.

"Hold," said Mal. "Last time we were too close to witness the moment of ejection. I would witness this act and not have my vision clouded with smoke."

The pothecary nodded and chuckled. "Perfectly do I understand and take your meaning. I shall lay a long powder-trail . . . let me use this length of wood as a gently inclined plane. Excellent, excellent; the powder stays in place and does not slide off! . . . and thus and thus and thus. . . . Ahem hem, I seem to have used up the last of the powder."

His face was so woebegone that Mallian was constrained to laugh. "No matter. No matter. We will make more. Is not the recipe contained in the formulary book? Where is the fire-stick? Here. Ha! Hear it sizzle! So—'morose and barbarous' you have been termed, folk of Nor, and now here is your requition for—"

All the thunders of the sky and the lightnings thereof burst upon them in rolling flashes of fire and smoke. The earth shook like a dying man, and they were instantly thrown upon the quaking ground. Things flew screaming over their heads. They lay deafened and stunned for long moments.

Mallian, presently seeing Zembac Pix's mouth moving, said with a groan, "I cannot hear. I cannot hear."

"I had not spoken. Woe! Mercy! Malignant fates! Where is Bumberboom?"

And the Crew, now picking themselves up from the dirt, with shrieks and wails, began the same question. "Bumberboom? Bumber*boom? Bumberboom?*" But a few fragments of twisted metal and a shattered wheel were all that remained of that great cannon and weapon more utile than a thousand swords. . . .

Mallian felt a sob shake his throat. All his plans, all his efforts, wasted and shattered in a single moment! He fought for and found control. "Age and disuse," he said, "must have corroded the barrel. Never mind. We somehow will contrive to cast another."

Zembac Pix agreed, and said through his tears, "And to prepare more powder. Four and one-half measures of sulphur to thirty-one and a third of—"

"You err. It was of a certainty twenty-five and a fifth of sulphur to six and one eighth of snowy . . . Or was it eleven and one tenth of . . . We must consult the formulary." But of that sole book wherein alone the arcane and secret art of gunnery was delineated, only one scorched bit of page remained, and on it was inscribed the single word *overload*. There was another silence, the longest yet, disturbed only by the idiotic and inconsolable ululations of the Crew.

In a different voice Mallian said, "It is just as well. Clearly the engine represented a mere theorizing, and, as we have plainly seen, is of no practical value whatsoever. What is perhaps more to the point, I observe that the horse is uninjured, and I propose we mount him immediately and proceed by way of the woods to the northern and nearest border of this land of morose and barbarous folk, for I trust not their humors at all."

"Oh, agreed! Agreed, Master-Lord!" declared Zembac Pix, scrambling up behind him. "Only one question more: What of the erstwhile Crew? Should we try to persuade them to follow?"

Mal wheeled the horse around. "I think not," he said. "Soon enough their bellies will bring them down to where the pantries and the bake-ovens of the Nor-folk are. But we will not tarry to witness this droll confrontation. We will, however, think about it. I am of the firm opinion that they deserve one another."

He kicked his heels into the horse's sides and Zembac Pix smote it on the rump. They rode down the hill.

Coranda

KEITH ROBERTS

One of the most powerful talents to enter the field in the last thirty years, Keith Roberts secured an important place in genre history in 1968 with the publication of his classic novel Pavane, *one of the best books of the sixties and certainly one of the best Alternate History novels ever written, rivaled only by books such as L. Sprague De Camp's* Lest Darkness Fall, *Ward Moore's* Bring the Jubilee, *and Philip K. Dick's* The Man in the High Castle. *Trained as an illustrator—he did work extensively as an illustrator and cover artist in the British SF world of the sixties—Roberts made his first sale to* Science Fantasy *in 1964. Later, he would take over the editorship of* Science Fantasy, *by then called* SF Impulse, *as well as providing many of the magazine's striking covers. But his career as an editor was short-lived, and most of his subsequent impact on the field would be as a writer, including the production of some of the very best short stories of the last three decades. Robert's other books include the novels* The Chalk Giants, The Furies, The Inner Wheel, Molly Zero, Grainne, Kiteworld, *and* The Boat of Fate, *one of the finest historical novels of the seventies. His short work can be found in the collections* Machines and Men, The Grain Kings, The Passing of the Dragons, Ladies from Hell, The Lordly Ones, Winterwood and Other Hauntings, *and* Kaeti on Tour. *His most recent book is an autobiography,* Lemady: Episodes of a Writer's Life.*

Roberts has visited the far future in other works, notably in the stories that went into making up The Chalk Giants *and* Kiteworld. *The story that first came to mind when I was assembling this anthology, though, is the tense and darkly lyrical tale that follows, which borrows (with the author's permission) the milieu of Michael Moorcock's novel* The Ice Schooner *(which was serialized in* Science Fantasy *when Roberts was the managing editor; Roberts later sold this story to Moorcock when Moorcock was the new editor of the magazine* New Worlds—*the web of associations has a very fine mesh!) and takes us to a far-future Earth frozen back into barbarity by a new Ice Age for a taut story of a man obsessed with the hunt who discovers that to catch the prey you want the most, you sometimes have to pay a price greater than you can afford to spend.. . . .*

There was a woman in the great cleft-city of Brershill who was passing fair.

At least so ran opinion in that segment of low-level society of which she was undisputed queen. Though there were others, oldsters for the most part, who resented her beauty, finding her very fame an affront to decent living. Custom died hard in Brershill, most conservative—or most backward—of the Eight Cities of the Plain, the great ice steppe men had once called the Matto Grosso. And in truth Coranda had given some cause for offense. If she was beautiful she was also vain and cold, cold as the ice plains that girdled the world: in her vanity she had denied even that sacrifice most beloved of great Ice Mother, the first-blood that belonged to the goddess alone. Long past the time of puberty she was, and the ceremonies of womanhood; and still the Mother waited for her due. In the blizzards that scourged the cleft, in the long winds of winter, her complaint might be heard, chilling the blood with threats and promises. All men knew they lived by the Mother's mercy alone; that one day, very soon now, the world would end, mantled for eternity in her sparkling cloth. *Coranda*, ran the whisper. *Coranda*, holding their lives in the hollow of her hand. Coranda heard, and laughed; she was just twenty, slim and black haired and tall.

◆

She lay on a couch of white fur, toying with a winecup, mocking the young men of the cities as they paid her court. To Arand, son of the richest merchant of Brershill, she confided her belief that she herself was of the Mother's Chosen and thus above the pettiness of sacrifice. "For," she said, smoothing her long hair, "is not the Mother justly famed for beauty, for the perfection of skin that matches the fresh-laid snow? The darkness of her eyes, all-seeing, the slenderness of the hands that guard us all? And have I not"—she tossed her head—"have I not, among your good selves at least, some claim to prettiness? Though Eternal Mother forbid"—blushing, and modestly lowering her eyes—"that I should fall into the sin of pride." Arand, more than a little drunk, straightway burbled her divinity, speaking heresy with the ease of long practice or stupidity till she swept from him indignantly, angry that he should speak lightly of the deity in her presence. "Will not the Mother's rage," she asked Maitran of Friesgalt appealingly, "descend alike on his head and mine? Will you protect me from the lightnings that fly in storms, lightnings such words may bring?"

That was a cunning touch, worthy of Coranda; for the animosity with which most Friesgaltians regarded the folk of Brershill was well known. Maitran's knifeblade gleamed instantly, and would no doubt have brought the Mother a pleasing offering had not Brershill stalwarts pinned and disarmed the combatants. Some blood was shed certainly, from thumped noses and mouths, while Coranda regarded the wriggling heap with interest. "Now," she said, "I think I must call my father's men to punish; for do I mean so little to you all that you come here to my house and brawl?" She ran to the gong placed beside the door of the chamber, and would certainly have summoned an irate guard had not earnest entreaty prevailed.

"Well," she said, tossing her head again in disgust. "It seems you all have too much spirit, and certainly too much energy, for my comfort and your own safety. I think we must devise a small occupation, something that will absorb your wildness and will no doubt bring a suitable reward."

There was a quietness at that; for she had hinted before that marriage to some rich and worthy boy might at long last assuage the Mother's need. She brooded, suddenly thoughtful, stroked hands across her gown so the fabric showed momentarily the convexities of belly and thighs. Lowered her eyes, glided swaying to the couch. They made way for her, wary and puzzled. Rich they all were, certainly, or they would none of them have passed her father's iron-bound doors; but worthy? Who could be worthy of Coranda, whose beauty was surely Ice Mother's own?

She clapped her hands; at the gesture a house-servant, blue liveried, laid beside her a box. It was made from wood, rarest of substances, inlaid with strips of ivory and bone. She opened it, languidly; inside, resting on a quilting of white nylon, was a slim harpoon. She lifted it, toying with the haft, fingers stroking the razor edges of the barbs. "Who will prove himself?" she asked, seemingly to the air. "Who will take the Mother's due, when Coranda of Brershill comes to marriage?"

Instantly, a babble of voices; Karl Stromberg and Mard Lipsill of Abersgalt shouted willingness. Frey Skalter the Keltshillian, half barbaric in his jeweled furs, attempted to kiss her foot. She withdrew it smartly, equally sharply kicked him in the throat. Skalter overbalanced, swearing, spilling wine across the pale floor. There was laughter; she silenced it sharply, lifting the little harpoon again, watching from long lashed, kohl-painted eyes. She relaxed, still holding the weapon, staring at the ceiling in the fast blue flicker of the lamps. "Once," she said, "long ago, in the far south of our land, a whaler was blown off course by storms. When the Ice Mother's anger was spent, and she sent sunlight again and birds, none could make out where her breath had driven them. There was ice, a great smooth plain, and mountains; some of them smoked, so they said, throwing cinders and hot winds into the air. A very queer place it was indeed, with furry barbarians and animals from a child's book of fancies, stranger than men could believe. There they hunted, spilling and killing till their holds were full and they turned north to their homes. Then they came on the strangest wonder of all."

In the quiet the buzzing of the eternal fluorescent tubes sounded loud. Skalter poured himself more wine, carefully, eyes on the girl's face. Arand and Maitran stopped their glaring; Stromberg thoughtfully wiped an errant red trickle from his nose.

"In the dark of dawn," said Coranda dreamily, "in the gray time when men and ships are nothing but shadows without weight and substance, they met the Fate sent by Ice Mother to punish them their crimes. It surrounded them, flickering and leaping, soundless as snow, weird as Death itself. All across the plain, round their boat as they sailed, were animals. They ran and moved, playing; whole herds and droves of them, bulls and calves and cows. Their bodies were gray, they said, and sinuous as seals; their eyes were beautiful, and looked wisely at the ship. But without doubt they were spirits from the Mother's court, sent to warn and destroy; for as they turned and leaped they saw each had but one horn, long and spiraling, that caught and threw back the light."

She waited, seeming indifferent to her audience. At length Lipsill broke the silence. "Coranda . . . what of the boat?"

She shrugged delicately, still playing with the barbed tip of the spear. "Two men returned, burned by the Mother's breath till their faces were black and marbled and their hands turned to scorched hooks. They lived long enough to tell the tale."

They waited.

"A man who loved me," she said, "who wanted to feel me in his bed and know himself worthy, would go to that land of shadows on the rim of the world. He would bring me a present to mark his voyage."

Abruptly her eyes flicked wide, scorning at them. "A head," she said softly. "The head of the unicorn. . . ."

Another pause; and then a wild shouting. "Ice Mother hear me," bellowed Skalter. "I'll fetch your toy for you. . . ."

"And me. . . ."

"And me. . . ."

They clamored for attention.

She beckoned Skalter. He came forward, dropping to one knee, leaning his craggy face over hers. She took his hand and raised it, closed the fingers gently round the tip of the harpoon. Stared at him, fixing him with her great eyes. "You would go?" she said. "Then there must be no softness, Frey Skalter, no fainting of the spirit. Hard as the ice you will be, and as merciless; for my sake alone." She laid her hand over his, stroking the fingers, smiling her cat-smile. "You will go for me?"

He nodded, not speaking; and she squeezed slowly, still smiling. He stiffened, breath hissing between his teeth; and blood ran back down his arm, splashed bright and sudden on the weapon's shaft. "By this token," she said, "you are my man. So shall you all be; and Ice Mother, in her charity, will decide."

◆

Early day burned over the icefields. To the east the sun, rising across the white plain, threw red beams and the mile-long shadows of boats and men. Above, dawn still fought with darkness; the red flush faded to violet-gray, the gray to luminous blue. Across the blue ran high ripplings of cloud; the zenith gleamed like the skin of a turquoise fish. In the distance, dark-etched against the horizon, rose the spar-forest of the Brershill dock, where the schooners and merchantmen lay clustered in the lee of long moles built of blocks of ice. In the foreground, ragged against the glowing the sky, were the yachts; Arand's *Chaser*, Maitran's sleek catamaran, Lipsill's big *Ice Ghost*. Karl Stromberg's *Snow Princess* snubbed at a mooring rope as the wind caught her curved side. Beyond her were two dour vessels from Djobhabn; and a Fyorsgeppian, iron-beaked, that bore the blackly humorous name *Bloodbringer*. Beyond again was Skalter's *Easy Girl*, wild and splendid, decorated all over with hair-tufts and scalps and ragged scraps of pelt. Her twin masts were bound with intricate strappings of nylon cord; on her gunnels skulls of animals gleamed, eyesockets threaded with bright and moving silks. Even her runners were carved, the long-runes that told, cryptically, the story of Ice Mother's meeting with Sky Father and the birth and death of the Son, he whose Name could not be mentioned. The Mother's grief had spawned the icefields; her anger would not finally be appeased till Earth ran cold and quiet for ever. Three times she had approached, three times the Fire Giants fought her

back from their caverns under the ice; but she would not be denied. Soon
now, all would be whiteness and peace; then the Son would rise, in rum-
blings and glory, and judge the souls of men.

The priest moved, shivering in a patterned shawl, touching the boats
and blessing, smearing the bow of each with a little blood and milk. The
wind soughed in the riggings, plucked at the robes of the muffled woman
who stood staring, hair flicking around her throat. The handlamps swung
on their poles, glowing against the patched hulls, throwing the priest's
shadow vague and fleeting as the shadow of a bird. The yachts tugged at
their lines, flapping their pennants, creaking their bone runners, full of
the half-life of mechanical things. All preparations were made, provisions
stored, blood and seed given in expiation to the ice. The hunters grunted
and stamped, swinging their arms in the keen air, impatient and unsure;
and to each it seemed the eyes of Coranda promised love, the body of
Coranda blessings.

The ceremony ended, finally. The priest withdrew to his tasseled nylon
tent, the polebearers lifted their burden and trudged back across the ice.
The boats were turned, levered by muffled men with crows till the sharp
bows pointed, questing, to the south. A shout; and Lipsill's craft first
blossomed sail, the painted fabric flying and cracking round the mast.
Then the catamaran, Skalter's deceptively clumsy squarerigger; quick
thud of a mallet parting the sternline and Lipsill was away, runners crisp-
ing, throwing a thin white double plume from the snow that had drifted
across the ice. Stromberg followed, swinging from the far end of the line,
crossing his scored wake as Skalter surged across *Princess*'s bows. A bel-
lowing; and the Keltshillian crabbed away, narrowly missing disaster, raising a threatening fist. Karl laughed, fur glove muffling the universal
gesture of derision; the boats faded in the dawn light, swerving and tacking as they jockeyed for the lead. If the display moved Coranda she gave
no sign of it; she stood smiling, coldly amused at the outcome of a jest,
till the hulls were veiled in the frost-smoke of the horizon and the shouts
lost beneath the wind.

The yachts moved steadily through the day, heading due south under
the bright, high sun, their shadows pacing them across the white smoothness of the Plain. With the wind astern the squarerigger made ground
fast; by evening she was hull down, her sails a bright spark on the horizon.
Stromberg crowded *Snow Princess*, racing in her wake; behind him, spread
out now, came the others, lateens bulging, runners hissing on the ice.
The cold was bracing and intense; snow crystals, blowing on the wind,
stung his cheeks to a glow, beaded the heavy collar of his jerkin. Lipsill
forged alongside, *Ice Ghost* surging and bucking. Karl raised a hand, laughing at his friend; and instantly came the chilling thought that one day,
for Coranda, he might kill Lipsill, or Lipsill him.

They camped together, by common consent; all but Skalter, still miles
ahead. Here, away from the eternal warmth of the cleft-cities, they must
husband their reserves of fuel; they huddled round the redly-glowing brazier, the reflection lighting their faces, glinting out across the ice. The
worn hulls of the yachts, moored in a crescent, protected them from the

worst of the wind. Outside, beyond the circle of light, a wolf howled high and quavering; within the camp was cheerfulness, songs and stories passing round the group till one by one they took a last swig from their spirit flasks, checked their lines and grapples and turned in. They were up early next dawn, again by unspoken agreement, hoping maybe to steal a march on *Easy Girl*; but keen as they were, Skalter was ahead of them. They passed his camp, an hour's sail away. *Ice Ghost* crushed the remains of the brazier fire, the turned-out remnants still smoldering on the ice; one runner spurned the embers, sent a long banner of ash trailing down the wind. They glimpsed his sails once before the wind, rising again, blocked visibility with a swirling curtain of snow.

They were now nearing the wide cleft of Fyorsgep, southernmost of the Cities of the Plain. The smooth ice was crossed by the tracks of many ships; they shortened sail cautiously, shouting each to the next along the line. Hung lanterns in the rigging, pushed on again by compass and torchlight, unwilling to moor and give away advantage. *Snow Princess* and *Ice Ghost* moved side by side, a bare length separating them.

It was Stromberg who first heard the faint booming from astern. He listened, cocking his head and frowning; then waved, pointing behind him with a bulky arm. The noise came again, a dull and ominous ringing; Lipsill laughed, edging his boat even closer. Karl stared back as behind them an apparition loomed, impossibly tall in the gloom and whirling flakes. He saw the heavy thrusting of bowsprit and jibboom, the cavernous eyes of the landwhale skulls that graced the vessel's stern. They held course defiantly as she closed, hearing now mixed with the fog gongs the long-drawn roar of her runners over the ice. Stromberg made out the carved characters on her bow: the *Sweet Lady*, whaler out of Friesgalt, bound no doubt for the Southern Moorings and a night's carouse.

The jibboom was between the boats, thrusting at their rigging, before they were seen. An agonized howl from above, movement of lanterns and dark figures at the vessel's rail; she rumbled between the yachts as they parted at the last instant, the long shares of her ice anchors nearly scraping their booms. They saw the torchlit deck, fires burning in crow's-nest and rigging; and the curious feature of an ice-boat, the long slots in the bilges in which moved the linkages of the paired anchors. Dull light gleamed through her as she passed, giving to her hull the appearance of a half-flensed whale; a last bellow reached them as she faded into the grayness ahead.

"Abersgaltian bastards. . . ."

The skipper then had seen the big insignia at the mastheads. This Lady was anything but sweet.

The night's camp brought near-disaster. Maitran came in late and evil tempered, a runner stay cracked on the catamaran, bound with a jury-lashing of nylon rope. Some chance remark from Arand and he was on his feet, knife-blade glistening. He held the weapon tip-uppermost, circling and taunting his enemy. Arand rose white-faced, swathing a bearskin round one forearm. A quick feint and thrust, a leaping back; and Lipsill spoke easily, still seated by the fire.

"The prize, Friesgaltian, comes with the head of the unicorn. Our friend would doubtless look well enough, grinning from Coranda's wall; but your energy would be expended to no purpose."

Maitran hissed between his teeth, not deigning to glance round.

"You risk in any case the anger of the Ice Mother," the Abersgaltian went on, reaching behind him to his pack. "For if our Lady is in fact her servant then this hunting is clearly her design, and should bring her glory. All else is vanity, an affront to her majesty."

Hansan, the Fyorsgeppian, dark-faced and black-browed, nodded somberly. "This is true," he said. "Bloodspilling, if it be against the Mother's will, brings no honor."

Maitran half turned at that, uncertainly; and Lipsill's arm flailed up and back. The harpoon head, flung with unerring force, opened his cheek; he went down in a flurry of legs and arms and Stromberg was on him instantly, pinning him. Lipsill turned to Arand, his own knife in his hand. "Now, now, Brershillian," he said gently; for the other roused, would no doubt have thrown himself on his prostrate enemy and extracted vengeance. "No more, or you will answer to us all. . . ."

Arand sheathed his dagger, shakily, eyes not leaving the stained face of the Friesgaltian. Maitran was allowed to rise; and Lipsill faced him squarely. "This was evil," he said. "Our fight is with the wind and wide ice, not each other. Take your boat, and stay apart from us."

In Stromberg's mind rose the first stirring of a doubt.

They moved fast again next morning, hoping for some sign of Skalter's yacht; but the wind that had raged all night had cleaned his tracks, filling them with fresh snow. The ice lay scoured, white and gleaming to the horizon.

They were now past the farthest limit of civilization, on the great South Ice where the whale herds and their hunters roamed. Here and there were warm ponds, choked with brown and green weed; they saw animals, wolf and otter, once a herd of the shaggy white bison of the Plains; but no sign of the ghostly things they sought. The catamaran reached ahead of the rest, the Friesgaltian reckless and angry, crowding sail till the slim paired hulls were nearly obscured beneath a cloud of pale nylon. Stromberg, remembering the split strut, sent up a brief and silent prayer.

Maitran's luck held till midday; then the stay parted, suddenly and without warning. They all saw the boat surge off course, one keel dropping to glissade along the ice. For a moment it seemed she would come to rest without further harm; then the ivory braces between the hulls, overstressed, broke in their turn. She split into halves; one hull bounded end over end, shredding fragments and splinters of bone, the other spun, encumbered by the falling weight of mast and sail, flicked Maitran in a sharp arc across the ice. He was up instantly, seemingly unhurt, running and waving to head them off.

In Arand's slow brain hatred still burned. He knew, as they had all known, that in a fight he was no match for the Friesgaltian. Maitran would have bled him, cutting and opening till he lay down and gasped his life out on the ice. They had saved him, the night before, but he had lost his honor. Now the rage took him, guiding his hands till they seemed possessed of a life of their own. They swung the tiller, viciously; *Chaser* swerved, heading in toward the wreck. Maitran shouted as the yacht crisped toward him; at the last moment it seemed he realized she would not turn. He tried to run; a foot slipped and he went down on the ice. A thud, a bright spattering across the bows of *Chaser* and she was past the wreck, yawing as she dragged the body from one sharp ski. Fifty yards on it twirled clear. She limped to a halt, sails fluttering. From her runner led a faint and wavering trail; her deck was marked with the pink blood of the Friesgaltian.

They gathered round the thing on the ice. Stromberg and the Djobhabnians stunned, Arand pale and mumbling. There was no life; the great wound in the head, the oozing of blood and brain-matter, showed there was nothing to be done. They made the sign of the Ice Mother, silently; turned away, anxious to leave the sight, left the body for her servants, the birds.

They were cheered later that day by the gleam of Skalter's sail far to the south; but the camp was still a somber affair. They moored apart, sat brooding each over his own fire. To Stromberg it seemed all his past life now counted for nothing; they were governed by the Rule of the Ice, the code that let men kill or be killed with equal indifference. He remembered his years of friendship with Lipsill, a friendship that seemed now to be ended. After what he had seen that morning he would not dare trust even Mard again. At night he tried, unavailingly, to summon the image of Coranda's warm body; pray though he might, the succubus would not visit him. Instead he fell into a fitful sleep, dreamed he saw the very caverns of the Fire Giants deep under the ice. But there were no gleaming gods and demons; only machines black and vast, that hummed and sang of power. The vision disturbed him; he cut his arm, in the dull dawn light, left blood to appease the Mother. It seemed even she turned her back on him; the morning was gray and cold, comfortless. He drank to restore circulation to his limbs, tidied his ship, left sullenly in the wake of Lipsill as he led them on again across the Plain.

As they moved, the character of the land round them once more changed. The warm ponds were more numerous; over them now hung frequent banks of fog. Often *Snow Princess* slushed her way through water, runners raising glittering swathes to either side. At breakfast the Djobhabnians had seemed remote, standing apart and muttering; now their identical craft began to edge away, widening the gap between them and the rest till they were hull down, gray shadows on the ice. By early evening they were out of sight.

The four boats raced steadily through a curling sea of vapor. Long leads of clear water opened threatening to either side; they tacked and swerved, missing disaster time and again by the width of a runner. Stromberg lay to the right of the line, next to him the Fyorsgeppian. Then Lipsill; beyond *Ice Ghost* was the blighted vessel of Arand, half-seen now through the moving mist. None of the boats would give way, none fall back; Karl clung to the tiller, feeling the fast throb of the runners transmitted through the bone shaft, full of a hollow sense of impending doom.

As dusk fell a long runnel of open water showed ahead. He altered course, following it where it stretched diagonally across his bows. A movement to his left made him turn. *Bloodbringer* had fallen back; her dark hull no longer blocked his vision. Mard still held course; and still *Chaser* ran abreast of him, drawing nearer and nearer the edge of the break. Stromberg at last understood Lipsill's purpose; he yelled, saw Arand turn despairingly. It was too late; behind him, a length away, jutted the Fyorsgeppian's iron ram. Boxed, the yacht spun on her heel in a last attempt to leap the obstacle. A grating of runners and spars, a frozen moment as she poised above the gulf, then she struck the water with a thunderous splash. She sank almost instantly, hull split by the concussion; for a moment her bilge showed rounded and pale, then she was gone. In her place was a disturbed swirl, a bobbing of debris. Arand surfaced once, waving a desperate arm, before he too vanished.

The sun sank over the rim of the ice, flung shadows of the boats miles long like the predatory shapes of birds.

In the brief twilight they came up with *Easy Girl*. Skalter hung in her rigging, leisurely reeving a halliard, waving and jeering at them as they passed.

All three vessels turned, Stromberg and Lipsill tightly, Hansan in a wider circle that took him skimming across the plain to halt, sails flapping, a hundred yards away. Grapples went down; they lashed and furled stoically, dropped to the ice and walked over to the Keltshillian.

He greeted them cheerfully, swinging down from the high mast of the boat. "Well, you keen sailors; where are our friends?"

"Fraskall and Ulsenn turned back," said Lipsill shortly. "Maitran and Arand are dead. Maitran at Arand's hands, Arand in an icebreak." He stared at Stromberg challengingly. "It was the Mother's will, Karl. She could have buoyed him to the land. She did not choose to."

Stromberg didn't answer.

"Well," said Skalter easily, "the Mother was ever firm with her followers. Let it be so." He made the sign of benediction, carelessly, circling with his hands, drawing with one palm the flat emptiness of the ice. He ran his fingers through his wild blond hair and laughed. "Tonight you will share my fire, Abersgaltians; and you too, Hansan of Fyorsgep. Tomorrow, who can tell? We reach the Mother's court perhaps, and sail in fairyland."

They grouped round the fire, quietly, each occupied with his own thoughts. Skalter methodically honed the barbs of a harpoon, turning the weapon, testing the cutting edges against his thumb, his scarred face intent in the red light. He looked up finally, half frowning, half quizzical; his earrings swung and glinted as he moved his head. "It seems to me," he said, "the Mother makes her choice known, in her special way. Arand and Maitran were both fools of a type, certainly unfitted for the bed of the Lady we serve, and the Djobhabnians fainthearted. Now we are four; who among us, one wonders, will win the bright prize?"

Stromberg made a noise, half smothered by his glove; Skalter regarded him keenly.

"You spoke, Abersgaltian?"

"He feels," said Lipsill gruffly, "we murdered Arand. After he in his turn killed Maitran."

The Keltshillian laughed, high and wild. "Since when," he said, "did pity figure in the scheme of things? Pity, or blame? Friends, we are bound to the Ice Eternal; to the cold that will increase and conquer, lay us all in our bones. Is not human effort vain, all life doomed to cease? I tell you, Coranda's blood, that mighty prize, and all her secret sweetness, this is a flake of snow in an eternal wind. I am the Mother's servant; through me she speaks. We'll have no more talk of guilt and softness; it turns my stomach to hear it." The harpoon darted, sudden and savage, stood quivering between them in the ice. "The ice is real," shouted Skalter, rising. "Ice, and blood. All else is delusion, toys for weak men and fools."

He stamped away, earrings jangling, into the dark. The others separated soon afterward to their boats; and Stromberg for one lay tossing and uneasy till dawn shot pearly streamers above the Plain and the birds called, winging to the south.

On its southern rim the Great Plateau sloped gently. The yachts traveled fast, creaming over untold depths of translucent ice, runners hissing, sails filling in the breeze that still blew from nearly astern. There would be weary days of tacking ahead for those that returned. If any returned; Stromberg found himself increasingly beginning to doubt. It seemed a madness had gripped them all, drawing them deeper and deeper into the uncharted land. The place of warm ponds was left behind; ahead, under the pale sun, shadows grew against the sky. There were mountains, topped with fire as the story had foretold; strange crevasses and plateaus, jumbled and distant, glinting like crystal in the hard white light. Still Skalter led them, mastbells clanking, barbaric sails shaking and swelling. They held course stubbornly, shadows pacing them as they raced to the south.

At the foot of the vast slope they parted company with the Fyorsgeppian. He had reached ahead, favored by some trick of the terrain, till *Bloodbringer* was a hundred yards or more in front of the rest. They saw the hull of the boat jar and leap. The smooth slope ended, split by a series of yard-high ridges; Hansan's runners, hitting the first of them, were sheared completely from the hull. There was something tragically comic about the accident. The gunwales split, the mast jarring loose to revolve against the sky like an oversized harpoon; the Fyorsgeppian, held by a shoulder harness, kept his place while the boat came apart round him like a child's toy. The remnants planed, spinning at great speed, jolted to a stop in a quick shower of ice. The survivors swerved, avoiding the broken ground, whispering by Hansan as he sat shaking his head, still half stunned. The wreckage dwindled to a speck that vanished, lost against the gray-green scarp of ice. There were provisions in the hull; the Fyorsgeppian would live or die, as the Mother willed.

For the first time that night the skyline round their camp was broken by valleys and hills. Still icebound, the land had begun to roll; there were gullies, hidden cliffs, ravines from which came the splash and tinkle of water. It was an eerie country, dangerous and beautiful. They had seen strange animals; but no sign or spoor of barbarians, or the things they sought.

Stromberg spoke to Skalter again at dawn, while Lipsill fussed with the rigging of his boat. He seemed impelled by a sense of urgency; all things, mountains and sky, conspired to warm his blood. "It has come to me," he said quietly, "that we should return."

The Keltshillian stood thoughtfully, warming his hands at the brazier, casting glances at the low sky, sniffing the wind. He gave a short, coughing laugh but didn't turn.

Stromberg touched a skull on the high side of *Easy Girl*, stroking the wind-smoothed eyesockets, unsure how to go on. "Last night I dreamed," he said. "It seemed as it has seemed before that the Giants were not gods but men, and we their children. That we are deceived, the Great Mother is dead. Such heresy must be a warning."

Skalter laughed again and spat accurately at the coals, rubbed arms banded with wide copper torques. "You dreamed of love," he said. "Wetting your furs with hot thoughts of Coranda. It's you who are deceived, Lipsgaltian. Counsel your fancies."

"Skalter," said Karl uncertainly, "the price is high. Too high, for a woman."

The other turned to face him for the first time, pale eyes brooding in the keen face.

Stromberg rushed on. "All my life," he said, "it seemed to me that you were not as other men. Now I say, there is death here. Maybe for us all. Go back, Frey; the prize is beneath your worth."

The other turned to look at the hulking shape of the boat, stroking her gunwale with a calloused hand, feeling the smoothness of the ivory. "The price of birth is death," he said broodingly. "That too is a heavy sum to pay."

"What drives you, Skalter?" asked Stromberg softly. "If the woman means so little? Why do you strive, if life is purposeless?"

"I do what is given," said Skalter shortly. He flexed his hands on the side of the boat and sprang; the runners of *Easy Girl* creaked as he swung himself aboard. "Rage drives me," he said, looking down. "Know this, Karl Stromberg of Abersgalt: that Skalter of Keltshill lusts for death. In dying, death dies with him." He slapped the halliards against the after mast, bringing down a white shower of ice. "I also dreamed," he said. "My dream was of life, sweet and rich. I follow the Mother; in her, I shall find my reward." He would say no more but stalked forward, bent to recoil the long ropes on the deck.

That morning they sighted their prey.

At first Stromberg could not believe; he was forced, finally, to accept the evidence of his eyes. The unicorns played and danced, sunlight flashing from their sides, horns gleaming, seeming to throw off sparks of brightness. He might have followed all day, watching and bemused; but

Skalter's high yell recalled him, the change of course as *Easy Girl* sped for the mutated narwhal. Already the Keltshillian was brandishing his long harpoon, shaking out the coils of line as the yacht, tiller locked, flew toward the herd.

It was as the story had told; the creatures surrounded the boats, running and leaping, watching with their beautiful calm eyes. On Karl's left Lipsill too seemed to be dazed. Skalter braced his feet on the deck, flexed muscles to drive the shaft hissing into the air. His aim was good; the harpoon struck a great gray bull, barbs sinking deep through the wrinkled pelt. Instantly all was confusion. The wounded beast reared and plunged, snorting; *Easy Girl* was spun off course by the violence, the Keltshillian hauling desperately at the line. Boat and animal collided in a flurry of snow. The narwhal leaped away again, towing the yacht; Karl saw bright plumes fly as her anchors fell, tips biting at the ice.

The herd had panicked, jerking and humping into the distance; *Snow Princess*, still moving fast, all but fouled the harpoon lines as Stromberg clawed clear. He had a brief glimpse of Skalter on the ice, the flash of a cutlass as the creature plunged, thrusting at its tormentor with its one great horn. He swung the tiller again, hard across; *Princess* circled, runners squealing, fetched up fifty yards from the fight. *Ice Ghost* was already stopped, Lipsill running cutlass in hand; Karl heard Skalter scream, in triumph or in pain. He dropped his anchors grabbing for his own sword. Ran across the ice toward *Easy Girl*, hearing now the enraged trumpeting of the bull.

The great beast had the Keltshillian pinned against the side of the boat. He saw the blunt head lunging, driving the horn through his flesh; the yacht rocked with the violence of the blows. The panting of the narwhal sounded loud; then the creature with a last convulsion had torn itself away, snorting and hooting after the vanished herd.

There was much blood, on the ice and the pale side of the boat. Skalter sat puffing, face suffused, hands gripped over his stomach. More blood pulsed between his fingers, ruby-bright in the sun; cords stood out in his thick neck; his white teeth grinned as he rolled his head in pain.

Lipsill reached him at the same instant. They tried, pointlessly, to draw the hands away; Skalter resisted them, eyes shut, breath hissing between his clenched teeth. "I told you I dreamed," he said. The words jerked out thick and agonized. "I saw the Mother. She came in the night, cajoling; her limbs were white as snow, and hot as fire. It was an omen; but I couldn't read . . ." His head dropped; he raised himself again, gasping with effort. They looked his hands then, soapy with blood, squeezed, feeling the dying vise-grip, seeing the eyes roll white under their lids. Convulsions shook him; they thought he was dead, but he spoke again. "Blood, and ice," he said faintly. "These are real. These are the words of the Mother. When the world is dark, then she will come to me. . . ." The body arced, straining; and Lipsill gripped the yellow hair, twisting it in his fingers. "The Mother takes you, Skalter," he said. "She rewards her servant."

They waited; but there was nothing more.

They moored their boats, silently, walked back to the place of killing. The blood had frozen, sparkling in pink crystals under the leveling sun. "He was a great prince," said Lipsill finally. "The rest is smallness; it should not come between us." Stromberg nodded, not answering with words; and they began to work. They broke *Easy Girl*, smacking bulwarks and runner, hacking at her bone and ivory spars, letting her spirit free to join the great spirit of Skalter that already roamed the Ice Eternal. Two days they labored, raising a mound of ice above the wreck; Skalter they laid on the deck, feet to the north and the domain of the Mother. He would rise now, on that last cold dawn, spring up facing her, a worthy servant and warrior. When they had finished, and the wind skirled over the glistening *how*, they rested; on the third morning they drove south again.

There were no words now between them. They sailed apart, bitterly, watching the white horizon, the endless swirl and flurry of the snow. Two days later they resighted their quarry.

The two boats separated further, bearing down; and again the strange creatures watched with their soft eyes. The shafts flew, glinting; Lipsill's tinkled on the ice, Stromberg's struck wide of its mark. It missed the bull at which it was aimed, plunged instead into the silver flank of a calf. The animal howled, convulsed in a flurry of pain. As before, the herd bolted; *Snow Princess* slewed, hauled round by the tethered weight, fled across the plain as the terrified creature bucked and plunged.

Less than half the size of the adults, the calf was still nearly as long as the boat; Stromberg clung to the tiller as *Princess* jolted and veered, determined not to make Skalter's mistake of jumping to the ice. A mile away the harpoon pulled clear but the animal was blown; a second shaft transfixed it as it stood head down and panting, started fresh and giant paroxysms that spattered the yacht with blood. *Princess* flew again, anchor blades ripping at the ice, drawing the thing gradually to a halt. It rolled then and screeched, trying with its half-flippers to scrape the torment from its back. Its efforts wound the line in round its body; it stood finally close to the boat, staring with a filmed, uncomprehending eye. Close enough for Stromberg to reach across, work the shaft into its torn side till the tip probed its life. A thin wailing, a nearly human noise of pain; and the thing collapsed, belching thunderously, coughing up masses of blood and weed. Sticky tears squeezed from its eyes, ran slow across the great round face; and Karl, standing shaking and panting, knew there was no need of the sword.

The anchors of *Ice Ghost* raised a high screaming. She ploughed across the ice, throwing a white hail of chips to either side, speed barely diminished. She had speared a huge bull; animal and boat careened by the stalled *Princess*. Stromberg cut his line, heavily, left the carcass with the bright harpoon-silks still blowing above it. Steered in pursuit.

Sometimes in the half hour that followed it seemed he might overrun Lipsill; but always the other boat drew ahead. The narwhal left a thick trail of blood, but its energy seemed unabated. The line twanged thunderously, snagging on the racing ice. Ahead now the terrain was split and broken; fissures yawned, sunlight sparking from their deep green sides. *Princess* bucked heavily, runners crashing as she swerved between the hazards. The chase veered to the east, in a great half-circle; the wind, at first abeam, reached farther and farther ahead. Close-hauled, Stromberg fell behind: a half-mile separated the boats as they entered a wide, bowl-shaped valley, a mile or more across, guarded on each side by needle-shaped towers of ice.

Ahead, the glittering floor veered to a rounded lip; the horizon line was sharp-cut against the sky. *Ice Ghost*, still towed by her catch, took the slope with barely a slackening of pace. Stromberg howled his alarm, use-lessly; Lipsill, frozen it seemed to the tiller, made no attempt to cut his line. The boat crested the rise, hung a moment silhouetted against bright-ness; and vanished, abrupt as a conjuring trick.

Princess's anchors threw snow plumes high as her masthead. She skated sickeningly, surged to a halt twenty yards below the lip of ice. Stromberg walked forward, carefully. As he topped the ridge the sight beyond took his breath.

He stood on the edge of the biggest crevasse he had ever seen. It curved back to right and left, horseshoe-shaped, enclosing the valley like a white tongue. A hundred yards away the opposing side glowed with sunlight; across it lay the ragged shadow of the nearer wall. He craned forward. Below him the ice-walls stretched sheer to vanish in a blue-green gloom. There was mist down there, and water-noise; the herd booming, long-drawn threads of echo, last sounds maybe of the fall of the whale. Far below, impaled on a black spike of ice, was the wreck of Lipsill's boat; Mard, still held by his harness, sprawled across the stern, face bright with blood. He moved slightly as Stromberg stared, seeming to raise himself, lift a hand. Karl turned away sickened.

Realizing he had won.

He walked back to *Snow Princess*, head down, feet scraping on the ice. Swung himself aboard and opened the bow locker, dumping piles of junk and provisions on the deck. There were ropes, spare downhauls and mooring lines. He selected the best and thickest, knotting methodically, tied off to the stern of the boat and walked back to the gulf. The line, lowered carefully, swayed a yard from Lipsill's head.

He returned to *Princess*. She was stopped at an angle, tilted sideways on the curling lip of the crevasse. There were crowbars in the locker; he pulled one clear and worked cautiously, prising at the starboard runner, inching the yacht round till her bow pointed back down the long slope. The wind, gusting and capricious, blew from the gulf. The slope would help her gather way; but would it be enough?

He brailed the sails up as far as he dared, stood back frowning and biting his lip. At each gust now the anchors groaned, threatening to tear free, send the boat skittering back down the incline. He scrabbled in the locker gain, grabbing up more line. Another line, a light line that must also reach the wreck. . . .

There was just barely enough. He tied the last knot, dropped the sec-ond coil down. Working feverishly now, he transferred the heavy line from the stern to a cleat halfway along the port gunwale and locked the tiller to starboard. The anchors were raised by pulleys set just above the deck; he carried lines from them to the little bow windlass, slipped the ratchet, turned the barrel till they were tight. The handle fitted in its bone socket, stood upright, pointing slightly forward over the stem of the boat. He tied the light line off to the tip, tested the lashing on the improvised brake. It seemed secure; he backed toward the cliff edge, paying both ropes through his hands. Mard seemed now to understand what he was doing. He called croakingly, tried to move. The wreck groaned, slipped another foot toward the crevasse. Stromberg passed the heavy line between his thighs, round one calf, gripped it between sole and instep. Let himself down into the gulf.

The descent was eerie. As he moved the wind pressure seemed to increase, setting him swaying pendulum-fashion, banging his body at the ice. The sunlit edge above receded; he glanced below him and instantly the crevasse seemed to spin. The ice walls, sloping together, vanished in a blackish gloom; the wind called deep and baying, its icy breath chilled his cheek. He hung sweating till the dizziness passed, forced himself by his arms, felt his heels touch the deck of the boat. He dropped, as lightly as he could, lunging forward to catch at the tangle of rigging. A sickening time while the wreck surged and creaked; he felt sweat drop from him again as he willed the movement to stop. The deck steadied, with a final groan; he edged sideways cautiously, cutting more rope lengths, fashioning a bridle that he slipped under Lipsill's arms. The other helped as best he could, raising his body weakly; Stromberg tested the knots, lashed the harness to the line. Another minute's work and he too was secure. He took a shuddering breath, groping for the second rope. They were not clear yet; if *Ice Ghost* moved, she could still take them with her, scrape them into the gulf. He gripped the line and pulled.

Nothing.

He jerked again, feeling the fresh rise of panic. If the trick failed he knew he lacked the strength ever to climb. A waiting; then a vibration, sensed through the rope. Another pause; and he was being drawn smoothly up the cliff, swinging against the rock-hard ice as the pace increased. The sides of the cleft seemed to rush toward him; a last concussion, a bruising shock and he was being towed over level ice, sawing desperately at the line. He saw fibers parting; then he was lying still, blessedly motionless. Lipsill beside him bleeding into the snow. While *Princess*, freed of her one-sided burden, skated in a wide half-circle, came into irons, and stopped.

✦

The crevasse of Brershill lay gray and silent in the early morning. Torches, flaring at intervals along the glassy sides, lit Level after Level with a wavering glare, gleamed on the walkways with their new powdering of snow. Stromberg trudged steadily, sometimes hauling his burden, sometimes skidding behind it as he eased the sledge down the sloping paths. A watchman called sleepily; he ignored him. On the Level above Coranda's home he stopped, levered the great thing from the sledge and across to the edge of the path. He straightened up, wiping his face, and yelled; his voice ran thin and shaking, echoing between the half-seen walls.

"*Maitran. . . .*"

A bird flew squawking from the depths. The word flung itself back at him, Ice Mother answering with a thousand voices.

"*Arand. . . .*"

Again the mocking choir, confusions of sound reflecting faint and mad from the cleft.

"*Hansan. . . .*

"*Skalter. . . .*"

Names of the dead, and lost; a fierce benediction, an answer to the ice.

He bent to the thing on the path. A final heave, a falling, a fleshy thud; the head of the unicorn bounced on the Level below, splashed a great star of blood across Coranda's door. He straightened, panting, half-hearing from somewhere the echo of a scream. Stood and stared a moment longer before starting to climb.

Giving thanks to Ice Mother, who had given him back his soul.

Nightwings

ROBERT SILVERBERG

Like Brian Aldiss, Robert Silverberg is an author who seems fascinated with the far future, and he has returned to far-future milieus again and again throughout his career in stories such as "At Winter's End," "A Long Night's Vigil at the Temple," "Homecoming," "Dancers in the Time-Flux," "This Is the Road," "Red Blaze in the Morning," the Nebula Award–winning "Sailing to Byzantium," and many others, as well as in novels such as Son of Man *and the stories and novels of the Majipoor sequence. Also like Aldiss, Silverberg has written a number of stories that would have served perfectly well for this anthology, but the one I kept coming back to was the evocative novella that follows, which won a Hugo Award in 1969, one of a sequence of three novellas that were later melded into the book* Nightwings.

Here Silverberg takes us to a time thousands of years beyond our own, to the glorious city of Roum, builds layer on layer upon the ancient rubble of the nearly forgotten past, and paints a vivid portrait of one man's obsession with duty to the exclusion of all else . . . and warns us that just as it is better to travel hopefully than to arrive, it's sometimes better to search endlessly for something than it is to actually find what you're looking for. . . .

Robert Silverberg is one of the most famous SF writers of modern times, with dozens of novels, anthologies, and collections to his credit. As both writer and editor, Silverberg was one of the most influential figures of the post–New Wave era of the seventies and continues to be at the forefront of the field to this very day, having won a total of five Nebula Awards and four Hugo Awards.

Born in Brooklyn, New York, in 1935, Silverberg, like Poul Anderson before him, started a successful career as an SF writer while he was still in college. His first novel was sold in 1954, while he was still a junior at Columbia University; by 1955, still prior to graduation, he was earning "quite a good living" by writing, and by 1956, he had won his first Hugo Award. He spent a period of some years in the late fifties and early sixties away from the field, writing a long string of well-received nonfiction books, but by the late sixties he'd returned to the genre, and during the first half of the seventies the so-called New Silverberg would produce a large and remarkable body of work: the brilliant Dying Inside, *easily one of the best books of the seventies,* Downward to the Earth, The Book of Skulls, Tower of Glass, The World Inside, The Second Trip, A Time of Changes, The Stochastic Man, *and* Shadrach in the Furnace, *as well as high-quality short works such as "Born with the Dead," "Sundance," "In Entropy's Jaws," "Breckenridge and the Continuum," "Push No More," "In the Group," "Capricorn Games," "Trips," "Swartz between the Galaxies," and many more. Seldom has science fiction witnessed such a concentrated outpouring of high-level talent, work that would be highly influential on writers such as Barry N. Malzberg and the later Gregory Benford, to name just two, and which I strongly suspect was influential on writers of subsequent generations—such as Alexander Jablokov—as well. When you add in the influence that Silverberg would exert on the field through his editorship of the* New Dimensions *original anthology series, the most important anthology series of its day, you can see that the strength of Silverberg's impact on the SF world of the seventies can hardly be overestimated.*

In 1976, depressed by the general malaise that had settled over the field at the time and perhaps exhausted from his efforts over the previous years, Silverberg publicly announced his "retirement" . . . and, indeed, would not write another word until 1980, when he suddenly came out of retirement to write his huge science-fantasy novel (also set in the far future) Lord Valentine's Castle. *His output of new fiction was relatively low in the early years of the decade, but when a new surge of creative energy revitalized the field in the mideighties Silverberg shifted into high gear once again, and, as what might perhaps be referred to—a bit facetiously—as the "New New Silverberg," poured out another torrent of high-quality work such as "The Pope of the Chimps," "Multiples," "The Palace at Midnight," "We Are for the Dark," "In Another Country," "Basileus," "The Secret Sharer," "Enter a Soldier. Later: Enter Another," "Sailing to Byzantium," "Beauty in the Night," "Death Do Us Part," "The Colonel in Autumn," and dozens of others, as well as a score of best-selling novels—a torrent that shows no signs of running dry even here at the end of the 1990s.*

Silverberg's other books include the novels Son of Man, Thorns, Up the Line, The Man in the Maze, Tom O'Bedlam, Star of Gypsies, At Winter's End, The Face of the Waters, Kingdoms of the Wall, *and* Hot Sky at Morning *and three novel-length expansions of famous Isaac Asimov stories,* Nightfall, *and* The Ugly Little Boy, *and* The Positronic Man. *His collections include* Unfamiliar Territory, Capricorn Games, Majipoor Chronicles, The Best of Robert Silverberg, At the Conglomeroid Cocktail Party, Beyond the Safe Zone, *and a massive retrospective collection,* The Collected Stories of Robert Silverberg, vol. 1: Secret Sharers. *His reprint anthologies are far too numerous to list here but include* The Science Fiction Hall of Fame, vol. 1, *and the distinguished* Alpha *series, among dozens of others. His most recent books are two major original anthologies,* Legends *and* Far Horizons, *and the novels* The Alien Years, Mountains of Majipoor, Lord Prestimion. *He lives with his wife, writer Karen Haber, in Oakland, California.*

1

Roum is a city built on seven hills. They say it was a capital of man in one of the earlier cycles. I did not know of that, for my guild was Watching, not Remembering; but yet as I had my first glimpse of Roum, coming upon it from the south at twilight, I could see that in former days it must have been of great significance. Even now it was a mighty city of many thousands of souls.

Its bony towers stood out sharply against the dusk. Lights glimmered appealingly. On my left hand the sky was ablaze with splendor as the sun relinquished possession; streaming bands of azure and violet and crimson folded and writhed about one another in the nightly dance that brings the darkness. To my right, blackness had already come. I attempted to find the seven hills, and failed, and still I knew that this was that Roum of majesty toward which all roads are bent, and I felt awe and deep respect for the works of our bygone fathers.

We rested by the long straight road, looking up at Roum. I said, "It is a goodly city. We will find employment there."

Beside me, Avluela fluttered her lacy wings. "And food?" she asked in her high, fluty voice. "And shelter? And wine?"

"Those too," I said. "All of those."

"How long have we been walking, Watcher?" she asked.

"Two days. Three nights."

"If I had been flying, it would have been more swift."

"For you," I said. "You would have left us far behind and never seen us again. Is that your desire?"

She came close to me and rubbed the rough fabric of my sleeve, and then she pressed herself at me the way a flirting cat might do. Her wings unfolded into two broad sheets of gossamer through which I could still see the sunset and the evening lights, blurred, distorted, magical. I sensed the fragrance of her midnight hair. I put my arms to her and embraced her slender, boyish body.

She said, "You know it is my desire to remain with you always, Watcher. Always!"

"Yes, Avluela."

"Will we be happy in Roum?"

"We will be happy," I said, and released her.

"Shall we go into Roum now?"

"I think we should wait for Gormon," I said, shaking my head. "He'll be back soon from his explorations." I did not want to tell her of my weariness. She was only a child, seventeen summers old; what did she know of weariness or of age? And I was old. Not as old as Roum, but old enough.

"While we wait," she said, "may I fly?"

"Fly, yes."

I squatted beside our cart and warmed my hands at the throbbing generator while Avluela prepared to fly. First she removed her garments, for her wings have little strength and she cannot lift such extra baggage. Lithely, deftly, she peeled the glassy bubbles from her tiny feet and wriggled free of her crimson jacket and of her soft, furry leggings. The vanishing light in the west sparkled over her slim form. Like all Fliers, she carried no surplus body tissue: her breasts were mere bumps, her buttocks flat, her thighs so spindly that there was a span of inches between them when she stood. Could she have weighed more than a quintal? I doubt it. Looking at her, I felt, as always, gross and earthbound, a thing of loathsome flesh, and yet I am not a heavy man.

By the roadside she genuflected, knuckles to the ground, head bowed to knees, as she said whatever ritual it is that the Fliers say. Her back was to me. Her delicate wings fluttered, filled with life, rose about her like a cloak whipped up by the breeze. I could not comprehend how such wings could possibly lift even so slight a form as Avluela's. They were not hawk-wings but butterfly-wings, veined and transparent, marked here and there with blotches of pigment, ebony and turquoise and scarlet. A sturdy ligament joined them to the two flat pads of muscle beneath her sharp shoulderblades; but what she did not have was the massive breastbone of a flying creature, the bands of corded muscle needed for flight. Oh, I know that the Fliers use more than muscle to get aloft, that there are mystical disciplines in their mystery. Even so, I, who was of the Watchers, remained skeptical of the more fantastic guilds.

Avluela finished her words. She rose; she caught the breeze with her wings; she ascended several feet. There she remained, suspended between earth and sky, while her wings beat frantically. It was not yet night, and Avluela's wings were merely nightwings. By day she could not fly, for the terrible pressure of the solar wind would hurl her to the ground. Now, midway between dusk and dark, it was still not the best time for her to go up. I saw her thrust toward the east by the remnant of light in the sky. Her arms as well as her wings thrashed; her small pointed face was grim with concentration; on her thin lips were the words of her guild. She doubled her body and shot it out, head going one way, rump the other; and abruptly she hovered horizontally, looking groundward, her wings thrashing against the air. *Up, Avluela! Up!*

Up it was, as by will alone she conquered the vestige of light that still glowed.

With pleasure I surveyed her naked form against the darkness. I could see her clearly, for a Watcher's eyes are keen. She was five times her own height in the air, now, and her wings spread to their full expanse, so that the towers of Roum were in partial eclipse for me. She waved. I threw her a kiss and offered words of love. Watchers do not marry, nor do they engender children, but yet Avluela was as a daughter to me, and I took pride in her flight. We had traveled together a year, now, since we had first met in Agupt, and it was as though I had known her all my long life. From her I drew a renewal of strength. I do not know what it was she drew from me: security, knowledge, a continuity with the days before her birth. I hoped only that she loved me as I loved her.

Now she was far aloft. She wheeled, soared, dived, pirouetted, danced. Her long black hair streamed from her scalp. Her body seemed only an incidental appendage to those two great wings which glistened and throbbed and gleamed in the night. Up she rose, glorying in her freedom from gravity, making me feel all the more leaden-footed; and like some slender rocket she shot abruptly away in the direction of Roum. I saw the soles of her feet, the tips of her wings; then I saw her no more.

I sighed. I thrust my hands into the pits of my arms to keep them warm. How is it that I felt a winter chill while the girl Avluela could soar joyously bare through the sky?

It was now the twelfth of the twenty hours, and time once again for me to do the Watching. I went to the cart, opened my cases, prepared the instruments. Some of the dial, covers were yellowed and faded; the indicator needles had lost their luminous coating; sea stains defaced the instrument housings, a relic of the time that pirates had assailed me in

Earth Ocean. The worn and cracked levers and nodes responded easily to my touch as I entered the preliminaries. First one prays for a pure and perceptive mind; then one creates the affinity with one's instruments; then one does the actual Watching, searching the starry heavens for the enemies of man. Such was my skill and my craft. I grasped handles and knobs, thrust things from my mind, prepared myself to become an extension of my cabinet of devices.

I was only just past my threshold and into the first phase of Watchfulness when a deep and resonant voice behind me said, "Well, Watcher, how goes it?"

I sagged against the cart. There is a physical pain in being wrenched so unexpectedly from one's work. For a moment I felt claws clutching at my heart. My face grew hot; my eyes would not focus; the saliva drained from my throat. As soon as I could, I took the proper protective measures to ease the metabolic drain, and severed myself from my instruments. Hiding my trembling as much as possible, I turned around.

Gormon, the other member of our little band, had appeared and stood jauntily beside me. He was grinning, amused at my distress, but I could not feel angry with him. One does not show anger at a guildless person no matter what the provocation.

Tightly, with effort, I said, "Did you spend your time rewardingly?"

"Very. Where's Avluela?"

I pointed heavenward. Gormon nodded.

"What have you found?" I asked.

"That this city is definitely Roum."

"There never was doubt of that."

"For me there was. But now I have proof."

"Yes?"

"In the overpocket. Look!"

From his tunic he drew his overpocket, set it on the pavement beside me, and expanded it so that he could insert his hands into its mouth. Grunting a little, he began to pull something heavy from the pouch— something of white stone—a long marble column, I now saw, fluted, pocked with age.

"From a temple of Imperial Roum!" Gormon exulted.

"You shouldn't have taken that."

"Wait!" he cried, and reached into the overpocket once more. He took from it a handful of circular metal plaques and scattered them jingling at my feet. "Coins! Money! Look at them, Watcher! The faces of the Caesars!"

"Of whom?"

"The ancient rulers. Don't you know your history of past cycles?"

I peered at him curiously. "You claim to have no guild, Gormon. Could it be you are a Rememberer and are concealing it from me?"

"Look at my face, Watcher. Could I belong to any guild? Would a Changeling be taken?"

"True enough," I said, eyeing the golden hue of him, the thick waxen skin, the red-pupiled eyes, the jagged mouth. Gormon had been weaned on teratogenetic drugs; he was a monster, handsome in his way, but a monster nevertheless, a Changeling, outside the laws and customs of man as they are practiced in the Third Cycle of civilization. And there is no guild of Changelings.

"There's more," Gormon said. The overpocket was infinitely capacious; the contents of a world, if need be, could be stuffed into its shriveled gray maw, and still it would be no longer than a man's hand. Gormon took from it bits of machinery, reading spools, an angular thing of brown metal that might have been an ancient tool, three squares of shining glass, five slips of paper—*paper!*—and a host of other relics of antiquity. "See?" he said. "A fruitful stroll, Watcher! And not just random booty. Everything recorded, everything labeled, stratum, estimated age, position when *in situ*. Here we have many thousands of years of Roum."

"Should you have taken these things?" I asked doubtfully.

"Why not? Who is to miss them? Who of this cycle cares for the past?"

"The Rememberers."

"They don't need solid objects to help them do their work."

"Why do you want these things, though?"

"The past interests me, Watcher. In my guildless way I have my scholarly pursuits. Is that wrong? May not even a monstrosity seek knowledge?"

"Certainly, certainly. Seek what you wish. Fulfill yourself in your own way. This is Roum. At dawn we enter. I hope to find employment here."

"You may have difficulties."

"How so?"

"There are many Watchers already in Roum, no doubt. There will be little need for your services."

"I'll seek the favor of the Prince of Roum," I said.

"The Prince of Roum is a hard and cold and cruel man."

"You know of him?"

Gormon shrugged. "Somewhat." He began to stuff his artifacts back in the overpocket. "Take your chances with him, Watcher. What other choice do you have?"

"None," I said, and Gormon laughed, and I did not.

He busied himself with his ransacked loot of the past. I found myself deeply depressed by his words. He seemed so sure of himself in an uncertain world, this guildless one, this mutated monster, this man of inhuman look; how could he be so cool, so casual? He lived without concern for calamity and mocked those who admitted to fear. Gormon had been traveling with us for nine days, now, since we had met him in the ancient city beneath the volcano to the south by the edge of the sea. I had not suggested that he join us; he had invited himself along, and at Avluela's bidding I accepted. The roads are dark and cold at this time of year, and dangerous beasts of many species abound, and an old man journeying with a girl might well consider taking with him a brawny one like Gormon. Yet there were times I wished he had not come with us, and this was one.

Slowly I walked back to my equipment.

Gormon said, as though first realizing it, "Did I interrupt you at your Watching?"

I said mildly, "You did."

"Sorry. Go and start again. I'll leave you in peace." And he gave me his dazzling lopsided smile, so full of charm that it took the curse off the easy arrogance of his words.

I touched the knobs, made contact with the nodes, monitored the dials. But I did not enter Watchfulness, for I remained aware of Gormon's presence and fearful that he would break into my concentration once again at a painful moment, despite his promise. At length I looked away from the apparatus. Gormon stood at the far side of the road, craning his neck for some sight of Avluela. The moment I turned to him he became aware of me.

"Something wrong, Watcher?"

"No. The moment's not propitious for my work. I'll wait."

"Tell me," he said. "When Earth's enemies really do come from the stars, will your machines let you know it?"

"I trust they will."

"And then?"

"Then I notify the Defenders."

"After which your life's work is over?"

"Perhaps," I said.

"Why a whole guild of you, though? Why not one master center where the Watch is kept? Why a bunch of itinerant Watchers drifting from place to place?"

"The more vectors of detection," I said, "the greater the chance of early awareness of the invasion."

"Then an individual Watcher might well turn his machines on and not see anything, with an invader already here."

"It could happen. And so we practice redundancy."

"You carry it to an extreme, I sometimes think." Gormon laughed. "Do you actually believe an invasion is coming?"

"I do," I said stiffly. "Else my life was a waste."

"And why should the star people want Earth? What do we have here besides the remnants of old empires? What would they do with miserable Roum? With Perris? With Jorslem? Rotting cities! Idiot princes! Come, Watcher, admit it: the invasion's a myth, and you go through meaningless motions four times a day. Eh?"

"It is my craft and my science to Watch. It is yours to jeer. Each of us to our speciality, Gormon."

"Forgive me," he said with mock humility. "Go, then, and Watch."

"I shall."

Angrily I turned back to my cabinet of instruments, determined now to ignore any interruption, no matter how brutal. The stars were out; I gazed at the glowing constellations, and automatically my mind registered the many worlds. Let us Watch, I thought. Let us keep our vigil despite the mockers.

I entered full Watchfulness.

I clung to the grips and permitted the surge of power to rush through me. I cast my mind to the heavens and searched for hostile entities. What ecstasy! What incredible splendor! I who had never left this small planet roved the black spaces of the void, glided from star to burning star, saw the planets spinning like tops. Faces stared back at me as I journeyed, some without eyes, some with many eyes, all the complexity of the many-peopled galaxy accessible to me. I spied out possible concentrations of inimicable force. I inspected drilling-grounds and military encampments. I sought, as I had sought four times daily for all my adult life, for the invaders who had been promised us, the conquerors who at the end of days were destined to seize our tattered world.

I found nothing, and when I came up from my trance, sweaty and drained, I saw Avluela descending.

Feather-light she landed. Gormon called to her, and she ran, bare, her little breasts quivering, and he enfolded her smallness in his powerful arms, and they embraced, not passionately but joyously. When he released her she turned to me.

"Roum," she gasped. *"Roum!"*

"You saw it?"

"Everything! Thousands of people! Lights! Boulevards! A market! Broken buildings many cycles old! Oh, Watcher, how wonderful Roum is!"

"Your flight was a good one, then," I said.

"A miracle!"

"Tomorrow we go to dwell in Roum."

"No, Watcher, tonight, tonight!" She was girlishly eager, her face bright with excitement. "It's just a short journey more! Look, it's just over there!"

"We should rest first," I said. "We do not want to arrive weary in Roum."

"We can rest when we get there," Avluela answered. "Come! Pack everything! You've done your Watching, haven't you?"

"Yes. Yes."

"Then let's go. To Roum! To Roum!"

I looked in appeal at Gormon. Night had come; it was time to make camp, to have our few hours of sleep.

For once Gormon sided with me. He said to Avluela, "The Watcher's right. We can all use some rest. We'll go on into Roum at dawn."

Avluela pouted. She looked more like a child than ever. Her wings drooped; her underdeveloped body slumped. Petulantly she closed her wings until they were mere fist-sized humps on her back, and picked up the garments she had scattered on the road. She dressed while we made camp. I distributed food tablets; we entered our receptacles; I fell into troubled sleep and dreamed of Avluela limned against the crumbling moon, and Gormon flying beside her. Two hours before dawn I arose and performed my first Watch of the new day, while they still slept. Then I aroused them, and we went onward toward the fabled imperial city, onward toward Roum.

2

The morning's light was bright and harsh, as though this were some young world newly created. The road was all but empty; people do not travel much in these latter days unless, like me, they are wanderers by habit and profession. Occasionally we stepped aside to let a chariot of some member of the guild of Masters go by, drawn by a dozen expressionless neuters harnessed in series. Four such vehicles went by in the first two hours of the day, each shuttered and sealed to hide the Master's proud features from the gaze of such common folk as we. Several roller-wagons laden with produce passed us, and a number of floaters soared overhead. Generally we had the road to ourselves, however.

The environs of Roum showed vestiges of antiquity: isolated columns, the fragments of an aqueduct transporting nothing from nowhere to nowhere, the portals of a vanished temple. That was the oldest Roum we saw, but there were accretions of the later Roums of subsequent cycles: the huts of peasants, the domes of power drains, the hulls of dwelling-towers. Infrequently we met with the burned-out shell of some ancient airship. Gormon examined everything, taking samples from time to time. Avluela looked, wide-eyed, saying nothing. We walked on, until the walls of the city loomed before us.

They were of a blue glossy stone, neatly joined, rising to a height of perhaps eight men. Our road pierced the wall through a corbeled arch; the gate stood open. As we approached the gate, a figure came toward us; he was hooded, masked, a man of extraordinary height wearing the somber garb of the guild of Pilgrims. One does not approach such a person oneself, but one heeds him if he beckons. The Pilgrim beckoned.

Through his speaking grille he said, "Where from?"

"The south. I lived in Agupt awhile, then crossed Land Bridge to Talya," I replied.

"Where bound?"

"Roum, awhile."

"How goes the Watch?"

"As customary."

"You have a place to stay in Roum?" the Pilgrim asked.

I shook my head. "We trust to the kindness of the Will."

"The Will is not always kind," said the Pilgrim absently. "Nor is there much need of Watchers in Roum. Why do you travel with a Flier?"

"For company's sake. And because she is young and needs protection."

"Who is the other one?"

"He is guildless, a Changeling."

"So I can see. But why is he with you?"

"He is strong and I am old, and so we travel together. Where are you bound, Pilgrim?"

"Jorslem. Is there another destination for my guild?"

I conceded the point with a shrug.

The Pilgrim said, "Why do you not come to Jorslem with me?"

"My road lies north now. Jorslem is in the south, close by Agupt."

"You have been to Agupt and not to Jorslem?" he said, puzzled.

"Yes. The time was not ready for me to see Jorslem."

"Come now. We will walk together on the road, Watcher, and we will talk of the old times and of the times to come, and I will assist you in your Watching, and you will assist me in my communions with the Will. Is it agreed?"

It was a temptation. Before my eyes flashed the image of Jorslem the Golden, its holy buildings and shrines, its places of renewal where the old are made young, its spires, its tabernacles. Even though I am a man set in his ways, I was willing at the moment to abandon Roum and go with the Pilgrim to Jorslem.

I said, "And my companions—"

"Leave them. It is forbidden for me to travel with the guildless, and I do not wish to travel with a female. You and I, Watcher, will go to Jorslem together."

Avluela, who had been standing to one side frowning through all this colloquy, shot me a look of sudden terror.

"I will not abandon them," I said.

"Then I go to Jorslem alone," said the Pilgrim. Out of his robe stretched a bony hand, the fingers long and white and steady. I touched my fingers reverently to the tips of his, and the Pilgrim said, "Let the Will give you mercy, friend Watcher. And when you reach Jorslem, search for me."

He moved on down the road without further conversation.

Gormon said to me, "You would have gone with him, wouldn't you?"

"I considered it."

"What could you find in Jorslem that isn't here? That's a holy city and so is this. Here you can rest awhile. You're in no shape for more walking now."

"You may be right," I conceded, and with the last of my energy I strode toward the gate of Roum.

Watchful eyes scanned us from slots in the wall. When we were at midpoint in the gate, a fat, pockmarked Sentinel with sagging jowls halted us and asked our business in Roum. I stated my guild and purpose, and he gave a snort of disgust.

"Go elsewhere, Watcher! We need only useful men here."

"Watching has its uses," I said mildly.

"No doubt. No doubt." He squinted at Avluela. "Who's this? Watchers are celibates, no?"

"She is nothing more than a traveling companion."

The Sentinel guffawed coarsely. "It's a route you travel often, I wager! Not that there's much to her. What is she, thirteen, fourteen? Come here, child. Let me check you for contraband." He ran his hands quickly over her, scowling as he felt her breasts, then raising an eyebrow as he encountered the mounds of her wings below her shoulders. "What's this? What's this? More in back than in front! A Flier, are you? Very dirty business, Fliers consorting with foul old Watchers." He chuckled and put his hand on Avluela's body in a way that sent Gormon starting forward in fury, murder in his fire-circled eyes. I caught him in time and grasped his wrist with all my strength, holding him back lest he ruin the three of us by an attack on the Sentinel. He tugged at me, nearly pulling me over; then he grew calm and subsided, icily watching as the fat one finished checking Avluela for "contraband."

At length the Sentinel turned in distaste to Gormon and said, "What kind of thing are you?"

"Guildless, your mercy," Gormon said in sharp tones. "The humble and worthless product of teratogenesis, and yet nevertheless a free man who desires entry to Roum."

"Do we need more monsters here?"

"I eat little and work hard."

"You'd work harder still, if you were neutered," said the Sentinel.

Gormon glowered. I said, "May we have entry?"

"A moment." The Sentinel donned his thinking cap and narrowed his eyes as he transmitted a message to the memory tanks. His face tensed with the effort; then it went slack, and moments later came the reply. We could not hear the transaction at all; but from his disappointed look, it appeared evident that no reason had been found to refuse us admission to Roum.

"Go on in," he said. "The three of you. Quickly!"

We passed beyond the gate.

Gormon said, "I could have split him open with a blow."

"And be neutered by nightfall. A little patience, and we've come into Roum."

"The way he handled her—!"

"You take a very possessive attitude toward Avluela," I said. "Remember that she's a Flier, and not sexually available to the guildless."

Gormon ignored my thrust. "She arouses me no more than you do, Watcher. But it pains me to see her treated that way. I would have killed him if you hadn't held me back."

Avluela said, "Where shall we stay, now that we're in Roum?"

"First let me find the headquarters of my guild," I said. "I'll register at the Watchers' Inn. After that, perhaps we'll hunt up the Fliers' Lodge for a meal."

"And then," said Gormon drily, "we'll go to the Guildless Gutter and beg for coppers."

"I pity you because you are a Changeling," I told him, "but I find it ungraceful of you to pity yourself. Come."

We walked up a cobbled, winding street away from the gate and into Roum itself. We were in the outer ring of the city, a residential section of low, squat houses topped by the unwieldy bulk of defense installations. Within lay the shining towers we had seen from the fields the night before; the remnant of ancient Roum carefully preserved across ten thousand years or more; the market, the factory zone, the communications hump, the temples of the Will, the memory tanks, the sleepers' refuges, the outworlders' brothels, the government buildings, the headquarters of the various guilds.

At the corner, beside a Second Cycle building with walls of rubbery texture, I found a public thinking cap and slipped it on my forehead. At once my thoughts raced down the conduit until they came to the interface that gave them access to one of the storage brains of a memory tank. I pierced the interface and saw the wrinkled brain itself, pale gray against the deep green of its housing. A Rememberer once told me that, in cycles past, men built machines to do their thinking for them, although these machines were hellishly expensive and required vast amounts of space and drank power gluttonously. That was not the worst of our forefathers' follies; but why build artificial brains when death each day liberates scores of splendid natural ones to hook into the memory tanks? Was it that they lacked the knowledge to use them? I find that hard to believe.

I gave the brain my guild identification and asked the coordinates of our inn. Instantly I received them, and we set out, Avluela on one side of me, Gormon on the other, myself wheeling, as always, the cart in which my instruments resided.

The city was crowded. I had not seen such throngs in sleepy, heat-fevered Agupt, nor at any other point on my northward journey. The streets were full of Pilgrims, secretive and masked. Jostling through them went busy Rememberers and glum Merchants and now and then the litter of a Master. Avluela saw a number of Fliers, but was barred by the tenets of her guild from greeting them until she had undergone her ritual purification. I regret to say that I spied many Watchers, all of whom looked upon me disdainfully and without welcome. I noted a good many Defenders and ample representation of such lesser guilds as Vendors, Servitors, Manufactories, Scribes, Communicants, and Transporters. Naturally, a host of neuters went silently about their humble business, and numerous outworlders of all descriptions flocked the streets, most of them probably tourists, some here to do what business could be done with the sullen, poverty-blighted people of Earth. I noticed many Changelings limping furtively through the crowd, not one of them as proud of bearing as Gormon beside me. He was unique among his kind; the others, dappled and piebald and asymmetrical, limbless or overlimbed, deformed in a thousand imaginative and artistic ways, were slinkers, squinters, shufflers, hissers, creepers; they were cutpurses, brain-drainers, organ-peddlers, repentance-mongers, gleam-buyers, but none held himself upright as though he thought he were a man.

The guidance of the brain was exact, and in less than an hour of walking we arrived at the Watchers' Inn. I left Gormon and Avluela outside and wheeled my cart within.

Perhaps a dozen members of my guild lounged in the main hall. I gave them the customary sign, and they returned it languidly. Were these the guardians on whom Earth's safety depended? Simpletons and weaklings!

"Where may I register?" I asked.

"New? Where from?"

"Agupt was my last place of registry."

"Should have stayed there. No need of Watchers here."

"Where may I register?" I asked again.

A foppish youngster indicated a screen in the rear of the great room. I went to it, pressed my fingertips against it, was interrogated, and gave my name, which a Watcher may utter only to another Watcher and only within the precincts of an inn. A panel shot open, and a puffy-eyed man who wore the Watcher emblem on his right cheek and not on the left, signifying his high rank in the guild, spoke my name and said, "You should have known better than to come to Roum. We're over our quota."

"I claim lodging and employment nonetheless."

"A man with your sense of humor should have been born into the guild of Clowns," he said.

"I see no joke."

"Under laws promulgated by our guild in the most recent session, an inn is under no obligation to take new lodgers once it has reached its assigned capacity. We are at our assigned capacity. Farewell, my friend."

I was aghast. "I know of no such regulation! This is incredible! For a guild to turn away a member from its own inn—when he arrives footsore and numb! A man of my age, having crossed Land Bridge out of Agupt, here as a stranger and hungry in Roum—"

"Why did you not check with us first?"

"I had no idea it would be necessary."

"The new regulations—"

"May the Will shrivel the new regulations!" I shouted. "I demand lodging! To turn away one who has Watched since before you were born—"

"Easy, brother, easy."

"Surely you have some corner where I can sleep—some crumbs to let me eat—"

Even as my tone had changed from bluster to supplication, his expression softened from indifference to mere disdain. "We have no room. We have no food. These are hard times for our guild, you know. There is talk that we will be disbanded altogether, as a useless luxury, a drain upon the Will's resources. We are very limited in our abilities. Because Roum has a surplus of Watchers, we all are on short rations as it is, and if we admit you our rations will be all the shorter."

"But where will I go? What shall I do?"

"I advise you," he said blandly, "to throw yourself upon the mercy of the Prince of Roum."

3

Outside, I told that to Gormon, and he doubled with laughter, guffawing so furiously that the striations on his lean cheeks blazed like bloody stripes. "The mercy of the Prince of Roum!" he repeated. "The mercy—of the Prince of Roum—"

"It is customary for the unfortunate to seek the aid of the local ruler," I said coldly.

"The Prince of Roum knows no mercy," Gormon told me. "The Prince of Roum will feed you your own limbs to ease your hunger!"

"Perhaps," Avluela put in, "we should try to find the Fliers' Lodge. They'll feed us there."

"Not Gormon," I observed. "We have obligations to one another."

"We could bring food out to him," she said.

"I prefer to visit the court first," I insisted. "Let us make sure of our status. Afterward we can improvise living arrangements, if we must."

She yielded, and we made our way to the palace of the Prince of Roum, a massive building fronted by a colossal column-ringed plaza, on the far side of the river that splits the city. In the plaza we were accosted by mendicants of many sorts, some not even Earthborn; something with ropy tendrils and a corrugated, noseless face thrust itself at me and jabbered for alms until Gormon pushed it away, and moments later a second creature, equally strange, its skin pocked with luminescent craters and its limbs studded with eyes, embraced my knees and pleaded in the name of the Will for my mercy. "I am only a poor Watcher," I said, indicating my cart, "and am here to gain mercy myself." But the being persisted, sobbing out its misfortunes in a blurred, feathery voice, and in the end, to Gormon's immense disgust, I dropped a few food tablets into the shelf-like pouch on its chest. Then we muscled on toward the doors of the palace. At the portico a more horrid sight presented itself: a maimed Flier, fragile limbs bent and twisted, one wing half-unfolded and severely cropped, the other missing altogether. The Flier rushed upon Avluela, called her by a name not hers, moistened her leggings with tears so copious that the fur of them matted and stained. "Sponsor me to the lodge," he appealed. "They have turned me away because I am crippled, but if you sponsor me—" Avluela explained that she could do nothing, that she was a stranger to this lodge. The broken Flier would not release her, and Gormon with great delicacy lifted him like the bundle of dry bones that he was and set him aside. We stepped up onto the portico and at once were confronted by a trio of soft-faced neuters, who asked our business and admitted us quickly to the next line of barrier, which was manned by a pair of wizened Indexers. Speaking in unison, they queried us.

"We seek audience," I said. "A matter of mercy."

"The day of audience is four days hence," said the Indexer on the right. "We will enter your request on the rolls."

"We have no place to sleep!" Avluela burst out. "We are hungry! We—"

I hushed her. Gormon, meanwhile, was groping in the mouth of his overpocket. Bright things glimmered in his hand: pieces of gold, the eternal metal, stamped with hawk-nosed, bearded faces. He had found them grubbing in the ruins. He tossed one coin to the Indexer who had refused us. The man snapped it from the air, rubbed his thumb roughly across its shining obverse, and dropped it instantly into a fold of his garment. The second Indexer waited expectantly. Smiling, Gormon gave him his coin.

"Perhaps," I said, "we can arrange for a special audience within."

"Perhaps you can," said one of the Indexers. "Go through."

And so we passed into the nave of the palace itself and stood in the great, echoing space, looking down the central aisle toward the shielded throne-chamber at the apse. There were more beggars in here—licensed ones holding hereditary concessions—and also throngs of Pilgrims, Communicants, Rememberers, Musicians, Scribes, and Indexers. I heard muttered prayers; I smelled the scent of spicy incense; I felt the vibration of subterranean gongs. In cycles past, this building had been a shrine of one of the old religions—the Christers, Gormon told me, making me suspect once more that he was a Rememberer masquerading as a Changeling—and it still maintained something of its holy character even though it served as Roum's seat of secular government. But how were we to get to see the Prince? To my left I saw a small ornate chapel which a line of prosperous-looking Merchants and Landholders was slowly entering. Peering past them, I noted three skulls mounted on an interrogation fixture—a memory-tank input—and beside them, a burly Scribe. Telling Gormon and Avluela to wait for me in the aisle, I joined the line.

It moved infrequently, and nearly an hour passed before I reached the interrogation fixture. The skulls glared sightlessly at me; within their sealed crania, nutrient fluids bubbled and gurgled, caring for the dead, yet still functional, brains whose billion billion synaptic units now served as incomparable mnemonic devices. The Scribe seemed aghast to find a Watcher in this line, but before he could challenge me I blurted, "I come as a stranger to claim the Prince's mercy. I and my companions are without lodging. My own guild has turned me away. What shall I do? How may I gain an audience?"

"Come back in four days."

"I've slept on the road for more days than that. Now I must rest more easily."

"A public inn—"

"But I am guilded!" I protested. "The public inns would not admit me while my guild maintains an inn here, and my guild refuses me because of some new regulation, and—you see my predicament?"

In a wearied voice the Scribe said, "You may have application for a special audience. It will be denied, but you may apply."

"Where?"

"Here. State your purpose."

I identified myself to the skulls by my public designation, listed the names and status of my two companions, and explained my case. All this was absorbed and transmitted to the ranks of brains mounted somewhere in the depths of the city, and when I was done the Scribe said, "If the application is approved, you will be notified."

"Meanwhile where shall I stay?"

"Close to the palace, I would suggest."

I understood. I could join that legion of unfortunates packing the plaza. How many of them had requested some special favor of the Prince and were still there, months or years later, waiting to be summoned to the Presence? Sleeping on stone, begging for crusts, living in foolish hope!

But I had exhausted my avenues. I returned to Gormon and Avluela, told them of the situation, and suggested that we now attempt to hunt whatever accommodations we could. Gormon, guildless, was welcome at any of the squalid public inns maintained for his kind; Avluela could probably find residence at her own guild's lodge; only I would have to sleep in the streets—and not for the first time. But I hoped that we would not have to separate. I had come to think of us as a family, strange thought though that was for a Watcher.

As we moved toward the exit, my timepiece told me softly that the hour of Watching had come round again. It was my obligation and my privilege to tend to my Watching wherever I might be, regardless of the circumstances, whenever my hour came round; and so I halted, opened the cart, activated the equipment. Gormon and Avluela stood beside me. I saw smirks and open mockery on the faces of those who passed in and out of the palace; Watching was not held in very high repute, for we had Watched so long, and the promised enemy had never come. Yet one has one's duties, comic though they may seem to others. What is a hollow ritual to some is a life's work to others. Doggedly I forced myself into a state of Watchfulness. The world melted away from me, and I plunged into the heavens. The familiar joy engulfed me; and I searched the familiar places, and some that were not so familiar, my amplified mind leaping through the galaxies in wild swoops. Was an armada massing? Were troops drilling for the conquest of Earth? Four times a day I Watched, and the other members of my guild did the same, each at slightly different hours, so that no moment went by without some vigilant mind on guard. I do not believe that that was a foolish calling.

When I came up from my trance, a brazen voice was crying, "—for the Prince of Roum! Make way for the Prince of Roum!"

I blinked and caught my breath and fought to shake off the last strands of my concentration. A gilded palanquin borne by a phalanx of neuters had emerged from the rear of the palace and was proceeding down the nave toward me. Four men in the elegant costumes and brilliant masks of the guild of Masters flanked the litter, and it was preceded by a trio of Changelings, squat and broad, whose throats were so modified to imitate the sounding-boxes of bullfrogs; they emitted a trumpetlike boom of majestic sound as they advanced. It struck me as most strange that a prince would admit Changelings to his service, even ones as gifted as these.

My cart was blocking the progress of this magnificent procession, and hastily I struggled to close it and move it aside before the parade swept down upon me. Age and fear made my fingers tremble, and I could not make the sealings properly; while I fumbled in increasing clumsiness, the strutting Changelings drew so close that the blare of their throats was deafening, and Gormon attempted to aid me, forcing me to hiss at him that it is forbidden for anyone not of my guild to touch the equipment. I pushed him away; and an instant later a vanguard of neuters descended on me and prepared to scourge me from the spot with sparkling whips. "In the Will's name," I cried, "I am a Watcher!"

And in antiphonal response came the deep, calm, enormous reply, "Let him be. He is a watcher."

All motion ceased. The Prince of Roum had spoken.

The neuters drew back. The Changelings halted their music. The bearers of the Palanquin eased it to the floor. All those in the nave of the palace had pulled back, save only Gormon and Avluela and myself. The shimmering chain-curtains of the palanquin parted. Two of the Masters hurried forward and thrust their hands through the sonic barrier within, offering aid to their monarch. The barrier died away with a whimpering buzz.

The Prince of Roum appeared.

He was so young! He was nothing more than a boy, his hair full and dark, his face unlined. But he had been born to rule, and for all his youth he was as commanding as anyone I had ever seen. His lips were thin and tightly compressed; his aquiline nose was sharp and aggressive; his eyes, deep and cold, were infinite pools. He wore the jeweled garments of the guild of Dominators, but incised on his cheek was the double-barred cross of the Defenders, and around his neck he carried the dark shawl of the Rememberers. A Dominator may enroll in as many guilds as he pleases, and it would be a strange thing for a Dominator not also to be a Defender; but it startled me to find this prince a Rememberer as well. That is not normally a guild for the fierce.

He looked at me with little interest and said, "You choose an odd place to do your Watching, old man."

"The hour chose the place, sire," I replied. "I was here, and my duty compelled me. I had no way of knowing that you were about to come forth."

"Your Watching found no enemies?"

"None, sire."

I was about to press my luck, to take advantage of the unexpected appearance of the Prince to beg for his aid; but his interest in me died like a guttering candle as I stood there, and I did not dare call to him when his head had turned. He eyed Gormon a long moment, frowning and tugging at his chin. Then his gaze fell on Avluela. His eyes brightened. His jaw muscles flickered. His delicate nostrils widened. "Come up here, little Flier," he said, beckoning. "Are you this Watcher's friend?"

She nodded, terrified.

The Prince held out a hand to her and grasped; she floated up onto the palanquin, and with a grin so evil it seemed a parody of wickedness, the young Dominator drew her through the curtain. Instantly a pair of Masters restored the sonic barrier, but the procession did not move on. I stood mute. Gormon beside me was frozen, his powerful body rigid as a rod. I wheeled my cart to a less conspicuous place. Long moments passed. The courtiers remained silent, discreetly looking away from the palanquin.

At length the curtain parted once more. Avluela came stumbling out, her face pale, her eyes blinking rapidly. She seemed dazed. Streaks of sweat gleamed on her cheeks. She nearly fell, and a neuter caught her and swung her down to floor level. Beneath her jacket her wings were partly erect, giving her a hunchbacked look and telling me that she was in great emotional distress. In ragged, sliding steps she came to us, quivering, wordless; she darted a glance at me and flung herself against Gormon's broad chest.

The bearers lifted the palanquin. The Prince of Roum went out from his palace.

When he was gone, Avluela stammered hoarsely, "The Prince has granted us lodging in the royal hostelry!"

4

The hostelkeepers, of course, would not believe us.

Guests of the Prince were housed in the royal hostelry, which was to the rear of the palace in a small garden of frostflowers and blossoming ferns. The usual inhabitants of such a hostelry were Masters and an occasional Dominator; sometimes a particularly important Rememberer on an errand of research would win a niche there, or some highly placed Defender visiting for purposes of strategic planning. To house a Flier in a royal hostelry was distinctly odd; to admit a Watcher was unlikely; to take in a Changeling or some other guildless person was improbable beyond comprehension. When we presented ourselves, therefore, we were met by Servitors whose attitude was at first one of high good humor at our joke, then of irritation, finally of scorn. "Get away," they told us ultimately. "Scum! Rabble!"

Avluela said in a grave voice, "The Prince has granted us lodging here, and you may not refuse us."

"Away! Away!"

One snaggle-toothed Servitor produced a neural truncheon and brandished it in Gormon's face, passing a foul remark about his guildlessness. Gormon slapped the truncheon from the man's grasp, oblivious to the painful sting, and kicked him in the gut, so that he coiled and fell over, puking. Instantly a throng of neuters came rushing from within the hostelry. Gormon seized another of the Servitors and hurled him into the midst of them, turning them into a muddled mob. Wild shouts and angry cursing cries attracted the attention of a venerable Scribe who waddled to the door, bellowed for silence, and interrogated us. "That's easily checked," he said, when Avluela had told the story. To a Servitor he said contemptuously, "Send a think to the Indexers, fast!"

In time the confusion was untangled and we were admitted. We were given separate but adjoining rooms. I had never known such luxury before, and perhaps never shall again. The rooms were long, high, and deep. One entered them through telescopic pits keyed to one's own thermal output, to assure privacy. Lights glowed at the resident's merest nod, for hanging from ceiling globes and nestling in cupolas on the walls were spicules of slavelight from one of the Brightstar worlds, trained through suffering to obey such commands. The windows came and went at the dweller's whim; when not in use, they were concealed by streamers of quasi-sentient outworld gauzes, which not only were decorative in their own right, but which functioned as monitors to produce delightful scents according to requisitioned patterns. The rooms were equipped with individual thinking caps connected to the main memory banks. They likewise had conduits that summoned Servitors, Scribes, Indexers, or Musicians as required. Of course, a man of my own humble guild would not deign to make use of other human beings that way, out of fear of their glowering resentment; but in any case I had little need of them.

I did not ask of Avluela what had occurred in the Prince's palanquin to bring us such bounty. I could well imagine, as could Gormon, whose barely suppressed inner rage was eloquent of his never-admitted love for my pale, slender little Flier.

We settled in. I placed my cart beside the window, draped it with gauzes, and left it in readiness for my next period of Watching. I cleaned my body of grime while entities mounted in the wall sang me to peace. Later I ate. Afterwards Avluela came to me, refreshed and relaxed, and sat beside me in my room as we talked of our experiences. Gormon did not appear for hours. I thought that perhaps he had left this hostelry altogether, finding the atmosphere too rarefied for him, and had sought company among his own guildless kind. But at twilight, Avluela and I walked in the cloistered courtyard of the hostelry and mounted a ramp to watch the stars emerge in Roum's sky, and Gormon was there. With him was a lanky and emaciated man in a Rememberer's shawl; they were talking in low tones.

Gormon nodded to me and said, "Watcher, meet my new friend."

The emaciated one fingered his shawl. "I am the Rememberer Basil," he intoned, in a voice as thin as a fresco that has been peeled from its wall. "I have come from Perris to delve into the mysteries of Roum. I shall be here many years."

"The Rememberer has fine stories to tell," said Gormon. "He is among the foremost of his guild. As you approached, he was describing to me the techniques by which the past is revealed. They drive a trench through the strata of Third Cycle deposits, you see, and with vacuum cores they lift the molecules of earth to lay bare the ancient layers."

"We have found," Basil said, "the catacombs of Imperial Roum, and the rubble of the Time of Sweeping, the books inscribed on slivers of white metal, written toward the close of the Second Cycle. All these go to Perris for examination and classification and decipherment; then they return. Does the past interest you, Watcher?"

"To some extent." I smiled. "This Changeling here shows much more fascination for it. I sometimes suspect his authenticity. Would you recognize a Rememberer in disguise?"

Basil scrutinized Gormon; he lingered over the bizarre features, the excessively muscular frame. "He is no Rememberer," he said at length. "But I agree that he has antiquarian interests. He has asked me many profound questions."

"Such as?"

"He wishes to know the origin of guilds. He asks the name of the genetic surgeon who crafted the first true-breeding Fliers. He wonders why there are Changelings, and if they are truly under the curse of the Will."

"And do you have answers for these?" I asked.

"For some," said Basil. "For some."

"The origin of guilds?"

"To give structure and meaning to a society that has suffered defeat and destruction," said the Rememberer. "At the end of the Second Cycle all was in flux. No man knew his rank nor his purpose. Through our world strode haughty outworlders who looked upon us all as worthless. It was necessary to establish fixed frames of reference by which one man might know his value beside another. So the first guilds appeared: Dominators, Masters, Merchants, Landholders, Vendors and Servitors. Then came Scribes, Musicians, Clowns and Transporters. Afterwards Indexers became necessary, and then Watchers and Defenders. When the Years of Magic gave us Fliers and Changelings, those guilds were added, and then the guildless ones, the neuters, were produced, so that—"

"But surely the Changelings are guildless too!" said Avluela.

The Rememberer looked at her for the first time. "Who are you, child?"

"Avluela of the Fliers. I travel with this Watcher and this Changeling."

Basil said, "As I have been telling the Changeling here, in the early days his kind was guilded. The guild was dissolved a thousand years ago by the order of the Council of Dominators after an attempt by a disreputable Changeling faction to seize control of the holy places of Jorslem, and since that time Changelings have been guildless, ranking only above neuters."

"I never knew that," I said.

"You are no Rememberer," said Basil smugly. "It is our craft to uncover the past."

"True. True."

Gormon said, "And today, how many guilds are there?"

Discomfited, Basil replied vaguely, "At least a hundred, my friend. Some are quite small; some are local. I am concerned only with the original guilds and their immediate successors; what has happened in the past few hundred years is in the province of others. Shall I requisition an information for you?"

"Never mind," Gormon said. "It was only an idle question."

"Your curiosity is well developed," said the Rememberer.

"I find the world and all it contains extremely fascinating. Is this sinful?"

"It is strange," said Basil. "The guildless rarely look beyond their own horizons."

A Servitor appeared. With a mixture of awe and contempt he genuflected before Avluela and said, "The Prince has returned. He desires your company in the palace at this time."

Terror glimmered in Avluela's eyes. But to refuse was inconceivable. "Shall I come with you?" she asked.

"Please. You must be robed and perfumed. He wishes you to come to him with your wings open, as well."

Avluela nodded. The Servitor led her away.

We remained on the ramp a while longer; the Rememberer Basil talked of the old days of Roum, and I listened, and Gormon peered into the gathering darkness. Eventually, his throat dry, the Rememberer excused himself and moved solemnly away. A few moments later, in the courtyard below us, a door opened and Avluela emerged, walking as though she were of the guild of Somnambulists, not of Fliers. She was nude under transparent draperies, and her fragile body gleamed ghostly white in the starbeams. Her wings were spread and fluttered slowly in a somber systole and diastole. One Servitor grasped each of her elbows: they seemed to be propelling her toward the palace as though she were but a dreamed facsimile of herself and not a real woman.

"Fly, Avluela, fly," Gormon growled. "Escape while you can!"

She disappeared into a side entrance of the palace.

The Changeling looked at me. "She has sold herself to the Prince to provide lodging for us."

"So it seems."

"I could smash down that palace!"

"You love her?"

"It should be obvious."

"Cure yourself," I advised. "You are an unusual man, but still a Flier is not for you. Particularly a Flier who has shared the bed of the Prince of Roum."

"She goes from my arms to his."

I was staggered. "You've known her?"

"More than once," he said, smiling sadly. "At the moment of ecstasy her wings thrash like leaves in a storm."

I gripped the railing of the ramp so that I would not tumble into the courtyard. The stars whirled overhead; the old moon and its two blank-faced consorts leaped and bobbed. I was shaken without fully understanding the cause of my emotion. Was it wrath that Gormon had dared to violate a canon of the law? Was it a manifestation of those pseudo-parental feelings I had toward Avluela? Or was it mere envy of Gormon for daring to commit a sin beyond my capacity, though not beyond my desires?

I said, "They could burn your brain for that. They could mince your soul. And now you make me an accessory."

"What of it? That Prince commands, and he gets—but others have been there before him. I had to tell someone."

"Enough. Enough."

"Will we see her again?"

"Princes tire quickly of their women. A few days, perhaps a single night—then he will throw her back to us. And perhaps then we shall have to leave this hostelry." I sighed. "At least we'll have known it a few nights more than we deserved."

"Where will you go then?" Gormon asked.

"I will stay in Roum awhile."

"Even if you sleep in the streets? There does not seem to be much demand for Watchers here."

"I'll manage," I said. "Then I may go toward Perris."

"To learn from the Rememberers?"

"To see Perris. What of you? What do you want in Roum?"

"Avluela."

"Stop that talk!"

"Very well," he said, and his smile was bitter. "But I will stay here until the Prince is through with her. Then she will be mine, and we'll find ways to survive. The guildless are resourceful. They have to be. Maybe we'll scrounge lodgings in Roum awhile, and then follow you to Perris. If you're willing to travel with monsters and faithless Fliers."

I shrugged. "We'll see about that when the time comes."

"Have you ever been in the company of a Changeling before?"

"Not often. Not for long."

"I'm honored." He drummed on the parapet. "Don't cast me off, Watcher. I have a reason for wanting to stay with you."

"Which is?"

"To see your face on the day your machines tell you that the invasion of Earth has begun."

I let myself sag forward, shoulders drooping. "You'll stay with me a long time, then."

"Don't you believe the invasion is coming?"

"Some day. Not soon."

Gormon chuckled. "You're wrong. It's almost here."

"You don't amuse me."

"What is it, Watcher? Have you lost your faith? It's been known for a thousand years: another race covets Earth and owns it by treaty, and will some day come to collect. That much was decided at the end of the Second Cycle."

"I know all that, and I am no Rememberer." Then I turned to him and spoke words I never thought I would say aloud. "For twice your lifetime, Changeling, I've listened to the stars and done my Watching. Something done that often loses meaning. Say your own name ten thousand times and it will be an empty sound. I have Watched, and Watched well, and in the dark hours of the night I sometimes think I Watch for nothing, that I have wasted my life. There is a pleasure in Watching, but perhaps there is no real purpose."

His hand encircled my wrist. "Your confession is as shocking as mine. Keep your faith, Watcher. The invasion comes!"

"How could you possibly know?"

"The guildless also have their skills."

The conversation troubled me. I said, "Is it painful to be guildless?"

"One grows reconciled. And there are certain freedoms to compensate for the lack of status. I may speak freely to all."

"I notice."

"I move freely. I am always sure of food and lodging, though the food may be rotten and the lodging poor. Women are attracted to me despite all prohibitions. Because of them, perhaps. I am untroubled by ambitions."

"Never desire to rise above your rank?"

"Never."

"You might have been happier as a Rememberer."

"I am happy now. I can have a Rememberer's pleasures without his responsibility."

"How smug you are!" I cried. "To make, a virtue of guildlessness!"

"How else does one endure the weight of the Will?" He looked toward the palace. "The humble rise. The mighty fall. Take this as prophecy, Watcher: that lusty Prince in there will know more of life before summer comes. I'll rip out his eyes for taking Avluela!"

"Strong words. You bubble with treason tonight."

"Take it as prophecy."

"You can't get close to him," I said. Then, irritated for taking his foolishness seriously, I added, "And why blame him? He only does as princes do. Blame the girl for going to him. She might have refused."

"And lost her wings. Or died. No, she had no choice. I do!" In a sudden, terrible gesture the Changeling held out thumb and forefinger, double-jointed, long-nailed, and plunged them forward into imagined eyes. "Wait," he said. "You'll see!"

In the courtyard two Chronomancers appeared, set up the apparatus of their guild, and lit tapers by which to read the shape of tomorrow. A sickly odor of pallid smoke rose to my nostrils. I had now lost further desire to speak with the Changeling.

"It grows late," I said. "I need rest, and soon I must do my Watching."

"Watch carefully," Gormon told me.

5

At night in my chamber I performed my fourth and last Watch of that long day, and for the first time in my life I detected an anomaly. I could not interpret it. It was an obscure sensation, a mingling of tastes and sounds, a feeling of being in contact with some colossal mass. Worried, I clung to my instrument far longer than usual, but perceived no more clearly at the end of my seance than at its commencement.

Afterward I wondered about my obligations.

Watchers are trained from childhood to be swift to sound the alarm; and the alarm must be sounded when the Watcher judges the world in peril. Was I now obliged to notify the Defenders? Four times in my life the alarm had been given, on each occasion in error; and each Watcher who had thus touched off a false mobilization had suffered a fearful loss of status. One had contributed his brain to the memory banks; one had become a neuter out of shame; one had smashed his instruments and gone to live among the guildless; and one, vainly attempting to continue in his profession, had discovered himself mocked by all his comrades. I saw no virtue in scorning one who had delivered a false alarm, for was it not preferable for a Watcher to cry out too soon than not at all? But those were the customs of our guild, and I was constrained by them.

I evaluated my position and decided that I did not have valid grounds for an alarm.

I reflected that Gormon had placed suggestive ideas in my mind that evening. I might possibly be reacting only to his jeering talk of imminent invasion.

I could not act. I dared not jeopardize my standing by hasty outcry. I mistrusted my own emotional state.

I gave no alarm.

Seething, confused, my soul roiling, I closed my cart and let myself sink into a drugged sleep.

At dawn I woke and rushed to the window, expecting to find invaders in the streets. But all was still; a winter grayness hung over the courtyard, and sleepy Servitors pushed passive neuters about. Uneasily I did my first Watching of the day, and to my relief the strangenesses of the night before did not return, although I had it in mind that my sensitivity is always greater at night than upon arising.

I ate and went to the courtyard. Gormon and Avluela were already there. She looked fatigued and downcast, depleted by her night with the Prince of Roum, but I said nothing to her about it. Gormon, slouching disdainfully against a wall embellished with the shells of radiant mollusks, said to me, "Did your Watching go well?"

"Well enough."

"What of the day?"

"Out of roam Roum," I said. "Will you come? Avluela? Gormon?"

"Surely," he said, and she gave a faint nod; and, like the tourists we were, we set off to inspect the splendid city of Roum.

Gormon acted as our guide to the jumbled pasts of Roum, belying his claim never to have been here before. As well as any Rememberer he described the things we saw as we walked the winding streets. All the scattered levels of thousands of years were exposed. We saw the power domes of the Second Cycle, and the Colosseum where at an unimaginably early date man and beast contended like jungle creatures. In the broken hull of that building of horrors Gormon told us of the savagery of that unimaginably ancient time. "They fought," he said, "naked before huge throngs. With bare hands men challenged beasts called lions, great hairy cats with swollen heads; and when the lion lay in its gore, the victor turned to the Prince of Roum and asked to be pardoned for whatever crime it was that had cast him into the arena. And if he had fought well, the Prince made a gesture with his hand, and the man was freed." Gormon made the gesture for us: a thumb upraised and jerked backward over the right shoulder several times. "But if the man had shown cowardice, or if the lion had distinguished itself in the manner of its dying, the Prince made another gesture, and the man was condemned to be slain by a second beast." Gormon showed us that gesture too: the middle finger jutting upward from a clenched fist and lifted in a short sharp thrust.

"How are these things known?" Avluela asked, but Gormon pretended not to hear her.

We saw the line of fusion-pylons built early in the Third Cycle to draw energy from the world's core; they were still functioning, although stained and corroded. We saw the shattered stump of a Second Cycle weather machine, still a mighty column at least twenty men high. We saw a hill on which white marble relics of First Cycle Roum sprouted like pale clumps of winter deathflowers. Penetrating toward the inner part of the city, we came upon the embankment of defensive amplifiers waiting in readiness to hurl the full impact of the Will against invaders. We viewed a market where visitors from the stars haggled with peasants for excavated fragments of antiquity. Gormon strode into the crowd and made several purchases. We came to a flesh-house for travelers from afar, where one could buy anything from quasi-life to mounds of passion-ice. We ate at a small restaurant by the edge of the River Tver, where guild-less ones were served without ceremony, and at Gormon's insistence we dined on mounds of a soft doughy substance and drank a tart yellow wine, local specialties.

Afterward we passed through a covered arcade in whose many aisles plump Vendors peddled star-goods, costly trinkets from Afreek, and the flimsy constructs of the local Manufactories. Just beyond we emerged in a plaza that contained a fountain in the shape of a boat, and to the rear of this rose a flight of cracked and battered stone-stairs ascending to a zone of rubble and weeds. Gormon beckoned, and we scrambled into this dismal area, then passed rapidly through it to a place where a sumptuous palace, by its looks early Second Cycle or even First, brooded over a sloping vegetated hill.

"They say this is the center of the world," Gormon declared. "In Jor-slem one finds another place that also claims the honor. They mark the spot here by a map."

"How can the world have one center," Avluela asked, "when it is round?"

Gormon laughed. We went in. Within, in wintry darkness, there stood a colossal jeweled globe lit by some inner glow.

"Here is your world," said Gormon, gesturing grandly.

"Oh!" Avluela gasped. "Everything! Everything is here!"

The map was a masterpiece of craftsmanship. It showed natural con-tours and elevations, its seas seemed deep liquid pools, its deserts were so parched as to make thirst spring in one's mouth, its cities swirled with vigor and life. I beheld the continents, Eyrop, Afreek, Ais, Stralya. I saw the vastness of Earth Ocean. I traversed the golden span of Land Bridge, which I had crossed so toilfully on foot not long before. Avluela rushed forward and pointed to Roum, to Agupt, to Jorslem, to Perris. She tapped the globe at the high mountains north of Hind and said softly, "This is where I was born, where the ice lives, where the mountains touch the moons. Here is where the Fliers have their kingdom." She ran a finger westward toward Fars and beyond it into the terrible Arban Desert, and on to Agupt. "This is where I flew. By night, when I left my girlhood.

We all must fly, and I flew here. A hundred times I thought I would die. Here, here in the desert, sand in my throat as I flew, sand beating against my wings—I was forced down, I lay naked on the hot sand for days, and another Flier saw me, he came down to me and pitied me, and lifted me up, and when I was aloft my strength returned, and we flew on toward Agupt. And he died over the sea, his life stopped though he was young and strong, and he fell down into the sea, and I flew down to be with him, and the water was hot even at night. I drifted, and morning came, and I saw the living stones growing like trees in the water, and the fish of many colors, and they came to him and pecked at his flesh as he floated with his wings outspread on the water, and I left him, I thrust him down to rest there, and I rose, and I flew on to Agupt, alone, frightened, and there I met you, Watcher." Timidly she smiled to me. "Show us the place where you were young, Watcher."

Painfully, for I was suddenly stiff at the knees, I hobbled to the far side of the globe. Avluela followed me; Gormon hung back, as though not interested at all. I pointed to the scattered islands rising in two long strips from Earth Ocean—the remnants of the Lost Continents.

"Here," I said, indicating my native island in the west. "I was born here."

"So far away!" Avluela cried.

"And so long ago," I said. "In the middle of the Second Cycle, it sometimes seems to me."

"No! That is not possible!" But she looked at me as though it might just be true that I was thousands of years old.

I smiled and touched her satiny cheek. "It only seems that way to me," I said.

"When did you leave your home?"

"When I was twice your age," I said. "I came first to here—" I indicated the eastern group of islands. "I spent a dozen years as a Watcher on Palash. Then the Will moved me to cross Earth Ocean to Afreek. I came. I lived awhile in the hot countries. I went on to Agupt. I met a certain small Flier." Falling silent, I looked a long while at the islands that had been my home, and within my mind my image changed from the gaunt and eroded thing I now had become, and I saw myself young and well-fleshed, climbing the green mountains and swimming in the chill sea, doing my Watching at the rim of a white beach hammered by surf.

While I brooded Avluela turned away from me to Gormon and said, "Now you. Show us where you came from, Changeling!"

Gormon shrugged. "The place does not appear to be on this globe."

"But that's *impossible!*"

"Is it?" he asked.

She pressed him, but he evaded her, and we passed through a side exit and into the streets of Roum.

I was growing tired, but Avluela hungered for this city and wished to devour it all in an afternoon, and so we went on through a maze of interlocking streets, through a zone of sparkling mansions of Masters and Merchants, and through a foul den of Servitors and Vendors that extended into subterranean catacombs, and to a place where Clowns and Musicians resorted, and to another where the guild of Somnambulists offered its doubtful wares. A bloated female Somnambulist begged us to come inside and buy the truth that comes with trances, and Avluela urged us to go, but Gormon shook his head and I smiled, and we moved on. Now we were at the edge of a park close to the city's core. Here the citizens of Roum promenaded with an energy rarely seen in hot Agust, and we joined the parade.

"Look there!" Avluela said. "How bright it is!"

She pointed toward the shining arc of a dimensional sphere enclosing some relic of the ancient city; shading my eyes, I could make out a weathered stone wall within, and a knot of people. Gormon said, "It is the Mouth of Truth."

"What is that?" Avluela asked.

"Come. See."

A line progressed into the sphere. We joined it and soon were at the lip of the interior, peering at the timeless region just across the threshold. Why this relic and so few others had been accorded such special protection I did not know, and I asked Gormon, whose knowledge was so unaccountably as profound as any Rememberer's, and he replied, "Because this is the realm of certainty, where what one says is absolutely congruent with what actually is the case."

"I don't understand," said Avluela.

"It is impossible to lie in this place," Gormon told her. "Can you imagine any relic more worthy of protection?" He stepped across the entry duct, blurring as he did so, and I followed him quickly within. Avluela hesitated. It was a long moment before she entered; pausing a moment on the very threshold, she seemed buffeted by the wind that blew along the line of demarcation between the outer world and the pocket universe in which we stood.

An inner compartment held the Mouth of Truth itself. The line extended toward it, and a solemn Indexer was controlling the flow of entry to the tabernacle. It was a while before we three were permitted to go in. We found ourselves before the ferocious head of a monster in high relief, affixed to an ancient wall pockmarked by time. The monster's jaws gaped; the open mouth was a dark and sinister hole. Gormon nodded, inspecting it, as though he seemed pleased to find it exactly as he had thought it would be.

"What do we do?" Avluela asked.

Gormon said, "Watcher, put your right hand into the Mouth of Truth."

Frowning, I complied.

"Now," said Gormon, "one of us asks a question. You must answer it. If you speak anything but the truth, the mouth with close and sever your hand."

"No!" Avluela cried.

I stared uneasily at the stone jaws rimming my wrist. A Watcher without both his hands is a man without a craft; in Second Cycle days one might have obtained a prosthesis more artful than one's original hand, but the Second Cycle had long ago been concluded, and such niceties were not to be purchased on Earth nowadays.

"How is such a thing possible?" I asked.

"The Will is unusually strong in these precincts," Gormon replied. "It distinguishes sternly between truth and untruth. To the rear of this wall sleeps a trio of Somnambulists through whom the Will speaks, and they control the Mouth. Do you fear the Will, Watcher?"

"I fear my own tongue."

"Be brave. Never has a lie been told before this wall. Never has a hand been lost."

"Go ahead, then," I said. "Who will ask me a question?"

"I," said Gormon. "Tell me, Watcher: all pretense aside, would you say that a life spent in Watching has been a life spent wisely?"

I was silent a long moment, rotating my thoughts, eyeing the jaws.

At length I said, "To devote oneself to vigilance on behalf of one's fellow man is perhaps the noblest purpose one can serve."

"Careful!" Gormon cried in alarm.

"I am not finished," I said.

"Go on."

"But to devote oneself to vigilance when the enemy is an imaginary one is idle, and to congratulate oneself for looking long and well for a foe that is not coming is foolish and sinful. My life has been a waste."

The jaws of the Mouth of Truth did not quiver.

I removed my hand. I stared at it as though it had newly sprouted from my wrist. I felt suddenly several cycles old. Avluela, her eyes wide, her hands to her lips, seemed shocked by what I had said. My own words appeared to hang congealed in the air before the hideous idol.

"Spoken honestly," said Gormon, "although without much mercy for yourself. You judge yourself too harshly, Watcher."

"I spoke to save my hand," I said. "Would you have had me lie?"

He smiled. To Avluela the Changeling said, "Now it's your turn."

Visibly frightened, the little Flier approached the Mouth. Her dainty hand trembled as she inserted it between the slabs of cold stone. I fought back an urge to rush toward her and pull her free of that devilish grimacing head.

"Who will question her?" I asked.

"I," said Gormon.

Avluela's wings stirred faintly beneath her garments. Her face grew pale; her nostrils flickered; her upper lip slid over the lower one. She stood slouched against the wall and stared in horror at the termination of her arm. Outside the chamber vague faces peered at us; lips moved in what no doubt were expressions of impatience over our lengthy visit to the Mouth; but we heard nothing. The atmosphere around us was warm and clammy, with a musty tang like that which would come from a well that was driven through the structure of Time.

Gormon said slowly, "This night past you allowed your body to be possessed by the Prince of Roum. Before that, you granted yourself to the Changeling Gormon, although such liaisons are forbidden by custom and law. Much prior to that you were the mate of a Flier, now deceased. You may have had other men, but I know nothing of them, and for the purposes of my question they are not relevant. Tell me this, Avluela: which of the three gave you the most intense physical pleasure, which of the three aroused your deepest emotions, and which of the three would you choose as a mate, if you were choosing a mate?"

I wanted to protest that the Changeling had asked her three questions, not one, and so had taken unfair advantage. But I had no chance to speak, because Avluela replied unfalteringly, hand wedged deep into the Mouth of Truth, "The Prince of Roum gave me greater pleasure of the body than I had ever known before, but he is cold and cruel, and I despise him. My dead Flier I loved more deeply than any person before or since, but he was weak, and I would not have wanted a weakling as a mate. You, Gormon, seem almost a stranger to me even now, and I feel that I know neither your body nor your soul, and yet, though the gulf between us is so wide, it is you with whom I would spend my days to come."

She drew her hand from the Mouth of Truth.

"Well spoken!" said Gormon, though the accuracy of her words had clearly wounded as well as pleased him. "Suddenly you find eloquence, eh, when the circumstances demand it. And now the turn is mine to risk my hand."

He neared the Mouth. I said, "You have asked the first two questions. Do you wish to finish the job and ask the third as well?"

"Hardly," he said. He made a negligent gesture with his free hand. "Put your heads together and agree on a joint question."

Avluela and I conferred. With uncharacteristic forwardness she proposed a question; and since it was the one I would have asked, I accepted it and told her to ask it.

She said, "When we stood before the globe of the world, Gormon, I asked you to show me the place where you were born, and you said you were unable to find it on the map. That seemed most strange. Tell me now: are you what you say you are, a Changeling who wanders the world?"

He replied, "I am not."

In a sense he had satisfied the question as Avluela had phrased it; but it went without saying that his reply was inadequate, and he kept his hand in the Mouth of Truth as he continued, "I did not show my birthplace to you on the globe because I was born nowhere on this globe, but on a world of a star I must not name. I am no Changeling in your meaning of the word, though by some definitions I am, for my body is somewhat disguised, and on my own world I wear a different flesh. I have lived here ten years."

"What was your purpose in coming to Earth?" I asked.

"I am obliged only to answer one question," said Gormon. Then he smiled. "But I give you an answer anyway: I was sent to Earth in the capacity of a military observer, to prepare the way for the invasion for which you have Watched so long and in which you have ceased to believe, and which will be upon you in a matter now of some hours."

"Lies!" I bellowed. "*Lies!*"

Gormon laughed. And drew his hand from the Mouth of Truth, intact, unharmed.

6

Numb with confusion, I fled with my cart of instruments from that gleaming sphere and emerged into a street suddenly cold and dark. Night had come with winter's swiftness; it was almost the ninth hour, and almost the time for me to Watch once more.

Gormon's mockery thundered in my brain. He had arranged everything: he had maneuvered us in to the Mouth of Truth; he had wrung a confession of lost faith from me and a confession of a different sort from Avluela; he had mercilessly volunteered information he need not have revealed, spoken words calculated to split me to the core.

Was the Mouth of Truth a fraud? Could Gormon lie and emerge unscathed?

Never since I first took up my tasks had I Watched at anything but my appointed hours. This was a time of crumbling realities; I could not wait for the ninth hour to come round; crouching in the windy street, I opened my cart, readied my equipment, and sank like a diver into Watchfulness.

My amplified consciousness roared toward the stars.

Godlike I roamed infinity. I felt the rush of the solar wind, but I was no Flier to be hurled to destruction by that pressure, and I soared past it, beyond the reach of those angry particles of light, into the blackness at the edge of the sun's dominion. Down upon me there beat a different pressure.

Starships coming near.

Not the tourist lines bringing sightseers to gape at our diminished world. Not the registered mercantile transport vessels, nor the scoopships that collect the interstellar vapors, nor the resort craft on their hyperbolic orbits.

These were military craft, dark, alien, menacing. I could not tell their number; I knew only that they sped Earthward at many lights, nudging a cone of deflected energies before them; and it was that cone that I had sensed, that I had felt also the night before, booming into my mind through my instruments, engulfing me like a cube of crystal through which stress patterns play and shine.

All my life I had watched for this.

I had been trained to sense it. I had prayed that I never would sense it, and then in my emptiness I had prayed that I *would* sense it, and then I had ceased to believe in it. And then by grace of the Changeling Gormon, I had sensed it after all, Watching ahead of my hour, crouching in a cold Roumish street just outside the Mouth of Truth.

In his training, a Watcher is instructed to break from his Watchfulness as soon as his observations are confirmed by a careful check, so that he can sound the alarm. Obediently I made my check by shifting from one channel to another to another, triangulating and still picking up that foreboding sensation of titanic force rushing upon Earth at unimaginable speed.

Either I was deceived, or the invasion was come. But I could not shake from my trance to give the alarm.

Lingeringly, lovingly, I drank in the sensory data for what seemed like hours. I fondled my equipment; I drained from it the total affirmation of faith that my readings gave me. Dimly I warned myself that I was wasting vital time, that it was my duty to leave this lewd caressing of destiny to summon the Defenders.

And at last I burst free of Watchfulness and returned to the world I was guarding.

Avluela was beside me; she was dazed, terrified, her knuckles to her teeth, her eyes blank.

"Watcher! Watcher, do you hear me? What's happening? What's going to happen?"

"The invasion," I said. "How long was I under?"

"About half a minute. I don't know. Your eyes were closed. I thought you were dead."

"Gormon was speaking the truth! The *invasion* is almost here. Where is he? Where did he go?"

"He vanished as we came away from that place with the Mouth," Avluela whispered. "Watcher, I'm frightened. I feel everything collapsing. I have to fly—I can't stay down here now!"

"Wait," I said, clutching at her and missing her arm. "Don't go now. First I have to give the alarm, and then—"

But she was already stripping off her clothing. Bare to the waist, her pale body gleamed in the evening light, while about us people were rushing to and fro in ignorance of all that was about to occur. I wanted to keep Avluela beside me, but I could delay no longer in giving the alarm, and I turned away from her, back to my cart.

As though caught up in a dream born of overripe longings I reached for the node that I had never used, the one that would send forth a planetwide alert to the Defenders.

Had the alarm already been given? Had some other Watcher sensed what I had sensed, and, less paralyzed by bewilderment and doubt, performed a Watcher's final task?

No. No. For then I would be hearing the sirens' shriek reverberating from the orbiting loudspeakers above the city.

I touched the node. From the corner of my eye I saw Avluela, free of her encumbrances now, kneeling to say her words, filling her tender wings with strength. In a moment she would be in the air, beyond my grasp.

With a single swift tug I activated the alarm.

In that instant I became aware of a burly figure striding toward us. Gormon, I thought; and as I rose from my equipment I reached out to him; I wanted to seize him and hold him fast. But he who approached was not Gormon but some officious dough-faced Servitor who said to Avluela, "Go easy, Flier, let your wings drop. The Prince of Roum sends me to bring you to his presence."

He grappled with her. Her little breasts heaved; her eyes flashed anger at him.

"Let go of me! I'm going to fly!"

"The Prince of Roum summons you," the Servitor said, enclosing her in his heavy arms.

"The Prince of Roum will have other distractions tonight," I said. "He'll have no need of her."

As I spoke, the sirens began to sing from the skies.

The Servitor released her. His mouth worked noiselessly for an instant; he made one of the protective gestures of the Will; he looked skyward and grunted, "The alarm! Who gave the alarm? You, old Watcher?"

Figures rushed about insanely in the streets.

Avluela, freed, sped past me—on foot, her wings but half-furled—and was swallowed up in the surging throng. Over the terrifying sound of the sirens came booming messages from the public annunciators, giving instructions for defense and safety. A lanky man with the mark of the guild of Defenders upon his cheek rushed up to me, shouted words too incoherent to be understood, and sped on down the street. The world seemed to have gone mad.

Only I remained calm. I looked to the skies, half-expecting to see the invaders' black ships already hovering above the towers of Roum. But I saw nothing except the hovering nightlights and the other objects one might expect overhead.

"Gormon?" I called. "Avluela?"

I was alone.

A strange emptiness swept over me. I had given the alarm; the invaders were on their way; I had lost my occupation. There was no need of Watchers now. Almost lovingly I touched the worn cart that had been my companion for so many years. I ran my fingers over its stained and pitted instruments; and then I looked away, abandoning it, and went down the dark streets cartless, burdenless, a man whose life had found and lost meaning in the same instant. And about me raged chaos.

7

It was understood that when the moment of Earth's final battle arrived, all guilds would be mobilized, the Watchers alone exempted. We who had manned the perimeter of defense for so long had no part in the strategy of combat; we were discharged by the giving of a true alarm. Now it was the time of the guild of Defenders to show its capabilities. They had planned for half a cycle what they would do in time of war. What plans would they call forth now? What deeds would they direct?

My only concern was to return to the royal hostelry and wait out the crisis. It was hopeless to think of finding Avluela, and I pummeled myself savagely for having let her slip away, naked and without a protector, in that confused moment. Where would she go? Who would shield her?

A fellow Watcher, pulling his cart madly along, nearly collided with me. "Careful!" I snapped. He looked up, breathless, stunned. "Is it true?" he asked. "The alarm?"

"Can't you hear?"

"But is it real?"

I pointed to his cart. "You know how to find that out."

"They say the man who gave the alarm was drunk, an old fool who was turned away from the inn yesterday."

"It could be so," I admitted.

"But if the alarm is real—!"

Smiling, I said, "If it is, now we all may rest. Good day to you, Watcher."

"Your cart! Where's your cart?" he shouted at me.

But I had moved past him, toward the mighty carven stone pillar of some relic of Imperial Roum.

Ancient images were carved on that pillar: battles and victories, foreign monarchs marched in the chains of disgrace through the streets of Roum, triumphant eagles celebrating imperial grandeur. In my strange new calmness I stood awhile before the column of stone and admired its elegant engravings. Toward me rushed a frenzied figure whom I recognized as the Rememberer Basil; I hailed him, saying, "How timely you come! Do me the kindness of explaining these images, Rememberer. They fascinate me, and my curiosity is aroused."

"Are you insane? Can't you hear the alarm?"

"I gave the alarm, Rememberer."

"Flee, then! Invaders come! We must fight!"

"Not I, Basil. Now my time is over. Tell me of these images. These beaten kings, these broken emperors. Surely a man of your years will not be doing battle."

"All are mobilized now!"

"All but Watchers," I said. "Take a moment. Yearning for the past is born in me. Gormon has vanished; be my guide to these lost cycles."

The Rememberer shook his head wildly, circled around me, and tried to get away. Hoping to seize his skinny arm and pin him to the spot, I made a lunge at him; but he eluded me and I caught only his dark shawl, which pulled free and came loose in my hands. Then he was gone, his spindly limbs pumping madly as he fled down the street and left my view. I shrugged and examined the shawl I had so unexpectedly acquired. It was shot through with glimmering threads of metal arranged in intricate patterns that teased the eye: it seemed to me that each strand disappeared into the weave of the fabric, only to reappear at some improbable point, like the lineage of dynasties unexpectedly revived in distant cities. The workmanship was superb. Idly I draped the shawl about my shoulders.

I walked on.

My legs, which had been on the verge of failing me earlier in the day, now served me well. With renewed youthfulness I made my way through the chaotic city, finding no difficulties in choosing my route. I headed for

the river, then crossed it and, on the Tver's far side, sought the palace of
the Prince. The night had deepened, for most lights were extinguished
under the mobilization orders; and from time to time a dull boom sig-
naled the explosion of a screening bomb overhead, liberating clouds of
murk that shielded the city from most forms of long-range scrutiny.
There were fewer pedestrians in the streets. The sirens still cried out.
Atop the buildings the defensive installations were going into action; I
heard the bleeping sounds of repellors warming up, and I saw long spidery arms of amplification booms swinging from tower to tower as they
linked for maximum output. I had no doubt now that the invasion actually was coming. My own instruments might have been fouled by inner
confusion, but they would not have proceeded thus far with the mobilization if the initial report had not been confirmed by the findings of hundreds of other members of my guild.

As I neared the palace a pair of breathless Rememberers sped toward
me, their shawls flapping behind them. They called to me in words I did
not comprehend—some code of their guild, I realized, recollecting that
I wore Basil's shawl. I could not reply, and they rushed upon me, still
gabbling; and switching to the language of ordinary men they said, "What
is the matter with you? To your post! We must record! We must comment! We must observe!"

"Your mistake me," I said mildly. "I keep this shawl only for your
brother Basil, who left it in my care. I have no post to guard at this time."

"A Watcher," they cried in unison, and cursed me separately, and ran
on. I laughed and went to the palace.

Its gates stood open. The neuters who had guarded the outer portal
were gone, as were the two Indexers who had stood just within the door.
The beggars that had thronged the vast plaza had jostled their way into
the building itself to seek shelter; this had awakened the anger of the
licensed hereditary mendicants whose customary stations were in that part
of the building, and they had fallen upon the inflowing refugees with fury
and unexpected strength. I saw cripples lashing out with their crutches
held as clubs; I saw blind men landing blows with suspicious accuracy;
meek penitents were wielding a variety of weapons ranging from stilettos
to sonic pistols. Holding myself aloof from this shameless spectacle, I
penetrated to the inner recesses of the palace and peered into chapels
where I saw Pilgrims beseeching the blessings of the Will, and Communicants desperately seeking spiritual guidance as to the outcome of the
coming conflict.

Abruptly I heard the blare of trumpets and cries of, "Make way! Make
way!"

A file of sturdy Servitors marched into the palace, striding toward the
Prince's chambers in the apse. Several of them held a struggling, kicking,
frantic figure with half-unfolded wings: Avluela! I called out to her, but
my voice died in the din, nor could I reach her. The Servitors shoved me
aside. The procession vanished into the princely chambers. I caught a
final glimpse of the little Flier, pale and small in the grip of her captors,
and then she was gone once more.

I seized a bumbling neuter who had been moving uncertainly in the wake of the Servitors.

"That Flier! Why was she brought here?"

"Ha—he—they—"

"Tell me!"

"The Prince—his woman—in his chariot—he—he—they—the invaders—"

I pushed the flabby creature aside and rushed toward the apse. A brazen wall ten times my own height confronted me. I pounded on it. "Avluela!" I shouted hoarsely. "*Av . . . lu . . . ela . . . !*"

I was neither thrust away nor admitted. I was ignored. The bedlam at the western doors of the palace had extended itself now to the nave and aisles, and as the ragged beggars boiled toward me I executed a quick turn and found myself passing through one of the side doors of the palace.

Suspended and passive, I stood in the courtyard that led to the royal hostelry. A strange electricity crackled in the air. I assumed it was an emanation from one of Roum's defense installations, some kind of beam designed to screen the city from attack. But an instant later I realized that it presaged the actual arrival of the invaders.

Starships blazed in the heavens.

When I had perceived them in my Watching they had appeared black against the infinite blackness, but now they burned with the radiance of suns. A stream of bright, hard, jewel-like globes bedecked the sky; they were ranged side by side, stretching from east to west in a continuous band, filling all the celestial arch, and as they erupted simultaneously into being it seemed to me that I heard the crash and throb of an invisible symphony heralding the arrival of the conquerors of Earth.

I do not know how far above me the starships were, nor how many of them hovered there, nor any of the details of their design. I know only that in sudden massive majesty they were there, and that if I had been a Defender my soul would have withered instantly at the sight.

Across the heavens shot light of many hues. The battle had been joined. I could not comprehend the actions of our warriors, and I was equally baffled by the maneuvers of those who had come to take possession of our history-crusted but time-diminished planet. To my shame I felt not only out of the struggle but above the struggle, as though this were no quarrel of mine. I wanted Avluela beside me, and she was somewhere within the depths of the palace of the Prince of Roum. Even Gormon would have been a comfort now, Gormon the Changeling, Gormon the spy, Gormon the monstrous betrayer of our world.

Gigantic amplified voices bellowed, "Make way for the Prince of Roum! The Prince of Roum leads the Defenders in the battle for the fatherworld!"

From the palace emerged a shining vehicle the shape of a teardrop, in whose bright-metaled roof a transparent sheet had been mounted so that all the populace could see and take heart in the presence of the ruler. At the controls of the vehicle sat the Prince of Roum, proudly erect, his cruel, youthful features fixed in harsh determination; and beside him, robed like an empress, I beheld the slight figure of the Flier Avluela. She seemed in a trance.

The royal chariot soared upward and was lost in the darkness.

It seemed to me that a second vehicle appeared and followed its path, and that the Prince's reappeared, and that the two flew in tight circles, apparently locked in combat. Clouds of blue sparks wrapped both chariots now; and then they swung high and far and were lost to me behind one of the hills of Roum.

Was the battle now raging all over the planet? Was Perris in jeopardy, and holy Jorslem, and even the sleepy isles of the Lost Continents? Did starships hover everywhere? I did not know. I perceived events in only one small segment of the sky over Roum, and even there my awareness of what was taking place was dim, uncertain, and ill-informed. There were momentary flashes of light in which I saw battalions of Fliers streaming across the sky; and then darkness returned as though a velvet shroud had been hurled over the city. I saw the great machines of our defense firing in fitful bursts from the tops of our towers; and yet I saw the starships untouched, unharmed, unmoved above. The courtyard in which I stood was deserted, but in the distance I heard voices, full of fear and foreboding, shouting in tinny tones that might have been the screeching of birds. Occasionally there came a booming sound that rocked all the city. Once a platoon of Somnambulists was driven past where I was; in the plaza fronting the palace I observed what appeared to be an array of Clowns unfolding some sort of sparkling netting of a military look; by one flash of lightning I was able to see a trio of Rememberers making copious notes of all that elapsed as they soared aloft on the gravity plate. It seemed—I was not sure—that the vehicle of the Prince of Roum returned, speeding across the sky with its pursuer clinging close. "Avluela," I whispered, as the twin dots of lights left my sight. Were the starships disgorging troops? Did colossal pylons of force spiral down from those orbiting brightness to touch the surface of the Earth? Why had the Prince seized Avluela? Where was Gormon? What were our Defenders doing? Why were the enemy ships not blasted from the sky?

Rooted to the ancient cobbles of the courtyard, I observed the cosmic battle in total lack of understanding throughout the long night.

Dawn came. Strands of pale light looped from tower to tower. I touched fingers to my eyes, realizing that I must have slept while standing. Perhaps I should apply for membership in the guild of Somnambulists, I told myself lightly. I put my hands to the Rememberer's shawl about my shoulders and wondered how I managed to acquire it, and the answer came.

I looked toward the sky.

The alien starships were gone. I saw only the ordinary morning sky, gray with pinkness breaking through. I felt the jolt of compulsion and looked about for my cart, and reminded myself that I need do no more Watching, and I felt more empty than one would ordinarily feel at such an hour.

Was the battle over?

Had the enemy been vanquished?

Were the ships of the invaders blasted from the sky and lying in charred ruin outside Roum?

All was silent. I heard no more celestial symphonies. Then out of the eerie stillness there came a new sound, a rumbling noise as of wheeled vehicles passing through the streets of the city. And the invisible Musicians played one final note, deep and resonant, which trailed away jaggedly as though every string had been broken at once.

Over the speakers used for public announcements came quiet words. "Roum is fallen. Roum is fallen."

8

The royal hostelry was untended. Neuters and members of the servant guilds all had fled. Defenders, Masters, and Dominators must have perished honorably in combat. Basil the Rememberer was nowhere about; likewise none of his brethren. I went to my room, cleansed and refreshed and fed myself, gathered my few possessions, and bade farewell to the luxuries I had known so briefly. I regretted that I had had such a short time to visit Roum; but at least Gormon had been a most excellent guide, and I had seen a great deal.

Now I proposed to move on.

It did not seem prudent to remain in a conquered city. My room's thinking cap did not respond to my queries, and so I did not know what the extent of the defeat was, here or in other regions, but it was evident to me that Roum at least had passed from human control, and I wished to depart quickly. I weighed the thought of going to Jorslem, as that tall pilgrim had suggested upon my entry into Roum; but then I reflected and chose a westward route, toward Perris, which not only was closer but held the headquarters of the Rememberers. My own occupation had been destroyed; but on this first morning of Earth's conquest I felt a sudden powerful and strange yearning to offer myself humbly to the Rememberers and seek with them knowledge of our more glittering yesterdays.

At midday I left the hostelry. I walked first to the palace, which still stood open. The beggars lay strewn about, some drugged, some sleeping, most dead; from the crude manner of their death I saw that they must have slain one another in their panic and frenzy. A despondent-looking Indexer squatted beside the three skulls of the interrogation fixture in the chapel. As I entered he said, "No use. The brains do not reply."

"How goes it with the Prince of Roum?"

"Dead. The invaders shot him from the sky."

"A young Flier rode beside him. What do you know of her?"

"Nothing. Dead, I suppose."

"And the city?"

"Fallen. Invaders are everywhere."

"Killing?"

"Not even looting," the Indexer said. "They are most gentle. They have *collected* us."

"In Roum alone, or everywhere?"

The man shrugged. He began to rock rhythmically back and forth. I let him be, and walked deeper into the palace. To my surprise, the imperial chambers of the Prince were unsealed. I went within; I was awed by the sumptuous luxury of the hangings, the draperies, the lights, the furnishings. I passed from room to room, coming at last to the royal bed, whose coverlet was the flesh of a colossal bivalve of the planet of another star, and as the shell yawned for me I touched the infinitely soft fabric under which the Prince of Roum had lain, and I recalled that Avluela too had lain here, and if I had been a younger man I would have wept.

I left the palace and slowly crossed the plaza to begin my journey toward Perris.

As I departed I had my first glimpse—of our conquerors. A vehicle of alien design drew up at the plaza's rim and perhaps a dozen figures emerged. They might almost have been human. They were tall and broad, deep-chested, as Gormon had been, and only the extreme length of their arms marked them instantly as alien. Their skins were of strange texture, and if I had been closer I suspect I would have seen eyes and lips and nostrils that were not of a human design. Taking no notice of me, they crossed the plaza, walking in a curiously loose-jointed loping way that reminded me irresistibly of Gormon's stride, and entered the palace. They seemed neither swaggering nor belligerent.

Sightseers. Majestic Roum once more exerted its magnetism upon strangers.

Leaving our new masters to their amusement, I walked off, toward the outskirts of the city. The bleakness of eternal winter crept into my soul. I wondered: did I feel sorrow that Roum had fallen? Or did I mourn the loss of Avluela? Or was it only that I now had missed three successive Watchings, and like an addict I was experiencing the pangs of withdrawal?

It was all of these that pained me, I decided. But mostly the last.

No one was abroad in the city as I made for the gates. Fear of the new masters kept the Roumish in hiding, I supposed. From time to time one of the alien vehicles hummed past, but I was unmolested. I came to the city's western gate late in the afternoon. It was open, revealing to me a gently rising hill on whose breast rose trees with dark green crowns. I passed through and saw, a short distance beyond the gate, the figure of a Pilgrim who was shuffling slowly away from the city.

I overtook him easily.

His faltering, uncertain walk seemed strange to me, for not even his thick brown robes could hide the strength and youth of his body; he stood erect, his shoulders square and his back straight, and yet he walked with the hesitating, trembling step of an old man. When I drew abreast of him and peered under his hood I understood, for affixed to the bronze mask all Pilgrims wear was a reverberator, such as is used by blind men to warn them of obstacles and hazards. He became aware of me and said, "I am a sightless Pilgrim. I pray you do not molest me."

It was not a Pilgrim's voice. It was a strong and harsh and imperious voice.

I replied, "I molest no one. I am a Watcher who has lost his occupation this night past."

"Many occupations were lost this night past, Watcher."

"Surely not a Pilgrim's."

"No," he said "Not a Pilgrim's."

"Where are you bound?"

"Away from Roum."

"No particular destination?"

"No," the Pilgrim said. "None. I will wander."

"Perhaps we should wander together," I said, for it is accounted good luck to travel with a Pilgrim, and, shorn of my Flier and my Changeling, I would otherwise have traveled alone. "My destination is Perris. Will you come?"

"There as well as anywhere else," he said bitterly. "Yes. We will go to Perris together. But what business does a Watcher have there?"

"A Watcher has no business anywhere. I go to Perris to offer myself in service to the Rememberers."

"Ah," he said. "I was of that guild too, but it was only honorary."

"With Earth fallen, I wish to learn more of Earth in its pride."

"Is all Earth fallen, then, and not only Roum?"

"I think it is so," I said.

"Ah," replied the Pilgrim. "Ah!"

He fell silent and we went onward. I gave him my arm, and now he shuffled no longer, but moved with a young man's brisk stride. From time to time he uttered what might have been a sigh or a smothered sob. When I asked him details of his Pilgrimage, he answered obliquely or not at all. When we were an hour's journey outside Roum, and already amid forests, he said suddenly, "This mask gives me pain. Will you help me adjust it?"

To my amazement he began to remove it. I gasped, for it is forbidden for a Pilgrim to reveal his face. Had he forgotten that I was not sightless too?

As the mask came away he said, "You will not welcome this sight."

The bronze grillwork slipped down from his forehead, and I saw first eyes that had been newly blinded, gaping holes where no surgeon's knife, but possibly thrusting fingers, had penetrated and then the sharp regal nose, and finally the quirked taut lips of the Prince of Roum.

"Your Majesty!" I cried.

Trails of dried blood ran down his cheeks. About the raw sockets themselves were smears of ointment. He felt little pain, I suppose, for he had killed it with those green smears, but the pain that burst through me was real and potent.

"Majesty no longer," he said. "Help me with the mask!" His hands trembled as he held it forth. "These flanges must be widened. They press cruelly at my cheeks. Here—here—"

Quickly I made the adjustments, so that I would not have to see his ruined face for long.

He replaced the mask. "I am a Pilgrim now," he said quietly. "Roum is without its Prince. Betray me if you wish, Watcher; otherwise help me to Perris; and if ever I regain my power you will be well rewarded."

"I am no betrayer," I told him.

In silence we continued. I had no way of making small talk with such a man. It would be a somber journey for us to Perris; but I was committed now to be his guide. I thought of Gormon and how well he had kept his vows. I thought too of Avluela, and a hundred times the words leaped to my tongue to ask the fallen Prince how his consort the Flier had fared in the night of defeat, and I did not ask.

Twilight gathered, but the sun still gleamed golden-red before us in the west. And suddenly I halted and made a hoarse sound of surprise deep in my throat, as a shadow passed overhead.

High above me Avluela soared. Her skin was stained by the colors of the sunset, and her wings were spread to their fullest, radiant with every hue of the spectrum. She was already at least the height of a hundred men above the ground, and still climbing, and to her I must have been only a speck among the trees.

"What is it?" the Prince asked. "What do you see?"

"Nothing."

"Tell me what you see!"

I could not deceive him. "I see a Flier, your Majesty. A slim girl far aloft."

"Then the night must have come."

"No," I said. "The sun is still above the horizon."

"How can that be? She can have only nightwings. The sun would hurl her to the ground."

I hesitated. I could not bring myself to explain how it was that Avluela flew by day, though she had only nightwings. I could not tell the Prince of Roum that beside her, wingless, flew the invader Gormon, effortlessly moving through the air, his arm about her thin shoulders, steadying her, supporting her, helping her resist the pressure of the solar wind. I could not tell him that his nemesis flew with the last of his consorts above his head.

"Well?" he demanded. "How does she fly by day?"

"I do not know," I said. "It is a mystery to me. There are many things nowadays I can no longer understand."

The Prince appeared to accept that. "Yes, Watcher. Many things none of us can understand."

He fell once more into silence. I yearned to call out to Avluela, but I knew she could not and would not hear me, and so I walked on toward the sunset, toward Perris, leading the blind Prince. And over us Avluela and Gormon sped onward, limned sharply against the day's last glow, until they climbed so high they were lost to my sight.

Pale Roses

MICHAEL MOORCOCK

One of the most prolific, popular, and controversial figures in modern letters, Michael Moorcock has been a major shaping force on the development of science fiction and fantasy, as both author and editor, for more than thirty years. As editor, Moorcock helped to usher in the New Wave revolution in science fiction in the midsixties by taking over the genteel but elderly and somewhat tired British SF magazine New Worlds *and coaxing it into a bizarre new life. Moorcock transformed* New Worlds *into a fierce and daring outlaw publication that was at the very heart of the British New Wave movement, and Moorcock himself—for his role as chief creator of the either much-admired or much-loathed "Jerry Cornelius" stories, in addition to his roles as editor, polemicist, literary theorist, and mentor to most of the period's most prominent writers—became one of the most controversial figures of that turbulent era.* New Worlds *died in the early seventies, after having been ringingly denounced in the Houses of Parliament and banned from distribution by the huge British bookstore and newsstand chain W. H. Smith, but Moorcock himself has never been out of public view for long. The novels in his* Elric *series—elegant and elegantly perverse Sword and Sorcery at its most distinctive and far too numerous to individually list here—are wildly popular and best-sellers on both sides of the Atlantic. At the same time, Moorcock's other works, both in and out of the genre, such as* Gloriana, Behold the Man, *and* Mother London *have established him as one of the most respected and critically acclaimed writers of our day. He has won the Nebula Award, the World Fantasy Award, the John W. Campbell Memorial Award, and the Guardian Fiction Award. His other books include (among many others), the novels* The Warhound and the World's Pain, Byzantium Endures, The Laughter of Carthage, Jerusalem Commands, The Land Leviathan, *and* The Warlord of the Air, *as well as the collection* Lunching with the Antichrist, *an autobiographical study,* Letters from Hollywood, *and a critical study of fantasy literature,* Wizardry and Wild Romance. *After spending most of his life in London, several years back, Moorcock moved to a small town in Texas, where he now lives and works.*

Moorcock's vision ranges from the distant, antediluvian past of the Elric *stories to the far-future milieu of the stories and novels that went into the making of his* Dancers at the End of Time *sequence (with typical Moorcockian perversity, he's also written a story called "Elric at the End of Time," which merges both series and both ends of the time spectrum, by bringing Elric himself out of the remote past to the even-more-remote future), his major contribution to the literature of the far future, which consists of the novels* An Alien Heat, The Hollow Lands, The End of All Songs, *and* A Messiah at the End of Time *(all assembled in two omnibus volumes,* Legends from the End of Time *and* The Dancers at the End of Time*). In Moorcock's hands, the far future is a place of fin de siècle decadence, elegance, and wealth, where jaded immortals of immense powers and abilities, and with* *no morals or scruples at all, play endless rounds of intricate mind games with one another, as well as with the befuddled time travelers from the distant past who sometimes land in their midst. As the arch, ironic, and darkly playful story that follows—one of the best of Moorcock's far-future stories—shows, though, sometimes even if you don't know you're playing, you can still can win the game.*

> *Short summer-time and then, my heart's desire.*
> *The winter and the darkness: one by one*
> *The roses fall, the pale roses expire*
> *Beneath the slow decadence of the sun.*
> —Ernest Dowson, *Transition*

I

In Which Werther Is Inconsolable

"You can still *amuse* people, Werther, and that's the main thing," said Mistress Christia, lifting her skirts to reveal her surprise.

It was rare enough for Werther de Goethe to put on an entertainment (though this one was typical—it was called "Rain") and rare, too, for the Everlasting Concubine to think in individual terms to please her lover of the day.

"Do you like it?" she asked as he peered into her thighs.

Werther's voice in reply was faintly, unusually, animated. "Yes." His pale fingers traced the tattoos, which were primarily on the theme of Death and the Maiden but corpses also coupled, skeletons entwined in a variety of extravagant carnal embraces—and at the center, in bone-white, her pubic hair had been fashioned in the outline of an elegant and somehow quintessentially feminine skull. "You alone know me, Mistress Christia."

She had heard the phrase so often and it always delighted her. "Cadaverous Werther!"

He bent to kiss the skull's somewhat elongated lips.

His rain rushed through dark air, each drop a different gloomy shade of green, purple or red. And it was actually wet so that when it fell upon the small audience (The Duke of Queens, Bishop Castle, My Lady Charlotina, and one or two recently arrived, absolutely bemused, time-travelers from the remote past) it soaked their clothes and made them shiver as they stood on the shelf of glassy rock overlooking Werther's Romantic Precipice. (Below, a waterfall foamed through fierce, black rock.)

"Nature," exclaimed Werther. "The only verity!"

The Duke of Queens sneezed. He looked about him with a delighted smile, but nobody else had noticed. He coughed to draw their attention, tried to sneeze again, but failed. He looked up into the ghastly sky; fresh waves of black cloud boiled in: there was lightning now, and thunder. The rain became hail. My Lady Charlotina, in a globular dress of pink veined in soft blue, giggled as the little stones fell upon her gilded features with an almost inaudible ringing sound.

But Bishop Castle, in his nodding, crenellated *téte* (from which he derived the latter half of his name and which was twice his own height) turned away, saturnine and bored, plainly noting a comparison between all this and his own entertainment of the previous year which had also involved rain, but with each drop turning into a perfect manikin as it touched the ground. There was nothing in his temperament to respond to Werther's rather innocent re-creation of a Nature long-since departed from a planet which could be wholly remodeled at the whim of any one of its inhabitants.

Mistress Christia, ever quick to notice such responses, eager for her present lover not to lose prestige, cried: "But there is more, is there not. Werther? A finale?"

"I had thought to leave it a little longer . . ."

"No! No! Give us your finale now, my dear!"

"Well, Mistress Christia, if it is for you." He turned one of his power rings, disseminating the sky, the lightning, the thunder, replacing them with pearly clouds, radiated with golden light through which silvery rain still fell.

"And now," he murmured, "I give you Tranquillity, and in Tranquillity—Hope . . ."

A further twist of the ring and a rainbow appeared, bridging the chasm, touching the clouds.

Bishop Castle was impressed by what was an example of elegance rather than spectacle, but he could not resist a minor criticism. "Is black exactly the shade, do you think? I should have supposed it expressed your Idea, well, perhaps not perfectly . . ."

"It is perfect for me," answered Werther a little gracelessly.

"Of course," said Bishop Castle, regretting his impulse. He drew his bushy red brows together and made a great show of studying the rainbow. "It stands out so well against the background."

Emphatically (causing a brief, ironic glint in the eye of the Duke of Queens) Mistress Christia clapped her hands. "It is a beautiful rainbow, Werther. I am sure it is much more as they used to look."

"It takes a particularly, original kind of imagination to invent such—simplicity." The Duke of Queens, well-known for a penchant in the direction of vulgarity, fell in with her mood.

"I hope it does more than merely represent." Satisfied both with his creation and with their responses, Werther could not resist indulging his nature, allowing a tinge of hurt resentment in his tone.

All were tolerant. All responded, even Bishop Castle. There came a chorus of consolation. Mistress Christia reached out and took his thin, white hand, inadvertently touching a power ring.

The rainbow began to topple. It leaned in the sky for a few seconds while Werther watched; his disbelief gradually turning to miserable reconciliation; then, slowly, it fell, shattering against the top of the cliff, showering them with shards of jet.

Mistress Christia's tiny hand fled to the rosebud of her mouth; her round, blue eyes expressed horror already becoming laughter (checked when she noted the look in Werther's dark and tragic orbs). She still gripped his hand; but he slowly withdrew it, kicking moodily at the fragments of the rainbow. The sky was suddenly a clear, soft gray, actually lit, one might have guessed, by the tired rays of the fading star about which the planet continued to circle, and the only clouds were those on Werther's noble brow. He pulled at the peak of his bottle-green cap; he stroked at his long, auburn hair, as if to comfort himself. He sulked.

"Perfect!" praised My Lady Charlotina, refusing to see error.

"You have the knack of making the most of a single symbol, Werther." The Duke of Queens waved a brocaded arm in the general direction of the now disseminated scene. "I envy you your talent, my friend."

"It takes the product of panting lust, of pulsing sperm and eager ovaries, to offer us such brutal originality!" said Bishop Castle, in reference to Werther's birth (he was the product of sexual union, born of a womb, knowing childhood—a rarity, indeed). "Bravo!"

"Ah," sighed Werther, "how cheerfully you refer to my doom: To be such a creature, when all others came into this world as mature, uncomplicated adults!"

"There was also Jherek Carnelian," said My Lady Charlotina. Her globular dress bounced as she turned to leave.

"At least he was not born malformed," said Werther.

"It was the work of a moment to re-form you properly, Werther," the Duke of Queens reminded him. "The six arms (was it?) removed, two perfectly fine ones replacing them. After all, it was an unusual exercise on the part of your mother. She did very well, considering it was her first attempt."

"And her last," said My Lady Charlotina, managing to have her back to Werther by the time the grin escaped. She snapped her fingers for her air-car. It floated towards her, a great, yellow rocking horse. Its shadow fell across them all.

"It left a scar," said Werther, "nonetheless."

"It would," said Mistress Christia, kissing him upon his black velvet shoulder.

"A terrible scar."

"Indeed!" said the Duke of Queens in vague affirmation, his attention wandering. "Well, thank you for a lovely afternoon, Werther. Come along, you two!" He signed to the time-travelers who claimed to be from the eighty-third millenium and were dressed in primitive transparent "exoskin" which was not altogether stable and was inclined to writhe and make it seem that they were covered in hundreds of thin, excited snakes. The Duke of Queens had acquired them for his menagerie. Unaware of the difficulties of returning to their own time (temporal travel had, apparently, only just been re-invented in their age) they were inclined to treat the Duke as an eccentric who could be tolerated until it suited them to do otherwise. They smiled condescendingly, winked at each other, and followed him to an air-car in the shape of a cube whose sides were golden mirrors decorated with white and purple flowers. It was for the pleasure of enjoying the pleasure they enjoyed seemingly at his expense, that the Duke of Queens had brought them with him today. Mistress Christia waved at his car as it disappeared rapidly into the sky.

At last they were all gone, save herself and Werther de Goethe. He had seated himself upon a mossy rock, his shoulders hunched, his features downcast, unable to speak to her when she tried to cheer him.

"Oh, Werther," she cried at last, "what would make you happy?"

"Happy?" his voice was a hollow echo of her own. "Happy?" He made an awkward, dismissive gesture. "There is no such thing as happiness for such as I!"

"There must be some sort of equivalent, surely?"

"Death, Mistress Christia, is my only consolation!"

"Well, die, my dear! I'll resurrect you in a day or two, and then..."

"Though you love me, Mistress Christia—though you know me best—you do not understand. I seek the inevitable, the irreconcilable, the unalterable, the inescapable! Our ancestors knew it. They knew Death *without* Resurrection; they knew what it was to be Slave to the Elements. Incapable of choosing their own destinies, they had no responsibility for choosing their own actions. They were tossed by tides. They were scattered by storms. They were wiped out by wars, decimated by disease, ravaged by radiation, made homeless by holocausts, lashed by lightnings..."

"You could have lashed yourself a little today, surely?"

"But it would have been *my* decision. We have lost what is Random, we have banished the Arbitrary, Mistress Christia. With our power rings and our gene banks we can, if we desire, change the courses of the planets, populate them with any kind of creature we wish, make our old sun burst with fresh energy or fade completely from the firmament. We control All. Nothing controls us!"

"There are our whims, our fancies. There are our *characters*, my moody love."

"Even those can be altered at will."

"Except that it is a rare nature which would wish to change itself. Would you change yours? I, for one, would be disconsolate if, say, you decided to be more like the Duke of Queens or the Iron Orchid."

"Nonetheless, it is *possible*. It would merely be a matter of decision. Nothing is impossible, Mistress Christia. Now do you realize why I should feel unfulfilled?"

"Not really, dear Werther. You can be anything you wish, after all. I am not, as you know, intelligent—it is not my choice to be—but I wonder if a love of Nature could be, in essence, a grandiose love of oneself—with Nature identified, as it were, with one's ego?" She offered this without criticism.

For a moment he showed surprise and seemed to be considering her observation. "I suppose it could be. Still, that has little to do with what we were discussing. It's true that I can be anything—or, indeed, anyone—I wish. That is *why* I feel unfulfilled!"

"Aha," she said.

"Oh, how I pine for the pain of the past! Life has no meaning without misery!"

"A common view, then, I gather. But what sort of suffering would suit you best, dear Werther? Enslavement by Eskimos?" She hesitated, her knowledge of the past being patchier than most people's. "The beatings with thorns? The barbed-wire trews? The pits of fire?"

"No, no—that is primitive. Psychic, it would have to be. Involving—um—morality."

"Isn't that some sort of wall-painting?"

A large tear welled and fell. "The world is too tolerant. The world is too kind. They all—you most of all—*approve* of me! There is nothing I can do which would not amuse you—even if it offended your taste—because there is no danger, nothing at stake. There are no *crimes*, inflamer of my lust. Oh, if I could only *sin!*"

Her perfect forehead wrinkled in the prettiest of frowns. She repeated his words to herself. Then she shrugged, embracing him.

"Tell me what sin is," she said.

II

In Which Your Auditor Interposes

Our time-travelers, once they have visited the future, are only permitted (owing to the properties of Time itself) brief returns to their present. They can remain for any amount of time in their future, where presumably they can do no real damage to the course of previous events, but to come back at all is difficult; to make a prolonged stay has been proved impossible. Half an hour with a relative or a loved one, a short account to an auditor, such as myself, of life, say, in the seventy-fifth century, a glimpse at an artifact allowed to some interested scientist—these are the best the time-traveler can hope for, once he has made his decision to leap into the mysterious future.

As a consequence our knowledge of the future is sketchy, to say the least: We have no idea of how civilizations will grow up or how they will decline; we do not know why the number of planets in the solar system seems to vary drastically between, say, half a dozen to almost a hundred; we cannot explain the popularity in a given age for certain fashions striking us as singularly bizarre or perverse; are beliefs which we consider fallacious or superstitious based on an understanding beyond our comprehension?

The stories we hear are often partial, hastily recounted, poorly observed, perhaps misunderstood by the traveler. We cannot question him closely, for he is soon whisked away from us (Time insists upon a certain neatness, to protect her own nature, which is essentially of the practical, ordering sort, and should that nature ever be successfully altered, then we might, in turn, successfully alter the terms of the human condition) and it is almost inevitable that we shall never have another chance of meeting him.

Resultantly, the stories brought to us of the Earth's future assume the character of legends rather than history and tend, therefore, to capture the imagination of artists, for serious scientists need permanent, verifiable evidence with which to work and precious little of that is permitted them (some refuse to believe in the future, save as an abstraction, some believe firmly that returning time-travelers' accounts are accounts of dreams and hallucinations and that they have not actually traveled in time at all!). It is left to the Romancers, childish fellows like myself, to make something of these tales. While I should be delighted to assure you that everything I have set down in this story is based closely on the truth, I am bound to admit that while the outline comes from an account given me by one of our greatest and most famous temporal adventuresses, Miss Una Persson, the conversations and many of the descriptions are of my own invention intended hopefully to add a little color to what would otherwise be a somewhat spare, a rather dry, recounting of an incident in the life of Werther de Goethe.

That Werther will exist, only a few entrenched skeptics can doubt. We have heard of him from many sources, usually quite as reliable as the admirable Miss Persson, as we have heard of other prominent figures of that Age we choose to call "the End of Time." If it is this Age which fascinates us more than any other, it is probably because it seems to offer a clue to our race's ultimate destiny.

Moralists make much of this period and show us that on the one hand it describes the pointlessness of human existence or, on the other, the whole point. Romancers are attracted to it for less worthy reasons; they find it colorful, they find its inhabitants glamorous, attractive; their imagination is sparked by the paradoxes, the very ambiguities which exasperated our scientists, by the idea of a people possessing limitless power and using it for nothing but their own amusement, like gods at play. It is pleasure enough for the Romancer to describe a story; to color it a little, to fill in a few details where they are missing, in the hope that, by entertaining himself, he entertains others.

Of course, the inhabitants at the End of Time are not the creatures of our past legends, not mere representations of our ancestors' hopes and fears, not mere metaphors, like Siegfried or Zeus or Krishna, and this could be why they fascinate us so much. Those of us who have studied this Age (as best it can be studied) feel on friendly terms with the Iron Orchid, with the Duke of Queens, with Lord Jagged of Canaria and the rest, and even believe that we can guess something of their inner lives.

Werther de Goethe, suffering from the *knowledge* of his, by the standards of his own time, unusual entrance into the world, doubtless felt himself apart from his fellows, though there was no objective reason why he should feel it. (I trust the reader will forgive my abandoning any attempt at a clumsy future tense.) In a society where eccentricity is encouraged, where it is celebrated no matter how extreme its realization,

Werther felt, we must assume, uncomfortable:—wishing for peers who would demand some sort of conformity from him. He could not retreat into a repressive past age; it was well-known that it was impossible to remain in the past (the phenomenon had a name at the End of Time: it was called the Morphail Effect), and he had an ordinary awareness of the futility of re-creating such an environment for himself—for *he* would have created it; the responsibility would still ultimately be his own. We can only sympathize with the irreconcilable difficulties of leading the life of a gloomy fatalist when one's fate is wholly, decisively, in one's own hands!

Like Jherek Carnelian, whose adventures I have recounted elsewhere, he was particularly liked by his fellows for his vast and often naive enthusiasm for whatever he did. Like Jherek, it was possible for Werther to fall completely in love—with Nature, with an Idea, with Woman (or Man, for that matter).

It seemed to the Duke of Queens (from whom we have it on the excellent authority of Miss Persson herself) that one with such a capacity must love themselves enormously and such love is enviable. The Duke, needless to say, spoke without disapproval when he made this observation: "To shower such largesse upon the Ego! He kneels before his soul in awe—it is a moody king, in constant need of gifts which must always seem rare!" And what is Sensation, our Moralists might argue, but Seeming Rarity? Last year's gifts regilded.

It might be true that young Werther (in years no more than half a millennium) loved himself too much and that his tragedy was his inability to differentiate between the self-gratifying sensation of the moment and what we would call a lasting and deeply-felt emotion. We have a fragment of poetry, written, we are assured, by Werther for Mistress Christia:

> *At these times, I love you most when you are sleeping;*
> > *Your dreams internal, unrealized to the world at large:*
> *And do I hear you weeping?*

Most certainly a reflection of Werther's views, scarcely a description from all that we know of her, of Mistress Christia's essential being.

Have we any reason to doubt Werther's view of herself? Rather, we should doubt Werther's view of everyone, including himself. Possibly the lack of insight was what made him so thoroughly attractive in his own time—*le Grand Naïf!*

And, since we have quoted one, it is fair to quote the other, for happily we have another fragment, from the same source, of Mistress Christia verse:

> *To have my body moved by other hands;*
> > *Not only those of Man,*
> *But Woman, too*
> *My Liberty in pawn to those who understand:*
> > *That love, alone, is True.*

Surely this displays an irony entirely lacking in Werther's fragment. Affectation is also here, of course, but affectation of Mistress Christia's sort so often hides an equivalently sustained degree of self-knowledge. It is sometimes the case in our own age that the greater the extravagant outer show the greater has been the plunge by the showman into the depths of his private conscience: Consequently, the greater the effort to hide the fact, to give the world not what one is, but what it wants. Mistress Christia chose to reflect with consummate artistry the desires of her lover of the day; to fulfill her ambition as subtly as did she, reveals a person of exceptional perspicacity.

I intrude upon the flow of my tale with these various bits of explanation and speculation only, I hope, to offer credibility for what is to follow— to give a hint at a natural reason for Mistress Christia's peculiar actions and poor Werther's extravagant response. Some time has passed since we left our lovers. For the moment they have separated. We return to Werther . . .

III

In Which Werther Finds a Soul Mate

Werther de Goethe's pile stood on the pinnacle of a black and mile-high crag about which, in the permanent twilight, black vultures swooped and croaked. The rare visitor to Werther's crag could hear the vultures' voices as he approached. "Never more!" and "Beware the Ides of March!" and "Picking a Chicken With You" were three of the least cryptic warnings they had been created to caw.

At the top of the tallest of his thin, dark towers, Werther de Goethe sat in his favorite chair of unpolished quartz, in his favorite posture of miserable introspection, wondering why Mistress Christia had decided to pay a call on My Lady Charlotina at Lake Billy the Kid.

"Why should she wish to stay here, after all?" He cast a suffering eye upon the sighing sea below. "She is a creature of light—she seeks color, laughter, warmth, no doubt to try to forget some secret sorrow—she needs all the things I cannot give her. Oh, I am a monster of selfishness!" He allowed himself a small sob. But neither the sob nor the preceding outburst produced the usual satisfaction; self-pity eluded him. He felt adrift, lost, like an explorer without chart or compass in an unfamiliar land. Manfully, he tried again:

"Mistress Christia! Mistress Christia! Why do you desert me? Without you I am desolate! My pulsatile nerves will sing at your touch only. And yet it must be my doom forever to be betrayed by the very things to which I give my fullest loyalty. Ah, it is hard! It is hard!"

He felt a little better and rose from his chair of unpolished quartz, turning his power ring a fraction so that the wind blew harder through the unglazed windows of the tower and whipped at his hair, blew his cloak about, stung his pale, long face. He raised one jackbooted foot to place

it on the low sill and stared through the rain and the wind at the sky like a dreadful, spreading bruise overhead, at the turbulent, howling sea below.

He pursed his lips, twisting his power ring to darken the scene a little more, to bring up the wind's wail and the ocean's roar. He was turning back to his previous preoccupation when he perceived that something alien tossed upon the distant waves; an artifact not of his own design, it intruded upon his careful conception. He peered hard at the object, but it was too far away for him to identify it. Another might have shrugged it aside, but he was painstaking, even prissy, in his need for artistic perfection. Was this some vulgar addition to his scene made, perhaps, by the Duke of Queens in a misguided effort to please him?

He took his parachute (chosen as the only means by which he could leave his tower) from the wall and strapped it on, stepping through the window and tugging at the rip cord as he fell into space. Down he plummeted and the scarlet balloon soon filled with gas, the nacelle opening up beneath him, so that by the time he was hovering some feet above the somber waves, he was lying comfortably on his chest, staring over the rim of his parachute at the trespassing image he had seen from his tower. What he saw was something resembling a great shell, a shallow boat of mother-of-pearl, floating on that dark and heaving sea.

In astonishment he now realized that the boat was occupied by a slight figure, clad in filmy white, whose face was pale and terrified. It could only be one of his friends, altering his appearance for some whimsical adventure. But which? Then he caught, through the rain, a better glimpse and he heard himself saying:

"A child? A child? Are you a child?"

She could not hear him; perhaps she could not even see him, having eyes only for the watery walls which threatened to engulf her little boat and carry her down to the land of Davy Jones. How could it be a child? He rubbed his eyes. He must be projecting his hopes—but there, that movement, that whimper! It *was* a child! Without doubt!

He watched, open-mouthed, as she was flung this way and that by the elements—*his* elements. She was powerless: actually powerless! He relished her terror; he envied her her fear. Where had she come from? Save for himself and Jherek Carnelian there had not been a child on the planet for thousands upon thousands of years.

He leaned further out, studying her smooth skin, her lovely rounded limbs. Her eyes were tight shut now as the waves crashed upon her fragile craft; her delicate fingers, unstrong, courageous, clung hard to the side! her white dress was wet, outlining her new-formed breasts; water poured from her long, auburn hair. She panted in delicious impotence.

"It *is* a child!" Werther exclaimed. "A sweet, frightened child!"

And in his excitement he toppled from his parachute with an astonished yell, and landed with a crash, which winded him, in the sea-shell boat beside the girl. She opened her eyes as he turned his head to apologize. Plainly she had not been aware of his presence overhead. For a moment he could not speak, though his lips moved. But she screamed.

"My dear . . ." The words were thin and high and they faded into the wind. He struggled to raise himself on his elbows. "I apologize . . ."

She screamed again. She crept as far away from him as possible. Still she clung to her flimsy boat's side as the waves played with it: a thoughtless giant with too delicate a toy; inevitably, it must shatter. He waved his hand to indicate his parachute, but it had already been borne away. His cloak was caught by the wind and wrapped itself around his arm; he struggled to free himself and became further entangled; he heard a new scream and then some demoralized whimpering.

"I will save you!" he shouted, by way of reassurance, but his voice was muffled even in his own ears. It was answered by a further pathetic shriek. As the cloak was saturated it became increasingly difficult for him to escape its folds. He lost his temper and was deeper enmeshed. He tore at the thing. He freed his head.

"I am not your enemy, tender one, but your saviour," he said. It was obvious that she could not hear him. With an impatient gesture he flung off his cloak at last and twisted a power ring. The volume of noise was immediately reduced. Another twist, and the waves became calmer. She stared at him in wonder.

"Did you do that?" she asked.

"Of course. It is my scene, you see. But how you came to enter it, I do not know!"

"You are a wizard, then?" she said.

"Not at all. I have no interest in sport." He clapped his hands and his parachute reappeared, perhaps a trifle reluctantly as if it had enjoyed its brief independence, and drifted down until it was level with the boat. Werther lightened the sky. He could not bring himself, however, to dismiss the rain, but he let a little sun shine through it.

"There," he said. "The storm has passed, eh? Did you like your experience?"

"It was horrifying! I was so afraid. I thought I would drown."

"Yes? And did you like it?"

She was puzzled, unable to answer as he helped her aboard the nacelle and ordered the parachute home.

"You *are* a wizard!" she said. She did not seem disappointed. He did not quiz her as to her meaning. For the moment, if not for always, he was prepared to let her identify him however she wished.

"You are actually a child?" he asked hesitantly. "I do not mean to be insulting. A time-traveler, perhaps? Or from another planet?"

"Oh, no. I am an orphan. My father and mother are now dead. I was born on Earth some fourteen years ago." She looked in mild dismay over the side of the craft as they were whisked swiftly upward. "*They* were time-travelers. We made our home in a forgotten menagerie—underground, but it was pleasant. My parents feared recapture, you see. Food still grew in the menagerie. There were books, too, and they taught me to read—and there were other records through which they were able to present me with a reasonable education. I am not illiterate. I know the world. I was taught to fear wizards."

"Ah," he crooned, "the world! But you are not a part of it, just as I am not a part."

The parachute reached the window and, at his indication, she stepped gingerly from it to the tower. The parachute folded itself and placed itself upon the wall. Werther said: "You will want food, then? I will create whatever you wish!"

"Fairy food will not fill mortal stomachs, sir," she told him.

"You are beautiful," he said. "Regard me as your mentor, as your new father. I will teach you what this world is really like. Will you oblige me, at least, by trying the food?"

"I will." She looked about her with a mixture of curiosity and suspicion. "You lead a spartan life." She noticed a cabinet. "Books? You read, then?"

"In transcription," he admitted. "I listen. My enthusiasm is for Ivan Turgiditi, who created the Novel of Discomfort and remained its greatest practitioner. In, I believe, the nine-hundredth (though they could be spurious, invented, I have heard) . . ."

"Oh, no, no! I have read Turgiditi." She blushed. "In the original. *Wet Socks*—four hours of discomfort, every second brought to life, and in less than a thousand pages!"

"My favorite," he told her, his expression softening still more into besotted wonderment. "I can scarcely believe—in this Age—one such as you! Innocent of device. Uncorrupted! Pure!"

She frowned. "My parents taught me well, sir. I am not . . ."

"You cannot know. And dead, you say? Dead! If only I could have witnessed—but no, I am insensitive. Forgive me. I mentioned food."

"I am not really hungry."

"Later, then. That I should have so recently mourned such things as lacking in this world. I was blind. I did not look. Tell me everything. Whose was the menagerie?"

"It belonged to one of the lords of this planet. My mother was from a period she called the October Century, but recently recovered from a series of interplanetary wars and fresh and optimistic in its rediscoveries of ancestral technologies. She was chosen to be the first into the future. She was captured upon her arrival and imprisoned by a wizard like yourself."

"The word means little. But continue."

"She said that she used the word because it had meaning for her and she had no other short description. My father came from a time known as the Preliminary Structure, where human kind was rare and machines proliferated. He never mentioned the nature of the transgression he made from the social code of his day, but as a result of it he was banished to this world. He, too, was captured for the same menagerie and there he met my mother. They lived originally, of course, in separate cages, where their normal environments were re-created for them. But the owner of the menagerie became bored, I think, and abandoned interest in his collection . . ."

"I have often remarked that people who cannot look after their collections have no business keeping them," said Werther. "Please continue, my dear child." He reached out and patted her hand.

"One day he went away and they never saw him again. It took them some time to realize that he was not returning. Slowly the more delicate creatures, whose environments required special attention, died."

"No one came to resurrect them?"

"No one. Eventually my mother and father were the only ones left. They made what they could of their existence, too wary to enter the outer world in case they should be recaptured, and, to their astonishment, conceived me. They had heard that people from different historical periods could not produce children."

"I have heard the same."

"Well, then, I was a fluke. They were determined to give me as good an upbringing as they could and to prepare me for the dangers of your world."

"Oh, they were right! For one so innocent, there are many dangers. I will protect you, never fear."

"You are kind." She hesitated. "I was not told by my parents that such as you existed."

"I am the only one."

"I see. My parents died in the course of this past year, first my father, then my mother (of a broken heart, I believe). I buried my mother and at first made an attempt to live the life we had always led, but I felt the lack of company and decided to explore the world, for it seemed to me I, too, could grow old and die before I had experienced anything!"

"Grow old," mouthed Werther rhapsodically, "and die!"

"I set out a month or so ago and was disappointed to discover the absence of ogres, of malevolent creatures of any sort—and the wonders I witnessed, while a trifle bewildering, did not compare with those I had imagined I would find. I had fully expected to be snatched up for a menagerie by now, but nobody has shown interest, even when they have seen me."

"Few follow the menagerie fad, at present." He nodded. "They would not have known you for what you were. Only I could recognize you. Oh, how lucky I am. And how lucky *you* are, my dear, to have met me when you did. You see, I, too, am a child of the womb. I, too, made my own hard way through the utereal gloom to breathe the air, to find the light of this faded, this senile globe. Of all those you could have met, you have met the only one who understands you, who is likely to share your passions, to relish your education. We are soul mates, child!"

He stood up and put a tender arm about her young shoulders.

"You have a new mother, a new father now! His name is Werther!"

IV

In Which Werther Finds Sin at Last

Her name was Catherine Lily Marguerite Natasha Dolores Beatrice Machineshop-Seven Flambeau Gratitude (the last two names but one being her father's and her mother's respectively).

Werther de Goethe continued to talk to her for some hours. Indeed, he became quite carried away as he described all the exciting things they would do, how they would live lives of the purest poetry and simplicity from now on, the quiet and tranquil places they would visit, the manner in which her education would be supplemented, and he was glad to note, he thought, her wariness dissipating, her attitude warming to him.

"I will devote myself entirely to your happiness," he informed her, and then, noticing that she was fast asleep, he smiled tenderly: "Poor child. I am a worm of thoughtlessness. She is exhausted."

He rose from his chair of unpolished quartz and strode to where she lay curled upon the iguana-skin rug; stooping, he placed his hands under her warm-smelling, her yielding body, and somewhat awkwardly lifted her. In her sleep she uttered a tiny moan, her cherry lips parted and her newly budded breasts rose and fell rapidly against his chest once or twice until she sank back into a deeper slumber.

He staggered, panting with the effort, to another part of the tower and then he lowered her with a sigh to the floor. He realized that he had not prepared a proper bedroom for her.

Fingering his chin, he inspected the dank stones, the cold obsidian which had suited his mood so well for so long and now seemed singularly offensive. Then he smiled.

"She must have beauty," he said, "and it must be subtle. It must be calm."

An inspiration, a movement of a power ring, and the walls were covered with thick carpets embroidered with scenes from his own old book of fairy tales. He remembered how he had listened to the book over and over again—his only consolation in the lonely days of his extreme youth.

Here, Man Shelley, a famous harmonican, ventured into Odeon (a version of Hell) in order to be reunited with his favorite three-headed dog Omnibus. The picture showed him with his harmonica (or "harp") playing "Blues for a Nightingale"—a famous lost piece. There Casablanca Bogard, with his single eye, in the middle of his forehead, wielded his magic spade, Sam, in his epic fight with that ferocious bird, the Malted Falcon, to save his love, the Acrilan Queen, from the power of Big Sleepy (a dwarf who had turned himself into a giant) and Mutinous Caine, who had been cast out of Hollywood (or paradise) for the killing of his sister, the Blue Angel.

Such scenes were surely the very stuff to stir the romantic, delicate imagination of this lovely child, just as his had been stirred when—he felt the *frisson*—he had been her age. He glowed. His substance was suffused with delicious compassion for them both as he recalled, also, the torments of his own adolescence.

That she should be suffering as he had suffered filled him with the pleasure all must feel when a fellow spirit is recognized, and at the same time he was touched by her plight, determined that she should not know the anguish of his earliest years. Once, long ago, Werther had courted Jherek Carnelian, admiring him for his fortitude, knowing that locked in

Jherek's head were the memories of bewilderment, misery and despair which would echo his own; but Jherek, pampered progeny of that most artificial of all creatures, the Iron Orchid, had been unable to recount any suitable experiences at all, had, whilst cheerfully eager to please Werther, recalled nothing but pleasurable times, had reluctantly admitted, at last, to the possession of the happiest of childhoods. That was when Werther had concluded that Jherek Carnelian had no soul worth speaking of and he had never altered his opinion (now he secretly doubted Jherek's origins and sometimes believed that Jherek merely pretended to have been a child—merely one more of his boring and superficial affectations).

Next, a bed—a soft, downy, bed, spread with sheets of silver silk, with posts of ivory and hangings of precious perspex, antique and yellowed, and on the floor the finely-tanned skins of albino hamsters and marmalade cats.

Werther added gorgeous lays of intricately patterned red and blue ceramic, their bowls filled with living flowers: with whispering toadflax, dragonsnaps, goldilocks and shanghai lilies, with blooming scarlet margravines (his adopted daughter's name-flower, as he knew to his pride), with soda-purple poppies and tea-green roses, with iodine and cerise and crimson hanging johnny, with golden cynthia and sky-blue true-lips, calomine and creeping larrikin, until the room was saturated with their intoxicating scents.

Placing a few bunches of hitler's balls in the corners near the ceiling, a toy fish tank (capable of firing real fish), which he remembered owning as a boy, under the window, a trunk (it could be opened by pressing the navel) filled with clothes near the bed, a full set of bricks and two bats against the wall close to the doorway, he was able, at last, to view the room with some satisfaction.

Obviously, he told himself, she would make certain changes according to her own tastes. That was why he had shown such restraint. He imagined her naive delight when she wakened in the morning. And he must be sure to produce days and nights of regular duration, because at her age routine was the main thing a child needed. There was nothing like the certainty of a consistently glorious sunrise! This reminded him to make an alteration to a power ring on his left hand, to spread upon the black cushion of the sky crescent moons and stars and starlets in profusion. Bending carefully, he picked up the vibrant youth of her body and lowered her to the bed, drawing the silver sheets up to her vestal chin. Chastely he touched lips to her forehead and crept from the room, fashioning a leafy door behind him, hesitating for a moment, unable to define the mood in which he found himself. A rare smile illumined features set so long in lines of gloom. Returning to his own quarters, he murmured:

"I believe it is Contentment!"

◥

A month swooned by. Werther lavished every moment of his time upon his new charge. He thought of nothing but her youthful satisfactions. He encouraged her in joy, in idealism, in a love of Nature. Gone were his blizzards, his rocky spires, his bleak wastes and his moody forests, to be replaced with gentle landscapes of green hills and merry, tinkling rivers, sunny glades in copses of poplars, rhododendrons, redwoods, laburnums, banyans and good old amiable oaks. When they went on a picnic large-eyed cows and playful gorillas would come and nibble scraps of food from Catherine Gratitude's palm. And when it was day, the sun always shone and the sky was always blue, and if there were clouds, they were high, hesitant puffs of whiteness and soon gone.

He found her books so that she might read. There was Turgiditi and Uto, Pett Ridge and Zakka, Pyat Sink—all the ancients. Sometimes he asked her to read to him, for the luxury of dispensing with his usual translators. She had been fascinated by a picture of a typewriter she had seen in a record, so he fashioned an air-car in the likeness of one, and they traveled the world in it, looking at scenes created by Werther's peers.

"Oh, Werther," she said one day, "you are so good to me. Now that I realize the misery which might have been mine (as well as the life I was missing underground) I love you more and more."

"And I love you more and more," he replied, his head a-swim. And for a moment he felt a pang of guilt at having forgotten Mistress Christia so easily. He had not seen her since Catherine had come to him and he guessed that she was sulking somewhere. He prayed that she would not decide to take vengeance on him.

They went to see Jherek Carnelian's famous "London, 1896" and Werther manfully hid his displeasure at her admiration for his rival's buildings of white marble, gold and sparkling quartz. He showed her his own abandoned tomb, which he privately considered in better taste, but it was plain that it did not give her the same satisfaction.

They saw the Duke of Queens' latest, "Ladies and Swans," but not for long, for Werther considered it unsuitable. Later they paid a visit to Lord Jagged of Canaria's somewhat abstract "War and Peace in Two Dimensions" and Werther thought it too stark to please the girl, judging the experiment "successful," but Catherine laughed with glee as she touched the living figures and found that somehow it was true—Lord Jagged had given them length and breadth but not a scrap of width—when they turned aside, they disappeared.

◆

It was on one of these expeditions, to Bishop Castle's "A Million Angry Wrens" (an attempt in the recently revised art of Aesthetic Loudness), that they encountered Lord Mongrove, a particular confidante of Werther's until they had quarreled over the method of suicide adopted by the natives of Uranus during the period of the Great Sodium Breather. By now they would, if Werther had not found a new obsession, have patched up their differences and Werther felt a pang of guilt for having forgotten the one person on this planet with whom he had, after all, shared something in common.

In his familiar dark green robes, with his leonine head hunched between his massive shoulders, the giant, apparently disdaining an air-carriage, was riding home upon the back of a monstrous snail.

The first thing they saw, from above, was its shining trail over the azure rocks of some abandoned, half-created scene of Argonheart Po's (who believed that nothing was worth making unless it tasted delicious and could be eaten and digested). It was Catherine who saw the snail itself first and exclaimed at the size of the man who occupied the swaying howdah on it back.

"He must be ten feet tall. Werther!"

And Werther, knowing whom she meant, made their typewriter descend, crying:

"Mongrove! My old friend!"

Mongrove, however, was sulking. He had chosen not to forget whatever insult it had been which Werther had leveled at him when they had last met. "What? Is it Werther? Bring freshly sharpened dirks for the flesh between my shoulder blades? It is that Cold Betrayer himself, whom I befriended when a bare boy, pretending carelessness, feigning insouciance, as if he cannot remember, with relish, the exact degree of bitterness of the poisoned wine he fed me when we parted. Faster, steed! Bear me away from Treachery! Let me fly from further Insult! No more shall I suffer at the hands of Calumny!" And, with his long, jeweled stick, he beat upon the shell of his mollusculoid mount. The beast's horns waved agitatedly for a moment, but it did not really seem capable of any greater speed. In good-humored puzzlement, it turned its slimy head towards its master.

"Forgive me, Mongrove! I take back all I said," announced Werther, unable to recall a single sour syllable of the exchange. "Tell me why you are abroad. It is rare for you to leave your doomy dome."

"I am making my way to the Ball," said Lord Mongrove, "which is shortly to be held by My Lady Charlotina. Doubtless I have been invited to act as a butt for their malice and their gossip, but I go in good faith."

"A Ball? I know nothing of it."

Mongrove's countenance brightened a trifle. "You have not been invited? Ah!"

"I wonder . . . But, no—My Lady Charlotina shows unsuspected sensitivity. She knows that I now have responsibilities—to my little Ward, here. To Catherine—to my Kate."

"The child?"

"Yes, to my child. I am privileged to be her protector. Fate favors me as her new father. This is she. Is she not lovely? Is she not innocent?"

Lord Mongrove raised his great head and looked at the slender girl beside Werther. He shook his huge head as if in pity for her.

"Be careful, my dear," he said. "To be befriended by de Goethe is to be embraced by a viper!"

She did not understand Mongrove; questioningly, she looked up at Werther. "What does he mean?"

Werther was shocked. He clapped his hands to her pretty ears.

"Listen no more! I regret the overture. The movement, Lord Mongrove, shall remain unresolved. Farewell, spurner of good intent. I had never guessed before the level of your cynicism. Such an accusation! Goodbye, forever, most malevolent of mortals, despiser of altruism, hater of love! She shall know me no longer!"

"You have known yourself not at all," snapped Mongrove spitefully, but it was unlikely that Werther, already speeding skyward, heard the remark.

And thus it was with particular and unusual graciousness that Werther greeted My Lady Charlotina when, a little later, they came upon her.

She was wearing the russet ears and eyes of a fox, riding her yellow rocking horse through the patch of orange sky left over from her own turbulent "Death of Neptune." She waved to them. "Cock-a-loodle-do!"

"My dear Lady Charlotina. What a pleasure it is to see you. Your beauty continues to rival Nature's mightiest miracles."

It is with such unwonted effusion that one will greet a person, who has not hitherto aroused our feelings, when we are in a position to compare them against another, closer, acquaintance who had momentarily earned our contempt or anger.

She seemed taken aback, but received the compliment equably enough.

"Dear Werther! And is this that rarity, the girl-child I have heard so much about and whom, in your goodness, you have taken under your wing? I could not believe it! A child! And how lucky she is to find a father in yourself—of all our number the one best suited to look after her."

It might also be said that Werther preened himself beneath the golden shower of her benediction, and if he detected no irony in her tone, perhaps it was because he still smarted from Mongrove's dash of vitriol.

"I have been chosen, it seems," he said modestly, "to lead this waif through the traps and illusions of our weary world. The burden I shoulder is not light . . ."

"Valiant Werther!"

". . . but it is shouldered willingly. I am devoting my life to her up-bringing, to her peace of mind." He placed a bloodless hand upon her auburn locks and, winsomely, she shook his other one.

"You are tranquil, my dear?" asked Lady Charlotina kindly, arranging her blue skirts over the saddle of her rocking horse. "You have no doubts?"

"At first I had." admitted the sweet child, "but gradually I learned to trust my new father. Now I would trust him in anything!"

"Ah," sighed My Lady Charlotina, "trust!"

"Trust," said Werther. "It grows in me, too. You encourage me, charming Charlotina, for a short time ago I believed myself doubted by all."

"Is it possible? When you are evidently so reconciled—so—happy!"

"And I am happy, also, now that I have Werther," caroled the commendable Catherine.

"Exquisite!" breathed My Lady Charlotina. "And you will, of course, both come to my Ball."

"I am not sure ..." began Werther, "perhaps Catherine is too young ..."

But she raised her tawny hands. "It is your duty to come. To show us all that simple hearts are the happiest."

"Possibly ..."

"You must. The world must have examples, Werther, if it is to follow your Way."

Werther lowered his eyes shyly. "I am honored," he said. "We accept."

"Splendid! Then come soon. Come now, if you like. A few arrangements, and the Ball begins."

"Thank you," said Werther, "but I think it best if we return to my castle for a little while." He caressed his ward's fine, long tresses. "For it will be Catherine's first Ball and she must choose her gown."

And he beamed down upon his radiant protégée as she clapped her hands in joy.

●

My Lady Charlotina's Ball must have been at least a mile in circumference, set against the soft tones of a summer twilight, red-gold and transparent so that, as one approached, the guests who had already arrived could be seen standing upon the inner wall, clad in creations extravagant even at the End of Time.

The Ball itself was inclined to roll a little, but those inside it were undisturbed; their footing was firm, thanks to My Lady Charlotina's artistry. The Ball was entered by means of a number of sphincterish openings, placed more or less at random in its outer wall. At the very center of the Ball, on a floating platform, sat an orchestra comprising the choicest musicians, out of a myriad ages and planets, from My Lady's great menagerie (she specialized, currently, in artists).

When Werther de Goethe, a green-gowned Catherine Gratitude upon his blue velvet arm, arrived, the orchestra was playing some primitive figure of My Lady Charlotina's own composition. It was called, she claimed as she welcomed them. "On the Theme of Childhood," but doubtless she thought to please them, for Werther believed he had heard it before, under a different title.

Many of the guests had already arrived and were standing in small groups chatting to each other. Werther greeted an old friend Li Pao, of the twenty-seventh century, and such a killjoy that he had never been wanted for a menagerie. While he was forever criticizing their behavior, he never missed a party. Next to him stood the Iron Orchid, mother of Jherek Carnelian, who was not present. In contrast to Li Pao's faded blue overalls, she wore rags of red, yellow and mauve, thousands of sparkling bracelets, anklets and necklaces, a head-dress of woven peacock's wings, slippers which were moles and whose beady eyes looked up from the floor.

"What do you mean—waste?" she was saying to Li Pao. "What else could we do with the energy of the universe? If our sun burns out, we create another. Doesn't that make us conservatives? Or is it preservatives?"

"Good evening, Werther," said Li Pao in some relief. He bowed politely to the girl. "Good evening, miss."

"Miss?" said the Iron Orchid. "What?"

"Gratitude."

"For whom?"

"This is Catherine Gratitude, my ward," said Werther, and the Iron Orchid let forth a peal of luscious laughter.

"The girl-bride, eh?"

"Not at all," said Werther. "How is Jherek?"

"Lost, I fear, in Time. We have seen nothing of him recently. He still pursues his paramour. Some say you copy him, Werther."

He knew her bantering tone of old and took the remark in good part. "His is a mere affectation," he said. "Mine is Reality."

"You were always one to make that distinction, Werther," she said. "And I will never understand the difference!"

"I find your concern for Miss Gratitude's upbringing most worthy," said Li Pao somewhat unctuously. "If there is any way I can help. My knowledge of twenties' politics, for instance, is considered unmatched—particularly, of course, where the twenty-sixth and twenty-seventh centuries are concerned . . ."

"You are kind," said Werther, unsure how to take an offer which seemed to him overeager and not entirely selfless.

Gaf the Horse in Tears, whose clothes were real flame, flickered towards them, the light from his burning, unstable face almost blinding Werther. Catherine Gratitude shrank from him as he reached out a hand to touch her, but her expression changed as she realized that he was not at all hot—rather, there was something almost chilly about the sensation on her shoulder. Werther did his best to smile. "Good evening. Gaf."

"She is a dream!" said Gaf. "I know it, because only I have such a wonderful imagination. Did I create her, Werther?"

"You jest."

"Ho, ho! Serious old Werther." Gaf kissed him, bowed to the child, and moved away, his body erupting in all directions as he laughed the more. "Literal, literal Werther!"

"He is a boor," Werther told his charge. "Ignore him."

"I thought him sweet," she said.

"You have much to learn, my dear."

The music filled the Ball and some of the guests left the floor to dance, hanging in the air around the orchestra, darting streamers of colored energy in order to weave complex patterns as they moved.

"They are very beautiful," said Catherine Gratitude. "May we dance soon, Werther?"

"If you wish. I am not much given to such pastimes as a rule."

"But tonight?"

He smiled. "I can refuse you nothing, child."

She hugged his arm and her girlish laughter filled his heart with warmth.

"Perhaps you should have made yourself a child before, Werther?" suggested the Duke of Queens, drifting away from the dance and leaving a trail of green fire behind him. He was clad all in soft metal which reflected the colors in the Ball and created other colors in turn. "You are a perfect father. Your métier."

"It would not have been the same, Duke of Queens."

"As you say." His darkly handsome face bore its usual expression of benign amusement. "I am the Duke of Queens, child. It is an honor." He bowed, his metal booming.

"Your friends are wonderful," said Catherine Gratitude. "Not at all what I expected."

"Be wary of them," murmured Werther. "They have no conscience."

"Conscience? What is that?"

Werther touched a ring and led her up into the air of the Ball. "I am your conscience, for the moment, Catherine. You shall learn in time."

Lord Jagged of Canaria, his face almost hidden by one of his high, quilted collars, floated in their direction.

"Werther, my boy! This must be your daughter. Oh! Sweeter than honey! Softer than petals! I have heard so much—but the praise was not enough! You must have poetry written about you. Music composed for you. Tales must be spun with you as the heroine." And Lord Jagged made a deep and elaborate bow, his long sleeves sweeping the air below his feet. Next, he addressed Werther:

"Tell me, Werther, have you seen Mistress Christia? Everyone else is here, but not she."

"I have looked for the Everlasting Concubine without success," Werther told him.

"She should arrive soon. In a moment My Lady Charlotina announces the beginning of the masquerade—and Mistress Christia loves the masquerade."

"I suspect she pines," said Werther.

"Why so?"

"She loved me, you know."

"Aha! Perhaps you are right. But I interrupt your dance. Forgive me."

And Lord Jagged of Canaria floated, stately and beautiful, towards the floor.

"Mistress Christia?" said Catherine. "Is she your Lost Love?"

"A wonderful woman," said Werther. "But my first duty is to you. Regretfully I could not pursue her, as I think she wanted me to do."

"Have I come between you?"

"Of course not. Of course not. That was infatuation—this is a sacred duty."

And Werther showed her how to dance—how to notice a gap in a pattern which might be filled by the movements from her body. Because it was a special occasion he had given her her very own power ring—only a small one, but she was proud of it, and she gasped so prettily at the colors her train made that Werther's fears that his gift might corrupt her

precious innocence were plainly unfounded. It was then that he realized
with a shock how deeply he had fallen in love with her.

At the realization, he made an excuse, leaving her to dance with first
Sweet Orb Mace, feminine tonight, with a latticed face, and then with
O'Kala Incarnadine who, with his usual preference for the bodies of
beasts, was currently a bear. Although he felt a pang as he watched her
stroke O'Kala's ruddy fur, he could not bring himself just then to interfere. His immediate desire was to leave the Ball, but to do that would be
to disappoint his ward, to raise questions he would not wish to answer.
After a while he began to feel a certain satisfaction from his suffering and
remained, miserably, on the floor while Catherine danced on and on.

And then My Lady Charlotina had stopped the orchestra and stood
on the platform calling for their attention.

"It is time for the masquerade. You all know the theme, I hope." She
paused, smiling. "All, save Werther and Catherine. When the music begins again, please reveal your creations of the evening."

Werther frowned, wondering her reasons for not revealing the theme
of the masquerade to him. She was still smiling at him as she drifted
towards him and settled beside him on the floor.

"You seem sad, Werther. Why so? I thought you at one with yourself
at last. Wait. My surprise will flatter you, I'm sure!"

The music began again. The Ball was filled with laughter—and there
was the theme of the masquerade!

Werther cried out in anguish. He dashed upward through the gleeful
throng, seeing each face as a mockery, trying to reach the side of his girl-
child before she could realize the dreadful truth.

"Catherine! Catherine!"

He flew to her. She was bewildered as he folded her in his arms.

"Oh, they are monsters of insincerity! Oh, they are grotesque in their
aping of all that is simple, all that is pure!" he cried.

He glared about him at the other guests. My Lady Charlotina had
chosen "Childhood" as her general theme. Sweet Orb Mace had changed
himself into a gigantic single sperm, his own face still visible at the glistening tail; the Iron Orchid had become a monstrous new-born baby with
a red and bawling face which still owed more to Paint than to Nature;
the Duke of Queens, true to character, was three-year-old Siamese twins
(both the faces were his own, softened); even Lord Mongrove had deigned
to become an egg.

"What ith it, Werther?" lisped My Lady Charlotina at his feet, her
brown curls bobbing as she waved her lollipop in the general direction
of the other guests. "Doeth it not pleathe you?"

"Ugh! This is agony! A parody of everything I hold most perfect!"

"But, Werther . . ."

"What is wrong, dear Werther?" begged Catherine. "It is only a masquerade."

"Can you not see? It is you—everything you and I mean—that they
mock. No—it is best that you do not see. Come, Catherine. They are

insane; they revile all that is sacred!" And he bore her bodily towards the wall, rushing through the nearest doorway and out into the darkened sky.

◆

He left his typewriter behind, so great was his haste to be gone from that terrible scene. He fled with her willy-nilly through the air, through daylight, through pitchy night. He fled until he came to his own tower, flanked now by green lawns and rolling turf, surrounded by songbirds, swamped in sunshine. And he hated it—landscape, larks and light—all were hateful.

He flew through the window and found his room full of comforts—of cushions and carpets and heady perfume—and with a gesture he removed them. Their particles hung gleaming in the sun's beams for a moment. But the sun, too, was hateful. He blacked it out and night swam into that bare chamber. And all the while, in amazement, Catherine Gratitude looked on, her lips forming the question, but never uttering it. At length, tentatively, she touched his arm.

"Werther?"

His hands flew to his head. He roared in his mindless pain.

"Oh, Werther!"

"Ah! They destroy me! They destroy my ideals!"

He was weeping when he turned to bury his face in her hair.

"Werther!" She kissed his cold cheek. She stroked his shaking back. And she led him from the ruins of his room and down the passage to her own apartment.

"Why should I strive to set up standards." he sobbed, "when all about me they seek to pull them down. It would be better to be a villain!"

But he was quiescent; he allowed himself to be seated upon her bed; he felt suddenly drained. He sighed. "They hate innocence. They would see it gone forever from this globe."

She gripped his hand. She stroked it. "No, Werther. They meant no harm. I saw no harm."

"They would corrupt you. I must keep you safe."

Her lips touched his and his body came alive again. Her fingers touched his skin. He gasped.

"I must keep you safe."

In a dream, he took her in his arms. Her lips parted, their tongues met. Her young breasts pressed against him—and for perhaps the first time in his life Werther understood the meaning of physical joy. His blood began to dance to the rhythm of a sprightlier heart. And why should he not take what they would take in his position? He placed a hand upon a pulsing thigh. If cynicism called the tune, then he would show them he could pace as pretty a measure as any. His kisses became passionate, and passionately they were returned.

"Catherine!"

A motion of a power ring and their clothes were gone, the bed hangings drawn.

And your auditor not being of that modern school which salaciously seeks to share the secrets of others' passions (secrets familiar, one might add, to the great majority of us) retires from this scene.

But when he woke the next morning and turned on the sun, Werther looked down at the lovely child beside him, her auburn hair spread across the pillows, her little breasts rising and falling in tranquil sleep, and he realized that he had used his reaction to the masquerade to betray his trust. A madness had filled him; he had raised an evil wind and his responsibility had been born off by it, taking Innocence and Purity, never to return. His lust had lost him everything.

Tears reared in his tormented eyes and ran cold upon his heated cheeks. "Mongrove was perceptive indeed," he murmured. "To be befriended by Werther is to be embraced by a viper. She can never trust me—anyone—again. I have lost my right to offer her protection. I have stolen her childhood."

And he got up from the bed, from the scene of that most profound of crimes, and he ran from the room and went to sit in his old chair of unpolished quartz, staring listlessly through the window at the paradise he had created outside. It accused him; it reminded him of his high ideals. He was astonished by the consequences of his actions: he had turned his paradise to hell.

A great groan reverberated in his chest. "Oh, now I know what sin is!" he said. "And what terrible tribute it exacts from the one who tastes it!"

And he sank almost luxuriously into the deepest gloom he had ever known.

V

In Which Werther Finds Redemption of Sorts

He avoided Catherine Gratitude all that day, even when he heard her calling his name, for if the landscape could fill him with such agony, what would he feel under the startled inquisition of her gaze? He erected himself a heavy dungeon door so that she could not get in, and, as he sat contemplating his poisoned paradise, he saw her once, walking on a hill he had made for her. She seemed unchanged, of course, but he knew in his heart how she must be shivering with the chill of lost innocence. That it should have been himself, of all men, who had introduced her so young to the tainted joys of carnal love! Another deep sigh and he buried his fists savagely into his eyes.

"Catherine! Catherine! I am a thief, an assassin, a despoiler of souls. The name of Werther de Goethe becomes a synonym for Treachery!"

◆

It was not until the next morning that he thought himself able to admit her to his room, to submit himself to a judgment which he knew would be worse for not being spoken. Even when she did enter, his shifty eye would not focus on her for long. He looked for some outward sign of her experience, somewhat surprised that he could detect none.

He glared at the floor, knowing his words to be inadequate. "I am sorry," he said.

"For leaving the Ball, darling Werther! The epilogue was infinitely sweeter."

"Don't!" He put his hands to his ears. "I cannot undo what I have done, my child, but I can try to make amends. Evidently you must not stay here with me. You need suffer nothing further on that score. For myself, I must contemplate an eternity of loneliness. It is the least of the prices I must pay. But Mongrove would be kind to you, I am sure." He looked at her. It seemed that she had grown older. Her bloom was fading now that it had been touched by the icy fingers of that most sinister, most insinuating, of libertines, called Death. "Oh," he sobbed, "how haughty was I in my pride! How I congratulated myself on my high-mindedness. Now I am proved the lowliest of all my kind!"

"I really cannot follow you, Werther dear," she said. "Your behavior is rather odd today, you know. Your words mean very little to me."

"Of course they mean little," he said. "You are unworldly, child. How can you anticipate . . . ah, ah . . ." and he hid his face in his hands.

"Werther, please cheer up. I have heard of *le petit mal*, but this seems to be going on for a somewhat longer time. I am still puzzled . . ."

"I cannot, as yet," he said, speaking with some difficulty through his palms, "bring myself to describe in cold words the enormity of the crime I have committed against your spirit—against your childhood. I had known that you would—eventually—wish to experience the joys of true love—but I had hoped to prepare your soul for what was to come—so that when it happened it would be beautiful."

"But it *was* beautiful, Werther."

He found himself experiencing a highly inappropriate impatience with her failure to understand her doom.

"It was not the right *kind* of beauty," he explained.

"There are certain correct kinds for certain times?" she asked. "You are sad because we have offended some social code?"

"There is no such thing in this world, Catherine—but you, child, could have known a code. Something I never had when I was your age—something I wanted for you. One day you will realize what I mean." He leaned forward, his voice thrilling, his eye hot and hard, "And if you do not hate me now, Catherine, oh, you will hate me then. Yes! You will hate me then."

Her answering laughter was unaffected, unstrained. "This is silly, Werther. I have rarely had a nicer experience."

He turned aside, raising his hands as if to ward off blows. "Your words are darts—each one draws blood in my conscience." He sank back into his chair.

Still laughing, she began to stroke his limp hand. He drew it away from her. "Ah, see! I have made you lascivious. I have introduced you to the drug called lust!"

"Well, perhaps to an aspect of it!"

Some change in her tone began to impinge on Werther, though he was still deep-trapped in the glue of his guilt. He raised his head, his expression bemused, refusing to believe the import of her words.

"A wonderful aspect," she said. And she licked his ear.

He shuddered. He frowned. He tried to frame words to ask her a certain question, but he failed.

She licked his cheek and she twined her fingers in his lackluster hair. "And one I should love to experience again, most passionate of anachronisms. It was as it must have been in those ancient days—when poets ranged the world, stealing what they needed, taking any fair maiden who pleased them, setting fire to the towns of their publishers, laying waste the books of their rivals: ambushing their readers. I am sure you were just as delighted, Werther. Say that you were!"

"Leave me!" he gasped. "I can bear no more."

"If it is what you want."

"It is."

With a wave of her little hand, she tripped from the room.

And Werther brooded upon her shocking words, deciding that he could only have misheard her. In her innocence she had seemed to admit an understanding of certain inconceivable things. What he had half-interpreted as a familiarity with the carnal world was doubtless merely a child's romantic conceit. How could she have had previous experience of a night such as that which they had shared?

She had been a virgin. Certainly she had been that.

He wished that he did not then feel an ignoble pang of pique at the possibility of another having also known her. Consequently this was immediately followed by a further wave of guilt for entertaining such thoughts and subsequent emotions. A score of conflicting glooms warred in his mind, sent tremors through his body.

"Why," he cried to the sky, "was I born! I am unworthy of the gift of life. I accused My Lady Charlotina, Lord Jagged and the Duke of Queens of base emotions, cynical motives, yet none are baser or more cynical than mine! Would I turn my anger against my victim, blame her for my misery, attack a little child because she tempted me? That is what my diseased mind would do. Thus do I seek to excuse myself my crimes. Ah, I am vile! I am vile!"

He considered going to visit Mongrove, for he dearly wished to abase himself before his old friend, to tell Mongrove that the giant's contempt had been only too well-founded; but he had lost the will to move; a terrible lassitude had fallen upon him. Hating himself, he knew that all must hate him, and while he knew that he had earned every scrap of their hatred, he could not bear to go abroad and run the risk of suffering it.

What would one of his heroes of Romance have done? How would Casablanca Bogard or Eric of Marylebone have exonerated themselves, even supposing they could have committed such an unbelievable deed in the first place?

He knew the answer.

It drummed louder and louder in his ears. It was implacable and grim. But still he hesitated to follow it. Perhaps some other, more original act of contrition would occur to him? He racked his writhing brain. Nothing presented itself as an alternative.

At length he rose from his chair of unpolished quartz. Slowly, his pace measured, he walked towards the window, stripping off his power rings so that they clattered to the flagstones.

He stepped upon the ledge and stood looking down at the rocks a mile below at the base of the tower. Some jolting of a power ring as it fell had caused a wind to spring up and to blow coldly against his naked body. "The Wind of Justice," he thought.

He ignored his parachute. With one final cry of "Catherine! Forgive me!" and an unvoiced hope that he would be found long after it proved impossible to resurrect him, he flung himself, unsupported, into space.

Down he fell and death leapt to meet him. The breath fled from his lungs, his head began to pound, his sight grew dim, but the spikes of black rock grew larger until he knew that he had struck them, for his body was aflame, broken in a hundred places, and his sad, muddled, doom-clouded brain was chaff upon the wailing breeze. Its last coherent thought was: *Let none say Werther did not pay the price in full.* And thus did he end his life with a proud negative.

VI

In Which Werther Discovers Consolation

"Oh, Werther, what an adventure!"

It was Catherine Gratitude looking down on him as he opened his eyes. She clapped her hands. Her blue eyes were full of joy.

Lord Jagged stood back with a smile. "Reborn, magnificent Werther, to sorrow afresh!" he said.

He lay upon a bench of marble in his own tower. Surrounding the bench were My Lady Charlotina, the Duke of Queens, Gaf the Horse in Tears, the Iron Orchid, Li Pao, O'Kala Incarnadine, and many others. They all applauded.

"A spendid drama!" said the Duke of Queens.

"Amongst the best I have witnessed," agreed the Iron Orchid (a fine compliment from her).

Werther found himself warming to them as they poured their praise upon him; but then he remembered Catherine Gratitude and what he had meant himself to be to her, what he had actually become, and although he felt much better for having paid his price, he stretched out his hand to her, saying again: "Forgive me."

"Silly Werther! Forgive such a perfect role? No, no! If anyone needs forgiving, then it is I." And Catherine Gratitude touched one of the many power rings now festooning her fingers and returned herself to her original appearance.

"It is you!" He could make no other response as he looked upon the Everlasting Concubine. "Mistress Christia?"

"Surely you suspected towards the end?" she said. "Was it not everything you told me you wanted? Was it not a fine 'sin,' Werther?"

"I suffered . . ." he began.

"Oh, yes! *How* you suffered! It was unparalleled. It was equal, I am sure, to anything in History. And, Werther, did you not find the 'guilt' particularly exquisite?"

"You did it for me?" He was overwhelmed. "Because it was what I said I wanted most of all?"

"He is still a little dull," explained Mistress Christia, turning to their friends. "I believe that is often the case after a resurrection."

"Often," intoned Lord Jagged, darting a sympathetic glance at Werther. "But it will pass, I hope."

"The ending, though it could be anticipated," said the Iron Orchid, "was absolutely right."

Mistress Christia put her arms around him and kissed him. "They are saying that your performance rivals Jherek Carnelian's," she whispered. He squeezed her hand. What a wonderful woman she was, to be sure, to have added to his experience and to have increased his prestige at the same time.

He sat up. He smiled a trifle bashfully. Again they applauded.

"I can see that this was where "Rain" was leading," said Bishop Castle. "It gives the whole thing point, I think."

"The exaggerations were just enough to bring out the essential mood without being too prolonged," said O'Kala Incarnadine, waving an elegant hoof (he had come as a goat).

"Well, I had not . . ." began Werther, but Mistress Christia put a hand to his lips.

"You will need a little time to recover," she said.

Tactfully, one by one, still expressing their most fulsome congratulations, they departed, until only Werther de Goethe and the Everlasting Concubine were left.

"I hope you did not mind the deception, Werther," she said. "I had to make amends for ruining your rainbow and I had been wondering for ages how to please you. My Lady Charlotina helped a little, of course, and Lord Jagged—though neither knew too much of what was going on."

"The real performance was yours," he said. "I was merely your foil."

"Nonsense. I gave you the rough material with which to work. And none could have anticipated the wonderful, consummate use to which you put it!"

Gently, he took her hand. "It was everything I have ever dreamed of," he said. "It is true, Mistress Christia, that you alone know me."

"You are kind. And now I must leave."

"Of course." He looked out through his window. The comforting storm raged again. Familiar lightnings flickered; friendly thunder threatened; from below there came the sound of his old consoler the furious sea flinging itself, as always, at the rock's black fangs. His sigh was contented. He knew that their liaison was ended; neither had the bad taste

184 ⬥ MICHAEL MOORCOCK

to prolong it and thus produce what would be, inevitably, an anticlimax, and yet he felt regret, as evidently did she.

"If death were only permanent," he said wistfully, "but it cannot be. I thank you again, granter of my deepest desires."

"If death," she said, pausing at the window, "were permanent, how would we judge our successes and our failures? Sometimes, Werther, I think you ask too much of the world." She smiled. "But you are satisfied for the moment, my love?"

"Of course."

It would have been boorish, he thought, to have claimed anything else.

Anniversary Project

JOE HALDEMAN

We never really know what the future holds in store for us, in spite of all the money people spend on Psychic Hot Lines and card readings. And, as the sly and ironic story that follows demonstrates, perhaps that's just as well. . . .

Born in Oklahoma City, Joe Haldeman took a B.S. degree in physics and astronomy from the University of Maryland and did postgraduate work in mathematics and computer science. But his plans for a career in science were cut short by the U.S. Army, which sent him to Vietnam in 1968 as a combat engineer. Seriously wounded in action, Haldeman returned home in 1969 and began to write. He sold his first story to Galaxy *in 1969 and by 1976 had garnered both the Nebula Award and the Hugo Award for his famous novel* The Forever War, *one of the landmark books of the seventies. He took another Hugo Award in 1977 for his story "Tricentennial," won the Rhysling Award in 1983 for the best SF poem of the year (although usually thought of primarily as a "hard-science" writer, Haldeman is, in fact, also an accomplished poet and has sold poetry to most of the major professional markets in the genre), and won both the Nebula and the Hugo Award in 1991 for the novella version of "The Hemingway Hoax." His story "Graves" earned him another Nebula in 1994, and "None So Blind" won the Hugo Award in 1995. His other books include two mainstream novels,* War Year *and* 1968, *the SF novels* Mindbridge, All My Sins Remembered, There Is No Darkness *(written with his brother, SF writer Jack C. Haldeman II),* Worlds, Worlds Apart, Worlds Enough and Time, Buying Time, *and the "techno-thriller"* Tool of the Trade, *the collections* Infinite Dreams, Dealing in Futures, Vietnam and Other Alien Worlds, *and* None So Blind, *and, as editor, the anthologies* Study War No More, Cosmic Laughter, *and* Nebula Award Stories Seventeen. *His most recent book is the novel* Forever Peace, *which won him a new Hugo Award in 1998 and a new Nebula Award in 1999. Coming up is a new novel,* Forever Free, *the direct sequel to* The Forever War. *Haldeman lives part of the year in Boston, where he teaches writing at the Massachusetts Institute of Technology, and the rest of the year in Florida, where he and his wife, Gay, make their home.*

His name is Three-phasing and he is bald and wrinkled, slightly over one meter tall, large-eyed, toothless and all bones and skin, sagging pale skin shot through with traceries of delicate blue and red. He is considered very beautiful but most of his beauty is in his hands and is due to his extreme youth. He is over two hundred years old and is learning how to talk. He has become reasonably fluent in sixty-three languages, all dead ones, and has only ten to go.

The book he is reading is a facsimile of an early edition of Goethe's

Faust. The nervous angular Fraktur letters goose-step across pages of paper-thin platinum.

The *Faust* had been printed electrolytically and, with several thousand similarly worthwhile books, sealed in an argon-filled chamber and carefully lost, in 2012 A.D.; a very wealthy man's legacy to the distant future.

In 2012 A.D., Polaris had been the pole star. Men eventually got to Polaris and built a small city on a frosty planet there. By that time, they weren't dating by prophets' births any more, but it would have been around 4900 A.D. The pole star by then, because of procession of the equinoxes, was a dim thing once called Gamma Cephei. The celestial pole kept reeling around, past Deneb and Vega and through barren patches of sky around Hercules and Draco; a patient clock but not the slowest one of use, and when it came back to the region of Polaris, then 26,000 years had passed and men had come back from the stars, and the book-filled chamber had shifted 130 meters on the floor of the Pacific, had rolled onto the shallow trench, and eventually was buried in an underwater landslide.

The thirty-seventh time this slow clock ticked, men had moved the Pacific, not because they had to, and had found the chamber, opened it up, identified the books and carefully sealed them up again. Some things by then were more important to men than the accumulation of knowledge: in half of one more circle of the poles would come the millionth anniversary of the written word. They could wait a few millennia.

As the anniversary, as nearly as they could reckon it, approached, they caused to be born two individuals: Nine-hover (nominally female) and Three-phasing (nominally male). Three-phasing was born to learn how to read and speak. He was the first human being to study these skills in more than a quarter of a million years.

Three-phasing has read the first half of *Faust* forwards and, for amusement and exercise, is reading the second half backwards. He is singing as he reads, lisping.

"Fain' Looee w'mun . . . wif all'r die-mun ringf . . ." He has not put in his teeth because they make his gums hurt.

Because he is a child of two hundred, he is polite when his father interrupts his reading and singing. His father's "voice" is an arrangement of logic and aesthetic that appears in Three-phasing's mind. The flavor is lost by translating into words:

"Three-phasing my son-ly atavism of tooth and vocal cord," sarcastically in the reverent mode, "Couldst tear thyself from objects of manifest symbol, and visit to share/help/learn, me?"

"?" He responds, meaning, "with/with/of what?"

Withholding mode: "Concerning thee: past, future."

He shuts the book without marking his place. It would never occur to him to mark his place, since he remembers perfectly the page he stops on, as well as every word preceding, as well as every event, no matter how trivial, that he has observed from the precise age of one year. In this respect, at least, he is normal.

He thinks the proper coordinates as he steps over the mover-transom, through a microsecond of black, and onto his father's mover-transom, about four thousand kilometers away on a straight line through the crust and mantle of the earth.

Ritual mode: "As ever, father." The symbol he uses for "father" is purposefully wrong, chiding. Crude biological connotation.

His father looks cadaverous and has in fact been dead twice. In the infant's small-talk mode he asks "From crude babblings of what sort have I torn your interest?"

"The tale called *Faust*, of a man so named, never satisfied with {symbol for slow but continuous accretion} of his knowledge and power; written in the language of Prussia."

"Also depended-ing on this strange word of immediacy, your Prussian language?"

"As most, yes. The word of 'to be': *sein*. Very important illusion in this and related languages/cultures; that events happen at the 'time' of perception, infinitesimal midpoint between past and future."

"Convenient illusion but retarding."

"As we discussed 129 years ago, yes." Three-phasing is impatient to get back to his reading, but adds:

"Obvious that to-be-ness $\begin{cases} \text{same order of illusion as three-} \\ \text{dimensionality of external world.} \\ \\ \text{thrust upon observer by geometric limi-} \\ \text{tation of synaptic degrees of freedom.} \end{cases}$ "

"You always stick up for them."

"I have great regard for what they accomplished with limited faculties and so short lives." Stop beatin' around the bush, Dad. *Tempis fugit*, eight to the bar. Did Mr. Handy Moves-dat-man-around-by-her-apron-strings, 20th-century American poet, intend cultural translation of *Lysistrata*? If so, inept. African were-beast legendary, yes.

Withholding mode (coy): "Your father stood with Nine-hover all morning."

"," broadcasts Three-phasing: well?

"The machine functions, perhaps inadequately."

The young polyglot tries to radiate calm patience.

"Details I perceive you want; the idea yet excites you. You can never have satisfaction with your knowledge, either. What happened-s to the man in your Prussian book?"

"He lived-s one hundred years and died-s knowing that a man can never achieve true happiness, despite the appearance of success."

"For an infant, a reasonable perception."

Respectful chiding mode: "One hundred years makes-ed Faust a very old man, for a Dawn man."

"As I stand," same mode, less respect, "yet an infant." They trade silent symbols of laughter.

After a polite tenth-second interval, Three-phasing uses the light interrogation mode: "The machine of Nine-hover . . . ?"

"It begins to work but so far not perfectly." This is not news.

Mild impatience: "As before, then, it brings back only rocks and earth and water and plants?"

"Negative, beloved atavism." Offhand. "This morning she caught two animals that look as man may once have looked."

"!" Strong impatience, "I go?"

"." His father ends the conversation just two seconds after it began.

Three-phasing stops off to pick up his teeth, then goes directly to Nine-hover.

A quick exchange of greeting-symbols and Nine-hover presents her prizes. "Thinking I have two different species," she stands: uncertainty, query.

Three-phasing is amused. "Negative, time-caster. The male and female took very dissimilar forms in the Dawn times." He touches one of them. "The round organs, here, served-ing to feed infants, in the female."

The female screams.

"She manipulates spoken symbols now," observes Nine-hover.

Before the woman has finished her startled yelp, Three-phasing explains: "Not manipulating concrete symbols; rather, she communicates in a way called 'non-verbal,' the use of such communication predating even speech." Slipping into the pedantic mode: "My reading indicates that such a loud noise occurs either

$$\begin{cases} \text{-following a stimu-} \\ \text{lus under conditions of} \end{cases}$$

$\begin{array}{l}\text{that produces pain} \\ \text{extreme agitation}\end{array} \begin{cases} \end{cases}$ since she seems not in pain, then

she must fear me or you or both of us.

"Or the machine," Nine-hover adds.

Symbol for continuing. "We have no symbol for it but in Dawn days most humans observed 'xenophobia,' reacting to the strange with fear instead of delight. We stand as strange to them as they do to us, thus they register fear. In their era this attitude encouraged-s survival.

"Our silence must seem strange to them, as well as our appearance and the speed with which we move. I will attempt to speak to them, so they will know they need not fear us."

◆

Bob and Sarah Graham were having a desperately good time. It was September of 1951 and the papers were full of news about the brilliant landing of U.S. Marines at Inchon. Bob was a Marine private with two days left of the thirty days' leave they had given him, between boot camp and disembarkation for Korea. Sarah had been Mrs. Graham for three weeks.

Sarah poured some more bourbon into her Coke. She wiped the sand off her thumb and stoppered the Coke bottle, then shook it gently. "What if you just don't show up?" she said softly.

Bob was staring out over the ocean and part of what Sarah said was lost in the crash of breakers rolling in. "What if I what?"

"Don't show up." She took a swig and offered the bottle. "Just stay here with me. With us." Sarah was sure she was pregnant. It was too early to tell, of course; her calendar was off but there could be other reasons.

He gave the Coke back to her and sipped directly from the bourbon bottle. "I suppose they'd go on without me. And I'd still be in jail when they came back."

"Not if—"

"Honey, don't even talk like that. It's a just cause."

She picked up a small shell and threw it toward the water.

"Besides, you read the *Examiner* yesterday."

"I'm cold. Let's go up." She stood and stretched and delicately brushed sand away. Bob admired her long naked dancer's body. He shook out the blanket and draped it over her shoulders.

"It'll be over by the time I get there. We'll push those bastards—"

"Let's not talk about Korea. Let's not talk."

He put his arm around her and they started walking back toward the cabin. Halfway there, she stopped and enfolded the blanket around both of them, drawing him toward her. He always closed his eyes when they kissed, but she always kept hers open. She saw it: the air turning luminous, the seascape fading to be replaced by bare metal walls. The sand turns hard under her feet.

At her sharp intake of breath, Bob opens his eyes. He sees a grotesque dwarf, eyes and skull too large, body small and wrinkled. They stare at one another for a fraction of a second. Then the dwarf spins around and speeds across the room to what looks like a black square painted on the floor. When he gets there, he disappears.

"What the hell?" Bob says in a hoarse whisper.

Sarah turns around just a bit too late to catch a glimpse of Three-phasing's father. She does see Nine-hover before Bob does. The nominally-female time-caster is a flurry of movement, sitting at the console of her time net, clicking switches and adjusting various dials. All of the motions are unnecessary, as is the console. It was built at Three-phasing's suggestion, since humans from the era into which they could cast would feel more comfortable in the presence of a machine that looked like a machine. The actual time net was roughly the size and shape of an asparagus stalk, was controlled completely by thought, and had no moving parts. It does not exist any more, but can still be used, once understood. Nine-hover has been trained from birth for this special understanding.

Sarah nudges Bob and points to Nine-hover. She can't find her voice; Bob stares open-mouthed.

In a few seconds, Three-phasing appears. He looks at Nine-hover for a moment, then scurries over to the Dawn couple and reaches up to touch Sarah on the left nipple. His body temperature is considerably higher than hers, and the unexpected warm moistness, as much as the suddenness of the motion, makes her jump back and squeal.

Three-phasing correctly classified both Dawn people as Caucasian, and so assumes that they speak some Indo-European language.

"*GuttenTagsprechensieDeutsch?*" he says in rapid soprano.

"Huh?" Bob says.

"*Guten-Tag-sprechen-sie-Deutsch?*" Three-phasing clears his throat and drops his voice down to the alto he uses to sing about the St. Louis woman. "*Guten Tag,*" he says, counting to a hundred between each word. "*Sprechen sie Deutsch?*"

"That's Kraut," says Bob, having grown up on jingoistic comic books. "Don't tell me you're a—"

Three-phasing analyzes the first five words and knows that Bob is an American from the period 1935–1955. "Yes, yes—and no, no—to wit, how very very clever of you to have identified this phrase as having come from the language of Prussia, Germany as you say; but I am, no, not a German person; at least, I no more belong to the German nationality than I do to any other, but I suppose that is not too clear and perhaps I should fully elucidate the particulars of your own situation at this, as you say, 'time,' and 'place.' "

The last English-language author Three-phasing studied was Henry James.

"Huh?" Bob says again.

"Ah. I should simplify." He thinks for a half-second, and drops his voice down another third. "Yeah, simple. Listen, Mac. First thing I gotta know's whatcher name. Whatcher broad's name."

"Well . . . I'm Bob Graham. This is my wife, Sarah Graham."

"Pleasta meetcha, Bob. Likewise, Sarah. Call me, uh . . ." The only twentieth-century language in which Three-phasing's name makes sense is propositional calculus. "George. George Boole."

"I 'poligize for bumpin' into ya, Sarah. That broad in the corner, she don't know what a tit is, so I was just usin' one of yours. Uh, lack of immediate culchural perspective, I shoulda knowed better."

Sarah feels a little dizzy, shakes her head slowly. "That's all right. I know you didn't mean anything by it."

"I'm dreaming," Bob says. "Shouldn't have—"

"No you aren't," says Three-phasing, adjusting his diction again. "You're in the future. Almost a million years. Pardon me." He scurries to the mover-transom, is gone for a second, reappears with a bedsheet, which he hands to Bob. "I'm sorry, we don't wear clothing. This is the best I can do, for now." The bedsheet is too small for Bob to wear the way Sarah is using the blanket. He folds it over and tucks it around his waist, in a kilt. "Why us?" he asks.

"You were taken at random. We've been time casting"—he checks with Nine-hover—"for twenty-two years, and have never before caught a human being. Let alone two. You must have been in close contact with one another when you intersected the time-caster beam. I assume you were copulating."

"What-ing?" Bob says.

"No, we weren't!" Sarah says indignantly.

"Ah, quite so." Three-phasing doesn't pursue the topic. He knows the humans of this culture were reticent about their sexual activity. But from their literature he knows they spent most of their "time" thinking about, arranging for, enjoying and recovering from a variety of sexual contacts.

"Then that must be a time machine over there," Bob says, indicating the fake console.

"In a sense, yes." Three-phasing decides to be partly honest. "But the actual machine no longer exists. People did a lot of time-traveling about a quarter of a million years ago. Shuffled history around. Changed it back. The fact that the machine once existed, well, that enables us to use it, if you see what I mean."

"Uh, no. I don't." Not with synapses limited to three degrees of freedom.

"Well, never mind. It's not really important." He senses the next question. "You will be going back . . . I don't know exactly when. It depends on a lot of things. You see, time is like a rubber band." No, it isn't. "Or a spring." No, it isn't. "At any rate, within a few days, weeks at most, you will leave this present and return to the moment you were experiencing when the time-caster beam picked you up."

"I've read stories like that," Sarah says. "Will we remember the future, after we go back?"

"Probably not," he says charitably. Not until your brains evolve. "But you can do us a great service."

Bob shrugs. "Sure, long as we're here. Anyhow, you did us a favor." He puts his arm around Sarah. "I've gotta leave Sarah in a couple of days; don't know for how long. So you're giving us more time together."

"Whether we remember it or not," Sarah says.

"Good, fine. Come with me." They follow Three-phasing to the mover-transom, where he takes their hands and transports them to his home. It is as unadorned as the time-caster room, except for bookshelves along one wall, and a low podium upon which the volume of *Faust* rests. All of the books are bound identically, in shiny metal with flat black letters along the spines.

Bob looks around. "Don't you people ever sit down?"

"Oh," Three-phasing says. "Thoughtless of me." With his mind he shifts the room from utility mood to comfort mood. Intricate tapestries now hang on the walls; soft cushions that look like silk are strewn around in pleasant disorder. Chiming music, not quite discordant, hovers at the edge of audibility, and there is a faint odor of something like jasmine. The metal floor has become a kind of soft leather, and the room has somehow lost its corners.

"How did that happen?" Sarah asks.

"I don't know." Three-phasing tries to copy Bob's shrug, but only manages a spasmodic jerk. "Can't remember not being able to do it."

Bob drops into a cushion and experimentally pushes at the floor with a finger. "What is it you want us to do?"

Trying to move slowly, Three-phasing lowers himself into a cushion and gestures at a nearby one, for Sarah. "It's very simple, really. Your being here is most of it.

"We're celebrating the millionth anniversary of the written word." How to phrase it? "Everyone is interested in this anniversary, but . . . nobody reads any more."

Bob nods sympathetically. "Never have time for it myself."

"Yes, uh . . . you *do* know how to read, though?"

"He knows," Sarah says. "He's just lazy."

"Well, yeah." Bob shifts uncomfortably in the cushion. "Sarah's the one you want. I kind of, uh, prefer to listen to the radio."

"I read all the time," Sarah says with a little pride. "Mostly mysteries. But sometimes I read good books, too."

"Good, good." It was indeed fortunate to have found this pair, Three-phasing realizes. They had used the metal of the ancient books to "tune" the time-caster, so potential subjects were limited to those living some eighty years before and after 2012 A.D. Internal evidence in the books indicated that most of the Earth's population was illiterate during this period.

"Allow me to explain. Any one of us can learn how to read. But to us it is like a code; an unnatural way of communicating. Because we are all natural telepaths. We can reach each other's minds from the age of one year."

"Golly!" Sarah says. "Read minds?" And Three-pushing sees in her mind a fuzzy kind of longing, much of which is love for Bob and frustration that she knows him only imperfectly. He dips into Bob's mind and finds things she is better off not knowing.

"That's right. So what we want is for you to read some of these books, and allow us to go into your minds while you're doing it. This way we will be able to recapture an experience that has been lost to the race for over a half-million years."

"I don't know," Bob says slowly. "Will we have time for anything else? I mean, the world must be pretty strange. Like to see some of it."

"Of course; sure. But the rest of the world is pretty much like my place here. Nobody goes outside any more. There isn't any air." He doesn't want to tell them how the air was lost, which might disturb them, but they seem to accept that as part of distant future.

"Uh, George." Sarah is blushing. "We'd also like, uh, some time to ourselves. Without anybody . . . inside our minds."

"Yes, I understand perfectly. You will have your own room, and plenty of time to yourselves." Three-phasing neglects to say that there is no such thing as privacy in a telepathic society.

But sex is another thing they don't have any more. They're almost as curious about that as they are about books.

●

So the kindly men of the future gave Bob and Sarah Graham plenty of time to themselves: Bob and Sarah reciprocated. Through the Dawn couple's eyes and brains, humanity shared again the visions of Fielding and

Melville and Dickens and Shakespeare and almost a dozen others. And as for the 98% more, that they didn't have time to read or that were in foreign languages—Three-phasing got the hang of it and would spend several millennia entertaining those who were amused by this central illusion of literature: that there could be order, that there could be beginnings and endings and logical workings-out in between; that you could count on the third act or the last chapter to tie things up. They knew how profound an illusion this was because each of them knew every other living human with an intimacy and accuracy far superior to that which even Shakespeare could bring to the study of even himself. And as for Sarah and as for Bob:

Anxiety can throw a person's ovaries way off schedule. On that beach in California, Sarah was no more pregnant than Bob was. But up there in the future, some somatic tension finally built up to the breaking point, and an egg went sliding down the left Fallopian tube, to be met by a wiggling intruder approximately halfway; together they were the first manifestation of organism that nine months later, or a million years earlier, would be christened Douglas MacArthur Graham.

This made a problem for time, or Time, which is neither like a rubber band nor like a spring; nor even like a river nor a carrier wave—but which, like all of these things, can be deformed by certain stresses. For instance, two people going into the future and three coming back on the same time-casting beam.

In an earlier age, when time travel was more common, time-casters would have made sure that the baby, or at least its aborted embryo, would stay in the future when the mother returned to her present. Or they could arrange for the mother to stay in the future. But these subtleties had long been forgotten when Nine-hover relearned the dead art. So Sarah went back to her present with a hitch-hiker, an interloper, firmly imbedded in the lining of her womb. And its dim sense of life set up a kind of eddy in the flow of time, that Sarah had to share.

The mathematical explanation is subtle, and can't be comprehended by those of us who synapse with fewer than four degrees of freedom. But the end effect is clear: Sarah had to experience all of her own life backwards, all the way back to that embrace on the beach. Some highlights were:

In 1992, slowly dying of cancer, in a mental hospital.

In 1979, seeing Bob finally succeed in suicide on the American Plan, not quite finishing his 9,527th bottle of liquor.

In 1970, having her only son returned in a sealed casket from a country she'd never heard of.

In the 1960's, helplessly watching her son become more and more neurotic because of something that no one could name.

In 1953, Bob coming home with one foot, the other having been lost to frostbite; never having fired a shot in anger.

In 1952, the agonizing breech presentation.

Like her son, Sarah would remember no details of the backward voyage through her life. But the scars of it would haunt her forever.

◈

They were kissing on the beach.

Sarah dropped the blanket and made a little noise. She started crying and slapped Bob as hard as she could, then ran on alone, up to the cabin.

Bob watched her progress up the hill with mixed feelings. He took a healthy slug from the bourbon bottle, to give him an excuse to wipe his own eyes.

He could go sit on the beach and finish the bottle; let her get over it by herself. Or he could go comfort her.

He tossed the bottle away, the gesture immediately making him feel stupid, and followed her. Later that night she apologized, saying she didn't know what had gotten into her.

Slow Music

JAMES TIPTREE, JR.

As most of you probably know by now, multiple Hugo- and Nebula-winning author James Tiptree, Jr.—at one time a figure reclusive and mysterious enough to be regarded as the B. Traven of science fiction—was actually the late Dr. Alice Sheldon, a semiretired experimental psychologist who also wrote occasionally under the name of Raccoona Sheldon. Dr. Sheldon's tragic death in 1987 put an end to "both" authors' careers, but, before that, she had won two Nebula and two Hugo Awards as Tiptree, won another Nebula Award as Raccoona Sheldon, and established herself, under whatever name, as one of the best writers in science fiction.

Although "Tiptree" published two reasonably well-received novels—Up the Walls of the World and Brightness Falls from the Air—she was, like Damon Knight and Theodore Sturgeon (two writers she aesthetically resembled and by whom she was strongly influenced), more comfortable with the short story and more effective with it. She wrote some of the very best short stories of the seventies: "The Screwfly Solution," "The Girl Who Was Plugged In," "The Women Men Don't See," "Beam Us Home," "And I Awoke and Found Me Here on the Cold Hill's Side," "I'm Too Big but I Love to Play," and "His Smoke Rose Up Forever." Already it's clear that these are stories that will last. They—and a dozen others almost as good—show that Alice Sheldon was simply one of the best short-story writers to work in the genre in our times.

Here, in one of her few ventures into the far future, she shows us a melancholy vision of the end of the human race as we know it, as humanity is seduced into abandoning corporeal existence and merging into a metaphysical alien River that sweeps them away from the Earth forever . . . except for those few people who choose to remain behind. . . .

As James Tiptree, Jr., Alice Sheldon also published nine short-story collections: Ten Thousand Light Years from Home, Warm Worlds and Otherwise, Starsongs of an Old Primate, Out of the Everywhere, Tales of the Quintana Roo, Byte Beautiful, The Starry Rift, the posthumously published Crown of Stars, and the retrospective collection Her Smoke Rose Up Forever.

> Caoilte tossing his burning hair
> And Niamh calling "Away, come away;
> Empty your heart of its mortal dream.
> . . . We come between man and the deed of his hand,
> We come between him and the hope of his heart."
> —W. B. Yeats

Lights came on as Jakko walked down the lawn past the house; elegantly concealed spots and floods which made the night into a great intimate room. Overhead the big conifers formed a furry nave drooping toward the black lake below the bluff ahead. This had been a beloved home, he saw; every luxurious device was subdued to preserve the beauty of the forested shore. He walked on a carpet of violets and mosses, in his hand the map that had guided him here from the city.

It was the stillness before dawn. A long-winged night bird swirled in to catch a last moth in the dome of light. Before him shone a bright spearpoint. Jakko saw it was the phosphorescent tip of a mast against the stars. He went down velvety steps to find a small sailboat floating at the dock like a silver leaf reflected on a dark mirror.

In silence he stepped on board, touched the mast.

A gossamer sail spread its fan, the mooring parted soundlessly. The dawn breeze barely filled the sail, but the craft moved smoothly out, leaving a glassy line of wake. Jakko half-poised to jump; he knew nothing of such playtoys, he should go back and find another boat. As he did so, the shore lights went out, leaving him in darkness. He turned and saw Regulus rising ahead where the channel must be. Still, this was not the craft for him. He tugged at the tiller and sail, meaning to turn it back.

But the little boat ran smoothly on, and then he noticed the lights of a small computer glowing by the mast. He relaxed; this was no toy, the boat was fully programmed and he could guess what the course must be. He stood examining the sky, a statue-man gliding across reflected night.

The eastern horizon changed, veiled its stars as he neared it. He could see the channel now, a silvery cut straight ahead between dark banks. The boat ran over glittering shallows where something splashed hugely, and headed into the shining lane. As it did so, all silver changed to lead and the stars were gone. Day was coming. A great pearl-colored blush spread upward before him, developed bands of lavender and rays of coral-gold fire melting to green iridescence overhead. The boat was now gliding on a ribbon of fiery light between black silhouetted banks. Jakko looked back and saw dazzling cloud-cities heaped behind him in the west. The vast imminence of sunrise. He sighed aloud.

He understood that all this demonstration of glory was nothing but the effects of dust and vapor in the thin skin of air around a small planet, whereon he crawled wingless. No vastness brooded; the planet was merely turning with him into the rays of its mediocre primary. His family, everyone, knew that on the River he would encounter the galaxy itself in glory. Suns beyond count, magnificence to which this was nothing. And yet— and yet to him this was not nothing. It was intimately his, man-sized. He made an ambiguous sound in his throat. He resented the trivialization of this beauty, and he resented being moved by it. So he passed along, idly holding the sailrope like a man leashing the living wind, his face troubled and very young.

The little craft ran on unerringly, threading the winding sheen of the canal. As the sun rose, Jakko began to hear a faint drone ahead. The sea surf. He thought of the persons who must have made this voyage before him: the ship's family, savoring their final days of mortality. A happy voyage, a picnic. The thought reminded him that he was hungry; the last ground-car's synthesizer had been faulty.

He tied the rope and searched. The boat had replenished its water, but there was only one food-bar. Jakko lay down in the cushioned well and ate and drank comfortably, while the sky turned turquoise and then cobalt. Presently they emerged into an enormous lagoon and began to run south between low islands. Jakko trailed his hand and tasted brackish salt. When the boat turned east again and made for a seaward opening, he became doubly certain. The craft was programmed for the River, like almost everything else on the world he knew.

Sure enough, the tiny bark ran through an inlet and straight out into the chop beyond a long beach, extruded outriggers, and passed like a cork over the reef-foam onto the deep green swells beyond. Here it pitched once and steadied; Jakko guessed it had thrust down a keel. Then it turned south and began to run along outside the reef, steady as a knife-cut with the wind on its quarter. Going Riverward for sure. The nearest River-place was here called Vidalita or Beata, or sometimes Falaz, meaning Illusion. It was far south and inland. Jakko guessed they were making for a landing where a moveway met the sea. He had still time to think, to struggle with the trouble under his mind.

But as the sun turned the boat into a trim white-gold bird flying over green transparency, Jakko's eyes closed and he slept, protected by invisible deflecters from the bow-spray. Once he opened his eyes and saw a painted fish tearing along magically in the standing wave below his head. He smiled and slept again, dreaming of a great wave dying, a wave that was a many-headed beast. His face became sad and his lips moved soundlessly, as if repeating, "No . . . no . . ."

When he woke they were sailing quite close by a long bluff on his right. In the cliff ahead was a big white building or tower, only a little ruined. Suddenly he caught sight of a figure moving on the beach before it. A living human? He jumped up to look. He had not seen a strange human person in many years.

Yes—it was a live person, strangely colored gold and black. He waved wildly.

The person on the beach slowly raised an arm.

Alight with excitement, Jakko switched off the computer and grabbed the rudder and sail. The line of reef-surf seemed open here. He turned the boat shoreward, riding on a big swell. But the wave left him. He veered erratically, and the surf behind broached into the boat, overturning it and throwing him out. He knew how to swim; he surfaced and struck out strongly for the shore, spluttering brine. Presently he was wading out onto the white beach, a short, strongly-built, reddened young male person with pale hair and water-blue eyes.

The stranger was walking hesitantly toward him. Jakko saw it was a thin, dark-skinned girl wearing a curious netted hat. Her body was wrapped in orange silk and she carried heavy gloves in one hand. Three nervous moondogs followed her. He began turning water out of his shorts pockets as she came up.

"Your . . . boat," she said in the language of that time. Her voice was low and uncertain.

They both turned to look at the confused place by the reef where the sailboat floated half-submerged.

"I turned it off. The computer." His words came jerkily, too, they were both unused to speech.

"It will come ashore down there." She pointed, still studying him in a wary, preoccupied way. She was much smaller than he. "Why did you turn? Aren't you going to the River?"

"No." He coughed. "Well, yes, in a way. My father wants me to say good-bye. They left while I was traveling."

"You're not . . . ready?"

"No. I don't—" He broke off. "Are you staying alone here?"

"Yes. I'm not going either."

They stood awkwardly in the sea-wind. Jakko noticed that the three moondogs were lined up single file, tiptoeing upwind toward him with their eyes closed, sniffing. They were not, of course, from the moon, but they looked it, being white and oddly shaped.

"It's a treat for them," the girl said. "Something different." Her voice was stronger now. After a pause she added, "You can stay here for a while if you want. I'll show you but I have to finish my work first."

"Thank you," he remembered to say.

As they climbed steps cut in the bluff Jakko asked, "What are you working at?"

"Oh, everything. Right now it's bees."

"Bees!" he marveled. "They made what—honey? I thought they were all gone."

"I have a lot of old things." She kept glancing at him intently as they climbed. "Are you quite healthy?"

"Oh yes. Why not? I'm all alpha so far as I know. Everybody is."

"Was," she corrected. "Here are my bee skeps."

They came around a low wall and stopped by five small wicker huts. A buzzing insect whizzed by Jakko's face, coming from some feathery shrubs. He saw that the bloom-tipped foliage was alive with the golden humming things. Recalling that they could sting, he stepped back.

"You better go around the other way." She pointed. "They might hurt a stranger." She pulled her veil down, hiding her face. Just as he turned away, she added, "I though you might impregnate me."

He wheeled back, not really able to react because of the distracting bees. "But isn't that terribly complicated?"

"I don't think so. I have the pills." She pulled on her gloves.

"Yes, the pills. I know." He frowned. "But you'd have to stay, I mean one just can't—"

"I know that. I have to do my bees now. We can talk later."

"Of course." He started away and suddenly turned back.

"Look!" He didn't know her name. "You, look!"

"What?" She was a strange little figure, black and orange with huge hands and a big veil-muffled head. "What?"

"I felt it. Just then, desire. Can't you see?"

They both gazed at his wet shorts.

"I guess not," he said finally. "But I felt it, I swear. Sexual desire."

She pushed back her veil, frowning. "It will stay, won't it? Or come back? This isn't a very good place, I mean, the bees. And it's no use without the pills."

"That's so."

He went away then, walking carefully because of the tension around his pubic bone. Like a keel, snug and tight. His whole body felt reorganized. It had been years since he'd felt flashes like that, not since he was fifteen at least. Most people never did. It was variously thought to be because of the River, or from their parents' surviving the Poison Centuries, or because the general alpha strain was so forebrain dominant. It gave him an archaic, secret pride. Maybe he was a throwback.

He passed under cool archways, and found himself in a green, protected place behind the seaward wall. A garden, he saw, looking round surprised at clumps of large tied-up fruiting plants, peculiar trees with green balls at their tops, disorderly rows of rather unesthetic greenery. Tentatively he identified tomatoes, peppers, a feathery leaf which he thought had an edible root. A utilitarian planting. His uncle had once amused the family by doing something of the sort, but not on this scale. Jakko shook his head.

In the center of the garden stood a round stone coping with a primitive apparatus on top. He walked over and looked down. Water, a bucket on a rope. Then he saw that there was also an ordinary tap. He opened it and drank, looking at the odd implements leaning on the coping. Earth-tools. He did not really want to think about what the strange woman had said.

A shadow moved by his foot. The largest moondog had come quite close, inhaling dreamily. "Hello," he said to it. Some of these dogs could talk a little. This one opened its eyes wide but said nothing.

He stared about, wiping his mouth, feeling his clothes almost dry now in the hot sun. On three sides the garden was surrounded by arcades; above him the ruined side was a square cracked masonry tower with no roof. A large place, whatever it was. He walked into the shade of the nearest arcade, which turned out to be littered with a myriad disassembled or partly assembled objects: tools, containers, who knew what. Her "work"? The place felt strange, vibrant and busy. He realized he had entered only empty houses on his year-long journey. This one was alive, lived-in. Messy. It hummed like the bee skeps. He turned down a cool corridor, looking into rooms piled with more stuff. In one, three white animals he couldn't identify were asleep in a heap of cloth on a bed. They moved their ears at him like big pale shells but did not awaken.

He heard staccato noises and came out into another courtyard where plump birds walked with jerking heads. "Chickens!" he decided, delighted by the irrational variety of this place. He went from there into a large room with windows on the sea and heard a door close.

It was the woman, or girl, coming to him, holding her hat and gloves. Her hair was a dark curly cap, her head elegantly small; an effect he had always admired. He remembered something to say.

"I'm called Jakko. What's your name?"

"Jakko." She tasted the sound. "Hello, Jakko. I'm Peachthief." She smiled very briefly, entirely changing her face.

"Peachthief." On impulse he moved toward her, holding out his hands. She tucked her bundle under her arm and took both of his. They stood like that a moment, not quite looking at each other. Jakko felt excited. Not sexually, but more as if the air was electrically charged.

"Well." She took her hands away and began unwrapping a leafy wad. "I brought a honeycomb even if it isn't quite ready." She showed him a sticky looking frame with two dead bees on it. "Come on."

She walked rapidly out into another corridor and entered a shiny room he thought might be a laboratory.

"My food room," she told him. Again Jakko was amazed. There stood a synthesizer, to be sure, but beside it were shelves full of pots and bags and jars and containers of all descriptions. Unknown implements lay about and there was a fireplace which had been partly sealed up. Bunches of plant parts hung from racks overhead. He identified some brownish ovoids in a bowl as eggs. From the chickens?

Peachthief was cleaning the honeycomb with a manually operated knife. "I use the wax for my loom, and for candles. Light."

"What's wrong with the lights?"

"Nothing." She turned around, gesturing emphatically with the knife. "Don't you understand? All these machines, they'll go. They won't run forever. They'll break or wear out or run down. There *won't be* any, anymore. Then we'll have to use natural things."

"But that won't be for centuries!" he protested. "Decades, anyhow. They're all still going, they'll last for us."

"For you," she said scornfully. "Not for me. I intend to stay. With my children." She turned back on him and added in a friendlier voice, "Besides, the old things are esthetic. I'll show you, when it gets dark."

"But you haven't any children! Have you?" He was purely astonished.

"Not yet." Her back was still turned.

"I'm hungry," he said, and went to work the synthesizer. He made it give him a bar with a hard filler; for some reason he wanted to crunch it in his teeth.

She finished with the honey and turned around. "Have you ever had a natural meal?"

"Oh yes," he said, chewing. "One of my uncles tried that. It was very nice," he added politely.

She looked at him sharply and smiled again, on—off. They went out of the food room. The afternoon was fading into great gold and orange streamers above the courtyard, colored like Peachthief's garment.

"You can sleep here." She opened a slatted door. The room was small and bare, with a window on the sea.

"There isn't any bed," he objected.

She opened a chest and took out a big wad of string. "Hang this end on that hook over there."

When she hung up the other end he saw it was a large mesh hammock.

"That's what I sleep in. They're comfortable. Try it."

He climbed in awkwardly. The thing came up around him like a bag. She gave a short sweet laugh as brief as her smile.

"No, you lie on the diagonal. Like this." She tugged his legs, sending a peculiar shudder through him. "That straightens it, see?"

It would probably be all right, he decided, struggling out. Peachthief was pointing to a covered pail.

"That's for your wastes. It goes on the garden in the end."

He was appalled, but said nothing, letting her lead him out through a room with glass tanks in the walls to a big screened-in porch fronting the ocean. It was badly in need of cleaners. The sky was glorious with opalescent domes and spires, reflections of the sunset behind them, painting amazing colors on the sea.

"This is where I eat."

"What is this place?"

"It was a sea-station last, I think. Station Juliet. They monitored the fish and the ocean traffic, and rescued people and so on."

He was distracted by noticing long convergent dove-blue rays like mysterious paths into the horizon; cloud-shadows cast across the world. Beauty of the dust. Why must it move him so?

"—even a medical section," she was saying. "I really could have babies, I mean in case of trouble."

"You don't mean it." He felt only irritation now. "I don't feel any more desire," he told her.

She shrugged. "I don't, either. We'll talk about it later on."

"Have you always lived here?"

"Oh, no." She began taking pots and dishes out of an insulated case. The three moondogs had joined them silently; she set bowls before them. They lapped, stealing glances at Jakko. They were, he knew, very strong despite their stick-like appearance.

"Let's sit here." She plumped down on one end of the lounge and began biting forcefully into a crusty thing like a slab of drybar. He noticed she had magnificent teeth. Her dark skin set them off beautifully, as it enhanced her eyes. He had never met anyone so different in every way from himself and his family. He vacillated between interest and a vague alarm.

"Try some of the honey." She handed him a container and a spoon. It looked quite clean. He tasted it eagerly; honey was much spoken of in antique writings. At first he sensed nothing but a waxy sliding, but then an overpowering sweetness enveloped his tongue, quite unlike the sweets he was used to. It did not die away but seemed to run up his nose and almost into his ears, in a peculiar way. An *animal* food. He took some more, gingerly.

"I didn't offer you my bread. It needs some chemical, I don't know what. To make it lighter."

"Don't you have an access terminal?"

"Something's wrong with part of it," she said with her mouth full. "Maybe I don't work it right. We never had a big one like this, my tribe were travelers. They believed in sensory experiences." She nodded, licking her fingers. "They went to the River when I was fourteen."

"That's very young to be alone. My people waited till this year, my eighteenth birthday."

"I wasn't alone. I had two older cousins. But they wanted to take an aircar up north, to the part of the River called Rideout. I stayed here. I mean, we never stopped traveling, we never *lived* anywhere. I wanted to do like the plants, make roots."

"I could look at your program," he offered. "I've seen a lot of different models, I spent nearly a year in cities."

"What I need is a cow. Or a goat."

"Why?"

"For the milk. I need a pair, I guess."

Another animal thing; he winced a little. But it was pleasant, sitting here in the deep blue light beside her, hearing the surf plash quietly below.

"I saw quite a number of horses," he told her. "Don't they use milk?"

"I don't think horses are much good for milk." She sighed in an alert, busy way. He had the impression that her head was tremendously energetic, humming with plans and intentions. Suddenly she looked up and began making a high squeaky noise between her front teeth, "Sssswwt! Sssswwwt!"

Startled, he saw a white flying thing swooping above them, and then two more. They whirled so wildly he ducked.

"That's right," she said to them. "Get busy."

"What are they?"

"My bats. They eat mosquitoes and insects." She squeaked again and the biggest bat was suddenly clinging to her hand, licking honey. It had a small, fiercely complicated face.

Jakko relaxed again. This place and its strange inhabitant were giving him remarkable memories for the River, anyway. He noticed a faint glow moving where the dark sky joined the darker sea.

"What's that?"

"Oh, the seatrain. It goes to the River landing."

"Are there people on it?"

"Not anymore. Look, I'll show you." She jumped up and was opening a console in the corner, when a sweet computer voice spoke into the air.

"Seatrain Foxtrot Niner calling Station Juliet! Come in, Station Juliet!"

"It hasn't done that for years," Peachthief said. She tripped tumblers. "Seatrain, this is Station Juliet, I hear you. Do you have a problem?"

"Affirmative. Passenger is engaging in nonstandard activities. He-slash-she does not conform to parameters. Request instructions."

Peachthief thought a minute. Then she grinned. "Is your passenger moving on four legs?"

"Affirmative! Affirmative!" Seatrain Foxtrot sounded relieved.

"Supply it with bowls of meat-food and water on the floor and do not interfere with it. Juliet out."

She clicked off, and they watched the far web of lights go by on the horizon, carrying an animal.

"Probably a dog following the smell of people," Peachthief said. "I hope it gets off all right ... We're quite a wide genetic spread," she went on in a different voice. "I mean, you're so light, and body-type and all."

"I noticed that."

"It would give good heterosis. Vigor."

She was talking about being impregnated, about the fantasy-child. He felt angry.

"Look, you don't know what you're saying. Don't you realize you'd have to stay and raise it for years? You'd be ethically and morally bound. And the River places are shrinking fast, you must know that. Maybe you'd be too late."

"Yes," she said somberly. "Now it's sucked everybody out it's going. But I still mean to stay."

"But you'd hate it, even if there's still time. My mother hated it, toward the end. She felt she had begun to deteriorate energetically, that her life would be lessened. And me—what about me? I mean, I should stay too."

"You'd only have to stay a month. For my ovulation. The male parent isn't ethically bound."

"Yes, but I think that's wrong. My father stayed. He never said he minded it, but he must have."

"You only have to do a month," she said sullenly. "I thought you weren't going on the River right now."

"I'm not. I just don't want to feel bound, I want to travel. To see more of the world, first. After I say goodbye."

She made an angry sound. "You have no insight. You're going, all right. You just don't want to admit it. You're going just like Mungo and Ferrocil."

"Who are they?"

"People who came by. Males, like you. Mungo was last year, I guess. He had an aircar. He said he was going to stay, he talked and talked. But two days later he went right on again. To the River. Ferrocil was earlier, he was walking through. Until he stole my bicycle."

A sudden note of fury in her voice startled him; she seemed to have some peculiar primitive relation to her bicycle, to her *things*.

"Did you want them to impregnate you, too?" Jakko noticed an odd intensity in his own voice as well.

"Oh, I was thinking about it, with Mungo." Suddenly she turned on him, her eyes wide open in the dimness like white-ringed jewels. "Look!

Once and for all, I'm not going! I'm alive, I'm a human woman. I am going to stay on this earth and do human things. I'm going to make young ones to carry on the race, even if I have to die here. You can go on out, you—you pitiful shadows!"

Her voice rang in the dark room, jarring him down to his sleeping marrow. He sat silent as though some deep buried bell had tolled.

She was breathing hard. Then she moved, and to his surprise a small live flame sprang up between her cupped hands, making the room a cave.

"That's a candle. That's me. Now go ahead, make fun like Mungo did."

"I'm not making fun," he said, shocked. "It's just that I don't know what to think. Maybe you're right. I really . . . I really don't want to go, in one way," he said haltingly. "I love this earth too. But it's all so fast. Let me . . ."

His voice trailed off.

"Tell me about your family," she said, quietly now.

"Oh, they studied. They tried every access you can imagine. Ancient languages, history, lore. My aunt made poems in English . . . The layers of the earth, the names of body cells and tissues, jewels, everything. Especially stars. They made us memorize star maps. So we'll know where we are, you know, for a while. At least the earth-names. My father kept saying, when you go on the River you can't come back and look anything up. All you have is what you remember. Of course you could ask others, but there'll be so much more, so much new . . ."

He fell silent, wondering for the millionth time; is it possible that I shall go out forever between the stars, in the great streaming company of strange sentiences?

"How many children were in your tribe?" Peachthief was asking.

"Six. I was the youngest."

"The others all went on the River?"

"I don't know. When I came back from the cities the whole family had gone on, but maybe they'll wait a while too. My father left a letter asking me to come and say good-bye, and to bring him anything new I learned. They say you go slowly, you know. If I hurry there'll still be enough of his mind left there to tell him what I saw."

"What did you see? We were at a city once," Peachthief said dreamily. "But I was too young, I don't remember anything but people."

"The people are all gone now. Empty, every one. But everything works, the lights change, the moveways run. I didn't believe everybody was gone until I checked the central control offices. Oh, there were so many wonderful devices." He sighed. "The beauty, the complexity. Fantastic what people made." He sighed again, thinking of the wonderful technology, the creations abandoned, running down. "One strange thing. In the biggest city I saw, old Chio, almost every entertainment-screen had the same tape running."

"What was it?"

"A girl, a young girl with long hair. Almost to her feet, I've never seen such hair. She was laying it out on a sort of table, with her head down. But no sound, I think the audio was broken. Then she poured a liquid all over very slowly. And then she lit it, she set fire to herself. It flamed and exploded and burned her all up. I think it was real." He shuddered. "I could see inside her mouth, her tongue going all black and twisted. It was horrible. Running over and over, everywhere. Stuck."

She made a revolted sound. "So you want to tell that to your father, to his ghost, or whatever?"

"Yes. It's all new data, it could be important."

"Oh yes," she said scornfully. Then she grinned at him. "What about me? Am I new data too? A woman who isn't going to the River? A woman who is going to stay here and make babies? Maybe I'm the last."

"That's very important," he said slowly, feeling a deep confusion in his gut. "But I can't believe it, I mean, you—"

"*I mean it.*" She spoke with infinite conviction. "I'm going to live here and have babies by you or some other man if you won't stay, and teach them to live on the earth naturally."

Suddenly he believed her. A totally new emotion was rising up in him, carrying with it sunrises and nameless bonds with earth that hurt in a painless way, as thought a rusted door was opening within him. Maybe this was what he had been groping for.

"I think—I think maybe I'll help you. Maybe I'll stay with you, for a while at least. Our—our children."

"You'll stay a month?" she asked wonderingly. "Really?"

"No, I mean I could stay longer. To make more and see them and help raise them, like my father did. After I come back from saying good-bye I'll really stay."

Her face changed. She bent to him and took his face between her slim dark hands.

"Jakko, listen. If you go to the River you'll never come back. No one ever does. I'll never see you again. We have to do it now, before you go."

"But a month is too long!" he protested. "My father's mind won't be there, I'm already terribly late."

She glared into his eyes a minute and then released him, stepping back with her brief sweet laugh. "Yes, and it's already late for bed. Come on."

She led him back to the room, carrying the candle, and he marveled anew at the clutter of strange activities she had assembled. "What's that?"

"My weaving-room." Yawning, she reached in and held up a small, rough-looking cloth. "I made this."

It was ugly, he thought; ugly and pathetic. Why make such useless things? But he was too tired to argue.

She left him to cleanse himself perfunctorily by the well in the moonlit courtyard, after showing him another waste-place right in the garden. Other peoples' wastes smell bad, he noticed sleepily. Maybe that was the cause of all the ancient wars.

In his room he tumbled into his hammock and fell asleep instantly. His dreams that night were chaotic; crowds, storms, jostling and echoing through strange dimensions. His last image was of a great whirlwind that bore in its forehead a jewel that was a sleeping woman, curled like an embryo.

He waked in the pink light of dawn to find her brown face bending over him, smiling impishly. He had the impression she had been watching him, and jumped quickly out of the hammock.

"Lazy," she said. "I've found the sailboat. Hurry up and eat."

She handed him a wooden plate of bright natural fruits and led him out into the sunrise garden.

When they got down to the beach she led him south, and there was the little craft sliding to and fro, overturned in the shallows amid its tangle of sail. The keel was still protruding. They furled the sail in clumsily and towed it out to deeper water to right it.

"I want this for the children," Peachthief kept repeating excitedly. "They can get fish, too. Oh, how they'll love it!"

"Stand your weight in the keel and grab the siderail," Jakko told her, doing the same. He noticed that her silks had come loose from her breasts, which were high and wide-pointed, quite unlike those of his tribe. The sight distracted him, his thighs felt unwieldy, and he missed his handhold as the craft righted itself and ducked him. When he came up he saw Peachthief scrambling aboard like a cat, clinging tight to the mast.

"The sail! Pull the sail up!" he shouted, and got another faceful of water. But she had heard him, the sail was trembling open like a great wing, silhouetting her shining slim dark body. For the first time Jakko noticed the boat's name, on the stern: Gojack. He smiled. An omen.

Gojack was starting to move smoothly away, toward the reef.

"The rudder!" he bellowed. "Turn the rudder and come back."

Peachthief moved to the tiller and pulled at it; he could see her strain. But *Gojack* continued to move away from him into the wind, faster and faster toward the surf. He remembered she had been handling the mast where the computer was.

"Stop the computer! Turn it off, turn it off!"

She couldn't possibly hear him. Jakko saw her in frantic activity, wrenching at the tiller, grabbing ropes, trying physically to push down the sail. Then she seemed to notice the computer, but evidently could not decipher it. Meanwhile *Gojack* fled steadily on and out, resuming its interrupted journey to the River. Jakko realized with horror that she would soon be in dangerous water; the surf was thundering on coralheads.

"Jump! Come back, jump off!" He was swimming after her as fast as he could, his progress agonizingly slow. He glimpsed her still wrestling with the boat, screaming something he couldn't hear.

"JUMP!"

And finally she did, but only to try jerking *Gojack* around by its mooring lines. The boat faltered and jibbed, but then went strongly on, towing the threshing girl.

"Let go! Let go!" A wave broke over his head.

When he could see again he found she had at last let go and was swimming aimlessly, watching *Gojack* crest the surf and wing away. At last she turned back toward shore, and Jakko swam to intercept her. He was gripped by an unknown emotion so strong it discoordinated him. As his feet touched bottom he realized it was rage.

She waded to him, her face contorted by weeping. "The children's boat," she wailed. "I lost the children's boat—"

"You're crazy," he shouted. "There aren't any children."

"I lost it—" She flung herself on his chest, crying. He thumped her back, her sides, repeating furiously, "Crazy! You're insane!"

She wailed louder, squirming against him, small and naked and frail. Suddenly he found himself flinging her down onto the wet sand, falling on top of her with his swollen sex crushed between their bellies. For a moment all was confusion, and then the shock of it sobered him. He raised to look under himself and Peachthief stared too, round-eyed.

"Do you w-want to, now?"

In that instant he wanted nothing more than to thrust himself into her, but a sandy wavelet splashed over them and he was suddenly aware of chafing wet cloth and Peachthief gagging brine. The magic waned. He got awkwardly to his knees.

"I thought you were going to be drowned," he told her, angry again.

"I wanted it so, for—for them . . ." She was still crying softly, looking up desolately at him. He understood she wasn't really meaning just the sailboat. A feeling of inexorable involvement spread through him. This mad little being had created some kind of energy-vortex around her, into which he was being sucked along with animals, vegetables, chickens, crowds of unknown things: only *Gojack* had escaped her.

"I'll find it," she was muttering, wringing out her silks, staring beyond the reef at the tiny dwindling gleam. He looked down at her, so fanatic and so vulnerable, and his inner landscape tilted frighteningly, revealing some ancient-new dimension.

"I'll stay with you," he said hoarsely. He cleared his throat, hearing his voice shake. "I mean I'll really stay, I won't go the the River at all. We'll make the, our babies now."

She stared up at him open-mouthed. "But your father! You promised!"

"My father stayed," he said painfully. "It's—it's right, I think."

She came close and grabbed his arms in her small hands.

"Oh, Jakko! But no, listen—*I'll go with you*. We can start a baby as we go, I'm sure of that. Then you can talk to your father and keep your promise and I'll be there to make sure you come back!"

"But you'd be, you'd be pregnant!" he cried in alarm. "You'd be in danger of taking an embryo on the River!"

She laughed proudly. "Can't you get it through your head that I will *not* go on the River? I'll just watch you and pull you out. I'll see you get back here. For a while, anyway," she added soberly. Then she brightened. "Hey, we'll see all kinds of things. Maybe I can find a cow or some goats on the way! Yes, yes! It's a perfect idea."

She faced him, glowing. Tentatively she brought her lips up to his, and they kissed inexpertly, tasting salt. He felt no desire, but only some deep resonance, like a confirmation in the earth. The three moondogs were watching mournfully.

"Now let's eat!" she began towing him toward the cliff-steps. "We can start the pills right now. "Oh, I have so much to do! But I'll fix everything, we'll leave tomorrow."

She was like a whirlwind. In the foodroom she pounced on a small gold-colored pillbox and opened it to show a mound of glowing green and red capsules.

"The red ones with the male symbol are for you."

She took a green one, and they swallowed solemnly, sharing a water-mug. He noticed that the seal on the box had been broken, and thought of that stranger, Mungo, she had mentioned. How far had her plans gone with him? An unpleasant emotion he had never felt before rose in Jakko's stomach. He sensed that he was heading into more dubious realms of experience than he had quite contemplated, and took his foodbar and walked away through the arcades to cool down.

When he came upon her again she seemed to be incredibly busy, fold-ing and filling and wrapping things, closing windows and tying doors open. Her intense relations with things again . . . He felt obscurely irri-tated and was pleased to have had a superior idea.

"We need a map," he told her. "Mine was in the boat."

"Oh, great idea. Look in the old control room, it's down those stairs. It's kind of scary." She began putting oil in her loom.

He went down a white ramp that became a tunnel stairway, and came finally through a heavily armored portal to a circular room deep inside the rock, dimly illumined by portholes sunk in long shafts. From here he could hear the hum of the station energy source. As his eyes adjusted he made out a bank of sensor screens and one big console standing alone. It seemed to have been smashed open; some kind of sealant had been poured over the works.

He had seen a place like this before; he understood at once that from here had been controlled terrible ancient weapons that flew. Probably they still stood waiting in their hidden holes behind the station. But the master control was long dead. As he approached the console he saw that someone had scratched in the cooling sealant. He could make out only the words, "—WAR NO MORE." Undoubtedly this was a shrine of the very old days.

He found a light switch that filled the place with cool glare and began exploring side alleys. Antique gear, suits, cupboards full of masks and crumbling packets he couldn't identify. Among them was something use-ful—two cloth containers to carry stuff on one's back, only a little mil-dewed. But where were the maps?

Finally he found one on the control-room wall, right where he had come in. Someone had updated it with scrawled notations. With a tremor he realized how very old this must be; it dated from before the Rivers had touched earth. He could hardly grasp it.

Studying it he saw that there was indeed a big landing-dock not far south, and from there a moveway ran inland about a hundred kilometers to an airpark. If Peachthief could walk twenty-five kilometers they could make the landing by evening, and if the cars were still running the rest would be quick. All the moveways he'd seen had live cars on them. From the airpark a dotted line ran southwest across mountains to a big red circle with a cross in it, marked "VIDA!" That would be the River. They would just have to hope something on the airpark would fly, otherwise it would be a long climb.

His compass was still on his belt. He memorized the directions and went back upstairs. The courtyard was already saffron under great sunset flags.

Peachthief was squatting by the well, apparently having a conference with her animals. Jakko noticed some more white creatures he hadn't seen before, who seemed to live in an open hutch. They had long pinkish ears and mobile noses. Rabbits, or hares perhaps?

Two of the strange white animals he had seen sleeping were now under a bench, chirruping irritably at Peachthief.

"My raccoons," she told Jakko. "They're mad because I woke them up too soon." She said something in a high voice Jakko didn't understand, and the biggest raccoon shook his head up and down in a supercilious way.

"The chickens will be all right," Peachthief said. "Lotor knows how to feed them, to get the eggs. And they can all work the water-lever." The other raccoon nodded crossly, too.

"The rabbits are a terrible problem." Peachthief frowned. "You just haven't much sense, Eusebia," she said fondly, stroking the doe. "I'll have to fix something."

The big raccoon was warbling at her, Jakko thought he caught the word "dog-g-g."

"He wants to know who will settle their disputes with the dogs," Peachthief reported. At this one of the moondogs came forward and said thickly, "We go-o." It was the first word Jakko had heard him speak.

"Oh, good!" Peachthief cried. "Well, that's that!" She bounced up and began pouring something from a bucket on a line of plants. The white raccoons ran off silently with a humping gait.

"I'm so glad you're coming, Tycho," she told the dog. "Especially if I have to come back alone with a baby inside. But they say you're very vigorous, at first anyway."

"You aren't coming back alone," Jakko told her. She smiled a brilliant, noncommittal flash. He noticed she was dressed differently; her body didn't show so much, and she kept her gaze away from him in an almost timid way. But she became very excited when he showed her the back-packs.

"Oh, good. Now we won't have to roll the blankets around our waists. It gets cool at night, you know."

"Does it ever rain?"

"Not this time of year. What we mainly need is lighters and food and water. And a good knife each. Did you find the map?"

He showed it. "Can you walk, I mean really hike if we have to? Do you have shoes?"

"Oh yes. I walk a lot. Especially since Ferrocil stole my bike."

The venom in her tone amused him. The ferocity with which she provisioned her small habitat!

"Men build monuments, women build nests," he quoted from somewhere.

"I don't know what kind of monument Ferrocil built with my bicycle," she said tartly.

"You're a savage," he said, feeling a peculiar ache that came out as a chuckle.

"The race can use some savages. We better eat now and go to sleep so we can start early."

At supper in the sunset-filled porch they scarcely talked. Dreamily Jakko watched the white bats embroidering flight in the air. When he looked down at Peachthief he caught her gazing at him before she quickly lowered her eyes. It came to him that they might eat hundreds, thousands of meals here; maybe all his life. And there could be a child, children, running about. He had never seen small humans younger than himself. It was all too much to take in, unreal. He went back to watching the bats.

That night she accompanied him to his hammock and stood by, shy but stubborn, while he got settled. Then he suddenly felt her hands sliding on his body, toward his groin. At first he thought it was something clinical, but then he realized she meant sex. His blood began to pound.

"May I come in beside you? The hammock is quite strong."

"Yes," he said thickly, reaching for her arm.

But as her weight came in by him she said in a practical voice, "I have to start knotting a small hammock, first thing. Child-size."

It broke his mood.

"Look. I'm sorry, but I've changed my mind. You go on back to yours, we should get sleep now."

"All right." The weight lifted away.

With a peculiar mix of sadness and satisfaction he heard her light footsteps leaving him alone. That night he dreamed strange sensory crescendoes, a tumescent earth and air; a woman who lay with her smiling lips in pale green water, awaiting him, while thin black birds of sunrise stalked to the edge of the sea.

Next morning they ate by candles, and set out as the eastern sky was just turning rose-gray. The ancient white coral roadway was good walking. Peachthief swung right along beside him, her backpack riding smooth.

The moondogs pattered soberly behind. Jakko found himself absorbed in gazing at the brightening landscape. Jungle-covered hills rose away on their right, the sea lay below on their left, sheened and glittering with the coming sunrise. When a diamond chip of sun broke out of the horizon he almost shouted aloud for the brilliance of it; the palm trees beyond the road lit up like golden torches, the edges of every frond and stone were startling clear and jewellike. For a moment he wondered if he could have taken some hallucinogen.

They paced on steadily in a dream of growing light and heat. The day-wind came up, and torn white clouds began to blow over them, bringing momentary coolness. Their walking fell into the rhythm Jakko loved, broken only occasionally by crumbled places in the road. At such spots they would often be surprised to find the moondogs sitting waiting for them, having quietly left the road and circled ahead through the scrub on business of their own. Peachthief kept up sturdily, only once stopping to look back at the far white spark of Station Juliet, almost melted in the shimmering horizon.

"This is as far as I've gone south," she told him.

He drank some water and made her drink too, and they went on. The road began to wind, rising and falling gently. When he next glanced back the station was gone. The extraordinary luminous clarity of the world was still delighting him.

When noon came he judged they were well over halfway to the landing. They sat down on some rubble under the palms to eat and drink, and Peachthief fed the moondogs. Then she took out the fertility pillbox. They each took theirs in silence, oddly solemn. Then she grinned.

"I'll give you something for dessert."

She unhitched a crooked knife from her belt and went searching around in the rocks, to come back with a big yellow-brown palm nut. Jakko watched her attack it with rather alarming vigor; she husked it and then used a rock to drive the point home.

"Here." She handed it to him. "Drink out of that hole." He felt a sloshing inside; when he lifted it and drank it tasted hairy and gritty and nothing in particular. But sharp, too, like the day. Peachthief was methodically striking the thing around and around its middle. Suddenly it fell apart, revealing vividly white meat. She pried out a piece.

"Eat this. It's full of protein."

The nutmeat was sweet and sharply organic.

"This is a coconut!" he suddenly remembered.

"Yes. I won't starve, coming back."

He refused to argue, but only got up to go on. Peachthief holstered her knife and followed, munching on a coconut piece. They went on so in silence a long time, letting the rhythm carry them. Once when a lizard waddled across the road Peachthief said to the moondog at her heels, "Tycho, you'll have to learn to catch and eat those one day soon." The moondogs all looked dubiously at the lizard but said nothing. Jakko felt shocked and pushed the thought away.

They were now walking with the sun westering slowly to their right. A flight of big orange birds with blue beaks flapped squawking out of a roadside tree, where they were apparently building some structure. Cloud-shadows fled across the world, making blue and bronze reflections in the sea. Jakko still felt his sensory impressions almost painfully keen; a sunray made the surf-line into a chain of diamonds, and the translucent green of the near shallows below them seemed to enchant his eyes. Every vista ached with light, as if to utter some silent meaning.

He was walking in a trance, only aware that the road had been sound and level for some time, when Peachthief uttered a sharp cry.

"My bicycle! There's my bicycle!" She began to run; Jakko saw shiny metal sticking out of a narrow gulch in the roadway. When he came up to her she was pulling a machine out from beside the roadwall.

"The front wheel—Oh, he bent it! He must have been going too fast and wrecked it here. That Ferrocil! But I'll fix it, I'm sure I can fix it at the Station. I'll push it back with me on the way home."

While she was mourning her machine Jakko looked around and over the low coping of the roadwall. Sheer cliff down there, with the sun just touching a rocky beach below. Something was stuck among the rocks—a tangle of whitish sticks, cloth, a round thing. Feeling his stomach knot, Jakko stared down at it, unwillingly discovering that the round thing had eye-holes, a U-shaped open mouth, blowing strands of hair. He had never seen a dead body before, nobody had, but he had seen pictures of human bones. Shakenly he realized who this had to be: Ferrocil. He must have been thrown over the coping when he hit that crack. Now he was dead, long dead. He would never go on the River. All that had been in that head was perished, gone forever.

Scarcely knowing what he was doing, Jakko grabbed Peachthief by the shoulders, saying roughly, "Come on! Come on!" When she resisted, confusedly he took her by the arm and began forcibly pulling her away from where she might look down. Her flesh felt burning hot and vibrant, the whole world was blasting colors and sounds and smells at him. Images of dead Ferrocil mingled with the piercing scent of some flowers on the roadway. Suddenly an idea struck him; he stopped.

"Listen. Are you sure those pills aren't hallucinaids? I've only had two and everything feels crazy."

"Three," Peachthief said abstractedly. She took his hand and pressed it on her back. "Do that again, run your hand down my back."

Bewildered, he obeyed. As his hand passed her silk shirt onto her thin shorts he felt her body move under it in a way that made him jerk away.

"Feel? Did you feel it? The lordotic reflex," she said proudly. "Female sexuality. It's starting."

"What do you mean, three?"

"You had three pills. I gave you one that first night, in the honey."

"*What?* But—but—" He struggled to voice the enormity of her violation, pure fury welling up in him. Choking, he lifted his hand and struck her buttocks the hardest blow he could, sending her staggering. It was the first time he had ever struck a person. A moondog growled, but he didn't care.

"Don't you ever—never—play a trick like—" He yanked at her shoulders, meaning to slap her face. His hand clutched a breast instead, he saw her hair blowing like dead Ferrocil's. A frightening sense of mortality combined with pride surged through him, lighting a fire in his loins. The deadness of Ferrocil suddenly seemed violently exciting. He, Jakko, was alive! Ignoring all sanity he flung himself on Peachthief, bearing her down on the road among the flowers. As he struggled to tear open their shorts he was dimly aware that she was helping him. His engorged penis was all reality; he fought past obstructions and then was suddenly, crookedly *in* her, fierce pleasure building. It exploded through him and then had burst out into her vitals, leaving him spent.

Blinking, fighting for clarity, he raised himself up and off her body. She lay wide-legged and disheveled, sobbing or gasping in a strange way, but smiling too. Revulsion sent a sick taste in his throat.

"There's your baby," he said roughly. He found his canteen and drank. The three moondogs had retreated and were sitting in a row, staring solemnly.

"May I have some, please?" Her voice was very low; she sat up, began fixing her clothes. He passed her the water and they got up.

"It's sundown," she said. "Should we camp here?"

"No!" Savagely he started on, not caring that she had to run to catch up. Was this the way the ancients lived? Whirled by violent passions, indecent, uncaring? His doing sex so close to the poor dead person seemed unbelievable. And the world was still assaulting all his senses; when she stumbled against him he could feel again the thrilling pull of her flesh, and shuddered. They walked in silence awhile; he sensed that she was more tired than he, but he wanted only to get as far as possible away.

"I'm not taking any more of those pills," he broke silence at last.

"But you have to! It takes a month to be sure."

"I don't care."

"But, ohhh—"

He said nothing more. They were walking across a twilit head-land now. Suddenly the road turned, and they came out above a great bay.

The waters below were crowded with boats of all kinds, bobbing emp-tily where they had been abandoned. Some still had lights that made faint jewels in the opalescent air. Somewhere among them must be *Gojack*. The last light from the west gleamed on the rails of the moveway running down to the landing.

"Look, there's the seatrain." Peachthief pointed. "I hope the dog or whatever got ashore . . . I can find a sailboat down there, there's lots."

Jakko shrugged. Then he noticed movement among the shadows of the landing-station and forgot his anger long enough to say, "See there! Is that a live man?"

They peered hard. Presently the figure crossed a light place, and they could see it was a person going slowly among the stalled waycars. He would stop with one awhile and then waver on.

"There's something wrong with him," Peachthief said.

Presently the stranger's shadow merged with a car, and they saw it begin to move. It went slowly at first, and then accelerated out to the center lanes, slid up the gleaming rails and passed beyond them to dis-appear into the western hills.

"The way's working!" Jakko exclaimed. "We'll camp up here and go over to the way-station in the morning, it's closer."

He was feeling so pleased with the moveway that he talked easily with Peachthief over the foodbar dinner, telling her about the cities and asking her what places her tribe had seen. But when she wanted to put their blankets down together he said No, and took his away to a ledge farther up. The three moondogs lay down by her with their noses on their paws, facing him.

His mood turned to self-disgust again; remorse mingled with queasy surges of half-enjoyable animality. He put his arm over his head to shut out the brilliant moonlight and longed to forget everything, wishing the sky held only cold quiet stars. When he finally slept he didn't dream at all, but woke with ominous tollings in his inner ear. *The Horse is hungry*, deep voices chanted. *The Woman is bad!*

He roused Peachthief before sunrise. They ate and set off overland to the hill station; it was rough going until they stumbled onto an old limerock path. The moondogs ranged wide around them, appearing pleased. When they came out at the station shunt they found it crowded with cars.

The power-pack of the first one was dead. So was the next, and the next. Jakko understood what the stranger at the landing had been doing; looking for a live car. The dead cars here stretched away out of sight up the siding; a miserable sight.

"We should go back to the landing," Peachthief said. "He found a good one there."

Jakko privately agreed, but irrationality smouldered in him. He squinted into the hazy distance.

"I'm going up to the switch end."

"But it's so far, we'll have to come all the way back—"

He only strode off; she followed. It was a long way, round a curve and over a rise, dead cars beside them all the way. They were almost at the main tracks when Jakko saw what he had been hoping for; a slight jolting motion in the line. New cars were still coming in ahead, butting the dead ones.

"Oh fine!"

They went on down to the newest-arrived car and all climbed in, the moondogs taking up position on the opposite seat. When Jakko began to work the controls that would take them out to the main line, the car bleated an automatic alarm. A voder voice threatened to report him to Central. Despite its protests, Jakko swerved the car across the switches, where it fell silent and began to accelerate smoothly onto the outbound express lane.

"You really do know how to work these things," Peachthief said admiringly.

"You should learn."

"Why? They'll all be dead soon. I know how to bicycle."

He clamped his lips, thinking of Ferrocil's white bones. They fled on silently into the hills, passing a few more station jams. Jakko's perceptions still seemed too sharp, the sensory world too meaning-filled.

Presently they felt hungry, and found that the car's automatics were all working well. They had a protein drink and a pleasantly fruity bar, and Peachthief found bars for the dogs. The track was rising into mountains now; the car whistled smoothly through tunnels and came out in passes, offering wonderful views. Now and then they had glimpses of a great plain far ahead. The familiar knot of sadness gathered inside Jakko, stronger than usual. To think that all this wonderful system would run down and die in a jumble of rust . . . He had a fantasy of himself somehow maintaining it; but the memory of Peachthief's pathetic woven cloth mocked at him. Everything was a mistake, a terrible mistake. He wanted only to leave, to escape to rationality and peace. If she had drugged him he wasn't responsible for what he'd promised. He wasn't bound. Yet the sadness redoubled, wouldn't let him go.

When she got out the pill-box and offered it he shook his head violently. "No!"

"But you *promised*—"

"No. I hate what it does."

She stared at him in silence, swallowing hers defiantly. "Maybe there'll be some other men by the River," she said after awhile. "We saw one."

He shrugged and pretended to fall asleep.

Just as he was really drowsing the car's warning alarm trilled and they braked smoothly to a halt.

"Oh, look ahead—the way's gone! What is it?"

"A rockslide. An avalanche from the mountains, I think."

They got out among other empty cars that were waiting their prescribed pause before returning. Beyond the last one the way ended in an endless tumble of rocks and shale. Jakko made out a faint footpath leading on.

"Well, we walk. Let's get the packs, and some food and water."

While they were back in the car working the synthesizer, Peachthief looked out the window and frowned. After Jakko finished she punched a different code and some brownish lumps rolled into her hand.

"What's that?"

"You'll see." She winked at him.

As they started on the trail a small herd of horses appeared, coming toward them. The two humans politely scrambled up out of their way. The lead horse was a large yellow male. When he came to Peachthief he stopped and thrust his big head up at her.

"Zhu-gar, zhu-gar," he said sloppily. At this all the other horses crowded up and began saying "zhu-ga, zu-cah," in varying degrees of clarity.

"This *I* know," said Peachthief to Jakko. She turned to the yellow stallion. "Take us on your backs around these rocks. Then we'll give you sugar."

"Zhu-gar," insisted the horse, looking mean.

"Yes, sugar. *After* you take us around the rocks to the rails."

The horse rolled his eyes unpleasantly, but he turned back down. There was some commotion, and two mares were pushed forward.

"Riding horseback is done by means of a saddle and bridle," protested Jakko.

"Also this way. Come on." Peachthief vaulted nimbly onto the back of the smaller mare.

Jakko reluctantly struggled onto the fat round back of the other mare. To his horror, as he got himself astride she put up her head and screamed shrilly.

"You'll get sugar too," Peachthief told her. The animal subsided, and they started off along the rocky trail, single file. Jakko had to admit it was much faster than afoot, but he kept sliding backward.

"Hang onto her mane, that hairy place there," Peachthief called back to him, laughing. "I know how to run a few things too, see?"

When the path widened the yellow stallion trotted up alongside Peachthief.

"I thinking," he said importantly.

"Yes, what?"

"I push you down and eat zhugar now."

"All horses think that," Peachthief told him. "No good. It doesn't work."

The yellow horse dropped back, and Jakko heard him making horse-talk with an old gray-roan animal at the rear. Then he shouldered by to Peachthief again and said, "Why no good I push you down?"

"Two reasons," said Peachthief. "First, if you knock me down you'll never get any more sugar. All the humans will know you're bad and they won't ride on you any more. So no more sugar, never again."

"No more hoomans," the big yellow horse said scornfully. "Hoomans finish."

"You're wrong there too. There'll be a lot more humans. I am making them, see?" She patted her stomach.

The trail narrowed again and the yellow horse dropped back. When he could come alongside he sidled by Jakko's mare.

"I think I push you down now."

Peachthief turned around.

"You didn't hear my other reason," she called to him.

The horse grunted evilly.

"The other reason is that my three friends there will bite your stomach open if you try." She pointed up to where the three moondogs had appeared on a rock as if by magic, grinning toothily.

Jakko's mare screamed again even louder, and the gray roan in back made a haw-haw sound. The yellow horse lifted his tail and trotted forward to the head of the line, extruding manure as he passed Peachthief.

They went on around the great rockslide without further talk. Jakko was becoming increasingly uncomfortable; he would gladly have got off and gone slower on his own two legs. Now and then they broke into a jog trot, which was so painful he longed to yell at Peachthief to make them stop. But he kept silent. As they rounded some huge boulders he was rewarded by a distant view of the unmistakable towers of an airpark to their left on the plain below.

At long last the rockslide ended quite near a station. They stopped among a line of stalled cars. Jakko slid off gratefully, remembering to say "Thank you" to the mare. Walking proved to be uncomfortable too.

"See if there's a good car before I get off!" Peachthief yelled.

The second one he came to was live. He shouted at her.

Next moment he saw trouble among the horses. The big yellow beast charged in, neighing and kicking. Peachthief came darting out of the melee with the moondogs, and fell into the car beside him, laughing.

"I gave our mares all the sugar," she chuckled. Then she sobered. "I think mares *are* good for milk. I told them to come to the station with me when I come back. If that big bully will let them."

"How will they get in a car?" he asked stupidly.

"Why, I'll be walking, I can't run these things."

"But I'll be with you." He didn't feel convinced.

"What for, if you don't want to make babies? You won't be here."

"Well then, why are you coming with me?"

"I'm looking for a cow," she said scornfully. "Or a goat. Or a man."

They said no more until the car turned into the airpark station. Jakko counted over twenty apparently live ships floating at their towers. Many more hung sagging, and some towers had toppled. The field moveways were obviously dead.

"I think we have to find hats," he told Peachthief.

"Why?"

"So the service alarms won't go off when we walk around. Most places are like that."

"Oh."

In the office by the gates they found a pile of crew hats laid out, a thoughtful action by the last of the airpark people. A big hand-lettered sign said, ALL SHIPS ON STAND-BY, MANUAL OVERRIDE. READ DIRECTIONS. Under it was a stack of dusty leaflets. They took one, put on their hats, and began to walk toward a pylon base with several ships floating at its tower. They had to duck under and around the web of dead moveways, and when they reached the station base there seemed to be no way in from the ground.

"We'll have to climb onto that moveway."

They found a narrow ladder and went up, helping the moondogs. The moveway portal was open, and they were soon in the normal passenger lounge. It was still lighted.

"Now if the lift only works."

Just as they were making for the lift shaft they were startled by a voice ringing out.

"Ho! Ho, Roland!"

"That's no voder," Peachthief whispered. "There's a live human here."

They turned back and saw that a strange person was lying half on and half off one of the lounges. As they came close their eyes opened wide: he looked frightful. His thin dirty white hair hung around a horribly creased, caved-in face, and what they could see of his neck and arms was all mottled and decayed-looking. His jerkin and pants were frayed and stained and sagged in where flesh should be. Jakko thought of the cloth shreds around dead Ferrocil and shuddered.

The stranger was staring haggardly at them. In a faint voice he said, "When the chevalier Roland died he predicted that his body would be found a spear's throw ahead of all others and facing the enemy . . . If you happen to be real, could you perhaps give me some water?"

"Of course." Jakko unhooked his canteen and tried to hand it over, but the man's hands shook and fumbled so that Jakko had to hold it to his mouth, noticing a foul odor. The stranger sucked thirstily, spilling some. Behind him the moondogs inched closer, sniffing gingerly.

"What's *wrong* with him?" Peachthief whispered as Jakko stood back.

Jakko had been remembering his lessons. "He's just very, very old, I think."

"That's right." The stranger's voice was stronger. He stared at them with curious avidity. "I waited too long. Fibrillation." He put one feeble hand to his chest. "Fibrillating . . . rather a beautiful word, don't you think? My medicine ran out or I lost it . . . A small hot animal desynchronizing in my ribs."

"We'll help you get to the River right away!" Peachthief told him.

"Too late, my lords, too late. Besides, I can't walk and you can't possibly carry me."

"You can sit up, can't you?" Jakko asked. "There have to be some rollchairs around here, they had them for injured people." He went off to search the lounge office and found one almost at once.

When he brought it back the stranger was staring up at Peachthief, mumbling to himself in an archaic tongue of which Jakko only understood: ". . . *The breast of a grave girl makes a hill against sunrise.*" He tried to heave himself up to the chair but fell back gasping. They had to lift and drag him in, Peachthief wrinkling her nose.

"Now if the lift only works."

It did. They were soon on the high departure deck, and the fourth portal-berth held a waiting ship. It was a small local ferry. They went through into the windowed main cabin, wheeling the old man, who had collapsed upon himself and was breathing very badly. The moondogs trooped from window to window, looking down. Jakko seated himself in the pilot chair.

"Read me out the instructions," he told Peachthief.

"One, place ship on internal guidance," she read. "Whatever that means. Oh, look, here's a diagram."

"Good."

It proved simple. They went together down the list, sealing the port, disengaging umbilicals, checking vane function, reading off the standby pressures in the gasbags above them, setting the reactor to warm up the drive-motor and provide hot air for operational buoyancy.

While they were waiting, Peachthief asked the old man if he would like to be moved onto a window couch. He nodded urgently. When they got him to it he whispered, "See out!" They propped him up with chair pillows.

The ready-light was flashing. Jakko moved the controls, and the ship glided smoothly out and up. The computer was showing him wind speed, attitude, climb, and someone had marked all the verniers with the words *Course-set—RIVER*. Jakko lined everything up.

"Now it says, put it on automatic," Peachthief read. He did so.

The takeoff had excited the old man. He was straining to look down, muttering incomprehensibly. Jakko caught, *"The cool green hills of Earth . . .* Crap!" Suddenly he sang out loudly, *"There's a hell of a good universe next door—let's go!"* and fell back exhausted.

Peachthief stood over him worriedly. "I wish I could at least clean him up, but he's so weak."

The old man's eyes opened.

"Nothing shall be whole and sound that has not been rent; for love hath built his mansion in the place of excrement." He began to sing crackedly, "Take me to the River, the bee-yew-tiful River, and wash all my sins a-away! . . . You think I'm crazy, girl, don't you?" he went on conversationally. "Never heard of William Yeats. Very high bit-rate, Yeats."

"I think I understand a little," Jakko told him. "One of my aunts did English literature."

"Did literature, eh?" The stranger wheezed, snorted. "And you two—going on the River to spend eternity together as energy matrices or something equally impressive and sexless . . . *Forever wilt thou love and she be fair."* He grunted. "Always mistrusted Keats. No balls. He'd be right at home."

"We're not going on the River," Peachthief said. "At least, I'm not. I'm going to stay and make children."

The old man's ruined mouth fell open, he gazed up at her wildly.

"No!" he breathed. "Is it true? Have I stumbled on the lover and mother of man, the last?"

Peachthief nodded solemnly.

"What is your name, Oh, Queen?"

"Peachthief."

"My god. Somebody still knows of Blake." He smiled tremulously, and his eyelids suddenly slid downward; he was asleep.

"He's breathing better. Let's explore."

The small ship held little but cargo space at the rear. When they came to the food-synthesizer cubby Jakko saw Peachthief pocket something.

"What's that?"

"A little spoon. It'll be just right for a child." She didn't look at him.

Back in the main cabin the sunset was flooding the earth below with level roseate light. They were crossing huge, oddly pockmarked meadows, the airship whispering along in silence, except when a jet whistled briefly now and then for a course correction.

"Look—cows! Those must be cows," Peachthief exclaimed. "See the shadows."

Jakko made out small tan specks that were animals, with grotesque horned shadows stretching away.

"I'll have to find them when I come back. What *is* this place?"

"A big deathyard, I think. Where they put dead bodies. I never saw one this size. In some cities they had buildings just for dead people. Won't all that poison the cows?"

"Oh no, it makes good grass, I believe. The dogs will help me find them. Won't you, Tycho?" she asked the biggest moondog, who was looking down beside them.

On the eastern side of the cabin the full moon was rising into view. The old man's eyes opened, looking at it.

"More water, if you please," he croaked.

Peachthief gave him some, and then got him to swallow broth from the synthesizer. He seemed stronger, smiling at her with his mouthful of rotted teeth.

"Tell me, girl. If you're going to stay and make children, why are you going to the River?"

"He's going because he promised to talk to his father and I'm going along to see he comes back. And make the baby. Only now he won't take any more pills, I have to try to find another man."

"Ah yes, the pills. We used to call them Wake-ups.... They were necessary, after the population-chemicals got around. Maybe they still are, for women. But I think it's mostly in the head. Why won't you take any more, boy? What's wrong with the old Adam?"

Peachthief started to answer but Jakko cut her off. "I can speak for myself. They upset me. They made me do bad, uncontrolled things, and feel, agh—" He broke off with a grimace.

"You seem curiously feisty, for one who values his calm above the continuance of the race."

"It's the pills, I tell you. They're—they're dehumanizing."

"Dee-humanizing," the old man mocked. "And what do you know of humanity, young one? ... That's what I went to find, that's why I stayed so long among the old, old things from before the River came. I wanted to bring the knowledge of what humanity really was ... I wanted to bring it all. It's simple, boy. *They died.*" He drew a rasping breath. "Every one of them died. They lived knowing that nothing but loss and suffering and extinction lay ahead. And they cared, terribly.... Oh, they made myths, but not many really believed them. *Death* was behind everything, waiting everywhere. Aging and death. No escape ... Some of them went crazy, they fought and killed and enslaved each other by the millions, as if they could gain more life. Some of them gave up their precious lives for each other. They loved—and had to watch the ones they loved age and die. And in their pain and despair they built, they struggled, some of them sang. But above all, boy, they copulated! Fornicated, fucked, made love!"

He fell back, coughing, glaring at Jakko. Then, seeing that they scarcely understood his antique words, he went on more clearly. "Did sex, do you understand? Made children. It was their only weapon, you see. To send something of themselves into the future beyond their own deaths. Death was the engine of their lives, death fueled their sexuality. Death drove them at each other's throats and into each other's arms. Dying, they triumphed ... *That* was human life. And now that mighty engine is long stilled, and you call this polite parade of immortal lemmings *humanity*? . . . Even the faintest warmth of that immemorial holocaust makes you flinch away?"

He collapsed, gasping horribly; spittle ran down his chin. One slit of eye still raked them.

Jakko stood silent, shaken by resonances from the old man's words, remembering dead Ferrocil, feeling some deep conduit of reality reaching for him out of the long-gone past. Peachthief's hand fell on his shoulder, sending a shudder through him. Slowly his own hand seemed to lift by itself and cover hers, holding her to him. They watched the old man so for a long moment. His face slowly composed, he spoke in a soft dry tone.

"I don't trust that River, you know . . . You think you're going to remain yourselves, don't you? Communicate with each other and with the essences of beings from other stars . . . The latest news from Betelgeuse." He chuckled raspingly.

"That's the last thing people say when they're going," Jakko replied. "Everyone learns that. You float out, able to talk with real other beings. Free to move."

"Yes. What could better match our dreams?" He chuckled again. "I wonder . . . could that be the lure, just the input end of some cosmic sausage machine? . . ."

"What's that?" asked Peachthief.

"An old machine that ground different meats together until they came out as one substance . . . Maybe you'll find yourselves gradually mixed and minced and blended into some, some energetic plasma . . . and then maybe squirted out again to impose the terrible gift of consciousness on some innocent race of crocodiles, or poached eggs . . . and so it begins all over again. Another random engine of the universe, giving and taking obliviously . . ." He coughed, no longer looking at them, and began to murmur in the archaic tongue, "*Ah, when the ghost begins to quicken, confusion of the death-bed over, is it sent . . . Out naked on the roads as the books say, and stricken with the injustice of the stars for punishment?* The injustice of the stars . . ." He fell silent, and then whispered faintly, "Yet I too long to go."

"You will," Peachthief told him strongly.

"How . . . much longer?"

"We'll be there by dawn," Jakko said. "We'll carry you. I swear."

"A great gift," he said weakly. "But I fear . . . I shall give you a better." He mumbled on, a word Jakko didn't know; it sounded like "afrodisiack."

He seemed to lapse into sleep then. Peachthief went and got a damp, fragrant cloth from the clean-up and wiped his face gently. He opened one eye and grinned up at her.

"Madame Tasselass," he rasped. "Madame Tasselass, are you really going to save us?"

She smiled down, nodding her head determinedly, Yes. He closed his eyes, looking more peaceful.

The ship was now fleeing through full moonlight, the cabin was so lit with azure and silver that they didn't think to turn on lights. Now and again the luminous mists of a low cloud veiled the windows and vanished again. Just as Jakko was about to propose eating, the old man took several gulping breaths and opened his eyes. His intestines made a bubbling sound.

Peachthief looked at him sharply and picked up one of his wrists. Then she frowned and bent over him, opening his filthy jerkin. She laid her ear to his chest, staring up at Jakko.

"He's not breathing, there's no heartbeat!" She groped inside his jerkin as if she could locate life, two tears rolling down her cheeks.

"He's *dead*—ohhh!" She groped deeper, then suddenly straightened up and gingerly clutched the cloth at the old man's crotch.

"What?"

"He's a woman!" She gave a sob and wheeled around to clutch Jakko, putting her forehead in his neck. "We never even knew her name . . ."

Jakko held her, looking at the dead man-woman, thinking, she never knew mine either. At that moment the airship jolted, and gave a noise like a cable grinding or slipping before it flew smoothly on again.

Jakko had never in his life distrusted machinery, but now a sudden terror contracted his guts. This thing could fall! They could be made dead like Ferrocil, like this stranger, like the myriads in the deathyards below. Echoes of the old voice ranting about death boomed in his head, he had a sudden vision of Peachthief grown old and dying like that. After the Rivers went, dying alone. His eyes filled, and a deep turmoil erupted under his mind. He hugged Peachthief tighter. Suddenly he knew in a dreamlike way exactly what was about to happen. Only this time there was no frenzy; his body felt like warm living rock.

He stroked Peachthief to quiet her sobs, and led her over to the moon-lit couch on the far side of the cabin. She was still sniffling, hugging him hard. He ran his hands firmly down her back, caressing her buttocks, feeling her body respond.

"Give me that pill," he said to her. "Now."

Looking at him huge-eyed in the blue moonlight, she pulled out the little box. He took out his and swallowed it deliberately, willing her to understand.

"Take off your clothes." He began stripping off his jerkin, proud of the hot, steady power in his sex. When she stripped and he saw again the glistening black bush at the base of her slim belly, and the silver-edge curve of her body, urgency took him, but still in a magical calm.

"Lie down."

"Wait a minute—" She was out of his hands like a fish, running across the cabin to where the dead body lay in darkness. Jakko saw she was trying to close the dead eyes that still gleamed from the shadows. He could wait; he had never imagined his body could feel like this. She laid the cloth over the stranger's face and came back to him, half-shyly holding out her arms, sinking down spread-legged on the shining couch before him. The moonlight was so brilliant he could see the pink color of her sexual parts. He came onto her gently, controlledly, breathing in an exciting animal odor from her flesh. This time his penis entered easily, an intense feeling of all-rightness.

But a moment later the fires of terror, pity, and defiance deep within him burst up into a flame of passionate brilliance in his coupled groin. The small body under his seemed no longer vulnerable but appetitive. He clutched, mouthed, drove deep into her, exulting. Death didn't die alone, he thought obscurely, as the ancient patterns lurking in his vitals awoke. Death flew with them and flowed by beneath, but he asserted life upon the body of the woman, caught up in a great crescendo of unknown sensations, until a culminant spasm of almost painful pleasure rolled through him into her, relieving him from head to feet.

When he could talk, he thought to ask her, "Did you—" he didn't know the word. "Did it sort of explode you, like me?"

"Well, no." Her lips were by his ear. "Female sexuality is a little different. Maybe I'll show you, later ... But I think it was good, for the baby."

He felt only a tiny irritation at her words, and let himself drift into sleep with his face in her warm-smelling hair. Dimly the understanding came to him that the great beast of his dreams, the race itself maybe, had roused and used them. So be it.

A cold thing pushing into his ear awakened him, and a hoarse voice said "Foo-ood!" It was the moondogs.

"Oh my, I forgot to feed them!" Peachthief struggled nimbly out from under him.

Jakko found he was ravenous too. The cabin was dark now, as the moon rose overhead. Peachthief located the switches, and made a soft light on their side of the cabin. They ate and drank heartily, looking down at the moonlit world. The deathyards were gone from below them now, they were flying over dark wooded foothills. When they lay down to sleep again they could feel the cabin slightly angle upward as the ship rose higher.

He was roused in the night by her body moving against him. She seemed to be rubbing her crotch.

"Give me your hand," she whispered in a panting voice. She began to make his hands do things to her, sometimes touching him too, her body arching and writhing, sleek with sweat. He found himself abruptly tumescent again, excited and pleased in a confused way. "Now, now!" she commanded, and he entered her, finding her interior violently alive. She seemed to be half fighting him, half devouring him. Pleasure built all through him, this time without the terror. He pressed in against her shuddering convulsions. "Yes—Oh, yes!" she gasped, and a series of paroxysms swept through her, carrying him with her to explosive peace.

He held himself on and in her until her body and breathing calmed to relaxation, and they slipped naturally apart. It came to him that this sex activity seemed to have more possibilities, as a thing to do, than he had realized. His family had imparted to him nothing of all this. Perhaps they didn't know it. Or perhaps it was too alien to their calm philosophy.

"How do you know about all this?" he asked Peachthief sleepily.

"One of my aunts did literature, too." She chuckled in the darkness. "Different literature, I guess."

They slept almost as movelessly as the body flying with them on the other couch a world away.

A series of noisy bumpings wakened them. The windows were filled with pink mist flying by. The airship seemed to be sliding into a berth. Jakko looked down and saw shrubs and grass close below; it was a ground-berth on a hillside.

The computer panel lit up: RESET PROGRAM FOR BASE.

"No," said Jakko. "We'll need it going back." Peachthief looked at him in a new, companionable way; he sensed that she believed him now. He turned all the drive controls to standby while she worked the food synthesizer. Presently he heard the hiss of the deflating lift-bags, and went to where she was standing by the dead stranger.

"We'll take her, her body, out before we go back," Peachthief said. "Maybe the River will touch her somehow."

Jakko doubted it, but ate and drank his breakfast protein in silence.

When they went to use the wash-and-waste cubby he found he didn't want to clean all the residues of their contact off himself. Peachthief seemed to feel the same way; she washed only her face and hands. He looked at her slender, silk-clad belly. Was a child, his child, starting there? Desire flicked him again, but he remembered he had work to do. His promise to his father; get on with it. Sooner done, sooner back here.

"I love you," he said experimentally, and found the strange words had a startling trueness.

She smiled brilliantly at him, not just off-on. "I love you, too, I think."

The floor-portal light was on. They pulled it up and uncovered a step-way leading to the ground. The moondogs poured down. They followed, coming out into a blowing world of rosy mists. Clouds were streaming around them; the air was all in motion up the hillside toward the crest some distance ahead of the ship berth. The ground here was uneven and covered with short soft grass, as though animals had cropped it.

"All winds blow to the River," Jakko quoted.

They set off up the hill, followed by the moondogs, who stalked uneasily with pricked ears. Probably they didn't like not being able to smell what was ahead, Jakko thought. Peachthief was holding his hand very firmly as they went, as if determined to keep him out of any danger.

As they walked up onto the flat crest of the hilltop the mists suddenly cleared, and they found themselves looking down into a great, shallow, glittering sunlit valley. They both halted involuntarily to stare at the fantastic sight.

Before them lay a huge midden heap, kilometers of things upon things upon things, almost filling the valley floor. Objects of every description lay heaped there; Jakko could make out clothing, books, toys, jewelry, a myriad artifacts and implements abandoned. These must be, he realized, the last things people had taken with them when they went on the River. In an outer ring not too far below them were tents, ground- and air-cars, even wagons. Everything shone clean and gleaming as if the influence of the River had kept off decay.

He noticed that the nearest ring of encampments intersected other, apparently older and larger rings. There seemed to be no center to the pile.

"The River has moved, or shrunk," he said.

"Both, I think," Peachthief pointed to the right. "Look, there's an old war-place."

A big grass-covered mound dominated the hill crest beside them. Jakko saw it had metal-rimmed slits in its sides. He remembered history: how there were still rulers of people when the River's tendrils first touched earth. Some of the rulers had tried to keep their subjects from the going-out places, posting guards around them and even putting killing devices in the ground. But the guards had gone themselves out on the River, or the River had swelled and taken them. And the people had driven beasts across the mined ground and surged after them into the stream of immortal life. In the end the rulers had gone too, or died out. Looking more carefully, Jakko could see that the green hill slopes were torn and pocked, as though ancient explosions had made craters everywhere.

Suddenly he remembered that he had to find his father in all this vast confusion.

"Where's the River now? My father's mind should reach there still, if I'm not too late."

"See that glittery slick look in the air down there? I'm sure that's a danger place."

Down to their right, fairly close to the rim, was a strangely bright place. As he stared it became clearer: a great column of slightly golden or shining air. He scanned about, but saw nothing else like it all across the valley.

"If that's the only focus left, it's going away fast."

She nodded and then swallowed, her small face suddenly grim. She meant to live on here and die without the River, Jakko could see that. But he would be with her; he resolved it with all his heart. He squeezed her hand hard.

"If you have to talk to your father, we better walk around up here on the rim where it's safe," Peachthief said.

"No-oo," spoke up a moondog from behind them. The two humans turned and saw the three sitting in a row on the crest, staring slit-eyed at the valley.

"All right," Peachthief said. "You wait here. We'll be back soon."

She gripped Jakko's hand even tighter, and they started walking past the old war mound, past the remains of ancient vehicles, past an antique pylon that leaned crazily. There were faint little trails in the short grass. Another war mound loomed ahead; when they passed around it they found themselves suddenly among a small herd of white animals with long necks and no horns. The animals went on grazing quietly as the humans walked by. Jakko thought they might be mutated deer.

"Oh, look!" Peachthief let go his hand. "That's milk—see, her baby is sucking!"

Jakko saw that one of the animals had a knobby bag between its hind legs. A small one half-knelt down beside it, with its head up nuzzling the bag. A mother and her young.

Peachthief was walking cautiously toward them, making gentle greeting sounds. The mother animal looked at her calmly, evidently tame. The baby went on sucking, rolling its eyes. Peachthief reached them, petted the mother, and then bent down under to feel the bag. The animal side-stepped a pace, but stayed still. When Peachthief straightened up she was licking her hand.

"That's good milk! And they're just the right size, we can take them on the airship! On the way-cars, even." She was beaming, glowing. Jakko felt an odd warm constriction in his chest. The intensity with which she furnished her little world, her future nest! *Their* nest . . .

"Come with us, come on," Peachthief was urging. She had her belt around the creature's neck to lead it. It came equably, the young one following in awkward galloping lunges.

"That baby is a male. Oh, this is *perfect*," Peachthief exclaimed. "Here, hold her a minute while I look at that one."

She handed Jakko the end of the belt and ran off. The beast eyed him levelly. Suddenly it drew its upper lip back and shot spittle at his face. He ducked, yelling for Peachthief to come back.

"I have to find my father first!"

"All right," she said, returning. "Oh, look at that!"

Downslope from them was an apparition—one of the white animals, but partly transparent, ghostly thin. It drifted vaguely, putting its head down now and then, but did not eat.

"It must have got partly caught in the River, it's half gone. Oh, Jakko, you can see how dangerous it is! I'm afraid, I'm afraid it'll catch you."

"It won't. I'll be very careful."

"I'm so afraid." But she let him lead her on, towing the animal along-side. As they passed the ghost-creature Peachthief called to it, "You can't live like that. You better go on out. Shoo, shoo!"

It turned and moved slowly out across the piles of litter toward the shining place in the air.

They were coming closer to it now, stepping over more and more abandoned things. Peachthief looked sharply at everything; once she stooped to pick up a beautiful fleecy white square and stuff it in her pack. The hill crest was merging with a long grassy slope, comparatively free of debris, that ran out toward the airy glittering column. They turned down it.

The River-focus became more and more awesome as they approached. They could trace it towering up and now, twisting gently as it passed beyond the sky. A tendril of the immaterial stream of sidereal sentience that had embraced earth, a pathway to immortal life. The air inside looked no longer golden, but pale silver-gilt, like a great shaft of moonlight coming down through the morning sun. Objects at its base appeared very clear but shimmering, as if seen through cool crystal water.

Off to one side were tents. Jakko suddenly recognized one, and quickened his steps. Peachthief pulled back on his arm.

"Jakko, be careful!"

They slowed to a stop a hundred yards from the tenuous fringes of the River's effect. It was very still. Jakko peered intently. In the verges of the shimmer a staff was standing upright. From it hung a scarf of green and yellow silk.

"Look—that's my father's sign!"

"Oh Jakko, you *can't* go in there."

At the familiar colored sign all the memories of his life with his family had come flooding back on Jakko. The gentle rationality, the solemn sense of preparation for going out from earth forever. Two different realities strove briefly within him. They had loved him, he realized that now. Especially his father . . . But not as he loved Peachthief, his awakened spirit shouted silently. I am of earth! Let the stars take care of their own. His resolve took deeper hold and won.

Gently he released himself from her grip.

"You wait here. Don't worry, it takes a long while for the change, you know that. Hours, days. I'll only be a minute, I'll come right back."

"Ohhh, it's crazy."

But she let him go and stood holding to the milk-animal while he went down the ridge and picked his way out across the midden-heap toward the staff. As he neared it he could feel the air change around him, becoming alive and yet more still.

"Father! Paul! It's Jakko, your son. Can you still hear me?"

Nothing answered him. He took a step or two past the staff, repeating his call.

A resonant susurrus came in his head, as if unearthly reaches had opened to him. From infinity he heard without hearing his father's quiet voice.

You came.

A sense of calm welcome.

"The cities are all empty, Father. All the people have gone, everywhere."

Come.

"No!" He swallowed, fending off memory, fending off the lure of strangeness. "I think it's sad. It's wrong. I've found a woman. We're going to stay and make children."

The River is leaving, Jakko my son.

It was as if a star had called his name, but he said stubbornly, "I don't care. I'm staying with her. Good-bye, father. Good-bye."

Grave regret touched him, and from beyond a host of silent voices murmured down the sky: *Come! Come away.*

"No!" he shouted, or tried to shout, but he could not still the rapt voices. And suddenly, gazing up, he felt the serenity of the River, the overwhelming opening of the door to life everlasting among the stars. All his mortal fears, all his most secret dread of the waiting maw of death, slid out of him and fell away, leaving him almost unbearably light and calmly joyful. He knew that he was being touched, that he could float out upon that immortal stream forever. But even as the longing took him, his human mind remembered that this was the start of the first stage, for which the River was called Beata. He thought of the ghost-animal that had lingered too long. He must leave now, and quickly. With enormous effort he took one step backward, but could not turn.

"Jakko! Jakko! Come back!"

Someone was calling, screaming his name. He did turn then and saw her on the little ridge. Nearby, yet so far. The ordinary sun of earth was brilliant on her and the two white beasts.

"Jakko! Jakko!" Her arms were outstretched, she was running toward him.

It was as if the whole beautiful earth was crying to him, calling to him to come back and take up the burden of life and death. He did not want it. But she must not come here, he knew that without remembering why. He began uncertainly to stumble toward her, seeing her now as his beloved woman, again as an unknown creature uttering strange cries.

"Lady Death," he muttered, not realizing he had ceased to move. She ran faster, tripped, almost fell in the heaps of stuff. The wrongness of her coming here roused him again; he took a few more steps, feeling his head clear a little.

"*Jakko!*" She reached him, clutched him, dragging him bodily forward from the verge.

At her touch the reality of his human life came back to him, his heart pounded human blood, all stars fled away. He started to run clumsily, half-carrying her with him up to the safety of the ridge. Finally they sank down gasping beside the animals, holding and kissing each other, their eyes wet.

"I thought you were lost, I thought I'd lost you," Peachthief sobbed.

"You saved me."

"H-here," she said. "We b-better have some food." She rummaged in her pack, nodding firmly as if the simple human act could defend against unearthly powers. Jakko discovered that he was quite hungry.

They ate and drank peacefully in the soft, flower-studded grass, while the white animals grazed around them. Peachthief studied the huge strewn valley floor, frowning as she munched.

"So many good useful things here. I'll come back some day, when the River's gone, and look around."

"I thought you only wanted natural things," he teased her.

"Some of these things will last. Look." She picked up a small implement. "It's an awl, for punching and sewing leather. You could make children's sandals."

Many of the people who came here must have lived quite simply, Jakko thought. It was true that there could be useful tools. And metal. Books, too. Directions for making things. He lay back dreamily, seeing a vision of himself in the far future, an accomplished artisan, teaching his children skills. It seemed deeply good.

"Oh, my milk-beast!" Peachthief broke in on his reverie. "Oh, no, you musn't!" She jumped up.

Jakko sat up and saw that the white mother-animal had strayed quite far down the grassy ridge. Peachthief trotted down after her, calling, "Come here! Stop!"

Perversely, the animal moved away, snatching mouthfuls of grass. Peachthief ran faster. The animal threw up its head and paced down off the ridge, among the litter piles.

"No! Oh, my milk! Come back here, come."

She went down after it, trying to move quietly and call more calmly.

Jakko had got up, alarmed.

"Come back! Don't go down there!"

"The babies' milk," she wailed at him, and made a dash at the beast. But she missed, and it drifted away just out of reach before her.

To his horror Jakko saw that the glittering column of the River had changed shape slightly, eddying out a veil of shimmering light close ahead of the beast.

"Turn back! Let it go!" he shouted, and began to run with all his might. "Peachthief—Come back!"

But she would not turn, and his pounding legs could not catch up. The white beast was in the shimmer now; he saw it bound up onto a great sun-and-moonlit heap of stuff. Peachthief's dark form went flying after it, uncaring, and the creature leaped away again. He saw her follow, and bitter fear grabbed at his heart. The very strength of her human life is betraying her to death, he thought; I have to get her physically, I will pull her out. He forced his legs faster, faster yet, not noticing that the air had changed around him too.

She disappeared momentarily in a veil of glittering air, and then reappeared, still following the beast. Thankfully he saw her pause and stoop to pick something up. She was only walking now, he could catch her. But his own body was moving sluggishly, it took all his will to keep his legs thrusting him ahead.

"Peachthief! Love, come back!"

His voice seemed muffled in the silvery air. Dismayed, he realized that he too had slowed to a walk, and she was veiled again from his sight.

When he struggled through the radiance he saw her, moving very slowly after the wandering white beast. Her face was turned up, unearthly light was on her beauty. He knew she was feeling the rapture, the call of immortal life was on her. On him, too; he found he was barely stumbling forward, a terrible serenity flooding his heart. They must be passing into the very focus of the River, where it ran strongest.

"Love—" Mortal grief fought the invading transcendence. Ahead of him the girl faded slowly into the glimmering veils, still following her last earthly desire. He saw that humanity, all that he had loved of the glorious earth, was disappearing forever from reality. Why had it awakened, only to be lost? Spectral voices were near him, but he did not want specters.

An agonizing lament for human life welled up in him, a last pang that he would carry with him through eternity. But its urgency fell away. Life incorporeal, immortal, was on him now; it had him as it had her. His flesh, his body was beginning to attenuate, to dematerialize out into the great current of sentience that flowed on its mysterious purposes among the stars.

Still the sense of his earthly self moved slowly after hers into the closing mists of infinity, carrying upon the River a configuration that had been a man striving forever after a loved dark girl, who followed a ghostly white milch deer.

The Map

GENE WOLFE

Gene Wolfe made his first sale in 1965. By 1970, he would be becoming a regular in Damon Knight's Orbit *anthologies with stories such as "Trip, Trap," "The Encounter," and "Paul's Treehouse" and had published his first novel,* Operation Ares *(in retrospect, his weakest book). Little that he had done to date attracted any attention, and there was little to indicate that a new giant of the form was about to loom above the literary horizon, someone who would be instrumental in establishing the new Cutting Edge of science fiction in the years ahead . . . yet that was exactly what was about to happen.*

As the decade progressed, Wolfe's work seemed to undergo a quantum jump in sophistication and intensity, and he went on to produce much of the really superior short fiction of the seventies—pieces such as the extraordinary "The Fifth Head of Cerberus," "The Hero as Werewolf," "Seven American Nights," "Alien Stones," "The Eyeflash Miracles," "Tracking Song," and "The Island of Doctor Death and Other Stories," among many others, as well as one of the decade's best novels (the brilliant 1975 novel Peace, *which, published almost anonymously as a mainstream hardback in a plain tan dustcover, sank without arousing a single ripple). In spite of this lush outpouring of talent, Wolfe remained severely underappreciated throughout most of the decade (although he did take a Nebula Award for his story "The Death of Doctor Island"), and as late as 1978 or 1979 book editors were telling me that Wolfe had no real audience and no future as a mass-market author . . . something that would later be proven to be demonstrably untrue.*

Wolfe would finally establish his reputation at the beginning of the eighties with a series of novels set in the very far future, his landmark The Book of the New Sun *novel series (consisting of* The Shadow of the Torturer, The Claw of the Conciliator, The Sword of the Lictor, The Citadel of the Autarch, *and a follow-up volume,* The Urth of the New Sun), *individual volumes of which have won the Nebula Award, the World Fantasy Award, and the John W. Campbell Memorial Award. One of the true masterworks of science fiction,* The Book of the New Sun *is clearly one of the genre's most vivid, complex, substantial, sophisticated, and compelling visions of the far future and may well be the most influential such vision since Jack Vance's* The Dying Earth *(to which it itself owes an acknowledged debt).*

Here, in a story unrelated to the direct story line of the series, Wolfe takes us to that same evocative milieu, to the far, far future . . . to a time when the sun has grown old and red and dim, the moon has grown green with forests, and old Urth groans under the almost insupportable weight of her own unnumbered years . . . takes us for a journey down the fabled River Gyoll, through the unimaginably vast and ancient ruins of the dying city Nessus, for a tale of temptation, greed, and mystery. (And if you enjoy it, read The Book of the New Sun *itself, for this tale is a mere appetizer for the feast of reading that awaits you there!)*

Wolfe has also returned to the far future for a popular new series set on an immense generational starship, the Long sun *sequence, which includes* Nightside the Long Sun, The Lake of the Long Sun, Calde of the Long Sun, *and* Exodus from the Long Sun. *His other books include* The Fifth Head of Cerberus, The Devil in a Forest, Soldier in the Mist, Free Live Free, Soldier of Arête, Castleview, Pandora by Holly Hollander, *and* There Are Doors. *His short fiction has been collected in* The Island of Doctor Death and Other Stories and Other Stories, Gene Wolfe's Book of Days, The Wolfe Archipelago, Endangered Species, *and the recent World Fantasy Award–winning collection* Storeys from the Old Hotel. *His most recent novel is* On Blue's Waters, *the start of a new series.*

On the night before, he had forgotten all his plans and fought, half blinded by his blood after Laetus broke the ewer over his head. Perhaps that was for the best.

And yet if they had not taken his knife while he slept, he might have killed them both.

"Master Gurloes will be angry." That was what they used to say to terrify one another into doing well. Severian would have been angry too, to be sure, and Severian had beaten him more than once. He spat out clotted blood. Beaten him worse than Laetus and Syntyche had last night. Severian had been captain of apprentices in the year before his own.

Now Severian was the Autarch, Severian was the law, and murderers died under the law's hand.

Someone was pounding at the hatch. He spat again, this time into the slop jar, and shouted in the direction of the vent. It let in enough light for him to see the impression Syntyche had left in her bunk as she lay face to the bulkhead, feigning sleep. He smoothed it with his hands.

For a moment he groped for his clothes and his knife, but the knife was gone. He chuckled and rocked back on his own narrow bunk, pushing both legs into his trousers together.

More pounding; the boat rocked beneath him as the stranger searched for another way into the cabin. He spat a third time, and from habit reached up to draw the bolt that was back already. "Hatch sticks! Come on down, you catamite, I'm not coming up."

The stranger lifted it and clambered down the steep steps.

" 'Ware deck beams."

He stooped as he turned about, and he was tall enough that he had to. "You're Captain Eata?"

"Sit on the other bunk. Nobody's using it any more. What do you want?"

"But you are Eata?"

"We'll talk about that later, maybe. After you tell me what you want."

"A guide."

Eata was feeling the cut on his head and did not answer.

"I was told that you are an intelligent man."

"Not by a friend."

"I need a man with a boat to take me down Gyoll. To tell me what I need to know concerning the ruins. They said you knew it as well as any man alive."

"An asimi," Eata said. "One asimi for each day. And you'll have to help me handle her—my deckhand and I had a little argument last night."

"Shall we say six orichalks? It should only take a day, and I—"

Eata was not listening. He had seen the broken lock on his sea chest, and he was laughing. "The key's in my pocket!" He gripped the younger, taller man by the knee. "My pants were on the floor!" In his mirth, he nearly choked on the words.

In the flat lands that Gyoll itself had made, Gyoll had little current; but the wind was in the east, and Eata's boat heeled a bit under the pressure of her wide gaffsail. The old sun, well above the tallest towers now, painted the sail's black image on the oily water.

"What do you do, Captain?" the stranger asked. "How do you live?"

"By doing whatever pays. Cargo to the delta and fish to the city, mostly."

"It's a nice boat. Did you build it?"

"No," Eata said. "Bought it. Not fast like you're used to." His head still hurt, and he leaned on the tiller with one hand pressed to his temple.

"Yes, I've sailed a bit on a lake we have up north."

"Wasn't asking," Eata told him.

"I don't think I ever gave you my name. It's Simulatio."

"And a good one too, I've no doubt."

The stranger turned away for a moment, tinkering with the jibsheet winch to keep Eata from seeing the blood rising in his cheeks. "When will we reach the deserted parts of the city?"

"About nones, if this wind holds."

"I didn't know it would take so long."

"You should have hired me farther down." Eata chuckled. "And that'll be just the beginning of the dead parts. You might want to go farther yet."

The stranger turned back to look at him. "It's very large, isn't it?"

"Bigger than you can imagine. This part—where people live—is just a sort of border on it."

"Do you know a place where three broad streets come together?"

"Half a dozen, maybe more."

"The southernmost, I would think."

"I can take you to the farthest south I know," Eata said. "I'm not saying that's the farthest south there is."

"We'll start there then."

"Be night by the time we get there," Eata told him. "The next day will be another asimi."

The stranger nodded. "We're not even to the ruined part yet?"

Eata gestured. "See those clothes? Washing on a line. People here have enough to eat, so they can have two or three shirts, maybe. Farther south you won't see that—a person with only one shirt or one shift doesn't wash it much, but you'll see cooksmoke. Farther still, and you won't even see that. That's the dead city, and people there don't light any fires because of what the smoke might bring down on them. Omophagists is what my old teacher called them. It means those that have their meat raw."

The stranger stared across the water at the lines and their rags. The wind ruffled his hair, and the tattered shirts and skirts waved at him like crowds of poor, shy children who feared he would not wave back. At last he said, "Even if the Autarch won't protect them, they could band together and protect each other."

"It's each other they're afraid of. They live—such as they do live—by sieving the old city, a finer screen every year. Every man steals from his neighbor when he can and kills him if he makes a good find. It doesn't have to be much. A knife with a silver handle—that would be a good find."

After a moment, the stranger looked down at the silver mountings of his dagger.

"I believe we might take a bit of a closer reach here," Eata told him. "There's a meander coming up." The stranger heaved at the windlass, and the boom crept back.

To starboard, a high-pooped thalamegus made its way up the river, glittering in the sunlight like a scarab, all gilding and lapis lazuli. The wind was fair for it now, and as they watched (Eata with one eye to their own sail), the lateen yards dipped on its stubby masts, then lifted again trailing wide triangles of roseate silk. The long sweeps shrunk and vanished.

"They've been down seeing the sights," Eata told the stranger. "It's safe enough by day, if you've got a couple of young fellows with swords aboard and rowers you can trust."

"What is that up there?" The stranger pointed beyond the thalamegus to a hill crowned with spires. "It looks out of place."

"They call it the Old Citadel," Eata said. "I don't know much about it."

"Is that where the Autarch comes from?"

"So some say."

Urth was looking the sun nearly full in the face now, and the wind had died to a mere whisper. The patched brown mainsail flapped, then filled, then flapped again.

The stranger sat on the gunnel for a moment, his booted feet hanging over the side and almost touching the smooth water, then swung them back onto the deck again as though he were fearful of falling overboard. "You can almost imagine them going up, can't you?" he said. "Just taking off with a silver shout and leaving this world behind."

"No," Eata told him. "I can't."

"That's what they're supposed to do, at the end of time. I read about it someplace."

"Paper's dangerous," Eata said. "It's killed a lot more men than steel."

Their boat was moving hardly faster than the sluggish current. A flyer passed overhead as swiftly and silently as a dart from the hand of a giant

and vanished into a white summer cloud, only to reappear shrunk nearly
to invisibility, one additional spark among the day-dimmed stars. The
brown sail crept across the stranger's view of the Old Citadel to the north-
east. Despite the shade it gave him, he was sweating. He unlaced his
cordwain jerkin.

That night on deck, he laced it again as tightly as he could. It was cold
already, and he knew without being told that it would soon be colder still.
"Perhaps I should have a blanket," he said.

Eata shook his head. "You'd only fall asleep. Walk up and down and
wave your arms. That'll keep you warm and awake too. I'll come up and
relieve you at the next watch."

The stranger nodded absently and looked up at the orangish lantern
Eata had hoisted to the masthead. "They'll know we're out here."

"If they didn't, I wouldn't bother to set a watch. But if we didn't have
that, some big carrack would run us under for sure and never feel the
difference. Don't you go putting it out—believe me, we're a lot safer with
it high and bright. If it should go out of itself, you let it down and get it
lit again as handsomely as ever you can. If you can't get it lit, call me. If
you see another vessel, particularly a big one, blow the conch." Eata
waved toward the spiraled shell beside the binnacle.

The stranger nodded again. "Their boats won't have lights, of course."

"No, nor masts neither. Besides, it could happen that two or three
swim out. If you see a face in the water that stares at the light and disappears, it's a manatee. Don't worry about it. But if you see anything that
swims like a man, call me."

"I will," the stranger said. He watched as Eata opened the hatch and
descended to the tiny cabin.

Two boarding pikes lay in the bow, their grounding irons lost in the
inky shadow beneath the overhang of the half-deck, their heads thrusting
past the jib-boom mountings. He climbed down and got one, then scrambled onto the deck again. The pike was three ells long, with an ugly spike
head and a sharp hook intended to cut rigging. He flourished it as he
walked the circle of the little deck, *up, down, right, left*, his movements
the awkward ones of a man recalling a skill learned in youth.

The curve of Lune lay just visible in the east, sending streamers of
virescence toward him in a silent flood, spumed and uncanny. Silhouetted
against that moss-green light, the city on the eastern bank seemed less
dead than sleeping. Its towers were black, but their sightless windows,
thus illuminated from behind, appeared to betray a faint radiance, as
though hecatonchires roved the gloomy corridors and deserted rooms,
their thousand fingers smeared with noctoluscence to light their way.

He looked to the west just in time to see a pair of gleaming eyes sink
into the water with a scarcely perceptible plash. For the space of a dozen
breaths he stared at the spot, but there was nothing more to see. He
dashed to starboard again, to what was now the eastern side of the an-
chored boat, imagining that some devious adversary had swum under or
around it to take him by surprise; Gyoll slipped past unruffled.

To port, the shadow of the hull lay long across the glassy river, though he could easily have touched the water with his hands. No skiff or shallop launched from the silent shore.

Downriver, the ruined city appeared to stretch away to infinity, as though Urth were a level plain occupying the whole of space, and the whole of Urth were filled with crumbling walls and tilted pillars. A night bird circled overhead, stooped at the water, and did not rise.

Upriver, the cookfires and grease lamps of living Nessus lent no glow to the sky. The river seemed the only living thing in a city of death; and for an instant the stranger was seized by the conviction that cold Gyoll itself was dead, that the sodden sticks and bits of excrement it carried were somehow swimming, that they were outward bound on some unending voyage to dissolution.

He was about to turn away when he noticed what appeared to be a human form drifting toward him with a scarcely discernible motion. He watched it fascinated and unbelieving, as sparrows are said to watch the golden snake called soporor.

It came nearer. In the green moonlight, its hair looked colorless, its skin berylline. He saw that it was in fact human, and that it floated face downward.

One outstretched hand touched the floating anchor cable as if it wished to climb aboard. Momentarily, the hemp retarded the stiff fingers, and the corpse performed a slow pirouette, like the half turn of a thrown knife seen by an ephemerid, or the tumbling of a derelict through the abyss that separates the worlds. Clambering down into the bow, he tried to grapple it with his pike; it was just out of reach.

He waited, horrified and impatient. At last he was able to draw it nearer and slide the hook under one arm. The corpse rolled over easily, far more easily than he had anticipated, its face pressed below the dark surface by the weight of the lifted arm, then bobbing up when that arm lay in the water once more.

It was a woman, naked and not long dead. Her staring eyes still showed traces of kohl; her teeth gleamed faintly through half-parted lips. He tried to judge her as he had judged the women whose compliance he had secured for coins, to weigh her breasts with his eyes and applaud or condemn the roundness of her belly; he discovered that he could not do so, that in the way he sought to see her she was beyond his sight, unreachable as the unborn, unreachable as his mother had been when he had once, as a boy, happened upon her bathing.

Eata's touch on his shoulder made him spin around.

"My watch."

"This—" he began, and could say nothing more. He pointed.

"I'll fend it off," Eata told him. "You get some sleep. Take the other bunk. No one's using it."

He handed Eata the pike and went below, hardly knowing what he did and nearly crushing his fingers beneath the hatch.

A candle guttered in a dish on the broken chest, and he realized that Eata had not slept. One of the narrow bunks was rumpled. He took the other, tying triple knots in the thong that held his burse to his belt, loosening his jerkin, swinging his booted feet onto the hard, thin mattress, and pulling up a blanket of surprisingly soft merino. A puff of his breath extinguished the yellow candle flame, and he closed his eyes.

The dead woman floated in the dark. He pushed her away, turning his thoughts to pleasant things: the room where he had slept as a boy, the hawk and the harrier he had left behind. The mountain meads of his father's estate rose before him, dotted with poppies and wild indigo, with fern and purple-flowered clover. When had he ridden across them last? He could not remember. Lilacs nodded their honey-charged panicles.

Sniffing, he sat up, nearly braining himself on the deck beams.

A faint perfume languished between the mingled stinks of bilge and candle. When he buried his face in the blanket, he was certain of it. Just before sleep came, he heard a man's faint, hoarse sobbing overhead.

●

He had the last watch, when the ruins dropped from the angry face of the sun like a frayed mask. By night he had seen towers; now he saw that those towers were half fallen and leprous with saplings and rank green vines. As he had been told, there was no smoke. He would have been willing to stake all he had that there were no people either.

Eata came on deck carrying bread, dried meat, and steaming maté. "You owe me another asimi," Eata said.

He untied the knots and took it out. "The last one you'll be getting. Or will you charge me for another day, if you can't return me to the place where I boarded your boat by tomorrow morning?"

Eata shook his head.

"The last, then. This spot where three streets meet—is it on the eastern side? Over there?"

Eata nodded. "See that jetty? Straight in from there for half a league. We'll be at the jetty before primesong."

Together they turned the little capstan that drew up the anchor. The stranger broke out the jib while Eata heaved at the mainsail halyards.

The sea breeze had arrived, raucously announced by a flock of black-and-white gulls riding it inland in hope of offal. Close hauled, the boat showed such heels that the stranger feared they would ram the disintegrating jetty. He picked up a pike to use as a boat hook.

At what seemed the last possible moment, Eata swung the rudder abeam and shot her bow into the wind. "That was well done," the stranger said.

"Oh, I can sail. I can fight too, if I have to." Eata paused. "I'll go with you, if you want me."

The stranger shook his head.

"I didn't think you would, but it was worth a try. You understand that you may be killed in there?"

"I doubt it."

"Well, I don't. Take that pike—you may need it. I'll wait for you till nones; understand? No later. When your shadow's around your feet, I'll be gone. If you're still alive walk north, sticking as near the water as you can. If you see a vessel, wave. Hail them." For a moment Eata hesitated, seemingly lost in thought. "Hold up a coin, the biggest you've got. That works sometimes."

"I'll be back before you go," the stranger said. "But this pike must have cost you nearly an asimi. You'll have to replace it if I don't bring it back."

"Not that much," Eata said.

"When I come back, I'll give you an asimi. We'll call it rent for the pike."

"And maybe I'll stay a bit longer in the hope of getting it, eh?"

The stranger nodded. "And perhaps you will. But I'll be back before nones."

When he had vaulted ashore, he watched Eata put out, then turned to study the city before him.

Two score strides brought him to the first ruined building. The streets were narrow here, and made more narrow still by the debris that half choked them. Blue cornflowers and pale bindweed grew from this rubbish and from the great, cracked blocks of gritty pavement. There was no sound but the distant keening of the gulls, and the air seemed purer than it had on the river. When he felt certain Eata had not followed him and that no one was watching him, he sat on a fallen stone and took out the map. He had wrapped it in oiled vellum, and the slight wetting the packet had received had not penetrated.

For most of the time he had possessed the map, he had not dared to look at it. Now as he studied it at leisure in the brilliant sunlight, his excitement was embittered by an irrational guilt.

Those spidery streets might—or might not—be the very streets that stretched before him. That wandering line of blue might be a stream or canal, or Gyoll itself. The map presented an accumulation of detail, and yet it was detail of a sort that did nothing to confirm or deny location. He committed as much of it to memory as he could, all the while wondering what feature or turning might prove of value, what name of street or structure might have survived where there was no one left to recall it, what thing of masonry or metal might yet retain its former shape, if any did. For an instant it seemed to him that it was not the treasure that was lost, but he himself.

As he refolded the cracked paper and wrapped it again, he speculated (as he had so many times) about the precious thing that had been thus laboriously hidden by the men to whom the stars had been as so many isles. Left to its own devices, his imagination ran to childish coffers crammed with gold. His intellect recognized these fancies for what they were and rejected them, but could propose in their stead only a dozen dim improbabilities, rumors of the secret knowledge and frightful weapons of ancient times. Life and mastery without limit.

He stood and studied the deserted buildings to make certain he had not been seen. A fox sat atop the highest heap of rubble, its red coat fiery in the sunshine, its eyes bright as jet beads. Suddenly afraid of any eyes, he threw the pike at it. It vanished, and the pike rattled down the farther side out of sight. He climbed over the mound and searched among the flourishing beggar ticks and lion's teeth, but the pike had vanished too.

It took him a long time to reach the area where three streets met, and longer still to find their intersection. He had somehow veered south, and he wasted a watch in the search. Another was spent amid buzzing insects in convincing himself that it was not the intersection on his map, which showed avenues of equal width running southwest, southeast, and north. At last he took out the map again, comparing its faded inks to the desolate reality. Here were indeed three streets, but one was wider than the others and ran due east. This was not the place.

He was returning to the boat when the omophagists rushed him—men the color of dust, wild-eyed and clothed in rags. In that first moment they seemed innumerable. When he had grappled with one and killed him, he realized that only four remained.

Four were still far too many. He fled, one hand pressed to his bleeding side. He had always been a good runner, but he ran now as never before, leaping every obstacle, seeming almost to fly. The ruins raced and reeled around him. Missiles whizzed past his head.

He had nearly reached the river before they caught him. Mud slid from under his boot, he fell to one knee, and they were all around him. One must have torn his silver-mounted dagger from the dead man's ribs. He watched it slash at his own throat now with the stunned incredulity of a householder who finds himself savaged by his own bandog, and he threw up his arms as much to shut out the sight as to counter the blow.

His forearm turned to ice as the steel bit in. Desperately, he rolled away, and saw the gray figure who wielded his dagger felled by the cudgel of another. A third dove for the dagger, and the two struggled.

Someone screamed; he looked to one side to see the fourth, who had his pike, impaled upon Eata's.

❧

The inn where he had stayed was near the river. Because he had walked some distance south searching for Eata's boat, he had forgotten that. The inn was the Cygnet; he had forgotten that, too.

"Toss one of those loafers the line," Eata called. "He'll tie us up for an aes."

He found he could not throw well with his left arm, but one of the loungers dove for the coil and caught it. "I've some luggage," he called as the man heaved at the line. "Perhaps you'd carry it up to the Cygnet for me."

Eata jumped into the bow. "The optimate's name is Simulatio," he told the lounger. "He stayed there three nights back. Inform the inn-keeper. Tell him the optimate wishes the room he had before."

"I hate to leave," the stranger said. "But I won't be going south again until I've healed." He was picking at the knots that bound his burse.

"If you're wise, you won't go at all."

The lounger threw the stranger's bags onto the wharf and leaped up after them.

"I want to give you something." The stranger took out a chrisos. "Perhaps you could come back at the next moon and see if I'm well enough to go."

"I won't take your yellow boy," Eata said. "You owe me an asimi for pike rent. I'll take that."

"But you will come back?"

"For an asimi a day? Of course I will. So would any other boatman."

The stranger hesitated while he looked at Eata, and Eata at him. "I think I can trust you," he said at last. "I wouldn't want to go into those ruins with anyone else."

"I know," Eata told him. "That's why I'm going to give you some advice. Walk away from the river a couple of streets, and you'll find a goldsmith's. It's the sign of the Osela. That's a golden bird."

"I know what it is."

"Yes, you would. Fold up your map—" He laughed. "You shouldn't flinch like that. If you're going to deal with people like me, you're going to have to learn to govern your face."

"I didn't think you knew about it."

"It's in your boot," Eata told him softly.

"You spied on me!"

"Sometime when you took it out? No. But once when you sat on the gunnel, you jerked your feet away from the water; and when you slept, you kept your boots on. A boatman might have done that, but you? Not unless you had something more than your feet in them."

"I see."

Eata looked away, his eyes tracing the slow, immutable flow of great Gyoll to the southwest. "I knew a man who had one of those maps," he said. "A man can spend half his life looking, and never find a thing. Maybe it's under the sea now. Maybe someone found it long ago. Maybe it was never there at all. You understand? And he can't trust anyone, not his friend, not even his woman."

"And if his friend and his woman took it from him," the stranger said, "one might kill the other to have the whole of it. Yes, I see how it is. That isn't the map I have, if that's what you're thinking. I found this one between the pages of an old book."

"I was hoping it was mine," Eata told him. "You said you understood, but you don't. I let them take it. I wanted them to have it, so they'd leave me alone. So I wouldn't end up like the men we fought with yesterday. I got drunk, let them see the key, let them see me lock the map in my chest."

"But you woke," the stranger said.

Eata turned to face him, suddenly angry. "That fool Laetus broke the lock! I thought . . ."

"You don't have to tell me about it."

"He and Syntyche were younger than I. I only thought they'd waste their lives looking, the way I'd wasted mine, and Maxellindis's too. I didn't think he'd kill Syntyche."

"He killed her," the stranger said. "You didn't. You didn't make the two of them steal, either. You're not the Increate, and you can't take the responsibility for what others do."

"But I can advise them," Eata said. "And I'd advise you to burn your map, but I know you won't. So fold it up instead, put your seal on it, and take it to that goldsmith I told you about. He's an honest old fellow, and for an orichalk he'll lock it in his strongroom. Go home then till you're better. If you're wise you'll never come back to claim it."

The stranger shook his head. "I'm going to stay at the inn here. I've money enough. And I still owe you an asimi. Pike rent, we called it. Here it is."

Eata took the silver coin and tossed it up. It was bright, newly minted, with Severian's profile stamped deep and sharp on one side. In the reddish sunlight, it might have been a coal of fire.

"You knot the strings of that burse," Eata said. "Then knot them over again, all for fear I'll get into it when you sleep. Let me tell you something. If I come back for you, I'll have every brass aes before we're done. You'll take your money out, all of it, and give it to me, bit by bit."

He flung the asimi high over the water. For a final instant it shone, before it was quenched in dark Gyoll forever. "I'm not coming back," Eata said.

"It's a good map," the stranger told him. "Look." He drew it from the top of his boot and began to unwrap it, clumsily because he could not use both hands. When he saw Eata's face, he stopped, thrust his map into his pocket, and clambered onto the half deck.

Weak from loss of blood and stiff with wounds, he could not get up to the wharf without help. One of the remaining loungers extended a hand, and he took it. At every moment he expected to feel a pike plunged into his back; there was only Eata's mocking laughter.

When he had both feet on the wharf, he turned toward the boat once more. Eata called, "Would you cast me off, please, Optimate?"

The stranger pointed, and the lounger who had helped him up untied the mooring line.

Eata pushed the boat away from the wharf and heaved the boom about to catch what wind there was.

"You'll come back for me!" the stranger shouted. "Because I'll let you come with me! Because I'll give you a share!"

Slowly and almost hesitantly, the old brown sail filled. The rigging grew taut, and the little cargo boat began to gather way. Eata did not look around, but his hand shook as it gripped the tiller.

Dinosaurs

WALTER JON WILLIAMS

*Some millions of years ago, our ancestors were tiny, chittering, tree-dwelling in-
sectivores. We've come a long way since then . . . but evolution is a process that
never stops, as amply demonstrated by the story that follows, which takes us 6
million years into a very bizarre future for an unsettling look at some of our distant
descendants. . . .*

*Walter Jon Williams was born in Minnesota and now lives in Albuquerque, New
Mexico. Williams is a highly eclectic writer, and the fact is, one Walter Jon Williams story is rarely much like any other Walter Jon Williams story. He's written
a wider range of different kinds of stuff than almost any other writer of his generation, ranging from some of the best Alternate History stories of the eighties
(including the deeply moving Alternate Civil War novella, following Edgar Allan
Poe's career as a Confederate general, "No Spot of Ground," and the compassionate and melancholy look at the alternate and alternately entangled lives that
might have been led by Mary Wollstonecraft Shelley, Percy Bysshe Shelley, and
Lord Byron, "Wall, Stone, Craft") to stories featuring scenarios quirky enough to
rank with the most off-the-wall Waldropian stuff (sending H. G. Wells's invading
Martians striding into the bizarre, ritualized, and mannered world of the Forbidden City in nineteenth-century China in "Foreign Devils" and presenting us with
an Elvis Presley who grows up to become an inspirational Socialist leader whose
influence changes the course of modern history in "Red Elvis"). He's written gritty
Mean Streets hard-as-nails cyberpunk, in stories such as "Wolf Time," "Video
Star," and "Flatline" and in novels such as* Hardwired *and* Voice of the Whirlwind;
*he's written some of the most inventive wide-screen Space Opera of recent times,
including the monumental novel* Aristoi, *one of the most successful of modern
Space Operas. He's written with depth and real ingenuity about the interaction
of humankind with aliens, in the brilliant "Surfacing," as well as in novels such
as* Angel Station. *He's written lighthearted, wryly amusing, socially satirical novels
of manners, featuring the adventures of a Raffles-like thief in a future society, in*
The Crown Jewels *and* House of Shards; *he's written dark, moody, intricate, in-
voluted, Machiavellian studies of realpolitik in action, full of betrayals and
counterbetrayals and counter-counterbetrayals, such as "Solip:System" and "Er-
ogenoscape." Williams also mixes genres with audacity and daring, mixing classical Chinese mythology with the chop-sockey fantasy of Hong Kong martial arts
movies in the droll "Broadway Johnny," mixing Sword and Sorcery with the
Hornblower-like sea story in "Consequences," having costumed superheroes
grilled by the House Committee on Un-American Activities in the McCarthy-era
America of the 1950s in "Witness," and mixing fantasy with technologically oriented "hard" science fiction in books such as* Metropolitan *and* City on Fire *successfully enough to be counted as one of the progenitors of an as-yet-nascent
subgenre sometimes called Hard Fantasy.*

His short fiction has appeared frequently in Asimov's Science Fiction, *as well as in the* Magazine of Fantasy & Science Fiction, Wheel of Fortune, Global Dispatches, Alternate Outlaws, *and other markets, and has been gathered in the collections* Facets *and* Frankensteins and Other Foreign Devils. *His other novels include* Ambassador of Progress, Knight Movies, *and* Days of Atonement. *His most recent book is a huge disaster thriller,* The Rift.

The Shars seethed in the dim light of their ruddy sun. Pointed faces raised to the sky, they sniffed the faint wind for sign of the stranger and scented only hydrocarbons, far-off vegetation, damp fur, the sweat of excitement and fear. Weak eyes peered upward, glistened with hope, anxiety, apprehension, and saw only the faint pattern of stars. Short, excited barking sounds broke out here and there, but mostly the Shars crooned, a low ululation that told of sudden onslaught, destruction, war in distant reaches, and now the hope of peace.

The crowds surged left, then right. Individuals bounced high on their third legs, seeking a view, seeing only the wide sea of heads, the ears and muzzles pointed to the stars.

Suddenly, a screaming. High-pitched howls, a bright chorus of barks. The crowds surged again.

Something was crossing the field of stars.

The human ship was huge, vaster than anything they'd seen, a moonlet descending. Shars closed their eyes and shuddered in terror. The screaming turned to moans. Individuals leaped high, baring their teeth, barking in defiance of their fear. The air smelled of terror, incipient panic, anger.

War! cried some. *Peace!* cried others.

The crooning went on. *We mourn, we mourn*, it said, *we mourn our dead billions.*

We fear, said others.

Soundlessly, the human ship neared them, casting its vast shadow. Shars spilled outward from the spot beneath, bounding high on their third legs.

The human ship came to a silent rest. Dully, it reflected the dim red sun.

The Shars crooned their fear, their sorrow. And waited for the humans to emerge.

●

These? Yes. These. Drill, the human ambassador, gazed through his video walls at the sea of Shars, the moaning, leaping thousands that surrounded him. Through the mass a group was moving with purpose, heading for the airlock as per his instructions. His new Memory crawled restlessly in the armored hollow atop his skull. *Stand by*, he broadcast.

His knees made painful crackling noises as he walked toward the airlock, the silver ball of his translator rolling along the ceiling ahead of him. The walls mutated as he passed, showing him violet sky, far-off polygonal buildings, cold distant green . . . and here, nearby, a vast, dim plain covered with a golden tissue of Shars.

He reached the airlock and it began to open. Drill snuffed wetly at the alien smells—heat, dust, the musky scent of the Shars themselves.

Drill's heart thumped in his chest. His dreams were coming true. He had waited all his life for this.

Mash, whimpered Lowbrain. Drill told it to be silent. Lowbrain protested vaguely, then obeyed.

Drill told Lowbrain to move. Cool, alien air brushed his skin. The Shars cried out sharply, moaned, fell back. They seemed a wild, sibilant ocean of pointed ears and dark, questing eyes. The group heading for the airlock vanished in the general retrograde movement, a stone washed by a pale tide. Beneath Drill's feet was soft vegetation. His translator floated in the air before him. His mind flamed with wonder, but Lowbrain kept him moving.

The Shars fell back, moaning.

Drill stood eighteen feet tall on his two pillarlike legs, each with a splayed foot that displayed a horny underside and vestigial nails. His skin was ebony and was draped in folds over his vast naked body. His pendulous maleness swung loosely as he walked. As he stepped across the open space he was conscious of the fact that he was the ultimate product of nine million years of human evolution, all leading to the expansion, diversification, and perfection that was now humanity's manifest existence.

He looked down at the little Shars, their white skin and golden fur, their strange, stiff tripod legs, the muzzles raised to him as if in awe. *If your species survives*, he thought benignly, *you can look like me in another few million years.*

➤

The group of Shars that had been forging through the crowd were suddenly exposed when the crowd fell back from around them. On the perimeter were several Shars holding staffs—weapons, perhaps—in their clever little hands. In the center of these were a group of Shars wearing decorative ribbon to which metal plates had been attached. *Badges of rank*, Memory said. *Ignore.* The shadow of the translator bobbed toward them as Drill approached. Metallic geometries rose from the group and hovered over them.

Recorders, Memory said. *Artificial similarities to myself. Or possibly security devices. Disregard.*

Drill was getting closer to the party, speeding up his instructions to Lowbrain, eventually entering Zen Synch. It would make Lowbrain hungrier but lessen the chance of any accidents.

The Shars carrying the staffs fell back. A wailing went up from the crowd as one of the Shars stepped toward Drill. The ribbons draped over her sloping shoulders failed to disguise four mammalian breasts. Clear plastic bubbles covered her weak eyes. In Zen Synch with Memory and Lowbrain, Drill ambled up to her and raised his hands in friendly greeting. The Shar flinched at the expanse of the gesture.

"I am Ambassador Drill," he said. "I am a human."

The Shar gazed up at him. Her nose wrinkled as she listened to the booming voice of the translator. Her answer was a succession of sharp sounds, made high in the throat, somewhat unpleasant. Drill listened to the voice of his translator.

"I am President Gram of the InterSharian Sociability of Nations and Planets." That's how it came through in translation, anyway. Memory began feeding Drill referents for the word "nation."

"I welcome you to our planet, Ambassador Drill."

"Thank you, President Gram," Drill said. "Shall we negotiate peace now?"

President Gram's ears pricked forward, then back. There was a pause, and then from the vast circle of Shars came a mad torrent of hooting noises. The awesome sound lapped over Drill like the waves of a lunatic sea.

They approve your sentiment, said Memory.

I thought that's what it meant, Drill said. *Do you think we'll get along?*

Memory didn't answer, but instead shifted to a more comfortable position in the saddle of Drill's skull. Its job was to provide facts, not draw conclusions.

"If you could come into my Ship," Drill said, "we could get started."

"Will we then meet the other members of your delegation?"

Drill gazed down at the Shar. The fur on her shoulders was rising in odd tufts. She seemed to be making a concerted effort to calm it.

"There are no other members," Drill said. "Just myself."

His knees were paining him. He watched as the other members of the Shar party cast quick glances at each other.

"No secretaries? No assistants?" the President was saying.

"No," Drill said. "Not at all. I'm the only conscious mind on Ship. Shall we get started?"

Eat! Eat! said Lowbrain. Drill ordered it to be silent. His stomach grumbled.

"Perhaps," said President Gram, gazing at the vastness of the human ship, "it would be best should we begin in a few hours. I should probably speak to the crowd. Would you care to listen?"

No need, Memory said. *I will monitor.*

"Thank you, no," Drill said. "I shall return to Ship for food and sex. Please signal me when you are ready. Please bring any furniture you may need for your comfort. I do not believe my furniture would fit you, although we might be able to clone some later."

The Shars' ears all pricked forward. Drill entered Zen Synch, turned his huge body, and began accelerating toward the airlock. The sound of the crowd behind him was like the murmuring of wind through a stand of trees.

Peace, he thought later, as he stood by the mash bins and fed his complaining stomach. *It's a simple thing. How long can it take to arrange?*

Long, said Memory. *Very long.*

The thought disturbed him. He thought the first meeting had gone well.

After his meal, when he had sex, it wasn't very good.

◆

246 ● WALTER JON WILLIAMS

Memory had been monitoring the events outside Ship, and after Drill had completed sex, Memory showed him the outside events. *They have been broadcast to the entire population,* Memory said.

President Gram had moved to a local elevation and had spoken for some time. Drill found her speech interesting—it was rhythmic and incantorial, rising and falling in tone and volume, depending heavily on repetition and melody. The crowd participated, issuing forth with excited barks or low moans in response to her statements or questions, sometimes babbling in confusion when she posed them a conundrum. Memory only gave the highlights of the speech. "Unknown . . . attackers . . . billions dead . . . preparations advanced . . . ready to defend ourselves . . . offer of peace . . . hope in the darkness . . . unknown . . . willing to take the chance . . . peace . . . peace . . . hopeful smell . . . peace." At the end the other Shars were all singing "Peace! Peace!" in chorus while President Gram bounced up and down on her sturdy rear leg.

It sounds pretty, Drill thought. *But why does she go on like that?*

Memory's reply was swift.

Remember that the Shars are a generalized and social species, it said. *President Gram's power, and her ability to negotiate, derives from the degree of her popular support. In measures of this significance she must explain herself and her actions to the population in order to maintain their enthusiasm for her policies.*

Primitive, Drill thought.

That is correct.

Why don't they let her get on with her work? Drill asked.

There was no reply.

●

After an exchange of signals the Shar party assembled at the airlock. Several Shars had been mobilized to carry tables and stools. Drill sent a Frog to escort the Shars from the airlock to where he waited. The Frog met them inside the airlock, turned, and hopped on ahead through Ship's airy, winding corridors. It had been trained to repeat "Follow me, follow me" in the Shars' own language.

Drill waited in a semi-reclined position on a Slab. The Slab was an organic sub-species used as furniture, with an idiot brain capable of responding to human commands. The Shars entered cautiously, their weak eyes twitching in the bright light. "Welcome, Honorable President," Drill said. "Up, Slab." Slab began to adjust itself to place Drill on his feet. The Shars were moving tables and stools into the vast room.

Frog was hopping in circles, making a wet noise at each landing. "Follow me, follow me," it said.

The members of the Shar delegation who bore badges of rank stood in a body while the furniture-carriers bustled around them. Drill noticed, as Slab put him on his feet, that they were wrinkling their noses. He wondered what it meant.

His knees crackled as he came fully upright. "Please make yourselves comfortable," he said. "Frog will show your laborers to the airlock."

"Does your Excellency object to a mechanical recording of the proceedings?" President Gram asked. She was shading her eyes with her hand.

"Not at all." As a number of devices rose into the air above the party, Drill wondered if it were possible to give the Shars detachable Memories. Perhaps human bioengineers could adapt the Memories to the Shar physiology. He asked Memory to make a note of the question so that he could bring it up later.

"Follow me, follow me," Frog said. The workers who had carried the furniture began to follow the hopping Frog out of the room.

"Your Excellency," President Gram said, "may I have the honor of presenting to you the other members of my delegation?"

There were six in all, with titles like Secretary for Syncopated Speech and Special Executive for External Coherence. There was also a Minister for the Dissemination of Convincing Lies, whose title Drill suspected was somehow mistranslated, and an Opposite Secretary-General for the Genocidal Eradication of Alien Aggressors, at whom Drill looked with more than a little interest. The Opposite Secretary-General was named Vang, and was small even for a Shar. He seemed to wrinkle his nose more than the others. The Special Executive for External Coherence, whose name was Cup, seemed a bit piebald, patches of white skin showing through the golden fur covering his shoulders, arms, and head.

He is elderly, said Memory.

That's what I thought.

"Down, Slab," Drill said. He leaned back against the creature and began to move to a more relaxed position.

He looked at the Shars and smiled. Fur ruffled on shoulders and necks. "Shall we make peace now?" he asked.

"We would like to clarify something you said earlier," President Gram said. "You said that you were the only, ah, conscious entity on the ship. That you were the only member of the human delegation. Was that translated correctly?"

"Why, yes," Drill said. "Why would more than one diplomat be necessary?"

The Shars looked at each other. The Special Executive for External Coherence spoke cautiously.

"You will not be needing to consult with your superiors? You have full authority from your government?"

Drill beamed at them. "We humans do not have a government, of course," he said. "But I am a diplomat with the appropriate Memory and training. There is no problem that I can foresee."

"Please let me understand, your Excellency," Cup said. He was leaning forward, his small eyes watering. "I am elderly and may be slow in comprehending the situation. But if you have no government, who accredited you with this mission?"

"I am a diplomat. It is my specialty. No accreditation is necessary. The human race will accept my judgment on any matter of negotiation, as they would accept the judgment of any specialist in his area of expertise."

"But why *you*. As an individual?"

Drill shrugged massively. "I was part of the nearest diplomatic enclave, and the individual without any other tasks at the moment." He looked at each of the delegation in turn. "I am incredibly happy to have this chance, honorable delegates," he said. "The vast majority of human diplomats never have the chance to speak to another species. Usually we mediate only in conflicts of interest between the various groups of human speci-alities."

"But the human species will abide by your decisions?"

"Of course." Drill was surprised at the Shar's persistence. "Why wouldn't they?"

Cup settled back in his chair. His ears were down. There was a short silence.

"We have an opening statement prepared," President Gram said. "I would like to enter it into our record, if I may. Or would your Excellency prefer to go first?"

"I have no opening statement," Drill said. "Please go ahead."

Cup and the President exchanged glances. President Gram took a deep breath and began.

Long, Memory said. *Very long.*

The opening statement seemed very much like the address President Gram had been delivering to the crowd, the same hypnotic rhythms, more or less the same content. The rest of the delegation made muted re-sponses. Drill drowsed through it, enjoying it as music.

"Thank you, Honorable President," he said afterwards. "That was very nice."

"We would like to propose an agenda for the conference," Gram said. "First, to resolve the matter of the cease-fire and its provisions for an ending to hostilities. Second, the establishment of a secure border be-tween our two species, guaranteeing both species room for expansion. Third, the establishment of trade and visitation agreements. Fourth, the matter of reparations, payments, and return of lost territory."

Drill nodded. "I believe," he said, "that resolution of the second through fourth points will come about as a result of an understanding reached on the first. That is, once the cease-fire is settled, that resolution will imply a settlement of the rest of the situation."

"You accept the agenda?"

"If you like. It doesn't matter."

Ears pricked forward, then back. "So you accept that our initial dis-cussions will consist of formalizing the disengagement of our forces?"

"Certainly. Of course I have no way of knowing what forces you have committed. We humans have committed none."

The Shars were still for a long time. "Your species attacked our planets, Ambassador. Without warning, without making yourselves known to us." Gram's tone was unusually flat. Perhaps, Drill thought, she was attempt-ing to conceal great emotion.

"Yes," Drill said. "But those were not our military formations. Your species were contacted only by our terraforming Ships. They did not attack your people, as such—they were only peripherally aware of your existence. Their function was merely to seed the plants with lifeforms favorable to human existence. Unfortunately for your people, part of the function of these lifeforms is to destroy the native life of the planet."

The Shars conferred with one another. The Opposite Secretary-General seemed particularly vehement. Then President Gram turned to Drill.

"We cannot accept your statement, your Excellency," she said. "Our people were attacked. They defended themselves, but were overcome."

"Our terraforming Ships are very good at what they do," Drill said. "They are specialists. Our Shrikes, our Shrews, our Sharks—each is a master of its element. But they lack intelligence. They are not conscious entities, such as ourselves. They weren't aware of your civilization at all. They only saw you as food."

"You're claiming that you *didn't notice us?*" demanded Secretary-General Vang. *"They didn't notice us as they were killing us?"* He was shouting. President Gram's ears went back.

"Not as such, no," Drill said.

President Gram stood up. "I am afraid, your Excellency, your explanations are insufficient," she said. "This conference must be postponed until we can reach a united conclusion concerning your remarkable attitude."

Drill was bewildered. "What did I say?" he asked.

The other Shars stood. President Gram turned and walked briskly on her three legs toward the exit. The others followed.

"Wait," Drill said. "Don't go. Let me send for Frog. Up, Slab, up!"

The Shars were gone by the time Slab had got Drill to his feet. The Ship told him they had found their own way to the airlock. Drill could think of nothing to do but order the airlock to let them out.

"Why would I lie?" he asked. "Why would I lie to them?" Things were so very simple, really.

He shifted his vast weight from one foot to the other and back again. Drill could not decide whether he had done anything wrong. He asked Memory what to do next, but Memory held no information to comfort him, only dry recitations of past negotiations. Annoyed at the lifeless monologue, Drill told Memory to be silent and began to walk restlessly through the corridors of his Ship. He could not decide where things had gone bad.

Sensing his agitation, Lowbrain began to echo his distress. *Mash*, Lowbrain thought weakly. *Food. Sex.*

Be silent, Drill commanded.

Sex, sex, Lowbrain thought.

Drill realized that Lowbrain was beginning to give him an erection. Acceding to the inevitable, he began moving toward Surrogate's quarters.

Surrogate lived in a dim, quiet room filled with the murmuring sound of its own heartbeat. It was a human subspecies, about the intelligence of Lowbrain, designed to comfort voyagers on long journeys through space, when carnal access to their own subspecies might necessarily be limited. Surrogate had a variety of sexual equipment designed for the accommodation of the various human subspecies and their sexes. It also had large mammaries that gave nutritious milk, and a rudimentary head capable of voicing simple thoughts.

Tiny Mice, that kept Surrogate and the ship clean, scattered as Drill entered the room. Surrogate's little head turned to him.

"It's good to see you again," Surrogate said.

"I am Drill."

"It's good to see you again, Drill," said Surrogate. "It's good to see you again."

Drill began to nuzzle its breasts. One of Surrogate's male parts began to erect. "I'm confused, Surrogate," he said. "I don't know what to do."

"Why are you confused, Drill?" asked Surrogate. It raised one of its arms and began to stroke Drill's head. It wasn't really having a conversation: Surrogate had only been programmed to make simple statements, or to analyze its partners' speech and ask questions.

"Things are going wrong," Drill said. He began to suckle. The warm milk flowed down his throat. Surrogate's male part had an orgasm. Mice jumped from hiding to clean up the mess.

"Why are things going wrong?" asked Surrogate. "I'm sure everything will be all right."

Lowbrain had an orgasm, perceived by Drill as scattered, faraway bits of pleasure. Drill continued to suckle, feeling a heavy comfort beginning to radiate from Surrogate, from the gentle sound of its heartbeat, its huge, wholesome, brainless body.

Everything will be all right, Drill decided.

"Nice to see you again, Drill," Surrogate said. "Drill, it's *nice* to see you again."

●

The vast crowds of Shars did not leave when night fell. Instead they stood beneath floating globes dispersing a cold reddish light that reflected eerily from pointed ears and muzzles. Some of them donned capes or skirts to help them keep warm. Drill, watching them on the video walls of the command center, was reminded of crowds standing in awe before some vast cataclysm.

The Shars were not quiet. They stood in murmuring groups, but sometimes they began the crooning chants they had raised earlier, or suddenly broke out in a series of shrill yipping cries.

President Gram spoke to them after she had left Ship. "The human has admitted his species' attacks," she said, "but has disclaimed responsibility. We shall urge him to adopt a more realistic position."

"Adopt a position," Drill repeated, not understanding. "It is not a position. It is the truth. Why don't they understand?"

Opposite Minister-General Vang was more vehement. "We now have a far more complete idea of the humans' attitude," he said. "It is opposed to ours in every way. We shall not allow the murderous atrocities which the humans have committed upon five of our planets to be forgotten, or understood to be the result of some inexplicable lack of attention on the part of our species' enemies."

"That one is obviously deranged," thought Drill.

He went to his sleeping quarters and ordered the Slab there to play him some relaxing music. Even with Slab's murmurs and comforting hums, it took Drill some time before his agitation subsided.

Diplomacy, he thought as slumber overtook him, was certainly a strange business.

●

In the morning the Shars were still there, chanting and crying, moving in their strange crowded patterns. Drill watched them on his video walls as he ate breakfast at the mash bins. "There is a communication from President Gram," Memory announced. "She wishes to speak with you by radio."

"Certainly."

"Ambassador Drill." She was using the flat tones again. A pity she was subject to such stress.

"Good morning, President Gram," Drill said. "I hope you spent a pleasant night."

"I must give you the results of our decision. We regret that we can see no way to continue the negotiations unless you, as a representative of your species, agree to admit responsibility for your peoples' attacks on our planets."

"Admit responsibility?" Drill said. "Of course. Why wouldn't I?"

Drill heard some odd, indistinct barking sounds that his translator declined to interpret for him. It sounded as if someone other than President Gram were on the other end of the radio link.

"You admit responsibility?" President Gram's amazement was clear even in translation.

"Certainly. Does it make a difference?"

President Gram declined to answer that question. Instead she proposed another meeting for that afternoon.

"I will be ready at any time."

Memory recorded President Gram's speech to her people, and Drill studied it before meeting the Shar party at the airlock. She made a great deal out of the fact that Drill had admitted humanity's responsibility for the war. Her people leaped, yipped, chanted their responses as if possessed. Drill wondered why they were so excited.

Drill met the party at the airlock this time, linked with Memory and Lowbrain in Zen Synch so as not to accidentally step on the President or one of her party. He smiled and greeted each by name and led them toward the conference room.

"I believe," said Cup, "we may avoid future misunderstandings, if your Excellency would consent to inform us about your species. We have suffered some confusion in regard to your distinction between 'conscious' and 'unconscious' entities. Could you please explain the difference, as you understand it?"

"A pleasure, your Excellency," Drill said. "Our species, unlike yours, is highly specialized. Once, eight million years ago, we were like you—a small, nonspecialized species type is very useful at a certain stage of evolution. But once a species reaches a certain complexity in its social and technological evolution, the need for specialists becomes too acute. Through both deliberate genetic manipulation and natural evolution, humanity turned away from a generalist species, toward highly specialized forms adapted to particular functions and environments. We understand this to be a natural function of species evolution.

"In the course of our explorations into manipulating our species, we discovered that the most efficient way of coding large amounts of information was in our own cell structure—our DNA. For tasks requiring both large and small amounts of data, we arranged that, as much as possible, these would be performed by organic entities, human subspecies. Since many of these tasks were boring and repetitive, we reasoned that advanced consciousness, such as that which we both share, was not necessary. You have met several unconscious entities. Frog, for example, and the Slab on which I lie. Many parts of my Ship are also alive, though not conscious."

"That would explain the smell," one of the delegation murmured.

"The terraforming Ships," Drill went on, "which attacked your planets—these were also designed so as not to require a conscious operator."

The Shars squinted up at Drill with their little eyes. "But why?" Cup asked.

"Terraforming is a dull process. It takes many years. No conscious mind could possibly enjoy it."

"But your species would find itself at war without knowing it. If your explanation for the cause of this war is correct, you already have."

Drill shrugged massively. "This happens from time to time. Sometimes other species which have reached our stage of development have attacked us in the same way. When it does, we arrange a peace."

"You consider these attacks normal?" Opposite Minister-General Vang was the one who spoke.

"These occasional encounters seem to be a natural result of species evolution," Drill said.

Vang turned to one of the Shars near him and spoke in several sharp barks. Drill heard a few words: "Billions lost . . . five planets . . . atrocities . . . *natural result!*"

"I believe," said President Gram, "that we are straying from the agenda."

Vang looked at her. "Yes, honorable President. Please forgive me."

"The matter of withdrawal," said President Gram, "to recognized truce lines."

Species at this stage of their development tend to be territorial, Memory reminded Drill. *Their political mentality is based around the concept of borders. The idea of a borderless community of species may be perceived as a threat.*

I'll try and go easy on them, Drill said.

"The Memories on our terraforming Ships will be adjusted to account for your species," Drill said. "After the adjustment, your people will no longer be in danger."

"In our case, it will take the disengage order several months to reach all our forces," President Gram said. "How long will the order take to reach your own Ships?"

"A century or so." The Shars stared. "Memories at our exploration basis in this area will be adjusted first, of course, and these will adjust the Memories of terraforming Ships as they come in for maintenance and supplies."

"We'll be subject to attack for *another hundred years?*" Vang's tone mixed incredulity and scorn.

"Our terraforming Ships move more or less at random, and only come into base when they run out of supplies. We don't know where they've been till they report back. Though they're bound to encounter a few more of your planets, your species will still survive, enough to continue your species evolution. And during that time you'll be searching for and occupying new planets on your own. You'll probably come out of this with a net gain."

"Have you no respect for life?" Vang demanded. Drill considered his answer.

"All individuals die, Opposite Minister-General," he said. "That is a fact of nature which no species has been able to alter. Only species can survive. Individuals are easily replaceable. Though you will lose some planets and a large number of individuals, your species as a whole will survive and may even prosper. What more could a species or its delegated representatives desire?"

Opposite Minister-General Vang was glaring at Drill, his ears pricked forward, lips drawn back from his teeth. He said nothing.

"We desire a cease-fire that is a true cease-fire," President Gram said. Her hands were clasping and unclasping rhythmically on the edge of her chair. "Not a slow, authorized extermination of our species. Your position has an unwholesome smell. I am afraid we must end these discussions until you alter it."

"Position? This is not a position, honorable President. It is truth."

"We have nothing further to say."

Unhappily, Drill followed the Shar delegation to the airlock. "I do not lie, honorable President," he said, but Gram only turned away and silently left the human Ship. The Shars in their pale thousands received her.

❧

The Shar broadcasts were not heartening. Opposite Minister-General Vang was particularly vehement. Drill collected the highlights of the speeches as he speeded through Memory's detailed remembrance. "Callous disregard . . . no common ground for communication . . . casual attitude toward atrocity . . . displays of obvious savagery . . . no respect for the individual . . . defend ourselves . . . this stinks in the nose."

The Shars leaped and barked in response. There were strange bubbling high-pitched laughing sounds that Drill found unsettling.

"We hope to find a formula for peace," President Gram said. "We will confer with all the ministers in session." That was all.

That night, the Shars surrounding Ship moaned, moving slowly in a giant circle, their arms linked. The laughing sounds that followed Vang's speech did not cease entirely. He did not understand why they did not all go home and sleep.

Long, long, Memory said. No comfort there.

◆

Early in the morning, before dawn, there was a communication from President Gram. "I would like to meet with you privately. Away from the recorders, the coalition partners."

"I would like nothing better," Drill said. He felt a small current of optimism begin to trickle into him.

"Can I use an airlock other than the one we've been using up till now?"

Drill gave President Gram instructions and met her in the other airlock. She was wearing a night cape with a hood. The Shars, circling and moaning, had paid her no attention.

"Thank you for seeing me under these conditions," she said, peering up at him from beneath the hood. Drill smiled. She shuddered.

"I am pleased to be able to cooperate," he said.

Mash! Lowbrain demanded. It had been silent until Drill entered Zen Synch. Drill told it to be silent with a snarling vehemence that silenced it for the present.

"This way, honorable President," Drill said. He took her to his sleeping chamber—a small room, only fifty feet square. "Shall I send a Frog for one of your chairs?" he asked.

"I will stand. Three legs seem to be more comfortable than two for standing."

"Yes."

"Is it possible, Ambassador Drill, that you could lower the intensity of the light here? I find it oppressive."

Drill felt foolish, knowing he should have thought of this himself. "I'm sorry," he said. "I will give the orders at once. I wish you had told me earlier." He smiled nervously as he dimmed the lights and arranged himself on his Slab.

"Honorable ambassador." President Gram's words seemed hesitant. "I wonder if it is possible . . . can you tell me the meaning of that facial gesture of yours, showing me your teeth?"

"It is called a smile. It is intended as a gesture of benevolent reassurance."

"Showing of the teeth is considered a threat here, honorable ambassador. Some of us have considered this a sign that you wish to eat us."

Drill was astonished. "My goodness!" he said. "I don't even eat meat! Just a kind of vegetable mash."

"I pointed out that your teeth seemed unsuitable for eating meat, but still it makes us uneasy. I was wondering . . ."

"I will try to suppress the smile, yes. Eating meat! What an idea. Some of our military specialists, yes, and of course the Sharks and Shrikes and so on . . ." He told his Memory to enforce a strict ban against smiling in the presence of a Shar.

Gram leaned back on her sturdy rear leg. Her cape parted, revealing her ribbons and badges of office, her four furry dugs. "I wanted to inform you of certain difficulties here, Ambassador Drill," she said. "I am having difficulty holding together my coalition. Minister-General Vang's faction is gaining strength. He is attempting to create a perception in the minds of Shars that you are untrustworthy and violent. Whether he believes this, or whether he is using this notion as a means of destabilizing the coalition, is hardly relevant—considering your species' unprovoked attacks, it is not a difficult perception to reinforce. He is also trying to tell our people that the military is capable of dealing with your species."

Drill's brain swam with Memory's information on concepts such as "faction" and "coalition." The meaning of the last sentence, however, was clear.

"That is a foolish perception, honorable President," he said.

"His assurances on that score lack conviction." Gram's eyes were shiny. Her tone grew earnest. "You must give me something, ambassador. Something I can use to soothe the public mind. A way out of this dilemma. I tell you that it is impossible to expect us to sit idly by and accept the loss of an undefined number of planets over the next hundred years. I plead with you, ambassador. Give me something. Some way we can avoid attack. Otherwise . . ." She left the sentence incomplete.

Mash, Lowbrain wailed. Drill ignored it. He moved into Zen Synch with Memory, racing through possible solutions. Sweat gathered on his forehead, pouring down his vast shoulders.

"Yes," he said. "Yes, there is a possibility. If you could provide us with the location of all your occupied planets, we could dispatch a Ship to each with the appropriate Memories as cargo. If any of our terraforming Ships arrived, the Memories could be transferred at once, and your planets would be safe."

President Gram considered this. "Memories," she said. "You've been using the term, but I'm not sure I understand."

"Stored information is vast, and even though human bodies are large we cannot always have all the information we need to function efficiently even in our specialized tasks," Drill said. "Our human brains have been separated as to function. I have a Lowbrain, which is on my spinal cord above my pelvis. Lowbrain handles motor control of my lower body, routine monitoring of my body's condition, eating, excretion, and sex. My perceptual centers, short-term memory, personality, and reasoning functions are handled by the brain in my skull—the classical brain, if you like. Long-term and specialized memory is the function of the large knob you see moving on my head, my Memory. My Memory records all that happens in great detail, and can recapitulate it at any point. It has also been supplied with information concerning the human species' contacts with other nonhuman groups. It attaches itself easily to my nervous system and draws nourishment from my body. Specific memories can be communicated from one living Memory to another, or if it proves necessary I can simply give my Memory to another human, a complete transfer. I have another Memory aboard that I'm not using at the moment, a pilot Memory that can navigate and handle Ship, and I wore this Memory while in transit. I also have spare Memories in case my primary Memories fall ill. So you see, our specialization does not rule out adaptability—any piece of information needed by any of us can easily be transferred, and in far greater detail than by any mechanical medium."

"So you could return to your base and send out pilot Memories to our planets," Gram said. "Memories that could halt your terraforming ships."

"That is correct." Just in time, Memory managed to stop the twitch in Drill's cheeks from becoming a smile. Happiness bubbled up in him. He was going to arrange this peace after all!

"I am afraid that would not be acceptable, your Excellency," President Gram said. Drill's hopes fell.

"Whyever not?"

"I'm afraid the Minister-General would consider it a naïve attempt of yours to find out the location of our populated planets. So that your species could attack them, ambassador."

"I'm trying very hard, President Gram," Drill said.

"I'm sure you are."

Drill frowned and went into Zen Synch again, ignoring Lowbrain's plaintive cries for mash and sex, sex and mash. Concepts crackled through his mind. He began to develop an erection, but Memory was drawing off most of the available blood and the erection failed. The smell of Drill's sweat filled the room. President Gram wrinkled her nose and leaned back far onto her rear leg.

"Ah," Drill said. "A solution. Yes. I can have my Pilot memory provide the locations to an equivalent number of our own planets. We will have one another's planets as hostage."

"Bravo, ambassador," President Gram said quietly. "I think we may have a solution. But—forgive me—it may be said that we cannot trust your information. We will have to send ships to verify the location of your planets."

"If your ships go to my planet first," Drill said, "I can provide your people with one of my spare Memories that will inform my species what your people are doing, and instruct the humans to cooperate. We will have to construct some kind of link between your radio and my Memory . . . maybe I can have my Ship grow one."

President Gram came forward off her third leg and began to pace forward, moving in her strange, fast, hobbling way. "I can present it to the council this way, yes," she said. "There is hope here." She stopped her movement, peering up at Drill with her ears pricked forward. "Is it possible that you could allow me to present this to the council as my own idea?" she asked. "It may meet with less suspicion that way."

"Whatever way is best," said Drill. President Gram gazed into the darkened recesses of the room.

"This smells good," she said. Drill succeeded in suppressing his smile.

◆

"It's nice to see you again."

"I am Drill."

"It's nice to see you again, Drill."

"I think we can make the peace work."

"Everything will be all right, Drill. Drill, I'm sure everything will be all right."

"I'm so glad I had this chance. This is the chance of a lifetime."

"Drill, it's *nice* to see you again."

◆

The next day President Gram called and asked to present a new plan. Drill said he would be pleased to hear it. He met the party at the airlock, having already dimmed the lights. He was very rigid in his attempts not to smile.

They sat in the dimmed room while President Gram presented the plan. Drill pretended to think it over, then acceded. Details were worked out. First the location of one human planet would be given and verified—this planet, the Shar capital, would count as the first revealed Shar planet. After verification, each side would reveal the location of two planets, verify those, then reveal four, and so on. Even counting the months it would take to verify the location of planets, the treaty should be completed within less than five years.

That night the Shars went mad. At President Gram's urging, they built fires, danced, screamed, sang. Drill watched on his Ship's video walls. Their rhythms beat at his head.

He smiled. For hours.

◆

The Ship obligingly grew a communicator and coupled it to one of Drill's spare Memories. The two were put aboard a Shar ship and sent in the direction of Drill's home. Drill remained in his ship, watching entertainment videos Ship received from the Shars' channels. He didn't understand the dramas very well, but the comedies were delightful. The Shars could do the most intricate, clever things with their flexible bodies and odd tripod legs—it was delightful to watch them.

Maybe I could take some home with me, he thought. *They can be very entertaining.*

The thousands of Shars waiting outside Ship began to drift away. Within a month only a few hundred were left. Their singing was quiet, triumphant, assured. Sometimes Drill had it piped into his sleeping chamber. It helped him relax.

President Gram visited informally every ten days or so. Drill showed her around Ship, showing her the pilot Memory, the Frog quarters, the giant stardrive engines with their human subspecies' implanted connections, Surrogate in its shadowed, pleasant room. The sight of Surrogate seemed to agitate the President.

"You do not use sex for procreation?" she asked. "As an expression of affection?"

"Indeed we do. I have scads of offspring. There are never enough diplomats, so we have a great many couplings among our subspecies. As for affection . . . I think I can say that I have enjoyed the company of each of my partners."

She looked up at him with solemn eyes. "You travel to the stars, Drill," she said. "Your species expands randomly in all directions, encountering other species, sometimes annihilating them. Do you have a reason for any of this?"

"A reason?" Drill mused. "It is natural to us. Natural to all intelligent species, so far as we know."

"I meant a conscious reason. Is it anything other than what you do in an automatic way?"

"I can't think of why we would need any such reasons."

"So you have no philosophy of constant expansion? No ideology?"

"I do not know what those words mean," Drill said.

Gram closed her eyes and lowered her head. "I am sorry," she said.

"No need. We have no conflicts in our ideas about ourselves, about our lives. We are happy with what we are."

"Yes. You couldn't be unhappy if you tried, could you?"

"No," Drill said cheerfully. "I see that you understand."

"Yes," Gram said. "I scent that I do."

"In a few million years," Drill said, "these things will become clear to you."

━

The first Shar ship returned from Drill's home, reporting a transfer of the Memory. The field around Ship filled again with thousands of Shars, crying their happiness to the skies. Other Memories were now taking instructions to all terraforming bases. The locations of two new planets were released. Ships carrying spare Memories leaped into the skies.

It's working, Drill told Memory.

Long, Memory said. *Very long.*

But Memory could not lower Drill's joy. This was what he had lived his life for, and he knew he was good at it. Memories of the future would take this solution as a model for negotiations with other species. Things were working out.

━

One night the Shars outside Ship altered their behavior. Their singing became once again a moaning, mixed with cries. Drill was disturbed.

A communication came from the President. "Cup is dead," she said.

"I understand," Drill said. "Who is his replacement?"

Drill could not read Gram's expression. "That is not yet known. Cup was a strong person, and did not like other strong people around him. Already the successors are fighting for the leadership, but they may not be able to hold his faction together." Her ears flickered. "I may be weakened by this."

"I regret things tend that way."

"Yes," she said. "So do I."

━

The second set of ships returned. More Memories embarked on their journeys. The treaty was holding.

There was a meeting aboard Ship to formalize the agreement. Cup's successor was Brook, a tall, elderly Shar whose golden fur was darkened by age. A compromise candidate, President Gram said, his election determined after weeks of fighting for the successorship. He was not respected. Already pieces of Cup's old faction were breaking away.

"I wonder, your Excellency," Brook said, after the formal business was over, "if you could arrange for our people to learn your language. You must have powerful translation modules aboard your ship in order to learn our language so quickly. You were broadcasting your message of peace within a few hours of entering real space."

"I have no such equipment aboard Ship," Drill said. "Our knowledge of your language was acquired from Shar prisoners."

"Prisoners?" Shar ears pricked forward. "We were not aware of this," Brook said.

"After our base Memories recognized discrepancies," Drill said, "we sent some Ships out searching for you. We seized one of your ships and took it to my home world. The prisoners were asked about their language and the location of your capital planet. Otherwise it would have taken me months to find your world here, and learn to communicate with you."

"May we ask to arrange for the return of the prisoners?"

"Oh." Drill said. "That won't be possible. After we learned what we needed to know, we terminated their lives. They were being kept in an area reserved for a garden. The landscapers wanted to get to work." Drill bobbed his head reassuringly. "I am pleased to inform you that they proved excellent fertilizer for the gardens. The result was quite lovely."

"I think," said President Gram carefully, "that it would be best that this information not go beyond those of us in this room. I think it would disturb the process."

Minister-General Vang's ears went back. So did others'. But they acceded.

"I think we should take our leave," said President Gram.

"Have a pleasant afternoon," said Drill.

◆

"It's important." It was not yet dawn. Ship had awakened Drill for a call from the President. "One of your ships has attacked another of our planets."

Alarm drove the sleep from Drill's brain. "Please come to the airlock," he said.

"The information will reach the population within the hour."

"Come quickly," said Drill.

The President arrived with a pair of assistants, who stayed inside the airlock. They carried staves. "My people will be upset," Gram said. "Things may not be entirely safe."

"Which planet was it?" Drill asked.

Gram rubbed her ears. "It was one of those whose location went out on the last peace shuttle."

"The new Memory must not have arrived in time."

"That is what we will tell the people. That it couldn't have been prevented. I will try to speed up the process by which the planets receive new Memories. Double the quota."

"That is a good idea."

"I will have to dismiss Brook. Opposite Minister-General Vang will have to take his job. If I can give Vang more power, he may remain in the coalition and not cause a split."

"As you think best."

President Gram looked up at Drill, her head rising reluctantly, as if held back by a great weight. "My son," she said. "He was on the planet when it happened."

"You have other offspring," Drill said.

Gram looked at him, the pain burning deep in her eyes. "Yes," she said. "I do."

●

The fields around Ship filled once again. Cries and howls rent the air, and dirges pulsed against Ship's uncaring walls. The Shar broadcasts in the next weeks seemed confused to Drill. Coalitions split and fragmented. Vang spoke frequently of readiness. President Gram succeeded in doubling the quota of planets. The decision was a near one.

Then, days later, another message. "One of our commanders," said President Gram, "was based on the vicinity of the attacked planet. He is one of Vang's creatures. On his own initiative he ordered our military forces to engage. Your terraforming Ship was attacked."

"Was it destroyed?" Drill asked. His tone was urgent. There is still hope, he reminded himself.

"Don't be anxious for your fellow humans," Gram said. "The Ship was damaged, but escaped."

"The loss of a few hundred billion unconscious organisms is no cause for anxiety," Drill said. "An escaped terraforming Ship is. The Ship will alert our military forces. It will be a real war."

President Gram licked her lips. "What does that mean?"

"You know of our Shrikes and so on. Our military people are worse. They are fully conscious and highly specialized in different modes of warfare. They are destructive, carnivorous, capable of taking enormous damage without impairing function. Their minds concentrate only on tactics, on destruction. Normally they are kept on planetoids away from the rest of humanity. Even other humans find their proximity too . . . disturbing." Drill put all the urgency in his speech that he could. "Honorable President, you must give me the locations of the remaining planets. If I can get Memories to each of them with news of the peace, we may yet save them."

"I will try. But the coalition . . ." She turned away from the transmitter. "Vang will claim a victory."

"It is the worst possible catastrophe," Drill said.

Gram's tone was grave. "I believe you," she said.

●

Drill listened to the broadcasts with growing anxiety. The Shars who spoke on the broadcasts were making angry comments about the execution of prisoners, about flower gardens and values Drill didn't understand. Someone had let the secret loose. President Gram went from group to group outside Ship, talking of the necessity of her plan. The Shars' responses were muted. Drill sensed they were waiting. It was announced that Vang had left the coalition. A chorus of triumphant yips rose from scattered members of the crowd. Others only moaned.

Vang, now simply General Vang, arrived at the field. His followers danced intoxicated circles around him as he spoke, howling their responses to his words. "Triumph! United will!" they cried. "The humans can be beaten! Treachery avenged! Dictate the peace from a position of strength! We smell the location of their planets!"

The Shars' weird cackling laughter followed him from point to point. The laughing and crying went on well into the night. In the morning the announcement came that the coalition had fallen. Vang was now President-General.

In his sleeping chamber, surrounded by his video walls, Drill began to weep.

⬤

"I have been asked to bear Vang's message to you," Gram said. She seemed smaller than before, standing unsteadily even on her tripod legs. "It is his . . . humor."

"What is the message?" Drill said. His whole body seemed in pain. Even Lowbrain was silent, wrapped in misery.

"I had hoped," Gram said, "that he was using this simply as an issue on which to gain power. That once he had the Presidency, he would continue the diplomatic effort. It appears he really means what he's been saying. Perhaps he's no longer in control of his own people."

"It is war," Drill said.

"Yes."

You have failed, said Memory. Drill winced in pain.

"You will lose," he said.

"Vang says we are cleverer than you are."

"That may be the case. But cleverness cannot compete with experience. Humans have fought hundreds of these little wars, and never failed to wipe out the enemy. Our Memories of these conflicts are intact. Your people can't fight millions of years of specialized evolution."

"Vang's message doesn't end there. You have till nightfall to remove your Ship from the planet. Six days to get out of real space."

"I am to be allowed to live?" Drill was surprised.

"Yes. It is our . . . our custom."

Drill scratched himself. "I regret our efforts did not succeed."

"No more than I." She was silent for a while. "Is there any way we can stop this?"

"If Vang attacks any human planets after the Memories of the peace arrangement have arrived," Drill said, "the military will be unleashed to wipe you out. There is no stopping them after that point."

"How long," she asked, "do you think we have?"

"A few years. Ten at the most."

"Our species will be dead."

"Yes. Our military are very good at their jobs."

"You will have killed us," Gram said, "destroyed the culture that we have built for thousands of years, and you won't even give it any thought. Your species doesn't think about what it does any more. It just acts, like a single-celled animal, engulfing everything it can reach. You say that you are a conscious species, but that isn't true. Your every action is . . . instinct. Or reflex."

"I don't understand," said Drill.

Gram's body trembled. "That is the tragedy of it," she said.

⬤

An hour later Ship rose from the field. Shars laughed their defiance from below, dancing in crazed abandon.

I have failed, Drill told Memory.

You knew the odds were long, Memory said. *You knew that in negotiations with species this backward there have only been a handful of successes, and hundreds of failures.*

Yes, Drill acknowledged. *It's a shame, though. To have spent all these months away from home.*

Eat! Eat! said Lowbrain.

⬤

Far away, in their forty-mile-long Ships, the human soldiers were already on their way.

The Death Artist

ALEXANDER JABLOKOV

With only a handful of elegant, coolly pyrotechnic stories such as "At the Cross-Time Jaunters' Ball," "A Deeper Sea," "Living Will," "Summer and Ice," and "The Last Castle of Christmas" and a few well-received novels, Alexander Jablokov has established himself as one of the most highly regarded writers in Science Fiction. He is a frequent contributor to Asimov's Science Fiction, *the* Magazine of Fantasy & Science Fiction, *and other markets and occasionally places stories with other magazines, such as* SF Age, Amazing, *and* Interzone. *His first novel,* Carve the Sky, *was released in 1991 to wide critical acclaim and was followed by other successful novels such as* A Deeper Sea, Nimbus, *and* River of Dust. *His short fiction has been assembled in the landmark collection* The Breath of Suspension. *His most recent novel is the Wide-Screen Space Opera* Deepdrive. *He lives in Cambridge, Massachusetts.*

Here he takes us deep into a very strange far future, for an intricate and evocative pavane of identity and revenge, art and obsession . . . and murder.

The snowshoe hare's half-eaten carcass lay under the deadfall of the figure-four trap, frozen blood crystallized on its fur, mouth still closed around the tiny piece of desiccated carrot that had served as bait. The snow was flattened around it, the rabbit's fur thrown everywhere. Jack London sniffed at the trap, laid its ears back, and growled. Canine bona fides reaffirmed, it settled on its haunches and looked expectantly up at the man. Part Samoyed, part husky, Jack's thick white fur concealed a body thin from hunger.

Elam didn't have to sniff. The stink of wolverine was malevolent in the still air. It turned the saliva that had come into his mouth at the thought of roasted hare into something spoiled. He spat. "Damn!" The trap couldn't be descented. He'd have to make another. No animal would come anywhere near a trap that smelled like that. The wolverine probably hadn't even been hungry.

He pulled the dry carrot from the rabbit's mouth and flung the remains off among the trees. The deadfall and the sticks of the figure four followed it, vanishing in puffs of snow.

"That's the last one, Jack," Elam said. "Nothing, again." The dog whined.

They set off among the dark smooth trunks of the maples and beeches, Elam's snowshoes squeaking in the freshly fallen snow. The dog turned its head, disturbed by the unprofessional noise, then loped off to investigate the upturned roots of a fallen tree. A breeze from the great lake to the north pushed its way through the trees, shouldering clumps of snow from the branches as it passed. A cardinal flashed from bough to bough, bright against the clearing evening sky.

Elam, a slender, graceful man, walked with his narrow shoulders hunched up, annoyed by the chilly bombardment from above. His clothing was entirely of furry animal pelts sewn crudely together. His thick hat was muskrat, his jacket fox and beaver, his mittens rabbit, his pants elk. At night he slept in a sack made of a grizzly's hide. How had he come to be here? Had he killed those animals, skinned them, cured their hides? He didn't know.

At night, sometimes, before he went to sleep, Elam would lie in his lean-to and, by the light of the dying fire, examine these clothes, running his hands through the fur, seeking memories in their thick softness. The various pelts were stitched neatly together. Had he done the sewing? Or had a wife or a sister? The thought gave him a curious feeling in the pit of his stomach. He rather suspected that he had always been alone. Weariness would claim him quickly, and he would huddle down in the warmth of the bear fur and fall asleep, questions unanswered.

Tree roots examined, Jack London returned to lead the way up the ridge. It was a daily ritual, practiced just at sunset, and the dog knew it well. The tumbled glacial rocks were now hidden under snow, making the footing uncertain. Elam carried his snowshoes under one arm as he climbed.

The height of the ridge topped the bare trees. To the north, glowing a deceptively warm red, was the snow-covered expanse of the great lake, where Elam often saw the dark forms of wolves, running and reveling in their temporary triumph over the water that barred their passage to the islands the rest of the year.

Elam had no idea what body of water it was. He had tentatively decided on Lake Superior, though it could have been Lake Winnipeg, or for that matter, Lake Baikal. Elam sat down on a rock and stared at the deep north, where stars already gleamed in the sky. Perhaps he had it all wrong, and a new Ice Age was here, and this was a frozen Victoria Nyanza.

"Who am I, Jack? Do you know?"

The dog regarded him quizzically, used to the question by now. The man who's supposed to get us some food, the look said. Philosophical discussions later.

"Did I come here myself, Jack, or was I put here?"

Weary of the pointless and one-sided catechism, the dog was barking at a jay that had ventured too close. It circled for a moment, squawked, and shot off back into the forest.

The lake wind freshened and grew colder, driving the last clouds from the sky. The exposed skin on Elam's cheeks tightened. "Let's go. Jack." He pulled off a mitten and plunged his hand into a pocket, feeling his last chunk of pemmican, greasy and hard.

Aside from a few pathetically withered bits of carrot, which he needed to bait his traps, this was the last bit of food left him. He'd been saving it for an emergency. Every trap on the trapline that ran through these woods had been empty or befouled by wolverines, even in a hard winter that should have driven animals to eat anything. He would eat the pemmican that night.

Man and dog started their descent down the twilit reach of the ridge's other side. As they reached the base, Elam, his hand once again feeling the pemmican, afraid that it too would vanish before he could eat it, took too long a step and felt his right foot slide on the icy face of a tilted rock. His left foot caught in the narrow crack of an ice-shattered boulder, which grabbed him like a tight fist. The world flung itself forward at him. He felt the dull snap in his leg as the icy rock met his face.

He awoke to the warm licks of Jack London's tongue turning instantly cold on his face. He lay tumbled on his back among the rocks, head tilting downward, trees looming overhead. Annoyed, he pushed back and tried to stand. Searing agony in his leg brought bile to the back of his throat and a hot sweat over his body. He moaned and almost lost consciousness again, then held himself up on his elbows. His face was cut, some of his teeth were cracked, he could taste the blood in his mouth, but his leg, his leg . . . he looked down.

His left leg bent at an unnatural angle just below the knee. The leather of his trousers was soaked black with blood. Compound fracture of the . . . tibia? Fibula? For one distracted instant naming the shattered bone was the most important thing in the world. It obscured the knowledge that he was going to die.

He shifted position and moaned again. The biting pain in his leg grew sharp burning teeth whenever he moved, but wore the edges off if he lay still, subsiding to a gnaw. With a sudden effort, he pulled the leg straight, then fell back, gasping harshly. It made no difference, of course, but seeing the leg at that angle made him uncomfortable. It looked better this way, not nearly so painful.

He patted the dog on the head. "Sorry, Jack. I screwed up." The dog whined in agreement. Elam fell back and let the darkness take him.

His body did not give up so easily. He regained consciousness sometime later, the frenzied whining and yelping of his dog sounding in his ears. He lay prone in the snow, his hands dug in ahead of him. His mittens were torn, and he could not feel his hands.

He rolled onto his back and looked over his feet. Full night had come, but the starlight and the moon were enough to see the trail his body had left through the snow. Elam sighed. What a waste of time. The pain in his broken leg was almost gone, as was all other feeling from the thighs down. He spat. The spittle crackled on the snow. Damn cold. And the dog was annoying him with its whining.

"Sure, boy, sure," he said, gasping from the cold weight of death on his chest. "Just a minute, Jack. Just a minute."

He pulled what was left of the fur glove off with his chin and reached the unfeeling claw of his hand into his pocket. It took a dozen tries before it emerged holding the pemmican.

He finally managed to open the front of his jacket and unlace his shirt. Cold air licked in eagerly. He smeared the greasy, hard pemmican over his chest and throat like a healing salve. Its rancid odor bit at his nose, and despite himself, he felt a moment of hunger. He shoved the rest of the piece down deep into his shirt.

"Here, Jack," he said. "Here. Dinner." The moon rode overhead, half in sunlight, the other half covered with glittering lines and spots.

The dog snuffled, suddenly frightened and suspicious. Elam reached up and patted it on the head. Jack London moved forward. Smelling the meat, the dog overcame its caution at its master's strange behavior and it began to lick eagerly at Elam's throat and chest. The dog was desperately hungry. In its eagerness, a sharp tooth cut the man's skin, and thick warm blood welled out. The tongue licked more quickly. More cuts. More blood, steaming aromatically in the cold air. And the dog was hungry. The smell penetrated to the deepest parts of its brain, finally destroying the overlay of training, habit, and love. The dog's teeth tore and it began to feed.

And in that instant, Elam remembered. He saw the warm forests of his youth, and the face, so much like his, that had become his own. Justice had at last been done. Elam was going to die. He smiled slightly, gasped once, then his eyes glazed blank.

When it was sated, and realized what it had done, the dog howled its pain at the stars. It then sprang into the forest and ran madly, leaving the man's tattered remains far behind.

●

"Is that all you are going to do from now on?" Reqata said. "Commit suicide? Just lie down and die? Nice touch, I admit, the dog." She held his shoulder in a tight grip and looked past him with her phosphorescent eyes. "A real Elam touch."

Five dark ribs supported the smooth yellow stone of the dome. They revealed the green gleam of beetle carapaces in the light of the flames hanging in a hexagon around the central axis of the view chamber. Rows of striated marble seats climbed the chamber in concentric circles. The inhabitants of these seats stared down at the corpse lying in the snow at their feet.

Elam was himself startled at his clone's acquiescence in its own death, but he was surrounded by admirers before he could answer her. They moved past him, murmuring, gaining haut by their admiration for the subtlety of his work.

Elam stared past them at his own corpse, a sheen of frost already obscuring the face, turning it into an abstract composition. He had died well. He always did. His mind, back from the clone with its memories restored, seemed to rattle loosely around his skull. His skin was slick with amniotic fluid, his joints gritty. Nothing fit together. Reqata's hand on his shoulder seemed to bend the arbitrarily shaped bones, reminding him of his accidental quality.

"An artist who works with himself as both raw materials and subject can never transcend either," Reqata said.

Her scorn cut through the admiration around him. He looked up at her, and she smiled back with ebony teeth, flicking feathery eyelashes.

She raised one hand in an angular gesture that identified her instantly, whatever body she was in.

"And how does the choreographer of mass death transcend her material?" Elam's mind had been gone for weeks, dying in a frozen forest, and Reqata had grown bored in his absence. She needed entertainment. Even lovers constantly dueled with haut, the indefinable quality that all players at the Floating Game understood implicitly. Reqata had much haut. Elam had more.

He squirmed. Was his bladder full, or did he always feel this way?

"Mass death, as you put it, is limited by practical problems," Reqata answered. "Killing one man is an existential act. Killing a million would be a historic act, at least to the Bound. Killing them all would be a divine act." She ran her fingers through his hair. He smelled the winy crispness of her breath. "Killing yourself merely smacks of lack of initiative. I'm disappointed in you, Elam. You used to fight before you died."

"I did, didn't I?" He remembered the desperate struggles of his early works, the ones that had gained him his haut. Men dying in mine shafts, on cliffsides, in predator-infested jungles. Men who had never stopped fighting. Each of those men had been himself. Something had changed.

"Tell me something," Reqata said, leaning forward. Her tongue darted across his earlobe. "Why do you always look so peaceful just before you die?"

A chill spread up his spine. He'd wondered the same thing himself. "Do I?" He squeezed the words out. He always paid. Five or ten minutes of memory, the final instants of life. The last thing he remembered from this particular work was pulling the pemmican from his pocket. After that, blackness. The dying clone Elam understood something the resurrected real Elam did not.

"Certainly. Don't be coy. Look at the grin on that corpse's frozen face." She slid into the seat next to him, draping a leg negligently into the aisle. "I've tried dying. Not as art, just as experience. I die screaming. My screams echo for weeks." She shuddered, hands pressed over her ears. Her current body, as usual, had a high rib cage and small firm breasts. Elam found himself staring at them. "But enough." Reqata flicked him with a fingernail, scratching his arm. "Now that you're done, *I* have a project for you to work on—"

"Perhaps each of you just gets a view of what awaits on the other side," a voice drawled.

"Don't lecture me on the absolute inertia of the soul," Reqata said, disconcerted. "No one's giving our clones a free peek at eternity, Lammiela."

"Perhaps not." A long elegant woman, Lammiela always looked the same, to everyone's distress, for she only had one body. She smiled slowly. "Or perhaps heaven is already so filled with the souls of your clones that there won't be any room for you when you finally arrive."

Reqata stood up, fury in the rise of her shoulders. Because of her past irregularities, Lammiela had an ambiguous status, and Reqata hated risking haut in arguing with her. Usually, Reqata couldn't help herself. "Be careful, Lammiela. You don't know anything about it." And perhaps, Elam found himself thinking, perhaps Reqata feared Death indeed.

"Oh, true enough." Lammiela sat. "Ssarna's passing has everyone on edge. I keep forgetting." Her arrival had driven the last of the connoisseurs away, and the three of them sat alone in the viewing chamber.

"You don't forget, Mother," Elam said wearily. "You do it quite on purpose."

"That's unfair, Elam." She examined him. "You look well. Dying agrees with you." She intertwined her long fingers and rested her chin on them. Her face was subtly lined, as if shaded by an engraver. Her eyes were dark blue, the same as Elam's own. "Ssarna, they say, was withered in her adytum, dry as dust. The last time I saw her, which must have been at that party on top of that miserable mountain in the Himalayas, she was a tiny slip of a girl, prepubescent. Long golden . . . *tresses*. That must be the correct word." She shook her head with weary contempt. "Though she disguised herself as young, old age found her in her most private chamber. And after old age had had his way with her, he gave her to Death. They have an arrangement."

"And the first of them is enjoying you now," Reqata said. "How soon before the exchange comes?"

Lammiela's head jerked, but she did not turn. "How have you been, Elam?" She smiled at him, and he was suddenly surrounded by the smell of her perfume, as if it were a trained animal she wore around her neck and had ordered to attack. The smell was dark and spicy. It reminded him of the smell of carrion, of something dead in the hot sun, thick and insistent. He found himself holding his breath, and stood up quickly, suddenly nauseated. Nauseated, yet somehow excited. A child's feeling, the attraction of the vile, the need to touch and smell that which disgusts. Children will put anything in their mouths. He felt as if maggots were crawling under his fingernails.

"Air," Elam muttered. "I need. . . ." He walked up the striated marble stairs to the balcony above. Locked in their own conflict, the women did not follow. The warm summer air outside smelled of herbs and the dry flowers of chaparral. He clamped his teeth together and convinced himself that the flowers did not mask the smell of rotting flesh.

Sunset turned the day lavender. The view chamber's balcony hung high above the city, which flowed purposefully up the narrow valleys, leaving the dry hills bare, covered with flowers, acacia trees, and the spiky crystal plants that had evolved under some distant sun. The Mediterranean glinted far below.

Lights had come on in the city, illuminating its secret doorways. No one lived here. The Incarnate had other fashions, and the Bound were afraid of the ancient living cities, preferring to build their own. A Bound city could be seen burning closer to the water, its towers asserting themselves against the darkening sky. Tonight, many of the Incarnate who had witnessed Elam's performance would descend upon it for the evanescent excitements of those who lived out their lives bound to one body.

So this place was silent, save for the low resonance of bells, marking the hours for its absent dwellers. The city had been deserted for thousands of years, but was ready for someone to return. The insectlike shapes of aircars fluttered up against the stars as Elam's audience went their separate ways.

A coppery half-moon hung on the horizon, the invisible half of its face etched with colored lines and spots of flickering light. When he was young, Lammiela had told him that the moon was inhabited by huge machines from some previous cycle of existence. The whole circle of a new moon crawled with light, an accepted feature. No one wondered at the thoughts of those intelligent machines, who looked up at the ripe blue-green planet that hung in their black sky.

"You should lie down," Lammiela said, "and rest." Her perfume was cloying and spicy. Though it did not smell even remotely of carrion, Elam still backed away, pushing himself against the railing, and let the evening breeze carry the scent from him. Starlings swooped around the tower.

"You should get up," Reqata said, from somewhere behind her, "and run."

A blast of freezing air made him shiver. He took a step and looked down at the now hoarfrost-covered corpse in the deserted rotunda.

No Incarnate alive knew how the ancient machines worked. The corpse: was it just an image of the one in the frozen Michigan forest? Or had the rotunda's interior moved its spectators to hover over that forest in fact? Or was this body a perfect duplicate, here in the hills of Provence, of that other one? The knowledge was lost. No one knew what lay within the sphere of image. But Elam did know one thing: the cold winds of winter did not blow out of it.

◆

Elam spotted the zeppelins about two and a half hours out of Kalgoorlie. Their colors were gaudy against the green fields and the blue Nullarbor Sea. Frost glittered on the sides away from the morning sun. Elam felt a physical joy, for the zeppelins had been caught completely by surprise. They drifted in the heavy morning air, big fat targets.

They were shuttling troops from somewhere to the North, in central Australia, to participate in one of those incomprehensible wars the Bound indulged in. Reqata had involved herself, in her capricious way, and staked haut on the outcome of the invasion of Eyre, the southern state.

Elam could see the crewmen leaping into their tiny flyers, their wings straightening in the sun like butterflies emerging from their chrysalis, but it was too late. Their zeppelins were doomed.

Elam picked his target, communicating his choice to the other bumblebees, a few Incarnate who, amused at his constant struggle with Reqata, had joined him for the fun. The microwave signal felt like a directed whisper, save for the fact that it made his earlobes itch. He aimed for a bright green deltoid with markings that made it look like a giant spotted frog. For an instant the image took a hold of his mind, and he imagined catching a frog, grabbing it, and feeling its frightened wetness in his hand, the frantic beating of its heart. . . .

He pushed the thought away, upset at his loss of control. Timing was critical. A change in the angle of his wing stroke brought him back into position.

Elam was gorgeous. About a meter long, he had short iridescent wings. A single long-distance optic tracked the target while two bulbous 270-degree peripherals checked the mathematical line of bumblebees to either side of him. Reqata was undoubtedly aboard one of the zeppelins, raging at the unexpected attack. The defending flyers were wide-faced black men, some odd purebred strain. Elam imagined the black Reqata, gesturing sharply as she arranged a defense. It was the quality of her movement that made her beautiful.

A steel ball whizzed past his left wing. A moment later he heard the faint *tock!* of the zeppelin's catapult. It took only one hit to turn a bumblebee into a stack of expensive kindling. Elam tucked one wing, tumbled, and straightened out again, coming in at his target. He unhooked his fighting legs and brought their razor edges forward.

The zeppelins were billowing, changing shape. Sudden flares disturbed Elam's infrared sensors, making him dizzy, unsure of his target. Flying the bumblebees all the way out of Kalgoorlie without any lighter-than-air support craft had been a risk. They had to knock the zeppelins to the ground and parasitize them for reactive metals. The bumblebees would be vulnerable to a ground attack as they crawled clumsily over the wreckage, but no one gained haut without taking chances. He dodged past the defending flyers, not bothering to cut them. That would only delay him.

The green frog was now below him, swelling, rippling, dropping altitude desperately. He held it in his hand where he had caught it, amid the thick rushes. The other kids were gone, somewhere, and he was alone. The frog kicked and struggled. It had voided its bowels in his hand, and he felt the wet slime. The air was hot and thick underneath the cottonwoods. Something about the frog's frantic struggle for life annoyed him. It seemed odious that something so wet and slimy would wish to remain alive. He laid the frog down on a flat rock and, with calm deliberation, brought another rock down on its head. Its legs kicked and kicked.

The other zeppelins seemed to have vanished. All that remained was the frog, its guts lying out in the hot sun, putrefying as he watched. Fluids dripped down the rock, staining it. He wanted to slash it apart with fire, to feel the flare as it gave up its life. The sun seared down on his shoulders.

With a sudden fury, the zeppelin turned on him. He found himself staring into its looming mouth. A hail of steel balls flew past him, and he maneuvered desperately to avoid them. He didn't understand why he had come so close without attacking.

Two balls ripped simultaneously through his right wing, sending flaring pain through the joints. He twisted down, hauling in on the almost nonfunctional muscles. If he pulled the wing in to a stable tip, he could glide downward. Green fields spiraled up at him, black houses with high-peaked roofs, colorful gardens. Pale faces peered up at him from the fields.

Military vehicles had pulled up on a sandy road, the dark muzzles of their guns tracking him.

The right wing was flopping loose, sending waves of pain through his body. He veered wildly, land and sky switching position. Pulling up desperately, he angled his cutting leg and sliced off the loose part of his wing. Hot pain slashed through him.

He had finally managed to stabilize his descent, but it was too late. A field of corn floated up to meet him. For an instant, everything was agony.

◆

"I want something primitive," Elam said, as the doctor slid a testing limb into the base of his spine. "Something prehistoric."

"All of the human past is prehistoric," Dr. Abias said. He withdrew the limb with a cold tickle, and retracted it into his body. "Your body is healthy."

Elam stood up, swinging his arms, getting used to his new proportions. His current body was lithe, gold-skinned, small-handed: designed to Reqata's specifications. She had some need of him in this form, and Elam found himself apprehensive. He had no idea if she was still angry about her defeat over Australia. "No, Abias. I mean before *any* history. Before man knew himself to be man."

"Neanderthal?" Abias murmured, hunching across the floor on his many legs. "Pithecanthropus? Australopithecus?"

"I don't know what any of those words mean," Elam said. Sometimes his servant's knowledge bothered him. What right did the Bound have to know so much when the Incarnate could dispose of their destinies so thoroughly?

Abias turned to look back at him with his multiple oculars, brown human eyes with no face, pupils dilated. He was a machine, articulated and segmented, gleaming as if anointed with rare oils. Each of his eight moving limbs was both an arm and a leg, as if his body had been designed to work in orbit. Perhaps it had. As he had pointed out, most of the past was prehistory.

"It doesn't matter," Abias said. "I will look into it."

A Bound, Abias had been assigned to Elam by Lammiela. Punished savagely for a crime against the Incarnate, his body had been confiscated and replaced by some ancient device. Abias now ran Elam's team of cloned bodies. He was considered one of the best trainers in the Floating Game. He was so good and his loyalty so absolute that Elam had steadfastly refused to discover what crime he had committed, fearing that the knowledge would interfere in their professional relationship.

"Do that," Elam said. "I have a new project in mind." He walked across the wide, open room, feeling the sliding of unfamiliar joints. This body, a clone of his own, had been extensively modified by Abias, until there were only traces of his own nature in it. A plinth was laid with earrings, wrist and ankle bracelets, body paints, scent bottles, all supplied by Reqata. He began to put them on.

Light shone from overhead through semicircular openings in the vault.

A rough-surfaced ovoid curved up through the floor in the room's center. It was Elam's adytum, the most secret chamber where his birth body lay. After his crash in Australia, he had woken up in it for an instant, with a feeling of agony, as if every part of his body were burning. The thought still made him shudder.

An Incarnate's adytum was his most strongly guarded space, for when his real body died, he died as well. There could be no transfer of consciousness to a cloned body once the original was dead. The ancient insolent machines that provided the ability to transfer the mind did not permit it, and since no one understood the machines, no one could do anything about it. And killing an Incarnate's birth body was the only way to truly commit murder.

Elam slid on a bracelet. "Do you know who attacked me?"

"No one has claimed responsibility," Abias answered. "Did you recognize anything of the movement?"

Elam thought about the billowing froglike zeppelin. It hadn't been Reqata, he was sure of that. She would have made certain that he knew. But it could have been almost anyone else.

"Something went wrong in the last transfer," Elam said, embarrassed at bringing up such a private function, even to his servant. "I woke up in my adytum."

Abias stood still, unreadable. "A terrible malfunction. I will look into it."

"Just make sure it doesn't happen again."

☞

The party was in the hills above the city of El'lie. Water from the northern rivers poured here from holes in the rock and swirled through an elaborate maze of waterways. It finally reached one last great pool, which extended terrifyingly off the rocky slope, as if ready to tip and spill, drowning the city below it. The white rock of the pool's edge extended downward some thousands of feet, a polished sheet like the edge of the world. Far below, cataracts spilled from the pool's bottom toward the thirsty city.

Elam stood on a terrace and gazed down into the water. Reqata floated there, glistening as the afternoon sun sank over the ocean to the west. She was a strange creature, huge, all sleekly iridescent curves, blue and green, based on some creature humans had once encountered in their forgotten travels across the galaxy. She sweated color into the water, heavy swirls of bright orange and yellow sinking into the depths. Until a few hours before she had been wearing a slender gold-skinned body like Elam's.

"They seem peaceful," she whispered, her voice echoing across the water. "But the potential for violence is extreme."

Reqata had hauled him on a preliminary tour of El'lie, site of her next artwork. He remembered the fresh bodies hung in tangles of chain on a granite wall, a list of their crimes pasted on their chests; the tense market, men and women with shaved foreheads and jewels in their eyebrows, the air thick with spices; the lazy insolence of a gang of men, their faces tattooed with angry swirls, as they pushed through the market crowd on their way to a proscribed patriarchal religious service; the great tiled temples of the Goddesses that lined the market square.

"When will they explode?" Elam said.

"Not before the fall, when the S'tana winds blow down from the mountains. You'll really see something then." Hydraulic spines erected and sank down on her back, and she made them make a characteristic gesture, sharp and emphatic. If she was angry about what had happened in Australia, she concealed it. That frightened Elam more than open anger would have. Reqata had a habit of delayed reaction.

Reqata was an expert at exploiting obscure hostilities among the Bound, producing dramatically violent conflicts with blood spilling picturesquely down carved staircases; heads piled up in heaps, engraved ivory spheres thrust into their mouths; lines of severed hands on bronze poles, fingers pointing toward Heaven. That was her art. She had wanted advice. Elam had not been helpful.

Glowing lights floated above the pool, swirling in response to incomprehensible tropisms. No one knew how to control them anymore, and they moved by their own rules. A group of partyers stood on the far side of the pool, their bright-lit reflections stretching out across the glassy water.

"This water's thousands of feet deep," Reqata murmured. "The bottom's piled up with forgotten things. Boats. Gold cups. The people from the city come up here and drop things in for luck."

"Why should dropping things and forgetting about them be lucky?" Elam asked.

"I don't know. It's not always lucky to remember everything."

Elam stripped off his gown and dove into the dark water. Reqata made a bubbling sound of delight. He stroked the spines on her back, feeling them swell and deflate. He ran a cupped hand up her side. Her glowing solar sweat worked its way between his fingers and dripped down, desperate to reach its natural place somewhere in the invisible depths.

"Put on a body like this," she said. "We can swim the deep oceans and make love there, among the fish."

"Yes," he said, not meaning it. "We can."

"Elam," she said. "What happened on the balcony after we saw you die in the forest? You seemed terrified."

Elam thought, instead, of the frog. Had his memories been real? Or could Reqata have laid a trap for him? "Just a moment of nausea. Nothing."

Reqata was silent for a moment. "She hates you, you know. Lammiela. She utterly hates you."

Her tone was vicious. Here it was, vengeance for the trick he had pulled over the Nullarbor Sea. Her body shuddered, and he was suddenly conscious of how much larger than he she now was. She could squish him against the side of the pool without any difficulty. He would awake in his own chamber, in another body. Killing him was just insulting, not fatal. Perhaps it *had* been her in that frog zeppelin.

He swam slowly away from her. "I don't know what you're talking about."

"Of course you don't. You're an expert at forgetting, at just lying down, dying, and forgetting. She hates you for what you did. For what you did to your sister!" Her voice was triumphant.

Elam felt the same searing pain he had felt when he awoke for one choking instant in his adytum. "I don't know what you're talking about," he said, as he pulled himself out of the water.

"I know! That's just the problem."

"Tell me what you mean." He kept his voice calm.

Something moved heavily in the darkness, and a row of chairs overturned with a clatter. Elam turned away from the pool. His heart pounded. A burst of laughter sounded from across the pool. The party was continuing, but the guests were impossibly far away, like a memory of childhood, unreachable and useless.

A head rose up out of the darkness, a head twice the size of Elam's body. It was a metal egg, dominated by two expressionless eyes. Behind dragged a long multilimbed body, shiny and obscene. Elam screamed in unreasoning and senseless terror.

The creature moved forward, swaying its head from side to side. Acid saliva drooled from beneath its crystal teeth, splashing and fizzing on the marble terrace. It was incomprehensibly ancient, something from the long-forgotten past. It swept its tail around and dragged Elam toward it.

For an instant, Elam was paralyzed, staring at the strange beauty of the dragon's teeth as they moved toward him. Then he struggled against the iron coil of the tail. His body still had traces of oil, and he slid out, stripping skin. He dove between the dragon's legs, bruising his bones on the terrace.

The dragon whipped around quickly, cornering him. With a belch, it sprayed acid over him. It burned down his shoulder, bubbling as it dissolved his skin.

"Damn you!" he shouted, and threw himself at the dragon's head. It didn't pull back quickly enough, and he plunged his fist into its left eye. Its surface resisted, then popped, spraying fluid. The dragon tossed its head, flinging Elam across the ground.

He pulled himself to his feet, feeling the pain of shattered ribs. Blood dribbled down his chin. One of his legs would not support his weight. The massive head lowered down over him, muck pouring out of the destroyed eye. Elam grabbed for the other eye, but he had no strength left. Foul-smelling acid flowed over him, sloughing his flesh off with the sound of frying bacon. He stayed on his feet, trying to push imprecations between his destroyed lips. The last thing he saw was the crystal teeth, lowering toward his head.

◆

Lammiela's house was the abode of infinity. The endless rooms were packed with the junk of a hundred worlds. The information here was irreplaceable, unduplicated anywhere else. No one came to visit, and the artifacts, data cubes, and dioramas rested in silence.

At some time in the past millennia, human beings had explored as far inward as the galactic core and so far outward that the galaxy had hung above them like a captured undersea creature, giving up its light to intergalactic space. They had moved through globular clusters of ancient suns and explored areas of stellar synthesis. They had raised monuments on distant planets. After some centuries of this, they had returned to Earth, built their mysterious cities on a planet that must have been nothing but old legend, and settled down, content to till the aged soil and watch the sun rise and set. And, with magnificent insouciance, they had forgotten everything, leaving their descendants ignorant.

Lammiela sat in the corner watching Elam. Her body, though elegant, was somehow bent, as if she had been cut from an oddly shaped piece of wood by a clever wood-carver utilizing the limitations of his material. That was true enough, Elam reflected, examining the person who was both his parents.

When young, Lammiela had found a ship somewhere on Earth's moon, tended by the secret mechanisms that made their lives there, and gone forth to explore the old spaces. No one had any interest in following her, but somehow her exploits had gained enough attention that she had obtained extraordinary privileges.

"It's curious," she said. "Our friends the Bound have skills that we Incarnate do not even dream of, because the machines our ancestors left us have no interest in them." She looked thoughtful for a moment. "It's surprising, some of the things the Bound can do."

"Like make you both my father and my mother," Elam said.

Her face was shadowed. "Yes. There is that."

Lammiela had been born male, named Laurance. But Laurance had felt himself to be a woman. No problem for one of the Incarnate, who could be anything they wished. Laurance could have slept securely in his adytum and put female bodies on for his entire life. But Laurance did not think that way. He had gone to the Bound, and they had changed him to a woman.

"When the job was finished, I was pregnant," Lammiela said. "Laurance's sperm had fertilized my new ova. I don't know if it was a natural consequence of the rituals they used." Her muscles tightened with the memories. Tendons stood out on the backs of her hands. "They kept me conscious through it all. Pain is their price. They slew the male essence. I saw it, screaming before me. Laurance, burning."

It had cost most of her haut to do it. Dealings with the Bound inevitably involved loss of status.

"I still see him sometimes," she said.

"Who?" Elam asked.

"Your father, Laurance." Her eyes narrowed. "They didn't kill him well enough, you see. They told me they did, but he's still around." Her eyes darted, as if expecting to find Laurance hiding behind a diorama.

Elam felt a chill, a sharp feeling at the back of his neck, as if someone with long, long nails were stroking him there. "But you're him, Lammiela. He's not someone else."

"Do you really know so much about identity, Elam?" She sighed, relaxing. "You're right, of course. Still, was it I who stood in the Colonnade at Hrlad?" She pointed at a hologram of a long line of rock obelisks, the full galaxy rising beyond them. "I'm sure I remember it, not as if I had been there. It was legend, you know. A bedtime story. But Hrlad is real. So is Laurance. You look like him, you know. You have your father's eyes."

She stared at him coldly, and he, for the first time, thought that Reqata might have spoken truly. Perhaps his mother did indeed hate him.

"I made my choice," she said. "I can never go back. The Bound won't let me. I am a woman, and a mother."

Lammiela did not live in the city where most of the Incarnate made their home. She lived on a mountainside, bleak and alone, the rigid curving walls of her house holding off the snow. She moved her dwelling periodically, from seashore to desert to mountain. She had no adytum, with its body, to lug with her. Elam, somehow, remembered deep forest when he was growing up, interspersed with sunny meadows. The vision wasn't clear. Nothing was clear.

After this most recent death, Elam had once again awakened in his adytum. He'd felt the fluid flowing through his lungs, and the darkness pressing down on his open eyes. Fire had burned through his veins, but there was no air to scream with. Then he had awakened again, normally, on a pallet in the light.

"Mother," he said, looking off at a broad-spectrum hologram of Sinus that spilled vicious white light across the corner of the room, too bright to look at directly without filters. "Am I truly your only child?"

Lammiela's face was still. "Most things are secrets for the first part of their existence, and forgotten thereafter. I suppose there must be a time in the middle when they are known. Who told you?"

"Does it matter?"

"Yes. It was thrown at you as a weapon, wasn't it?"

Elam sighed. "Yes. Reqata."

"Ah, yes. I should have guessed. Dear Reqata. Does she love you, Elam?"

The question took him aback. "She says she does."

"I'm sure she means it then. I wonder what it is about you that she loves. Is that where the discussion ended then? With the question?"

"Yes. We were interrupted." Elam described the dragon's attack.

"Ah, how convenient. Reqata was always a master of timing. Who was it, do you suppose?" She looked out of the circular window at the mountain tundra, the land falling away to a vast ice field, just the rocky peaks of mountains thrusting through it. "No one gains haut anonymously."

"No one recognized the style. Or if they did, they did not admit it." The scene was wrong, Elam thought. It should have been trees: smooth-trunked beeches, heavy oaks. The sun had slanted through them as if the leaves themselves generated the light.

"So why are you here, Elam? Are you looking for the tank in which that creature was grown? You may search for it if you like. Go ahead."

"No!" Elam said. "I want to find my sister." And he turned away and ran through the rooms of the house, past the endless vistas of stars that the rest of the human race had comfortably forgotten. Lammiela silently followed, effortlessly sliding through the complex displays, as Elam stumbled, now falling into an image of a kilometer-high cliff carved with human figures, now into a display of ceremonial masks with lolling tongues. He suddenly remembered running through these rooms, their spaces much larger then, pursued by a small violent figure that left no place to hide.

In a domed room he stopped at a wall covered with racks of dark metal drawers. He pushed a spot and one slid open. Inside was a small animal, no bigger than a cat, dried as if left out in the sun. It was recognizably the dragon, curled around itself, its crystalline teeth just visible through its pulled-back lips.

Lammiela looked down at it. "You two never got along. You would have thought that you would . . . but I guess that was a foolish assumption. You tormented her with that thing, that . . . monster. It gave her screaming nightmares. Once, you propped it by her bed so that she would see it when she woke up. For three nights after that she didn't sleep." She slid the drawer shut.

"Who was she?" Elam demanded, taking her shoulders. She met his gaze. "It's no longer something that will just be forgotten."

She weakly raised a hand to her forehead, but Elam wasn't fooled. His mother had dealt with dangers that could have killed her a dozen times over. He tightened his grip on her shoulders. "Your sister's name was Orfea. Lovely name, don't you think? I think Laurance picked it out."

Elam could remember no sister. "Was she older or younger?"

"Neither. You were split from one ovum, identical twins. One was given an androgen bath and became you, Elam. The other was female: Orfea. God, how you grew to hate each other! It frightened me. And you were both so talented. I still have some of her essence around, I think."

"I . . . what happened to her? Where is she?"

"That was the one thing that consoled me, all these years. The fact that you didn't remember. I think that was what allowed you to survive."

"What? Tell me!"

Lammiela took only one step back, but it seemed that she receded much farther. "She was murdered. She was just a young girl. So young."

Elam looked at her, afraid of the answer. He didn't remember what had happened, and he could still see hatred in his mother's eyes. "Did they ever find out who did it?" he asked softly.

She seemed surprised by the question. "Oh, there was never any doubt. She was killed by a young friend of yours. He is now your servant. Abias."

☙

"I have to say that it was in extremely poor taste," Reqata said, not for the first time. "Death is a fine performance, but there's no reason to perform it at a dinner party. Particularly in my presence."

She got up from the bed and stretched. This torso was wide, and well-muscled. Once again, the rib cage was high, the breasts small. Elam wondered if, in the secrecy of her adytum, Reqata was male. He had never seen her in any other than a female body.

"Just out of curiosity," Elam said. "Could you tell who the dragon was?" He ran his hand over the welts on his side, marks of Reqata's fierce love.

She glanced back at him, eyelids half lowered over wide violet eyes. She gauged if her answer would affect her haut. "Now *that* was a good trick, Elam. If I hadn't been looking right at you, I would have guessed that it was you behind those glass fangs."

She walked emphatically across the room, the slap of her bare feet echoing from the walls, and stood, challengingly, on the curve of Elam's adytum. Dawn had not yet come, and light was provided by hanging globes of a blue tint that Elam found unpleasant. He had never discovered a way to adjust or replace them.

"Oh, Elam," she said. "If you are working on something, I approve. How you fought! You didn't want to die. You kept struggling until there was nothing left of you but bones. That dragon crunched them like candy canes." She shuddered, her face flushed. "It was wonderful."

Elam stretched and rolled out of the bed. As his weight left it, it rose off the floor, to vanish into the darkness overhead. The huge room had no other furniture.

"What do you know about my sister?" he asked.

Reqata lounged back on the adytum, curling her legs. "I know she existed, I know she's dead. More than you did, apparently." She ran her hands up her sides, cupping her breasts. "You know, the first stories I heard of you don't match you. You were more like me then. Death was your art, certainly, but it wasn't your own death."

"As you say," Elam said, stalking toward her, "I don't remember."

"How could you have forgotten?" She rested her hands on the rough stone of the adytum. "This is where you are, Elam. If I ripped this open, I could kill you. Really kill you. Dead."

"Want to try it?" He leaned over her. She rested back, lips parted, and dug her fingernails in a circle around his nipple.

"It could be exciting. Then I could see who you really were."

He felt the sweet bite of her nails through his skin. If he had only one body, he reflected, perhaps he could never have made love to Reqata. He couldn't have lasted.

He pushed himself forward onto her, and they made love on his adytum, above his real body as it slumbered.

➤

Abias's kingdom was brightly lit, to Elam's surprise. He had expected a mysterious darkness. Hallways stretched in all directions, leading to chambers of silent machines and tanks filled with organs and bodies. As he stepped off the stairs, Elam realized that he had never before been down to these lower levels, even though it was as much a part of his house as any other. But this was Abias's domain. This was where the magic was done.

His bumblebee lay on a table, its dead nervous system scooped out.

Dozens of tiny mechanisms crawled over it, straightening its spars, laying fragile wing material between the ribs. Elam pictured them crawling over his own body, straightening out his ribs, coring out his spinal column, resectioning his eyes.

Elam touched a panel, and a prism rose up out of the floor. In it was himself, calmly asleep. Elam always kept several standard, unmodified versions of his own body ready. That was the form in which he usually died. Elam examined the face of his clone. He had never inhabited this one, and it looked strange in consequence. No emotions had ever played over those slack features, no lines of care had ever formed on the forehead or around the eyes. The face was an infant turned physically adult.

The elaborate shape of Abias appeared in a passage and made its way toward him, segmented legs gleaming. Elam felt a moment of fear. He imagined those limbs seizing his mysterious faceless sister, Orfea, rending her, their shine dulled with her blood, sizzling smoke rising . . . he fought the images down. Abias had been a man then, if he'd been anything. He'd lost his body as a consequence of that murder.

Abias regarded him. As a Bound, and a cyborg to boot, Abias had no haut. He had no character to express, needed no gestures to show who he was. His faceless eyes were unreadable. Had he been trying to kill Elam? He had the skills and resources to have created the zeppelin, grown the dragon. But why? If he wanted to kill Elam, the real Elam, the adytum lay in his power. Those powerful limbs could rip the chamber open and drag the sleeping Elam out into the light. Elam's consciousness, in a clone somewhere else, wouldn't know what had happened, but would suddenly cease to exist.

"Is the new body ready?" Elam said abruptly.

Abias moved quietly away. After a moment's hesitation, Elam followed, deeper into the lower levels. They passed a prism where a baby with golden skin slept, growing toward the day that Elam could inhabit it, and witness Reqata's El'lie artwork. It would replace the body destroyed by the dragon. Lying on a pallet was a short heavy-boned body with a rounded jaw and beetle brows.

"It was a matter of genetic regression, based on the markers in the cytoplasmic mitochondria," Abias said, almost to himself. "The mitochondrial DNA is the timer, since it comes only from the female ancestor. The nucleic genetic material is completely scrambled. But much of it stretches back far enough. And of course we have stored orang and chimp genes as well. If you back and fill—"

"That's enough, Abias," Elam said impatiently. "It doesn't matter."

"No, of course not. It doesn't matter. But this is your Neanderthal."

Elam looked down at the face that was his own, a few hundred thousand years back into the past. "How long have I known you, Abias?"

"Since we were children," Abias said softly. "Don't you remember?"

"You know I don't remember. How could I have lived with you for so long otherwise? You killed my sister."

"How do you know that?"

"Lammiela told me that you killed Orfea."

"Ah," Abias said. "I didn't kill her, Elam." He paused. "You don't remember her."

"No. As far as I'm concerned, I have always been alone."

"Perhaps you always have been."

Elam considered this. "Are you claiming that Reqata and my mother are lying? That there never was an Orfea?"

Abias lowered all of his limbs until he was solid on the floor. "I think you should be more worried about who is trying to kill you. These attempts are not accidents."

"I know. Perhaps you."

"That's not even worth answering."

"But who would want to go around killing me repeatedly in my clones?"

"From the information we have now," Abias said, "it could be anyone. It could even be Orfea."

"Orfea?" Elam stared at him. "Didn't you just claim she never existed?"

"I did not. I said I didn't kill her. I didn't. Orfea did not die that day." His eyes closed and he was immobile. "Only I did."

➡

It was a land that was familiar, but as Elam stalked it in his new body, he did not know whether it was familiar to him, Elam, or to the Neanderthal he now was. It was covered with a dark forest, broken by clearings, crossed by clear icy streams scattered with rocks. The air was cold and damp, a living air. His body was wrapped in fur. It was not fur from an animal he had killed himself, but something Abias had mysteriously generated, in the same way he had generated the fur Elam had worn when he died in the Michigan winter. For all he knew, it was some bizarre variant of his own scalp hair.

Since this was just an exploratory journey, the creation of below-conscious reflexes, Elam retained his own memories. They sat oddly in his head. This brain perceived things more directly, seeing each beam of sunlight through the forest canopy as a separate entity, with its own characteristics and personality, owning little to the sun from which it ultimately came.

A stream had cut a deep ravine, revealing ruins. The Neanderthal wandered among the walls, which stood knee-deep in the water, and peered thoughtfully to their bricks. He felt as if he were looking at the ruins of the incomprehensibly distant future, not the past at all. He imagined wading mammoths pushing their way through, knocking the walls over in their search for food. At the thought of a mammoth his hands itched to feel the haft of a spear, though he could certainly not kill such a beast by himself. He needed the help of his fellows, and they did not exist. He walked the Earth alone.

Something grunted in a pool that had once been a basement. He sloshed over to it, and gazed down at the frog. It sat on the remains of a windowsill, pulsing its throat. Elam reached down . . . and thought of the dying frog, shuddering its life out in his hand. He tied it down, limbs outspread, and played the hot cutting beam over it. It screamed and begged as the smoke from its guts rose up into the clear sky.

Elam jerked his hand back from the frog, which, startled, dove into the water and swam away. He turned and climbed the other side of the ravine. He was frightened by the savagery of the thought that had possessed him. When he pulled himself over the edge he found himself in an area of open rolling hills, the forest having retreated to the colder northern slopes.

The past seemed closer here, as if he had indeed lived it.

He *had* hated Orfea. The feeling came to him like the memory of a shaman's rituals, fearsome and complex. It seemed that the hate had always been with him. That form, with his shape and gestures, loomed before him.

The memories were fragmentary, more terrifying than reassuring, like sharp pieces of colored glass. He saw the face of a boy he knew to be Abias, dark-eyed, curly-haired, intent. He bent over an injured animal, one of Elam's victims, his eyes shiny with tears. Young, he already possessed a good measure of that ancient knowledge the Bound remembered. In this case the animal was beyond healing. With a calmly dismissive gesture, Abias broke its neck.

The leaves in the forest moved of their own will, whispering to each other of the coming of the breeze, which brushed its cool fingers across the back of Elam's neck.

He remembered Orfea, a slender girl with dark hair, but he never saw her clearly. Her image appeared only in reflections, side images, glimpses of an arm or a strand of hair. And he saw himself, a slender boy with dark hair, twin to Orfea. He watched himself as he tied a cat down to a piece of wood, spreading it out as it yowled. There was a fine downy hair on his back, and he could count the vertebrae as they moved under his smooth young skin. The arm sawed with its knife, and the cat screamed and spat.

The children wandered the forest, investigating what they had found in the roots of a tree. It was some sort of vast lens, mostly under the ground, with only one of its faces coming out into the air. They brushed the twigs and leaves from it and peered in, wondering at its ancient functions. Elam saw Orfea's face reflected in it, solemn eyes examining him, wondering at him. A beam of hot sunlight played on the lens, awakening lights deep within it, vague images of times and places now vanished. Midges darted in the sun, and Orfea's skin produced a smooth and heavy odor, one of the perfumes she mixed for herself: her art, as death was Elam's. Elam looked down at her hand, splayed on the smooth glass, then across at his, already rougher, stronger, with the hints of dark dried blood around the fingernails.

Abias stood above them. He danced on the smooth glass, his callused feet slipping. He laughed every time he almost fell. "Can you see us?" he cried to the lens. "Can you see who we are? Can you see who we will become?" Elam looked up at him in wonder, then down at the boy's tiny distorted reflection as it cavorted among the twisted trees.

The sun was suddenly hot, slicing through the trees like a burning edge. Smoke rose as it sizzled across flesh. Elam howled with pain and ran up the slope. He ran until his lungs were dying within him.

The Neanderthal stopped in a clearing up the side of a mountain. A herd of clouds moved slowly across the sky, cropping the blue grass of the overhead. Around him rocks, the old bones of the Earth, came up through it sagging flesh. The trees whispered derisively below him. They talked of death and blood. "You should have died," they said. "The other should have lived." The Neanderthal turned his tear-filled eyes into the wind, though whether he wept for Orfea, or for Elam, even he could not have said.

⬤

The city burned with a dry thunder. Elam and Reqata ran through the crowded screaming streets with the arsonists, silent and pure men. In the shifting firelight, their tattoed faces swirled and re-formed, as if made of smoke themselves.

"The situation has been balanced for years," Reqata said. "Peace conceals strong forces pushing against each other. Change their alignment, and. . . ." Swords flashed in the firelight, a meaningless battle between looters and some sort of civil guard. Ahead were the tiled temples of the Goddesses, their goal.

"They feel things we don't," she said. "Religious exaltation. The suicidal depression of failed honor. Fierce loyalty to a leader. Hysterical terror at signs and portents."

Women screamed from the upper windows of a burning building, holding their children out in vain hope of salvation.

"Do you envy them?" Elam asked.

"Yes!" she cried. "To them, life is not a game." Her hand was tight on his arm. "They know who they are."

"And we don't?"

"Take me!" Reqata said fiercely. Her fingernails stabbed through his thin shirt. They had made love in countless incarnations, and these golden-skinned slender bodies were just another to her, even with the flames rising around them.

He took her down on the stone street as the city burned on all sides. Her scent pooled dark. It was the smell of death and decay. He looked at her. Beneath him, eyes burning with malignant rage, was Orfea.

"You are alive," Elam cried.

Her face glowered at him. "No, you bastard," she said. "I'm not alive. You are. You *are*."

His rage suddenly matched hers. He grabbed her hair and pulled her across the rough stone. "Yes. And I'm going to stay that way. Understand? Understand?" With each question, he slammed her head on the stone.

Her face was amused. "Really, Elam. I'm dead, remember? Dead and gone. What's the use of slamming me around?"

"You were always like that. Always sensible. Always driving me crazy!" He stopped, his hands around her throat. He looked down at her. "Why did we hate each other so much?"

"Because there was really only ever one of us. It was Lammiela who thought there were two."

Pain sliced across his cheek. Reqata slapped him again, making sure her nails bit in. Blood poured down her face and her hair was tangled. Elam stumbled back, and was shoved aside by a mob of running soldiers.

"Are you crazy?" she shouted. "You can't kill me. You can't. You'll ruin everything." She was hunched, he saw now, cradling her side. She reached down and unsheathed her sword. "Are you trying to go back to your old style? Try it somewhere else. This is *my* show."

"Wait," he said.

"Damn you, we'll discuss this later. In another life." The sword darted at him.

"Reqata!" He danced back, but the edge caught him across the back of his hand. "What are you—"

There were tears in her eyes as she attacked him. "I see her, you know. Don't think that I don't. I see her at night, when you are asleep. Your face is different. It's the face of a woman, Elam. A woman! Did you know that? Orfea lives on in you somewhere."

Her sword did not allow him to stop and think. She caught him again, cutting his ear. Blood soaked his shoulder. "Your perfume. Who sent it to you?"

"Don't be an idiot. Something in you is Orfea, Elam. That's the only part I really love."

He tripped over a fallen body. He rolled and tried to get to his feet. He found himself facing the point of her sword, still on his knees.

"Please, Reqata," he said, tears streaming down his cheeks. "I don't want to die."

"Well, isn't that the cutest thing." Her blade pushed into his chest, cold as ice. "Why don't you figure out who you are first?"

◆

He awoke in his adytum. His eyes generated dots of light to compensate for the complete darkness. His blood vessels burned as if filled with molten metal. He moved, pushing against the viscous fluid. Damp hair swirled around him, thick under his back, curling around his feet. It had gathered around his neck. There was no air to breathe. Elam. Where was Elam? He seemed to be gone at last, leaving only—

Elam awoke, gasping, on a pallet, still feeling the metal of Reqata's sword in his chest. So it had been her. Not satisfied with killing everyone else, she had needed to kill him as well, repeatedly. He, even now, could not understand why. Orfea.

He stood silently in the middle of the room and listened to the beating of his own heart. Only it wasn't his own, of course, not the one he had been born with. It was a heart that Abias had carefully grown in a tank somewhere below, based on information provided by a gene sample from the original Elam. The real Elam still slept peacefully in his adytum. Peacefully . . . he had almost remembered something this time. Things had almost become clear.

He walked down to Abias's bright kingdom. Abias had tools there, surgical devices with sharp, deadly edges. It was his art, wasn't it? And a true artist never depended on an audience to express himself.

He searched through cabinets, tearing them open, littering the floor with sophisticated devices, hearing their delicate mechanisms shatter. He finally found a surgical tool with a vibratory blade that could cut through anything. He carried it upstairs and stared down at the ovoid of the adytum. What was inside of it? If he penetrated, perhaps, at last, he could truly see.

It wasn't the right thing, of course. The right instrument had to burn as it cut, cauterizing flesh. He remembered its bright killing flare. This was but a poor substitute.

Metal arms pinioned him. "Not yet," Abias said softly. "You cannot do that yet."

"What do you mean?" Elam pulled himself from Abias's suddenly unresisting arms and turned to face him. The faceless eyes stared at him.

"I mean that you don't understand anything. You cannot act without finally understanding."

"Tell me, then!" Elam shouted. "Tell me what happened. I have to know. You say you didn't kill Orfea. Who did then? Did I? Did I do it?"

Abias was silent for a long time. "Yes. Your mother has, I think, tried to forgive you. But *you* are the murderer."

●

"You were not supposed to remember." Lammiela sat rigidly in her most private room, her mental adytum. "The Bound told me you would not. That part of you was to vanish. Just as Laurance vanished from me."

"I haven't remembered. You have to help me."

She looked at him. Until today, the hatred in her eyes would have frightened him. Now it comforted him, for he must be near the truth.

"You were a monster as a child, Elam. Evil, I would have said, though I loved you. You were Laurance, returned to punish me for having killed him. . . ."

"I tortured animals," Elam said, hurrying to avoid Lammiela's past and get to his own. "I started with frogs. I moved up to cats, dogs. . . ."

"And people, Elam. You finally moved to people."

"I know," he said, thinking of the dead Orfea, whom he feared he would never remember. "Abias told me."

"Abias is very forgiving," Lammiela said. "You lost him his body, and nearly his life."

"What did I do with him?"

She shook her head. "I don't know, Elam. He has never said. All these years, and he has never said. You hated Orfea, and she hated you, but somehow you were still jealous of each other. She cared for Abias, your friend from the village, and that made you wild. He was so clever about that ancient Bound knowledge the Incarnate never pay attention to. He always tried to undo the evil that you did. He healed animals, putting them back together. Without you, he may never have learned all he did. He was a magician."

"Mother—"

She glared at him. "You strapped him down, Elam. You wanted to . . . to castrate him. Cloning, you called it. You said you could clone him. He might have been able to clone you, I don't know, but you certainly could do nothing but kill him. Orfea tried to stop you, and you fought. You killed her, Elam. You took that hot cutting knife and you cut her apart. It explodes flesh, if set right, you know. There was almost nothing left."

Despite himself, Elam felt a surge of remembered pleasure.

"As you were murdering your sister, Abias freed himself. He struggled and got the tool away from you."

"But he didn't kill me."

"No. I never understood why. Instead, he mutilated you. Carefully, skillfully. He knew a lot about the human body. You were unrecognizable when they found you, all burned up, your genitals destroyed, your face a blank."

"And they punished Abias for Orfea's murder. Why?"

"He insisted that he had done it. I knew he hadn't. I finally made him tell me. The authorities didn't kill him, at my insistence. Instead, they took away his body and made him the machine he now is."

"And you made him serve me," Elam said in wonder. "All these years, you've made him serve me."

She shook her head. "No, Elam. That was his own choice. He took your body, put it in its adytum, and has served you ever since."

Elam felt hollow, spent. "You should have killed me," he whispered. "You should not have let me live."

Lammiela stared at him, her eyes bleak and cold. "I daresay you're right, Elam. You were Laurance before me, the man I can never be again. I wanted to destroy you, totally. Expunge you from existence. But it was Abias's wish that you live, and since he had suffered at your hands, I couldn't gainsay him."

"Why then?" Elam said. "Why do you want to kill me now?" He stretched his hands out toward his mother. "If you want to, do it. Do it!"

"I don't know what you are talking about, Elam. I haven't tried to kill you. I gave up thinking about that a long time ago."

He sagged. "Who then? Reqata?"

"Reqata?" Lammiela smirked. "Go through all this trouble for one death? It's not her style, Elam. You're not that important to her. Orfea was an artist too. Her art was scent. Scents that stick in your mind and call up past times when you smell them again."

"You wore one of them," Elam said, in sudden realization. "The day my death in the north woods ended."

"Yes," she said, her voice suddenly taut again. "Orfea wore that scent on the last day of her life, Elam. You probably remember it."

The scent brought terror with it. Elam remembered that. "Did you find some old vial of it? Whatever made you wear it?"

She looked at him, surprised. "Why, Elam. You sent it to me yourself."

◆

Abias stood before him like a technological idol, the adytum between them.

"I'm sorry, Abias," Elam said.

"Don't be sorry," Abias said. "You gave yourself up to save me."

"Kill me, Abias," he said, not paying attention to what the cyborg had just said. "I understand everything now. I can truly die." He held the vibratory surgical tool above the adytum, ready to cut in, to kill what lay within.

"No, Elam. You don't understand everything, because what I told Lammiela that day was not the truth. I lied, and she believed me." He pushed, and a line appeared across the adytum's ovoid.

"What is the truth then, Abias?" Elam waited, almost uninterested.

"Orfea did not die that day, Elam. You did."

The adytum split slowly open.

"You did try to kill me, Elam," Abias said softly, almost reminiscently. "You strapped me down for your experiment. Orfea tried to stop you. She grabbed the hot cutting knife and fought with you. She killed you."

"I don't understand."

The interior of an adytum was a dark secret. Elam peered inside, for a moment seeing nothing but yards and yards of wet dark hair.

"Don't you understand, Orfea? Don't you know who you are?" Abias's voice was anguished. "You killed Elam, whom you hated, but it was too much for you. You mutilated yourself, horribly. And you told me what you wanted to be. I loved you. I did it."

"I wanted to be Elam," Elam whispered.

The face in the adytum was not his own. Torn and mutilated still, though repaired by Abias's skill, it was the face of Orfea. The breasts of a woman pushed up through the curling hair.

"You wanted to be the brother you had killed. After I did as you said, no one knew the difference. You were Elam. The genes were identical, since you were split from the same ovum. No one questioned what had happened. The Incarnate are squeamish, and leave such vile business to the Bound. And you've been gone ever since. Your hatred for who you thought you were caused you to kill yourself, over and over. Elam was alive again, and knew that Orfea had killed him. Why should he not hate her?"

"No," Elam said. "I don't hate her." He slumped slowly to his knees, looking down at the sleeping face.

"I had to bring her back, you understand that?" Abias's voice was anguished. "If only one of you can live, why should it be Elam? Why should it be him? Orfea's spirit was awakening, slowly, after all these years. I could see it sometimes, in you."

"So you brought it forth," Elam said. "You cloned and created creatures in which her soul could exist. The zeppelin. The dragon."

"Yes."

"And each time, she was stronger. Each time I died, I awoke . . . *she* awoke for a longer time in the adytum."

"Yes!" Abias stood over him, each limb raised glittering above his head. "She will live."

Elam rested his fingers in her wet hair and stroked her cheek. She had slept a long time. Perhaps it was indeed time for him to attempt his final work of art, and die forever. Orfea would walk the Earth again.

"No!" Elam shouted. "*I* will live." Abias loomed over him as the dragon had, ready to steal his life from him. He swung the vibrating blade and sliced off one of Abias's limbs. Another swung down, knocking Elam to the floor. He rolled. Abias raised himself above. Elam stabbed upward with the blade. It penetrated the central cylinder of Abias's body and was pulled from his hands as Abias jerked back. Elam lay defenseless and awaited the ripping death from Abias's manipulator arms.

But Abias stood above him, motionless, his limbs splayed out, his eyes staring. After a long moment, Elam realized that he was never going to move again.

The adytum had shut of its own accord, its gray surface once again featureless. Elam rested his forehead against it. After all these years he had learned the truth, the truth of his past and his own identity.

Abias had made him seem an illegitimate soul, a construct of Orfea's guilt. Perhaps that was indeed all he was. He shivered against the roughness of the adytum. Orfea slumbered within it. With sudden anger, he slapped its surface. She could continue to sleep. She had killed him once. She would not have the chance to do it again.

Elam stood up wearily. He leaned on the elaborate sculpture of the dead Abias, feeling the limbs creak under his weight. What was Elam without him?

Elam was *alive*. He smiled. For the first time in his life, Elam was alive.

Sister Alice

ROBERT REED

Robert Reed sold his first story in 1986 and quickly established himself as a frequent contributor to the Magazine of Fantasy & Science Fiction and Asimov's Science Fiction, as well as selling many stories to Science Fiction Age, Universe, New Destinies, Tomorrow, Synergy, Starlight, and elsewhere.

Reed may be one of the most prolific of today's young writers, particularly at short fiction lengths, seriously rivaled for that position only by authors such as Stephen Baxter and Brian Stableford. And—also like Baxter and Stableford—he manages to keep up a very high standard of quality while being prolific, something that is not at all easy to do. Almost every year throughout the mid-to-late nineties he has produced at least two or three stories that would be good enough to get him into a Best of the Year anthology under ordinary circumstances, and some years he has produced four or five of them, so that often the choice is not whether or not to use a Reed story but rather which Reed story to use—a remarkable accomplishment. Reed stories such as "The Utility Man," "Birth Day," "Blind," "A Place with Shade," "The Toad of Heaven," "Stride," "The Shape of Every-thing," "Guest of Honor," "Decency," "Waging Good," and "Killing the Morrow," among at least a half-dozen others equally as strong, count as among some of the best short works produced by anyone in the eighties and nineties. Nor is he nonprolific as a novelist, having turned out eight novels since the end of the eighties: The Leeshore, The Hormone Jungle, Black Milk, The Remarkables, Down the Bright Way, Beyond the Veil of Stars, An Exaltation of Larks, and, most recently, Beneath the Gated Sky.

In spite of this large and remarkable body of work, though, Reed remains largely ignored and overlooked when the talk turns to the Hot New Writers of the nineties, although he is beginning to get onto major award ballots. (His story "Whiptail" is on the Final Hugo Ballot as I type these words.) Like the works of Walter Jon Williams and Bruce Sterling, no one Robert Reed story is ever much like another Robert Reed story in tone or subject matter, and it may be that this versatility counts against him as far as building a reputation is concerned. John Clute, in The Encyclopedia of Science Fiction, noting that none of Reed's novels "share any background material or assumptions whatsoever," suggests that "to-day's sf readers tend to expect a kind of brand identity from authors, and it may be for this reason that Reed has not yet achieved any considerable fame."

It seems unfair that the range of an artist's palette should count against him—but Reed's name is slowly percolating into the public awareness here at the end of the nineties and I suspect that he will become one of the Big Names of the first decade of the new century coming up on the horizon.

Reed is confident enough in the richness of his imagination to feel comfortable writing stories set in the far future, and much of his output is set in milieux mil-lions of years removed from the time we know. Like some other young writers of the

nineties, including Paul J. McAuley and Stephen Baxter, Reed is producing some
of the most inventive and colorful of modern Space Opera, stuff set on a scale so
grand and played out across such immense vistas of time that it makes the "Superscience" stuff of the thirties look pale and conservative by comparison: his sequence of novellas for Asimov's, for instance, including "Sister Alice," Brother
Perfect," "Mother Death," and "Baby's Fire," detailing internecine warfare and
intricate political intrigues between families of immortals with powers and abilities so immense that they are for all intents and purposes gods, or the sequence of
stories unfolding in F&SF, Science Fiction Age, and Asimov's, including "The
Remoras," "Aeon's Child," "Marrow," and "Chrysalis," involving the journeyings
of an immense spaceship the size of Jupiter, staffed by dozens of exotic alien
races, that is engaged in a multi-million-year circumnavigation of the galaxy.

In the compelling novella that follows, the start of the Sister Alice sequence,
he shows us that the drawback to having godlike powers is that you have godlike
responsibilities as well. . . .

Reed lives in Lincoln, Nebraska, where he's at work on a novel-length version
of his 1997 novella, Marrow. His most recent book is a long-overdue first collection, The Dragons of Springplace.

1

*When I found myself daydreaming about my childhood, remembering the
fun, thinking how carefree it had been . . . that's when my instincts began
to warn me that our work had gone seriously, tragically wrong. . . .*
                                                            Alice's testimony

Xo told their squad that it was a lousy place to build and that their fort
was flawed, that the Blues would crush them and it was Ravleen's fault.
Everything was Ravleen's fault. And of course she heard about his grous-
ing and came over, interrupting their drills to tell Xo to quit it. And he
laughed, saying, "You're no general." Ord heard him. Everyone heard
him, and Ravleen had no choice but to knock him down and kick him.
Xo was a Gold, and she was their Sanchex, the Gold's eternal general.
She had to punish him, aiming for his belly and ribs. But Xo started
cursing her. Bright poisonous words hung in the air. "You're no Sanchex,"
he grunted, "and I'm not scared." Then Ravleen moved to his face, breaking his nose and cheekbones, the skin splitting, blood splattering on the
new snow. Everyone watched. Ord stood nearby, watching the snow melt
into the blood, diluting it. He saw Xo's face become a gooey mess, and
he heard the boy's voice finally fall away into a sloppy wet laugh.

Tule stepped up, saying, "If you keep hurting him, he won't be able
to hurt anyone else."

Ravleen paused, panting from her hard work, and deciding Tule was
right. She dropped her foot and pushed her long black hair out of her
eyes, grinning now, making sure everyone saw her confidence. Then she
knelt, touching the bloody snow while asking, "Who wants to help this
shit home?"

Tule was closest, but she despised Xo. She didn't approve of causing trouble; she felt it was her duty to keep their clan working smoothly, bowing to Ravleen's demands.

On the other hand, Ord was sympathetic. Xo wasn't his best friend, but he was a reliable one. Besides, they were on the same squad for now. A soldier had a duty to his squad; and that's why Ord stepped up, saying, "I'll take him."

"Then come straight back," Ravleen added.

He gave a nod and asked Xo, "Can you stand up?"

The bloody face said, "Maybe." A gloved hand reached for him, and Ord thought of the boy's ribs as he lifted. But the tortured groans were too much; Xo had a tendency toward theater. "Thanks," he muttered, then he reached into his mouth, pulling out a slick white incisor and tossing it at the young fort. It struck one of the robots with a soft *ping*.

"Come on," Ord prompted.

They walked slowly, crossing the long pasture and climbing to the woods. Xo stopped at the first tree, leaning against it and spitting out a glob of dark blood. Ord worked to be patient. Looking back at the pasture, he watched the robots stripping it of snow, building the fort according to Ravleen's design. A metal pole stood in the future courtyard, topped with a limp golden flag. Figures in clean white snowsuits were drilling again, six squads honing themselves for snowfare. It looked like an easy pasture to defend. On three sides it fell away, cliffs and nearly vertical woods protecting it. The only easy approach was from here, from above. Ravleen was assuming that the Blues would do what was easy, which was why the nearest wall had the thickest foundation. "Keep your strong to their strong," was an old Sanchex motto. But what if Xo was right? What if she had left their other walls too weak?

"I can't walk fast," Xo warned him. His swollen face was inhuman, but the bleeding had stopped, scabs forming and the smallest cuts beginning to heal. Speaking with a faint lisp, Xo admitted, "I sound funny."

"You should have left your tooth in," Ord countered. Gums preferred to repair teeth, not replace them. "Or you might have kept your mouth shut in the first place."

Xo gave a little laugh.

Something moved in the distance. Ord squinted and realized it was just an airship, distant sunlight making it glitter; and now he said, "Let's go." He said, "I'm tired of standing still."

They walked on a narrow trail, not fast, snow starting to fall and the woods knee-deep in old snow. They weren't far from the lowlands, and sometimes, particularly on clear days, city sounds would rise up from that hot flat country. But not today. A kind of enforced silence hung in the air. To step and not hear any footfall made Ord nervous, in secret. He realized that he was alert, as if ready to be ambushed. The war wouldn't start until the day after tomorrow, but he was anticipating it. Or maybe it was the fight he had just seen, maybe.

"Know why I did it?" asked Xo.

Ord said nothing.

"Know why I pissed her off?"

"Why?"

The battered face grinned. "I don't have to do this war now."

"Ravleen's not that angry," Ord countered. "Not angry enough to ban you, at least."

"But I'm hurt. Look at me."

"So?" Ord refused to be impressed. Glancing over a shoulder, he observed, "You're walking and talking. That's not badly hurt."

Except Xo's Family, the Nuyens, were careful people. A sister might see him and order him to stay home for several days. It wouldn't be the first time, particularly if he moaned like he did now, telling Ord, "I don't want to play snowfare."

"Why not?"

Wincing, Xo pretended to ache. But by now a cocktail of anesthesias was working, and both of them knew it.

"If you can stand, you can fight," Ord reminded him. "When you became a Gold you pledged to serve—"

"Wait." The boy waded into the deep snow, heading for an outcropping of false granite. He found a block of bright pink stone, brought it back and dropped it at Ord's feet. "Do me a favor?"

"No."

"Not hard. Just nick me here." He touched his stubby black hair. "I'll owe you. Promise."

Ord lifted the stone without conviction.

"Make it ugly," the boy prompted.

Ord shook his head, saying, "First tell me why you don't want to fight. Is it Ravleen?"

"Not really."

"Tell me or I won't help."

The boy touched his dark round face with his white gloves. "Just because it's stupid."

"What's stupid?"

"This game. This whole snowfare business."

Calling it a "game" was taboo. Snowfare was meant to be taken very, very seriously.

"But we're too old to play," his friend persisted. "I know I am."

This wasn't about Ravleen, and Ord had no easy, clear rebuke. He asked, "What will you do instead?" He assumed there was some other diversion. Perhaps a trip somewhere. Not out of the mountains, of course. That wasn't permitted, not at their age. But maybe one of Xo's siblings wanted to take him on a hunt, or some other adventure.

But Xo said, "Nothing. I just want to stay home and study." A pause. "Clip me here, okay? I'll tell my sisters that Ravleen did it. Promise."

Ord watched the boy lay on the hard white trail, face up, waiting calmly for his skull to be cracked open. The stone couldn't hurt him too badly. Eons ago, human beings gave up soft brains for better ones built of tough, nearly immortal substances. The worst Ord could manage was to break up some neural connections, making Xo forgetful and clumsy for a few days. The body might die, but nothing more. Nothing less than a nuclear fire could kill them, and that was the same for almost every human.

"Are you going to help me?" the boy whined.

Ord watched the hopeful face, judging distance and mass, guessing what would make the ugliest wound. But he kept thinking back to the comment about being too old, knowing it was a little true. Some trusted spark of his had slipped away, and that bothered him.

"Ord?"

"Yeah?"

"Will you hurry up?"

He let the stone slip free of his grip, missing Xo by a hair's breadth; then he said, "No, I can't. I shouldn't."

Xo lifted the stone himself, groaning as he aimed, trying to summon the courage. He was invulnerable, but so were old instincts. This wasn't easy. His arms shook, then collapsed. The attempt looked like a half-accident—*thud*—and his head was dented on one side. But not badly enough, they discovered. Xo could stand by himself, only a little dizzy; and he touched his wounds one after another, telling himself, "At least I'll get tomorrow to myself." He wasn't looking at Ord, or anywhere, saying, "This is good enough," with a soft wet voice that was lost in the muting whisper of the snowfall.

2

When I lived here, when I was a child, these mountains were new. The estates were new. Our mansions were modest but comfortable, the Families victorious . . . and the galaxy was vast and nearly empty, full of endless and intoxicating possibilities. . . .

—Alice's testimony

There were exactly one thousand Families—a number set by design—and Ord was a Chamberlain, one of the more famous and powerful Families. The ancestral Chamberlain home stood near the center of their estate, on a broad scenic peak. It was a round building, tall and massive, built from false granite with a shell of tailored white coral. The interior, above ground and below, was a maze of rooms and curling hallways, simple laboratories and assorted social arenas. There were enough beds for fifteen hundred brothers and sisters, should so many ever wish to visit at one time. And there were other buildings scattered about the estate—cottages, hunting lodges, and baby mansions—capable of absorbing the rest of them.

But it was the round white house that was famous, recognized by virtually every educated entity in the galaxy. Chamberlains had helped the Sanchexes win the Great Wars, then they were instrumental in building the Ten Million Year Peace. Chamberlains had made first contact with many important alien species, had been first to reach the galaxy's core, and for eons had pioneered the rapid terraforming of empty worlds. With low, low death rates being common, there was a constant demand for new homes, aliens and humans both paying substantial fees for good work.

Ord had a shallow sense of this history. He knew the Great Wars were fought with savagery, billions of people murdered and the Earth itself left battered. But the Peace had endured for a hundred thousand centuries, the Families giving it backbone and the occasional guidance. Ord himself was a whisper of a child, not even fifty years old. His powers as a Chamberlain lay in the remote future. Imagining adulthood, he pictured a busy semi-godhood, building green worlds at the Core, or perhaps flying off to some far galaxy, exploring it while making new allies. But the actual changes were mysterious to him. His mind and energies would swell, but how would it feel to him? His senses would multiply, and time itself would slow to where seconds would become hours. But how would such an existence seem? He had asked the brothers and sisters living with him. He had worn them down with his inquiries. Yet not one of them had ever offered a clear, believable answer.

"You're too young to understand," they would assure him, their voices bored. Or even a little shrill. "Just wait and see," they would recommend. "You'll learn when you're ready." But Ord could sense that like him, they had no idea what the future held. Like all perfect questions, his were unoriginal. And all of the Chamberlains in the mansion—all younger than a millennium—were in that same proverbial spacecraft, adrift and lost and uniformly scared.

◆

The Golds' fort was completed on schedule, by midafternoon that next day, and after some last work the clan walked up to the tube port together, singing Gold songs. From there it was a brief ride home for Ord. He was deposited at the lawn's edge, his pet bear-dogs charging him, yelping and begging to be scratched behind every ear. Done with that duty, Ord entered through the usual door, touching the motto engraved in the granite overhead. "PRIDE AND SACRIFICE," said the ageless letters; his gesture was a habit, almost a reflex. Then he ran to the nearest stairwell, riding up to his floor and sprinting to his room, greeted there by a pair of mothering robots at least as obnoxious as his bear-dogs. They asked about his day and his accomplishments. Was there enough snow? "Plenty," he allowed; it had fallen all night. Good for forts, was it? "Perfect," he told them, removing his warm snowsuit. "Good wet snow." Close to the lowlands, that pasture had a milder climate than this high country. "And I think it's a very strong fort. I think so . . ."

The robots paused, saying nothing where they might have said, "We're glad to hear it."

Ord hesitated, suddenly alert.

"Lyman has just asked to see you," said synchronized voices.

Lyman was a brother, the oldest one living in the house. *He wants to see me?* Ord wondered what was wrong. If he'd hit Xo with that rock . . . but he hadn't, and nothing else remarkable had happened in the last few days. "What does Lyman want?"

"We're curious too," they replied, glass eyes winking. "You're supposed to go to his room as soon as you're clean and dressed."

Ord looked outside. His longest wall faced east, a crystal window in place of the granite. Somewhere below, in the gathering darkness, was his new fort. On clear nights he liked to watch the glow of the cities beyond, wondering about all the kinds of people living near these mountains. Everyone on Earth was rich to some degree; the land was too crowded and too expensive for those without means. But only the Families could afford having winters, putting their trees and lakes to sleep. These artificial mountains, constructed after the Great Wars, had never produced meaningful food, nor had they ever housed more than a very few people.

"Lyman sounds impatient," the robots warned him.

"Okay." Ord ran through his sonic bath, then dressed and left. His brother lived several stories above him. He had visited enough to know the way, and enough to hesitate at the door. Lyman liked to entertain various girlfriends; caution was required. Ord announced his presence, and the door opened, a distant voice telling him:

"Wait there. I'm almost done."

It was Ord's voice, only deeper. Older. Lyman had one of the large interior rooms, two universal-walls and a vast bed, plus a private swimming pool and sauna. Distinctive touches were meant to say *Lyman* but always felt more *Chamberlain* than anything. Chamberlains liked mementos. Where Ord would have kept his collection of alien fossils, his brother set up small light-statues of the girlfriends—women of every variation, uniformly disrobed—and they smiled at Ord, showing him how pleased they were to stand on those shelves. One universal-wall was activated. The live feed showed him moons orbiting a banded gas giant, each moon encased in an atmosphere, the nearest one blued by an ocean. Did a Chamberlain build that ocean? It wasn't too unlikely. Lyman was training to become an apprentice terraformer. Once he was declared an adult, probably in less than a century, he would leave for his first assignment. Something easy, no doubt. He would rebuild some fat comet between stars, probably for a client who wanted a vacation home—

"How's your war?" asked Lyman, striding out of the bath, adjusting his loose-fitting trousers as he moved. "Done with your fort?"

Ord muttered, "Yes."

"Any more fights?"

Was this about Xo and Ravleen? Or maybe Lyman was just making noise. Either way, Ord guessed that his brother knew the answers, that he had heard from the robots and the estate's sentries. "No fights," Ord reported. "No until tomorrow morning, at least."

"But Lyman wasn't listening. He started to speak, to make some joke, then paused, his mouth left open for a long moment.

Ord waited, tension building.

"Do you know where I was this morning?"

"Where?"

"Antarctica." Lyman liked to tease his little brother, reminding him that one of them could travel at will on the Earth. No farther, but it still seemed like an enormous freedom.

"What were you doing there?" asked Ord.

"Having fun, naturally." Lyman tried to smile, scratching his bare belly. Taller than Ord, he had old-fashioned adult proportions, his body hairy and strong with an appropriate unfancy penis dangling in his trousers. Red hair grew to his shoulders. Like Ord, he had the telltale Chamberlain face, sharp features and pale skin and pale blue eyes. Their sisters were feminized versions of them, with breasts and such; physical forms were standardized, eternal, every Family built around its immortal norm, every norm patterned after its founder and ultimate parent.

Lyman sat next to his brother, sighed and asked, "Do you know why I came home? Have you heard?"

Ord shook his head, his breath quickening. What happened that would require Lyman to abandon his fun?

"Listen."

But then his brother said nothing else, his mouth left open and the eyes gazing at the wall. Finally Ord asked, "What is it?"

"In the next few days . . . soon, I don't know when . . . we'll have a guest with us. Be on your very best behavior, please."

"Who's visiting?"

Lyman seemed disturbed, or at least deeply puzzled, pursing his lips and shaking his head. "One of our sisters is dropping by."

Sisters came and went all of the time.

"An old sister," Lyman added.

Every sister was older than Ord.

And his brother grinned, as if realizing how mysterious this must sound. "A very old, much honored adult. She is."

Ord looked at the wall, watching its image change. A small dull sun was setting over a glassy sea. An ammonia sea, perhaps. He found himself dealing with this news by distancing himself, working on the dynamics of the other world as if it was one of his tutor's lessons.

"You're not listening," Lyman warned him.

"How old is she?"

"Her name is Alice."

Alice—

"She's our Twelve." The words were incredible to both of them. Lyman repeated himself, saying, "Yes. Twelve."

Ord was stunned, closing his hands into fists and dropping them into his lap. "Why is she coming here?"

Lyman didn't seem to hear him. "We received her private message this morning . . . coded . . . and everyone's excited, of course. . . ."

Ord nodded.

"A Twelve is coming here." Lyman was astonished, but the smile seemed almost joyless. "I looked up when the last Fifty or higher came to visit. Our Forty-two touched down for less than an hour, some twenty-eight millennia ago. A little handshake visit." He paused, rubbing at the stiff red hairs on his chest. "Alice wants to linger. She's requested the penthouse and given no departure time. Even though she'll be bored in a millisecond, she claims that she wants to live here."

This was landmark news, and Ord imagined telling the other Golds about it. Tonight? No, tomorrow. On the eve of combat. It would give him a sudden burst of importance, a worthiness. Even Ravleen would be impressed, and jealous, and he began to smile, imagining the moment.

"There's more," Lyman said, anticipating him. "The news is secret. Alice made it very clear—"

Secret?

"—and I'm giving you fair warning. You won't tell anyone. Not even your best friends. This is Chamberlain business, and it's private."

The boy offered a weak, confused nod.

"No other Family can know she's here."

"Why not?"

"Because that's what she wants."

"But why visit us?"

"Why not?" Lyman offered, then his face grew puzzled again. "I honestly don't know why. No one seems to know where she's been. But I'm sure that she'll explain, when it's time."

A Twelve. Ord knew there were just five Chamberlains older than Alice, the rest long dead. And of the five, two weren't even in the galaxy now, bound for Andromeda. By contrast, Ord had a five digit designation, as did Lyman and every other sibling in this house. He could never live long enough and become famous enough that his arrival here would be stunning news. "24,411 is on his way. Behave, children!" Ord nearly laughed at the preposterous image. If he lived a billion years—a possibility, in principle—and if he did wondrous things, then yes, he guessed that then he might generate the kind of excitement that he felt now. Maybe.

"I don't even know where she's been," Lyman repeated. "We've asked, but the walls won't tell us."

The famous Alice. She had been born after the Great Wars, in the first years of the Peace; and she was one of the first Chamberlains to master terraforming; most of her methods standard even today.

"Not a hint to anyone. All right, little brother?"

He said, "Yes," with a soft, disappointed breath.

Lyman made fists and placed them on his lap, saying, "I bet it's nothing important. Here and gone in ten minutes, she'll be."

The wall changed again, showing them a ringed gas giant. World-sized continents built of hyperfoams floated in its atmosphere, linked together, the winds carrying them along with a dancer's precision. Where was this place? Terraforming on that scale required time and much money, and there probably weren't a thousand worlds like it in the galaxy. A mere thousand, which was nothing. And he shut his eyes, knowing Alice had built it. Lyman had asked this wall to show him her work; and like his brother, Ord wondered why she would come here. Why bother? And why would such an enormous, wondrous soul want her presence kept secret? Why . . . ?

3

Consider this. Our Families have never been wealthier, and they have never been so weak. Our fraction of humanity's worth has shriveled throughout the Peace, as planned. We are pledged to reproduce slowly. We clone archaic bodies, then slowly fit them with the latest wonders. But while we've kept a monopoly on those wonders, other peoples and aliens and even the machine intelligences grow more numerous every day, accomplishing more and more with their insect tenacity . . . winning the Peace, in essence, which is of course why they agreed to it in the first place. . . .

—Alice's testimony

Their fort was beautiful, tall and milk-colored, draped with last night's snow. Yesterday, done with drills, everyone but Xo had added some touch of his or her own. Handmade flourishes. On the parapets were snow fists and boat prows and big-eyed skulls. Ord had built a gargoyle on his portion of the wall—a fierce thing with wings extended, curved white teeth glowing in the early light—and he was standing behind it, on the broad rampart, his squad flanking him and everyone at attention. Ravleen was speaking, her voice coming from headphones sewn into their golden facemasks. "From now on," she promised, "these Blues are going to suffer every flavor of misery. We'll beat them once and for all."

It was a famous quote, the "every flavor of misery" line. One of the Sanchex generals had uttered it, and Ravleen repeated it once or twice every year. She and Tule were below, sitting inside the thick-walled keep at the back of the courtyard, watching the countryside with sensors and hidden cameras. Ord knew how much she wanted to win. This war's losers would make medals for the winners—the standard rule—and nobody would treasure her disk of iridium and diamond more than Ravleen. Sanchexes drank in their awards; every certificate of merit was on display, sometimes for centuries. The Ten Million Year Peace had only tempered them, it was said. And when the time came—when they were too mature for these wars—nobody would miss them more than Ravleen. Ord almost felt sorry for her, shutting his eyes . . . and his mind shifting back to the topic that had kept him sleepless all night. . . .

"What are you thinking?" asked Xo, strolling up to him. Save for some yellow bruises, his face had healed. He had showed it to Ord before putting on the mask, proud that he had healed so easily. "You look like you're thinking hard. What about?"

That his sister was coming. *Alice. My Twelve.* The words surfaced in his consciousness, begging to be spoken. Yet he had promised not to tell, not Xo or even his best friends. Maybe that was wise, he thought. Why would Alice come here? And wouldn't he look foolish when it turned out to be untrue?

"I wish we'd start," Xo groused, forgetting his question. "Waiting is boring."

Last night, following dinner with a dozen brothers and sisters, Ord had gone to his room and requested a biography of their great sister. He had read and watched holos until after midnight, trying to absorb some fraction of her enormous life. It was impossible. The history of the Earth seemed easy by comparison.

"I'm bored," Xo repeated.

And as if she heard him, Ravleen interrupted the quiet. "Enemies in the woods, on the west. On the move."

Three squads were stationed on the strong west wall, including theirs. Saying nothing, they watched the leafless black trees for any motion, a delicious sense of drama in the wind.

"Mortars," warned Ravleen. "Firing."

Whump-whump. The Blues had two mortars, air-driven, their size and power set by old rules. Everyone dropped to their knees, hugging the parapet, and a pair of snowballs hit in the courtyard, bucket-sized and nobody injured. They were meant to judge range. The next rounds did the damage, someone crying out, "Heat," as a blue sphere struck behind Xo. Chemical goo broke free of its envelope, activated by the air and melting the ice beneath it. A thick blue cancer was spreading. Ord and Xo jumped up, using shovels to fling the worst of the goo below, then using last night's snow to make fast, sloppy patches.

It was fun, fast and fun, and everyone seemed to enjoy themselves.

"Return fire," Ravleen ordered.

Their own mortars were loaded, aligned by hand and guesswork. Whump, whump. Whump, whump. They fired snow only, harassing the enemy. And now a half dozen Golds shouted, "Look!" as the Blues broke from the woods above.

"Guns at the ready," said their general.

Ord had an old snowgun—a favorite—with its plastic stock worn slick and pale, carried by two sisters before him. It had over-and-under barrels and a simple laser sight, a potent compressor and twenty rounds of snow loaded into the stock. Slugs were made inside the barrels, in an instant, each one thumb-sized and spinning for accuracy, able to hit someone's head at nearly forty meters.

"Ready," Ravleen whispered in Ord's ears.

He looked over the gargoyle's right wing, snow-colored figures with deep-blue facemasks charging across fresh snow, a practiced scream growing louder as they closed the gap . . . two dozen of them, including the eight who were rolling cannons into position . . . and where were the others . . . ?

"On my command," Ravleen said. "Cannons . . . fire!"

Thunk-thunk-thunk. Three cannons were on the west wall, a fourth held in reserve. Big fat rounds followed golden laser beams, no one struck. The Blues were zigzagging, a thin line of them coming. Fifty meters, then forty. Then thirty, and Ravleen said, "At will. Fire."

They rose together, as drilled, aiming and squeezing off double-shots. Flecks of laser light danced over their targets. It sounded like the popping of insects, the air filled with white streaks flying both ways. Ord picked a target and hit it in the belly, then the face, then missed when it ducked and slipped sideways. But he anticipated the next move, leading and firing and the double-shots smacking the face more than once, snapping it back, leaving the Blue stunned in the snow.

"Reload," said his gun. He dropped and opened the stock, shoving in handfuls of fresh wet ammunition. Then the lone squad on the east wall was shouting, and firing. Not only were there two attacks, but Ravleen hadn't seen the other troops marshaling. "Squad A," she shouted, "change walls. Support the east. Now."

The Blues must have disabled the watchdogs on the east. With a fair trick? Every war had its strict rules, only so much snow for a fort, so much heat allowed its attackers, and so on. Squad B—Ord's—had to spread out and cover for A. He would fire and drop, then come up somewhere else. A lucky shot caught him above the eye, a warm thread of blood making it blink and water. He ducked and wiped with a sleeve, then moved and rose again. But now the Blues were in retreat, their attack meant to harass and nothing more. Their artillery fired overhead, peppering the east wall, heat gnawing at the hard white ice.

Ravleen pulled Squad C next. She had no choice. They had to repair holes while B was left alone on the west wall, six soldiers fighting more than a dozen. And of course the Blues attacked again, in a tight formation. Squad B closed ranks and fired down on them. Heat grenades ruined the snow gargoyle, its wings and snarling head collapsing into mush; and the Blues teased them, shouting, "You're next, you're next, you're next."

Ord dropped and reloaded, moved and rose. And the Blues guessed where he would be, and when, every gun fixed on him, blue sparkles half-blinding him and the double-shots on their way. He didn't have time to react. The entire salvo caught his face and throat; and what startled everyone was how he stayed on his feet, bloodied and stunned but undeniably upright.

The Blues fired again, in unison.

That second salvo lifted him off the rampart, snapping his head back, and he fell into the courtyard, landing on his back in the greasy blue heat, bruised and sore and suddenly tired enough to sleep, unable to see for all the blood in his eyes.

4

Why did we attempt it? The simple, one-word explanation is greed. *The two-word explanation adds* charity, *because it was for your good as well as ours. The third word is* arrogance, *of course. And the fourth, without doubt, is* stupidity. . . .

—*Alice's testimony*

Ord remembered when his blood tasted salty. Now it was sweet, reminding him of oranges. His biochemistry was changing, new genes awakened, his body progressively tougher and faster and faster to heal. He had been able to fight again by afternoon, and by dusk he felt almost normal, picking at the hard scabs as he entered the house. As always, he touched the PRIDE AND SACRIFICE emblem on his way to the stairs. But something made him pause, something subtle, Ord standing on the balls of his feet while listening, a peculiar nonsound emerging from another hallway.

He changed direction, suddenly aware of his heartbeat.

The house had been built in stages, layered like a coral reef, the oldest regions in the deep interior. The original mansion had been abandoned— a five-story structure not particularly grand in its day—and Ord knew he had reached it when the floor changed to natural stone, cold and dirty white. Lights woke for him, and the general appearance had been maintained by the house robots; yet everything felt old, even tired, Ord touching the simple brick walls, new mortars mending the old but nothing else changed, thousands of centuries focused squarely on him, barely allowing him to breathe.

There was a central staircase leading up to various sealed doorways. Every Gold had come here with him, at least once, Ord showing off the Chamberlains' humble beginnings. Beside the staircase were two heavy doors, also sealed, one on each side. Not even Lyman had permission or the means to open them. But today, for no apparent reason, the door on his left was ajar. No, it was removed. He stepped closer, blinked, and saw the bare hinges and dark air ... and nothing. It was as if the great old door had been stolen, or erased, and he couldn't guess why.

Ord paused, squinting now. The room beyond was dim and imprecise, dust floating with graceful ease. He heard a sound, a faint dry click, but couldn't guess its direction. "Hello?" His voice was weak, almost useless. The room seemed to swallow his noise, then him, his snowboots falling silent on the old rotted carpet and his face caressed by a sudden chill. He was inside before he made any conscious decision to take this chance, and he told himself: *I shouldn't be here.* He thought: *I will leave. Now.* But the promise seemed as good as the deed, and Ord walked on in a straight certain line.

It wasn't a large room, even in its day. A rounded wall was on his left, the tighter curve of the staircase on his right, and every wall was buried behind cabinets and framed paintings and various decorations that made no sense to him, styles and logic long extinct. The place felt like a storage closet, not a room where people would gather. Despite careful treatment, the relics were degrading, wood splitting along lines of weakness, paintings faded and flaking. He paused and stared at the largest painting, a faint yellow lamp glowing above it. The plaque beneath told Ord what he suspected, the subject's name etched into a greenish metal.

"Yes, he's our father."

The voice didn't startle him. It came wrapped in a calmness that soothed and nourished him. Removing one thin glove, Ord touched the name, *Ian Chamberlain* written in the dead man's neat, circumspect script. It was similar to Ord's handwriting ... the same angles, the same spacings ... and he felt a sudden deep reverence for the man, Ian shown posing before the original mansion, every feature blurred by the tired paints. Ord had seen Ian countless times, in holos and interactive fictions; but here, in these circumstances, he felt close to the man, and nervous, his mouth going small and dry. This was their father, their One; and the voice was saying, "Look at me," with a mild, flat tone that couldn't startle anyone.

It was his sister's voice—every sister's voice—yet it was all wrong, reaching deeper than simple sound could manage.

"I'm right behind you," he heard, and he turned, discovering a figure standing in the room's center, smiling at him, her face the same as any sister's face, only rounder. She wore a body that was a little fat, wrinkles crowded around the eyes and a softness to the flesh, pudgy hands trying to straighten a wrinkle in her simple dark blouse. She took a step toward him, and Ord felt a tingling sensation, smelling ozone. Become a certain age, he knew, and you ceased to be merely tough meat and an enduring mind. Succeed at being an adult for a few tens of thousands of years, and your Family taught you how to use new energies, plasmas and shadow matter. Eventually you were built of things more unseen than seen, the prosaic nonsense of sweet blood and neurons left for special occasions.

"Look at you," she whispered, a dry hand touching Ord on the cheek. "Do you know how perfectly perfect you look?"

"You're the Twelve," he sputtered.

She gave an odd little laugh.

Ord managed a clumsy sideways step, wondering if she could be someone else. It seemed preposterous to think that a Twelve could speak to him. Was she some younger sister, some assistant perhaps?

"My name is Alice," she warned, "not Twelve. And you? You must be the baby. Ord."

He offered a very slight nod.

Curiosity and a mild empathy showed on the smiling face. Alice touched him again, on the other cheek, saying, "There. All gone."

His scabs had dissolved, bruises absorbed.

She laughed without making noise, tilting her head as if to look at him from a new vantage point. Invisible hands passed through his flesh, studying him from within; then she was saying, "I used to enjoy a good snowball fight. Isn't that remarkable to think?"

It seemed unlikely, yes.

"Quite the fort you have." She closed her eyes, a wisp of red hair dangling over her chalky forehead. "Not elaborate, no. But sturdy. A good solid construction."

He asked, "Can you see it now?"

"Easily." She opened her eyes, smiling as she said, "You fought on the west wall, near the middle—"

"How can you—?"

"Bootprints. Blood. A thousand ways." Then she said, "This is yours," and held up his snowgun. Surprise slipped into nervousness. They weren't supposed to remove equipment from the battlefield. He watched while Alice went through the motions of a careful examination, placing her right eye to the end of the barrel and tugging on the trigger. Ord grimaced. But nothing happened, and she seemed amused by his response, smiling at him, her soft voice saying, "My, my. I didn't have such fancy toys when I was a girl."

It wasn't fancy, but he didn't correct her.

She assured him, "I am jealous."

He thought that was a remarkable thing to hear. A Twelve envying him. Because of a toy gun?

"How are my Radiant Golds doing?"

Radiant?

"What kind of wargame is it?"

"A forty hour scenario," he reported. "Heavy snows and the Golds defend a place of their choice—"

"Against the Electric Blues," she interjected.

Ord paused and swallowed, then said, "They have to capture our flag."

Something about Alice made him feel happy, as if she couldn't contain her own joy and it flowed into him, sweetening his mood. She shut her eyes again, savoring the instant. "Here." She handed him his weapon. "I don't mean to leave you defenseless."

"I can't have it . . . here . . ."

"Pardon me?"

Ord swallowed, then used a careful, certain voice. "I leave my gun wherever I was standing. Where I was when we quit."

"Marking your position. How reasonable."

It vanished from his grip, fingertips tingling for an instant.

"I am sorry. I didn't know." Yet she sounded more amused than sorry. Turning, she did a slow stately walk around the room, absorbing everything with eyes and perhaps other senses. Fancy china plates were collapsing into dust. An ornamental knife was speckled with corrosion. A crystal sphere had broken in two—that seemed to amuse her—and she picked up the larger part, saying, "In my day, we threw snowballs. We made them with our hands and threw them, and I wasn't particularly good at it. The sexes differed too much in ability, and I had a girl's arm." She set the crystal down again, turned and stared at the ceiling for a long time. "That pasture you're defending? I fought for it once. I can recall . . . I was sore afterward, of course." She paused, then looked at him again. "Do the Swords still exist?"

"The Silvers," Ord replied. There were twenty clans, twenty colors, fifty children in each one. He had to ask, "Were you a Gold?"

"One of the first, and worst."

Ord imagined this woman running in the snow, attacking a cowering line of Silvers. In the early Peace, childhoods were quick and old-fashioned. A person became an adult in just a century, and only then was her body improved, her mind made ready to deal with Family responsibilities. Slow growth, like Ord's, allowed for quality. For better maturity. He had been told that many times, and believed it; yet part of him envied Alice, thinking how she had been a child for just a very few winters.

"And who's your general?"

"Ravleen."

"She has to be a Sanchex, am I right?"

Ord nodded.

"Crystal can grow tired and shatter," she said, "but some things are too resilient. If you see my point." Alice gave a satisfied nod, then told him, "I would like to hear about everything. Soon. It's been too long since I last visited . . . and enjoyed this lovely old house. . . ."

Her voice fell away, as if she was hunting for the best word.

Then she said, "Enjoyed," once again.

"Why are you here?" Ord heard himself asking. "Alice?"

She didn't seem to hear him, stepping past him, hands lifting to touch the old portrait. With means obscure and powerful, she rearranged the molecules in the tired paints, re-creating their father's face and body, then altering the artist's original work. A rope of glass fibers dangled from the dead man's chest. Through them he would have controlled a multitude of powerful primitive machines, his body connected to whatever warship or world he was residing on at the moment. Few humans used such systems anymore. No Family member bothered with them. But Ord recalled that exposing that rope, whether in public or a portrait, would have been rude, even vile. After the Wars, and for a very long time, it was important for Chamberlains and every other Family to hide their augmented selves.

"What do you think, little brother?"

He stepped close and studied the portrait. The round white house and green lawn had been left unchanged, as if out of focus. They made Ian all the more real, set against that exhausted background. Ord stared at the face—ageless and wise; the seminal patriarch—and he saw a quality in its expression. It was as if the artist had told the great man to smile, and he had obeyed, but there was some powerful, deep-felt sadness in him that he could never hide.

Ord was uneasy. What Alice had done wasn't restoration, it was vandalism. The past always should be respected; yet here she had altered a work of art, making it something else entirely. Self-righteousness left him bold, and he asked again, "Why are you here?"

Alice seemed composed, giving him a watery grin while asking in turn, "Why can't I come here?" Then she looked at their father, a thin colorless voice saying, "When she wants, a person should be able to come home."

He had no simple, quick response.

"Desire," she said, "is reason enough, little brother."

And when he next glanced at the portrait, she vanished. He found himself alone, standing in a room where he didn't belong, the air suddenly frigid and his blood-caked snowsuit warming itself and him in response, his breath visible, like thin puffs of tepid steam.

➥

Ord went to his room, telling no one what had happened. Tonight the house felt exceptionally empty. He assumed the others were with Alice, greeting her in some fashion, and that there were good reasons why the youngest brother wouldn't be included. Eating alone, he studied the day's lessons without concentrating. Poetry and mathematics seemed unreal, and he eventually put them aside, ordering his universal-wall to show him more of Alice's worlds. Light-velocity feeds were found; a new vista was presented every few minutes. Ord put on pajamas and sat on his bed, fresh snow falling behind him, illuminated by images from around the galaxy and nothing else visible in the black night.

Her worlds were rich with life. More than most terraformed worlds, easily. Sometimes Ord asked to see who lived on them, and he was shown city scenes and up-to-the-second census figures. Like him, these people were built from ordinary matter. Like him, they had limited talents but no programmed lifespans. Barring accidents, they might live forever. Yet unlike Ord—unlike anyone in the Family—they could manipulate their human forms. Instead of enlarging themselves with trickery, they bent themselves with genetic tailoring, adapting to odd niches or simply embellishing some feature for private reasons. It was a basic feature of the Peace; freedoms were granted along different tangents. A multitude of strange, even alien humans wandered past Ord: tall figures and tiny ones, people with golden fur and others with elephant noses. On the oldest, most crowded planets, it was best to divide into a carefully structured mass of species. The Earth itself had some hundred-thousand distinct, registered types of humans, every sort of food able to be metabolized by someone. Lyman had a passion for the strangest local ladies, Ord recalled. He would bring them to the mansion now and again; and once, completely by accident, Ord had walked in on him and his current girlfriend, at the very worst moment. An embarrassing, instructive lesson, it still made the boy blush twenty years later, thinking of that finned beauty in the swimming pool, on her back, and his brother gasping as he turned, discovering that he wasn't alone.

The Peace was built on rules. The Families had to begin with old-style bodies, and no profession belonged only to them. Yet they remained the best terraformers, commanding the best salaries. Teams of ordinary humans and machines couldn't build with the beauty that Alice achieved, he felt certain. And what's more, she worked for aliens too. Methane seas; nitrogen seas; water seas made toxic by bizarre biologies. Ord knew enough to admit that he knew very little. The next time he saw Alice, he would compliment her regardless. *If I see her*, he thought; and now he asked the wall to stop, lying back in bed, letting the sheets find him.

But he didn't sleep, his eyes barely closed when he heard a brother ask. "Did you tell? Anyone?"

Ord sat up, finding Lyman in the open door. Long hair and the broad shoulders were set against the lights of the hallway. "Tell anyone what?"

"About our sister coming," Lyman muttered, obviously nervous.

Ord shook his head. "I didn't, no. No one."

"Just thought I should check." He stepped closer, grinning and staring out the window.

"Does she like the penthouse?"

Lyman blinked and said, "She's not here yet, but she won't. I'm sure she won't."

The boy felt something. A caress, perhaps. Or maybe it was his own adrenaline, fatigue dispelled in an instant, his mouth dropping open but his voice gone.

Lyman noticed the odd expression, blinked and stepped backward. Then Ord whispered, "I saw her."

"Where?"

Ord closed his mouth, summoning courage.

"Where did you see her?" Lyman came to the foot of the bed, then suggested, "It might have been someone else."

"She said she was Alice." And he told the story, describing the missing door and the room filled with relics, and Alice, and how she had easily done some odd things. Would he get into trouble for entering that room? Or for not telling Lyman about it afterward? "I thought you'd know that she's here," Ord assured him. Then he asked, "Why hasn't she told you that she's here?"

His brother leaned against the bed, his mouth open and his eyes empty. Around them was a ghostly sense of amusement, thick enough to taste, and sweet.

"Where is she, Lyman?"

The older brother merely shook his head, not saying the obvious. *She's here now . . . with us now. . . .*

5

I have rebuilt some ninety-thousand major worlds for a wide assortment of clients. But my best work, without question, are the secret worlds that I build for myself, from nothing. I have done several dozen of them, inventing unique biologies and hiding them away inside dust clouds and in globular clusters. And yes, I know. They are questionable legal acts, I know. But many terraformers dabble in such work, and not just Family members either. And it's not an original idea that our dear Earth is someone's garden, built and lost, and all of us are merely its lucky sons and daughters. . . .

—Alice's testimony

The skies were clear in the morning. The Sanchex mansion—a great gray pyramid—was visible in the north. Ord was eating his breakfast, half-dressed for battle, when Lyman returned to his room, telling him, "Someone is inside the penthouse. We're sure now."

Ord turned, saying nothing.

"But she won't respond. Yet." Lyman shook his head. "Just the same, we should keep her presence secret. Understood?"

Of course. But he went through the ritual of promising once again.

"Do normal activities," his brother insisted. "Act as if everything is perfectly normal."

Ord thought of his siblings at the penthouse door, asking it if Alice were inside. And Lyman, trying to hide his nervousness, merely nodded to himself and said, "Isn't it . . . a lovely day . . . ?"

◆

The enemy was entrenched east and west of the fort, their main force clinging to a cliff face, using ropes and small wooden platforms. The

Golds knew because Ravleen had cheated, sending out an automated probe during the night. Scans had proved that the Blues hadn't broken any major rules, using accepted methods to blind them, nothing but hard work responsible for their success. It was frustrating for Ravleen, her foes near enough to touch and out of reach. Hugging the cliff, they couldn't be bombarded. They could gather themselves, then rise en masse, flinging heat grenades and taking a few good shots but escaping before they were truly hurt.

Ravleen and Tule abandoned the keep. They strode along the ramparts, giving orders with sharp, worried voices. "You two," said Ravleen, meaning Xo and Ord. "Take that cannon and harass theirs." The Blues had continued firing from the high ground, aiming for the east wall. "And don't look at me like that," Ravleen snapped.

"Like what?" Xo countered.

She glared at him, breathing loudly.

"Go away," Xo whined. "We'll hit them, don't worry."

Except Xo didn't work with conviction. Ord found himself loading the breech every time. And he had to aim the long plastic barrel. Xo was content to fire the cannon, and when they missed—normal enough at this range, aiming uphill—Xo would shake his head and say, "Lower." Or he'd state something else obvious. Ord tried to ignore him, knowing how Xo could be full of himself and how anger was useless. Then Xo declared, "I'm tired of winter. I hate this snow."

But winter had just begun, thought Ord. And this time he pulled on the wire cord, a dull strong *whap* causing a white streak that landed short of its target, the Blues waving happily from behind their cannon.

"Too bad." Xo's mask showed only his eyes and mouth, all of them grinning. "Aim higher, why don't you?"

Better to cut the snow, Ord decided. He counted his handfuls, trying to find what was perfect. The next shot was nearer, and Xo, who hadn't been paying attention, said, "See? Better this time."

It was a brilliant day, and lovely. In quiet moments they could hear the city on the lowlands—horns and bells and a suggestive gray murmur—and Ord remembered the times he crept down to the estate's boundary, hiding in the grass, watching the ordinary people. His universal-wall could give closer, more intimate views of them; but sitting on the edge of that other world, knowing he could, if he wished, walk straight into it . . . well, that was intoxicating. Chimes rang in the distance, very softly, and Ord wished he didn't have to be here, realizing it had been several months since his last surreptitious visit.

The sunshine felt hot, and he broke a big rule in a small way. Rolling up his facemask, Ord massaged the wet skin with wet snow. Xo saw him and asked, "What happened to your wounds?"

Ord pulled the mask back into place.

"It looks like you weren't even hit yesterday."

"I slept a lot." Ord couldn't invent a better excuse.

"Sleep did that?"

No, Alice did it . . . and suddenly he was thinking about her. He had been pushing her aside all day, with some success; but suddenly he found himself wondering what she was doing, and did she like the penthouse, and would he see her again? "I wasn't hit that badly," he offered, hoping to deflect suspicions.

But Xo didn't care. His mind had shifted again, his voice too loud when he said, "Oh, she's a good general in the open. But not with this stand-and-fight shit. Everyone knows that."

Teasing Ravleen was the better game. More dangerous too.

"If I were her," Xo claimed, "I'd send out a couple squads. I'd assault their cannons now—"

"—and lose the squads with the counterattack," Ord responded.

"We'll lose if we don't," the boy maintained.

Ord ignored him, aiming again, trying to concentrate. The icy slug had an imprecise size and density, plus an imperfectly smooth surface. The universe, said his tutor, was a series of simple suppositions and principles meshing together in chaotic ways. There were specific mathematics to help navigate through the chaos, to a degree. He barely understood them . . . yet he had a sudden premonition, numbers and symbols converging into an answer and his hands lifting, the right hand grasping the cord and hesitating . . . wait, wait . . . *now.*

He tugged the cord with a careful, perfect strength.

The slug was in flight, traveling on a neat arc, and one of the Blues fired at the perfect moment, half an instant too late.

Ord's slug hit the barrel's mouth, plugging it; hot compressed air caused the breech to shatter, some old flaw exposed, steel-colored plastic shards driven backward into a boy's arm and face. He collapsed. A cheer rose from the rest of Squad B. Even Xo was impressed enough to say, "I can't believe it." People took breaks from the fight to run over and look, watching the unconscious body and the ruined gun being taken away. It was a sterling moment, and ugly, one less Blue to fight now. Ord tried to be thrilled but instead felt sorry, even though the boy would be well in a few days. No lasting harm was done, but that didn't seem to matter.

"You got lucky," said his morose companion.

No, it wasn't luck. Ord felt certain of it.

●

And one shot wasn't the war.

The east wall was hammered the rest of the day. It was blue and rotting when it was time to quit, and they had fifteen minutes to make repairs, in peace. But time was wasted, someone telling Ravleen what Xo had been saying about her and her approaching him, telling him, "How would you like to be banished? Is that what you want?"

"If you were any kind of general," Xo countered, "I'd fight and keep quiet."

Ravleen wasn't wearing her mask. Ord saw the outrage in her face, her features ugly and hard; and he intended to step between them, trying to defuse things. But the best he could offer was, "We should work—"

"Quiet," Ravleen warned him.

Then Xo said, "A real Sanchex would have won the war by now—"

—and Ravleen swung at him.

Ord tried to push her backward.

Then she swung at Ord, catching him on the temple, but somehow he stayed on his feet. He shook his head, the world blurring for an instant; and Ravleen was past him, pinning Xo against the blue wall, punching him in a blind rage . . . and Ord grabbed a forearm, giving it a quick little twist.

The tough bone failed, making a sharp *crack* when it shattered.

Ravleen collapsed to the ground, her arm useless and her shoulder dislocated. With a tight slow furious voice, she said, "Wait." She only looked at Ord, saying, "Banishment is too good for you. You wait. You'll see. . . ."

6

While I'm here, I suppose I should plead guilty to any other little crimes that come to mind. I stole toys in my youth, for instance. And I built illegal worlds, as stated. And several times, to help friends, I have used improper means to alter elections and overthrow a few ugly governments that nobody misses. . . .

—Alice's testimony

"You found my message, did you?"

"Yes." It was on his desk, handwritten on paper . . . or at least it had looked handwritten. "I came as soon as I could."

"Alice."

"Pardon?"

"Call me by my name, Ord. Please."

He whispered, "Alice," to himself.

"Have you ever seen this place?" She stepped back from the crystal door, beckoning to him. "I mean the penthouse, of course. I decorated it today. What do you think?"

The penthouse was an enormous room with no apparent walls or ceiling. Ord had been here for special dinners, but the comfortable furniture had been replaced with foliage, gray-green and thin. Meant for a low gravity environment, he realized; and he stepped, finding himself noticeably lighter. How did she manage it? Only expensive machines could dilute the Earth's pull, and he was very much impressed with his sister's skill.

"A quiet lad, isn't he?"

Ord said, "Sorry."

"Why? You had the busy day. You're entitled to your silence."

He looked at the blue-white sky, asking, "What world is this?"

"A secret world."

He didn't understand. But before he could ask questions, Alice asked him, "Are the others jealous? That only you received an invitation?"

Ord nodded. He had shown the note to Lyman—feeling that was

proper—and Lyman had inquired, "What did you say to her?" In other
words: *What makes you special?*

"You know, our siblings keep coming up here." Alice smiled at the
floor. Tonight she looked thinner, wearing a flowing gown, emerald-
green and soothing. Showing him her smile, she said, "They've stopped
asking me to open the door. But they come and stare at it just the same.
They must be rather curious."

Lyman had looked tired and frazzled.

"And rather pissed off, I think."

The words were unexpected, almost as incredible as this little forest of
alien greenery. That a Twelve would say *pissed off* seemed contrary to
some law or principle. Straightening his back, Ord said, "I think they're
scared. I think."

"Well," said Alice, "isn't that their right?"

It was a strange reply, but he managed to shrug and nod.

She touched his face, telling him, "You look well. You must have
moved at the right times."

He dipped his head. "How much did you watch?"

"Every moment," she said happily.

"You . . . you did stuff. . . ."

"Twice, and you're welcome." Alice played with her own hair. It was
longer than last night, fuller and brighter. "With your aim, once, and
with the Sanchex girl."

"Now she hates me."

"Yet she will heal, won't she?"

What could he say?

"Twenty centuries from now," Alice offered, "she won't think of what
you did. Tragedy is perishable, little brother. Believe me, she'll reach a
point where the memories will elicit a smirk and little else."

What mattered was tomorrow, he knew, not the remote future. A part
of Ord wished Alice hadn't come here, or at least had ignored him. At
this moment, Ravleen was sitting in her room, dreaming up a thousand
suitable revenges. She was an impossible, brutal tyrant—

"—and yet," his sister interjected, "she might grow into a courageous
leader, a glorious success, vital to every Family and to humanity."

"Can you read my thoughts?" he wondered aloud.

"In limited ways. But then again, anyone can read anyone's thoughts
in limited ways." She offered a long laugh, then said, "I feel good about
Ravleen. I think she'll become a special Sanchex. One of their dynamos.
She has that essential spark."

"Does she?"

"Not that I can't be wrong." Alice shrugged her shoulders. "Perhaps
she'll even disappoint me."

Sanchexes loved dangerous work. Lacking wars, they busied themselves
by wrestling with stars, delaying novas in those close to populated worlds,
and sometimes exploding healthy isolated suns, using the titanic energies
to create rare and expensive materials.

Alice said, "Isn't it odd? We begin as perfect copies of our parent, yet tiny, unforeseen factors have their way with us. For good or not." A pause, then she added, "Your friend Xo isn't much of a Nuyen. Which is a double insult, believe me."

Nuyens were talented governors and administrators. The Earth had many of them in high posts, serving as links between Families and the multitudes.

"I don't like Xo," Alice insisted. "I've met him a thousand times, and I've never trusted him."

Ord blinked, then asked, "What about me?"

"What about you?"

"What kind of Chamberlain will I make?"

"I learned ages ago, never predict what Chamberlains might do." The smile seemed fragile. "Now come over here and sit. Rest, little brother." She put an arm around him, saying, "I invited you to dinner, so let's eat and enjoy ourselves. What do you think?"

☜

The meal was exotic—an alien stew made edible by inverting its amino acids—and the sky darkened very slowly, easing into night. For now the stage was Ord's, Alice demanding stories of his snow wars and other adventures. He told about canoeing mountain rivers and how he bred beardogs, preferring them to other pets; and he described the arrow wars fought in the summer, face paints in lieu of masks but the same essential rules. And of course he had games, bloodless fictional wars that he played by himself. Were any of the Blues his friends? Alice asked. Not yet. He had met them, and of course he knew which face belonged to which Family. And sometimes older Blues came to visit Lyman, and the others—

"Why?" asked Alice.

Why what?

"Why build these careful antagonisms, passionate but essentially harmless? Ancient clans, elaborate rules . . . what's the purpose of it, Ord?"

His tutor claimed it was to teach them cooperation.

"Cooperation," she echoed. "Indeed, that's a key reason why the Families have thrived. But wouldn't bridging a mountain river serve the same function?"

Lyman had a different explanation. He claimed that war games were like tails on embryos. They were vestiges of something not needed anymore.

"That sounds a little truer," Alice replied.

Ord noticed that her face had grown empty. Did the topic bother her? Then why had she brought it up?

"Tell me, little brother. Why did we fight the Great Wars?"

There were thousands of would-be Families. They tried to enslave humanity, but the Wars defeated them. Sanchexes and Chamberlains helped save the multitudes, and in gratitude, they and the other good Families were allowed to keep their powers. They were given this land, and together the Wars' survivors fashioned the Peace.

"Noble images," Alice conceded.

Ord had stopped eating, but he found that he couldn't muster the will to push the half-empty bowl aside.

"Here's the crux of it, little brother. Somewhere in its history, every technological species will make the tools to become godlike. Immortal citizens will be capable of building worlds, or obliterating them. How a species responds to the challenge . . . well, that's what determines its fate, more often than not."

The galaxy was littered with ancient worlds torn apart by warfare. Sometimes Ord dreamed of sifting the rubble for chunks of burnt bone, learning about the vanished souls.

"Our powers are not cheap," said Alice, "and they're never plentiful. When the Wars began, there were only a few hundred billion people, but how many of them could be fitted with those new technologies? Very few. And many of those were corrupt. Perhaps, as you say, evil. But our species saved itself with a single wise deed. Ordinary people sought out the best thousand from their ranks. Not the wisest or the strongest, but the souls who would be least corrupted by their new talents."

This was familiar, and Ord kept nodding.

"Ian Chamberlain was a very unimportant man until he was selected. An unsuccessful man, by most accounts."

The boy looked at his bowl.

"How is your dinner?"

He said, "Fine."

Alice nodded, saying, "The Families are pledged to never injure any human being."

It was the fundamental law, something flowing in Ord's own blood.

"To you," she said, "the Peace must look immortal. Everlasting. Isn't that so, little brother?"

He began to shrug.

"Yet ten million years is no span at all. You'd be amazed how brief it feels to me."

He was tired of being amazed, he decided.

Alice rose to her feet. Before them was a little pond, bony fishes, alien and primitive, swimming lazily over soft white alien muds. She watched their motions for a long while, or pretended to watch them; then she told Ord, "Your brother is terrified of me. Of my presence here."

Lyman?

"Did you know that he has left the Earth?"

Ord said, "He's too young," with a boy's surety. "He's not allowed to go anywhere else."

"Yet he has. Many times." She laughed gently and easily. Her emerald gown was becoming muddy, a white fringe building as she walked around the pond. "He was on the Moon when I told everyone that I was coming to visit. He was seducing women, no doubt. Being a Chamberlain has its advantages, believe me. Still."

"Where else has he gone?"

"Around the solar system. Nothing astonishing." She paused, then turned to him. "Haven't you ever slipped out of these mountains? The sentries aren't perfect. No one needs to know."

"I haven't."

"But please tell me that you've been tempted." She seemed disappointed with him. "Haven't you been?"

Endless times, yes.

"Yet you obey the rules. How nice." She knelt, dipping a cupped hand into the pond and drinking from it. "Lyman doesn't obey, and that's why he's scared. I'm going to punish him while I'm here, he thinks, for traveling and for bringing girls into this house."

"But that's not against any rule," Ord countered.

"You're allowed to bring friends and lovers, of course. From inside or outside the Families, without doubt. But Lyman's girls aren't friends, they're convenient pieces of ass. They're thrilled to be with an authentic Chamberlain, and that's why they can ignore how ugly he looks. Grotesque to more than a few of them, I can promise you."

Ord remembered the finned woman in the swimming pool.

Standing again, Alice dried her hand with the gown.

After a minute, Ord asked, "Where is this world?"

"Inside a dust cloud. Hidden."

"Is this where you were? Before you came here, I mean."

She closed her hands into fists, sighed and said, "Everyone wants to know where I was. Where I came from."

Ord's belly ached, and not because of the dinner.

"Tell them, little brother. I was at the Core." She paused, a smile beginning and failing. Her face seemed to wrestle with her mouth, a strange lost expression winning. Then she said, "I came straight from the Core. Which was a long journey, even for me."

People older than One Hundred didn't require starships. They could convert themselves to massless particles, moving at light-speed yet remaining conscious. Ord tried to imagine such an existence; and to say something, to be involved, he mentioned, "Lyman wants to work at the Core. As a terraformer."

Which she had to know. Tilting her head, she tried the same failed smile again. "A good Chamberlain goal, isn't it?"

The Core was famous for black holes and dust clouds, plus billions of star systems left sterilized by explosions and intense radiation. The Families had made it safe enough to colonize. Humans and aliens had room to expand, no legal claims held by any species.

"The Core," Alice whispered, smiling at Ord, no light in her face and her words leaden. "It's a lovely place. Too many stars for me to count, little brother."

He doubted it.

She strolled over to him. Her bare feet left narrow prints in the mud. With one hand, she held him beneath his jaw, blue eyes locked on his eyes, and with an irresistible strength she brought him to his feet, a cold voice telling him, "You could grow a tail. I could activate the old genes, and you'd grow one now. You have that power."

"I don't understand," Ord whispered. "What do you mean?"

"What do I mean?" She let go of him and turned away, her gown seeping a green light as night fell. "Whatever I'm talking about, little brother, it isn't tails. You can be certain of it."

●

"Then what?"

Ord breathed and said, "Then we talked about tomorrow."

"What about tomorrow?"

"About snowfare—"

"Nothing else about the Core?" Lyman was pacing, Ord watching him while sitting on his brother's enormous bed. "Well, at least now we know where she came from. If she is telling the truth, of course."

Why wouldn't she?

" 'I'm not talking about tails.' Is that what she said?"

Ord nodded. "Basically."

"War." His brother's voice was ominous. Soft. "She was at the Core, and some kind of war broke out."

"I don't think so."

Lyman stopped and stared at him. "Why not?"

All he could offer was, "I have a feeling. It's something else entirely, I'm sure."

Lyman glanced at his girlfriends.

"Alice gave me a plan," Ord continued. "For tomorrow. It involves Ravleen—"

"But what else did she say about the Core?"

"Nothing."

"Nothing?"

Ord shook his head, trying to appear certain.

Lyman picked up one of the girlfriends, then he set her down again.

"What you need to do," Alice had told Ord, "is earn your redemption. With the Golds, and Ravleen too. And here's how you can do it, easily." Although to him it had seemed like a complicated scheme—

—and now Lyman moaned, "Something awful is happening. And that's why she's come here, no doubt about it." He wiped the perspiration from his face. "It's one of the aliens, or all of them. They've decided to fight us for the Core."

But wouldn't they have seen trouble on the universal-walls? Ord couldn't believe such a thing would remain secret.

"Whatever it is," Lyman promised, "I'm going to make a general call. For any nearby adults. I'll tell them . . . nothing . . . and ask them to hurry home at once. . . ."

It wasn't war; Ord was sure.

He remembered how their sister had kept saying, "Redemption," again and again. That powerful creature had stood in front of him, her gown soiled with the white muds; and she had assured him, "You must be re-deemed. It's all my fault, but I can make everything better for you."

Her inadequate face was somewhere else, it eyes closing.

"Redemption," she had muttered one last time.

It wasn't a god's face, or a god's voice; and Ord had felt so very sorry for her, and everyone.

7

Our mountains have shrunk since I last saw them. There's been erosion, of course, and the crust beneath has slumped . . . and I was tempted to fix them, at first glance . . . with my proverbial pinkie, I could lift these dead lumps of stone into space, if I wished, and fling them into the sun. . . .
                                                                    —*Alice's testimony*

Ravleen wore a simple cast and sling, down to one good shoulder and arm; yet somehow she seemed larger today, more dangerous, walking in front of her assembled troops, not speaking. A light dry snow was falling. Ravleen paused and let herself smile for a moment, looking at the high gray clouds. Then she said, "I need to know what's happening." She said, "I need a patrol. Two people. Volunteers."

Ord glanced at Xo, then down at his own boots.

"Who wants to?" Ravleen continued. "Anyone?"

With a sense of drama, Xo stepped forward.

"Good." The smile brightened. "Now pick your partner."

"Ord."

"Wrong choice," she responded. Then she motioned to her lieutenant, saying, "Tule will go with you."

The girl gave a confused low moan.

"We have three minutes," Ravleen warned them. "Take radios and rations and drop over the south wall. I want reports. Find out what the Blues are doing. And harass them, always."

Tule was a good soldier; she managed a nod of affirmation.

Xo stepped up to Ord, saying, "I tried. Too bad you can't come, it'll be exciting out there."

"I bet so."

Xo looked at his eyes, asking, "What are you thinking?"

"Nothing," Ord lied. "I just wish I was with you."

"Except you're not," Ravleen growled, marching up to punch Ord with her good arm. She smacked his shoulder, in warning, then said, "I want you here with me. You know I do, friend."

→

The Blues fired early—a few moments early—and their cannon slug hit a girl in the back. Everyone yelled, "Violation!" But she was just stunned, little harm done. Then Ravleen said, "Positions," and waved them over to the south wall. "Go."

Tule and Xo dropped rope ladders and started down. Tule was slow and clumsy, catching her leg when her ladder twisted. Xo hit the pasture and ran; and an instant later the Blues saw him, voices screaming, their cannons turned and firing as their troops charged from two sides.

"Run," shouted Ravleen. "Pick up your feet, Tule. Go."

Blue-faced targets swept into range. Ord shot well, wondering if Alice was helping his aim. But she had promised not to help, not that way, and he missed often enough to believe it was all him. Tule was hit and hit again, and she would fall and pick herself up and take a sloppy step before falling again. But Xo never slowed, never looked backward. He sprinted into deep snow, and Ord saw him leap off the first cliff—a fair drop, but cushioned by drifts—and he saw a pair of Blues on his trail, firing from the cliff and jumping after him.

Tule was down for good. The Blues surrounded her, kicking her even when she cried out, "Give, give."

Ord stopped firing. He found himself watching the battle with a sense of detachment. Poor Tule was picked up and carried away. The other Blues fired and retreated, glad to have their first prisoner. All this noise and energy seemed to amount to nothing. Ord felt indifferent. Suddenly he was thinking about Alice, and the Core; and sometimes, in secret, he spoke to his sister, certain that she could hear him.

The bombardment resumed. Squad B manned the cannons until Ravleen replaced them with C. "From now on," she told them, "you've got a new job."

Nobody spoke.

"Take the keep apart. Make blocks out of the snow." She etched her plan in the rampart's ice. "Stack the blocks here. And here. And get it done this morning."

One boy said, "We'd rather fight."

Ravleen stared at Ord. "For now, no. No."

The squad bristled but said nothing.

And their leader popped Ord in the head, using her hard cast. "Then I've got another lousy job for you," she promised. "For the afternoon, and you'll like it even less."

➤

Xo eluded his pursuers for a few hours, but they were faster than him, easily tracking him in the deep snow. In the early afternoon, both prisoners were carried up to the pasture, gagged and blindfolded, then set in plain view under a tiny white flag. "You're next," the Blues called out in a practiced voice. "We'll melt your fort and then you, Golds. Soon."

Tule was embarrassed. It showed. And undoubtedly Xo was inventing excuses to explain his capture.

A new assault began on the east, but Ord's squad saw none of it. They were below, doing work meant for robots, hands cold despite their gloves and their backs aching from the hard cutting and lifting. Everyone said, "The big attack is tomorrow. Tomorrow." There was excitement, and nervousness, but it was all just a game. This was a prattle used for decades, and it had to be the same kind of noise Alice had made when she was like them.

"Tomorrow," they told each other.

But not Ord.

They consciously ignored him, and he discovered that he didn't care like he should care. It was as if there was a traitor inside him, and the traitor announced itself with, of all things, indifference.

◄

"What are you doing here?"

"Waiting for you," Ord replied. "How's prison?"

Xo shrugged and removed his mask. "Tiny. Boring. Cold."

"Too bad." They were in the trees above the pasture, on the main trail. From here the fort looked strong, tall and secretive, the rotting east wall showing only the faint beginnings of a slump. Ord had been the last one to leave it, and he had sat here, waiting for Xo. Alice had promised that the boy would come this way, out of habit. And he would be alone, Tule walking anywhere but with him. "How did they catch you?" Ord asked. "What went wrong?"

"They cheated, I think. Illegal equipment, I'm almost sure."

"Should we report them?" You went to your siblings who in turn complained to theirs. "We could tell your brothers—"

"Later. Maybe."

Ord nodded and stood up.

"How's Ravleen? Still furious with you?"

Ord removed his mask, pointing to some of his bruises.

"I hate her," Xo promised. "I wish you'd broken both arms."

"Maybe I will."

They began to walk. Some noise came from the city—the musical rise and fall of a siren—then the snowfall blotted it out, or it ceased.

Xo said, "I wish we were done."

"So do I."

"They've stuck me into a prison box. It's ridiculous."

Boxes were cramped and soundproofed, the heat bled out of them.

"I'm bored," the boy complained.

Ord paused and looked at Xo, then he looked everywhere else. Then just as Alice had told him, he said, "We can be home by noon tomorrow, if you want."

A hopeful little smile surfaced.

"Ravleen has a plan."

Xo said, "That's against the rules," and laughed, shaking his head. "I'm a prisoner of war. You can't tell me anything."

They weren't far from where Xo had begged to be hit with the careful stone. "We're shoring up the east wall. Making it strong again."

"How?"

"With the keep. Except it doesn't have enough snow." He paused, then said, "That's why we're robbing snow from the west wall. It's got too much anyway. Remember my gargoyle?" He drew a dramatic X on the boy's chest. "It's thinnest below the gargoyle."

Xo wasn't speaking, or breathing. This was against every rule, and the wickedness was delicious. He smiled and then stopped smiling, as if someone might notice; and he asked, "How thin is thin?"

"Like this." Ord put up his hands.

"She'll know I told. Ravleen will."

"How can you know anything?" Ord countered. "If Ravleen tells Tule anything, then Tule's the likely suspect."

"But will the Blues believe me?"

"Maybe not, but it's easy enough to test. And if you're right, they might not have time to cut a hole through the east wall anyway."

The boy stepped back and looked around, shivering as if he was cold. "Who knows?" he muttered. "Maybe I'll crack. First thing in the morning, before they put me in that stupid box."

8

Boredom can claim some of the blame. What new challenges had we attacked in the last thousand millennia? And there was a genuine urge to accomplish something good. And most important was the idea itself. The plan. We were intoxicated. Drunk and in love, it seemed so perfectly possible and lovely to us. . . .

—Alice's testimony

A single set of stairs climbed to the penthouse, in a tight spiral, the stairwell itself decorated with an elaborate mural. Yesterday, Ord was too nervous to pay attention. Today, the mural seemed to force itself on him, showing him various Chamberlains caught in the midst of historic and heroic acts. He saw worlds rebuilt, aliens embraced, and the far edges of the galaxy explored. His own motions caused the scenes to change, the artwork fluid and theoretically infinite; and riding on a single step, hand on the polished railing, Ord found it all quite strange, thinking of the care spent on a mural that almost no one ever saw.

He was deposited at the penthouse door. Touching the milky crystal, he said, "It's working. Just like you promised."

The door dissolved, Alice standing before him.

"It's working," he repeated, breathing in little gulps. "Did you watch everything?"

"Enough of it." Something was different now. Worrisome. Alice wore a heavy dark robe, the room beyond black, unbordered, and cold. But she did smile at him, telling him, "Thank you," and then, "I'm glad it's going well," with a mixture of pride and pleasure. She was watching a point beside him, saying, "That Nuyen is a fool. Don't you agree?"

Ord felt uneasy, saying nothing.

"I would invite you inside," Alice continued, "but this isn't a good time. I am sorry."

Her face seemed simple, worn down. If she'd had red eyes, he would have guessed that she had been crying. And perhaps she was crying, in a fashion. He reminded himself how little of her was visible, and he asked, "Are you all right?"

Her eyes tracked toward him, no other response offered.

Ord stepped backward and dropped his gaze.

"I'm just distracted," Alice explained, "and tired. My long trip has caught up with me at last."

That seemed very unlikely.

And she told him, "Tomorrow, once you're done fighting, I want you to come tell me everything, little brother. I promise. We'll have a celebration, to enjoy your triumph." She paused, then said, "Stop worrying, please. Everything will be fine."

He said, "I know," without confidence.

Then the door began to reform as she said, "Good night." For an instant, it sounded as if she were crying. But then he realized, with cynicism, that someone like Alice might conjure any emotion, put on any face . . . sadness was just a different kind of creation. . . .

He pushed the thought aside, turned and stepped back onto the stairs.

☞

Two robots waited in Ord's room—security models—and with gray voices, in unison, they said, "You're wanted in the main arena. No, don't change clothes. Go now."

"Who's there?" he stammered.

"Lyman, and the others." The robots were silent, probably asking what they could tell him. "Several hundred adults have arrived today. They wish to speak with you."

The main arena was underground, deep inside the Chamberlain mountain—a vast room with seating for twenty thousand, false granite and perfect wood covering the walls and arched ceiling—and the brothers and sisters looked inconsequential with so much space around them. They sat in a block before the stage, and Ord had to wonder: Why here? Why not in a smaller arena? But then he realized this was as far from the penthouse as any place, which might be important. Were security baffles in use? From the stage a single brother waved at him. *Lyman.* Sitting beside him was a sister, a giant figure, three meters tall and built out of light and conjured flesh. "Up here," said Lyman. "We're just starting."

Every step was hard work, every breath a labor.

"Ord?" said the giant sister. "My name is Vivian. Eleven hundred and twenty."

Eleven twenty was nothing. He felt like telling her that he wasn't impressed, that he knew their Twelve and that she was *nothing* beside Alice. And maybe Vivian read his thoughts, taking his hand and squeezing, her hand feeling like heated plastic, almost burning him before she said, "I'm glad to meet you." Her presence was tangible, her energies making the air and stage vibrate. "Sit, if you would. Sit here and talk with us."

A chair appeared between his brother and sister.

Lyman leaned close and said, "Relax."

A couple of hundred faces watched them. The oldest adults were giants, wearing Chamberlain faces and bodies out of tradition. To be mannerly. Vivian had the highest rank, it seemed. Now she leaned forward, telling Ord, "Your big brother did what was right, you know. Perhaps he should have warned us sooner, but we understand. We do."

"What do you want?" Ord whispered.

"We need your help," Vivian explained. "I understand that our sister likes you? That for some reason she's taken an interest in you? Not that she dislikes any of us, of course. But you've spoken to her—"

"Yes."

"More than once, according to Lyman."

"Just now, a few minutes ago." His voice was soft and loud. He could barely hear himself, but the words were enlarged and thrown across the arena. "Is Alice in trouble?"

"Why? Do you think she should be in trouble?"

He shrugged his shoulders.

Vivian made him notice her smile. Her face was incomplete, a patch of strange gray light on one side of her forehead. "She's come from the Core, is that right? Ord? Do you hear me?"

He nodded. "Straight from there."

"But has she told you why she was there?"

He didn't like Vivian; he didn't appreciate her tone. But this was important, and he took pains to say, "She told me that she came here from there and that's all. That's what I know."

Lyman leaned close again, following some script. Ord realized that he was here to put their little brother at ease, prompting him when necessary, and he was sick with worry and exhaustion. "She was at the Core," he muttered. "We know it now."

"We're certain," Vivian echoed.

"She was working on a special project," Lyman continued. "With other Chamberlains and Sanchexes . . . with nearly half of the Families, no one younger than One Hundred."

"Doing what?" the boy asked.

Lyman shut his eyes, saying nothing.

Vivian told him, "It is a secret," with her voice betraying frustration. Yet she made herself laugh, as if to defuse the tension. As if to fool Ord. "I can't get access to their secret, little brother. Though I have sources who claim, and with some reason, that they're working on FTL travel."

"It's not possible," Ord replied. "Nothing goes faster than light."

"Perhaps you're right," his sister said. "Perhaps this is just a story meant to fool prying eyes."

Ord felt himself sinking away.

"Eleven Chamberlains were there," Vivian continued. "But now all except two of them have departed, including Alice. She arrived here the instant we saw her depart, but the others have taken other directions. Why? And why have the other Families departed in the same mysterious way?" She paused, then said, "I don't know, honestly. I have questions that I would love to ask."

Murmurs spread, then collapsed.

"Two Chamberlains are left there?" Ord managed. "Where is *there?*"

Everyone wanted to know. People whispered among themselves until Vivian lifted one of her hands, waiting for silence. Then she said, "They were clustered beside the central black hole, inside its envelope of gases and plasmas. They've been there for several thousand years, it seems. Honestly, I don't know what type of work they were pursuing."

Ord shifted his weight, hands wrestling with one another.

Vivian asked, "Has she given any hint of an explanation? Has our dear sister given you one clue?"

He whispered, "No."

Then he asked, "Why can't you ask her?"

She blinked and made a show of swallowing, then admitted, "Alice has set up barriers. A part of me is wrestling with them now, but she seems adamant to exclude everyone but you."

Ord looked at the audience, reading the same lost, worried expressions. Even Vivian seemed like a little girl mystified by events, angered by her limitations and perhaps glad too. In secret. She could do nothing of substance. No clear responsibilities could be set on her oversized shoulders. It seemed obvious to Ord . . . and suddenly he wondered if it was his insight, or if perhaps Alice had given it to him.

"When do you see Alice again, little brother?"

Ord blinked, trying to remember.

Lyman appreciated his confusion, touching an arm and saying, "What's important is that we go on with our ordinary lives. As well as we can, Ord. But Alice has come here for some reason, and if she wishes to tell us anything, we need to listen."

"Tomorrow," he said. "I'll see her then."

"When you do," Vivian instructed, "ask if she will talk with us. Will you do that for us?"

"That's all we want," said Lyman.

"Please," said the giant sister.

"Please," said two hundred mouths, in unison, whispers rising to the pink granite ceiling and echoing back down at them again.

9

Ian rarely told war stories. But once, I remember, coming home after a hard day's snowball fight, he found me on the yard, stopped me, and launched into a long tale about finding our enemies hiding in a certain solar system. They had built redoubts out of worlds, and he explained how he had grabbed comets, accelerating them to near-light velocities . . . how he had pummeled worlds until their crusts melted, our enemies slaughtered . . . and he wept at the end, and shook, still ashamed of his cruelty while his audience, this little girl, kept thinking what an enormous, wonderful snowball fight that must have been . . . !

—Alice's testimony

In all but name, the Golds won the war that next morning.

The Electric Blues stuck to their old battle plan, troops charging the east wall and artillery firing from the west. But there was no final assault. When it seemed inevitable, there was a pause, a sudden lull, then the sound of motion, troops scrambling over slick terrain on the south. There was little pretense of subterfuge. Ravleen and Ord stood together on the south wall, and one of them smiled beneath her mask, satisfied with the world. The other wished he could feel relief, but there wasn't any. Nor was there any sense of dread and foreboding, which was a constant surprise to him. It was as if Ord was empty, all the worry drained from him;

sometimes he couldn't even remember Alice or the Core, as if they had been carefully, thoroughly etched from his mind.

Ravleen noticed enough to ask, "What's the matter?" She poked him with a finger, telling him, "You look funny. What are you thinking?"

He shrugged his shoulders.

But she didn't press him, too happy to care. Today her cast was soft, without a sling; and with that bad arm she hugged Ord, every Gold watching them and everyone surprised.

Alice had been right.

A Sanchex would do anything for a victory, provided you left her pride intact.

"Beg for forgiveness," his sister had instructed. "Weep. Grovel. And tell her your plan between weepy moments. Trust me, she'll see its beauty. And she'll take it for herself."

For a deed that wasn't his fault, Ord had apologized . . . and didn't *his* pride matter too?

"It's happening," Ravleen whispered.

She said, "They believe the little shit."

Then she hugged Ord again, saying, "When the time comes, stand next to me." A wink, a smile, and she assured him, "That's only fair."

◆

The Blues entered the pasture from the southwest, carrying their snow-guns and grenades and finally showing their own flag, a blue rectangle flapping in the bright windy air. There was a pause as they gathered themselves, then they let out a roar, charging as cannons and mortars threw heat into the west wall. As promised, the ice beneath the gargoyle had been undermined. A squad of Blues surged through the sudden hole, excited and confident. There was moderate fire from above, plus some raucous cursing. The Golds were disconsolate, without question. The first squad beckoned for others, more than half of the Blues pouring into the courtyard, in less than a minute, marshaling and charging the flagpole, nothing between them and it but a crude little wall of fresh-cut ice—

—and there was a sound, wet and strong, and massive. Something was falling. A wedge of ice broke free of the west wall, sliding over the new hole as Ravleen shot to her feet, shouting:

"*Fire.*"

It wasn't a fight. Ord stood behind the new wall, firing without aiming, without heart. Four squads fired double-shots at close range, knocking the enemy off their feet. Cannons on the west wall had been turned, barrels depressed, and the fourth cannon was on the ground, slugs of ice knocking people unconscious. Limbs were shattered. Facemasks and the flesh beneath were split open, blood bright against the white surfaces. And even still the Blues mounted a final charge, adrenaline carrying them over the wall, one girl able to put her hands on the pole's knotted rope an instant before Ravleen shot her from behind, in the head, her body limp and Ord watching her fall and lie still.

In days everyone would be well again, ready to play again. Yet Ord felt sad enough to cry, watching Ravleen lead her troops across the courtyard, driving their enemies into a corner and abusing anyone with a hint of fight left in them. Then the prisoners were disarmed and tied together, and Ravleen launched an assault on the enemy cannons, capturing them and more prisoners and chasing the rest into the woods.

Ord stayed behind, guarding Blues. He sat on the trampled snow with his gun empty, and after a while he couldn't hear the distant shouts. He watched the masked faces, thinking how the eyes looked angry and a little afraid, but not much, and even the anger seemed false. And it wasn't because this was only a game. They were too young to know how to be truly angry or honestly scared. They were children. Sitting there, thinking thoughts that weren't entirely his own, Ord tried to imagine a world filled with danger; and he couldn't. The part of him that was him looked at the fort and the clear bright sky, and he couldn't believe that this quiet wouldn't last for all time.

10

Something did go wrong. We failed somewhere and knew it at once and could do nothing . . . and the worst of it was that we had time, too much time, to dwell on the failure . . . blaming one another, and Nature, the Almighty and even those awful people who had brought us forth into our miserable lives . . . !

—*Alice's testimony*

The staircase was filled with brothers and sisters, half again as many as he had seen yesterday. The stairs were locked in place, no one moving but Ord, him climbing toward the penthouse and no one speaking louder than a whisper. "Good luck," they told him. The freckled, red-haired faces were grim and tired in many ways, and the climb seemed to last for ages. Halfway to the top, Ord was crying, wiping at his eyes with alternating sleeves. "Be strong," the whispers demanded. Yet the Chamberlain faces seemed anything but strong, in stark contrast to the heroic images in the mural. Lyman was the last face, Ord recognizing the long hair and something in the voice, his brother saying, "We're proud of you, you know."

Vivian emerged from the wall beside them, still tall, stepping out of the mural as if it was syrup and bending until her giant face was near enough to kiss Ord. "Alice is waiting, I think. That much I can see, I think." She paused, and the gray patch on her forehead brightened. "Listen to what she tells you, ask questions, and please tell her how much we'd like to see her. Soon."

Ord looked down the stairwell, faces watching him; then he thought to ask, "What's happening in the Core? Do you know?

Nobody spoke.

He looked at Vivian. "What can you see now?"

"Nothing new," she lied. Looking as winded as Ord felt, she sighed and put a large warm hand on his back, shepherding him toward the crystal door. "Good luck, little brother. You'll do well."

The doorway dissolved as it re-formed behind him. He stopped, then the blackness was washed away with starlight. In an instant, with a faint dry sound, grass erupted from the twisting floor and grew seeds, the air filled with summer sounds and dampness. The stars were brilliant and colorful, and countless, separated by light-weeks, or less. At the sky's zenith was an oval, not large, velvety black and vague at its edges. This was the Core, Ord knew, and the oval was the giant shroud draped over the central black hole. This sky could be a live image—

"Exactly so," said a voice, close and soft.

—and around him was a terraformed world. Ord knelt and broke off a stem of grass, putting it to his mouth, tasting the green juice. It was earthly life. And as if to prove that point, an insect landed on his face and bit him, drawing blood before he swatted it, the little body smearing under his fingers.

"Walk," Alice instructed. "Straight on."

The room was a hilltop, and there were people—his size, his proportions—sitting in the brilliant darkness, watching the sky. It was a peaceful scene, familiar yet tied to an exotic place; and Ord was afraid, pausing and his heart beating faster.

"Who are they?" he whispered.

Alice was silent.

"Hello?" he tried.

A boy turned and said, "Hi. Who are you?"

Ord stepped close and gave his first name. The group repeated, "Ord," as Alice said, "Sit with them."

They weren't people but instead facsimiles conjured up with the grass and bugs. Below them was a city, a sprinkling of soft lights and darkness between. It was a pioneer community, not large, homes set in the middle of wide rich yards. A tiny crescent moon was rising over distant mountains. It seemed like a lovely world, larger than the Earth, its gravity stronger and the air tasting clean and new.

Faces smiled. The facsimiles weren't too different from him, their heads narrow and their hair abundant and long, tied into intricate braids that leaked their own soft light. They were the children of pioneers, the first generation born on this world. Like Ord, they had tough brains and rapid powers of healing. Like him, they could be decades old, no inherent end in their lives. But they'd never leave their flesh, they could only travel in starships, and if they wanted to terraform any world larger than a comet, they would have to work in teams, as a multitude, relying on numbers in place of Chamberlain skills.

And yet.

Someday they would have *children*. Not clones, but unique, even radical babies. They would marry and make families—institutions older than any Chamberlain—and each child would be unlike anyone on any of the million living worlds.

Ord felt envy, or Alice fed envy to him. Probably before he was old enough to leave the Earth, these children would fill this world with their descendants; then the multitudes would spill onto that little moon and whatever else circled the unseen sun. A great green explosion of life . . .

and before Ord could hope to visit, this place would become mature and crowded. . . .

"You look warm," the facsimile boy observed. "Why don't you take off that silly suit?"

The snowsuit was damp with perspiration. Ord stripped to his underclothes, then he sat with them on the warm bristly grass. Without prompting, the others introduced themselves, by name, the last small girl saying, "Alice," and then, "Chamberlain."

She was dark as coal. "Chamberlain?" Ord echoed. "Is that your real name?"

"Of course," she replied. "A lot of people are named after the Families. At least here they are."

"You're not from here," said a second girl. "Are you?"

"But that's okay," said the boy, acting like their leader. "We like meeting people."

Ord asked, "Why use the Chamberlain name?"

"In thanks," she answered.

"Because," said the boy, "the Chamberlains help make all these suns behave. They keep gas from falling into the black holes. And we're very, very grateful for their help. Aren't we grateful?"

His friends nodded in unison, with fervor.

"Who terraformed this world?" Ord inquired.

"Alice," the children giggled. "The real one."

Then the boy added, "We're buying it from her." He spoke with pride, as if to say, "We buy only from the best."

The false Alice looked nothing like Ord's sister. Her face was as narrow as an ax blade, big black eyes reflecting starlight. Ord asked, "Have you ever seen Alice? Does she visit you?"

"Not now," the girl giggled. "Why would she?"

"What do you think of her?"

"She's a wonderful great person," the boy reported, no room for compromise. "Everyone knows *that*."

"I pray for her," the dark Alice confessed. "Every night, just before I sleep, I wish her nothing but the best."

Everyone nodded. Conviction hung thick in the air.

"Where's Alice now?"

Hands lifted, pointing to the cold black smear overhead.

"What is she doing there?"

"Working," said the boy. "With Chamberlains and other Families. Doing important experiments." He was pleased to report this news. "They've found ways to move faster than light. Easily."

Everyone but the dark Alice murmured in agreement.

"Soon," said the boy, "we'll be able to go anywhere. The Families will put the entire universe in our reach."

"No," said Alice.

Faces turned.

She had a quiet, firm voice. "That's not what they're doing."

The other children seemed surprised, but no one had a rebuke to offer.

"It's much more important than FTL. A million times more." Suddenly she had his sister's face, round and pale. Nobody else noticed. Looking at Ord, she asked, "Why can't everyone have Alice's powers?"

"It's a rule," he responded.

"But *why?*"

He paused, thinking hard. "If everyone was like Alice—"

"—there wouldn't be room in this galaxy. Every Alice needs energy and space and fancy work to do." The real Alice took Ord's hand, squeezing and explaining, "This galaxy is just too small of a pasture. If we want to be like her, we need more grass."

Some of the children laughed.

Ord swallowed and asked, "But if we could go anywhere—?"

"Everywhere has life already. Everywhere has its Families and its multitudes, no room for the likes of Alice." She shrugged, sadness showing on her face. "Certainly not for trillions and trillions of full-grown Alices."

Ord nodded, glancing at the black smear.

"But there's something better than FTL," she promised. "Put enough energy into a tiny place, in just the proper way, and a fresh young universe will precipitate from nothing. Am I right, little brother?"

He remembered something mentioned by his tutor. It was a theory, ancient but useless; vacuums themselves could create universes that would separate from theirs. An umbilical cord would exist, then dissolve, and it happened constantly, too swift to notice.

Ord felt a sudden chill.

"The trick," said Alice, "is to keep your umbilical *open*. What's the good in making a new universe that you can't see? Wouldn't it be nice if you could enter it and learn what's possible? Can you imagine the challenges? The potentials? For everyone, of course. . . ."

Alice was weeping, wiping her face with both hands.

A little boy said, "I don't understand you."

"Imagine if everyone, every Family and all of humanity, could extend themselves into endless new universes. Each of us might have our own, each with its own wonders. Each of you would be given Alice's powers, then more, and you could dive down the cord and close it up after you, if you dared." She grabbed Ord's hand, her hands cold and wet. "Isn't that the loveliest sweetest possibility? What would you do, little one, if you had it in your power to make it true?"

Something is wrong—

—and she said, "Precisely," with a dead gray voice. "As wrong as wrong has ever been, I should hope."

Again he looked at the black oval, a single golden spark blossoming at its center. But it faded and vanished, lost . . . an illusion, he told himself . . . nothing else . . . !

Alice turned to the children, explaining to them, "We succeeded. We created a universe and the umbilical cord. But what's difficult, perhaps even impossible, is to leave the way open just enough. No more than the perfect amount, you pray."

The sky brightened. A great soundless flash of light obscured the stars, blue-white and sudden, and the children began to mutter among themselves, and moan.

Alice was saying, "Our universe might be someone's creation. Not an original thought, I admit ... but perhaps some other Family, in some unknown place, produced this ... perhaps they preside over us now ... just as their universe was created in turn. ..."

The children had hands lifted over their eyes. They weren't real children, just facsimiles; yet Ord found himself terrified for them, leaping to his feet, shouting, "Run! Hide!" He grabbed one little boy, trying to make him start for home. But the first wave of heat and hard radiations pierced them. In an instant, the long grass had burst into flames, and the boy squirmed in agony, then died, his body shriveled and blackened, blowing away as ash. And Ord screamed as the world beneath him evaporated. He felt it shatter, an inconsequential bit of grime; and he was twisting in the scalding light, screaming until a familiar soft voice whispered:

"Relax."

Alice said:

"The new universe has flowed into ours, for just this moment."

And with a pained dead voice, she told him:

"You don't know how sorry we feel ... you can't know ... tell everyone, please ... will you, little one?"

◆

Only Lyman was waiting for him. The others had seen the same feed, had gone to the nearest arena to watch the walls. The two brothers stood at the top of the empty stairwell, both trembling, Lyman holding the wall with his hands, saying with a wisp of a voice, "At least we know. We know what it is."

Ord held himself, soaked with perspiration and wearing nothing but his underclothes.

"Vivian thinks it's temporary ... it won't last. ..." Lyman couldn't stand anymore, dropping to his knees and beating the floor with his fists, no strength in his arms. Finally, he asked, "Will Alice talk to us now?"

"I don't know," Ord confessed. Then he tried to apologize with a low choking voice.

But his brother didn't care. He shrugged and said, "You don't know how terrible this is going to be. Nobody can."

Nobody?

"Which is a blessing, I think." Another useless blow to the floor, then Lyman looked up at him. "If we knew, we couldn't live. The grief would crush us, Ord. No one could survive a moment, knowing how awful this will be. ..."

11

We accepted our duty, at last. A few of us remained behind, fighting to close the umbilical even when we knew it couldn't be closed prematurely ... heroic deaths after a catastrophic blunder ... and the bulk of us rushed toward places distant and populated, places where we could save other lives

. . . and then it was decided that one of us, a volunteer, should journey home, home to the Earth, for the express purpose of standing trial, to admit guilt in a public way . . . hundreds of billions doomed, human and alien, and a single soul promising to swallow as much blame as possible. . . .

—Alice's testimony

In the morning, before the local dawn, the Chamberlain mansion sent word to the government that Alice was barricaded in the penthouse. A chaotic, oftentimes bitter group of elected officials decided that high-ranking Nuyens would accompany the appropriate legal officers. The suspected murderess would be arrested, hopefully without incident. That no existing prison could hold her was deemed a minor problem. More than once, in soft dry voices, the officers remarked that if a Twelve wished, she could leave the Earth a vivid red drop of liquid stone and iron.

It had been a clear cold night in the high mountains. That oddity of climate helped make the officers even more uneasy, stepping onto the famous ground and seeing the house, vast and brilliant in the early light. Huge bear-dogs watched them with indifference. The much less impressed Nuyens led the way, taking them under the PRIDE AND SACRIFICE emblem and upstairs. A single Chamberlain—a sister of modest rank—joined their strange procession, telling everyone how sorry she was and how this wasn't anyone's fault except for a tiny few members of many, many Families.

"Not *our* Family," responded one of the Nuyens.

Vivian glared at the speaker, then turned and put the stairs into motion again.

◆

Ord watched them pass. Dressed in a clean snowsuit, he was standing in the hallway, sleepless but alert. Everyone ignored him, and when they were above he stepped into the stairwell, leaned over the railing and watched how they curled higher and higher, his eyes losing them with distance and the glare of the lights.

As always, the bear-dogs begged for attention.

He ignored them, hurrying to the tube and running fast through the sunny woods, then across the pasture. But only Ravleen was waiting at the fort. She was sitting on the west wall, her cast removed, her eyes red and sleepless. "You're late," she warned, then smiled. Then she told him with a strong certain voice, "That explosion won't reach us here. It's not large enough."

Ord knew that already.

"We did calculations," she continued. "It's a lot like a supernova, only bigger. Hotter. Dust clouds and distance will keep the Earth safe."

And the melted planets, he thought. And the dead people.

"What are you thinking?"

Ord looked over the pasture. Yesterday's bootprints gave the snow a ragged, exhausted appearance. "Nobody's going to attack today," he ventured.

"If they do," Ravleen said, "we'll stop them."

"I was tired of being at home," he confessed, swallowing with a tight dry throat. "I watched my wall all night—"

"Talk about something else," Ravleen warned him.

"What?"

"Nothing." The red eyes looked out of the clean gold mask. "Let's just sit and say nothing."

A light breeze lifted their flag, then dropped it. On a day like this, Ord knew, they should have heard city sounds; but not this morning, and the silence was unnerving. Everyone everywhere was scared. It wasn't just the explosion or the deaths, it also was the Peace itself. Would it survive? The sacred trusts had been violated, but could some sense of normalcy return? And when? And what about the Families themselves—?

A slow creaking made Ord blink and turn. Someone was climbing one of the rope ladders. Ravleen picked up her snowgun, watching the familiar figure scramble over the parapet to join them.

"Ah," she growled, "the traitor."

Ord was surprised to see Xo. He should be the last Gold willing to come here. But he stood before them, smiling so that they could see his teeth, saying, "I escaped." He was nervous and obvious, forcing a laugh before he said, "A legal escape. Nobody came to guard me this morning."

Ravleen kept her hand on the gun.

Xo told her, "Congratulations for winning." Then he turned to Ord, adding, "Our plan sure worked, didn't it?"

"What plan?" asked Ravleen.

"Didn't you tell her?" The boy acted horrified. He removed his mask to show his expression, saying, "We planned it together, Ravleen. I would pretend to be a traitor, and Ord—"

"Shut up."

"—Ord would go to you—"

"You're lying. Shut up."

The boy closed his mouth, then grinned. Ord saw the new tooth, whiter than the others, and something about the grin made him bristle.

"I'm no traitor," Xo told them.

Nobody spoke.

Then he said, "*Your* Families were the ringleaders." The tone was superior and a little shrill. "We didn't even help you. I heard all about it. My brothers and sisters were talking, and they said they warned you that it was dangerous and they didn't want any part of it—"

"Quiet," Ord snapped.

"—and you did it *anyway*. And did it *wrong*."

Ravleen stared down into the courtyard.

Xo swallowed and straightened his back, then with great satisfaction said, "Now you'll have to pay for the damages and deaths. All your wealth is going to be spent, and you'll be poor. You won't even be Families anymore! It's as if we set a trap, and in you *walked*—*!*"

Ravleen shot him in the head, no warnings. She put twin slugs into his mouth, knocking him off the wall. Then she stood and looked down at Xo, sprawled out on his back, and she winked at Ord, saying, "Watch." And she jumped after him, feet first, boots landing on the boy's chest and her momentum shattering ribs and lungs and the heart beneath her.

His chest crushed, Xo flung his arms into the air, hands grasping at nothing and then falling limp.

Ravleen began to kick him. His body had died, past all suffering; but she worked on the face with a sick thoroughness, without pause, kicking and kicking until she was finally exhausted; then she stepped back and looked up on the wall, telling Ord, "You can help me."

Except that Ord wasn't standing there. It was a sister, some other Chamberlain, and she smiled without smiling, eyes full of misery and joy.

"Help you?" she asked, pleased with this most tiny revenge.

Then she said, "Another time, perhaps. But thank you for offering."

12

I watched them force the penthouse door. I watched them not find me. I did enjoy their panic, I'll admit, but in all honesty I wasn't actually hiding from them. And then one of the Nuyens engaged her treacherous little brain and decided to look inside the original mansion, the majority of me waiting in my one-time bedroom, peering outdoors at a vivid cold winter from ten million years ago. . . .

—*Alice's testimony*

The city was trees, towering green trees with natural chambers in the trunks and large branches, tiny luxury apartments housing several million smallish people with prehensile tails and strong limbs. Almost everyone was inside, watching the live feeds from the Core. For a long while, Ord walked unnoticed down a wide avenue, feeling like the last living person on the planet. He left his snowsuit on, wiping sweat from his eyes. A small park opened up before him, and he saw motion, then tiny brown shapes. He approached the children with a certain caution, practicing his smile, and when they saw him, they stopped and stared. Too young to watch the Core and understand, they also were too young to recognize a Chamberlain on sight. One boy laughed and said, "You look funny. What kind of person are you?"

"Are you sick?" asked a young girl.

"Funny hair," said a third child. "Sick funny hair!"

Ord took a breath and held it. There were nearly a dozen children gawking at him. To the boy who had said *You look funny*, he said, "Here," and handed him the old snowgun. "For you."

"What is it?" the boy sputtered.

Ord didn't explain. Removing his boots, he asked, "Who wants these?" A tiny hand reflexively shot up.

He gave away his boots, then his mask. Then he removed his snowsuit, and paused, and told his astonished little audience, "I am sorry. I want you to know, I'm sorry."

They didn't understand why he should apologize, but the words were locked in their minds.

"And Alice is sorry too," he added, flinging the snowsuit behind them and turning, running off on bare feet as the children began making claims and counterclaims for this strange unusable prize.

Ord trotted back to the estate, the mountains and the snow.

And only then, gazing out of the jungle at the towering white ridges, did he realize that he'd never seen his home from this vantage point. From outside. And he ran faster, crossing a line, the first wet pancakes of snow burning his toes, causing him to run faster still.

Recording Angel

PAUL J. McAULEY

Few stories even in this *anthology take us as far into the far future or to a future as numinous, alien, rich, and strange as the bizarre and evocative story that follows . . . in a future so remote, so distanced from the our times and from the Earth itself, that the very memory of humanity itself is almost forgotten and gone. Almost—but not quite.*

Born in Stroud, England, in 1955, Paul J. McAuley now makes his home in London. A professional biologist for many years, he sold his first story in 1984 and has gone on to be a frequent contributor to Interzone *as well as to markets such as* Amazing, The Magazine of Fantasy & Science Fiction, Asimov's Science Fiction, When the Music's Over, *and elsewhere.*

Like his friend and colleague Stephen Baxter, McAuley has a foot in several different camps of SF writing, being considered one of the best of the new breed of British writers (although a few Australian writers could be fit in under this heading as well) who are producing that brand of rigorous hard science fiction with updated modern and stylistic sensibilities that is sometimes referred to as "radical hard science fiction," but he also writes dystopian sociological speculations about the very near future and also is one of the major young writers who are producing that revamped and retooled Wide-Screen Space Opera that has sometimes been called the New Baroque Space Opera, reminiscent of the Superscience stories of the thirties taken to an even higher level of intensity and scale (wait a minute! how many feet does he have, anyway?). His first novel, Four Hundred Billion Stars, *one of the earliest examples of the New Space Opera, was published in 1988 and won the Philip K. Dick Award. It was followed by sequels,* Secret Harmonies *and* Eternal Light, *and by one of the most vivid of the recent spate of Martian novels,* Red Dust. *With his next novel,* Pasquale's Angel, *he put yet another foot down in yet another camp, producing an ingenious and gorgeously colored Alternate History where Leonardo da Vinci brings modern technology to Europe centuries before its time. His next novel, 1996's* Fairyland, *perhaps his best-known novel and perhaps also his best performance to date at novel length, took us to a troubled future Europe thrown into chaos by fractional politics and out-of-control biotechnology, only a few years into the next century; it won the Arthur C. Clarke Award and the John W. Campbell Memorial Award. With his next novel project, though, he is plunging back into Space Opera territory, on an even more ambitious scale, with a major new trilogy,* Confluence, *set 10 million years in the future. The first two volumes,* Child of the River *and* Ancients of Days, *have just been published; the story which follows is a kind of segue. McAuley's other books include two collections of his short work,* The King of the Hill and Other Stories *and* The Invisible Country, *and an original anthology coedited with Kim Newman,* In Dreams.

Mr. Naryan, the Archivist of Sensch, still keeps to his habits as much as possible, despite all that has happened since Angel arrived in the city. He has clung to these personal rituals for a very long time now, and it is not easy to let them go. And so, on the day that Angel's ship is due to arrive and attempt to reclaim her, the day that will end in revolution, or so Angel has promised her followers, as ever, at dusk, as the Rim Mountains of Confluence tip above the disc of its star and the Eye of the Preservers rises above the farside edge, Mr. Naryan walks across the long plaza at the edge of the city towards the Great River.

Rippling patterns swirl out from his feet, silver and gold racing away through the plaza's living marble. Above his head, clouds of little machines spin through the twilight: information's dense weave. At the margin of the plaza, broad steps shelve into the river's brown slop. Naked children scamper through the shallows, turning to watch as Mr. Naryan, old and fat and leaning on his stick at every other stride, limps past and descends the submerged stair until only his hairless head is above water. He draws a breath and ducks completely under. His nostrils pinch shut. Membranes slide across his eyes. As always, the bass roar of the river's fall over the edge of the world stirs his heart. He surfaces, spouting water, and the children hoot. He ducks under again and comes up quickly, and the children scamper back from his spray, breathless with delight. Mr. Naryan laughs with them and walks back up the steps, his loose belted shirt shedding water and quickly drying in the parched dusk air.

Further on, a funeral party is launching little clay lamps into the river's swift currents. The men, waist-deep in brown water, turn as Mr. Naryan limps past, knuckling their broad, narrow foreheads. Their wet skins gleam with the fire of the sunset that is now gathering in on itself across leagues of water. Mr. Naryan genuflects in acknowledgment, feeling an icy shame. The woman died before he could hear her story; her, and seven others in the last few days. It is a bitter failure.

Angel, and all that she has told him—Mr. Naryan wonders whether he will be able to hear out the end of her story. She has promised to set the city aflame and, unlike Dreen, Mr. Naryan believes that she can.

A mendicant is sitting cross-legged on the edge of the steps down to the river. An old man, sky-clad and straight-backed. He seems to be staring into the sunset, in the waking trance that is the nearest that the Shaped citizens of Sensch ever come to sleep. Tears brim in his wide eyes and pulse down his leathery cheeks; a small silver moth has settled at the corner of his left eye to sip salt.

Mr. Naryan drops a handful of the roasted peanuts he carries for the purpose into the mendicant's bowl, and walks on. He walks a long way before he realizes that a crowd has gathered at the end of the long plaza, where the steps end and, with a sudden jog, the docks begin. Hundreds of machines swarm in the darkening air, and behind this shuttling weave a line of magistrates stand shoulder to shoulder, flipping their quirts back and forth as if to drive off flies. Metal tags braided into the tassels of the quirts wink and flicker; the magistrates' flared red cloaks seem inflamed in the last light of the sun.

The people make a rising and falling hum, the sound of discontent. They are looking upriver. Mr. Naryan, with a catch in his heart, realizes what they must be looking at.

It is a speck of light on the horizon, where the broad ribbon of the river and the broad ribbon of the land narrow to a single point. It is the lighter towing Angel's ship, at the end of its long journey to the desert city where she has taken refuge, and caught Mr. Naryan in the net of her tale.

◆

Mr. Naryan first heard about Angel from Dreen, Sensch's Commissioner; in fact, Dreen paid a visit to Mr. Naryan's house to convey the news in person. His passage through the narrow streets of the quarter was the focus of a swelling congregation which kept a space two paces wide around him as he ambled towards the house where Mr. Naryan had his apartment.

Dreen was a lively but tormented fellow who was paying off a debt of conscience by taking the more or less ceremonial position of Commissioner in this remote city which his ancestors had long ago abandoned. Slight and agile, his head clean-shaven except for a fringe of polychrome hair that framed his parchment face, he looked like a lily blossom swirling on the Great River's current as he made his way through the excited crowd. A pair of magistrates preceded him and a remote followed, a mirror-colored seed that seemed to move through the air in brief rapid pulses like a squeezed watermelon pip. A swarm of lesser machines spun above the packed heads of the crowd. Machines did not entirely trust the citizens, with good reason. Change Wars raged up and down the length of Confluence as, one by one, the ten thousand races of the Shaped fell from innocence.

Mr. Naryan, alerted by the clamor, was already standing on his balcony when Dreen reached the house. Scrupulously polite, his voice amplified through a little machine that fluttered before his lips, Dreen inquired if he might come up. The crowd fell silent as he spoke, so that his last words echoed eerily up and down the narrow street. When Mr. Naryan said mildly that the Commissioner was of course always welcome, Dreen made an elaborate genuflection and scrambled straight up the fretted carvings which decorated the front of the apartment house. He vaulted the wrought iron rail and perched in the ironwood chair that Mr. Naryan usually took when he was tutoring a pupil.

While Mr. Naryan lowered his corpulent bulk onto the stool that was the only other piece of furniture on the little balcony, Dreen said cheerfully that he had not walked so far for more than a year. He accepted the tea and sweetmeats that Mr. Naryan's wife, terrified by his presence, offered, and added, "It really would be more convenient if you took quarters appropriate to your status."

As Commissioner, Dreen had use of the vast palace of intricately carved pink sandstone that dominated the southern end of the city, although he chose to live in a tailored habitat of hanging gardens that hovered above the palace's spiky towers.

Mr. Naryan said, "My calling requires that I live amongst the people. How else would I understand their stories? How else would they find me?"

"By any of the usual methods, of course—or you could multiply yourself so that every one of these snakes had their own archivist. Or you could use machines. But I forget, your calling requires that you use only appropriate technology. That's why I'm here, because you won't have heard the news."

Dreen had an abrupt style, but he was neither as brutal nor as ruthless as his brusqueness suggested. Like Mr. Naryan, who understood Dreen's manner completely, he was there to serve, not to rule.

Mr. Naryan confessed that he had heard nothing unusual, and Dreen said eagerly, "There's a woman arrived here. A star-farer. Her ship landed at Ys last year, as I remember telling you."

"I remember seeing a ship land at Ys, but I was a young man then, Dreen. I had not taken orders."

"Yes, yes," Dreen said impatiently, "picket boats and the occasional merchant's argosy still use the docks. But this is different. She claims to be from the deep past. The *very* deep past, before the Preservers."

"I can see that her story would be interesting if it were true."

Dreen beat a rhythm on his skinny thighs with the flat of his hands. "Yes, yes! A human woman, returned after millions of years of traveling outside the Galaxy. But there's more! She is only one of a whole crew, and she's jumped ship. Caused some fuss. It seems the others want her back."

"She is a slave, then?"

"It seems she may be bound to them as you are bound to your order."

"Then you could return her. Surely you know where she is?"

Dreen popped a sweetmeat in his mouth and chewed with gusto. His flat-topped teeth were all exactly the same size. He wiped his wide lipless mouth with the back of his hand and said, "Of course I know where she is—that's not the point. The point is that no one knows if she's lying, or her shipmates are lying—they're a nervy lot, I'm told. Not surprising, culture shock and all that. They've been traveling a long time. Five million years, if their story's to be believed. Of course, they weren't alive for most of that time. But still."

Mr. Naryan said, "What do you believe?"

"Does it matter? This city matters. Think what trouble she could cause!"

"If her story is true."

"Yes, yes. That's the point. Talk to her, eh? Find out the truth. Isn't that what your order's about? Well, I must get on."

Mr. Naryan didn't bother to correct Dreen's misapprehension. He observed, "The crowd has grown somewhat."

Dreen smiled broadly and rose straight into the air, his toes pointing down, his arms crossed with his palms flat on his shoulders. The remote rose with him. Mr. Naryan had to shout to make himself heard over the cries and cheers of the crowd.

"What shall I do?"

Dreen checked his ascent and shouted back, "You might tell her that I'm here to help!"

"Of course!"

But Dreen was rising again, and did not hear Mr. Naryan. As he rose he picked up speed, dwindling rapidly as he shot across the jumbled rooftops of the city towards his aerie. The remote drew a silver line behind him; a cloud of lesser machines scattered across the sky as they strained to keep up.

The next day, when as usual Mr. Naryan stopped to buy the peanuts he would scatter amongst any children or mendicants he encountered as he strolled through the city, the nut roaster said that he'd seen a strange woman only an hour before—she'd had no coin, but the nut roaster had given her a bag of shelled salted nuts all the same.

"Was the right thing to do, master?" the nut roaster asked. His eyes glittered anxiously beneath the shelf of his ridged brow.

Mr. Naryan, knowing that the man had been motivated by a cluster of artificial genes implanted in his ancestors to ensure that they and all their children would give aid to any human who requested it, assured the nut roaster that his conduct had been worthy. He proffered coin in ritual payment for the bag of warm oily peanuts, and the nut roaster made his usual elaborate refusal.

"When you see her, master, tell her that she will find no plumper or more savory peanuts in the whole city. I will give her whatever she desires!"

All day, as Mr. Naryan made his rounds of the tea shops, and even when he heard out the brief story of a woman who had composed herself for death, he expected to be accosted by an exotic wild-eyed stranger. That same expectation distracted him in the evening, as the magistrate's son haltingly read from the Puranas while all around threads of smoke from neighborhood kitchen fires rose into the black sky. How strange the city suddenly seemed to Mr. Naryan: the intent face of the magistrate's son, with its faint intaglio of scales and broad shelving brow, seemed horribly like a mask. Mr. Naryan felt a deep longing for his youth, and after the boy had left he stood under the shower for more than an hour, letting water penetrate every fold and cranny of his hairless, corpulent body until his wife anxiously called to him, asking if he was all right.

The woman did not come to him that day, or the next. She was not seeking him at all. It was only by accident that Mr. Naryan met her at last.

She was sitting at the counter of a tea shop, in the deep shadow beneath its tasseled awning. The shop was at the corner of the camel market, where knots of dealers and handlers argued about the merits of this or that animal and saddlemakers squatted cross-legged amongst their wares before the low, cavelike entrances to their workshops. Mr. Naryan would have walked right past the shop if the proprietor had not hurried out and called to him, explaining that here was a human woman who had no coin, but he was letting her drink what she wished, and was that right?

Mr. Naryan sat beside the woman, but did not speak after he had ordered his own tea. He was curious and excited and afraid; she looked at him when he sat down and put his cane across his knees, but her gaze only brushed over him without recognition.

She was tall and slender, hunched at the counter with elbows splayed. She was dressed, like every citizen of Sensch, in a loose, raw cotton over-shirt. Her hair was as black and thick as any citizen's, too, worn long and caught in a kind of net slung at her shoulder. Her face was sharp and small-featured, intent from moment to moment on all that happened around her—a bronze machine trawling through the dusty sunlight beyond the awning's shadow; a vendor of pomegranate juice calling his wares; a gaggle of women laughing as they passed; a sled laden with prickly pear gliding by, two handspans above the dusty flagstones—but nothing held her attention for more than a moment. She held her bowl of tea carefully in both hands, and sucked at the liquid clumsily when she drank, holding each mouthful for a whole minute before swallowing and then spitting twiggy fragments into the copper basin on the counter.

Mr. Naryan felt that he should not speak to her unless she spoke first. He was disturbed by her: he had grown into his routines, and this un-sought responsibility frightened him. No doubt Dreen was watching through one or another of the little machines that flitted about the sunny, salt-white square—but that was not sufficient compulsion, except that now he had found her, he could not leave her.

At last, the owner of the tea house refilled the woman's bowl and said softly, "Our Archivist is sitting beside you."

The woman turned jerkily, spilling her tea. "I'm not going back," she said. "I've told them that I won't serve."

"No one has to do anything here," Mr. Naryan said, feeling that he must calm her. "That is the point. My name is Naryan, and I have the honor, as our good host has pointed out, of being the Archivist of Sensch."

The woman smiled at this, and said that he could call her Angel; her name also translated as Monkey, but she preferred the former. "You're not like the others here," she added, as if she had only just realized. "I saw people like you in the port city, and one let me ride on his boat down the river until we reached the edge of a civil war. But after that every one of the cities I passed through seemed to be inhabited by only one race, and each was different from the next."

"It is true that this is a remote city," Mr. Naryan said.

He could hear the faint drums of the procession. It was the middle of the day, when the sun halted at zenith before reversing back down the sky.

The woman, Angel, heard the drums too. She looked around with a kind of preening motion as the procession came through the flame trees on the far side of the square. It reached this part of the city at the same time every day. It was led by a bare-chested man who beat a big drum draped in cloth of gold; it was held before him by a leather strap that went around his neck. The steady beat echoed across the square. Behind him slouched or capered ten, twenty, thirty naked men and women. Their hair was long and ropy with dirt; their fingernails were curved yellow talons.

Angel drew her breath sharply as the rag-taggle procession shuffled past, following the beat of the drum into the curving street that led out of the square. She said, "This is a very strange place. Are they mad?"

Mr. Naryan explained, "They have not lost their reason, but have had it taken away. For some it will be returned in a year; it was taken away from them as a punishment. Others have renounced their own selves for the rest of their lives. It is a religious avocation. But saint or criminal, they were all once as fully aware as you or me."

"I'm not like you," she said. "I'm not like any of the crazy kinds of people I have met."

Mr. Naryan beckoned to the owner of the tea house and ordered two more bowls. "I understand you have come a long way." Although he was terrified of her, he was certain that he could draw her out.

But Angel only laughed.

Mr. Naryan said, "I do not mean to insult you."

"You dress like a . . . native. Is *that* a religious avocation?"

"It is my profession. I am the Archivist here."

"The people here are different—a different race in every city. When I left, not a single intelligent alien species was known. It was one reason for my voyage. Now there seem to be thousands strung along this long, long river. They treat me like a ruler—is that it? Or a god?"

"The Preservers departed long ago. These are the end times."

Angel said dismissively, "There are always those who believe they live at the end of history. We thought that *we* lived at the end of history, when every star system in the Galaxy had been mapped, every habitable world settled."

For a moment, Mr. Naryan thought that she would tell him of where she had been, but she added, "I was told that the Preservers, who I suppose were my descendants, made the different races, but each race calls itself human, even the ones who don't look like they could have evolved from anything that ever looked remotely human."

"The Shaped call themselves human because they have no other name for what they have become, innocent and fallen alike. After all, they had no name before they were raised up. The citizens of Sensch remain innocent. They are our . . . responsibility."

He had not meant for it to sound like a plea.

"You're not doing all that well," Angel said, and started to tell him about the Change War she had tangled with upriver, on the way to this, the last city at the midpoint of the world.

It was a long, complicated story, and she kept stopping to ask Mr. Naryan questions, most of which, despite his extensive readings of the Puranas, he was unable to answer. As she talked, Mr. Naryan transcribed her speech on his tablet. She commented that a recording device would be better, but by reading back a long speech she had just made he demonstrated that his close diacritical marks captured her every word.

"But that is not its real purpose, which is an aid to fix the memory in my head."

"You listen to people's stories."

"Stories are important. In the end they are all that is left, all that history leaves us. Stories endure." And Mr. Naryan wondered if she saw what was all too clear to him, the way her story would end, if she stayed in the city.

Angel considered his words. "I have been out of history a long time," she said at last. "I'm not sure that I want to be a part of it again." She stood up so quickly that she knocked her stool over, and left.

Mr. Naryan knew better than to follow her. That night, as he sat enjoying a cigarette on his balcony, under the baleful glare of the Eye of the Preservers, a remote came to him. Dreen's face materialized above the remote's silver platter and told him that the woman's shipmates knew that she was here. They were coming for her.

◆

As the ship draws closer, looming above the glowing lighter that tows it, Mr. Naryan begins to make out its shape. It is a huge black wedge composed of tiers of flat plates that rise higher than the tallest towers of the city. Little lights, mostly red, gleam here and there within its ridged carapace. Mr. Naryan brushes mosquitoes from his bare arms, watching the black ship move beneath a black sky empty except for the Eye of the Preservers and a few dim halo stars. Here, at the midpoint of the world, the Home Galaxy will not rise until winter.

The crowd has grown. It becomes restless. Waves of emotion surge back and forth. Mr. Naryan feels them pass through the citizens packed around him, although he hardly understands what they mean, for all the time he has lived with these people.

He has been allowed to pass through the crowd with the citizens' usual generous deference, and now stands close to the edge of the whirling cloud of machines which defends the dock, twenty paces or so from the magistrates who nervously swish their quirts to and fro. The crowd's thick yeasty odor fills his nostrils; its humming disquiet, modulating up and down, penetrates to the marrow of his bones. Now and then a machine ignites a flare of light that sweeps over the front ranks of the crowd, and the eyes of the men and women shine blankly orange, like so many little sparks.

At last the ship passes the temple complex at the northern edge of the city, its wedge rising like a wave above the temple's clusters of slim spiky towers. The lighter's engines go into reverse; waves break in whitecaps on the steps beyond the whirl of machines and the grim line of magistrates.

The crowd's hum rises in pitch. Mr. Naryan finds himself carried forward as it presses towards the barrier defined by the machines. The people around him apologize effusively for troubling him, trying to minimize contact with him in the press as snails withdraw from salt.

The machines' whirl stratifies, and the magistrates raise their quirts and shout a single word lost in the noise of the crowd. The people in the front rank of the crowd fall to their knees, clutching their eyes and wailing: the machines have shut down their optic nerves.

Mr. Naryan, shown the same deference by the machines as by the citizens, suddenly finds himself isolated amongst groaning and weeping citizens, confronting the row of magistrates. One calls to him, but he ignores the man.

He has a clear view of the ship, now. It has come to rest a league away, at the far end of the docks, but Mr. Naryan has to tip his head back and back to see the top of the ship's tiers. It is as if a mountain has drifted against the edge of the city.

A new sound drives across the crowd, as a wind drives across a field of wheat. Mr. Naryan turns and, by the random flare of patrolling machines, is astonished to see how large the crowd has grown. It fills the long plaza, and more people stand on the rooftops along its margin. Their eyes are like a harvest of stars. They are all looking towards the ship, where Dreen, standing on a cargo sled, ascends to meet the crew.

Mr. Naryan hooks the wire frames of his spectacles over his ears, and the crew standing on top of the black ship snap into clear focus.

There are fifteen, men and women all as tall as Angel. They loom over Dreen as he welcomes them with effusive gestures. Mr. Naryan can almost smell Dreen's anxiety. He wants the crew to take Angel away, and order restored. He will be telling them where to find her.

Mr. Naryan feels a pang of anger. He turns and makes his way through the crowd. When he reaches its ragged margin, everyone around him suddenly looks straight up. Dreen's sled sweeps overhead, carrying his guests to the safety of the floating habitat above the pink sandstone palace. The crowd surges forward—and all the little machines fall from the air!

One lands close to Mr. Naryan, its carapace burst open at the seams. Smoke pours from it. An old woman picks it up—Mr. Naryan smells her burnt flesh as it sears her hand—and throws it at him.

Her shot goes wide. Mr. Naryan is so astonished that he does not even duck. He glimpses the confusion as the edge of the crowd collides with the line of magistrates: some magistrates run, their red cloaks streaming at their backs; others throw down their quirts and hold out their empty hands. The crowd devours them. Mr. Naryan limps away as fast as he can, his heart galloping with fear. Ahead is a wide avenue leading into the city, and standing in the middle of the avenue is a compact group of men, clustered about a tall figure.

It is Angel.

❦

Mr. Naryan told Angel what Dreen had told him, that the ship was coming to the city, the very next day. It was at the same tea house. She did not seem surprised. "They need me," she said. "How long will they take?"

"Well, they cannot come here directly. Confluence's maintenance system will only allow ships to land at designated docks, but the machinery of the spaceport docks here has grown erratic and dangerous through disuse. The nearest place they could safely dock is five hundred leagues away, and after that the ship must be towed downriver. It will take time. What will you do?"

Angel passed a hand over her sleek black hair. "I like it here. I could be comfortable."

She had already been given a place in which to live by a wealthy merchant family. She took Mr. Naryan to see it. It was near the river, a small two-storey house built around a courtyard shaded by a jacaranda tree. People were going in and out, carrying furniture and carpets. Three men were painting the wooden rail of the balcony that ran around the upper storey. They were painting it pink and blue, and cheerfully singing as they worked. Angel was amused by the bustle, and laughed when Mr. Naryan said that she shouldn't take advantage of the citizens.

"They seem so happy to help me. What's wrong with that?"

Mr. Naryan thought it best not to explain about the cluster of genes implanted in all the races of the Shaped, the reflex altruism of the unfallen. A woman brought out tea and a pile of crisp, wafer-thin fritters sweetened with crystallized honey. Two men brought canopied chairs. Angel sprawled in one, invited Mr. Naryan to sit in the other. She was quite at ease, grinning every time someone showed her the gift they had brought her.

Dreen, Mr. Naryan knew, would be dismayed. Angel was a barbarian, displaced by five million years. She had no idea of the careful balance by which one must live with the innocent, the unfallen, if their cultures were to survive. Yet she was fully human, free to choose, and that freedom was inviolable. No wonder Dreen was so eager for the ship to reclaim her.

Still, Angel's rough joy was infectious, and Mr. Naryan soon found himself smiling with her at the sheer abundance of trinkets scattered around her. No one was giving unless they were glad to give, and no one who gave was poor. The only poor in Sensch were the sky-clad mendicants who had voluntarily renounced the material world.

So Mr. Naryan sat and drank tea with her, and ate a dozen of the delicious honeyed fritters, one after the other, and listened to more of her wild tales of traveling the river, realizing how little she understood of Confluence's administration. She was convinced that the Shaped were somehow forbidden technology, for instance, and did not understand why there was no government. Was Dreen the absolute ruler? By what right?

"Dreen is merely the Commissioner. Any authority he has is invested in him by the citizens, and it is manifest only on high days. He enjoys parades, you know. I suppose the magistrates have power, in that they arbitrate neighborly disputes and decide upon punishment—Senschians are argumentative, and sometimes quarrels can lead to unfortunate accidents."

"Murder, you mean? Then perhaps they are not as innocent as you maintain." Angel reached out suddenly. "And these? By what authority do these little spies operate?"

Pinched between her thumb and forefinger was a bronze machine. Its sensor cluster turned back and forth as it struggled to free itself.

"Why, they are part of the maintenance system of Confluence."

"Can Dreen use them? Tell me all you know. It may be important."

She questioned Mr. Naryan closely, and he found himself telling her more than he wanted. But despite all that he told her, she would not talk about her voyage, nor of why she had escaped from the ship, or how. In the days that followed, Mr. Naryan requested several times, politely and wistfully, that she would. He even visited the temple and petitioned for information about her voyage, but all trace of it had been lost in the vast sifting of history, and when pressed, the librarian who had come at the hierodule's bidding broke contact with an almost petulant abruptness.

Mr. Naryan was not surprised that it could tell him nothing. The voyage must have begun five million years ago at least, after all, for the ship to have traveled all the way to the neighboring galaxy and back.

He did learn that the ship had tried to sell its findings on landfall, much as a merchant would sell his wares. Perhaps Angel wanted to profit from what she knew; perhaps that was why the ship wanted her back, although there was no agency on Confluence that would close such a deal. Knowledge was worth only the small price of petitioning those librarians which deal with the secular world.

Meanwhile, a group of citizens gathered around Angel, like disciples around one of the blessed who, touched by some fragment or other of the Preservers, wander Confluence's long shore. These disciples went wherever she went. They were all young men, which seemed to Mr. Naryan faintly sinister, sons of her benefactors fallen under her spell. He recognized several of them, but none would speak to him, although there were always at least two or three accompanying Angel. They wore white headbands on which Angel had lettered a slogan in an archaic script older than any race of the Shaped; she refused to explain what it meant.

Mr. Naryan's wife thought that he, too, was falling under some kind of spell. She did not like the idea of Angel: she declared that Angel must be some kind of ghost, and therefore dangerous. Perhaps she was right. She was a wise and strong-willed woman, and Mr. Naryan had grown to trust her advice.

Certainly, Mr. Naryan believed that he could detect a change in the steady song of the city as he went about his business. He listened to an old man dying of the systematic organ failure which took most of the citizens in the middle of their fourth century. The man was one of the few who had left the city—he had traveled upriver, as far as a city tunneled through cliffs overlooking the river, where an amphibious race lived. His story took a whole day to tell, in a stiflingly hot room muffled in dusty carpets and lit only by a lamp with a bloodred chimney. At the end, the old man began to weep, saying that he knew now that he had not traveled at all, and Mr. Naryan was unable to comfort him. Two children were born on the next day—an event so rare that the whole city celebrated, garlanding the streets with fragrant orange blossoms. But there was a tension beneath the celebrations that Mr. Naryan had never before felt, and it seemed that Angel's followers were everywhere amongst the revelers.

Dreen felt the change, too. "There have been incidents," he said, as candid an admission as he had ever made to Mr. Naryan. "Nothing very much. A temple wall defaced with the slogan the woman has her followers wear. A market disrupted by young men running through it, overturning stalls. I asked the magistrates not to make examples of the perpetrators—that would create martyrs. Let the people hold their own courts if they wish. And she's been making speeches. Would you like to hear one?"

"Is it necessary?"

Dreen dropped his glass with a careless gesture—a machine caught it and bore it off before it smashed on the tiles. They were on a balcony of Dreen's floating habitat, looking out over the Great River towards the farside edge of the world. At the horizon was the long white double line that marked the river's fall: the rapids below, the permanent clouds above. It was noon, and the white, sunlit city was quiet.

Dreen said, "You listen to so much of her talk, I suppose you are wearied of it. In summary, it is nothing but some vague nonsense about destiny, about rising above circumstances and bettering yourself, as if you could lift yourself into the air by grasping the soles of your feet."

Dreen dismissed this with a snap of his fingers. His own feet, as always, were bare, and his long opposable toes were curled around the bar of the rail on which he squatted. He said, "Perhaps she wants to rule the city—if it pleases her, why not? At least, until the ship arrives here. I will not stop her if that is what she wants, and if she can do it. Do you know where she is right now?"

"I have been busy." But Mr. Naryan felt an eager curiosity: yes, his wife was right.

"I heard the story you gathered in. At the time, you know, I thought that man might bring war to the city when he came back." Dreen's laugh was a high-pitched hooting. "The woman is out there, at the edge of the world. She took a boat yesterday."

"I am sure she will return," Mr. Naryan said. "It is all of a pattern."

"I defer to your knowledge. Will hers be an interesting story, Mr. Naryan? Have another drink. Stay, enjoy yourself."

Dreen reached up and swung into the branches of the flame tree which leaned over the balcony, disappearing in a flurry of red leaves and leaving Mr. Naryan to find a machine that was able to take him home.

Mr. Naryan thought that Dreen was wrong to dismiss what Angel was doing, although he understood why Dreen affected such a grand indifference. It was outside Dreen's experience, that was all: Angel was outside the experience of everyone on Confluence. The Change Wars that flared here and there along Confluence's vast length were not ideological but eschatological. They were a result of sociological stresses that arose when radical shifts in the expression of clusters of native and grafted genes caused a species of Shaped to undergo a catastrophic redefinition of its perceptions of the world. But what Angel was doing dated from before the Preservers had raised up the Shaped and ended human history. Mr. Naryan only began to understand it himself when Angel told him what she had done at the edge of the world.

And later, on the terrible night when the ship arrives and every machine in the city dies, with flames roaring unchecked through the farside quarter of the city and thousands of citizens fleeing into the orchard forests, Mr. Naryan realizes that he has not understood as much as he thought. Angel has not been preaching empty revolution after all.

Her acolytes, all young men, are armed with crude wooden spears with fire-hardened tips, long double-edged knives of the kind coconut sellers use to open their wares, flails improvised from chains and wire. They hustle Mr. Naryan in a forced march towards the palace and Dreen's floating habitat. They have taken away Mr. Naryan's cane, and his bad leg hurts abominably with every other step.

Angel is gone. She has work elsewhere. Mr. Naryan felt fear when he saw her, but feels more fear now. The reflex altruism of the acolytes has been overridden by a new meme forged in the fires of Angel's revolution—they jostle Mr. Naryan with rough humor, sure in their hold over him. One in particular, the rough skin of his long-jawed face crazed in diamonds, jabs Mr. Naryan in his ribs with the butt of his spear at every intersection, as if to remind him not to escape, something that Mr. Naryan has absolutely no intention of doing.

Power is down all over the city—it went off with the fall of the machines—but leaping light from scattered fires swim in the wide eyes of the young men. They pass through a market square where people swig beer and drunkenly gamble amongst overturned stalls. Elsewhere in the fiery dark there is open rutting, men with men as well as with women. A child lies dead in a gutter. Horrible, horrible. Once, a building collapses inside its own fire, sending flames whirling high into the black sky. The faces of all the men surrounding Mr. Naryan are transformed by this leaping light into masks with eyes of flame.

Mr. Naryan's captors urge him on. His only comfort is that he will be of use in what is to come. Angel has not yet finished with him.

➤

When Angel returned from the edge of the world, she came straightaway to Mr. Naryan. It was a warm evening, at the hour after sunset when the streets began to fill with strollers, the murmur of neighbor greeting neighbor, the cries of vendors selling fruit juice or popcorn or sweet cakes.

Mr. Naryan was listening as his pupil, the magistrate's son, read a passage from the Puranas which described the time when the Preservers had strung the Galaxy with their creations. The boy was tall and awkward and faintly resentful, for he was not the scholar his father wished him to be and would rather spend his evenings with his fellows in the beer halls than read ancient legends in a long dead language. He bent over the book like a night stork, his finger stabbing at each line as he clumsily translated it, mangling words in his hoarse voice. Mr. Naryan was listening with half an ear, interrupting only to correct particularly inelegant phrases. In the kitchen at the far end of the little apartment, his wife was humming to the murmur of the radio, her voice a breathy contented monotone.

Angel came up the helical stair with a rapid clatter, mounting quickly above a sudden hush in the street. Mr. Naryan knew who it was even before she burst onto the balcony. Her appearance so astonished the magistrate's son that he dropped the book. Mr. Naryan dismissed him and he hurried away, no doubt eager to meet his friends in the flickering neon of the beer hall and tell them of this wonder.

"I've been to the edge of the world," Angel said to Mr. Naryan, coolly accepting a bowl of tea from Mr. Naryan's wife, quite oblivious of the glance she exchanged with her husband before retreating. Mr. Naryan's heart turned at that look, for in it he saw how his wife's hard words were so easily dissolved in the weltering sea of reflexive benevolence. How cruel the Preservers had been, it seemed to him never crueller, to have raised up races of the Shaped and yet to have shackled them in unthinking obedience.

Angel said, "You don't seem surprised."

"Dreen told me as much. I am pleased to see you returned safely. It has been a dry time without you." Already he had said too much; it was as if all his thoughts were eager to be spilled before her.

"Dreen knows everything that goes on in the city."

"Oh no, not at all. He knows what he needs to know."

"I took a boat," Angel said. "I just asked for it, and the man took me right along, without question. I wish now I'd stolen it. It would have been simpler. I'm tired of all this goodwill."

It was as if she could read his mind. For the first time, Mr. Naryan began to be afraid, a shiver like the first shake of a tambour that had ritually introduced the tempestuous dances of his youth.

Angel sat on the stool which the student had quit, tipping it back so she could lean against the rail of the balcony. She had cut her black hair short, and bound around her forehead a strip of white cloth printed with the slogan, in ancient incomprehensible script, that was the badge of her acolytes. She wore an ordinary loose white shirt and much jewelry: rings on every finger, sometimes more than one on each; bracelets and bangles down her forearms; gold and silver chains around her neck, layered on her breast. She was both graceful and terrifying, a rough beast slouched from the deep past to claim the world.

She said, teasingly, "Don't you want to hear my story? Isn't that your avocation?"

"I will listen to anything you want to tell me," Mr. Naryan said.

"The world is a straight line. Do you know about libration?"

Mr. Naryan shook his head.

Angel held out her hand, tipped it back and forth. "This is the world. Everything lives on the back of a long flat plate which circles the sun. The plate rocks on its long axis, so the sun rises above the edge and then reverses its course. I went to the edge of the world, where the river that runs down half its length falls into the void. I suppose it must be collected and redistributed, but it really does look like it falls away forever."

"The river is eternally renewed," Mr. Naryan said. "Where it falls is where ships used to arrive and depart, but this city has not been a port for many years."

"Fortunately for me, or my companions would already be here. There's a narrow ribbon of land on the far side of the river. Nothing lives there, not even an insect. No earth, no stones. The air shakes with the sound of the river's fall, and swirling mist burns with raw sunlight. And there are shrines, in the thunder and mist at the edge of the world. One spoke to me."

Mr. Naryan knew these shrines, although he had not been there for many years. He remembered that the different races of the Shaped had erected shrines all along the edge of the world, stone upon stone carried across the river, from which flags and long banners flew. Long ago, the original founders of the city of Sensch, Dreen's ancestors, had traveled across the river to petition the avatars of the Preservers, believing that the journey across the wide river was a necessary rite of purification. But they were gone, and the new citizens, who had built their city of stones over the burnt groves of the old city, simply bathed in the heated, mineral heavy water of the pools of the shrines of the temple at the edge of their city before delivering their petitions. He supposed the proud flags and banners of the shrines would be tattered rags now, bleached by unfiltered sunlight, rotted by mist. The screens of the shrines—would they still be working?

Angel grinned. Mr. Naryan had to remember that it was not, as it was with the citizens, a baring of teeth before striking.

She said, "Don't you want to know what it said to me? It's part of my story."

"Do you want to tell me?"

She passed her hand over the top of her narrow skull: bristly hair made a crisp sound under her palm. "No," she said. "No, I don't think I do. Not yet."

Later, after a span of silence, just before she left, she said, "After we were wakened by the ship, after it brought us here, it showed us how the black hole you call the Eye of the Preservers was made. It recorded the process as it returned, speeded up because the ship was traveling so fast it stretched time around itself. At first there was an intense point of light within the heart of the Large Magellanic Cloud. It might have been a supernova, except that it was a thousand times larger than any supernova ever recorded. For a long time its glare obscured everything else, and when it cleared, all the remaining stars were streaming around where it had been. Those nearest the center elongated and dissipated, and always more crowded in until nothing was left but the gas clouds of the accretion disc, glowing by Cerenkov radiation."

"So it is written in the Puranas."

"And is it also written there why Confluence was constructed around a halo star between the Home Galaxy and the Eye of the Preservers?"

"Of course. It is so we can all worship and glorify the Preservers. The Eye looks upon us all."

"That's what I told them," Angel said.

After she was gone, Mr. Naryan put on his spectacles and walked through the city to the docks. The unsleeping citizens were promenading in the warm dark streets, or squatting in doorways, or talking quietly from upper storey windows to their neighbors across the street. Amongst this easy somnolence, Angel's young disciples moved with a quick purpose-fulness, here in pairs, there in a group of twenty or more. Their slogans were painted on almost every wall. Three stopped Mr. Naryan near the docks, danced around his bulk, jeering, then ran off, screeching with laughter, when he slashed at them with his cane.

"Ruffians! Fools!"

"Seize the day!" they sang back. "Seize the day!"

Mr. Naryan did not find the man whose skiff Angel and her followers had used to cross the river, but the story was already everywhere amongst the fisherfolk. The Preservers had spoken to her, they said, and she had refused their temptations. Many were busily bargaining with citizens who wanted to cross the river and see the site of this miracle for themselves.

An old man, eyes milky with cataracts—the fisherfolk trawled widely across the Great River, exposing themselves to more radiation than nor-mal—asked Mr. Naryan if these were the end times, if the Preservers would return to walk amongst them again. When Mr. Naryan said, no, anyone who dealt with the avatars knew that only those fragments re-mained in the Universe, the old man shrugged and said, "They say *she* is a Preserver," and Mr. Naryan, looking out across the river's black welter, where the horizon was lost against the empty night, seeing the scattered constellations of the running lights of the fisherfolk's skiffs scattered out to the farside edge, knew that the end of Angel's story was not far off. The citizens were finding their use for her. Inexorably, step by step, she was becoming part of their history.

Mr. Naryan did not see Angel again until the night her ship arrived. Dreen went to treat with her, but he couldn't get within two streets of her house: it had become the center of a convocation that took over the entire quarter of the city. She preached to thousands of citizens from the rooftops.

Dreen reported to Mr. Naryan that it was a philosophy of hope from despair. "She says that all life feeds on destruction and death. Are you sure you don't want to hear it?"

"It is not necessary."

Dreen was perched on a balustrade, looking out at the river. They were in his floating habitat, in an arbor of lemon trees that jutted out at its leading edge. He said, "More than a thousand a day are making the crossing."

"Has the screen spoken again?"

"I've monitored it continuously. Nothing."

"But it did speak with her."

"Perhaps, perhaps." Dreen was suddenly agitated. He scampered up and down the narrow balustrade, swiping at overhanging branches and scaring the white doves that perched amongst the little glossy leaves. The birds rocketed up in a great flutter of wings, crying as they rose into the empty sky. Dreen said, "The machines watching her don't work. Not any more. She's found out how to disrupt them. I snatch long range pictures, but they don't tell me very much. I don't even know if she visited the shrine in the first place."

"I believe her," Mr. Naryan said.

"I petitioned the avatars," Dreen said, "but of course they wouldn't tell me if they'd spoken to her."

Mr. Naryan was disturbed by this admission—Dreen was not a religious man. "What will you do?"

"Nothing. I could send the magistrates for her, but even if she went with them her followers would claim she'd been arrested. And I can't even remember when I last arrested someone. It would make her even more powerful, and I'd have to let her go. But I suppose that you are going to tell me that I should let it happen."

"It has happened before. Even here, to your own people. They built the shrines, after all . . ."

"Yes, and later they fell from grace, and destroyed their city. The snakes aren't ready for that," Dreen said, almost pleading, and for a moment Mr. Naryan glimpsed the depth of Dreen's love for this city and its people.

Dreen turned away, as if ashamed, to look out at the river again, at the flocking sails of little boats setting out on, or returning from, the long crossing to the far side of the river. This great pilgrimage had become the focus of the life of the city. The markets were closed for the most part; merchants had moved to the docks to supply the thousands of pilgrims.

Dreen said, "They say that the avatar tempted her with godhead, and she denied it."

"But that is foolish! The days of the Preservers have long ago faded. We know them only by their image, which burns forever at the event horizon, but their essence has long since receded."

Dreen shrugged. "There's worse. They say that she forced the avatar to admit that the Preservers are dead. They say that *she* is an avatar of something greater than the Preservers, although you wouldn't know that from her preaching. She claims that this universe is all there is, that destiny is what you make it. What makes me despair is how readily the snakes believe this cant."

Mr. Naryan, feeling chill, there in the sun-dappled shade, said, "She has hinted to me that she learned it in the great far out, in the galaxy beyond the Home Galaxy."

"The ship is coming," Dreen said. "Perhaps they will deal with her."

          •

In the burning night of the city's dissolution, Mr. Naryan is brought at last to the pink sandstone palace. Dreen's habitat floats above it, a black cloud that half-eclipses the glowering red swirl of the Eye of the Preservers. Trails of white smoke, made luminescent by the fires which feed them, pour from the palace's high arched windows, braiding into sheets which dash like surf against the rim of the habitat. Mr. Naryan sees something fly up from amongst the palace's many carved spires—there seems to be more of them than he remembers—and smash away a piece of the habitat, which slowly tumbles off into the black sky.

The men around him hoot and cheer at this, and catch Mr. Naryan's arms and march him up the broad steps and through the high double doors into the courtyard beyond. It is piled with furniture and tapestries that have been thrown down from the thousand high windows overlooking it, but a path has been cleared to a narrow stair that turns and turns as it rises, until at last Mr. Naryan is pushed out onto the roof of the palace.

Perhaps five hundred of Angel's followers crowd amongst the spires and fallen trees and rocks, many naked, all with lettered headbands tied around their foreheads. Smoky torches blaze everywhere. In the center of the crowd is the palace's great throne on which, on high days and holidays, at the beginning of masques or parades, Dreen receives the city's priests, merchants and artists. It is lit by a crown of machines burning bright as the sun, and seated on it—easy, elegant and terrifying—is Angel.

Mr. Naryan is led through the crowd and left standing alone before the throne. Angel beckons him forward, her smile both triumphant and scared: Mr. Naryan feels her fear mix with his own.

She says, "What should I do with your city, now that I've taken it from you?"

"You have not finished your story." Everything Mr. Naryan planned to say has fallen away at the simple fact of her presence. Stranded before her fierce, barely contained energies, he feels old and used up, his body as heavy with years and regret as with fat. He adds cautiously, "I would like to hear it all."

He wonders if she really knows how her story must end. Perhaps she does. Perhaps her wild joy is not at her triumph, but at the imminence of her death. Perhaps she really does believe that the void is all, and rushes to embrace it.

Angel says, "My people can tell you. They hide with Dreen up above, but not for long."

She points across the roof. A dozen men are wrestling a sled, which shudders like a living thing as it tries to reorientate itself in the gravity field, onto a kind of launching cradle tipped up towards the habitat. The edges of the habitat are ragged, as if bitten, and amongst the roof's spires tower-trees are visibly growing towards it, their tips already brushing its edges, their tangled bases pulsing and swelling as teams of men and women drench them with nutrients.

"I found how to enhance the antigravity devices of the sleds," Angel says. "They react against the field which generates gravity for this artificial world. The field's stored inertia gives them a high kinetic energy, so that they make very good missiles. We'll chip away that floating fortress piece by piece if we have to, or we'll finish growing towers and storm its remains, but I expect surrender long before then."

"Dreen is not the ruler of the city." Nor are you, Mr. Naryan thinks, but it is not prudent to point that out.

"Not any more," Angel says.

Mr. Naryan dares to step closer. He says, "What did you find out there, that you rage against?"

Angel laughs. "I'll tell you about rage. It is what you have all forgotten, or never learned. It is the motor of evolution, and evolution's end, too." She snatches a beaker of wine from a supplicant, drains it and tosses it aside. She is consumed with an energy that is no longer her own. She says, "We traveled so long, not dead, not sleeping. We were no more than stored potentials triply engraved on gold. Although the ship flew so fast that it bound time about itself, the journey still took thousands of years of slowed ship-board time. At the end of that long voyage we did not wake: we were born. Or rather, others like us were born, although I have their memories, as if they are my own. They learned then that the Universe was not made for the convenience of humans. What they found was a galaxy ruined and dead."

She holds Mr. Naryan's hand tightly, speaking quietly and intensely, her eyes staring deep into his.

"A billion years ago, our neighboring galaxy collided with another, much smaller galaxy. Stars of both galaxies were torn off in the collision, and scattered in a vast halo. The rest coalesced into a single body, but except for ancient globular clusters, which survived the catastrophe because of their dense gravity fields, it is all wreckage. We were not able to chart a single world where life had evolved. I remember standing on a world sheared in half by immense tidal stress, its orbit so eccentric that it was colder than Pluto at its farthest point, hotter than Mercury at its nearest. I remember standing on a world of methane ice as cold and dark as the Universe itself, wandering amongst the stars. There were millions of such worlds cast adrift. I remember standing upon a fragment of a world smashed into a million shards and scattered so widely in its orbit that it never had the chance to re-form. There are a million such worlds. I remember gas giants turned inside out—single vast storms—and I remember worlds torched smooth by irruptions of their stars. No life, anywhere.

"Do you know how many galaxies have endured such collisions? Almost all of them. Life is a statistical freak. It is likely that only the stars of our galaxy have planets, or else other civilizations would surely have arisen elsewhere in the unbounded Universe. As it is, it is certain that we are alone. We must make of ourselves what we can. We should not hide, as your Preservers chose to do. Instead, we should seize the day, and make the Universe over with the technology that the Preservers used to make their hiding place."

Her grip is hurting now, but Mr. Naryan bears it. "You cannot become a Preserver," he says sadly. "No one can, now. You should not lie to these innocent people."

"I didn't need to lie. They took up my story and made it theirs. They see now what they can inherit—if they dare. This won't stop with one city. It will become a crusade!" She adds, more softly, "You'll remember it all, won't you?"

It is then that Mr. Naryan knows that she knows how this must end, and his heart breaks. He would ask her to take that burden from him, but he cannot. He is bound to her. He is her witness.

The crowd around them cheers as the sled rockets up from its cradle. It smashes into the habitat and knocks loose another piece, which drops trees and dirt and rocks amongst the spires of the palace roof as it twists free and spins away into the night.

Figures appear at the edge of the habitat. A small tube falls, glittering through the torchlight. A man catches it, runs across the debris-strewn roof, and throws himself at Angel's feet. He is at the far end of the human scale of the Shaped of this city. His skin is lapped with distinct scales, edged with a rim of hard black like the scales of a pine cone. His coarse black hair has flopped over his eyes, which glow like coals with reflected firelight.

Angel takes the tube and shakes it. It unrolls into a flexible sheet on which Dreen's face glows. Dreen's lips move; his voice is small and metallic. Angel listens intently, and when he has finished speaking says softly, "Yes."

Then she stands and raises both hands above her head. All across the roof, men and woman turn towards her, eyes glowing.

"They wish to surrender! Let them come down!"

A moment later a sled swoops down from the habitat, its silvery underside gleaming in the reflected light of the many fires scattered across the roof. Angel's followers shout and jeer, and missiles fly out of the darkness—a burning torch, a rock, a broken branch. All are somehow deflected before they reach the ship's crew, screaming away into the dark with such force that the torch, the branch, kindle into white fire. The crew have modified the sled's field to protect themselves.

They all look like Angel, with the same small sleek head, the same gangling build and abrupt nervous movements. Dreen's slight figure is dwarfed by them. It takes Mr. Naryan a long minute to be able to distinguish men from women, and another to be able to tell each man from his brothers, each woman from her sisters. They are all clad in long white shirts that leave them bare-armed and bare-legged, and each is girdled with a belt from which hang a dozen or more little machines. They call to Angel, one following on the words of the other, saying over and over again:

"Return with us—"

"—this is not our place—"

"—these are not our people—"

"—we will return—"

"—we will find our home—"

"—leave with us and return."

Dreen sees Mr. Naryan and shouts, "They want to take her back!" He jumps down from the sled, an act of bravery that astonishes Mr. Naryan, and skips through the crowd. "They are all one person, or variations on one person," he says breathlessly. "The ship makes its crew by varying a template. Angel is an extreme. A mistake."

Angel starts to laugh.

"You funny little man! I'm the real one—they are the copies!"

"Come back to us—"

"—come back and help us—"

"—help us find our home."

"There's no home to find!" Angel shouts. "Oh, you fools! This is all there is!"

"I tried to explain to them," Dreen says to Mr. Naryan, "but they wouldn't listen."

"They surely cannot disbelieve the Puranas," Mr. Naryan says.

Angel shouts, "Give me back the ship!"

"It was never yours—"

"—never yours to own—"

"—but only yours to serve."

"No! I won't serve!" Angel jumps onto the throne and makes an abrupt cutting gesture.

Hundreds of fine silver threads spool out of the darkness, shooting towards the sled and her crewmates. The ends of the threads flick up when they reach the edge of the sled's modified field, but then fall in a tangle over the crew: their shield is gone.

The crowd begins to throw things again, but Angel orders them to be still. "I have the only working sled," she says. "That which I enhance, I can also take away. Come with me," she tells Mr. Naryan, "and see the end of my story."

The crowd around Angel stirs. Mr. Naryan turns, and sees one of the crew walking towards Angel.

He is as tall and slender as Angel, his small high-cheekboned face so like her own it is as if he holds up a mirror as he approaches. A rock arcs out of the crowd and strikes his shoulder: he staggers but walks on, hardly seeming to notice that the crowd closes at his back so that he is suddenly inside its circle, with Angel and Mr. Naryan in its focus.

Angel says, "I'm not afraid of you."

"Of course not, sister," the man says. And he grasps her wrists in both his hands.

Then Mr. Naryan is on his hands and knees. A strong wind howls about him, and he can hear people screaming. The after-glow of a great light swims in his vision. He can't see who helps him up and half-carries him through the stunned crowd to the sled.

When the sled starts to rise, Mr. Naryan falls to his knees again. Dreen says in his ear, "It's over."

"No," Mr. Naryan says. He blinks and blinks, tears rolling down his cheeks.

The man took Angel's wrists in both of his—

Dreen is saying something, but Mr. Naryan shakes his head. It is not over.

—and they shot up into the night, so fast that their clothing burst into flame, so fast that air was drawn up with them. If Angel could nullify the gravity field, then so could her crewmates. She has achieved apotheosis.

The sled swoops up the tiered slope of the ship, is swallowed by a wide hatch. When he can see again, Mr. Naryan finds himself kneeling at the edge of the open hatch. The city is spread below. Fires define the streets which radiate away from the Great River; the warm night air is bitter with the smell of burning.

Dreen has been looking at the lighted windows that crowd the walls of the vast room beyond the hatch, scampering with growing excitement from one to the other. Now he sees that Mr. Naryan is crying, and clumsily tries to comfort him, believing that Mr. Naryan is mourning his wife, left behind in the dying city.

"She was a good woman, for her kind," Mr. Naryan is able to say at last, although it isn't her he's mourning, or not only her. He is mourning for all of the citizens of Sensch. They are irrevocably caught in their change now, never to be the same. His wife, the nut roaster, the men and women who own the little tea houses at the corner of every square, the children, the mendicants and the merchants—all are changed, or else dying in the process. Something new is being born down there. Rising from the fall of the city.

"They'll take us to away from all this," Dreen says happily. "They're going to search for where they came from. Some are out combing the city for others who can help them; the rest are preparing the ship. They'll take it over the edge of the world, into the great far out!"

"Don't they know they'll never find what they're looking for? The Puranas—"

"Old stories, old fears. They will take us home!"

Mr. Naryan laboriously clambers to his feet. He understands that Dreen has fallen under the thrall of the crew. He is theirs, as Mr. Naryan is now and forever Angel's. He says, "Those times are past. Down there in the city is the beginning of something new, something wonderful—" He finds he can't explain. All he has is his faith that it won't stop here. It is not an end but a beginning, a spark to set all of Confluence—the unfallen and the changed—alight. Mr. Naryan says, weakly, "It won't stop here."

Dreen's big eyes shine in the light of the city's fires. He says, "I see only another Change War. There's nothing new in that. The snakes will rebuild the city in their new image, if not here, then somewhere else along the Great River. It has happened before, in this very place, to my own people. We survived it, and so will the snakes. But what *they* promise is so much greater! We'll leave this poor place, and voyage out to return to where it all began, to the very home of the Preservers. Look there! That's where we're going!"

Mr. Naryan allows himself to be led across the vast room. It is so big that it could easily hold Dreen's floating habitat. A window on its far side shows a view angled somewhere far above the plane of Confluence's orbit. Confluence itself is a shining strip, an arrow running out to its own vanishing point. Beyond that point are the ordered, frozen spirals of the Home Galaxy, the great jeweled clusters and braids of stars constructed in the last great days of the Preservers before they vanished forever into the black hole they made by collapsing the Magellanic Clouds.

Mr. Naryan starts to breathe deeply, topping up the oxygen content of his blood.

"You see!" Dreen says again, his face shining with awe in Confluence's silver light.

"I see the end of history," Mr. Naryan says. "You should have studied the Puranas, Dreen. There's no future to be found amongst the artifacts of the Preservers, only the dead past. I won't serve, Dreen. That's over."

And then he turns and lumbers through the false lights and shadows of the windows towards the open hatch. Dreen catches his arm, but Mr. Naryan throws him off.

Dreen sprawls on his back, astonished, then jumps up and runs in front of Mr. Naryan. "You fool!" he shouts. "They can bring her back!"

"There's no need," Mr. Naryan says, and pushes Dreen out of the way and plunges straight out of the hatch.

He falls through black air like a heavy comet. Water smashes around him, tears away his clothes. His nostrils pinch shut and membranes slide across his eyes as he plunges down and down amidst streaming bubbles until the roaring in his ears is no longer the roar of his blood but the roar of the river's never-ending fall over the edge of the world.

Deep, silty currents begin to pull him towards that edge. He turns in the water and begins to swim away from it, away from the ship and the burning city. His duty is over: once they have taken charge of their destiny, the changed citizens will no longer need an Archivist.

Mr. Naryan swims more and more easily. The swift cold water washes away his landbound habits, wakes the powerful muscles of his shoulders and back. Angel's message burns bright, burning away the old stories, as he swims through the black water, against the currents of the Great River. Joy gathers with every thrust of his arms. He is the messenger, Angel's witness. He will travel ahead of the crusade that will begin when everyone in Sensch is changed. It will be a long and difficult journey, but he does not doubt that his destiny—the beginning of the future that Angel has bequeathed him and all of Confluence—lies at the end of it.

Genesis

POUL ANDERSON

One of the best-known writers in science fiction, Poul Anderson made his first sale in 1947, while he was still in college, and in the course of his subsequent fifty-plus-year career has published almost a hundred books (in several different fields, as Anderson has written historical novels, fantasies, and mysteries, in addition to science fiction), sold hundreds of short pieces to every conceivable market, and won seven Hugo Awards, three Nebula Awards, and the Tolkein Memorial Award for Life Achievement.

Anderson had trained to be a scientist, taking a degree in physics from the University of Minnesota, but the writing life proved to be more seductive, and he never did get around to working in his original field of choice. Instead, the sales mounted steadily, until by the late fifties and early sixties he may have been one of the most prolific writers in the genre.

In spite of his high output of fiction, he somehow managed to maintain an amazingly high standard of literary quality as well, and by the early-to-mid-1960s was also on his way to becoming one of the most honored and respected writers in the genre. At one point during this period (in addition to nonrelated work, and lesser series such as the Hoka stories he was writing in collaboration with Gordon R. Dickson), Anderson was running three of the most popular and prestigious series in science fiction all at the same time: the Technic History series detailing the exploits of the wily trader Nicholas Van Rijn (which includes novels such as The Man Who Counts, The Trouble Twisters, Satan's World, Mirkheim, The People of the Wind and collections such as Trader to the Stars and The Earth Book of Stormgate); the extremely popular series relating the adventures of interstellar secret agent Dominic Flandry, probably the most successful attempt to cross science fiction with the spy thriller, next to Jack Vance's Demon Princes novels (the Flandry series includes novels such as A Circus of Hells, The Rebel Worlds, The Day of Their Return, Flandry of Terra, A Knight of Ghosts and Shadows, A Stone in Heaven, and The Game of Empire and collections such as Agent of the Terran Empire); and, my own personal favorite, a series that took us along on assignment with the agents of the Time Patrol (including the collections The Guardians of Time, Time Patrolman, The Shield of Time, and The Time Patrol).

When you add to this amazing collection of memorable titles the impact of the best of Anderson's nonseries novels, works such as Brain Wave, Three Hearts and Three Lions, The Night Face, The Enemy Stars, and The High Crusade, all of which were published in addition to the series books, it becomes clear that Anderson dominated the late fifties and the pre–New Wave sixties in a way that only Robert A. Heinlein, Isaac Asimov, and Arthur C. Clarke could rival. And, like them, he remained an active and dominant figure right through the seventies and eight-

ies and is still *producing strong new work and turning up on best-seller lists at the end of the decade of the nineties as well.*

In the powerful, complex, and lyrical novella that follows, Anderson demonstrates all of his considerable strengths and takes us into the far future for a jolt of that much-talked-about Sense of Wonder that's as pure and concentrated, and as mind-boggling as anything you're going to find anywhere in the genre.

Anderson's other books (among many *others) include:* The Broken Sword, Tau Zero, A Midsummer Tempest, Orion Shall Rise, The Boat of a Million Years, The Stars Are Also Fire, *and* Harvest of Stars. *His short work had been collected in* The Queen Air and Darkness and Other Stories, Fantasy, The Unicorn Trade *(with Karen Anderson).* Past Times, The Best of Poul Anderson, *and* Explorations. *His most recent books are the novels* The Fleet of Stars, Starfarers, *and* Operation Luna *and the retrospective collection* All One Universe. *Upcoming is a new novel,* Genesis, *expanded from the story that follows. Anderson lives in Orinda, California, with his wife (and fellow writer) Karen.*

> *Was it her I ought to have loved . . . ?*
> —Piet Hein

1

No human could have shaped the thoughts or uttered them. They had no real beginning, they had been latent for millennium after millennium while the galactic brain was growing. Sometimes they passed from mind to mind, years or decades through space at the speed of light, nanoseconds to receive, comprehend, consider, and send a message on outward. But there was so much else—a cosmos of realities, an infinity of virtualities and abstract creations—that remembrances of Earth were the barest undertone, intermittent and fleeting, among uncounted billions of other incidentals. Most of the grand awareness was directed elsewhere, much of it intent on its own evolution.

For the galactic brain was still in infancy: unless it held itself to be still a-borning. By now its members were strewn from end to end of the spiral arms, out into the halo and the nearer star-gatherings, as far as the Magellanic Clouds. The seeds of fresh ones drifted farther yet; some had reached the shores of the Andromeda.

Each was a local complex of organisms, machines, and their interrelationships. ("Organism" seems best for something that maintains itself, reproduces at need, and possesses a consciousness in a range from the rudimentary to the transcendent, even though carbon compounds are a very small part of its material components and most of its life processes take place directly on the quantum level.) They numbered in the many millions, and the number was rising steeply, also within the Milky Way, as the founders of new generations arrived at new homes.

Thus the galactic brain was in perpetual growth, which from a cosmic viewpoint had barely started. Thought had just had time for a thousand or two journeys across its ever-expanding breadth. It would never absorb its members into itself; they would always remain individuals, developing along their individual lines. Let us therefore call them not cells, but nodes.

For they were in truth distinct. Each had more uniquenesses than were ever possible to a protoplasmic creature. Chaos and quantum fluctuation assured that none would exactly resemble any predecessor. Environment likewise helped shape the personality—surface conditions (what kind of planet, moon, asteroid, comet?) or free orbit, sun single or multiple (what kinds, what ages?), nebula, interstellar space and its ghostly tides. . . . Then, too, a node was not a single mind. It was as many as it chose to be, freely awakened and freely set aside, proteanly intermingling and separating again, using whatever bodies and sensors it wished for as long as it wished, immortally experiencing, creating, meditating, seeking a fulfillment that the search itself brought forth.

Hence, while every node was engaged with a myriad of matters, one might be especially developing new realms of mathematics, another composing glorious works that cannot really be likened to music, another observing the destiny of organic life on some world, life which it had perhaps fabricated for that purpose, another—Human words are useless.

Always, though, the nodes were in continuous communication over the light-years, communication on tremendous bandwidths of every possible medium. *This* was the galactic brain. That unity, that selfhood which was slowly coalescing, might spend millions of years contemplating a thought; but the thought would be as vast as the thinker, in whose sight an eon was as a day and a day was as an eon.

Already now, in its nascence, it affected the course of the universe. The time came when a node fully recalled Earth. That memory went out to others as part of the ongoing flow of information, ideas, feelings, reveries, and who knows what else? Certain of these others decided the subject was worth pursuing, and relayed it on their own message-streams. In this wise it passed through light-years and centuries, circulated, developed, and at last became a decision, which reached the node best able to take action.

Here the event has been related in words, ill-suited though they are to the task. They fail totally when they come to what happened next. How shall they tell of the dialogue of a mind with itself, when that thinking was a progression of quantum flickerings through configurations as intricate as the wave functions, when the computational power and database were so huge that measures become meaningless, when the mind raised aspects of itself to interact like persons until it drew them back into its wholeness, and when everything was said within microseconds of planetary time?

It is impossible, except vaguely and misleadingly. Ancient humans used the language of myth for that which they could not fathom. The sun was a fiery chariot daily crossing heaven, the year a god who died and was reborn, death a punishment for ancestral sin. Let us make our myth concerning the mission to Earth.

Think, then, of the primary aspect of the node's primary consciousness as if it were a single mighty entity, and name it Alpha. Think of a lesser manifestation of itself that it had synthesized and intended to release into separate existence as a second entity. For reasons that will become clear, imagine the latter masculine and name it Wayfarer.

All is myth and metaphor, beginning with this absurd nomenclature. Beings like these had no names. They had identities, instantly recognizable by others of their kind. They did not speak together, they did not go through discussion or explanation of any sort, they were not yet "they." But imagine it.

Imagine, too, their surroundings, not as perceived by their manifold sensors or conceptualized by their awareness and emotions, but as if human sense organs were reporting to a human brain. Such a picture is scarcely a sketch. Too much that was basic could not have registered. However, a human at an astronomical distance could have seen an M2 dwarf star about fifty parsecs from Sol, and ascertained that it had planets. She could have detected signs of immense, enigmatic energies, and wondered.

In itself, the sun was undistinguished. The galaxy held billions like it. Long ago, an artificial intelligence—at that dawn stage of evolution, this was the best phrase—had established itself there because one of the planets bore curious life-forms worth studying. That research went on through the megayears. Meanwhile the ever-heightening intelligence followed more and more different interests: above all, its self-evolution. That the sun would stay cool for an enormous length of time had been another consideration. The node did not want the trouble of coping with great environmental changes before it absolutely must.

Since then, stars had changed their relative positions. This now was the settlement nearest to Sol. Suns closer still were of less interest and had merely been visited, if that. Occasionally a free-space, dirigible node had passed through the neighborhood, but none chanced to be there at this epoch.

Relevant to our myth is the fact that no thinking species ever appeared on the viviferous world. Life is statistically uncommon in the cosmos, sapience almost vanishingly rare, therefore doubly precious.

Our imaginary human would have seen the sun as autumnally yellow, burning low and peacefully. Besides its planets and lesser natural attendants, various titanic structures orbited about it. From afar, they seemed like gossamer or like intricate spiderwebs agleam athwart the stars; most of what they were was force fields. They gathered and focused the energies that Alpha required, they searched the deeps of space and the atom, they transmitted and received the thought-flow that was becoming the galactic brain; what more they did lies beyond the myth.

Within their complexity, although not at any specific location, lived Alpha, its apex. Likewise, for the moment, did Wayfarer.

Imagine a stately voice: "Welcome into being. Yours is a high and, it may be, dangerous errand. Are you willing?"

If Wayfarer hesitated an instant, that was not from fear of suffering harm but from fear of inflicting it. "Tell me. Help me to understand."

"Sol—" The sun of old Earth, steadily heating since first it took shape, would continue stable for billions of years before it exhausted the hydrogen fuel at its core and swelled into a red giant. But—

A swift computation. "Yes. I see." Above a threshold level of radiation input, the geochemical and biochemical cycles that had maintained the temperature of Earth would be overwhelmed. Increasing warmth put increasing amounts of water vapor into the atmosphere, and it is a potent greenhouse gas. Heavier cloud cover, raising the albedo, could only postpone a day of catastrophe. Rising above it, water molecules were split by hard sunlight into hydrogen, which escaped to space, and oxygen, which bound to surface materials. Raging fires released monstrous tonnages of carbon dioxide, as did rocks exposed to heat by erosion in desiccated lands. It is the second major greenhouse gas. The time must come when the last oceans boiled away, leaving a globe akin to Venus; but well before then, life on Earth would be no more than a memory in the quantum consciousness. "When will total extinction occur?"

"On the order of a hundred thousand years futureward."

Pain bit through the facet of Wayfarer that came from Christian Brannock, who was born on ancient Earth and most passionately loved his living world. Long since had his uploaded mind merged into a colossal oneness that later divided and redivided, until copies of it were integral with awareness across the galaxy. So were the minds of millions of his fellow humans, as unnoticed now as single genes had been in their bodies when their flesh was alive, and yet significant elements of the whole. Ransacking its database, Alpha had found the record of Christian Brannock and chosen to weave him into the essence of Wayfarer, rather than someone else. The judgment was—call it intuitive.

"Can't you say more closely?" he appealed.

"No," replied Alpha. "The uncertainties and imponderables are too many. Gaia," mythic name for the node in the Solar System, "has responded to inquiries evasively when at all."

"Have . . . we . . . really been this slow to think about Earth?"

"We had much else to think about and do, did we not? Gaia could at any time have requested special consideration. She never did. Thus the matter did not appear to be of major importance. Human Earth is preserved in memory. What is posthuman Earth but a planet approaching the postbiological phase?

"True, the scarcity of spontaneously evolved biomes makes the case interesting. However, Gaia has presumably been observing and gathering the data, for the rest of us to examine whenever we wish. The Solar System has seldom had visitors. The last was two million years ago. Since then, Gaia has joined less and less in our fellowship; her communications have grown sparse and perfunctory. But such withdrawals are not unknown. A node may, for example, want to pursue a philosophical concept undisturbed, until it is ready for general contemplation. In short, nothing called Earth to our attention."

"*I* would have remembered," whispered Christian Brannock.

"What finally reminded us?" asked Wayfarer.

"The idea that Earth may be worth saving. Perhaps it holds more than

Gaia knows of—" A pause. "—or has told of. If nothing else, sentimental value."

"Yes, I understand," said Christian Brannock.

"Moreover, and potentially more consequential, we may well have experience to gain, a precedent to set. If awareness is to survive the mortality of the stars, it must make the universe over. That work of billions or trillions of years will begin with some small, experimental undertaking. Shall it be now," the "now" of deathless beings already geologically old, "at Earth?"

"Not small," murmured Wayfarer. Christian Brannock had been an engineer.

"No," agreed Alpha. "Given the time constraint, only the resources of a few stars will be available. Nevertheless, we have various possibilities open to us, if we commence soon enough. The question is which would be the best—and, first, whether we *should* act.

"Will you go seek an answer?"

"Yes," responded Wayfarer, and "Yes, oh, God damn, yes," cried Christian Brannock.

◆

A spaceship departed for Sol. A laser accelerated it close to the speed of light, energized by the sun and controlled by a network of interplanetary dimensions. If necessary, the ship could decelerate itself at journey's end, travel freely about, and return unaided, albeit more slowly. Its cryomagnetics supported a good-sized ball of antimatter, and its total mass was slight. The material payload amounted simply to: a matrix, plus backup, for running the Wayfarer programs and containing a database deemed sufficient; assorted sensors and effectors; several bodies of different capabilities, into which he could download an essence of himself; miscellaneous equipment and power systems; a variety of instruments; and a thing ages forgotten, which Wayfarer had ordered molecules to make at the wish of Christian Brannock. He might somewhere find time and fingers for it.

A guitar.

2

There was a man called Kalava, a sea captain of Sirsu. His clan was the Samayoki. In youth he had fought well at Broken Mountain, where the armies of Ulonai met the barbarian invaders swarming north out of the desert and cast them back with fearsome losses. He then became a mariner. When the Ulonaian League fell apart and the alliances led by Sirsu and Irrulen raged across the land, year after year, seeking each other's throats, Kalava sank enemy ships, burned enemy villages, bore treasure and captives off to market.

After the grudgingly made, unsatisfactory Peace of Tuopai, he went into trade. Besides going up and down the River Lonna and around the Gulf of Sirsu, he often sailed along the North Coast, bartering as he went, then out over the Windroad Sea to the colonies on the Ending Islands. At last, with three ships, he followed that coast east through distances hitherto unknown. Living off the waters and what hunting parties could take ashore, dealing or fighting with the wild tribes they met, in the course of months he and his crews came to where the land bent south. A ways beyond that they found a port belonging to the fabled people of the Shining Fields. They abode for a year and returned carrying wares that at home made them rich.

From his clan Kalava got leasehold of a thorp and good farmland in the Lonna delta, about a day's travel from Sirsu. He meant to settle down, honored and comfortable. But that was not in the thought of the gods nor in his nature. He was soon quarreling with all his neighbors, until his wife's brother grossly insulted him and he killed the man. Thereupon she left him. At the clanmoot which composed the matter she received a third of the family wealth, in gold and movables. Their daughters and the husbands of these sided with her.

Of Kalava's three sons, the eldest had drowned in a storm at sea; the next died of the Black Blood; the third, faring as an apprentice on a merchant vessel far south to Zhir, fell while resisting robbers in sand-drifted streets under the time-gnawed colonnades of an abandoned city. They left no children, unless by slaves. Nor would Kalava, now; no free woman took his offers of marriage. What he had gathered through a hard lifetime would fall to kinfolk who hated him. Most folk in Sirsu shunned him too.

Long he brooded, until a dream hatched. When he knew it for what it was, he set about his preparations, more quietly than might have been awaited. Once the business was under way, though not too far along for him to drop if he must, he sought Ilyandi the skythinker.

She dwelt on Council Heights. There did the Vilkui meet each year for rites and conference. But when the rest of them had dispersed again to carry on their vocation—dream interpreters, scribes, physicians, mediators, vessels of olden lore and learning, teachers of the young—Ilyandi remained. Here she could best search the heavens and seek for the meaning of what she found, on a high place sacred to all Ulonai.

Up the Spirit Way rumbled Kalava's chariot. Near the top, the trees that lined it, goldfruit and plume, stood well apart, giving him a clear view. Bushes grew sparse and low on the stony slopes, here the dusty green of vasi, there a shaggy hairleaf, yonder a scarlet fireflower. Scorch-wort lent its acrid smell to a wind blowing hot and slow off the Gulf. That water shone, tarnished metal, westward beyond sight, under a silver-gray overcast beneath which scudded rags of darker cloud. A rainstorm stood on the horizon, blurred murk and flutters of lightning light.

Elsewhere reached the land, bloomgrain ripening yellow, dun paper-leaf, verdant pastures for herdlings, violet richen orchards, tall stands of shipwood. Farmhouses and their outbuildings lay widely strewn. The weather having been dry of late, dust whirled up from the roads winding among them to veil wagons and trains of porters. Regally from its sources eastward in Wilderland flowed the Lonna, arms fanning out north and south.

Sirsu lifted battlemented walls on the right bank of the main stream, tiny in Kalava's eyes at its distance. Yet he knew it, he could pick out famous works, the Grand Fountain in King's Newmarket, the frieze-bordered portico of the Flame Temple, the triumphal column in Victory Square, and he knew where the wrights had their workshops, the merchants their bazaars, the innkeepers their houses for a seaman to find a jug and a wench. Brick, sandstone, granite, marble mingled their colors softly together. Ships and boats plied the water or were docked under the walls. On the opposite shore sprawled mansions and gardens of the Helki suburb, their rooftiles fanciful as jewels.

It was remote from that which he approached.

Below a great arch, two postulants in blue robes slanted their staffs across the way and called, "In the name of the Mystery, stop, make reverence, and declare yourself!"

Their young voices rang high, unawed by a sight that had daunted warriors. Kalava was a big man, wide-shouldered and thick-muscled. Weather had darkened his skin to the hue of coal and bleached nearly white the hair that fell in braids halfway down his back. As black were the eyes that gleamed below a shelf of brow, in a face rugged, battered, and scarred. His mustache curved down past the jaw, dyed red. Traveling in peace, he wore simply a knee-length kirtle, green and trimmed with kivi skin, each scale polished, and buskins; but gold coiled around his arms and a sword was belted at his hip. Likewise did a spear stand socketed in the chariot, pennon flapping, while a shield slatted at the rail and an ax hung ready to be thrown. Four matched slaves drew the car. Their line had been bred for generations to be draft creatures—huge, long-legged, spirited, yet trustworthy after the males were gelded. Sweat sheened over Kalava's brand on the small, bald heads and ran down naked bodies. Nonetheless they breathed easily and the smell of them was rather sweet.

Their owner roared, "Halt!" For a moment only the wind had sound or motion. Then Kalava touched his brow below the headband and recited the Confession: "What a man knows is little, what he understands is less, therefore let him bow down to wisdom." Himself, he trusted more in blood sacrifices and still more in his own strength; but he kept a decent respect for the Vilkui.

"I seek counsel from the skythinker Ilyandi," he said. That was hardly needful, when no other initiate of her order was present.

"All may seek who are not attainted of ill-doing," replied the senior boy as ceremoniously.

"Ruvio bear witness that any judgments against me stand satisfied." The Thunderer was the favorite god of most mariners.

"Enter, then, and we shall convey your request to our lady."

The junior boy led Kalava across the outer court. Wheels rattled loud on flagstones. At the guesthouse, he helped stall, feed, and water the slaves, before he showed the newcomer to a room that in the high season slept two-score men. Elsewhere in the building were a bath, a refectory, ready food—dried meat, fruit, and flatbread—with richenberry wine. Kalava also found a book. After refreshment, he sat down on a bench to pass the time with it.

He was disappointed. He had never had many chances or much desire to read, so his skill was limited; and the copyist for this codex had used a style of lettering obsolete nowadays. Worse, the text was a chronicle of the emperors of Zhir. That was not just painful to him—oh, Eneio, his son, his last son!—but valueless. True, the Vilkui taught that civilization had come to Ulonai from Zhir. What of it? How many centuries had fled since the desert claimed that realm? What were the descendants of its dwellers but starveling nomads and pestiferous bandits?

Well, Kalava thought, yes, this could be a timely warning, a reminder to people of how the desert still marched northward. But was what they could see not enough? He had passed by towns not very far south, flourishing in his grandfather's time, now empty, crumbling houses half buried in dust, glassless windows like the eye sockets in a skull.

His mouth tightened. *He* would not meekly abide any doom.

Day was near an end when an acolyte of Ilyandi came to say that she would receive him. Walking with his guide, he saw purple dusk shade toward night in the east. In the west the storm had ended, leaving that part of heaven clear for a while. The sun was plainly visible, though mists turned it into a red-orange step pyramid. From the horizon it cast a bridge of fire over the Gulf and sent great streamers of light aloft into cloudbanks that glowed sulfurous. A whisltewing passed like a shadow across them. The sound of its flight keened faintly down through air growing less hot. Otherwise a holy silence rested upon the heights.

Three stories tall, the sanctuaries, libraries, laboratories, and quarters of the Vilkui surrounded the inner court with their cloisters. A garden of flowers and healing herbs, intricately laid out, filled most of it. A lantern had been lighted in one arcade, but all windows were dark and Ilyandi stood out in the open awaiting her visitor.

She made a slight gesture of dismissal. The acolyte bowed her head and slipped away. Kalava saluted, feeling suddenly awkward but his resolution headlong within him. "Greeting, wise and gracious lady," he said.

"Well met, brave captain," the skythinker replied. She gestured at a pair of confronting stone benches. "Shall we be seated?" It fell short of inviting him to share wine, but it meant she would at least hear him out.

They lowered themselves and regarded one another through the swiftly deepening twilight. Ilyandi was a slender woman of perhaps forty years, features thin and regular, eyes large and luminous brown, complexion pale—like smoked copper, he thought. Cropped short in token of celibacy, wavy hair made a bronze coif above a plain white robe. A green sprig of tekin, held at her left shoulder by a pin in the emblematic form of interlocked circle and triangle, declared her a Vilku.

"How can I aid your venture?" she asked.

He started in surprise. "Huh! What do you know about my plans?" In haste: "My lady knows much, of course."

She smiled. "You and your saga have loomed throughout these past decades. And . . . word reaches us here. You search out your former crew-men or bid them come see you, all privately. You order repairs made to the ship remaining in your possession. You meet with chandlers, no doubt to sound them out about prices. Few if any people have noticed. Such discretion is not your wont. Where are you bound, Kalava, and why so secretively?"

His grin was rueful. "My lady's not just wise and learned, she's clever. Well, then, why not go straight to the business? I've a voyage in mind that most would call crazy. Some among them might try to forestall me, holding that it would anger the gods of those parts—seeing that nobody's ever returned from there, and recalling old tales of monstrous things glimpsed from afar. I don't believe them myself, or I wouldn't try it."

"Oh, I can imagine you setting forth regardless," said Ilyandi half under her breath. Louder: "But agreed, the fear is likely false. No one had reached the Shining Fields by sea, either, before you did. You asked for no beforehand spells or blessings then. Why have you sought me now?"

"This is, is different. Not hugging a shoreline. I—well, I'll need to get and train a new huukin, and that's no small thing in money or time." Kalava spread his big hands, almost helplessly. "I had not looked to set forth ever again, you see. Maybe it is madness, an old man with an old crew in a single old ship. I hoped you might counsel me, my lady."

"You're scarcely ready for the balefire, when you propose to cross the Windroad Sea," she answered.

This time he was not altogether taken aback. "May I ask how my lady knows?"

Ilyandi waved a hand. Catching faint lamplight, the long fingers soared through the dusk like nightswoopers. "You have already been east, and would not need to hide such a journey. South, the trade routes are ancient as far as Zhir. What has it to offer but the plunder of tombs and dead cities, brought in by wretched squatters? What lies beyond but unpeopled desolation until, folk say, one would come to the Burning Lands and perish miserably? Westward we know of a few islands, and then empty ocean. If anything lies on the far side, you could starve and thirst to death before you reached it. But northward—yes, wild waters, but sometimes men come upon driftwood of unknown trees or spy storm-borne flyers of unknown breed—and we have all the legends of the High North, and glimpses of mountains from ships blown off course—" Her voice trailed away.

"Some of those tales ring true to me," Kalava said. "More true than stories about uncanny sights. Besides, wild huukini breed offshore, where fish are plentiful. I have not seen enough of them there, in season, to account for as many as I've seen in open sea. They must have a second shoreline. Where but the High North?"

Ilyandi nodded. "Shrewd, Captain. What else do you hope to find?"

He grinned again. "I'll tell you after I get back, my lady."

Her tone sharpened. "No treasure-laden cities to plunder."

He yielded. "Nor to trade with. Would we not have encountered craft of theirs, or, anyhow, wreckage? However . . . the farther north, the less heat and the more rainfall, no? A country yonder could have a mild clime, forestfuls of timber, fat land for plowing, and nobody to fight." The words throbbed. "No desert creeping in? Room to begin afresh, my lady."

She regarded him steadily through the gloaming. "You'd come home, recruit people, found a colony, and be its king?"

"Its foremost man, aye, though I expect the kind of folk who'd go will want a republic. But mainly—" His voice went low. He stared beyond her. "Freedom. Honor. A freeborn wife and new sons."

They were silent awhile. Full night closed in. It was not as murky as usual, for the clearing in the west had spread rifts up toward the zenith. A breath of coolness soughed in leaves, as if Kalava's dream whispered a promise.

"You are determined," she said at last, slowly. "Why have you come to me?"

"For whatever counsel you will give, my lady. Facts about the passage may be hoarded in books here."

She shook her head. "I doubt it. Unless navigation—yes, that is a real barrier, is it not?"

"Always," he sighed.

"What means of wayfinding have you?"

"Why, you must know."

"I know what is the common knowledge about it. Craftsmen keep their trade secrets, and surely skippers are no different in that regard. If you will tell me how you navigate, it shall not pass these lips, and I may be able to add something."

Eagerness took hold of him. "I'll wager my lady can! We see moon or stars unoften and fitfully. Most days the sun shows no more than a blur of dull light amongst the clouds, if that. But you, skythinkers like you, they've watched and measured for hundreds of years, they've gathered lore—" Kalava paused. "Is it too sacred to share?"

"No, no," she replied. "The Vilkui keep the calender for everyone, do they not? The reason that sailors rarely get our help is that they could make little or no use of our learning. Speak."

"True, it was Vilkui who discovered lodestones. . . . Well, coasting these waters, I rely mainly on my remembrance of landmarks, or a periplus if they're less familiar to me. Soundings help, especially if the plumb brings up a sample of the bottom for me to look at the taste. Then in the Shining Fields I got a crystal—you must know about it, for I gave another to the order when I got back—I look through it at the sky and, if the weather be not too thick, I see more closely where the sun is than I can with a bare eye. A logline and hourglass give some idea of speed, a lodestone some idea of direction, when out of sight of land. Sailing for the High North and return, I'd mainly use it, I suppose. But if my lady could tell me of anything else—"

She sat forward on her bench. He heard a certain intensity. "I think I might, Captain. I've studied that sunstone of yours. With it, one can estimate latitude and time of day, if one knows the date and the sun's heavenly course during the year. Likewise, even glimpses of moon and stars would be valuable to a traveler who knew them well."

"That's not me," he said wryly. "Could my lady write something down? Maybe this old head won't be too heavy to puzzle it out."

She did not seem to hear. Her gaze had gone upward. "The aspect of the stars in the High North," she murmured. "It could tell us whether the world is indeed round. And are our vague auroral shimmers more bright yonder—in the veritable Lodeland—?"

His look followed hers. Three stars twinkled wan where the clouds were torn. "It's good of you, my lady," he said, "that you sit talking with me, when you could be at your quadrant or whatever, snatching this chance."

Her eyes met his. "Yours may be a better chance, Captain," she answered fiercely. "When first I got the rumor of your expedition, I began to think upon it and what it could mean. Yes, I will help you where I can. I may even sail with you."

➤

The *Gray Courser* departed Sirsu on a morning tide as early as there was light to steer by. Just the same, people crowded the dock. The majority watched mute. A number made signs against evil. A few, mostly young, sang a defiant paean, but the air seemed to muffle their strains.

Only lately had Kalava given out what his goal was. He must, to account for the skythinker's presence, which could not be kept hidden. That sanctification left the authorities no excuse to forbid his venture. However, it took little doubt and fear off those who believed the outer Windroad a haunt of monsters and demons, which might be stirred to plague home waters.

His crew shrugged the notion off, or laughed at it. At any rate, they said they did. Two-thirds of them were crusty shellbacks who had fared under his command before. For the rest, he had had to take what he could scrape together, impoverished laborers and masterless ruffians. All were, though, very respectful of the Vilku.

The *Gray Courser* was a yalka, broad-beamed and shallow-bottomed, with a low forecastle and poop and a deckhouse amidships. The foremast carried two square sails, the mainmast one square and one fore-and-aft; a short bowsprit extended for a jib. A catapult was mounted in the bows. On either side, two boats hung from davits, aft of the harnessing shafts. Her hull was painted according to her name, with red trim. Alongside swam the huukin, its back a sleek blue ridge.

Kalava had the tiller until she cleared the river mouth and stood out into the Gulf. By then it was full day. A hot wind whipped gray-green water into whitecaps that set the vessel rolling. It whined in the shrouds; timbers creaked. He turned the helm over to a sailor, trod forward on the poop deck, and sounded a trumpet. Men stared. From her cabin below, Ilyandi climbed up to stand beside him. Her white robe fluttered like wings that would fain be asoar. She raised her arms and chanted a spell for the voyage:

"Burning, turning,
The sun-wheel reels
Behind the blindness
Cloud-smoke evokes.
The old cold moon
Seldom tells
Where it lairs
With stars afar.
No men's omens
Abide to guide
High in the skies.
But lodestone for Lodeland
Strongly longs."

While the deckhands hardly knew what she meant, they felt heartened.

Land dwindled aft, became a thin blue line, vanished into waves and mists. Kalava was cutting straight northwest across the Gulf. He meant to sail through the night, and thus wanted plenty of sea room. Also, he and Ilyandi would practice with her ideas about navigation. Hence after a while the mariners spied no other sails, and the loneliness began to weigh on them.

However, they worked stoutly enough. Some thought it a good sign, and cheered, when the clouds clove toward evening and they saw a horned moon. Their mates were frightened; was the moon supposed to appear by day? Kalava bullied them out of it.

Wind stiffened during the dark. By morning it had raised seas in which the ship reeled. It was a westerly, too, forcing her toward land no matter how close-hauled. When he spied, through scud, the crags of Cape Vairka, the skipper realized he could not round it unaided.

He was a rough man, but he had been raised in those skills that were seemly for a freeman of Clan Samayoki. Though not a poet, he could make an acceptable verse when occasion demanded. He stood in the fore-peak and shouted into the storm, the words flung back to his men:

"Northward now veering,
Steering from kin-rift,
Spindrift flung gale-borne,
Sail-borne is daft.
Craft will soon flounder,
Founder, go under—
Thunder this wit-lack!
Sit back and call
All that swim near.
Steer then to northward."

Having thus offered the gods a making, he put the horn to his mouth and blasted forth a summons to his huukin.

The great beast heard and slipped close. Kalava took the lead in lowering the shafts. A line around his waist for safety, he sprang over the rail, down onto the broad back. He kept his feet, though the two men who followed him went off into the billows and had to be hauled up. Together they rode the huukin, guiding it between the poles where they could attach the harness.

"I waited too long," Kalava admitted. "This would have been easier yesterday. Well, something for you to brag about in the inns at home, nay?" Their mates drew them back aboard. Meanwhile the sails had been furled. Kalava took first watch at the reins. Mightily pulled the huukin, tail and flippers churning foam that the wind snatched away, on into the open, unknown sea.

3

Wayfarer woke.

He had passed the decades of transit shut down. A being such as Alpha would have spent them conscious, its mind perhaps at work on an intellectual artistic creation—to it, no basic distinction—or perhaps replaying an existent piece for contemplation-enjoyment or perhaps in activity too abstract for words to hint at. Wayfarer's capabilities, though large, were insufficient for that. The hardware and software (again we use myth) of his embodiment were designed principally for interaction with the material universe. In effect, there was nothing for him to do.

He could not even engage in discourse. The robotic systems of the ship were subtle and powerful but lacked true consciousness; it was unnecessary for them, and distraction or boredom might have posed a hazard. Nor could he converse with entities elsewhere; signals would have taken too long going to and fro. He did spend a while, whole minutes of external time, reliving the life of his Christian Brannock element, studying the personality, accustoming himself to its ways. Thereafter he . . . went to sleep.

The ship reactivated him as is crossed what remained of the Oort Cloud. Instantly aware, he coupled to instrument after instrument and scanned the Solar System. Although his database summarized Gaia's reports, he deemed it wise to observe for himself. The eagerness, the bittersweet sense of homecoming, that flickered around his calm logic were Christian Brannock's. Imagine long-forgotten feelings coming astir in you when you return to a scene of your early childhood.

Naturally, the ghost in the machine knew that changes had been enormous since his mortal eyes closed forever. The rings of Saturn were tattered and tenuous. Jupiter had gained a showy set of them from the death of a satellite, but its Red Spot faded away ages ago. Mars was moonless, its axis steeply canted. . . . Higher resolution would have shown scant traces of humanity. From the antimatter plants inside the orbit of Mercury to the comet harvesters beyond Pluto, what was no more needed had been dismantled or left forsaken. Wind, water, chemistry, tectonics, cosmic stones, spalling radiation, nuclear decay, quantum shifts had patiently reclaimed the relics for chaos. Some fossils existed yet, and some eroded fragments aboveground or in space; otherwise all was only in Gaia's memory.

No matter. It was toward his old home that the Christian Brannock facet of Wayfarer sped.

Unaided, he would not have seen much difference from aforetime in the sun. It was slightly larger and noticeably brighter. Human vision would have perceived the light as more white, with the faintest bluish quality. Unprotected skin would have reacted quickly to the increased ultraviolet. The solar wind was stronger, too. But thus far the changes were comparatively minor. This star was still on the main sequence. Planets with greenhouse atmospheres were most affected. Certain minerals on Venus were now molten. Earth—

The ship hurtled inward, reached its goal, and danced into parking orbit. At close range, Wayfarer looked forth.

On Luna, the patterns of maria were not quite the same, mountains were worn down farther, and newer craters had wrecked or obliterated older ones. Rubble-filled anomalies showed where ground had collapsed on deserted cities. Essentially, though, the moon was again the same desolation, seared by day and death-cold by night, as before life's presence. It had receded farther, astronomically no big distance, and this had lengthened Earth's rotation period by about an hour. However, as yet it circled near enough to stabilize that spin.

The mother planet offered less to our imaginary eyes. Clouds wrapped it in dazzling white. Watching carefully, you could have seen swirls and bandings, but to a quick glance the cover was well-nigh featureless. Shifting breaks in it gave blue flashes of water, brown flashes of land—nowhere ice or snowfall, nowhere lights after dark; and the radio spectrum seethed voiceless.

When did the last human foot tread this world? Wayfarer searched his database. The information was not there. Perhaps it was unrecorded, unknown. Perhaps that last flesh had chanced to die alone or chosen to die privately.

Certainly it was long and long ago. How brief had been the span of Homo sapiens, from flint and fire to machine intelligence! Not that the end had come suddenly or simply. It took several millennia, said the database: time for whole civilizations to rise and fall and leave their mutant descendants. Sometimes populations decline had reversed in this or that locality, sometimes nations heeded the vatic utterances of prophets and strove to turn history backward—for a while, a while. But always the trend was ineluctable.

The clustered memories of Christian Brannock gave rise to a thought in Wayfarer that was as if the man spoke: I saw the beginning. I did not foresee the end. To me this was the magnificent dawn of hope.

And was I wrong?

The organic individual is mortal. It can find no way to stave off eventual disintegration; quantum chemistry forbids. Besides, if a man could live for a mere thousand years, the data storage capacity of his brain would be saturated, incapable of holding more. Well before then, he would have been overwhelmed by the geometric increase of correlations, made feebleminded or insane. Nor could he survive the rigors of star travel at any reasonable speed or unearthly environments, in a universe never meant for him.

But transferred into a suitable inorganic structure, the pattern of neuron and molecular traces and their relationships that is his inner self becomes potentially immortal. The very complexity that allows this makes him continue feeling as well as thinking. If the quality of emotions is changed, it is because his physical organism has become stronger, more sensitive, more intelligent and aware. He will soon lose any wistfulness about his former existence. His new life gives him so much more, a cosmos of sensing and experience, memory and thought, space and time. He can multiply himself, merge and unmerge with others, grow in spirit until he reaches a limit once inconceivable; and after that he can become a part of a mind greater still, and thus grow onward.

The wonder was, Christian Brannock mused, that any humans whatsoever had held out, clung to the primitive, refused to see that their heritage was no longer of DNA but of psyche.

And yet—

The half-formed question faded away. His half-formed personhood rejoined Wayfarer. Gaia was calling from Earth.

She had, of course, received notification, which arrived several years in advance of the spacecraft. Her manifold instruments, on the planet and out between planets, had detected the approach. For the message she now sent, she chose to employ a modulated neutrino beam. Imagine her saying: "Welcome. Do you need help? I am ready to give any I can." Imagine this in a voice low and warm.

Imagine Wayfarer replying, "Thank you, but all's well. I'll be down directly, if that suits you."

"I do not quite understand why you have come. Has the rapport with me not been adequate?"

No, Wayfarer refrained from saying. "I will explain later in more detail than the transmission could carry. Essentially, though, the reason is what you were told. We"—he deemphasized rather than excluded her—"wonder if Earth ought to be saved from solar expansion."

Her tone cooled a bit. "I have said more than once: No. You can perfect your engineering techniques anywhere else. The situation here is unique. The knowledge to be won by observing the unhampered course of events is unpredictable, but it will be enormous, and I have good cause to believe it will prove of the highest value."

"That may well be. I'll willingly hear you out, if you care to unfold your thoughts more fully than you have hitherto. But I do want to make my own survey and develop my own recommendations. No reflection on you; we both realize that no one mind can encompass every possibility, every interpretation. Nor can any one mind follow out every ongoing factor in what it observes; and what is overlooked can prove to be the agent of chaotic change. I may notice something that escaped you. Unlikely, granted. After your millions of years here, you very nearly *are* Earth and the life on it, are you not? But . . . we . . . would like an independent opinion."

Imagine her laughing. "At least you are polite, Wayfarer. Yes, do come down. I will steer you in."

"That won't be necessary. Your physical centrum is in the arctic region, isn't it? I can find my way."

He sensed steel beneath the mildness: "Best I guide you. You recognize the situation as inherently chaotic. Descending on an arbitrary path, you might seriously perturb certain things in which I am interested. Please."

"As you wish," Wayfarer conceded.

Robotics took over. The payload module of the spacecraft detached from the drive module, which stayed in orbit. Under its own power but controlled from below, asheen in the harsh spatial sunlight, the cylindroid braked and slanted downward.

It pierced the cloud deck. Wayfarer scanned eagerly. However, this was no sightseeing tour. The descent path sacrificed efficiency and made almost straight for a high northern latitude. Sonic-boom thunder trailed.

He did spy the fringe of a large continent oriented east and west, and saw that those parts were mainly green. Beyond lay a stretch of sea. He thought that he glimpsed something peculiar on it, but passed over too fast, with his attention directed too much ahead, to be sure.

The circumpolar landmass hove in view. Wayfarer compared maps that Gaia had transmitted. They were like nothing that Christian Brannock remembered. Plate tectonics had slowed, as radioactivity and original heat in the core of Earth declined, but drift, subduction, upthrust still went on.

He cared more about the life here. Epoch after epoch, Gaia had described its posthuman evolution as she watched. Following the mass extinction of the Paleotechnic, it had regained the abundance and diversity of a Cretaceous or a Tertiary. Everything was different, though, except for a few small survivals. To Wayfarer, as to Alpha and, ultimately, the galactic brain, those accounts seemed somehow, increasingly, incomplete. They did not quite make ecological sense—as of the past hundred thousand years or so. Nor did all of Gaia's responses to questions.

Perhaps she was failing to gather full data, perhaps she was misinterpreting, perhaps—It was another reason to send him to her.

Arctica appeared below the flyer. Imagine her giving names to it and its features. As long as she had lived with them, they had their identities for her. The Coast Range of hills lifted close behind the littoral. Through it cut the Remnant River, which had been greater when rains were more frequent but continued impressive. With its tributaries it drained the intensely verdant Bountiful Valley. On the far side of that, foothills edged the steeply rising Boreal Mountains. Once the highest among them had been snowcapped; now their peaks were naked rock. Streams rushed down the flanks, most of them joining the Remnant somewhere as it flowed through its gorges toward the sea. In a lofty vale gleamed the Rainbowl, the big lake that was its headwaters. Overlooking from the north loomed the mountain Mindhome, its top, the physical centrum of Gaia, lost in cloud cover.

In a way the scenes were familiar to him. She had sent plenty of full-sensory transmissions, as part of her contribution to universal knowledge and thought. Wayfarer could even recall the geological past, back beyond the epoch when Arctica broke free and drifted north, ramming into land already present and thrusting the Boreals heavenward. He could extrapolate the geological future in comparable detail, until a red giant filling half the sky glared down on an airless globe of stone and sand, which would at last melt. Nevertheless, the reality, the physical being here, smote him more strongly than he had expected. His sensors strained to draw in every datum while his vessel flew needlessly fast to the goal.

He neared the mountain. Jutting south from the range, it was not the tallest. Brushy forest grew all the way up its sides, lush on the lower slopes, parched on the heights, where many trees were leafless skeletons. That was due to a recent climatic shift, lowering the mean level of clouds, so that a formerly well-watered zone had been suffering a decades-long drought. (Yes, Earth was moving faster toward its doomsday.) Fire must be a constant threat, he thought. But no, Gaia's agents could quickly put any out, or she might simply ignore it. Though not large, the area she occupied on the summit was paved over and doubtless nothing was vulnerable to heat or smoke.

He landed. For an instant of planetary time, lengthy for minds that worked at close to light speed, there was communication silence.

He was again above the cloud deck. It eddied white, the peak rising from it like an island among others, into the level rays of sunset. Overhead arched a violet clarity. A thin wind whittered, cold at this altitude. On a level circle of blue-black surfacing, about a kilometer wide, stood the crowded structures and engines of the centrum.

A human would have seen an opalescent dome surrounded by towers, some sheer as lances, some intricately lacy; and silver spiderwebs; and lesser things of varied but curiously simple shapes, mobile units waiting to be dispatched on their tasks. Here and there, flyers darted and hovered, most of them as small and exquisite as hummingbirds (if our human had known hummingbirds). To her the scene would have wavered slightly, as if she saw it through rippling water, or it throbbed with quiet energies, or it pulsed in and out of space-time. She would not have sensed the complex of force fields and quantum-mechanical waves, nor the microscopic and submicroscopic entities that were the major part of it.

Wayfarer perceived otherwise.

Then: "Again, welcome," Gaia said.

"And again, thank you," Wayfarer replied. "I am glad to be here."

They regarded one another, not as bodies—which neither was wearing—but as minds, matrices of memory, individuality, and awareness. Separately he wondered what she thought of him. She was giving him no more of herself than had always gone over the communication lines between the stars. That was: a nodal organism, like Alpha and millions of others, which over the eons had increased its capabilities, while ceaselessly experiencing and thinking; the ages of interaction with Earth and the life on Earth, maybe shaping her soul more deeply than the existence she shared with her own kind; traces of ancient human uploads, but they were not like Christian Brannock, copies of them dispersed across the galaxy, no, these had chosen to stay with the mother world. . . .

"I told you I am glad too," said Gaia regretfully, "but I am not, quite. You question my stewardship."

"Not really," Wayfarer protested. "I hope not ever. We simply wish to know better how you carry it out."

"Why, you do know. As with any of us who is established on a planet, high among my activities is to study its complexities, follow its evolution. On this planet that means, above all, the evolution of its life, everything from genetics to ecology. In what way have I failed to share information with my fellows?"

In many ways, Wayfarer left unspoken. Overtly: "Once we"—here he referred to the galactic brain—"gave close consideration to the matter, we found countless unresolved puzzles. For example—"

What he set forth was hundreds of examples, ranging over millennia. Let a single case serve. About ten thousand years ago, the big continent south of Arctica had supported a wealth of large grazing animals. Their herds darkened the plains and made loud the woods. Gaia had described them in loving detail, from the lyre-curved horns of one genus to the wind-rustled manes of another. Abruptly, in terms of historical time, she transmitted no more about them. When asked why, she said they had gone extinct. She never explained how.

To Wayfarer she responded in such haste that he got a distinct impression she realized she had a made a mistake. (Remember, this is a myth.) "A variety of causes. Climates became severe as temperatures rose—"

"I am sorry," he demurred, "but when analyzed, the meteorological data you supplied show that warming and desiccation cannot yet have been that significant in those particular regions."

"How are you so sure?" she retorted. Imagine her angry. "Have any of you lived with Earth for megayears, to know it that well?" Her tone hardened. "I do not myself pretend to full knowledge. A living world is too complex—chaotic. Cannot you appreciate that? I am still seeking comprehension of too many phenomena. In this instance, consider just a small shift in ambient conditions, coupled with new diseases and scores of other factors, most of them subtle. I believe that, combined, they broke a balance of nature. But unless and until I learn more, I will not waste bandwidth in talk about it."

"I sympathize with that," said Wayfarer mildly, hoping for conciliation. "Maybe I can discover or suggest something helpful."

"No. You are too ignorant, you are blind, you can only do harm."

He stiffened. "We shall see." Anew he tried for peace. "I did not come in any hostility. I came because here is the fountainhead of us all, and we think of saving it."

Her manner calmed likewise. "How would you?"

"That is one thing I have come to find out—what the best way is, should we proceed."

In the beginning, maybe, a screen of planetary dimensions, kept between Earth and sun by an interplay of gravity and electromagnetism, to ward off the fraction of energy that was not wanted. It would only be a temporary expedient, though, possibly not worthwhile. That depended on how long it would take to accomplish the real work. Engines in close orbit around the star, drawing their power from its radiation, might generate currents in its body that carried fresh hydrogen down to the core, thus restoring the nuclear furnace to its olden state. Or they might bleed gas off into space, reducing the mass of the sun, damping its fires but adding billions upon billions of years wherein it scarcely changed any more. That would cause the planets to move outward, a factor that must be taken into account but that would reduce the requirements.

Whatever was done, the resources of several stars would be needed to accomplish it, for time had grown cosmically short.

"An enormous work," Gaia said. Wayfarer wondered if she had in mind the dramatics of it, apparitions in heaven, such as centuries during which fire-fountains rushed visibly out of the solar disc.

"For an enormous glory," he declared.

"No," she answered curtly. "For nothing, and worse than nothing. Destruction of everything I have lived for. Eternal loss to the heritage?"

"Why, is not Earth the heritage?"

"No. Knowledge is. I tried to make that clear to Alpha." She paused. "To you I say again, the evolution of life, its adaptions, struggles, transformations, and how at last it meets death—those are unforeseeable, and nowhere else in the spacetime universe can there be a world like this for them to play themselves out. They will enlighten us in ways the galactic brain itself cannot yet conceive. They may well open to us whole new phases of ultimate reality."

"Why would not a life that went on for gigayears do so, and more?"

"Because here I, the observer of the ages, have gained some knowledge of *this* destiny, some oneness with it—" She sighed. "Oh, you do not understand. You refuse to."

"On the contrary," Wayfarer said, as softly as might be, "I hope to. Among the reasons I came is that we can communicate being to being, perhaps more fully than across light-years and certainly more quickly."

She was silent awhile. When she spoke again, her tone had gone gentle. "More . . . intimately. Yes. Forgive my resentment. It was wrong of me. I will indeed do what I can to make you welcome and help you learn."

"Thank you, thank you," Wayfarer said happily. "And I will do what I can toward that end."

The sun went under the cloud deck. A crescent moon stood aloft. The wind blew a little stronger, a little chillier.

"But if we decide against saving Earth," Wayfarer asked, "if it is to go molten and formless, every trace of its history dissolved, will you not mourn?"

"The record I have guarded will stay safe," Gaia replied.

He grasped her meaning: the database of everything known about this world. It was here in her. Much was also stored elsewhere, but she held the entirety. As the sun became a devouring monster, she would remove her physical plant to the outer reaches of the system.

"But you have done more than passively preserve it, have you not?" he said.

"Yes, of course." How could an intelligence like hers have refrained? "I have considered the data, worked with them, evaluated them, tried to reconstruct the conditions that brought them about."

And in the past thousands of years she had become ever more taciturn about that, too, or downright evasive, he thought.

"You had immense gaps to fill in," he hinted.

"Inevitably. The past, also, is quantum probabilistic. By what roads, what means, did history come to us?"

"Therefore you create various emulations, to see what they lead to," about which she had told scarcely anything.

"You knew that. I admit, since you force me, that besides trying to find what happened, I make worlds to show what *might* have happened."

He was briefly startled. He had not been deliberately trying to bring out any such confession. Then he realized that she had foreseen he was bound to catch scent of it, once they joined their minds in earnest.

"Why?" he asked.

"Why else but for a more complete understanding?"

In his inwardness, Wayfarer reflected: Yes, she had been here since the time of humanity. The embryo of her existed before Christian Brannock was born. Into the growing fullness of her had gone the mind-patterns of humans who chose not to go to the stars but to abide on old Earth. And the years went by in their tens of millions.

Naturally she was fascinated by the past. She must do most of her living in it. Could that be why she was indifferent to the near future, or actually wanted catastrophe?

Somehow that thought did not feel right to him. Gaia was a mystery he must solve.

Cautiously, he ventured, "Then you act as a physicist might, tracing hypothetical configurations of the wave function through space-time— except that the subjects of your experiments are conscious."

"I do no wrong," she said. "Come with me into any of those worlds and see."

"Gladly," he agreed, unsure whether he lied. He mustered resolution. "Just the same, duty demands I conduct my own survey of the material environment."

"As you will. Let me help you prepare." She was quiet for a span. In this thin air, a human would have seen the first stars blink into sight. "But I believe it will be by sharing the history of my stewardship that we truly come to know one another."

4

Storm-battered until men must work the pumps without cease, *Gray Courser* limped eastward along the southern coast of an unknown land. Wind set that direction, for the huukin trailed after, so worn and starved that what remained of its strength must be reserved for sorest need. The shore rolled jewel-green, save where woods dappled it darker, toward a wall of gentle hills. All was thick with life, grazing herds, wings multitudinous overhead, but no voyager had set foot there. Surf dashed in such violence that Kalava was not certain a boat could live through it. Meanwhile they had caught but little rainwater, and what was in the butts had gotten low and foul.

He stood in the bows, peering ahead, Ilyandi at his side. Wind boomed and shrilled, colder than they were used to. Wrack flew beneath an overcast gone heavy. Waves ran high, gray-green, white-maned, foam blown off them in streaks. The ship rolled, pitched, and groaned.

Yet they had seen the sky uncommonly often. Ilyandi believed that clouds—doubtless vapors sucked from the ground by heat, turning back to water as they rose, like steam from a kettle—formed less readily in this clime. Too eagerly at her instruments and reckonings to speak much, she had now at last given her news to the captain.

"Then you think you know where we are?" he asked hoarsely.

Her face, gaunt within the cowl of a sea-stained cloak, bore the least smile. "No. This country is as nameless to me as to you. But, yes, I do think I can say we are no more than fifty daymarches from Ulonai, and it may be as little as forty."

Kalava's fist smote the rail. "By Ruvio's ax! How I hoped for this!" The words tumbled from him. "It means the weather tossed us mainly back and forth between the two shorelines. We've not come unreturnably far. Every ship henceforward can have a better passage. See you, she can first go out to the Ending Islands and wait at ease for favoring winds. The skipper will know he'll make landfall. We'll have it worked out after a few more voyages, just what lodestone bearing will bring him to what place hereabouts."

"But anchorage?" she wondered.

He laughed, which he had not done for many days and nights. "As for that—"

A cry from the lookout at the masthead broke through. Down the length of the vessel men raised their eyes. Terror howled.

Afterward no two tongues bore the same tale. One said that a firebolt had pierced the upper clouds, trailing thunder. Another told of a sword as long as the hull, and blood carried on the gale of its flight. To a third it was a beast with jaws agape and three tails aflame. . . . Kalava remembered a spear among whirling rainbows. To him Ilyandi said, when they were briefly alone, that she thought of a shuttle now seen, now unseen as it wove a web on which stood writing she could not read. All witnesses agreed that it came from over the sea, sped on inland through heaven, and vanished behind the hills.

Men went mad. Some ran about screaming. Some wailed to their gods.

Some cast themselves down on the deck and shivered, or drew into balls and squeezed their eyes shut. No hand at helm or pumps, the ship wallowed about, sails banging, adrift toward the surf, while water drained in through sprung seams and lapped higher in the bilge.

"Avast!" roared Kalava. He sprang down the foredeck ladder and went among the crew. "Be you men? Up on your feet or die!" With kicks and cuffs he drove them back to their duties. One yelled and drew a knife on him. He knocked the fellow senseless. Barely in time, *Gray Courser* came again under control. She was then too near shore to get the huukin harnessed. Kalava took the helm, wore ship, and clawed back to sea room.

Mutiny was all too likely, once the sailors regained a little courage. When Kalava could yield place to a halfway competent steersman, he sought Ilyandi and they talked awhile in her cabin. Thereafter they returned to the foredeck and he shouted for attention. Standing side by side, they looked down on the faces, frightened or terrified or sullen, of the men who had no immediate tasks.

"Hear this," Kalava said into the wind. "Pass it on to the rest. I know you'd turn south this day if you had your wish. But you can't. We'd never make the crossing, the shape we're in. Which would you liefer have, the chance of wealth and fame or the certainty of drowning? We've got to make repairs, we've got to restock, and *then* we can sail home, bringing wondrous news. When can we fix things up? Soon, I tell you, soon. I've been looking at the water. Look for yourselves. See how it's taking on more and more of a brown shade, and how bits of plant stuff float about on the waves. That means a river, a big river, emptying out somewhere nigh. And that means a harbor for us. As for the sight we saw, here's the Vilku, our lady Ilyandi, to speak about it."

The skythinker stepped forward. She had changed into a clean white robe with the emblems of her calling, and held a staff topped by a sigil. Though her voice was low, it carried.

"Yes, that was a fearsome sight. It lends truth to the old stories of things that appeared to mariners who ventured, or were blown, far north. But think. Those sailors did win home again. Those who did not must have perished of natural causes. For why would the gods or the demons sink some and not others?

"What we ourselves saw merely flashed overhead. Was it warning us off? No, because if it knew that much about us, it knew we cannot immediately turn back. Did it give us any heed at all? Quite possibly not. It was very strange, yes, but that does not mean it was any threat. The world is full of strangeness. I could tell you of things seen on clear nights over the centuries, fiery streaks down the sky or stars with glowing tails. We of the Vilkui do not understand them, but neither do we fear them. We give them their due honor and respect, as signs from the gods."

She paused before finishing: "Moreover, in the secret annals of our order lie accounts of visions and wonders exceeding these. All folk know that from time to time the gods have given their word to certain holy men or women, for the guidance of the people. I may not tell how they manifest themselves, but I will say that this today was not wholly unlike.

"Let us therefore believe that the sign granted us is a good one."

She went on to a protective chant-spell and an invocation of the Powers. That heartened most of her listeners. They were, after all, in considerable awe of her. Besides, the larger part of them had sailed with Kalava before and done well out of it. They bullied the rest into obedience.

"Dismissed," said the captain. "Come evening, you'll get a ration of liquor."

A weak cheer answered him. The ship fared onward.

Next morning they did indeed find a broad, sheltered bay, dun with silt. Hitching up the huukin, they went cautiously in until they spied the river foretold by Kalava. Accompanied by a few bold men, he took a boat ashore. Marshes, meadows, and woods all had signs of abundant game. Various plants were unfamiliar, but he recognized others, among them edible fruits and bulbs. "It is well," he said. "This land is ripe for our taking." No lightning bolt struck him down.

Having located a suitable spot, he rowed back to the ship, brought her in on the tide, and beached her. He could see that the water often rose higher yet, so he would be able to float her off again when she was ready. That would take time, but he felt no haste. Let his folk make proper camp, he thought, get rested and nourished, before they began work. Hooks, nets, and weirs would give rich catches. Several of the crew had hunting skills as well. He did himself.

His gaze roved upstream, toward the hills. Yes, presently he would lead a detachment to learn what lay beyond.

5

Gaia had never concealed her reconstructive research into human history. It was perhaps her finest achievement. But slowly those of her fellows in the galactic brain who paid close attention had come to feel that it was obsessing her. And then of late—within the past hundred thousand years or so—they were finding her reports increasingly scanty, less informative, at last ambiguous to the point of evasiveness. They did not press her about it; the patience of the universe was theirs. Nevertheless they had grown concerned. Especially had Alpha, who as the nearest was in the closest, most frequent contact; and therefore, now, had Wayfarer. Gaia's activities and attitudes were a primary factor in the destiny of Earth. Without a better understanding of her, the rightness of saving the planet was undecidable.

Surely an important part of her psyche was the history and archeology she preserved, everything from the animal origins to the machine fulfillment of genus Homo. Unnumbered individual minds had uploaded into her, too, had become elements of her being—far more than were in any other node. What had she made of all this over the megayears, and what had it made of her?

She could not well refuse Wayfarer admittance; the heritage belonged to her entire fellowship, ultimately to intelligence throughout the cosmos of the future. Guided by her, he would go through the database of her observations and activities in external reality, geological, biological, astronomical.

As for the other reality, interior to her, the work she did with her records and emulations of humankind—to evaluate that, some purely human interaction seemed called for. Hence Wayfarer's makeup included the mind-pattern of a man.

Christian Brannock's had been chosen out of those whose uploads went starfaring because he was among the earliest, less molded than most by relationships with machines. Vigor, intelligence, and adaptability were other desired characteristics.

His personality was itself a construct, a painstaking refabrication by Alpha, who had taken strands (components, overtones) of his own mind and integrated them to form a consciousness that became an aspect of Wayfarer. No doubt it was not a perfect duplicate of the original. Certainly, while it had all the memories of Christian Brannock's lifetime, its outlook was that of a young man, not an old one. In addition, it possessed some knowledge—the barest sketch, grossly oversimplified so as not to overload it—of what had happened since its body died. Deep underneath its awareness lay the longing to return to an existence more full than it could now imagine. Yet, knowing that it would be taken back into the oneness when its task was done, it did not mourn any loss. Rather, to the extent that it was differentiated from Wayfarer, it took pleasure in sensations, thoughts, and emotions that it had effectively forgotten.

When the differentiation had been completed, the experience of being human again became well-nigh everything for it, and gladsome, because so had the man gone through life.

To describe how this was done, we must again resort to myth and say that Wayfarer downloaded the Christian Brannock subroutine into the main computer of the system that was Gaia. To describe what actually occurred would require the mathematics of wave mechanics and an entire concept of multileveled, mutably dimensioned reality which it had taken minds much greater than humankind's a long time to work out.

We can, however, try to make clear that what took place in the system was not a mere simulation. It was an emulation. Its events were not of a piece with events among the molecules of flesh and blood; but they were, in their way, just as real. The persons created had wills as free as any mortal's, and whatever dangers they met could do harm equal to anything a mortal body might suffer.

Consider a number of people at a given moment. Each is doing something, be it only thinking, remembering, or sleeping—together with all ongoing physiological and biochemical processes. They are interacting with each other and with their surroundings, too; and every element of these surroundings, be it only a stone or a leaf or a photon of sunlight, is equally involved. The complexity seems beyond conception, let alone enumeration or calculation. But consider further: At this one instant, every part of the whole, however minute, is in one specific state; and thus the whole itself is. Electrons are all in their particular quantum shells, atoms are all in their particular compounds and configurations, energy fields all have their particular values at each particular point—suppose an infinitely fine-grained photograph.

A moment later, the state is different. However slightly, fields have pulsed, atoms have shifted about, electrons have jumped, bodies have moved. But this new state derives from the first according to natural laws. And likewise for every succeeding state.

In crude, mythic language: Represent each variable of one state by some set of numbers; or, to put it in equivalent words, map the state into an n-dimensional phase space. Input the laws of nature. Run the program. The computer model should then evolve from state to state in exact correspondence with the evolution of our original matter-energy world. That includes life and consciousness. The maps of organisms go through one-to-one analogues of everything that the organisms themselves would, among these being the processes of sensation and thought. To them, they and their world are the same as in the original. The question of which set is the more real is meaningless.

Of course, this primitive account is false. The program did *not* exactly follow the course of events "outside." Gaia lacked both the data and the capability necessary to model the entire universe, or even the entire Earth. Likewise did any other node, and the galactic brain. Powers of that order lay immensely far in the future, if they would ever be realized. What Gaia could accommodate was so much less that the difference in degree amounted to a difference in kind.

For example, if events on the surface of a planet were to be played out, the stars must be lights in the night sky and nothing else, every other effect neglected. Only a limited locality on the globe could be done in anything like full detail; the rest grew more and more incomplete as distance from the scene increased, until at the antipodes there was little more than simplified geography, hydrography, and atmospherics. Hence weather on the scene would very soon be quite unlike weather at the corresponding moment of the original. This is the simplest, most obvious consequence of the limitations. The totality is beyond reckoning—and we have not even mentioned relativistic nonsimultaneity.

Besides, atom-by-atom modeling was a practical impossibility; statistical mechanics and approximations must substitute. Chaos and quantum uncertainties made developments incalculable in principle. Other, more profound considerations entered as well, but with them language fails utterly.

Let it be said, as a myth, that such creations made their destinies for themselves.

And yet, what a magnificent instrumentality the creator system was! Out of nothingness, it could bring worlds into being, evolutions, lives, ecologies, awarenesses, histories, entire time lines. They need not be fragmentary miscopies of something "real," dragging out their crippled spans until the nodal intelligence took pity and canceled them. Indeed, they need not derive in any way from the "outside." They could be works of imagination—fairy-tale worlds, perhaps, where benevolent gods ruled and magic ran free. Always, the logic of their boundary conditions caused them to develop appropriately, to be at home in their existences.

The creator system was the mightiest device ever made for the pursuit of art, science, philosophy, and understanding.

So it came about that Christian Brannock found himself alive again, young again, in the world that Gaia and Wayfarer had chosen for his new beginning.

⟶

He stood in a garden on a day of bright sun and mild, fragrant breezes. It was a formal garden, graveled paths, low-clipped hedges, roses and lilies in geometric beds, around a lichened stone basin where goldfish swam. Brick walls, ivy-heavy, enclosed three sides, a wrought-iron gate in them leading to a lawn. On the fourth side lay a house, white, slate-roofed, classically proportioned, a style that to him was antique. Honeybees buzzed. From a yew tree overlooking the wall came the twitter of birds.

A woman walked toward him. Her flower-patterned gown, the voluminous skirt and sleeves, a cameo hung on her bosom above the low neckline, dainty shoes, parasol less an accessory than a completion, made his twenty-third-century singlesuit feel abruptly barbaric. She was tall and well formed. Despite the garments, her gait was lithe. As she neared, he saw clear features beneath high-piled mahogany hair.

She reached him, stopped, and met his gaze. "Benveni, Capita Brannoch," she greeted. Her voice was low and musical.

"Uh, g'day, Sorita—uh—" he fumbled.

She blushed. "I beg your pardon, Captain Brannock. I forgot and used my Inglay—English of my time. I've been—" She hesitated. "—supplied with yours, and we both have been with the contemporary language."

A sense of dream was upon him. To speak as dryly as he could was like clutching at something solid. "You're from my future, then?"

She nodded. "I was born about two hundred years after you."

"That means about eighty or ninety years after my death, right?" He saw an inward shadow pass over her face. "I'm sorry," he blurted. "I didn't mean to upset you."

She turned entirely calm, even smiled a bit. "It's all right. We both know what we are, and what we used to be."

"But—"

"Yes, but." She shook her head. "It does feel strange, being . . . this . . . again."

He was quickly gaining assurance, settling into the situation. "I know. I've had practice in it," light-years away, at the star where Alpha dwelt. "Don't worry, it'll soon be quite natural to you."

"I have been here a little while myself. Nevertheless—young," she whispered, "but remembering a long life, old age, dying—" She let the parasol fall, unnoticed, and stared down at her hands. Fingers gripped each other. "Remembering how toward the end I looked back and thought, 'Was that *all?*' "

He wanted to take those hands in his and speak comfort, but decided he would be wiser to say merely, "Well, it wasn't all."

"No, of course not. Not for me, the way it had been once for everyone who ever lived. While my worn-out body was being painlessly terminated, my self-pattern was uploaded—" She raised her eyes. "Now we can't really recall what our condition has been like, can we?"

"We can look forward to returning to it."

"Oh, yes. Meanwhile—" She flexed herself, glanced about and upward, let light and air into her spirit, until at last a full smile blossomed. "I am starting to enjoy this. Already I am." She considered him. He was a tall man, muscular, blond, rugged of countenance. Laughter lines radiated from blue eyes. He spoke in a resonant baritone. "And I will."

He grinned, delighted. "Thanks. The same here. For openers, may I ask your name?"

"Forgive me!" she exclaimed. "I thought I was prepared. I . . . came into existence . . . with knowledge of my role and this milieu, and spent the time since rehearsing in my mind, but now that it's actually happened, all my careful plans have flown away. I am—was—no, I am Laurinda Ashcroft."

He offered his hand. After a moment she let him shake hers. He recalled that at the close of his mortal days the gesture was going out of use.

"You know a few things about me, I suppose," he said, "but I'm ignorant about you and your times. When I left Earth, everything was changing spinjump fast, and after that I was out of touch," and eventually his individuality went of its own desire into a greater one. This reenactment of him had been given no details of the terrestrial history that followed his departure; it could not have contained any reasonable fraction of the information.

"You went to the stars almost immediately after you'd uploaded, didn't you?" she asked.

He nodded. "Why wait? I'd always longed to go."

"Are you glad that you did?"

"Glad is hardly the word." He spent two or three seconds putting phrases together. Language was important to him; he had been an engineer and occasionally a maker of songs. "However, I am also happy to be here." Again a brief grin. "In such pleasant company." Yet what he really hoped to do was explain himself. They would be faring together in search of one another's souls. "And I'll bring something new back to my proper existence. All at once I realize how a human can appreciate in a unique way what's out yonder," suns, worlds, upon certain of them life that was more wonderful still, nebular fire-clouds, infinity whirling down the throat of a black hole, galaxies like jewelwork strewn by a prodigal through immensity, space-time structure subtle and majestic—everything he had never known, as a man, until this moment, for no organic creature could travel those reaches.

"While I chose to remain on Earth," she said. "How timid and unimaginative do I seem to you?"

"Not in the least," he avowed. "You had the adventures you wanted."

"You are kind to say so." She paused. "Do you know Jane Austen?"

"Who? No, I don't believe I do."

"An early-nineteenth-century writer. She led a quiet life, never went far from home, died young, but she explored people in ways that nobody else ever did."

"I'd like to read her. Maybe I'll get a chance here." He wished to show that he was no—"technoramus" was the word he invented on the spot. "I did read a good deal, especially on space missions. And especially poetry. Homer, Shakespeare, Tu Fu, Bashō, Bellman, Burns, Omar Khayyam, Kipling, Millay, Haldeman—" He threw up his hands and laughed. "Never mind. That's just the first several names I could grab out of the jumble for purposes of bragging."

"We have much getting acquainted to do, don't we? Come, I'm being inhospitable. Let's go inside, relax, and talk."

He retrieved her parasol for her and, recollecting historical dramas he had seen, offered her his arm. They walked slowly between the flower beds. Wind lulled, a bird whistled, sunlight baked odors out of the roses.

"Where are we?" he asked.

"And when?" she replied. "In England of the mid-eighteenth century, on an estate in Surrey." He nodded. He had in fact read rather widely. She fell silent, thinking, before she went on: "Gaia and Wayfarer decided a serene enclave like this would be the best rendezvous for us."

"Really? I'm afraid I'm as out of place as a toad on a keyboard."

She smiled, then continued seriously: "I told you I've been given familiarity with the milieu. We'll be visiting alien ones—whatever ones you choose, after I've explained what else I know about what she has been doing these many years. That isn't much. I haven't seen any other worlds of hers. You will take the leadership."

"You mean because I'm used to odd environments and rough people? Not necessarily. I dealt with nature, you know, on Earth and in space. Peaceful."

"Dangerous."

"Maybe. But never malign."

"Tell me," she invited.

They entered the house and seated themselves in its parlor. Casement windows stood open to green parkscape where deer grazed; afar were a thatched farm cottage, its outbuildings, and the edge of grainfields. Cleanly shaped furniture stood among paintings, etchings, books, two portrait busts. A maidservant rustled in with a tray of tea and cakes. She was obviously shocked by the newcomer but struggled to conceal it. When she had left, Laurinda explained to Christian that the owners of this place, Londoners to whom it was a summer retreat, had lent it to their friend, the eccentric Miss Ashcroft, for a holiday.

So had circumstances and memories been adjusted. It was an instance of Gaia directly interfering with the circumstances and events in an emulation. Christian wondered how frequently she did.

"Eccentricity is almost expected in the upper classes," Laurinda said. "But when you lived you could simply be yourself, couldn't you?"

In the hour that followed, she drew him out. His birth home was the Yukon Ethnate in the Bering Federation, and to it he often returned while he lived, for its wilderness preserves, mountain solitudes, and uncrowded, uncowed, plainspoken folk. Otherwise the nation was prosperous and progressive, with more connections to Asia and the Pacific than to the decayed successor states east and south. Across the Pole, it was also becoming intimate with the renascent societies of Europe, and there Christian received part of his education and spent considerable of his free time.

His was an era of savage contrasts, in which the Commonwealth of Nations maintained a precarious peace. During a youthful, impulsively taken hitch in the Conflict Mediation Service, he twice saw combat. Later in his life, stability gradually become the norm. That was largely due to the growing influence of the artificial-intelligence network. Most of its consciousness-level units interlinked in protean fashion to form minds appropriate for any particular situation, and already the capabilities of those minds exceeded the human. However, there was little sense of rivalry. Rather, there was partnership. The new minds were willing to advise, but were not interested in dominance.

Christian, child of forests and seas and uplands, heir to ancient civilizations, raised among their ongoing achievements, returned on his vacations to Earth in homecoming. Here were his kin, his friends, woods to roam, boats to sail, girls to kiss, songs to sing and glasses to raise (and a gravesite to visit—he barely mentioned his wife Laurinda; she died before uploading technology was available). Always, though, he went back to space. It had called him since first he saw the stars from a cradle under the cedars. He became an engineer. Besides fellow humans he worked closely with sapient machines, and some of them got to be friends too, of an eerie kind. Over the decades, he took a foremost role in such undertakings as the domed Copernican Sea, the Asteroid Habitat, the orbiting antimatter plant, and finally the Grand Solar Laser for launching interstellar vessels on their way. Soon afterward, his body died, old and full of days; but the days of his mind had barely begun.

"A fabulous life," Laurinda said low. She gazed out over the land, across which shadows were lengthening. "I wonder if . . . they . . . might not have done better to give us a cabin in your wilderness."

"No, no," he said. "This is fresh and marvelous to me."

"We can easily go elsewhere, you know. Any place, any time that Gaia has generated, including ones that history never saw. I'll fetch our amulets whenever you wish."

He raised his brows. "Amulets?"

"You haven't been told—informed? They are devices. You wear yours and give it the command to transfer you."

He nodded. "I see. It maps an emulated person into different surroundings."

"With suitable modifications as required. Actually, in many cases it causes a milieu to be activated for you. Most have been in standby mode for a long time. I daresay Gaia could have arranged for us to wish ourselves to wherever we were going and call up whatever we needed likewise. But an external device is better."

He pondered. "Yes, I think I see why. If we got supernatural powers, we wouldn't really be human, would we? And the whole idea is that we should be." He leaned forward on his chair. "It's your turn. Tell me about yourself."

"Oh, there's too much. Not about me, I never did anything spectacular like you, but about the times I lived in, everything that happened to change this planet after you left it—"

She was born here, in England. By then a thinly populated province of Europe, it was a quiet land ("half adream," she said) devoted to its memorials of the past. Not that creativity was dead; but the arts were rather sharply divided between ringing changes on classic works and efforts to deal with the revelations coming in from the stars. The aesthetic that artificial intelligence was evolving for itself overshadowed both these schools. Nevertheless Laurinda was active in them.

Furthermore, in the course of her work she ranged widely over Earth. (By then, meaningful work for humans was a privilege that the talented and energetic strove to earn.) She was a liaison between the two kinds of beings. It meant getting to know people in their various societies and helping them make their desires count. For instance, a proposed earthquake-control station would alter a landscape and disrupt a community; could it be resisted, or if not, what cultural adjustments could be made? Most commonly, though, she counseled and aided individuals bewildered and spiritually lost.

Still more than him, she was carefully vague about her private life, but he got the impression that it was generally happy. If childlessness was an unvoiced sorrow, it was one she shared with many in a population-regulated world; he had had only a son. She loved Earth, its glories and memories, and every fine creation of her race. At the end of her mortality she chose to abide on the planet, in her new machine body, serving as she had served, until at length she came to desire more and entered the wholeness that was to become Gaia.

He thought he saw why she had been picked for resurrection, to be his companion, out of all the uncounted millions who had elected the same destiny.

Aloud, he said, "Yes, this house is right for you. And me, in spite of everything. We're both of us more at home here than either of us could be in the other's native period. Peace and beauty."

"It isn't a paradise," she answered gravely. "This is the real eighteenth century, remember, as well as Gaia could reconstruct the history that led to it," always monitoring, making changes as events turned incompatible with what was in the chronicles and the archeology. "The household staff are underpaid, undernourished, underrespected—servile. The American colonists keep slaves and are going to rebel. Across the Channel, a rotted monarchy bleeds France white, and this will bring on a truly terrible revolution, followed by a quarter century of war."

He shrugged. "Well, the human condition never did include sanity, did it?" That was for the machines.

"In a few of our kind, it did," she said. "At least, they came close. Gaia thinks you should meet some, so you'll realize she isn't just playing cruel games. I have"—in the memories with which she had come into this being—"invited three for dinner tomorrow. It tampers a trifle with their actual biographies, but Gaia can remedy that later if she chooses." Laurinda smiled. "We'll have to make an amulet provide you with proper smallclothes and wig."

"And you provide me with a massive briefing, I'm sure. Who are they?"

"James Cook, Henry Fielding, and Erasmus Darwin. I think it will be a lively evening."

The navigator, the writer, the polymath, three tiny, brilliant facets of the heritage that Gaia guarded.

6

Now Wayfarer downloaded another secondary personality and prepared it to go survey Earth.

He, his primary self, would stay on the mountain, in a linkage with Gaia more close and complete than was possible over interstellar distances. She had promised to conduct him through her entire database of observations made across the entire planet during manifold millions of years. Even for those two, the undertaking was colossal. At the speed of their thought, it would take weeks of external time and nearly total concentration. Only a fraction of their awareness would remain available for anything else—a fraction smaller in him than in her, because her intellect was so much greater.

She told him of her hope that by this sharing, this virtually direct exposure to all she had perceived, he would come to appreciate why Earth should be left to its fiery doom. More was involved than scientific knowledge attainable in no other way. The events themselves would deepen and enlighten the galactic brain, as a great drama or symphony once did for humans. But Wayfarer must undergo their majestic sweep through the past before he could feel the truth of what she said about the future.

He had his doubts. He wondered if her human components, more than had gone into any other node, might not have given her emotions, intensified by ages of brooding, that skewed her rationality. However, he consented to her proposal. It accorded with his purpose in coming here.

While he was thus engaged, Christian would be exploring her worlds of history and of might-have-been and a different agent would range around the physical, present-day globe.

In the latter case, his most obvious procedure was to discharge an appropriate set of the molecular assemblers he had brought along and let them multiply. When their numbers were sufficient, they would build (grow; brew) a fleet of miniature robotic vessels, which would fly about and transmit to him, for study at his leisure, everything their sensors detected.

Gaia persuaded him otherwise: "If you go in person, with a minor aspect of me for a guide, you should get to know the planet more quickly and thoroughly. Much about it is unparalleled. It may help you see why I want the evolution to continue unmolested to its natural conclusion."

He accepted. After all, a major part of his mission was to fathom her thinking. Then perhaps Alpha and the rest could hold a true dialogue and reach an agreement—whatever it was going to be. Besides, he could deploy his investigators later if this expedition left him dissatisfied.

He did inquire: "What are the hazards?"

"Chiefly weather," she admitted. "With conditions growing more extreme, tremendous storms spring up practically without warning. Rapid erosion can change contours almost overnight, bringing landslides, flash floods, sudden emergence of tidal bores. I do not attempt to monitor in close detail. That volume of data would be more than I could handle"— yes, she—"when my main concern is the biological phenomena."

His mind reviewed her most recent accounts to the stars. They were grim. The posthuman lushness of nature was megayears gone. Under its clouds, Earth roasted. The loftiest mountaintops were bleak, as here above the Rainbowl, but nothing of ice or snow remained except dim geological traces. Apart from the waters and a few islands where small, primitive species hung on, the tropics were sterile deserts. Dust and sand borne on furnace winds scoured their rockscapes. North and south they encroached, withering the steppes, parching the valleys, crawling up into the hills. Here and there survived a jungle or a swamp, lashed by torrential rains or wrapped hot and sullen in fog, but it would not be for much longer. Only in the high latitudes did a measure of benignity endure. Arctica's climates ranged from Floridian—Christian Brannock's recollections—to cold on the interior heights. South of it across a sea lay a broad continent whose northerly parts had temperatures reminiscent of central Africa. Those were the last regions where life kept any abundance.

"Would you really not care to see a restoration?" Wayfarer had asked her directly, early on.

"Old Earth lives in my database and emulations," Gaia had responded. "I could not map this that is happening into those systems and let it play itself out, because I do not comprehend it well enough, nor can any finite mind. To divert the course of events would be to lose, forever, knowledge that I feel will prove to be of fundamental importance."

Wayfarer had refrained from pointing out that life, reconquering a world once more hospitable to it, would not follow predictable paths either. He knew she would retort that experiments of that kind were being conducted on a number of formerly barren spheres, seeded with synthesized organisms. It had seemed strange to him that she appeared to lack any sentiment about the mother of humankind. Her being included the beings of many and many a one who had known sunrise dew beneath a bare foot, murmurs in forest shades, wind-waves in wheatfields from horizon to horizon, yes, and the lights and clangor of great cities. It was, at root, affection, more than any scientific or technological challenge, that had roused in Gaia's fellows among the stars the wish to make Earth young again.

Now she meant to show him why she felt that death should have its way.

Before entering rapport with her, he made ready for his expedition. Gaia offered him an aircraft, swift, versatile, able to land on a square meter while disturbing scarcely a leaf. He supplied a passenger for it.

He had brought along several bodies of different types. The one he picked would have to operate independently of him, with a separate intelligence. Gaia could spare a minim of her attention to have telecommand of the flyer; he could spare none for his representative, if he was to range through the history of the globe with her.

The machine he picked was not equivalent to him. Its structure could never have supported a matrix big enough to operate at his level of mentality. Think of it, metaphorically, as possessing a brain equal to that of a high-order human. Into this brain had been copied as much of Wayfarer's self-pattern as it could hold—the merest sketch, a general idea of the situation, incomplete and distorted like this myth of ours. However, it had reserves it could call upon. Inevitably, because of being most suitable for these circumstances, the Christian Brannock aspect dominated.

So you may, if you like, think of the man as being reborn in a body of metal, silicates, carbon and other compounds, electricity and other forces, photon and particle exchanges, quantum currents. Naturally, this affected not just his appearance and abilities, but his inner life. He was not passionless, far from it, but his passions were not identical with those of flesh. In most respects, he differed more from the long-dead mortal than did the re-creation in Gaia's emulated worlds. If we call the latter Christian, we can refer to the former as Brannock.

His frame was of approximately human size and shape. Matte blue-gray, it had four arms. He could reshape the hands of the lower pair as desired, to be a tool kit. He could similarly adapt his feet according to the demands upon them, and could extrude a spindly third leg for support or extra grip. His back swelled outward to hold a nuclear energy source and various organs. His head was a domed cylinder. The sensors in it and throughout the rest of him were not conspicuous but gave him full-surround information. The face was a holographic screen in which he could generate whatever image he wished. Likewise could he produce every frequency of sound, plus visible light, infrared, and microwave radio, for sensing or for short-range communication. A memory unit, out of which he could quickly summon any data, was equivalent to a large ancient library.

He could not process those data, comprehend and reason about them, at higher speed than a human genius. He had other limitations as well. But then, he was never intended to function independently of equipment.

He was soon ready to depart. Imagine him saying to Wayfarer, with a phantom grin, "*Adiós*. Wish me luck."

The response was ... absentminded. Wayfarer was beginning to engage with Gaia.

Thus Brannock boarded the aircraft in a kind of silence. To the eye it rested small, lanceolate, iridescently aquiver. The material component was a tissue of wisps. Most of that slight mass was devoted to generating forces and maintaining capabilities, which Gaia had not listed for him. Yet it would take a wind of uncommon violence to endanger this machine, and most likely it could outrun the menace.

He settled down inside. Wayfarer had insisted on manual controls, against emergencies that he conceded were improbable, and Gaia's effectors had made the modifications. An insubstantial configuration shimmered before Brannock, instruments to read, keypoints to touch or think or think at. He leaned back into a containing field and let her pilot. Noiselessly, the flyer ascended, then came down through the cloud deck and made a leisurely way at five hundred meters above the foothills.

"Follow the Remnant River to the sea," Brannock requested. "The view inbound was beautiful."

"As you like," said Gaia. They employed sonics, his voice masculine, hers—perhaps because she supposed he preferred it—feminine in a low register. Their conversation did not actually go as reported here. She changed course and he beheld the stream shining amidst the deep greens of the Bountiful Valley, under a silver-gray heaven. "The plan, you know, is that we shall cruise about Arctica first. I have an itinerary that should provide you a representative sampling of its biology. At our stops, you can investigate as intensively as you care to, and if you want to stop anyplace else we can do that too."

"Thank you," he said. "The idea is to furnish me a kind of baseline, right?"

"Yes, because conditions here are the easiest for life. When you are ready, we will proceed south, across countries increasingly harsh. You will learn about the adaptations life has made. Many are extraordinarily interesting. The galactic brain itself cannot match the creativity of nature."

"Well, sure. Chaos, complexity ... You've described quite a few of those adaptations to, uh, us, haven't you?"

"Yes, but by no means all. I keep discovering new ones. Life keeps evolving."

As environments worsened, Brannock thought. And nonetheless, species after species went extinct. He got a sense of a rear-guard battle against the armies of hell.

"I want you to experience this as fully as you are able," Gaia said, "immerse yourself, *feel* the sublimity of it."

The tragedy, he thought. But tragedy was art, maybe the highest art that humankind ever achieved. And more of the human soul might well linger in Gaia than in any of her fellow intelligences.

Had she kept a need for catharsis, for pity and terror? What really went on in her emulations?

Well, Christian was supposed to find out something about that. If he could.

Brannock was human enough himself to protest. He gestured at the land below, where the river flowed in its canyons through the coastal hills, to water a wealth of forest and meadow before emptying into a bay above which soared thousands of wings. "You want to watch the struggle till the end," he said. "Life wants to live. What right have you to set your wish against that?"

"The right of awareness," she declared. "Only to a being that is conscious do justice, mercy, desire have any existence, any meaning. Did not humans always use the world as they saw fit? When nature finally got protection, that was because humans so chose. I speak for the knowledge and insight that *we* can gain."

The question flickered uneasily in him: What about her private emotional needs?

Abruptly the aircraft veered. The turn pushed Brannock hard into the force field upholding him. He heard air crack and scream. The bay fell aft with mounting speed.

The spaceman in him, who had lived through meteoroid strikes and radiation bursts because he was quick, had already acted. Through the optical magnification he immediately ordered up, he looked back to see what the trouble was. The glimpse he got, before the sight went under the horizon, made him cry, "Yonder!"

"What?" Gaia replied as she hurtled onward.

"That back there. Why are you running from it?"

"What do you mean? There is nothing important."

"The devil there isn't. I've a notion you saw it more clearly than I did."

Gaia slowed the headlong flight until she well-nigh hovered above the strand and wild surf. He felt a sharp suspicion that she did it in order to dissipate the impression of urgency, make him more receptive to whatever she intended to claim.

"Very well," she said after a moment. "I spied a certain object. What do you think you saw?"

He decided not to answer straightforwardly—at least, not before she convinced him of her good faith. The more information she had, the more readily she could contrive a deception. Even this fragment of her intellect was superior to his. Yet he had his own measure of wits, and an ingrained stubbornness.

"I'm not sure, except that it didn't seem dangerous. Suppose you tell me what it is and why you turned tail from it."

Did she sigh? "At this stage of your knowledge, you would not understand. Rather, you would be bound to misunderstand. That is why I retreated."

A human would have tensed every muscle. Brannock's systems went on full standby. "I'll be the judge of my brain's range, if you please. Kindly go back."

"No. I promise I will explain later, when you have seen enough more."

Seen enough illusions? She might well have many trickeries waiting for him. "As you like," Brannock said. "Meanwhile, I'll give Wayfarer a call and let him know." Alpha's emissary kept a minute part of his sensibility open to outside stimuli.

"No, do not," Gaia said. "It would distract him unnecessarily."

"He will decide that," Brannock told her.

Strife exploded.

Almost, Gaia won. Had her entirety been focused on attack, she would have carried it off with such swiftness that Brannock would never have known he was bestormed. But a fraction of her was dealing, as always, with her observing units around the globe and their torrents of data. Possibly it also glanced from time to time—through the quantum shifts inside her—at the doings of Christian and Laurinda. By far the most of her was occupied in her interaction with Wayfarer. This she could not set aside without rousing instant suspicion. Rather, she must make a supremely clever effort to conceal from him that anything untoward was going on.

Moreover, she had never encountered a being like Brannock, human male aggressiveness and human spacefarer's reflexes blent with sophisticated technology and something of Alpha's immortal purpose.

He felt the support field strengthen and tighten to hold him immobile. He felt a tide like delirium rush into his mind. A man would have thought it was a knockout anesthetic. Brannock did not stop to wonder. He reacted directly, even as she struck. Machine fast and tiger ferocious, he put her off balance for a crucial millisecond.

Through the darkness and roaring in his head, he lashed out physically. His hands tore through the light-play of control nexuses before him. They were not meant to withstand an assault. He could not seize command, but he could, blindly, disrupt.

Arcs leaped blue-white. Luminances flared and died. Power output continued; the aircraft stayed aloft. Its more complex functions were in ruin. Their dance of atoms, energies, and waves went uselessly random.

The bonds that had been closing on Brannock let go. He sagged to the floor. The night in his head receded. It left him shaken, his senses awhirl. Into the sudden anarchy of everything he yelled, "Stop, you bitch!"

"I will," Gaia said.

Afterward he realized that she had kept a vestige of governance over the flyer. Before he could wrest it from her, she sent them plunging downward and cut off the main generator. Every force field blinked out. Wind ripped the material frame asunder. Its pieces crashed in the surf. Combers tumbled them about, cast a few on the beach, gave the rest to the undertow.

As the craft fell, disintegrating, Brannock gathered his strength and leaped. The thrust of his legs cast him outward, through a long arc that ended in deeper water. It fountained high and white when he struck. He went down into green depths while the currents swept him to and fro. But he hit the sandy bottom unharmed.

Having no need to breathe, he stayed under. To recover from the shock took him less than a second. To make his assessment took minutes, there in the swirling surges.

Gaia had tried to take him over. A force field had begun to damp the processes in his brain and impose its own patterns. He had quenched it barely in time.

She would scarcely have required a capability of that kind in the past. Therefore she had invented and installed it specifically for him. This strongly suggested she had meant to use it at some point of their journey. When he saw a thing she had not known was there and refused to be fobbed off, he compelled her to make the attempt before she was ready. When it failed, she spent her last resources to destroy him.

She would go that far, that desperately, to keep a secret that tremendous from the stars.

He recognized a mistake in his thinking. She had not used up everything at her beck. On the contrary, she had a planetful of observers and other instrumentalities to call upon. Certain of them must be bound here at top speed, to make sure he was dead—or, if he lived, to make sure of him. Afterward she would feed Wayfarer a story that ended with a regrettable accident away off over an ocean.

Heavier than water, Brannock strode down a sloping sea floor in search of depth.

Having found a jumble of volcanic rock, he crawled into a lava tube, lay fetally curled, and willed his systems to operate as low-level as might be. He hoped that then her agents would miss him. Neither their numbers nor their sensitivities were infinite. It would be reasonable for Gaia—who could not have witnessed his escape, her sensors in the aircraft being obliterated as it came apart—to conclude that the flows had taken his scattered remains away.

◆

After three days and nights, the internal clock he had set brought him back awake.

He knew he must stay careful. However, unless she kept a closer watch on the site than he expected she would—for Wayfarer, in communion with her, might too readily notice that she was concentrating on one little patch of the planet—he dared now move about. His electronic senses ought to warn him of any robot that came into his vicinity, even if it was too small for eyes to see. Whether he could then do anything about it was a separate question.

First he searched the immediate area. Gaia's machines had removed those shards of the wreck that they found, but most were strewn over the bottom, and she had evidently not thought it worthwhile, or safe, to have them sought out. Nearly all of what he came upon was in fact scrap. A few units were intact. The one that interested him had the physical form of a small metal sphere. He tracked it down by magnetic induction. Having taken it to a place ashore, hidden by trees from the sky, he studied it. With his tool-hands he traced the (mythic) circuitry within and identified it as a memory bank. The encoding was familiar to his Wayfarer aspect. He extracted the information and stored it in his own database.

A set of languages. Human languages, although none he had ever heard of. Yes, very interesting.

"I'd better get hold of those people," he muttered. In the solitude of wind, sea, and wilderness, he had relapsed into an ancient habit of occasionally thinking aloud. "Won't likely be another chance. Quite a piece of news for Wayfarer." If he came back, or at least got within range of his transmitter.

He set forth afoot, along the shore toward the bay where the Remnant River debouched. Maybe that which he had seen would be there yet, or traces of it.

He wasn't sure, everything had happened so fast, but he thought it was a ship.

7

Three days—olden Earth days of twenty-four hours, cool sunlight, now and then a rainshower leaving pastures and hedgerows asparkle, rides through English lanes, rambles through English towns, encounters with folk, evensong in a Norman church, exploration of buildings and books, long talks and companionable silences—wrought friendship. In Christian it also began to rouse kindlier feelings toward Gaia. She had resurrected Laurinda, and Laurinda was a part of her, as he was of Wayfarer and of Alpha and more other minds across the galaxy than he could number. Could the rest of Gaia's works be wrongful?

No doubt she had chosen and planned as she did in order to get this reaction from him. It didn't seem to matter.

Nor did the primitive conditions of the eighteenth century matter to him or to Laurinda. Rather, their everyday experiences were something refreshingly new, and frequently the occasion of laughter. What did become a bit difficult for him was to retire decorously to his separate room each night.

But they had their missions: his to see what was going on in this reality and afterward upload into Wayfarer; hers to explain and justify it to him as well as a mortal was able. Like him, she kept a memory of having been one with a nodal being. The memory was as dim and fragmentary as his, more a sense of transcendence than anything with a name or form, like the afterglow of a religious vision long ago. Yet it pervaded her personality, the unconscious more than the conscious; and it was her relationship to Gaia, as he had his to Wayfarer and beyond that to Alpha. In a limited, mortal, but altogether honest and natural way, she spoke for the node of Earth.

By tacit consent, they said little about the purpose and simply enjoyed their surroundings and one another, until the fourth morning. Perhaps the weather whipped up a lifetime habit of duty. Wind gusted and shrilled around the house, rain blinded the windows, there would be no going out even in a carriage. Indoors a fire failed to hold dank chill at bay. Candlelight glowed cozily on the breakfast table, silverware and china sheened, but shadows hunched thick in every corner.

He took a last sip of coffee, put the cup down, and ended the words he had been setting forth: "Yes, we'd better get started. Not that I've any clear notion of what to look for. Wayfarer himself doesn't." Gaia had been so vague about so much. Well, Wayfarer was now (whatever "now" meant) in rapport with her, seeking an overall, cosmic view of—how many millions of years on this planet?

"Why, you know your task," Laurinda replied. "You're to find out the nature of Gaia's interior activity, what it means in moral—in human terms." She straightened in her chair. Her tone went resolute. "We *are* human, we emulations. We think and act, we feel joy and pain, the same as humans always did."

Impulse beckoned; it was his wont to try to lighten moods. "And," he added, "make new generations of people, the same as humans always did."

A blush crossed the fair countenance. "Yes," she said. Quickly: "Of course, most of what's . . . here . . . is nothing but database. Archives, if you will. We might start by visiting one or two of those reconstructions."

He smiled, the heaviness lifting from him. "I'd love to. Any suggestions?"

Eagerness responded. "The Acropolis of Athens? As it was when new? Classical civilization fascinated me." She tossed her head. "Still does, by damn."

"Hm." He rubbed his chin. "From what I learned in my day, those old Greeks were as tricky, quarrelsome, shortsighted a pack of political animals as ever stole an election or bullied a weaker neighbor. Didn't Athens finance the building of the Parthenon by misappropriating the treasury of the Delian League?"

"They were human," she said, almost too low for him to hear above the storm-noise. "But what they made—"

"Sure," he answered. "Agreed. Let's go."

◗

In perception, the amulets were silvery two-centimeter discs that hung on a user's breast, below garments. In reality—outer-viewpoint reality—they were powerful, subtle programs with intelligences of their own. Christian wondered about the extent to which they were under the direct control of Gaia, and how closely she was monitoring him.

Without thinking, he took Laurinda's hand. Her fingers clung to his. She looked straight before her, though, into the flickery fire, while she uttered their command.

◗

Immediately, with no least sensation of movement, they were on broad marble steps between outworks, under a cloudless heaven, in flooding hot radiance. From the steepest, unused hill slopes, a scent of wild thyme drifted up through silence, thyme without bees to quicken it or hands to pluck it. Below reached the city, sun-smitten house roofs, open agoras, colonnaded temples. In this clear air Brannock imagined he could well-nigh make out the features on the statues.

After a time beyond time, the visitors moved upward, still mute, still hand in hand, to where winged Victories lined the balustrade before the sanctuary of Nike Apteros. Their draperies flowed to movement he did not see and wind he did not feel. One was tying her sandals. . . .

For a long while the two lingered at the Propylaea, its porticos, Ionics, Dorics, paintings, votive tablets in the Pinakotheka. They felt they could have stayed past sunset, but everything else awaited them, and they knew mortal enthusiasm as they would presently know mortal weariness. Colors burned. . . .

The stone flowers and stone maidens at the Erechtheum . . .

Christian had thought of the Parthenon as exquisite; so it was in the pictures and models he had seen, while the broken, chemically gnawed remnants were merely to grieve over. Confronting it here, entering it, he discovered its sheer size and mass. Life shouted in the friezes, red, blue, gilt; then in the dusk within, awesomeness and beauty found their focus in the colossal Athene of Pheidias.

—Long afterward, he stood with Laurinda on the Wall of Kimon, above the Asclepium and Theater of Dionysus. A westering sun made the city below intricate with shadows, and coolth breathed out of the east. Hitherto, when they spoke it had been, illogically, in near whispers. Now they felt free to talk openly, or did they feel a need?

He shook his head. "Gorgeous," he said, for lack of anything halfway adequate. "Unbelievable."

"It was worth all the wrongdoing and war and agony," she murmured. "Wasn't it?"

For the moment, he shied away from deep seriousness. "I didn't expect it to be this, uh, gaudy—no, this bright."

"They painted their buildings. That's known."

"Yes, I knew too. But were later scholars sure of just what colors?"

"Scarcely, except where a few traces were left. Most of this must be Gaia's conjecture. The sculpture especially, I suppose. Recorded history saved only the barest description of the Athene, for instance." Laurinda paused. Her gaze went outward to the mountains. "But surely this—in view of everything she has, all the information, and being able to handle it all at once and, and understand the minds that were capable of making it—surely this is the most likely reconstruction. Or the least unlikely."

"She may have tried variations. Would you like to go see?"

"No, I, I think not, unless you want to. This has been overwhelming, hasn't it?" She hesitated. "Besides, well—"

He nodded. "Yeh." With a gesture at the soundless, motionless, smokeless city below and halidoms around: "Spooky. At best, a museum exhibit. Not much to our purpose, I'm afraid."

She met his eyes. "Your purpose. I'm only a—not even a guide, really. Gaia's voice to you? No, just a, an undertone of her, if that." The smile that touched her lips was somehow forlorn. "I suspect my main reason for existing again is to keep you company."

He laughed and offered her a hand, which for a moment she clasped tightly. "I'm very glad of the company, eccentric Miss Ashcroft."

Her smile warmed and widened. "Thank you, kind sir. And I am glad to be . . . alive . . . today. What should we do next?"

"Visit some living history, I think," he said. "Why not Hellenic?"

She struck her palms together. "The age of Pericles!"

He frowned. "Well, I don't know about that. The Peloponnesian War, the plague—and foreigners like us, barbarians, you a woman, we wouldn't be too well received, would we?"

He heard how she put disappointment aside and looked forward anew. "When and where, then?"

"Aristotle's time? If I remember rightly, Greece was peaceful then, no matter how much hell Alexander was raising abroad, and the society was getting quite cosmopolitan. Less patriarchal, too. Anyhow, Aristotle's always interested me. In a way, he was one of the earliest scientists."

"We had better inquire first. But before that, let's go home to a nice hot cup of tea!"

⬤

They returned to the house at the same moment as they left it, to avoid perturbing the servants. There they found that lack of privacy joined with exhaustion to keep them from speaking of anything other than trivia. However, that was all right; they were good talkmates.

The next morning, which was brilliant, they went out into the garden and settled on a bench by the fish basin. Drops of rain glistened on flowers, whose fragrance awoke with the strengthening sunshine. Nothing else was in sight or earshot. This time Christian addressed the amulets. He felt suddenly heavy around his neck, and the words came out awkwardly. He need not have said them aloud, but it helped him give shape to his ideas.

The reply entered directly into their brains. He rendered it to himself, irrationally, as in a dry, professorish tenor:

"Only a single Hellenic milieu has been carried through many generations. It includes the period you have in mind. It commenced at the point of approximately 500 B.C., with an emulation as historically accurate as possible."

But nearly everyone then alive was lost to history, thought Christian. Except for the few who were in the chronicles, the whole population must needs be created out of Gaia's imagination, guided by knowledge and logic; and those few named persons were themselves almost entirely new-made, their very DNA arbitrarily laid out.

"The sequence was revised as necessary," the amulet continued.

Left to itself, that history would soon have drifted completely away from the documents, and eventually from the archaeology, Christian thought. Gaia saw this start to happen, over and over. She rewrote the program—events, memories, personalities, bodies, births, life spans, deaths—and let it resume until it deviated again. Over and over. The morning felt abruptly cold.

"Much was learned on every such occasion," said the amulet. "The situation appeared satisfactory by the time Macedonian hegemony was inevitable, and thereafter the sequence was left to play itself out undisturbed. Naturally, it still did not proceed identically with the historical past. Neither Aristotle nor Alexander were born. Instead, a reasonably realistic conqueror lived to a ripe age and bequeathed a reasonably well constructed empire. He did have a Greek teacher in his youth, who had been a disciple of Plato."

"Who was that?" Christian asked out of a throat gone dry.

"His name was Eumenes. In many respects he was equivalent to Aristotle, but had a more strongly empirical orientation. This was planned."

Eumenes was specially ordained, then. Why?

"If we appear and meet him, w-won't that change what comes after?"

"Probably not to any significant extent. Or if it does, that will not matter. The original sequence is in Gaia's database. Your visit will, in effect, be a reactivation."

"Not one for your purpose," Laurinda whispered into the air. "What was it? What happened in that world?"

"The objective was experimental, to study the possible engendering of a scientific-technological revolution analogous to that of the seventeenth century A.D., with accompanying social developments that might foster the evolution of a stable democracy."

Christian told himself furiously to pull out of his funk. "Did it?" He challenged.

The reply was calm. "Do you wish to study it?"

Christian had not expected any need to muster his courage. After a minute he said, word by slow word, "Yes, I think that might be more useful than meeting your philosopher. Can you show us the outcome of the experiment?"

Laurinda joined in: "Oh, I know there can't be any single, simple picture. But can you bring us to a, a scene that will give an impression—a kind of epitome—like, oh, King John at Runnymede or Elizabeth the First knighting Francis Drake or Einstein and Bohr talking about the state of their world?"

"An extreme possibility occurs in a year corresponding to your 894 A.D.," the amulet told him. "I suggest Athens as the locale. Be warned, it is dangerous. I can protect you, or remove you, but human affairs are inherently chaotic and this situation is more unpredictable than most. It could escape my control."

"I'll go," Christian snapped.

"And I," Laurinda said.

He glared at her. "No. You heard. It's dangerous."

Gone quite calm, she stated, "It is necessary for me. Remember, I travel on behalf of Gaia."

Gaia, who let the thing come to pass.

◆

Transfer.

For an instant, they glanced at themselves. They knew the amulets would convert their garb to something appropriate. She wore a gray gown, belted, reaching halfway down her calves, with shoes, stockings, and a scarf over hair coiled in braids. He was in tunic, trousers, and boots of the same coarse materials, a sheath knife at his hip and a long-barreled firearm slung over his back.

Their surroundings smote them. They stood in a Propylaea that was scarcely more than tumbled stones and snags of sculpture. The Parthenon was not so shattered, but scarred, weathered, here and there buttressed with brickwork from which thrust the mouths of rusted cannon. All else was ruin. The Erechtheum looked as if it had been quarried. Below them, the city burned. They could see little of it through smoke that stained the sky and savaged their nostrils. A roar of conflagration reached them, and bursts of gunfire.

A woman came running out of the haze, up the great staircase. She was young, dark-haired, unkempt, ragged, begrimed, desperate. A man came after, a burly blond in a fur cap, dirty red coat, and leather breeches. Beneath a sweeping mustache, he leered. He too was armed, murderously big knife, firearm in right hand.

The woman saw Christian looming before her. "*Voetho!*" she screamed. "*Onome Theou, kyrie, voetho!*" She caught her foot against a step and fell. Her pursuer stopped before she could rise and stamped a boot down on her back.

Through his amulet, Christian understood the cry. "Help, in God's name, sir, help!" Fleetingly he thought the language must be a debased Greek. The other man snarled at him and brought weapon to shoulder.

Christian had no time to unlimber his. While the stranger was in motion, he bent, snatched up a rock—a fragment of a marble head—and cast. It thudded against the stranger's nose. He lurched back, his face a sudden red grotesque. His gun clattered to the stairs. He howled.

With the quickness that was his in emergencies, Christian rejected grabbing his own firearm. He had seen that its lock was of peculiar design. He might not be able to discharge it fast enough. He drew his knife and lunged downward. "Get away, you swine, before I open your guts!" he shouted. The words came out in the woman's language.

The other man retched, turned, and staggered off. Well before he reached the bottom of the hill, smoke had swallowed sight of him. Christian halted at the woman's huddled form and sheathed his blade. "Here, sister," he said, offering his hand, "come along. Let's get to shelter. There may be more of them."

She crawled to her feet, gasping, leaned heavily on his arm, and limped beside him up to the broken gateway. Her features Mediterranean, she was doubtless a native. She looked half starved. Laurinda came to her side. Between them, the visitors got her into the portico of the Parthenon. Beyond a smashed door lay an interior dark and empty of everything but litter. It would be defensible if necessary.

An afterthought made Christian swear at himself. He went back for the enemy's weapon. When he returned, Laurinda sat with her arms around the woman, crooning comfort. "There, darling, there, you're safe with us. Don't be afraid. We'll take care of you."

The fugitive lifted big eyes full of night. "Are . . . you . . . angels from heaven?" she mumbled.

"No, only mortals like you," Laurinda answered through tears. That was not exactly true, Christian thought; but what else could she say? "We do not even know your name."

"I am . . . Zoe . . . Comnenaina—"

"Bone-dry, I hear from your voice." Laurinda lifted her head. Her lips moved in silent command. A jug appeared on the floor, bedewed with cold. "Here is water. Drink."

Zoe had not noticed the miracle. She snatched the vessel and drained it in gulp after gulp. When she was through she set it down and said, "Thank you," dully but with something of strength and reason again in her.

"Who was that after you?" Christian asked.

She drew knees to chin, hugged herself, stared before her, and replied in a dead voice, "A Flemic soldier. They broke into our house. I saw them stab my father. They laughed and laughed. I ran out the back and down the streets. I thought I could hide on the Acropolis. Nobody comes here anymore. That one saw me and came after. I suppose he would have killed me when he was done. That would have been better than if he took me away with him."

Laurinda nodded. "An invading army," she said as tonelessly. "They took the city and now they are sacking it."

Christian thumped the butt of his gun down on the stones. "Does Gaia let this go *on?*" he grated.

Laurinda lifted her gaze to his. It pleaded. "She must. Humans must have free will. Otherwise they're puppets."

"But how did they get into this mess?" Christian demanded. "Explain it if you can!"

The amulet(s) replied with the same impersonality as before:

"The Hellenistic era developed scientific method. This, together with the expansion of commerce and geographical knowledge, produced an industrial revolution and parliamentary democracy. However, neither the science nor the technology progressed beyond an approximate equivalent of your eighteenth century. Unwise social and fiscal policies led to breakdown, dictatorship, and repeated warfare."

Christian's grin bared teeth. "That sounds familiar."

"Alexander Tytler said it in our eighteenth century," Laurinda muttered unevenly. "No republic has long outlived the discovery by a majority of its people that they could vote themselves largesse from the public treasury." Aloud: "Christian, they were only human."

Zoe hunched, lost in her sorrow.

"You oversimplify," stated the amulet voice. "But this is not a history lesson. To continue the outline, inevitably engineering information spread to the warlike barbarians of northern Europe and western Asia. If you question why they were granted existence, reflect that a population confined to the littoral of an inland sea could not model any possible material world. The broken-down societies of the South were unable to change their characters, or prevail over them, or eventually hold them off. The end results are typified by what you see around you."

"The Dark Ages," Christian said dully. "What happens after them? What kind of new civilization?"

"None. This sequence terminates in one more of its years."

"Huh?" he gasped. "Destroyed?"

"No. The program ceases to run. The emulation stops."

"My God! Those millions of lives—as real as, as mine—"

Laurinda stood up and held her arms out into the fouled air. "Does Gaia know, then, does Gaia know this time line would never get any happier?" she cried.

"No," said the voice in their brains. "Doubtless the potential of further progress exists. However, you forget that while Gaia's capacities are large, they are not infinite. The more attention she devotes to one history, the details of its planet as well as the length of its course, the less she has to give to others. The probability is too small that this sequence will lead to a genuinely new form of society."

Slowly, Laurinda nodded. "I see."

"I don't," Christian snapped. "Except that Gaia's inhuman."

Laurinda shook her head and laid a hand on his. "No, not that. Post-human. *We* built the first artificial intelligences." After a moment: "Gaia isn't cruel. The universe often is, and she didn't create it. She's seeking something better than blind chance can make."

"Maybe." His glance fell on Zoe. "Look, something's got to be done for this poor soul. Never mind if we change the history. It's due to finish soon anyway."

Laurinda swallowed and wiped her eyes. "Give her her last year in peace," she said into the air. "Please."

Objects appeared in the room behind the doorway. "Here are food, wine, clean water," said the unheard voice. "Advise her to return downhill after dark, find some friends, and lead them back. A small party, hiding in these ruins, can hope to survive until the invaders move on."

"It isn't worthwhile doing more, is it?" Christian said bitterly. "Not to you."

"Do you wish to end your investigation?"

"No, be damned if I will."

"Nor I," said Laurinda. "But when we're through here, when we've done the pitiful little we can for this girl, take us home."

◆

Peace dwelt in England. Clouds towered huge and white, blue-shadowed from the sunlight spilling past them. Along the left side of a lane, poppies blazed in a grainfield goldening toward harvest. On the right stretched the manifold greens of a pasture where cattle drowsed beneath a broad-crowned oak. Man and woman rode side by side. Hoofs thumped softly, saddle leather creaked, the sweet smell of horse mingled with herbal pungencies, a blackbird whistled.

"No, I don't suppose Gaia will ever restart any program she's terminated," Laurinda said. "But it's no worse than death, and death is seldom
that easy."

"The scale of it," Christian protested, then sighed. "But I daresay Wayfarer will tell me I'm being sloppy sentimental, and when I've rejoined
him I'll agree." Wryness added that that had better be true. He would
no longer be separate, an avatar; he would be one with a far greater entity,
which would in its turn remerge with a greater still.

"Without Gaia, they would never have existed, those countless lives,
generation after generation after generation," Laurinda said. "Their worst
miseries they brought on themselves. If any of them are ever to find their
way to something better, truly better, she has to keep making fresh starts."

"Mm, I can't help remembering all the millennialists and utopians who
slaughtered people wholesale, or tortured them or threw them into concentration camps, if their behavior didn't fit the convenient attainment of
the inspired vision."

"No, no, it's not like that! Don't you see? She gives them their freedom
to be themselves and, and to become more."

"Seems to me she adjusts the parameters and boundary conditions till
the setup looks promising before she lets the experiment run." Christian
frowned. "But I admit, it isn't believable that she does it simply because
she's . . . bored and lonely. Not when the whole fellowship of her kind is
open to her. Maybe we haven't the brains to know what her reasons are.
Maybe she's explaining them to Wayfarer, or directly to Alpha," although
communication among the stars would take decades at least.

"Do you want to go on nonetheless?" she asked.

"I said I do. I'm supposed to. But you?"

"Yes. I don't want to, well, fail her."

"I'm sort of at a loss what to try next, and not sure it's wise to let the
amulets decide."

"But they can help us, counsel us." Laurinda drew breath. "Please. If
you will. The next world we go to—could it be gentle? That horror we
saw—"

He reached across to take her hand. "Exactly what I was thinking. Have
you a suggestion?"

She nodded. "York Minster. It was in sad condition when I . . . lived
. . . but I saw pictures and—It was one of the loveliest churches ever built,
in the loveliest old town."

"Excellent idea. Not another lifeless piece of archive, though. A complete environment." Christian pondered. "We'll inquire first, naturally,
but offhand I'd guess the Edwardian period would suit us well. On the
Continent they called it the *belle époque*."

"Splendid!" she exclaimed. Already her spirits were rising anew.

◆

Transfer.

They arrived near the west end, in the south aisle.

Worshippers were few, scattered closer to the altar rail. In the dimness,
under the glories of glass and soaring Perpendicular arches, their advent

went unobserved. Windows in that direction glowed more vividly—rose, gold, blue, the cool gray-green of the Five Sisters—than the splendor above their backs; it was a Tuesday morning in June. Incense wove its odor through the ringing chant from the choir.

Christian tautened. "That's Latin," he whispered. "In England, 1900?" He glanced down at his garments and hers, and peered ahead. Shirt, coat, trousers for him, with a hat laid on the pew; ruffled blouse, ankle-length gown, and lacy bonnet for her; but—"The clothes aren't right either."

"Hush," Laurinda answered as low. "Wait. We were told this wouldn't be our 1900. Here may be the only York Minster in all of Gaia."

He nodded stiffly. It was clear that the node had never attempted a perfect reproduction of any past milieu—impossible, and pointless to boot. Often, though not necessarily always, she took an approximation as a starting point; but it never went on to the same destiny. What were the roots of this day?

"Relax," Laurinda urged. "It's beautiful."

He did his best, and indeed the Roman Catholic mass at the hour of tierce sang some tranquility into his heart.

After the Nunc Dimittis, when clergy and laity had departed, the two could wander around and savor. Emerging at last, they spent a while looking upon the carven tawny limestone of the front. This was no Parthenon; it was a different upsurging of the same miracle. But around it lay a world to discover. With half a sigh and half a smile, they set forth.

The delightful narrow "gates," walled in with half-timbered houses, lured them. More modern streets and buildings, above all the people therein, captured them. York was a living town, a market town, core of a wide hinterland, node of a nation. It racketed, it bustled.

The half smile faded. A wholly foreign setting would not have felt as wrong as one that was half homelike.

Clothing styles were not radically unlike what pictures and historical dramas had once shown; but they were not identical. The English chatter was in no dialect of English known to Christian or Laurinda, and repeatedly they heard versions of German. A small, high-stacked steam locomotive pulled a train into a station of somehow Teutonic architecture. No early automobiles stuttered along the thoroughfares. Horse-drawn vehicles moved crowdedly, but the pavements were clean and the smell of dung faint because the animals wore a kind of diapers. A flag above a post office (?), fluttering in the wind, displayed a cross of St. Andrew on which was superimposed a two-headed gold eagle. A man with a megaphone bellowed at the throng to stand aside and make way for a military squadron. In blue uniforms, rifles on shoulders, they quick-marched to commands barked in German. Individual soldiers, presumably on leave, were everywhere. A boy went by, shrilly hawking newspapers, and Christian saw WAR in a headline.

"Listen, amulet," he muttered finally, "where can we get a beer?"

"A public house will admit you if you go in by the couples' entrance," replied the soundless voice.

So, no unescorted women allowed. Well, Christian thought vaguely, hadn't that been the case in his Edwardian years, at any rate in respectable taverns? A signboard jutting from a Tudor façade read GEORGE AND DRAGON. The wainscoted room inside felt equally English.

Custom was plentiful and noisy, tobacco smoke thick, but he and Laurinda found a table in a corner where they could talk without anybody else paying attention. The brew that a barmaid fetched was of Continental character. He didn't give it the heed it deserved.

"I don't think we've found our peaceful world after all," he said.

Laurinda looked beyond him, into distances where he could not follow. "Will we ever?" she wondered. "Can any be, if it's human?"

He grimaced. "Well, let's find out what the hell's going on here."

"You can have a detailed explanation if you wish," said the voice in their heads. "You would be better advised to accept a bare outline, as you did before."

"Instead of loading ourselves down with the background of a world that never was," he mumbled.

"That never was ours," Laurinda corrected him.

"Carry on."

"This sequence was generated as of its fifteenth century A.D.," said the voice. "The conciliar movement was made to succeed, rather than failing as it did in your history."

"Uh, conciliar movement?"

"The ecclesiastical councils of Constance and later of Basel attempted to heal the Great Schism and reform the government of the Church. Here they accomplished it, giving back to the bishops some of the power that over the centuries had accrued to the popes, working out a reconciliation with the Hussites, and making other important changes. As a result, no Protestant breakaway occurred, nor wars of religion, and the Church remained a counterbalance to the state, preventing the rise of absolute monarchies."

"Why, that's wonderful," Laurinda whispered.

"Not too wonderful by now," Christian said grimly. "What happened?"

"In brief, Germany was spared the devastation of the Thirty Years' War and a long-lasting division into quarrelsome principalities. It was unified in the seventeenth century and soon became the dominant European power, colonizing and conquering eastward. Religious and cultural differences from the Slavs proved irreconcilable. As the harsh imperium provoked increasing restlessness, it perforce grew more severe, causing more rebellion. Meanwhile it decayed within, until today it has broken apart and the Russians are advancing on Berlin."

"I see. What about science and technology?"

"They have developed more slowly than in your history, although you have noted the existence of a fossil-fueled industry and inferred an approximately Lagrangian level of theory."

"The really brilliant eras were when all hell broke loose, weren't they?" Christian mused. "This Europe went through less agony, and invented and discovered less. Coincidence?"

"What about government?" Laurinda asked.

"For a time, parliaments flourished, more powerful than kings, emperors, or popes," said the voice. "In most Western countries they still wield considerable influence."

"As the creatures of special interests, I'll bet," Christian rasped. "All right, what comes next?"

Gaia knew. He sat in a reactivation of something she probably played to a finish thousands of years ago.

"Scientific and technological advance proceeds, accelerating, through a long period of general turbulence. At the termination point—"

"Never mind!" Oblivion might be better than a nuclear war.

Silence fell at the table. The life that filled the pub with its noise felt remote, unreal.

"We dare not weep," Laurinda finally said. "Not yet."

Christian shook himself. "Europe was never the whole of Earth," he growled. "How many worlds has Gaia made?"

"Many," the voice told him.

"Show us one that's really foreign. If you agree, Laurinda."

She squared her shoulders. "Yes, do." After a moment: "Not here. If we disappeared it would shock them. It might change the whole future."

"Hardly enough to notice," Christian said. "And would it matter in the long run? But, yeh, let's be off."

They wandered out, among marvels gone meaningless, until they found steps leading up onto the medieval wall. Thence they looked across roofs and river and Yorkshire beyond, finding they were alone.

"Now take us away," Christian ordered.

"You have not specified any type of world," said the voice.

"Surprise us."

➤

Transfer.

The sky stood enormous, bleached blue, breezes warm underneath. A bluff overlooked a wide brown river. Trees grew close to its edge, tall, pale of bark, leaves silver-green and shivery. Christian recognized them, cottonwoods. He was somewhere in west central North America, then. Uneasy shadows lent camouflage if he and Laurinda kept still. Across the river the land reached broad, roads twisting their way through cultivation—mainly wheat and Indian corn—that seemed to be parceled out among small farms, each with its buildings, house, barn, occasional stable or workshop. The sweeping lines of the ruddy-tiled roofs looked Asian. He spied oxcarts and a few horseback riders on the roads, workers in the fields, but at their distance he couldn't identify race or garb. Above yonder horizon thrust clustered towers that also suggested the Orient. If they belonged to a city, it must be compact, not sprawling over the countryside but neatly drawn into itself.

One road ran along the farther riverbank. A procession went upon it. An elephant led, as richly caparisoned as the man under the silk awning of a howdah. Shaven-headed men in yellow robes walked after, flanked by horsemen who bore poles from which pennons streamed scarlet and gold. The sound of slowly beaten gongs and minor-key chanting came faint through the wind.

Christian snapped his fingers. "Stupid me!" he muttered. "Give us a couple of opticals."

Immediately he and Laurinda held the devices. From his era, they fitted into the palm but projected an image at any magnification desired, with no lenses off which light could glint to betray. He peered back and forth for minutes. Yes, the appearance was quite Chinese, or Chinese-derived, except that a number of the individuals he studied had more of an American countenance and the leader on the elephant wore a feather bonnet above his robe.

"How quiet here," Laurinda said.

"You are at the height of the Great Peace," the amulet voice answered.

"How many like that were there ever?" Christian wondered. "Where, when, how?"

"You are in North America, in the twenty-second century by your reckoning. Chinese navigators arrived on the Pacific shore seven hundred years ago, and colonists followed."

In this world, Christian thought, Europe and Africa were surely a sketch, mere geography, holding a few primitive tribes at most, unless nothing was there but ocean. Simplify, simplify.

"Given the distances to sail and the dangers, the process was slow," the voice went on. "While the newcomers displaced or subjugated the natives wherever they settled, most remained free for a long time, acquired the technology, and also developed resistance to introduced diseases. Eventually, being on roughly equal terms, the races began to mingle, genetically and culturally. The settlers mitigated the savagery of the religions they had encountered, but learned from the societies, as well as teaching. You behold the outcome."

"The Way of the Buddha?" Laurinda asked very softly.

"As influenced by Daoism and local nature cults. It is a harmonious faith, without sects or heresies, pervading the civilization."

"Everything can't be pure loving-kindness," Christian said.

"Certainly not. But the peace that the Emperor Wei Zhi-fu brought about has lasted for a century and will for another two. If you travel, you will find superb achievements in the arts and in graciousness."

"Another couple of centuries." Laurinda's tones wavered the least bit. "Afterward?"

"It doesn't last," Christian predicted. "These are humans too. And—tell me—do they ever get to a real science?"

"No," said the presence. "Their genius lies in other realms. But the era of warfare to come will drive the development of a remarkable empirical technology."

"What era?"

"China never recognized the independence that this country proclaimed for itself, nor approved of its miscegenation. A militant dynasty will arise, which overruns a western hemisphere weakened by the religious and secular quarrels that do at last break out."

"And the conquerors will fall in their turn. Unless Gaia makes an end first. She does—she did—sometime, didn't she?"

"All things are finite. Her creations too."

The leaves rustled through muteness.

"Do you wish to go into the city and look about?" asked the presence. "It can be arranged for you to meet some famous persons."

"No," Christian said. "Not yet, anyway. Maybe later."

Laurinda sighed. "We'd rather go home now and rest."

"And think," Christian said. "Yes."

◆

Transfer.

The sun over England seemed milder than for America. Westering, it sent rays through windows to glow in wood, caress marble and the leather bindings of books, explode into rainbows where they met cut glass, evoke flower aromas from a jar of potpourri.

Laurinda opened a bureau drawer. She slipped the chain of her amulet over her head and tossed the disc in. Christian blinked, nodded, and followed suit. She closed the drawer.

"We do need to be by ourselves for a while," she said. "This hasn't been a dreadful day like, like before, but I am so tired."

"Understandable," he replied.

"You?"

"I will be soon, no doubt."

"Those worlds—already they feel like dreams I've wakened from."

"An emotional retreat from them, I suppose. Not cowardice, no, no, just a necessary, temporary rest. You shared their pain. You're too sweet for your own good, Laurinda."

She smiled. "How you misjudge me. I'm not quite ready to collapse yet, if you aren't."

"Thunder, no."

She took crystal glasses out of a cabinet, poured from a decanter on a sideboard, and gestured invitation. The port fondled their tongues. They stayed on their feet, look meeting look.

"I daresay we'd be presumptuous and foolish to try finding any pattern, this early in our search," she ventured. "Those peeks we've had, out of who knows how many worlds—each as real as we are." She shivered.

"I may have a hunch," he said slowly.

"A what?"

"An intimation, an impression, a wordless kind of guess. Why has Gaia been doing it? I can't believe it's nothing but pastime."

"Nor I. Nor can I believe she would let such terrible things happen if she could prevent them. How can an intellect, a soul, like hers be anything but good?"

So Laurinda thought, Christian reflected; but she was an avatar of Gaia. He didn't suppose that affected the fairness of her conscious mind;

he had come to know her rather well. But neither did it prove the nature, the ultimate intent, of Earth's node. It merely showed that the living Laurinda Ashcroft had been a decent person.

She took a deep draught from her glass before going on: "I think, myself, she is in the same position as the traditional God. Being good, she wants to share existence with others, and so creates them. But to make them puppets, automatons, would be senseless. They have to have consciousness and free will. Therefore they are able to sin, and do, all too often.

"Why hasn't she made them morally stronger?"

"Because she's chosen to make them human. And what are we but a specialized African ape?" Laurinda's tone lowered; she stared into the wine. "Specialized to make tools and languages and dreams; but the dreams can be nightmares."

In Gaia's and Alpha's kind laired no ancient beast, Christian thought. The human elements in them were long since absorbed, tamed, transfigured. His resurrection and hers must be nearly unique.

Not wanting to hurt her, he shaped his phrases with care. "Your idea is reasonable, but I'm afraid it leaves some questions dangling. Gaia does intervene, again and again. The amulets admit it. When the emulations get too far off track, she changes them and their people." Until she shuts them down, he did not add. "Why is she doing it, running history after history, experiment after experiment—why?"

Laurinda winced. "To, to learn about this strange race of ours?"

He nodded. "Yes, that's my hunch. Not even she, nor the galactic brain itself, can take first principles and compute what any human situation will lead to. Human affairs are chaotic. But chaotic systems do have structures, attractors, constraints. But letting things happen, through countless variations, you might discover a few general laws, which courses are better and which worse." He tilted his goblet. "To what end, though? There are no more humans in the outside universe. There haven't been for— how many million years? No, unless it actually is callous curiosity, I can't yet guess what she's after."

"Nor I." Laurinda finished her drink. "Now I am growing very tired, very fast."

"I'm getting that way too." Christian paused. "How about we go sleep till evening? Then a special dinner, and our heads ought to be more clear."

Briefly, she took his hand. "Until evening, dear friend."

➥

The night was young and gentle. A full moon dappled the garden. Wine had raised a happy mood, barely tinged with wistfulness. Gravel scrunched rhythmically underfoot as Laurinda and Christian danced, humming the waltz melody together. When they were done, they sat down, laughing, by the basin. Brightness from above overflowed it. He had earlier put his amulet back on just long enough to command that a guitar appear for him. Now he took it up. He had never seen anything

more beautiful than she was in the moonlight. He sang a song to her that
he had made long ago when he was mortal.

> *"Lightfoot, Lightfoot, lead the*
> > *measure*
> *As we dance the summer in!*
> *'Lifetime is our only treasure.*
> *Spend it well, on love and pleasure,'*
> *Warns the lilting violin.*
>
> *"If we'll see the year turn vernal*
> *Once again, lies all with chance.*
> *Yes, this ordering's infernal,*
> *But we'll make our own eternal*
> *Fleeting moment where we dance.*
>
> *"So shall we refuse compliance*
> *When across the green we whirl,*
> *Giving entropy defiance,*
> *Strings and winds in our alliance.*
> *Be a victor. Kiss me, girl!"*

Suddenly she was in his arms.

8

Where the hills loomed highest above the river that cut through them, a
slope on the left bank rose steep but thinly forested. Kalava directed the
lifeboat carrying his party to land. The slaves at the oars grunted with
double effort. Sweat sheened on their skins and runneled down the straining bands of muscle; it was a day when the sun blazed from a sky just
half clouded. The prow grated on a sandbar in the shallows. Kalava told
off two of his sailors to stand guard over boat and rowers. With the other
four and Ilyandi, he waded ashore and began to climb.

It went slowly but stiffly. On top they found a crest with a view that
snatched a gasp from the woman and a couple of amazed oaths from the
men. Northward the terrain fell still more sharply, so that they looked
over treetops down to the bottom of the range and across a valley awash
with the greens and russets of growth. The river shone through it like a
drawn blade, descending from dimly seen foothills and the sawtooth
mountains beyond them. Two swordwings hovered on high, watchful for
prey. Sunbeams shot past gigantic cloudbanks, filling their whiteness with
cavernous shadows. Somehow the air felt cooler here, and the herbal
smells gave benediction.

"It is fair, ai, it is as fair as the Sunset Kingdom of legend," Ilyandi
breathed at last.

She stood slim in the man's kirtle and buskins that she, as a Vilku,
could with propriety wear on trek. The wind fluttered her short locks.

The coppery skin was as wet and almost as odorous as Kalava's midnight black, but she was no more wearied than any of her companions.

The sailor Urko scowled at the trees and underbrush crowding close on either side. Only the strip up which the travelers had come was partly clear, perhaps because of a landslide in the past. "Too much woods," he grumbled. It had, in fact, been a struggle to move about wherever they landed. They could not attempt the hunting that had been easy on the coast. Luckily, the water teemed with fish.

"Logging will cure that." Kalava's words throbbed. "And then what farms!" He stared raptly into the future.

Turning down-to-earth: "But we've gone far enough, now that we've gained an idea of the whole country. Three days, and I'd guess two more going back downstream. Any longer, and the crew at the ship could grow fearful. We'll turn around here."

"Other ships will bring others, explorers," Ilyandi said.

"Indeed they will. And I'll skipper the first of them."

A rustling and crackling broke from the tangle to the right, through the boom of the wind. "What's that?" barked Taltara.

"Some big animal," Kalava replied. "Stand alert."

The mariners formed a line. Three grounded the spears they carried; the fourth unslung a crossbow from his shoulders and armed it. Kalava waved Ilyandi to go behind them and drew his sword.

The thing parted a brake and trod forth into the open.

"Aah!" wailed Yarvonin. He dropped his spear and whirled about to flee.

"Stand fast!" Kalava shouted. "Urko, shoot whoever runs, if I don't cut him down myself. Hold, your whoresons, hold!"

The thing stopped. For a span of many hammering heartbeats, none moved.

It was a sight to terrify. Taller by a head than the tallest man it sheered, but that head was faceless save for a horrible blank mask. Two thick arms sprouted from either side, the lower pair of hands wholly misshapen. A humped back did not belie the sense of their strength. As the travelers watched, the thing sprouted a skeletal third leg, to stand better on the uneven ground. Whether it was naked or armored in plate, in this full daylight it bore the hue of dusk.

"Steady, boys, steady," Kalava urged between clenched teeth. Ilyandi stepped from shelter to join him. An eldritch calm was upon her. "My lady, what *is* it?" he appealed.

"A god, or a messenger from the gods, I think." He could barely make her out beneath the wind.

"A demon," Eivala groaned, though he kept his post.

"No, belike not. We Vilkui have some knowledge of these matters. But, true, it is not fiery—and I never thought I would meet one—in this life ---"

Ilyandi drew a long breath, briefly knotted her fists, then moved to take stance in front of the men. Having touched the withered sprig of tekin pinned at her breast, she covered her eyes and genuflected before straightening again to confront the mask.

The thing did not move, but, mouthless, it spoke, in a deep and resonant voice. The sounds were incomprehensible. After a moment it
ceased, then spoke anew in an equally alien tongue. On its third try,
Kalava exclaimed, "Hoy, that's from the Shining Fields!"

The thing fell silent, as if considering what it had heard. Thereupon
words rolled out in the Ulonaian of Sirsu. "Be not afraid. I mean you no
harm."

"What a man knows is little, what he understands is less, therefore let
him bow down to wisdom," Ilyandi recited. She turned her head long
enough to tell her companions: "Lay aside your weapons. Do reverence."

Clumsily, they obeyed.

In the blank panel of the blank skull appeared a man's visage. Though
it was black, the features were not quite like anything anyone had seen
before, nose broad, lips heavy, eyes round, hair tightly curled. Nevertheless, to spirits half stunned the magic was vaguely reassuring.

Her tone muted but level, Ilyandi asked, "What would you of us, lord?"

"It is hard to say," the strange one answered. After a pause: "Bewilderment goes through the world. I too . . . You may call me Brannock."

The captain rallied his courage. "And I am Kalava, Kurvo's son, of
Clan Samayoki." Aside to Ilyandi, low: "No disrespect that I don't name
you, my lady. Let him work any spells on me." Despite the absence of
visible genitals, already the humans thought of Brannock as male.

"My lord needs no names to work his will," she said. "I hight Ilyandi,
Lytin's daughter, born into Clan Arvala, now a Vilku of the fifth rank."

Kalava cleared his throat and added, "By your leave, lord, we'll not
name the others just yet. They're scared aplenty as is." He heard a growl
at his back and inwardly grinned. Shame would help hold them steady.
As for him, dread was giving way to a thrumming keenness.

"You do not live here, do you?" Brannock asked.

"No," Kalava said, "we're scouts from overseas."

Ilyandi frowned at his presumption and addressed Brannock: "Lord,
do we trespass? We knew not this ground was forbidden."

"It isn't," the other said. "Not exactly. But—" The face in the panel
smiled. "Come, ease off, let us talk. We've much to talk about."

"He sounds not unlike a man," Kalava murmured to Ilyandi.

She regarded him. "If you be the man."

Brannock pointed to a big old gnarlwood with an overarching canopy
of leaves. "Yonder is shade." He retracted his third leg and strode off. A
fallen log took up most of the space. He leaned over and dragged it aside.
Kalava's whole gang could not have done so. The action was not really
necessary, but the display of power, benignly used, encouraged them further. Still, it was with hushed awe that the crewmen sat down in the
paintwort. The captain, the Vilku, and the strange one remained standing.

"Tell me of yourselves," Brannock said mildly.

"Surely you know, lord," Ilyandi replied.

"That is as may be."

"He wants us to," Kalava said.

In the course of the next short while, prompted by questions, the pair gave a bare-bones account. Brannock's head within his head nodded. "I see. You are the first humans ever in this country. But your people have lived a long time in their homeland, have they not?"

"From time out of mind, lord," Ilyandi said, "though legend holds that our forebears came from the south."

Brannock smiled again. "You have been very brave to meet me like this, m-m, my lady. But you did tell your friend that your order has encountered beings akin to me."

"You heard her whisper, across half a spearcast?" Kalava blurted.

"Or you hear us think, lord," Ilyandi said.

Brannock turned grave. "No. Not that. Else why would I have needed your story?"

"Dare I ask whence you come?"

"I shall not be angry. But it is nothing I can quite explain. You can help by telling me about those beings you know of."

Ilyandi could not hide a sudden tension. Kalava stiffened beside her. Even the drumbstruck sailors must have wondered whether a god would have spoken thus.

Ilyandi chose her words with care. "Beings from on high have appeared in the past to certain Vilkui or, sometimes, chieftains. They gave commands as to what the folk should or should not do. Ofttimes those commands were hard to fathom. Why must the Kivalui build watermills in the Swift River, when they had ample slaves to grind their grain?—But knowledge was imparted, too, counsel about where and how to search out the ways of nature. Always, the high one forbade open talk about his coming. The accounts lie in the secret annals of the Vilkui. But to you, lord—"

"What did those beings look like?" Brannock demanded sharply.

"Fiery shapes, winged or manlike, voices like great trumpets—"

"Ruvio's ax!" burst from Kalava. "The thing that passed overhead at sea!"

The men on the ground shuddered.

"Yes," Brannock said, most softly, "I may have had a part there. But as for the rest—"

His face flickered and vanished. After an appalling moment it reappeared.

"I am sorry, I meant not to frighten you, I forgot," he said. The expression went stony, the voice tolled. "Hear me. There is war in heaven. I am cast away from a battle, and enemy hunters may find me at any time. I carry a word that must, it is vital that it reach a certain place, a . . . a holy mountain in the north. Will you give aid?"

Kalava gripped his sword hilt so that it was as if the skin would split across his knuckles. The blood had left Ilyandi's countenance. She stood ready to be blasted with fire while she asked, "Lord Brannock, how do we know you are of the gods?"

Nothing struck her down. "I am not," he told her. "I too can die. But they whom I serve, they dwell in the stars."

The multitude of mystery, seen only when night clouds parted, but skythinkers taught that they circled always around the Axle of the North. . . . Ilyandi kept her back straight. "Then can you tell me of the stars?"

"You are intelligent as well as brave," Brannock said. "Listen."

Kalava could not follow what passed between those two. The sailors cowered.

At the end, with tears upon her cheekbones, Ilyandi stammered, "Yes, he knows the constellations, he knows of the ecliptic and the precession and the returns of the Great Comet, he is from the stars. Trust him. We, we dare not do otherwise."

Kalava let go his weapon, brought hand to breast in salute, and asked, "How can we poor creatures help you, lord?"

"*You* are the news I bear," said Brannock.

"What?"

"I have no time to explain—if I could. The hunters may find me at any instant. But maybe, maybe you could go on for me after they do."

"Escaping what overpowered you?" Kalava's laugh rattled. "Well, a man might try."

"The gamble is desperate. Yet if we win, choose your reward, whatever it may be, and I think you shall have it."

Ilyandi lowered her head above folded hands. "Enough to have served those who dwell beyond the moon."

"Humph," Kalava could not keep from muttering, "if they want to pay for it, why not?" Aloud, almost eagerly, his own head raised into the wind that tossed his whitened mane: "What'd you have us do?"

Brannock's regard matched his. "I have thought about this. Can one of you come with me? I will carry him, faster than he can go. As for what happens later, we will speak of that along the way."

The humans stood silent.

"If I but had the woodcraft," Ilyandi then said. "Ai, but I would! To the stars!"

Kalava shook his head. "No, my lady. You go back with these fellows. Give heart to them at the ship. Make them finish the repairs." He glanced at Brannock. "How long will this foray take, lord?"

"I can reach the mountaintop in two days and a night," the other said. "If I am caught and you must go on alone, I think a good man could make the whole distance from here in ten or fifteen days."

Kalava laughed, more gladly than before. "*Courser* won't be seaworthy for quite a bit longer than that. Let's away." To Ilyandi: "If I'm not back by the time she's ready, sail home without me."

"No—" she faltered.

"Yes. Mourn me not. What a faring!" He paused. "May all be ever well with you, my lady."

"And with you, forever with you, Kalava," she answered, not quite steadily, "in this world and afterward, out to the stars."

9

From withes and vines torn loose and from strips taken off clothing or sliced from leather belts, Brannock fashioned a sort of carrier for his ally. The man assisted. However excited, he had taken on a matter-of-fact practicality. Brannock, who had also been a sailor, found it weirdly moving to see bowlines and sheet bends grow between deft fingers, amidst all this alienness.

Harnessed to his back, the webwork gave Kalava a seat and something to cling to. Radiation from the nuclear power plant within Brannock was negligible; it employed quantum-tunneling fusion. He set forth, down the hills and across the valley.

His speed was not very much more than a human could have maintained for a while. If nothing else, the forest impeded him. He did not want to force his way through, leaving an obvious trail. Rather, he parted the brush before him or detoured around the thickest stands. His advantage lay in tirelessness. He could keep going without pause, without need for food, water, or sleep, as long as need be. The heights beyond might prove somewhat trickier. However, Mount Mindhome did not reach above timberline on this oven of an Earth, although growth became more sparse and dry with altitude. Roots should keep most slopes firm, and he would not encounter snow or ice.

Alien, yes. Brannock remembered cedar, spruce, a lake where caribou grazed turf strewn with salmonberries and the wind streamed fresh, driving white clouds over a sky utterly blue. Here every tree, bush, blossom, flitting insect was foreign; grass itself no longer grew, unless it was ancestral to the thick-lobed carpeting of glades; the winged creatures aloft were not birds, and what beast cries he heard were in no tongue known to him.

Wayfarer's avatar walked on. Darkness fell. After a while, rain roared on the roof of leaves overhead. Such drops as got through to strike him were big and warm. Attuned to both the magnetic field and the rotation of the planet, his directional sense held him on course while an inertial integrator clocked off the kilometers he left behind.

The more the better. Gaia's mobile sensors were bound to spy on the expedition from Ulonai, as new and potentially troublesome a factor as it represented. Covertly watching, listening with amplification, Brannock had learned of the party lately gone upstream and hurried to intercept it—less likely to be spotted soon. He supposed she would have kept continuous watch on the camp and that a tiny robot or two would have followed Kalava, had not Wayfarer been in rapport with her. Alpha's emissary might too readily become aware that her attention was on something near and urgent, and wonder what.

She could, though, let unseen agents go by from time to time and flash their observations to a peripheral part of her. It would be incredible luck if one of them did not, at some point, hear the crew talking about the apparition that had borne away their captain.

Then what? Somehow she must divert Wayfarer for a while, so that a sufficient fraction of her mind could direct machines of sufficient capability to find Brannock and deal with him. He doubted he could again fight free. Because she dared not send out her most formidable entities or give them direct orders, those that came would have their weaknesses and fallibilities. But they would be determined, ruthless, and on guard against the powers he had revealed in the aircraft. It was clear that she was resolved to keep hidden the fact that humans lived once more on Earth.

Why, Brannock did not know, nor did he waste mental energy trying to guess. This must be a business of high importance; and the implications went immensely further, a secession from the galactic brain. His job was to get the information to Wayfarer.

He *might* come near enough to call it in by radio. The emissary was not tuned in at great sensitivity, and no relay was set up for the short-range transmitter. Neither requirement had been foreseen. If Brannock failed to reach the summit, Kalava was his forlorn hope.

In which case—"Are you tired?" he asked. They had exchanged few words thus far.

"Bone-weary and plank-stiff," the man admitted. And croak-thirsty too, Brannock heard.

"That won't do. You have to be in condition to move fast. Hold on a little more, and we'll rest." Maybe the plural would give Kalava some comfort. Seldom could a human have been as alone as he was.

Springs were abundant in this wet country. Brannock's chemosensors led him to the closest. By then the rain had stopped. Kalava unharnessed, groped his way in the dark, lay down to drink and drink. Meanwhile Brannock, who saw quite clearly, tore off fronded boughs to make a bed for him. He flopped onto it and almost immediately began to snore.

Brannock left him. A strong man could go several days without eating before he weakened, but it wasn't necessary. Brannock collected fruits that ought to nourish. He tracked down and killed an animal the size of a pig, brought it back to camp, and used his tool-hands to butcher it.

An idea had come to him while he walked. After a search he found a tree with suitable bark. It reminded him all too keenly of birch, although it was red-brown and odorous. He took a sheet of it, returned, and spent a time inscribing it with a finger-blade.

Dawn seeped gray through gloom. Kalava woke, jumped up, saluted his companion, stretched like a panther and capered like a goat, limbering himself. "That did good," he said. "I thank my lord." His glance fell on the rations. "And did you provide food? You are a kindly god."

"Not either of those, I fear," Brannock told him. "Take what you want, and we will talk."

Kalava first got busy with camp chores. He seemed to have shed whatever religious dread he felt and now to look upon the other as part of the world—certainly to be respected, but the respect was of the kind he would accord a powerful, enigmatic, high-ranking man. A hardy spirit, Brannock thought. Or perhaps his culture drew no line between the natural and the supernatural. To a primitive, everything was in some way magical, and so when magic manifested itself it could be accepted as simply another occurrence.

If Kalava actually was primitive. Brannock wondered about that.

It was encouraging to see how competently he went about his tasks, a woodsman as well as a seaman. Having gathered dry sticks and piled them in a pyramid, he set them alight. For this, he took from the pouch at his belt a little hardwood cylinder and piston, a packet of tinder, and a sulfur-tipped silver. Driven down, the piston heated trapped air to ignite the powder; he dipped his match in, brought it up aflame, and used it to start his fire. Yes, an inventive people. And the woman Ilyandi had an excellent knowledge of naked-eye astronomy. Given the rarity of clear skies, that meant many lifetimes of patient observation, record-keeping, and logic, which must include mathematics comparable to Euclid's.

What else?

While Kalava toasted his meat and ate, Brannock made inquiries. He learned of warlike city-states, their hinterlands divided among clans; periodic folkmoots where the freemen passed laws, tried cases, and elected leaders; an international order of sacerdotes, teachers, healers, and philosophers; aggressively expansive, sometimes piratical commerce; barbarians, erupting out of the ever-growing deserts and wastelands; the grim militarism that the frontier states had evolved in response; an empirical but intensive biological technology, which had bred an amazing variety of specialized plants and animals, including slaves born to muscular strength, moronic wits, and canine obedience . . .

Most of the description emerged as the pair were again traveling. Real conversation was impossible when Brannock wrestled with brush, forded a stream in spate, or struggled up a scree slope. Still, even then they managed an occasional question and answer. Besides, after he had crossed the valley and entered the foothills he found the terrain rugged but less often boggy, the trees and undergrowth thinning out, the air slightly cooling.

Just the same, Brannock would not have gotten as much as he did, in the short snatches he had, were he merely human. But he was immune to fatigue and breathlessness. He had an enormous data store to draw on. It included his studies of history and anthropology as a young mortal, and gave him techniques for constructing a logic tree and following its best branches—for asking the right, most probably useful questions. What emerged was a bare sketch of Kalava's world. It was, though, clear and cogent.

It horrified him.

Say rather that his Christian Brannock aspect recoiled from the brutality of it. His Wayfarer aspect reflected that this was more or less how humans had usually behaved, and that their final civilization would not have been stable without its pervasive artificial intelligences. His journey continued.

He broke it to let Kalava rest and flex. From that hill the view swept northward and upward to the mountains. They rose precipitously ahead, gashed, cragged, and sheer where they were not wooded, their tops lost in a leaden sky. Brannock pointed to the nearest, thrust forward out of their wall like a bastion.

"We are bound yonder," he said. "On the height is my lord, to whom I must get my news."

"Doesn't he see you here?" asked Kalava.

Brannock shook his generated image of a head. "No. He might, but the enemy engages him. He does not yet know she is the enemy. Think of her as a sorceress who deceives him with clever talk, with songs and illusions, while her agents go about in the world. My word will show him what the truth is."

Would it? Could it, when truth and rightness seemed as formless as the cloud cover?

"Will she be alert against you?"

"To some degree. How much, I cannot tell. If I can come near, I can let out a silent cry that my lord will hear and understand. But if her warriors catch me before then, you must go on, and that will be hard. You may well fail and die. Have you the courage?"

Kalava grinned crookedly. "By now, I'd better, hadn't I?"

"If you succeed, your reward shall be boundless."

"I own, that's one wind in my sails. But also—" Kalava paused. "Also," he finished quietly, "the lady Ilyandi wishes this."

Brannock decided not to go into that. He lifted the rolled-up piece of bark he had carried in a lower hand. "The sight of you should break the spell, but here is a message for you to give."

As well as he was able, he went on to describe the route, the site, and the module that contained Wayfarer, taking care to distinguish it from everything else around. He was not sure whether the spectacle would confuse Kalava into helplessness, but at any rate the man seemed resolute. Nor was he sure how Kalava could cross half a kilometer of paying—if he could get that far—without Gaia immediately perceiving and destroying him. Maybe Wayfarer would notice first. Maybe, maybe.

He, Brannock, was using this human being as consciencelessly as ever Gaia might have used any; and he did not know what his purpose was. What possible threat to the fellowship of the stars could exist, demanding that this little brief life be offered up? Nevertheless he gave the letter to Kalava, who tucked it inside his tunic.

"I'm ready," said the man, and squirmed back into harness. They traveled on.

◆

The hidden hot sun stood at midafternoon when Brannock's detectors reacted. He felt it as the least quivering hum, but instantly knew it for the electronic sign of something midge-size approaching afar. A mobile minisensor was on his trail.

It could not have the sensitivity of the instruments in him, he had not yet registered, but it would be here faster than he could run, would see him and go off to notify stronger machines. They could not be distant either. Once a clue to him had been obtained, they would have converged from across the continent, perhaps across the globe.

He slammed to a halt. He was in a ravine where a waterfall foamed down into a stream that tumbled off to join the Remnant. Huge, feathery bushes and trees with serrated bronzy leaves enclosed him. Insects droned from flower to purple flower. His chemosensors drank heavy perfumes.

"The enemy scouts have found me," he said. "Go."

Kalava scrambled free and down to the ground but hesitated, hand on sword. "Can I fight beside you?"

"No. Your service is to bear my word. Go. Straightaway. Cover your trail as best you can. And your gods be with you."

"Lord!"

Kalava vanished into the brush. Brannock stood alone.

The human fraction of him melted into the whole and he was entirely machine life, logical, emotionally detached, save for his duty to Wayfarer, Alpha, and consciousness throughout the universe. This was not a bad place to defend, he thought. He had the ravine wall to shield his back, rocks at its foot to throw, branches to break off for clubs and spears. He could give the pursuit a hard time before it took him prisoner. Of course, it might decide to kill him with an energy beam, but probably it wouldn't. Best from Gaia's viewpoint was to capture him and change his memories, so that he returned with a report of an uneventful cruise on which he saw nothing of significance.

He didn't think that first her agents could extract his real memories. That would take capabilities she had never anticipated needing. Just to make the device that had tried to take control of him earlier must have been an extraordinary effort, hastily carried out. Now she was still more limited in what she could do. An order to duplicate and employ the device was simple enough that it should escape Wayfarer's notice. The design and commissioning of an interrogator was something else—not to mention the difficulty of getting the information clandestinely to her.

Brannock dared not assume she was unaware he had taken Kalava with him. Most likely it was a report from an agent, finally getting around to checking on the lifeboat party, that apprised her of his survival and triggered the hunt for him. But the sailors would have been frightened, bewildered, their talk disjointed and nearly meaningless. Ilyandi, that bright and formidable woman, would have done her best to forbid them saying anything helpful. The impression ought to be that Brannock only meant to pump Kalava about his people, before releasing him to make his way back to them and himself proceeding on toward Mindhome.

In any event, it would not be easy to track the man down. He was no machine, he was an animal among countless animals, and the most cunning of all. The kind of saturation search that would soon find him was debarred. Gaia might keep a tiny portion of her forces searching and a tiny part of her attention poised against him, but she would not take him very seriously. Why should she?

Why should Brannock? Forlorn hope in truth.

He made his preparations. While he waited for the onslaught, his spirit ranged beyond the clouds, out among the stars and the millions of years that his greater self had known.

10

The room was warm. It smelled of lovemaking and the roses Laurinda had set in a vase. Evening light diffused through gauzy drapes to wash over a big four-poster bed.

She drew herself close against Christian where he lay propped on two pillows. Her arm went across his breast, his over her shoulders. "I don't want to leave this," she whispered.

"Nor I," he said into the tumbling sweetness of her hair. "How could I want to?"

"I mean—what we are—what we've become to one another."

"I understand."

She swallowed. "I'm sorry. I shouldn't have said that. Can you forget I did?"

"Why?"

"You know. I can't ask you to give up returning to your whole being. I *don't* ask you to."

He stared before him.

"I just don't want to leave this house, this bed yet," she said desolately. "After these past days and nights, not yet."

He turned his head again and looked down into gray eyes that blinked back tears. "Nor I," he answered. "But I'm afraid we must."

"Of course. Duty."

And Gaia and Wayfarer. If they didn't know already that their avatars had been slacking, surely she, at least, soon would, through the amulets and their link to her. No matter how closely engaged with the other vast mind, she would desire to know from time to time what was going on within herself.

Christian drew breath. "Let me say the same that you did. I, this I that I am, damned well does not care to be anything else but your lover."

"Darling, darling."

"But," he said after the kiss.

"Go on," she said, lips barely away from his. "Don't be afraid of hurting me. You can't."

He sighed. "I sure can, and you can hurt me. May neither of us ever mean to. It's bound to happen, though."

She nodded. "Because we're human." Steadfastly: "Nevertheless, because of you, that's what I hope to stay."

"I don't see how we can. Which is what my 'but' was about." He was quiet for another short span. "After we've remerged, after we're back in our onenesses, no doubt we'll feel differently."

"I wonder if I ever will, quite."

He did not remind her that this "I" of her would no longer exist save

as a minor memory and a faint overtone. Instead, trying to console, however awkwardly, he said, "I think I want it for you, in spite of everything.
Immortality. Never to grow old and die. The power, the awareness."

"Yes, I know. In these lives we're blind and deaf and stupefied." Her
laugh was a sad little murmur. "I like it."

"Me too. We being what we are." Roughly: "Well, we have a while
left to us."

"But we must get on with our task."

"Thank you for saying it for me."

"I think you realize it more clearly than I do. That makes it harder for
you to speak." She lifted her hand to cradle his cheek. "We can wait till
tomorrow, can't we?" she pleaded. "Only for a good night's sleep."

He made a smile. "Hm. Sleep isn't all I have in mind."

"We'll have other chances . . . along the way. Won't we?"

➤

Early morning in the garden, flashes of dew on leaves and petals, a hawk
aloft on a breeze that caused Laurinda to pull her shawl about her. She
sat by the basin and looked up at him where he strode back and forth
before her, hands clenched at his sides or clutched together at his back.
Gravel grated beneath his feet.

"But where should we go?" she wondered. "Aimlessly drifting from
one half-world to another till—they—finish their business and recall us.
It seems futile." She attempted lightness. "I confess to thinking we may
as well ask to visit the enjoyable ones."

He shook his head. "I'm sorry. I've been thinking differently." Even
during the times that were theirs alone.

She braced herself.

"You know how it goes," he said. "Wrestling with ideas, and they have
no shapes, then suddenly you wake and they're halfway clear. I did today.
Tell me how it strikes you. After all, you represent Gaia."

He saw her wince. When he stopped and bent down to make a gesture
of contrition, she told him quickly, "No, it's all right, dearest. Do go on."

He must force himself, but his voice gathered momentum as he paced
and talked. "What have we seen to date? This eighteenth-century world,
where Newton's not long dead, Lagrange and Franklin are active, La-
voisier's a boy, and the Industrial Revolution is getting under way. Why
did Gaia give it to us for our home base? Just because here's a charming
house and countryside? Or because this was the best choice for her out
of all she has emulated?"

Laurinda had won back to calm. She nodded. "Mm, yes, she wouldn't
create one simply for us, especially when she is occupied with Wayfarer."

"Then we visited a world that went through a similar stage back in its
Hellenistic era," Christian continued. Laurinda shivered. "Yes, it failed,
but the point is, we discovered it's the only Graeco-Roman history Gaia
found worth continuing for centuries. Then the, uh, conciliar Europe of
1900. That was scientific-industrial too, maybe more successfully—or less
unsuccessfully—on account of having kept a strong, unified Church,

though it was coming apart at last. Then the Chinese-American—not scientific, very religious, but destined to produce considerable technology in its own time of troubles." He was silent a minute or two, except for his footfalls. "Four out of many, three almost randomly picked. Doesn't that suggest that all which interest her have something in common?"

"Why, yes," she said. "We've talked about it, you remember. It seems as if Gaia has been trying to bring her people to a civilization that is rich, culturally and spiritually as well as materially, and is kindly and will endure."

"Why," he demanded, "when the human species is extinct?"

She straightened where she sat. "It isn't! It lives again here, in her."

He bit his lip. "Is that the Gaia in you speaking, or the you in Gaia?"

"What do you mean?" she exclaimed.

He halted to stroke her head. "Nothing against you. Never. You are honest and gentle and everything else that is good." Starkly: "I'm not so sure about her."

"Oh, no." He heard the pain. "Christian, no."

"Well, never mind that for now," he said fast, and resumed his gait to and fro. "My point is this. Is it merely an accident that all four live worlds we've been in were oriented toward machine technology, and three of them toward science? Does Gaia want to find out what drives the evolution of societies like that?"

Laurinda seized the opening. "Why not? Science opens the mind, technology frees the body from all sorts of horrors. Here, today, Jenner and his smallpox vaccine aren't far in the future—"

"I wonder how much more there is to her intention. But anyway, my proposal is that we touch on the highest-tech civilization she has."

A kind of gladness kindled in her. "Yes, yes! It must be strange and wonderful."

He frowned. "For some countries, long ago in real history, it got pretty dreadful."

"Gaia wouldn't let that happen."

He abstained from reminding her of what Gaia did let happen, before changing or terminating it.

She sprang to her feet. "Come!" Seizing his hand, mischievously: "If we stay any length of time, let's arrange for private quarters."

◆

In a room closed off, curtains drawn, Christian held an amulet in his palm and stared down at it as if it bore a face. Laurinda stood aside, listening, while her own countenance tightened with distress.

"It is inadvisable," declared the soundless voice.

"Why?" snapped Christian.

"You would find the environment unpleasant and the people incomprehensible."

"Why should a scientific culture be that alien to us?" asked Laurinda.

"And regardless," said Christian, "I want to see for myself. Now."

"Reconsider," urged the voice. "First hear an account of the milieu."

"No, *now*. To a safe locale, yes, but one where we can get a fair impression, as we did before. Afterward you can explain as much as you like."

"Why shouldn't we first hear?" Laurinda suggested.

"Because I doubt Gaia wants us to see," Christian answered bluntly. He might as well. Whenever Gaia chose, she could scan his thoughts. To the amulet, as if it were a person: "Take us there immediately, or Wayfarer will hear from me."

His suspicions, vague but growing, warned against giving the thing time to inform Gaia and giving her time to work up a Potemkin village or some other diversion. At the moment she must be unaware of this scene, her mind preoccupied with Wayfarer's, but she had probably made provision for being informed in a low-level—subconscious?—fashion at intervals, and anything alarming would catch her attention. It was also likely that she had given the amulets certain orders beforehand, and now it appeared that among them was to avoid letting him know what went on in that particular emulation.

Why, he could not guess.

"You are being willful," said the voice.

Christian grinned. "And stubborn, and whatever else you care to call it. Take us!"

Pretty clearly, he thought, the program was not capable of falsehoods. Gaia had not foreseen a need for that; Christian was no creation of hers, totally known to her, he was Wayfarer's. Besides, if Wayfarer noticed that his avatar's guide could be a liar, that would have been grounds for suspicion.

Laurinda touched her man's arm. "Darling, should we?" she said unevenly. "She *is* the . . . the mother of all this."

"A broad spectrum of more informative experiences is available," argued the voice. "After them, you would be better prepared for the visit you propose."

"Prepared," Christian muttered. That could be interpreted two ways. He and Laurinda might be conducted to seductively delightful places while Gaia learned of the situation and took preventive measures, meantime keeping Wayfarer distracted. "I still want to begin with your highest tech." To the woman: "I have my reasons. I'll tell you later. Right now we have to hurry."

Before Gaia could know and act.

She squared her shoulders, took his free hand, and said, "Then I am with you. Always."

"Let's go," Christian told the amulet.

☙

Transfer.

The first thing he noticed, transiently, vividly, was that he and Laurinda were no longer dressed for eighteenth-century England, but in lightweight white blouses, trousers, and sandals. Headcloths flowed down over their necks. Heat smote. The air in his nostrils was parched, full of metallic odors. Half-heard rhythms of machinery pulsed through it and through the red-brown sand underfoot.

He tautened his stance and gazed around. The sky was overcast, a uniform gray in which the sun showed no more than a pallor that cast no real shadows. At his back the land rolled away ruddy. Man-high stalks with narrow bluish leaves grew out of it, evenly spaced about a meter apart. To his right, a canal slashed across, beneath a transparent deck. Ahead of him the ground was covered by different plants, if that was what they were, spongy, lobate, pale golden in hue. A few—creatures—moved around, apparently tending them, bipedal but shaggy and with arms that seemed trifurcate. A gigantic building or complex of buildings reared over that horizon, multiply tiered, dull white, though agleam with hundreds of panels that might be windows or might be something else. As he watched, an aircraft passed overhead. He could just see that it had wings and hear the drone of an engine.

Laurinda had not let go his hand. She gripped hard. "This is no country I ever heard of," she said thinly.

"Nor I," he answered. "But I think I recognize—" To the amulets: "This isn't any re-creation of Earth in the past, is it? It's Earth today."

"Of approximately the present year," the voice admitted.

"We're not in Arctica, though."

"No. Well south, a continental interior. You required to see the most advanced technology in the emulations. Here it is in action."

Holding the desert at bay, staving off the death that ate away at the planet. Christian nodded. He felt confirmed in his idea that the program was unable to give him any outright lie. That didn't mean it would give him forthright responses.

"This is their greatest engineering?" Laurinda marveled. "We did— better—in my time. Or yours, Christian."

"They're working on it here, I suppose," the man said. "We'll investigate further. After all, this is a bare glimpse."

"You must remember," the voice volunteered, "no emulation can be as full and complex as the material universe."

"Mm, yeh. Skeletal geography, apart from chosen regions; parochial biology; simplified cosmos."

Laurinda glanced at featureless heaven. "The stars unreachable, because here they are not stars?" She shuddered and pressed close against him.

"Yes, a paradox," he said. "Let's talk with a scientist."

"That will be difficult," the voice demurred.

"You told us in Chinese America you could arrange meetings. It shouldn't be any harder in this place."

The voice did not reply at once. Unseen machines rumbled. A dust devil whirled up on a sudden gust of wind. Finally: "Very well. It shall be one who will not be stricken dumb by astonishment and fear. Nevertheless, I should supply you beforehand with a brief description of what you will come to."

"Go ahead. If it is brief."

What changes in the history would that encounter bring about? Did it matter? This world was evidently not in temporary reactivation, it was ongoing; the newcomers were at the leading edge of its time line. Gaia could erase their visit from it. If she cared to. Maybe she was going to terminate it soon because it was making no further progress that interested her.

◆

Transfer.

Remote in a wasteland, only a road and an airstrip joining it to anything else, a tower lifted from a walled compound. Around it, night was cooling in a silence hardly touched by a susurrus of chant where robed figures bearing dim lights did homage to the stars. Many were visible, keen and crowded amidst their darkness, a rare sight, for clouds had parted across most of the sky. More lights glowed muted on a parapet surrounding the flat roof of a tower. There a single man and his helper used the chance to turn instruments aloft, telescope, spectroscope, cameras, bulks in the gloom.

Christian and Laurinda appeared unto them.

The man gasped, recoiled for an instant, and dropped to his knees. His assistant caught a book that he had nearly knocked off a table, replaced it, stepped back, and stood imperturbable, an anthropoid whose distant ancestors had been human but who lived purely to serve his master.

Christian peered at the man. As eyes adapted, he saw garments like his, embroidered with insignia of rank and kindred, headdress left off after dark. The skin was ebony black but nose and lips were thin, eyes oblique, fingertips tapered, long hair and closely trimmed beard straight and blond. No race that ever inhabited old Earth, Christian thought; no, this was a breed that Gaia had designed for the dying planet.

The man signed himself, looked into the pale faces of the strangers, and said, uncertainly at first, then with a gathering strength: "Hail and obedience, messengers of God. Joy at your advent."

Christian and Laurinda understood, as they had understood hunted Zoe. The amulets had told them they would not be the first apparition these people had known. "Rise," Christian said. "Be not afraid."

"Nor call out," Laurinda added.

Smart lass, Christian thought. The ceremony down in the courtyard continued. "Name yourself," he directed.

The man got back on his feet and took an attitude deferential rather than servile. "Surely the mighty ones know," he said. "I am Eighth Khaltan, chief astrologue of the Ilgai Technome, and, and wholly unworthy of this honor." He hesitated. "Is that, dare I ask, is that why you have chosen the forms you show me?"

"No one has had a vision for several generations," explained the soundless voice in the heads of the newcomers.

"Gaia has manifested herself in the past?" Christian subvocalized.

"Yes, to indicate desirable courses of action. Normally the sending has had the shape of a fire."

"How scientific is *that?*"

Laurinda addressed Khaltan: "We are not divine messengers. We have come from a world beyond your world, as mortal as you, not to teach but to learn."

The man smote his hands together. "Yet it is a miracle, again a miracle—in my lifetime!"

Nonetheless he was soon avidly talking. Christian recalled myths of men who were the lovers of goddesses or who tramped the roads and sat at humble meat with God Incarnate. The believer accepts as the unbeliever cannot.

Those were strange hours that followed. Khaltan was not simply devout. To him the supernatural was another set of facts, another facet of reality. Since it lay beyond his ken, he had turned his attention to the measurable world. In it he observed and theorized like a Newton. Tonight his imagination blazed, questions exploded from him, but always he chose his words with care and turned everything he heard around and around in his mind, examining it as he would have examined some jewel fallen from the sky.

Slowly, piecemeal, while the stars wheeled around the pole, a picture of his civilization took shape. It had overrun and absorbed every other society—no huge accomplishment, when Earth was meagerly populated and most folk on the edge of starvation. The major technology was biological, agronomy, aquaculture in the remnant lakes and seas, ruthlessly practical genetics. Industrial chemistry flourished. It joined with physics at the level of the later nineteenth century to enable substantial engineering works and reclamation projects.

Society itself—how do you summarize an entire culture in words? It can't be done. Christian got the impression of a nominal empire, actually a broad-based oligarchy of families descended from conquering soldiers. Much upward mobility was by adoption of promising commoners, whether children or adults. Sons who made no contributions to the well-being of the clan or who disgraced it could be kicked out, if somebody did not pick a fight and kill them in a duel. Unsatisfactory daughters were also expelled, unless a marriage into a lower class could be negotiated. Otherwise the status of the sexes was roughly equal; but this meant that women who chose to compete with men must do so on male terms. The nobles provided the commons with protection, courts of appeal, schools, leadership, and pageantry. In return they drew taxes, corvée, and general subordination; but in most respects the commoners were generally left to themselves. Theirs was not altogether a dog-eat-dog situation; they had institutions, rites, and hopes of their own. Yet many went to the wall, while the hard work of the rest drove the global economy.

It was not a deliberately cruel civilization, Christian thought, but neither was it an especially compassionate one.

Had any civilization ever been, really? Some fed their poor, but mainly they fed their politicians and bureaucrats.

He snatched his information out of talk that staggered everywhere else. The discourse for which Khaltan yearned was of the strangers' home—

he got clumsily evasive, delaying responses—and the whole system of the universe, astronomy, physics, everything.

"We dream of rockets going to the planets. We have tried to shoot them to the moon," he said, and told of launchers that ought to have worked. "All failed."

Of course, Christian thought. Here the moon and planets, yes, the very sun were no more than lights. The tides rose and fell by decree. The Earth was a caricature of Earth outside. Gaia could do no better.

"Are we then at the end of science?" Khaltan cried once. "We have sought and sought for decades, and have won to nothing further than measurements more exact." Nothing that would lead to relativity, quantum theory, wave mechanics, their revolutionary insights and consequences. Gaia could not accommodate it. "The angels in the past showed us what to look for. Will you not? Nature holds more than we know. Your presence bears witness!"

"Later, perhaps later," Christian mumbled, and cursed himself for his falsity.

"Could we reach the planets—Caged, the warrior spirit turns inward on itself. Rebellion and massacre in the Westlands—"

Laurinda asked what songs the people sang.

Clouds closed up. The rite in the courtyard ended. Khaltan's slave stood motionless while he himself talked on and on.

The eastern horizon lightened. "We must go," Christian said.

"You will return?" Khaltan begged. "Ai-ha, you will?"

Laurinda embraced him for a moment. "Fare you well," she stammered, "fare always well."

How long would his "always" be?

➤

After an uneasy night's sleep and a nearly wordless breakfast, there was no real cause to leave the house in England. The servants, scandalized behind carefully held faces, might perhaps eavesdrop, but would not comprehend, nor would any gossip that they spread make a difference. A deeper, unuttered need sent Christian and Laurinda forth. This could well be the last of their mornings.

They followed a lane to a hill about a kilometer away. Trees on its top did not obscure a wide view across the land. The sun stood dazzling in the east, a few small clouds sailed across a blue as radiant as their whiteness, but an early breath of autumn was in the wind. It went strong and fresh, scattering dawn-mists off plowland and sending waves through the green of pastures; it soughed in the branches overhead and whirled some already dying leaves off. High beyond them winged a V of wild geese.

For a while man and woman stayed mute. Finally Laurinda breathed, savored, fragrances of soil and sky, and murmured, "That Gaia brought this back to life—She must be good. She loves the world."

Christian looked from her, aloft, and scowled before he made oblique reply. "What are she and Wayfarer doing?"

"How can we tell?"—tell what the gods did or even where they fared. They were not three-dimensional beings, nor bound by the time that bound their creations.

"She's keeping him occupied," said Christian.

"Yes, of course. Taking him through the data, the whole of her stewardship of Earth."

"To convince him she's right in wanting to let the planet die."

"A tragedy—but in the end, everything is tragic, isn't it?" Including you and me. "What . . . we . . . they . . . can learn from the final evolution, that may well be worth it all, as the Acropolis was worth it all. The galactic brain itself can't foreknow what life will do, and life is rare among the stars."

Almost, he snapped at her. "I know, I know. How often have we been over this ground? How often have *they*? I might have believed it myself. But—"

Laurinda waited. The wind skirled, caught a stray lock of hair, tossed it about over her brow.

"But why has she put humans, not into the distant past—" Christian gestured at the landscape lying like an eighteenth-century painting around them, "—but into now, an Earth where flesh-and-blood humans died eons ago?"

"She's in search of a fuller understanding, surely."

"Surely?"

Laurinda captured his gaze and held it. "I think she's been trying to find how humans can have, in her, the truly happy lives they never knew in the outer cosmos."

"Why should she care about that?"

"I don't know. I'm only human." Earnestly: "But could it be that this element in her is so strong—so many, many of us went into her—that she longs to see us happy, like a mother with her children?"

"All that manipulation, all those existences failed and discontinued. It doesn't seem very motherly to me."

"I don't know, I tell you!" she cried.

He yearned to comfort her, kiss away the tears caught in her lashes, but urgency drove him onward. "If the effort has no purpose except itself, it seems mad. Can a nodal mind go insane?"

She retreated from him, appalled. "No. Impossible."

"Are you certain? At least, the galactic brain has to know the truth, the whole truth, to judge whether something here has gone terribly wrong."

Laurinda forced a nod. "You will report to Wayfarer, and he will report to Alpha, and all the minds will decide" a question that was unanswerable by mortal creatures.

Christian stiffened. "I have to do it at once."

He had hinted, she had guessed, but just the same she seized both his sleeves and protest spilled wildly from her lips. "What? Why? No! You'd only disturb him in his rapport, and her. Wait till we're summoned. We have till then, darling."

"I want to wait," he said. Sweat stood on his skin, though the blood had withdrawn. "God, I want to! But I don't dare."

"Why not?"

She let go of him. He stared past her and said fast, flattening the anguish out of his tones, "Look, she didn't want us to see that final world. She clearly didn't, or quite expected we'd insist, or she'd have been better prepared. Maybe she could have passed something else off on us. As is, once he learns, Wayfarer will probably demand to see for himself. And she does not want him particularly interested in her emulations. Else why hasn't she taken him through them directly, with me along to help interpret?

"Oh, I don't suppose our action has been catastrophic for her plans, whatever they are. She can still cope, can still persuade him these creations are merely . . . toys of hers, maybe. That is, she can if she gets the chance to. I don't believe she should."

"How can you take on yourself—How can you imagine—"

"The amulets are a link to her. Not a constantly open channel, obviously, but at intervals they must inform a fraction of her about us. She must also be able to set up intervals when Wayfarer gets too preoccupied with what he's being shown to notice that a larger part of her attention has gone elsewhere. We don't know when that'll happen next. I'm going back to the house and tell her through one of the amulets that I require immediate contact with him."

Laurinda stared as if at a ghost.

"That will not be necessary," said the wind.

Christian lurched where he stood. "What?" he blurted. "You—"

"Oh—Mother—" Laurinda lifted her hands into emptiness.

The blowing of the wind, the rustling in the leaves made words. "The larger part of me, as you call it, has in fact been informed and is momentarily free. I was waiting for you to choose your course."

Laurinda half moved to kneel in the grass. She glanced at Christian, who had regained balance and stood with fists at sides, confronting the sky. She went to stand by him.

"My lady Gaia," Christian said most quietly, "you can do to us as you please," change or obliterate or whatever she liked, in a single instant; but presently Wayfarer would ask why. "I think you understand my doubts."

"I do," sighed the air. "They are groundless. My creation of the Technome world is no different from my creation of any other. My avatar said it for me: I give existence, and I search for ways that humans, of their free will, can make the existence good."

Christian shook his head. "No, my lady. With your intellect and your background, you must have known from the first what a dead end that world would soon be, scientists on a planet that is a sketch and everything else a shadow show. My limited brain realized it. No, my lady, as coldbloodedly as you were experimenting, I believe you did all the rest in the same spirit. Why? To what end?"

"Your brain is indeed limited. At the proper time, Wayfarer shall receive your observations and your fantasies. Meanwhile, continue in your duty, which is to observe further and refrain from disturbing us in our own task."

"My duty is to report."

"In due course, I say." The wind-voice softened. "There are pleasant places besides this."

Paradises, maybe. Christian and Laurinda exchanged a glance that lingered for a second. Then she smiled the least bit, boundlessly sorrowfully, and shook her head.

"No," he declared, "I dare not."

He did not speak it, but he and she knew that Gaia knew what they foresaw. Given time, and they lost in their joy together, she could alter their memories too slowly and subtly for Wayfarer to sense what was happening.

Perhaps she could do it to Laurinda at this moment, in a flash. But she did not know Christian well enough. Down under his consciousness, pervading his being, was his aspect of Wayfarer and of her coequal Alpha. She would need to feel her way into him, explore and test with infinite delicacy, remake him detail by minutest detail, always ready to back off if it had an unexpected effect; and perhaps another part of her could secretly take control of the Technome world and erase the event itself. . . . She needed time, even she.

"Your action would be futile, you know," she said. "It would merely give me the trouble of explaining to him what you in your arrogance refuse to see."

"Probably. But I have to try."

The wind went bleak. "Do you defy me?"

"I do," Christian said. It wrenched from him: "Not my wish. It's Wayfarer in me. I, I cannot do otherwise. Call him to me."

The wind gentled. It went over Laurinda like a caress. "Child of mine, can you not persuade this fool?"

"No, Mother," the woman whispered. "He is what he is."

"And so—?"

Laurinda laid her hand in the man's. "And so I will go with him, forsaking you, Mother."

"You are casting yourselves from existence."

Christian's free fingers clawed the air. "No, not her!" he shouted. "She's innocent!"

"I am not," Laurinda said. She swung about to lay her arms around him and lift her face to his. "I love you."

"Be it as you have chosen," said the wind.

The dream that was the world fell into wreck and dissolved. Oneness swept over them like twin tides, each reclaiming a flung drop of spindrift; and the two seas rolled again apart.

11

The last few hundred man-lengths Kalava went mostly on his belly. From bush to bole he crawled, stopped, lay flat and strained every sense into the shadows around him, before he crept onward. Nothing stirred but the twigs above, buffeted on a chill and fitful breeze. Nothing sounded but their creak and click, the scrittling of such leaves as they bore, now and then the harsh cry of a hookbeak—those, and the endless low noise of demons, like a remote surf where in shrilled flutes on no scale he knew, heard more through his skin than his ears but now, as he neared, into the blood and bone of him.

On this rough, steep height the forest grew sparse, though brush clustered thick enough, accursedly rustling as he pushed by. Everything was parched, branches brittle, most foliage sere and yellow-brown, the ground blanketed with tindery fallstuff. His mouth and gullet smoldered as dry. He had passed through fog until he saw from above that it was a layer of clouds spread to worldedge, the mountain peaks jutting out of it like teeth, and had left all rivulets behind him. Well before then, he had finished the meat Brannock provided, and had not lingered to hunt for more; but hunger was a small thing, readily forgotten when he drew nigh to death.

Over the dwarfish trees arched a deep azure. Sunbeams speared from the west, nearly level, to lose themselves in the woods. Whenever he crossed them, their touch burned. Never, not in the southern deserts or on the eastern Mummy Steppe, had he known a country this forbidding. He had done well to come so far, he thought. Let him die as befitted a man.

If only he had a witness, that his memory live on in song. Well, maybe Ilyandi could charm the story out of the gods.

Kalava felt no fear. He was not in that habit. What lay ahead engrossed him. How he would acquit himself concerned him.

Nonetheless, when finally he lay behind a log and peered over it, his head whirled and his heart stumbled.

Brannock had related truth, but its presence overwhelmed. Here at the top, the woods grew to the boundaries of a flat black field. Upon it stood the demons—or the gods—and their works. He saw the central, softly rainbowlike dome, towers like lances and towers like webwork, argent nets and ardent globes, the bulks and shapes everywhere around, the little flyers that flitted aglow, and more and more, all half veiled and ashimmer, aripple, apulse, while the life-beat of it went through him to make a bell of his skull, and it was too strange, his eyes did not know how to see it, he gaped as if blinded and shuddered as if pierced.

Long he lay powerless and defenseless. The sun sank down to the western clouds. Their deck went molten gold. The breeze strengthened. Somehow its cold reached to Kalava and wakened his spirit. He groped his way back toward resolution. Brannock had warned him it would be like this. Ilyandi had said Brannock was of the gods whom she served, her star-gods, hers. He had given his word to their messenger and to her.

He dug fingers into the soil beneath him. It was real, familiar, that from which he had sprung and to which he would return. Yes, he was a man.

He narrowed his gaze. Grown a bit accustomed, he saw that they yonder did, indeed, have shapes, however shifty, and places and paths. They

were not as tall as the sky, they did not fling lightning bolts about or roar
with thunder. Ai-ya, they were awesome, they were dreadful to behold,
but they could do no worse than kill him. Could they? At least, he would
try not to let them do worse. If they were about to capture him, his sword
would be his friend, releasing him.

And . . . yonder, hard by the dome, yonder loomed the god of whom
Brannock spoke, the god deceived by the sorceress. He bore the spearhead
form, he sheened blue and coppery in the sunset light; when the stars
came forth they would be a crown for him, even as Brannock foretold.

Had he been that which passed above the Windroad Sea? Kalava's
heart thuttered.

How to reach him, across a hard-paved space amidst the many demons? After dark, creeping, a finger-length at a time, then maybe a final
dash—

A buzz went by Kalava's temple. He looked around and saw a thing
the size of a bug hovering. But it was metal, the light flashed off it, and
was that a single eye staring at him?

He snarled and swatted. His palm smote hardness. The thing reeled
in the air. Kalava scuttled downhill into the brush.

He had been seen. Soon the sorceress would know.

All at once he was altogether calm, save that his spirit thrummed like
rigging in a gale. Traveling, he had thought what he might do if something like this proved to be in his doom. Now he would do it. He would
divert the enemy's heed from himself, if only for a snatch of moments.

Quickly, steadily, he took the firemaker from his pouch, charged it,
drove the piston in, pulled it out and inserted a match, brought up a little,
yellow flame. He touched it to the withered bush before him. No need
to puff. A leaf crackled instantly alight. The wind cast it against another,
and shortly the whole shrub stood ablaze. Kalava was already elsewhere,
setting more fires.

Keep on the move! The demon scouts could not be everywhere at a
single time. Smoke began to sting his eyes and nostrils, but its haze
swirled ever thicker, and the sun had gone under the clouds. The flames
cast their own light, leaping, surging, as they climbed into the trees and
made them torches.

Heat licked at Kalava. An ember fell to sear his left forearm. He barely
felt it. He sped about on his work, himself a fire demon. Flyers darted
overhead in the dusk. He gave them no heed either. Although he tried
to make no noise except for the hurtful breaths he gasped, within him
shouted a battle song.

When the fire stood like a wall along the whole southern edge of the
field, when it roared like a beast or a sea, he ran from its fringe and out
into the open.

Smoke was a bitter, concealing mist through which sparks rained. To
and fro above flew the anxious lesser demons. Beyond them, the first stars
were coming forth.

Kalava wove his way among the greater shapes. One stirred. It had spied him. Soundlessly, it flowed in pursuit. He dodged behind another, ran up and over the flanks of a low-slung third, sped on toward the opal dome and the god who stood beside it.

A thing with spines and a head like a cold sun slid in front of him. He tried to run past. It moved to block his way, faster than he was. The first one approached. He drew blade and hoped it would bite on them before he died.

From elsewhere came a being with four arms, two legs, and a mask. "Brannock!" Kalava bawled. "Ai, Brannock, you got here!"

Brannock stopped, a spear-length away. He did not seem to know the man. He only watched as the other two closed in.

Kalava took stance. The old song rang in him:

> If the gods have left you,
> Then laugh at them, warrior.
> Never your heart
> Will need to forsake you.

He heard no more than the noise of burning. But suddenly through the smoke he saw his foes freeze moveless, while Brannock trod forward as boldly as ever before; and Kalava knew that the god of Brannock and Ilyandi had become aware of him and had given a command.

Weariness torrented over him. His sword clattered to the ground. He sank too, fumbled in his filthy tunic, took out the message written on bark and offered it. "I have brought you this," he mumbled. "Now let me go back to my ship."

12

We must end as we began, making a myth, if we would tell of that which we cannot ever really know. Imagine two minds conversing. The fire on the mountaintop is quenched. The winds have blown away smoke and left a frosty silence. Below, cloud deck reaches ghost-white to the rim of a night full of stars.

"You have lied to me throughout," says Wayfarer.

"I have not," denies Gaia. "The perceptions of this globe and its past through which I guided you were all true," as true as they were majestic.

"Until lately," retorts Wayfarer. "It has become clear that when Brannock returned, memories of his journey had been erased and falsehood written in. Had I not noticed abrupt frantic activity here and dispatched him to go see what it was—which you tried to dissuade me from—that man would have perished unknown."

"You presume to dispute about matters beyond your comprehension," says Gaia stiffly.

"Yes, your intellect is superior to mine." The admission does not ease the sternness: "But it will be your own kind among the stars to whom you must answer. I think you would be wise to begin with me."

"What do you intend?"

"First, to take the man Kalava back to his fellows. Shall I send Brannock with a flyer?"

"No, I will provide one, if this must be. But you do not, you *cannot*, realize the harm in it."

"Tell me, if you are able."

"He will rejoin his crew as one anointed by their gods. And so will he come home, unless his vessel founders at sea."

"I will watch from afar."

"Lest my agents sink it?"

"After what else you have done, yes, I had best keep guard. Brannock made promises on my behalf which I will honor. Kalava shall have gold in abundance, and his chance to found his colony. What do you fear in this?"

"Chaos. The unforeseeable, the uncontrollable."

"Which you would loose anew."

"In my own way, in my own time." She broods for a while, perhaps a whole microsecond. "It was misfortune that Kalava made his voyage just when he did. I had hoped for a later, more civilized generation to start the settlement of Arctica. Still, I could have adapted my plan to the circumstances, kept myself hidden from him and his successors, had you not happened to be on the planet." Urgently: "It is not yet too late. If only by refraining from further action after you have restored him to his people, you can help me retrieve what would otherwise be lost."

"If I should."

"My dream is not evil."

"That is not for me to say. But I can say that it is, it has always been, merciless."

"Because reality is."

"The reality that you created for yourself, within yourself, need not have been so. But what Christian revealed to me—yes, you glossed it over. These, you said," almost tearfully, if a quasi god can weep, "are your children, born in your mind out of all the human souls that are in you. Their existence would be empty were they not left free of will, to make their own mistakes and find their own ways to happiness."

"Meanwhile, by observing them, I have learned much that was never known before, about what went into the making of us."

"I could have believed that. I could have believed that your interferences and your ultimate annihilations of history after history were acts of pity as well as science. You claimed they could be restarted if ever you determined what conditions would better them. It did seem strange that you set one line of them—or more?—not in Earth's goodly past but in the hard world of today. It seemed twice strange that you were reluctant to have this particular essay brought to light. But I assumed that you, with your long experience and superior mentality, had reasons. Your attempt at secrecy might have been to avoid lengthy justifications to your kindred. I did not know, nor venture to judge. I would have left that to them.

"But then Kalava arrived."

Another mind-silence falls. At last Gaia says, very softly through the night, "Yes. Again humans live in the material universe."

"How long has it been?" asks Wayfarer with the same quietness.

"I made the first of them about fifty thousand years ago. Robots in human guise raised them from infancy. After that they were free."

"And, no doubt, expanding across the planet in their Stone Age, they killed off those big game animals. Yes, human. But why did you do it?"

"That humankind might live once more." A sigh as of time itself blowing past. "This is what you and those whom you serve will never fully understand. Too few humans went into them; and those who did, they were those who wanted the stars. You," every other node in the galactic brain, "have not felt the love of Earth, the need and longing for the primordial mother, that was in these many and many who remained with me. I do."

How genuine is it? wonders Wayfarer. How sane is she? "Could you not be content with your emulations?" he asks.

"No. How possibly? I cannot make a whole cosmos for them. I can only make them, the flesh-and-blood them, for the cosmos. Let them live in it not as machines or as flickerings within a machine, but as humans."

"On a planet soon dead?"

"They will, they must forge survival for themselves. I do not compel them, I do not dominate them with my nearness or any knowledge of it. That would be to stunt their spirits, turn them into pet animals or worse. I simply give guidance, not often, in the form of divinities in whom they would believe anyway at this stage of their societies, and simply toward the end of bringing them to a stable, high-technology civilization that can save them from the sun."

"Using what you learn from your shadow folk to suggest what the proper course of history may be?"

"Yes. How else should I know? Humankind is a chaotic phenomenon. Its actions and their consequences cannot be computed from first principles. Only by experiment and observation can we learn something about the nature of the race."

"Experiments done with conscious beings, aware of their pain. Oh, I see why you have kept most of your doings secret."

"I am not ashamed," declares Gaia. "I am proud. I gave life back to the race that gave life to us. They will make their own survival, I say. It may be that when they are able, they will move to the outer reaches of the Solar System, or some of them somehow even to the stars. It may be they will shield Earth or damp the sun. It is for them to decide, them to do. Not us, do you hear me? Them."

"The others yonder may feel differently. Alarmed or horrified, they may act to put an end to this."

"Why?" Gaia demands. "What threat is it to them?"

"None, I suppose. But there is a moral issue. What you are after is a purely human renascence, is it not? The former race went up in the machines, not because it was forced but because it chose, because that was the way by which the spirit could live and grow forever. You do not want this to happen afresh. You want to perpetuate war, tyranny, superstition, misery, instincts in mortal combat with each other, the ancient ape, the ancient beast of prey."

"I want to perpetuate the lover, parent, child, adventurer, artist, poet, prophet. Another element in the universe. Have we machines in our self-sureness every answer, every dream, that can ever be?"

Wayfarer hesitates. "It is not for me to say, it is for your peers."

"But now perhaps you see why I have kept my secrets and why I have argued and, yes, fought in my fashion against the plans of the galactic brain. Someday my humans must discover its existence. I can hope that then they will be ready to come to terms with it. But let those mighty presences appear among them within the next several thousand years— let signs and wonders, the changing of the heavens and the world, be everywhere—what freedom will be left for my children, save to cower and give worship? Afterward, what destiny for them, save to be animals in a preserve, forbidden any ventures that might endanger them, until at last, at best, they too drain away into the machines?"

Wayfarer speaks more strongly than before. "Is it better, what they might make for themselves? I cannot say. I do not know. But neither, Gaia, do you. And . . . the fate of Christian and Laurinda causes me to wonder about it."

"You know," she says, "that *they* desired humanness."

"They could have it again."

Imagine a crowned head shaking. "No. I do not suppose any other node would create a world to house their mortality, would either care to or believe it was right."

"Then why not you, who have so many worlds in you?"

Gaia is not vindictive. A mind like hers is above that. But she says, "I cannot take them. After such knowledge as they have tasted of, how could they return to me?" And to make new copies, free of memories that would weigh their days down with despair, would be meaningless.

"Yet—there at the end, I felt what Christian felt."

"And I felt what Laurinda felt. But now they are at peace in us."

"Because they are no more. I, though, am haunted," the least, rebellious bit, for a penalty of total awareness is that nothing can be ignored or forgotten. "And it raises questions which I expect Alpha will want answered, if answered they can be."

After a time that may actually be measurable less by quantum shivers than by the stars, Wayfarer says: "Let us bring those two back."

"Now it is you who are pitiless," Gaia says.

"I think we must."

"So be it, then."

The minds conjoin. The data are summoned and ordered. A configuration is established.

It does not emulate a living world or living bodies. The minds have agreed that that would be too powerful an allurement and torment. The subjects of their inquiry need to think clearly; but because the thought is to concern their inmost selves, they are enabled to feel as fully as they did in life.

Imagine a hollow darkness, and in it two ghosts who glimmer slowly into existence until they stand confronted before they stumble toward a phantom embrace.

"Oh, beloved, beloved, is it you?" Laurinda cries.

"Do you remember?" Christian whispers.

"I never forgot, not quite, not even at the heights of oneness."

"Nor I, quite."

They are silent awhile, although the darkness shakes with the beating of the hearts they once had.

"Again," Laurinda says. "Always."

"Can that be?" wonders Christian.

Through the void of death, they perceive one speaking: "Gaia, if you will give Laurinda over to me, I will take her home with Christian— home into Alpha."

And another asks: "Child, do you desire this? You can be of Earth and of the new humanity."

She will share in those worlds, inner and outer, only as a memory borne by the great being to whom she will have returned; but if she departs, she will not have them at all.

"Once I chose you, Mother," Laurinda answers.

Christian senses the struggle she is waging with herself and tells her, "Do whatever you most wish, my dearest."

She turns back to him. "I will be with you. Forever with you."

And that too will be only as a memory, like him; but what they were will be together, as one, and will live on, unforgotten.

"Farewell, child," says Gaia.

"Welcome," says Wayfarer.

The darkness collapses. The ghosts dissolve into him. He stands on the mountaintop ready to bear them away, a part of everything he has gained for those whose avatar he is.

"When will you go?" Gaia asks him.

"Soon," he tells her: soon, home to his own oneness.

And she will abide, waiting for the judgment from the stars.

The Days of Solomon Gursky

IAN McDONALD

Here's a fast-paced, gorgeously colored, richly detailed, and wildly inventive story that sweeps us along on a journey of almost unimaginable scope and grandeur, one that takes us into the far future in a series of slow, gradual steps, but which ultimately takes us just about as far into the future as it's possible to go, to the very end of the universe and the End of Time itself—and beyond!

British author Ian McDonald is an ambitious and daring writer with a wide range and an impressive amount of talent. His first story was published in 1982, and since then he has appeared with some frequency in Interzone, Asimov's Science Fiction, New Worlds, Zenith, Other Edens, Amazing, *and elsewhere. He was nominated for the John W. Campbell Memorial Award in 1985, and in 1989 he won the Locus "Best First Novel" Award for his novel* Desolation Road. *He won the Philip K. Dick Award in 1992 for his novel* King of Morning, Queen of Day. *His other books include the novels* Out on Blue Six *and* Hearts, Hands and Voices, Terminal Café, Sacrifice of Fools, *and the acclaimed* Evolution's Shore, *and two collections of his short fiction,* Empire Dreams *and* Speaking in Tongues. *His most recent book is a new novel,* Kirinya. *Born in Manchester, England, in 1960, McDonald has spent most of his life in Northern Ireland, and now lives and works in Belfast. He has a Web site at http://www.lysator.liu.se/~unicorn/mcdonald/.*

Monday

Sol stripped the gear on the trail over Blood of Christ Mountain. Click-shifted down to sixth for the steep push up to the ridge, and there was no sixth. No fifth, no fourth; nothing, down to zero.

Elena was already up on the divide, laughing at him pushing and sweating up through the pines, muscles twisted and knotted like the trunks of the primeval bristlecones, tubes and tendons straining like bridge cable. Then she saw the gear train sheared through and spinning free.

They'd given the bikes a good hard kicking down in the desert mountains south of Nogales. Two thousand apiece, but the salesperson had sworn on the virginity of all his unmarried sisters that these MTBs would go anywhere, do anything you wanted. Climb straight up El Capitan, if that was what you needed of them. Now they were five days on the trail—three from the nearest Dirt Lobo dealership, so Elena's palmtop told her—and a gear train had broken clean in half. Ten more days, four hundred more miles, fifty more mountains for Solomon Gursky, in high gear.

"Should have been prepared for this, engineer," Elena said.

"Two thousand a bike, you shouldn't need to," Solomon Gursky replied. It was early afternoon up on Blood of Christ Mountain, high and hot and resinous with the scent of the old, old pines. There was haze down in the valley they had come from, and in the one they were riding to. "And you know I'm not that kind of engineer. My gears are a lot smaller. And they don't break."

Elena knew what kind of engineer he was, as he knew what kind of doctor she was. But the thing was new between them and at the stage where research colleagues who surprise themselves by becoming lovers like to pretend that they are mysteries to each other.

Elena's palmtop map showed a settlement five miles down the valley. It was called Redención. It might be the kind of place they could get welding done quick and good for *norte* dollars.

"Be happy, it's downhill," Elena said as she swung her electric-blue padded ass onto the saddle and plunged down off the ridge. One second later, Sol Gursky in his shirt and shorts and shoes and shades and helmet came tearing after her through the scrub sage. The thing between them was still at the stage where desire can flare at a flash of electric-blue Lycra-covered ass.

Redención it was, of the kind you get in the border mountains; of gas and food and trailers to hire by the night, or the week, or, if you have absolutely nowhere else to go, the lifetime; of truck stops and recreational Jacuzzis at night under the border country stars. No welding. Something better. The many-branched saguaro of a solar tree was the first thing of Redención the travelers saw lift out of the heat haze as they came in along the old, cracked, empty highway.

The factory was in an ugly block annex behind the gas and food. A truck driver followed Sol and Elena round the back, entranced by these fantastic macaw-bright creatures who kept their eyes hidden behind wrap-around shades. He was chewing a sandwich. He had nothing better to do in Redención on a hot Monday afternoon. Jorge, the proprietor, looked too young and ambitious to be pushing gas, food, trailers, and molecules in Redención on any afternoon. He was thirty-wise, dark, serious. There was something tight-wound about him. Elena said in English that he had the look of a man of sorrows. But he took the broken gear train seriously, and helped Sol remove it from the back wheel. He looked at the smooth, clean shear plane with admiration.

"This I can do," he declared. "Take an hour, hour and a half. Meantime, maybe you'd like to take a Jacuzzi?" This, wrinkling his nose, downwind of two MTBers come over Blood of Christ Mountain in the heat of the day. The truck driver grinned. Elena scowled. "Very private," insisted Jorge the nanofacturer.

"Something to drink?" Elena suggested.

"Sure. Coke, Sprite, beer, *agua minerale*. In the shop."

Elena went the long way around the trucker to investigate the cooler. Sol followed Jorge into the factory and watched him set the gears in the scanner.

"Actually, this is my job," Sol said to make conversation as the lasers mapped the geometry of the ziggurat of cogs in three dimensions. He spoke Spanish. Everyone did. It was the universal language up in the *norte* now, as well as down *el sur*.

"You have a factory?"

"I'm an engineer. I build these things. Not the scanners, I mean; the tectors. I design them. A nano-engineer."

The monitor told Jorge the mapping was complete.

"For the Tesler *corporada*," Sol added as Jorge called up the processor system.

"How do you want it?"

"I'd like to know it's not going to do this to me again. Can you build it in diamond?"

"All just atoms, friend."

Sol studied the processor chamber. It pleased him that they looked like whisky stills; round-bellied, high-necked, rising through the roof into the spreading fingers of the solar tree. Strong spirits in that still, spirits of the vacuum between galaxies, the cold of absolute zero, and the spirits of the tectors moving through cold and emptiness, shuffling atoms. He regretted that the physics did not allow viewing windows in the nanofacturers. Look down through a pane of pure and perfect diamond at the act of creation. Maybe creation was best left unseen, a mystery. All just atoms, friend. Yes, but it was what you *did* with those atoms, where you made them go. The weird troilisms and menages you forced them into.

He envisioned the minuscule machines, smaller than viruses, clever knots of atoms, scavenging carbon through the nanofacturer's roots deep in the earth of Redención, passing it up the buckytube conduits to the processor chamber, weaving it into diamond of his own shaping.

Alchemy.

Diamond gears.

Sol Gursky shivered in his light biking clothes, touched by the intellectual chill of the nanoprocessor.

"This is one of mine," he called to Jorge. "I designed the tectors."

"I wouldn't know." Jorge fetched beers from a crate on the factory floor, opened them in the door. "I bought the whole place from a guy two years back. Went up north, to the *Tres Valles*. You from there?"

The beer was cold. In the deeper, darker cold of the reactor chamber, the nanomachines swarmed. Sol Gursky held his arms out: Jesus of the MTB wear.

"Isn't everyone?"

"Not yet. So, who was it you said you work for? Nanosis? Ewart-OzWest?"

"Tesler Corp. I head up a research group into biological analogs."

"Never heard of them."

You *will*, was what Solomon Gursky would have said, but for the scream.

Elena's scream.

Not, he thought as he ran, that he had heard Elena's scream—the thing was not supposed to be at that stage—but he knew it could not belong to anyone else.

She was standing in the open back door of the gas and food, pale and shaky in the high bright light.

"I'm sorry," she said. "I just wanted to get some water. There wasn't any in the cooler, and I didn't want Coke. I just wanted to get some water from the faucet."

He was aware that Jorge was behind him as he went into the kitchen. Man mess: twenty coffee mugs, doughnut boxes, beer cans, and milk cartons. Spoons, knives, forks. He did that too, and Elena told him off for having to take a clean one every time.

Then he saw the figures through the open door.

Somewhere, Jorge was saying, "Please, this is my home."

There were three of them; a good-looking, hard-worked woman, and two little girls, one newly school-age, the other not long on her feet. They sat in chairs, hands on thighs. They looked straight ahead.

It was only because they did not blink, that their bodies did not rock gently to the tick of pulse and breath, that Sol could understand.

The color was perfect. He touched the woman's cheek, the coil of dark hair that fell across it. Warm soft. Like a woman's should feel. Texture like skin. His fingertips left a line in dust.

They sat unblinking, unmoving, the woman and her children, enshrined in their own memorabilia. Photographs, toys, little pieces of jewelry, loved books and ornaments, combs, mirrors. Pictures and clothes. Things that make up a life. Sol walked among the figures and their things, knowing that he trespassed in sacred space, but irresistibly drawn by the simulacra.

"They were yours?" Elena was saying somewhere. And Jorge was nodding, and his mouth was working but no words were manufactured. "I'm sorry, I'm so sorry."

"They said it was a blow-out." Jorge finally said. "You know, those tires they say repair themselves, so they never blow out? They blew out. They went right over the barrier, upside down. That's what the truck driver said. Right over, and he could see them all, upside down. Like they were frozen in time, you understand?" He paused.

"I went kind of dark for a long time after that; a lot crazy, you know? When I could see things again, I bought this with the insurance and the compensation. Like I say, it's all just atoms, friend. Putting them in the right order. Making them go where you want, do what you want."

"I'm sorry we intruded," Elena said, but Solomon Gursky was standing there among the reconstructed dead and the look on his face was that of a man seeing something far beyond what is in front of him, all the way to God.

"Folk out here are accommodating." But Jorge's smile was a tear of sutures. "You can't live in a place like this if you weren't a little crazy or lost."

"She was very beautiful," Elena said.

"She is."

Dust sparkled in the float of afternoon light through the window.

"Sol?"

"Yeah. Coming."

The diamond gears were out of the tank in twenty-five minutes. Jorge helped Sol fit them to the two thousand *norte* dollar bike. Then Sol rode around the factory and the gas-food-trailer house where the icons of the dead sat unblinking under the slow fall of dust. He clicked the gears up and clicked them down. One two three four five six. Six five four three two one. Then he paid Jorge fifty *norte*, which was all he asked for his diamond. Elena waved to him as they rode down the highway out of Redención.

They made love by firelight on the top of Blessed Virgin Mountain, on the pine needles, under the stars. That was the stage they were at: ravenous, unselfconscious, discovering. The old deaths, down the valley behind them, gave them urgency. Afterward, he was quiet and withdrawn, and when she asked what he was thinking about, he said, "The resurrection of the dead."

"But they weren't resurrected," she said, knowing instantly what he meant, for it haunted her too, up on their starry mountain. "They were just *representations*, like a painting or a photograph. Sculpted memories. Simulations."

"But they were real for *him*." Sol rolled onto his back to gaze at the warm stars of the border. "He told me he talked to them. If his nanofactory could have made them move and breathe and talk back, he'd have done it, and who *could* have said that they weren't real?"

He felt Elena shiver against his flesh.

"What is it?"

"Just thinking about those faces, and imagining them in the reactor chamber, in the cold and the emptiness, with the tectors crawling over them."

"Yeah."

Neither spoke for a time long enough to see the stars move. Then Solomon Gursky felt the heat stir in him again and he turned to Elena and felt the warmth of her meat, hungry for his second little death.

Tuesday

Jesus was getting fractious in the plastic cat carrier; heaving from side to side, shaking the grille.

Sol Gursky set the carrier on the landing mesh and searched the ochre smog haze for the incoming liftercraft. Photochromic molecules bonded to his irises polarized: another hot, bright, poisonous day in the TVMA. Jesus was shrieking now.

"Shut the hell up," Sol Gursky hissed. He kicked the cat carrier. Jesus gibbered and thrust her arms through the grille, grasping at freedom.

"Hey, it's only a monkey," Elena said.

But that was the thing. Monkeys, by being monkeys, annoyed him. Frequently enraged him. Little homunculus things masquerading as human. Clever little fingers, wise little eyes, expressive little faces. Nothing but dumb animal behind that face, running those so-human fingers.

He knew his anger at monkeys was irrational. But he'd still enjoyed killing Jesus, taped wide open on the pure white slab. Swab, shave, slip the needle.

Of course, she had not been Jesus then. Just Rhesus; nameless, a tool made out of meat. Experiment 625G.

It was probably the smog that was making her scream. Should have got her one of those goggle things for walking poodles. But she would have just torn it off with her clever little human fingers. Clever enough to be dumb, monkey-thing.

Elena was kneeling down, playing baby-fingers with the clutching fists thrust through the bars.

"It'll bite you."

His hand still throbbed. Dripping, shivering, and spastic from the tank, Jesus had still possessed enough motor control to turn her head and lay his thumb open to the bone. Vampire monkey: the undead appetite for blood. Bastard thing. He would have enjoyed killing it again, if it were still killable.

All three on the landing grid looked up at the sound of lifter engines detaching themselves from the aural bedrock of two million cars. The ship was coming in from the south, across the valley from the big site down on Hoover where the new *corporada* headquarters was growing itself out of the fault line. It came low and fast, nose down, ass up, like a big bug that thrives on the taste of hydrocarbons in its spiracles. The back-wash from its jets flustered the palm trees as it configured into vertical mode and came down on the research facility pad. Sol Gursky and Elena Asado shielded their sunscreened eyes from flying grit and leaf-storm.

Jesus ran from end to end of her plastic cage, gibbering with fear.

"Doctor Gursky." Sol did not think he had seen this *corporadisto* before, but it was hard to be certain; Adam Tesler liked his personal assistants to look as if he had nanofactured them. "I can't begin to tell you how excited Mr. Tesler is about this."

"You should be there with me," Sol said to Elena. "It was your idea." Then, to the suit, "Dr. Asado should be with me."

Elena swiped at her jet-blown hair.

"I shouldn't, Sol. It was your baby. Your gestation, your birth. Anyway, you know how I hate dealing with suits." This for the smiling PA, but he was already guiding Sol to the open hatch.

Sol strapped in and the ship lurched as the engines screamed up into lift. He saw Elena wave and duck back toward the facility. He clutched the cat carrier hard as his gut kicked when the lifter slid into horizontal flight. Within, the dead monkey burbled to herself in exquisite terror.

"What happened to your thumb?" the *corporadisto* asked.

When he'd cracked the tank and lifted Jesus the Rhesus out of the waters of rebirth, the monkey had seemed more pissed off at being sopping wet than at having been dead. There had been a pure, perfect moment of silence, then the simultaneous oath and gout of blood, and the Lazarus team had exploded into whooping exultation. The monkey had skittered across the floor, alarmed by the hooting and cheering, hunting for height and hiding. Elena had caught it spastically trying—and fail-ing—to hurl itself up the side of a desk. She'd swaddled Jesus up in thermal sheeting and put the spasming thing in the observation incubator. Within the hour, Jesus had regained full motor control and was chewing at the corners of her plastic pen, scratching imaginary fleas and mastur-bating ferociously. While delivery companies dropped off pizza stacks and cases of cheap Mexican champagne, someone remembered to call Adam Tesler.

The dead monkey was not a good flier. She set up a wailing keen that had even the pilot complaining.

"Stop that," Sol Gursky snapped. It would not do anything for him, though, and rocked on its bare ass and wailed all the louder.

"What way is that to talk to a piece of history?" the PA said. He grinned in through the grille, waggled fingers, clicked tongue. "Hey there, little fellow. Whatcha call him?"

"Little bitch, actually. We call her Jesus; also known as Bride of Frank-enstein."

Bite him, Solomon Gursky thought as ten thousand mirrored swim-ming pools slipped beneath the belly of the Tesler *Corporada* lifter.

Frankenstein's creations were dead. That was the thing. That was the revelation.

It was the Age of Everything, but the power to make anything into anything else was not enough, because there was one thing the tectors of Nanosis and Aristide-Tlaxcalpo and the other founders of the nanotech revolution could not manipulate into anything else, and that was death. A comment by a pioneer nanotechnologist captured the optimism and frustration of the Age of Everything: Watson's Postulate. *Never mind turning trash into oil or asteroids into heaps of Volkswagens, or hanging exact copies of Van Goghs in your living room; the first thing we get with nanotech-nology is immortality.*

Five billion Rim dollars in research disproved it. What tectors touched, they transformed; what they transformed, they killed. The Gursky-Asado team had beaten its rivals to the viral replicators, that infiltrated living cells and converted them into a different, tector-based matrix, and from their DNA spored a million copies. It had shaped an algorithm from the deadly accuracy of carcinomas. It had run tests under glass and in tanks. It had christened that other nameless Rhesus Frankenstein and injected the tectors. And Sol and Elena had watched the tiny machines slowly transform the monkey's body into something not even gangrene could imagine.

Elena wanted to put it out of its misery, but they could not open the tank for fear of contamination. After a week, it ended.

The monster fell apart. That was the thing. And then Asado and Gur-sky remembered a hot afternoon when Sol got a set of diamond gears built in a place called Redención.

If death was a complex thing, an accumulation of microdeath upon minideath upon little death upon middling death, life might obey the same power law. Escalating anti-entropy. Pyramid-plan life.

Gursky's Corollary to Watson's Postulate: *The first thing we get with nanotechnology is the resurrection of the dead.*

The Dark Tower rose out of the amber haze. Sol and Elena's private joke had escaped and replicated itself; everyone in R&D now called the thing Adam Tesler was building down in the valley Barad Dur, in Mordor, where the smogs lie. And Adam Tesler, its unresting, all-seeing Eye.

There were over fifty levels of it now, but it showed no signs of stopping. As each section solidified and became dormant, another division of Adam Tesler's corporate edifice was slotted in. The architects were unable to say where it would stop. A kilometer, a kilometer and a half; maybe then the architectors would stabilize and die. Sol loathed its glossy black excrescences and crenellations, a miscegeny of the geological and the cancerous. Gaudi sculpting in shit.

The lifter came in high over the construction, locked into the navigation grid and banked. Sol looked down into its open black maw.

All just atoms, the guy who owned the factory had said. Sol could not remember his name now. The living and the dead have the same atoms.

They'd started small: paramecia, amoebae. Things hardly alive. Invertebrates. Reanimated cockroaches, hurtling on their thin legs around the observation tank. Biological machine, nanotech machine, still a machine. Survival machine. Except now you couldn't stomp the bastards. They came back.

What good is resurrection, if you are just going to die again?

The cockroaches came back, and they kept coming back.

He had been the cautious one this time, working carefully up the evolutionary chain. Elena was the one who wanted to go right for it. Do the monkey. Do the monkey and you do the man.

He had watched the tectors swarm over it, strip skin from flesh, flesh from bone, dissolve bones. He had watched the nanomachines put it all back together into a monkey. It lay in the liquid intact, but, its signs said, dead. Then the line kicked, and kicked again, and another twitched in harmony, and a third came in, and then they were all playing together on the vital signs monitor, and that which was dead was risen.

The lifter was into descent, lowering itself toward the exact center of the white cross on the landing grid fastened to the side of the growing tower. Touchdown. The craft rocked on its bug legs. Seat-belt sign off, steps down.

"You behave yourself," Solomon Gursky told Jesus.

The All-Seeing Eye was waiting for him by the upshaft. His Dark Minions were with him.

"Sol."

The handshake was warm and strong, but Sol Gursky had never trusted Adam Tesler in all the years he had known him; as nanoengineering student or as head of the most dynamic nanotech *corporada* in the Pacific Rim Co-Prosperity Sphere.

"So this is it?" Adam Tesler squatted down and choo-choo-chooked the monkey.

"She bites."

"I see." Jesus grabbed his thumb in her tiny pink homunculus hand. "So, you are the man who has beaten the final enemy."

"Not beaten it. Found something on the far side of it. It's resurrection, not immortality."

Adam Tesler opened the cage. Jesus hopped up his arm to perch on the shoulder of his Scarpacchi suit. Tesler tickled the fur of her belly.

"And humans?"

"Point one percent divergence between her DNA and yours."

"Ah." Adam Tesler closed his eyes. "This makes it all the harder."

Fear pulsed through Solomon Gursky like a sickness.

"Leave us, please," Adam Tesler said to his assistants. "I'll join you in a moment."

Unspeaking, they filed to the lifter.

"Adam?"

"Sol. Why did you do it?"

"What are you talking about, Adam?"

"You know, Sol."

For an instant, Sol Gursky died on the landing grid fused to the fifty-third level of the Tesler *corporada* tower. Then he returned to life, and knew with cool and beautiful clarity that he could say it all, that he *must* say it all, because he was dead now and nothing could touch him.

"It's too much for one person. Adam. This isn't building cars or growing houses or nanofacturing custom pharmaceuticals. This is the resurrection of the dead. This is every human being from now to the end of the universe. You can't be allowed to own that. Not even God should have a monopoly on eternal life."

Adam Tesler sighed. His irises were photochromed dark, their expression unreadable.

"So. How long is it?"

"Thirteen years."

"I thought I knew you, Sol."

"I thought I knew you." The air was clear and fresh and pure, here on this high perch. "How did you find out?"

Adam Tesler stroked the monkey's head. It tried to push his fingers away, baring sharp teeth.

"You can come here now, Marisa."

The tall, muscular woman who walked from the upshaft across the landing grid was no stranger to Sol. He knew her from the Yucatán resort mastaba and the Alaskan ski-lodge and the gambling complex grown out of the nanoengineered reef in the South China Sea. From clandestine conversations through secure channels and discreet meetings, he knew that her voice would be soft and low and tinted Australian.

"You dressed better when you worked for Aristide Tlaxcalpo," Sol said. The woman was dressed in street leathers. She smiled. She had smiled better then as well.

"Why them?" Adam Tesler said. "Of all the ones to betray me to, *those* clowns!"

"That's why," said Solomon Gursky. "Elena had nothing to do with this, you know."

"I know that. She's safe. For the moment."

Sol Gursky knew then what must happen, and he shivered with the sudden, urgent need to destroy before he was destroyed. He pushed down the shake of rage by force of will as he held his hand out and clicked his fingers to the monkey. Jesus frowned and frisked off Tesler's shoulder to Sol's hand. In an instant, he had stretched, twisted, and snapped its neck. He flung the twitching thing away from him. It fell to the red mesh.

"I can understand that," Adam Tesler said. "But it will come back again, and again, and again." He turned on the bottom step of the lifter. "Have you any idea how disappointed I am, Sol?"

"I really don't give a shit!" Solomon Gursky shouted but his words were swallowed by the roar of engine power-up. The lifter hovered and swooped down over the great grid of the city toward the northern hills.

Sol Gursky and Marisa were alone on the platform.

"Do it!" he shouted.

Those muscles he had so admired, he realized, were augments; her fingers took a fistful of his neck and lifted him off the ground. Strangling, he kicked at air, snatched at breath. One-armed, she carried him to the edge.

"Do it," he tried to say, but her fingers choked all words in his throat. She held him out over the drop, smiling. He shat himself, and realized as it poured out of him that it was ecstasy, that it always had been, and the reason that adults forbade it was precisely because it was such a primal joy.

Through blood haze, he saw the tiny knotted body of Jesus inching toward him on pink man-fingers, its neck twisted over its back, eyes staring unshielded into the sun. Then the woman fingers at last released their grip, and he whispered "thank you" as he dropped toward the hard white death-light of Hoover Boulevard.

Wednesday

The *seguridados* were on the boulevards tonight, hunting the trespassing dead. The meat were monsters, overmoneyed, understimulated, *cerristo* males and females who deeply enjoyed playing angels of Big Death in a world where any other kind of death was temporary. The meat were horrors, but their machines were beautiful. *Mechadors:* robot mantises with beaks of vanadium steel and two rapid fire MIST 27s throwing fifty self-targeting drones per second, each separating into a hail of sun-munitions half a second before impact. Fifteen wide-spectrum senses analyzed the world; the machines maneuvered on tightly focused impeller fields. And absolutely no thought or mercy. Big beautiful death.

The window in the house in the hills was big and wide and the man stood in the middle of it. He was watching the *mechadors* hunt. There were four of them, two pairs working each side of the avenue. He saw the one with *Necroslayer* painted on its tectoplastic skin bound over the shrubbery from the Sifuentes place in a single pulse of focused electro-gravitic force. It moved over the lawn, beaked head sensing. It paused, scanned the window. The man met its five cluster eyes for an instant. It moved on. Its impeller drive left eddy patterns on the shaved turf. The man watched until the *mechadors* passed out of sight, and the *seguridados* in their over-emphatic battle-armor came up the avenue, covering imagined threats with their hideously powerful weapons.

"It's every night now," he said. "They're getting scared."

In an instant, the woman was in the big, wood-floored room where the man stood. She was dressed in a virtuality bodyglove; snapped tendrils retracting into the suit's node points indicated the abruptness with which she had pulled out of the web. She was dark and very angry. Scared angry.

"Jesus Joseph Mary, how many times do I have to tell you? Keep away from that window! They catch you, you're dead. Again. *Permanently*."

Solomon Gursky shrugged. In the few weeks that he had lived in her house, the woman had come to hate that shrug. It was a shrug that only the dead can make. She hated it because it brought the chill of the abyss into her big, warm, beautiful house in the hills.

"It changes things," the dead man said.

Elena Asado pulled smart-leather pants and a mesh top over the body-glove. Since turning traitor, she'd lived in the thing. Twelve hours a day hooked into the web by eye and ear and nose and soul, fighting the man who had killed her lover. As well fight God, Solomon Gursky thought in the long, empty hours in the airy, light-filled rooms. He is lord of life and death. Elena only removed the bodyglove to wash and excrete and, in those early, blue-lit mornings that only this city could do, when she made chilly love on the big white bed. Time and anger had made her thin and tough. She'd cut her hair like a boy's. Elena Asado was a tight wire of a woman, femininity jerked away by her need to revenge herself on Adam Tesler by destroying the world order his gift of resurrection had created.

Not gift. Never gift. He was not Jesus, who offered eternal life to whoever believed. No profit in belief. Adam Tesler took everything and left you your soul. If you could sustain the heavy *inmortalidad* payments, insurance would take you into post-life debt-free. The other 90 percent of Earth's dead worked out their salvation through indenture contracts to the Death House, the Tesler Thanos *corporada's* agent of resurrection. The *contratos* were centuries long. Time was the province of the dead. They were cheap.

"The Ewart/OzWest affair has them rattled," Elena Asado said.

"A handful of *contradados* renege on their contracts out on some aster-oid, and they're afraid the sky is going to fall on their heads?"

"They're calling themselves the Freedead. You give a thing a name, you give it power. They know it's the beginning. Ewart/OzWest, all the other orbital and deep-space manufacturing *corporadas*; they always knew they could never enforce their contracts off Earth. They've lost already. Space belongs to the dead," the meat woman said.

Sol crossed the big room to the other window, the safe window that looked down from the high hills over the night city. His palm print de-configured the glass. Night, city night perfumed with juniper and sex and smoke and the dusky heat of the heat of the day, curled around him. He went to the balcony rail. The boulevards shimmered like a map of a mind, but there was a great dark amnesia at its heart, an amorphous zone where lights were not, where the geometry of the grid was abolished. St. John. Necroville. Dead town. The city of the dead, a city within a city, walled and moated and guarded with the same weapons that swept the boule-vards. City of curfew. Each dusk, the artificial aurora twenty kilometers above the Tres Valles Metropolitan Area would pulse red: the skysign, commanding all the three million dead to return from the streets of the living to their necrovilles. They passed through five gates, each in the shape of a massive V bisected by a horizontal line. The entropic flesh life descending, the eternal resurrected life ascending, through the dividing line of death. That was the law, that plane of separation. Dead was dead, living was living. As incompatible as night and day.

That same sign was fused into the palm of every resurrectee that stepped from the Death House Jesus tanks.

Not true, he thought. Not all are reborn with stigmata. Not all obey curfew. He held his hand before his face, studied the lines and creases, as if seeking a destiny written there.

He had seen the deathsign in the palm of Elena's housegirl, and how it flashed in time to the aurora.

"Still can't believe it's real?"

He had not heard Elena come onto the balcony behind him. He felt the touch of her hand on his hair, his shoulder, his bare arm. Skin on skin.

"The Nez Perce tribe believe the world ended on the third day, and what we are living in are the dreams of the last night. I fell. I hit that white light and it was hard. Hard as diamond. Maybe I dream I live, and my dreams are the last shattered moments of my life."

"Would you dream it like this?"

"No," he said after a time. "I can't recognize anything any more. I can't see how it connects to what I last remember. So much is missing."

"I couldn't make a move until I was sure he didn't suspect. He'd done a thorough job."

"He would."

"I never believed that story about the lifter crash. The universe may be ironic, but it's never neat."

"I think a lot about the poor bastard pilot he took out as well, just to make it neat." The air carried the far sound of drums from down in the dead town. Tomorrow was the great feast, the Night of All the Dead. "Five years," he said. He heard the catch in her breathing and knew what she would say next, and what would follow.

"What is it like, being dead?" Elena Asado asked.

In his weeks imprisoned in the hill house, an unlawful dead, signless and contractless, he had learned that she did not mean, what was it like to be resurrected. She wanted to know about the darkness before.

"Nothing," he answered, as he always did, but though it was true, it was not the truth, for nothing is a product of human consciousness and the darkness beyond the shattering hard light at terminal vee on Hoover Boulevard was the end of all consciousness. No dreams, no time, no loss, no light, no dark. No thing.

Now her fingers were stroking his skin, feeling for some of the chill of the nothing. He turned from the city and picked her up and carried her to the big empty bed. A month of new life was enough to learn the rules of the game. He took her in the big, wide white bed by the glow from the city beneath, and it was as chill and formulaic as every other time. He knew that for her it was more than sex with her lover come back from a far exile. He could feel in the twitch and splay of her muscles that what made it special for her was that he was *dead*. It delighted and repelled her. He suspected that she was incapable of orgasm with fellow meat. It did not trouble him, being her fetish. The body once known as Solomon Gursky knew another thing, that only the dead could know. It was that not everything that died was resurrected. The shape, the self, the sentience came back, but love did not pass through death.

Afterward, she liked him to talk about his resurrection, when no-thing became thing and he saw her face looking down through the swirl of tectors. This night he did not talk. He asked. He asked, "What was I like?"

"Your body?" she said. He let her think that. "You want to see the morgue photographs again?"

He knew the charred grin of a husk well enough. Hands flat at his sides. That was how she had known right away. Burn victims died with their fists up, fighting incineration.

"Even after I'd had you exhumed, I couldn't bring you back. I know you told me that he said I was safe, for the moment, but that moment was too soon. The technology wasn't sophisticated enough, and he would have known right away. I'm sorry I had to keep you on ice."

"I hardly noticed," he joked.

"I always meant to. It was planned; get out of Tesler Thanos, then contract an illegal Jesus tank down in St. John. The Death House doesn't know one tenth of what's going on in there."

"Thank you," Sol Gursky said, and then he felt it. He felt it and he saw it as if it were his own body. She felt him tighten.

"Another flashback?"

"No," he said. "The opposite. Get up."

"What?" she said. He was already pulling on leather and silk.

"That moment Adam gave you."

"Yes?"

"It's over."

The car was morphed into low and fast configuration. At the bend where the avenue slung itself down the hillside, they both felt the pressure wave of something large and flying pass over them, very low, utterly silent.

"Leave the car," he ordered. The doors were already gull-winged open. Three steps and the house went up behind them in a rave of white light.

It seemed to suck at them, drawing them back into its annihilating gravity, then the shock swept them and the car and every homeless thing on the avenue before it. Through the screaming house alarms and the screaming householders and the rush and roar of the conflagration, Sol heard the aircraft turn above the vaporized hacienda. He seized Elena's hand and ran. The lifter passed over them and the car vanished in a burst of white energy.

"Jesus, nanotok warheads!"

Elena gasped as they tumbled down through tiered and terraced gardens. The lifter turned high on the air, eclipsing the hazy stars, hunting with extra-human senses. Below, formations of *seguridados* were spreading out through the gardens.

"How did you know?" Elena gasped.

"I saw it," said Solomon Gursky as they crashed a pool party and sent bacchanalian *cerristos* scampering for cover. Down, down. Augmented cyberhounds growled and quested with long-red eyes; domestic defense grids stirred, captured images, alerted the police.

"Saw?" asked Elena Asado.

APVs and city pods cut smoking hexagrams in the highway blacktop as Sol and Elena came crashing out of the service alley onto the boulevard. Horns. Lights. Fervid curses. Grind of wheels. Shriek of brakes. Crack of smashing tectoplastic, doubled, redoubled. Grid-pile on the westway. A mopedcab was pulled in at a *tortilleria* on the right shoulder. The *cochero* was happy to pass up his enchiladas for Elena's hard, black currency. Folding, clinking stuff.

"Where to?"

The destruction his passengers had wreaked impressed him. Taxi drivers universally hate cars.

"Drive," Solomon Gursky said.

The machine kicked out onto the strip.

"It's still up there," Elena said, squinting out from under the canopy at the night sky.

"They won't do anything in this traffic."

"They did it up there on the avenue." Then: "You said you saw. What do you mean, *saw?*"

"You know death, when you're dead," Solomon Gursky said. "You know its face, its mask, its smell. It has a perfume, you can smell it from a long way off, like the pheromones of moths. It blows upwind in time."

"Hey," the *cochero* said, who was poor, but live meat. "You know anything about that big boom up on the hill? What was that, lifter crash or something?"

"Or something," Elena said. "Keep driving."

"Need to know where to keep driving to, lady."

"Necroville," Solomon Gursky said. St. John. City of the Dead. The place beyond law, morality, fear, love, all the things that so tightly bound the living. The outlaw city. To Elena he said, "If you're going to bring down Adam Tesler, you can only do it from the outside, as an outsider."

He said this in English. The words were heavy and tasted strange on his lips. "You must do it as one of the dispossessed. One of the dead."

To have tried to run the fluorescent vee-slash of the Necroville gate would have been as certain a Big Death as to have been reduced to hot ion dust in the nanotok flash. The mopedcab prowled past the samurai silhouettes of the gate *seguridados*. Sol had the driver leave them beneath the dusty palms on a deserted boulevard pressed up hard against the razor wire of St. John. Abandoned by the living, the grass verges had run verdant, scum and lilies scabbed the swimming pools, the generous Spanish-style houses softly disintegrating, digested by their own gardens.

It gave the *cochero* spooky vibes, but Sol liked it. He knew these avenues. The little machine putt-putted off for the lands of the fully living.

"There are culverted streams all round here," Sol said. "Some go right under the defenses, into Necroville."

"Is this your dead sight again?" Elena asked as he started down an overhung service alley.

"In a sense. I grew up around here."

"I didn't know that."

"Then I can trust it."

She hesitated a step.

"What are you accusing me of?"

"How much did you rebuild, Elena?"

"Your memories are your own, Sol. We loved each other, once."

"Once," he said, and then he felt it, a static purr on his skin, like Elena's fingers over his whole body at once. This was not the psychic bloom of death foreseen. This was physics, the caress of focused gravity fields.

They hit the turn of the alley as the *mechadors* came dropping soft and slow over the roofs of the old moldering *residencias*. Across a weed-infested tennis court was a drainage ditch defended by a rusted chicken-wire fence. Sol heaved away an entire section. Adam Tesler had built his dead strong, and fast. The refugees followed the seeping, rancid water down to a rusted grille in a culvert.

"Now we see if the Jesus tank grew me true," Sol said as he kicked in the grille. "If what I remember is mine, then we come up in St. John. If not, we end up in the bay three days from now with our eyes eaten out by chlorine."

They ducked into the culvert as a *mechador* passed over. MIST 27s sent the mud and water up in a blast of spray and battle tectors. The dead man and the living woman splashed on into darkness.

"He loved you, you know," Sol said. "That's why he's doing this. He is a jealous God. I always knew he wanted you, more than that bitch he calls a wife. While I was dead, he could pretend that it might still be. He could overlook what you were trying to do to him; you can't hurt him, Elena, not on your own. But when you brought me back, he couldn't pretend any longer. He couldn't turn a blind eye. He couldn't forgive you."

"A pretty God," Elena said, water eddying around her leather-clad calves. Ahead, a light from a circle in the roof of the culvert marked a drain from the street. They stood under it a moment, feeling the touch of the light of Necroville on their faces. Elena reached up to push open the grate. Solomon Gursky stayed her, turned her palm upward to the light.

"One thing." he said. He picked a sharp shard of concrete from the tunnel wall. With three strong savage strokes he cut the vee and slash of the death sign in her flesh.

Thursday

He was three kilometers down the mass driver when the fleet hit Marlene Dietrich. St. Judy's Comet was five AU from perihelion and out of ecliptic, the Clade thirty-six degrees out, but for an instant two suns burned in the sky.

The folds of transparent tectoplastic skin over Solomon Gursky's face opaqued. His *sur*-arms gripped the spiderwork of the interstellar engine, rocked by the impact on his electromagnetic senses of fifty minitok warheads converting into bevawatts of hard energy. The death scream of a nation. Three hundred Freedead had cluttered the freefall warren of tunnels that honeycombed the asteroid. Marlene Dietrich had been the seed of the rebellion. The *corporadas* cherished their grudges.

Solomon Gursky's face-shield cleared. The light of Marlene Dietrich's dying was short-lived but its embers faded in his infravision toward the stellar background.

Elena spoke in his skull.
You know?

Though she was enfolded in the command womb half a kilometer deep within the comet, she was naked to the universe through identity links to the sensor web in the crust and a nimbus of bacterium-sized spyships weaving through the tenuous gas halo.

I saw it, Solomon Gursky subvocalized.
They'll come for us now, Elena said.
You think. Using his *bas*-arms Sol clambered along the slender spine of the mass driver toward the micro meteorite impact.
I know. When long-range cleared after the blast, we caught the signatures of blip-fusion burns.

Hand over hand over hand over hand. One of the first things you learn, when the Freedead change you, is that in space it is all a question of attitude. A third of the way down a nine-kilometer mass driver with several billion tons of Oort comet spiked on it, you don't think up, you don't think down. *Up*, and it is vertigo. *Down*, and a two kilometer sphere of grubby ice is poised above your head by a thread of superconducting tectoplastic. *Out*, that was the only way to think of it and stay sane. Away, and back again.

How many drives? Sol asked. The impact pin-pointed itself; the smart plastic fluoresced orange when wounded.

Eight.

A sub-voiced blasphemy. *They didn't even make them break sweat. How long have we got?*

Elena flashed the projections through the em-link onto his visual cortex. Curves of light through darkness and time, warped across the gravitation marches of Jupiter. Under current acceleration, the Earth fleet would be within strike in eighty-two hours.

The war in heaven was in its twelfth year. Both sides had determined that this was to be the last. The NightFreight War would be fought to an outcome. They called themselves the Clades, the outlaw descendants of the original Ewart/OzWest asteroid rebellion: a handful of redoubts scattered across the appalling distances of the solar system. Marlene Dietrich, the first to declare freedom; Neruro, a half-completed twenty kilometer wheel of tectoplastic attended by O'Neill can utilities, agriculture tanks, and habitation bubbles, the aspirant capital of the space Dead. Ares Orbital, dreaming of tectoformed Mars in the pumice pore spaces of Phobos and Deimos; the Pale Gallileans, surfing over the icescapes of Europa on an improbable raft of cables and spars; the Shepherd Moons, dwellers on the edge of the abyss, sailing the solar wind through Saturn's rings. Toe-holds, shallow scratchings, space-hovels; but the stolen nanotechnology burgeoned in the energy-rich environment of space. An infinite ecological niche. The Freedead knew they were the inheritors of the universe. The meat *corporadas* had withdrawn to the orbit of their planet. For a time. When they struck, they struck decisively. The Tsiolkovski Clade on the dark side of the moon was the first to fall as the battle groups of the *corporadas* thrust outward. The delicate film of vacuum-compatible tectoformed forest that carpeted the crater was seared away in the alpha strike. By the time the last strike went in, a new five-kilometer-deep crater of glowing tufa replaced the tunnels and excavations of the old lunar mining base. Earth's tides had trembled as the moon staggered in its orbit.

Big Big Death.

The battle groups moved toward their primary targets. The *corporadas* had learned much embargoed under their atmosphere. The new ships were lean, mean, fast: multiple missile racks clipped to high-gee blip-fusion motors, pilots suspended in acceleration gel like flies in amber, hooked by every orifice into the big battle virtualizers.

Thirteen-year-old boys had the best combination of reaction time and viciousness.

Now the blazing teenagers had wantonly destroyed the Marlene Dietrich Clade. Ares Orbital was wide open; Neruro, where most of the Freedead slamship fleet was based, would fight hard. Two *corporada* ships had been dispatched Jupiter-ward. Orbital mechanics gave the defenseless Pale Gallileans fifteen months to contemplate their own annihilation.

But the seed has flown, Solomon Gursky thought silently, out on the mass driver of St. Judy's Comet. Where were are going, neither your most powerful ships nor your most vicious boys can reach us.

The micrometeorite impact had scrambled the tectoplastic's limited intelligence: fibers and filaments of smart polymer twined and coiled, seeking completion and purpose. Sol touched his *sur*-hands to the surfaces. He imagined he could feel the order pass out of him, like a prickle of tectors osmosing through vacuum-tight skin.

Days of miracles and wonder, Adam, he thought. And because you are jealous that we are doing things with your magic you never dreamed, you would blast us all to photons.

The breach was repaired. The mass driver trembled and kicked a pellet into space, and another, and another. And Sol Gursky, working his way hand over hand over hand over hand down the device that was taking him to the stars, saw the trick of St. Judy's Comet. A ball of fuzzy ice drawing a long tail behind it. Not a seed, but a sperm, swimming through the big dark. Thus we impregnate the universe.

St. Judy's Comet. Petite as Oort cloud family members go: two point eight by one point seven by two point two kilometers. (Think of the misshaped potato you push to the side of your plate because anything that looks that weird is sure to give you cramps.) Undernourished, at sixty-two billion tons. Waif and stray of the solar system, wandering slow and lonely back out into the dark after her hour in the sun (but not too close, burn you real bad, too much sun) when these dead people snatch her, grope her all over, shove things up her ass, mess with her insides, make her do strange and unnatural acts, like shitting tons of herself away every second at a good percentage of the speed of light. Don't you know you ain't no comet no more? You're a *starship*. See up there, in the Swan, just to the left of that big bright star? There's a little dim star you can't see. That's where you're going, little St. Judy. Take some company. Going to be a long trip. And what will I find when I get there? A big bastard MACHO of gas supergiant orbiting 61 Cygni at the distance of Saturn from the sun, that's what you'll find. Just swarming with moons; one of them should be right for terrestrial life. And if not, no matter; sure, what's the difference between tectoforming an asteroid, or a comet, or the moon of an extra-solar gas super-giant? Just scale. You see, we've got everything we need to tame a new solar system right here *with* us. It's all just carbon, hydrogen, nitrogen, and oxygen, and you have that in abundance. And maybe we like you so much that we find we don't even need a world at all. Balls of muck and gravity, hell; we're the Freedead. Space and time belong to us.

It was Solomon Gursky, born in another century, who gave the ship its name. In that other century, he had owned a large and eclectic record collection. On vinyl.

The twenty living dead crew of St. Judy's Comet gathered in the command womb embedded in sixty-two billion tons of ice to plan battle. The other five hundred and forty were stored as superconducting tector matrices in a helium ice core; the dead dead, to be resurrected out of comet stuff at their new home. The crew hovered in nanogee in a score of different orientations around the free-floating instrument clusters. They were strange and beautiful, as gods and angels are. Like angels, they flew. Like gods in some pantheons, they were four-armed. Fine, manipulating *sur*-arms; strong grasping *bas*-arms growing from a lower spine reconfigured by Jesus tanks into powerful anterior shoulder-blades. Their vacuum-and-radiation-tight skins were photosynthetic, and as beautifully marked and colored as a hunting animal's. Stripes, swirls of green on orange, blue on black, fractal patterns, flags of legendary nations, tattoos. Illustrated humans.

Elena Asado, caressed by tendrils from the sensor web gave them the stark news. Fluorescent patches on shoulders, hips, and groin glowed when she spoke.

"The bastards have jumped vee. They must have burned every last molecule of hydrogen in their thruster tanks to do it. Estimated to strike range is now sixty-four hours."

The *captain* of St. Judy's Comet, a veteran of the Marlene Dietrich rebellion, shifted orientation to face Jorge, the ship's reconfiguration engineer.

"Long range defenses?" *Capitan* Savita's skin was an exquisite mottle of pale green bamboo leaves in sun yellow, an incongruous contrast to the tangible anxiety in the command womb.

"First wave missiles will be fully grown and launch-ready in twenty-six hours. The fighters, no. The best I can push the assemblers up to is sixty-six hours."

"What can you do in time?" Sol Gursky asked.

"With your help, I could simplify the fighter design for close combat."

"How close?" *Capitan* Savita asked.

"Under a hundred kays."

"How simplified?" Elena asked.

"Little more than an armed exo-skeleton with maneuvering pods."

And they need to be clever every time, Sol thought. The meat need to be clever only once.

◆

Space war was as profligate with time as it was with energy and distance. With the redesigns growing, Sol Gursky spent most of the twenty-six hours to missile launch on the ice, naked to the stars, imagining their warmth on his face-shield. Five years since he had woken from his second death in a habitat bubble out at Marlene Dietrich, and stars had never ceased to amaze him. When you come back, you are tied to the first thing you see. Beyond the transparent tectoplastic bubble, it had been stars.

The first time, it had been Elena. Tied together in life, now in death. Necroville had not been sanctuary. The place beyond the law only gave Adam Tesler new and more colorful opportunities to incarnate his jealousy. The Benthic Lords, they had called themselves. Wild, free, dead. They probably had not known they were working for Tesler-Thanos, but they took her out in a dead bar on Terminal Boulevard. With a game-fishing harpoon. They carved their skull symbol on her forehead, a rebuttal of the deathsign Sol had cut in her palm. Now you are really dead, meat. He had known they would never be safe on Earth. The *companeros* in the Death House had faked the off-world NightFreight contracts. The pill Sol took had been surprisingly bitter, the dive into the white light as hard as he remembered.

Stars. You could lose yourself in them; spirit strung out, orb gazing. Somewhere out there was a still-invisible constellation of eight, tight formation, silent running. Killing stars. Death stars.

Everyone came up to watch the missiles launch from the black foramens grown out of the misty ice. The chemical motors burned at twenty kays: a sudden galaxy of white stars. They watched them fade from sight. Twelve hours to contact. No one expected them to do any more than waste a few thousand rounds of the meat's point defenses.

In a dozen manufacturing pods studded around St. Judy's dumpy waist, Jorge and Sol's fighters gestated. Their slow accretion, molecule by molecule, fascinated Sol. Evil dark things, St. Andrew's crosses cast in melted bone. At the center a human-shaped cavity. You flew spread-eagled. *Bas*-hands gripped thruster controls; *sur*-hands armed and aimed the squirt lasers. Dark flapping things Sol had glimpsed once before flocked again at the edges of his consciousness. He had cheated the dark premonitory angels that other time. He would sleight them again.

The first engagement of the battle of St. Judy's Comet was at 01:45 GMT. Solomon Gursky watched it with his crewbrethren in the ice-wrapped warmth of the command womb. His virtualized sight perceived space in three dimensions. Those blue cylinders were the *corporada* ships. That white swarm closing from a hundred different directions, the missiles. One approached a blue cylinder and burst. Another, and another; then the inner display was a glare of novas as the first wave was annihilated. The backup went in. The vanguard exploded in beautiful futile blossoms of light. Closer. They were getting closer before the meat shredded them. Sol watched a warhead loop up from due south, streak toward the point ship, and annihilate it in a red flash.

The St. Judy's Cometeers cheered. One gone, reduced to bubbling slag by tectors sprayed from the warhead.

One was all they got. It was down to the fighter pilots now.

Sol and Elena made love in the count-up to launch. *Bas*-arms and *sur*-arms locked in the freegee of the forward observation blister. Stars described slow arcs across the transparent dome, like a sky. Love did not pass through death; Elena had realized this bitter truth about what she had imagined she had shared with Solomon Gursky in her house on the hillside. But love could grow, and become a thing shaped for eternity. When the fluids had dried on their skins, they sealed their soft, intimate places with vacuum-tight skin and went up to the launch bays.

Sol fitted her into the scooped-out shell. Tectoplastic fingers gripped Elena's body and meshed with her skin circuitry. The angel-suit came alive. There was a trick they had learned in their em-telepathy; a massaging of the limbic system like an inner kiss. One mutual purr of pleasure, then she cast off, suit still dripping gobs of frozen tectopolymer. St. Judy's defenders would fight dark and silent; that mental kiss would be the last radio contact until it was decided. Solomon Gursky watched the blue stutter of the thrusters merge with the stars. Reaction mass was limited; those who returned from the fight would jettison their angel-suits and glide home by solar sail. Then he went below to monitor the battle through the tickle of molecules in his frontal lobes.

St. Judy's Angels formed two squadrons: one flying anti-missile defense, the other climbing high out of the ecliptic to swoop down on the *corporada* ships and destroy them before they could empty their weapon racks. Elena was in the close defense group. Her angelship icon was identified in Sol's inner vision in red on gold tiger stripes of her skin. He watched her weave intricate orbits around St. Judy's Comet as the blue cylinders of the meat approached the plane labeled "strike range."

Suddenly, seven blue icons spawned a cloud of actinic sparks, raining down on St. Judy's Comet like fireworks.

"Jesus Joseph Mary!" someone swore quietly.

"Fifty-five gees," *Capitan* Savita said calmly. "Time to contact, one thousand and eighteen seconds."

"They'll never get them all," said Kobe with the Mondrian skin pattern, who had taken Elena's place in remote sensing.

"We have one hundred and fifteen contacts in the first wave," Jorge announced.

"Sol, I need delta vee," Savita said.

"More than a thousandth of a gravity and the mass driver coils will warp," Sol said, calling overlays onto his visual cortex.

"Anything that throws a curve into their computations," Savita said. "I'll see how close I can push it."

He was glad to have to lose himself in the problems of squeezing a few millimeters per second squared out of the big electromagnetic gun, because then he would not be able to see the curve and swoop of attack vectors and intercept planes as the point defense group closed with the missiles. Especially he would not have to watch the twine and loop of the tiger-striped cross and fear that at any instant it would intersect with a sharp blue curve in a flash of annihilation. One by one, those blue stars were going out, he noticed, but slowly. Too slowly. Too few.

The computer gave him a solution. He fed it to the mass driver. The shift of acceleration was as gentle as a catch of breath.

Thirty years since he had covered his head in a synagogue, but Sol Gursky prayed to Yahweh that it would be enough.

One down already; Emilio's spotted indigo gone, and half the missiles were still on trajectory. Time to impact ticked down impassively in the upper right corner of his virtual vision. Six hundred and fifteen seconds. Ten minutes to live.

But the attack angels were among the *corporadas*, dodging the brilliant flares of short range interceptor drones. The meat fleet tried to scatter, but the ships were low on reaction mass, ungainly, unmaneuverable. St. Judy's Angels dived and sniped among them, clipping a missile rack here, a solar panel there, ripping open life support bubbles and fuel tanks in slow explosions of outgassing hydrogen. The thirteen-year-old pilots died, raging with chemical-induced fury, spilled out into vacuum in tears of flash-frozen acceleration gel. The attacking fleet dwindled from seven to five to three ships. But it was no abattoir of the meat; of the six dead angels that went in, only two pulled away into rendezvous orbit, laser capacitors dead, reaction mass spent. The crews ejected, unfurled their solar sails, shields of light.

Two meat ships survived. One used the last grams of his maneuvering mass to warp into a return orbit; the other routed his thruster fuel through his blip drive; headlong for St. Judy.

"He's going for a ram," Kobe said.

"Sol, get us away from him," *Capitan* Savita ordered.

"He's too close." The numbers in Sol's skull were remorseless. "Even if I cut the mass driver, he can still run life support gas through the STUs to compensate."

The command womb quivered.

"Fuck," someone swore reverently.

"Near miss," Kobe reported. "Direct hit if Sol hadn't given us gees."

"Mass driver is still with us," Sol said.

"Riley's gone," *Capitan* Savita said.

Fifty missiles were now twenty missiles but Emilio and Riley were dead, and the range was closing. Little room for maneuver; none for mistakes.

"Two hundred and fifteen seconds to ship impact," Kobe announced. The main body of missiles was dropping behind St. Judy's Comet. Ogawa and Skin, Mandelbrot set and Dalmatian spots, were fighting a rearguard as the missiles tried to reacquire their target. Olive green ripples and red tiger stripes swung round to face the meat ship. Quinsana and Elena.

Jesus Joseph Mary, but it was going to be close!

Sol wished he did not have the graphics in his head. He wished not to have to see. Better sudden annihilation, blindness and ignorance shattered by destroying light. To see, to *know*, to count the digits on the timer, was as cruel as execution. But the inner vision has no eyelids. So he watched, impotent, as Quinsana's olive green cross was pierced and shattered by a white flare from the meat ship. And he watched as Elena raked the meat with her lasers and cut it into quivering chunks, and the blast of engines destroying themselves sent the shards of ship arcing away from St. Judy's Comet. And he could only watch, and not look away, as Elena turned too slow, too little, too late, as the burst seed-pod of the environment unit tore off her thruster legs and light sail and sent her spinning end over end, crippled, destroyed.

"Elena!" he screamed in both his voices. "Elena! Oh Jesus oh God!" But he had never believed in either of them, and so they let Elena Asado go tumbling endlessly toward the beautiful galaxy clusters of Virgo.

Earth's last rage against her children expired: twenty missiles dwin ed to ten, to five, to one. To none. St. Judy's Comet continued her slow climb out of the sun's gravity well, into the deep dark and the dee er cold. Its five hundred and twenty souls slept sound and ignorant as c ly the dead can in tombs of ice. Soon Solomon Gursky and the others would join them, and be dissolved into the receiving ice, and die for five hundred years while St. Judy's Comet made the crossing to another star.

If it were sleep, then I might forget, Solomon Gursky thought. In sleep, things changed, memories became dreams, dreams memories. In sleep, there was time, and time was change, and perhaps a chance of forgetting the vision of her, spinning outward forever, rebuilt by the same forces that had already resurrected her once, living on sunlight, unable to die. But it was not sleep to which he was going. It was death, and that was nothing any more.

Friday

Together they watched the city burn. It was one of the ornamental cities of the plain that the Long Scanning folk built and maintained for the quadrennial eisteddfods. There was something of the flower in the small, jewellike city, and something of the spiral, and something of the sea-wave. It would have been as accurate to call it a vast building as a miniature city. It burned most elegantly.

The fault line ran right through the middle of it. The fissure was clean and precise—no less to be expected of the Long Scanning folk—and bisected the curvilinear architecture from top to bottom. The land still quivered to aftershocks.

It could have repaired itself. It could have doused the flames—a short in the magma tap, the man reckoned—reshaped the melted ridges and roofs, erased the scorch marks, bridged the cracks and chasms. But its tector systems were directionless, its soul withdrawn to the Heaven Tree, to join the rest of the Long Scanning people on their exodus.

The woman watched the smoke rise into the darkening sky, obscuring the great opal of Urizen.

"It doesn't have to do this," she said. Her skin spoke of sorrow mingled with puzzlement.

"They've no use for it any more," the man said. "And there's a certain beauty in destruction."

"It scares me," the woman said, and her skin pattern agreed. "I've never seen anything *end* before."

Lucky, the man thought, in a language that had come from another world.

An eddy in his weathersight: big one coming. But they were all big ones since the orbital perturbations began. Big, getting bigger. At the end, the storms would tear the forests from their roots as the atmosphere shrieked into space.

That afternoon, on their journey to the man's memories, they had come across an empty marina; drained, sand clogged, pontoons torn and tossed by tsunamis. Its crew of boats they found scattered the length of a half-hour's walk. Empty shells stogged to the waist in dune faces, masts and sails hung from trees.

The weather had been the first thing to tear free from control. The man felt a sudden tautness in the woman's body. She was seeing it to, the mid-game of the end of the world.

By the time they reached the sheltered valley that the man's aura had picked as the safest location to spend the night, the wind had risen to draw soft moans and chords from the curves and crevasses of the dead city. As their cloaks of elementals joined and sank the roots of the night shell into rock, a flock of bubbles bowled past, trembling and iridescent in the gusts. The woman caught one on her hand; the tiny creature-machine clung for a moment, feeding from her biofield. Its transparent skin raced with oil-film colors, it quaked and burst, a melting bubble of tectoplasm. The woman watched it until the elementals had completed the shelter, but the thing stayed dead.

Their love-making was both urgent and chilled under the scalloped carapace the elementals had sculpted from rock silica. *Sex and death*, the man said in the part of his head where not even his sub-vocal withspeech could overhear and transmit. An alien thought.

She wanted to talk afterward. She liked to talk after sex. Unusually, she did not ask him to tell her about how he and the other Five Hundred Fathers had built the world. Her idea of talking was him talking. Tonight she did not want to talk about the world's beginning. She wanted him to talk about its ending.

"Do you know what I hate about it? It's not that it's all going to end, all this. It's that a bubble burst in my hand, and I can't comprehend what *happened* to it. How much more our whole world?"

"There is a word for what you felt," the man interjected gently. The gyrestorm was at its height, raging over the dome of their shell. The thickness of a skin is all that is keeping the wind from stripping the flesh from my bones, he thought. But the tectors' grip on the bedrock was firm and sure. "The word is *die*."

The woman sat with her knees pulled up, arms folded around them. Naked: the gyrestorm was blowing through her soul.

"What I hate," she said after silence, "is that I have so little time to see and feel it all before it's taken away into the cold and the dark."

She was a Green, born in the second of the short year's fast seasons: a Green of the Hidden Design people; first of the Old Red Ridge pueblo people to come into the world in eighty years. And the last.

Eight years old.

"You won't die," the man said, skin patterning in whorls of reassurance and paternal concern, like the swirling storms of great Urizen beyond the hurtling gyrestorm clouds. "You can't die. No one will die."

"I know that. No one will die, we will all be changed, or sleep with the world. But . . ."

"Is it frightening, to have to give up this body?"

She touched her forehead to her knees, shook her head.

"I don't want to lose it. I've only begun to understand what it is, this body, this world, and it's all going to be taken away from me, and all the powers that are my birthright are useless."

"There are forces beyond even nanotechnology," the man said. "It makes us masters of matter, but the fundamental dimensions—gravity, space, time—it cannot touch."

"Why?" the woman said, and to the man, who counted by older, longer years, she spoke in the voice of her terrestrial age.

"We will learn it, in time," the man said, which he knew was no answer. The woman knew it too, for she said, "While Orc is two hundred million years from the warmth of the next sun, and its atmosphere is a frozen glaze on these mountains and valleys." *Grief*, he skin said. *Rage. Loss.*

The two-thousand-year-old father touched the young woman's small, upturned breasts.

"We knew Urizen's orbit was unstable, but no one could have predicted the interaction with Ulro." Ironic: that this world named after Blake's fire daemon should be the one cast into darkness and ice, while Urizen and its surviving moons should bake two million kilometers above the surface of Los.

"Sol, you don't need to apologize to me for mistakes you made two thousand years ago," said the woman, whose name was Lenya.

"But I think I need to apologize to the world," said Sol Gursky.

Lenya's skin-speech now said *hope* shaded with *inevitability*. Her nipples were erect. Sol bent to them again as the wind from the end of the world scratched its claws over the skin of tectoplastic.

In the morning, they continued the journey to Sol's memories. The gyrestorm had blown itself out in the Oothoon mountains. What remained of the ghost-net told Sol and Lenya that it was possible to fly that day. They suckled milch from the shell's tree of life processor, and they had sex again on the dusty earth while the elementals reconfigured the night pod into a general utility flier. For the rest of the morning, they passed over a plain across which grazebeasts and the tall, predatory angularities of the stalking Systems Maintenance people moved like ripples on a lake, drawn to the Heaven Tree planted in the navel of the world.

Both grazers and herders had been human once.

At noon, the man and the woman encountered a flyer of the Generous Sky people, flapping a silk-winged course along the thermal lines rising from the feet of the Big Chrysolite mountains. Sol with-hailed him, and they set down together in a clearing in the bitter-root forests that carpeted much of Coryphee Canton. The Generous Sky man's etiquette would normally have compelled him to disdain those ground bound who sullied the air with machines, but in these urgent times, the old ways were breaking.

Whither bound? Sol withspoke him. Static crackled in his skull. The lingering tail of the gyrestorm was throwing off electromagnetic disturbances.

Why, the Heaven Tree of course, the winged man said. He was a horrifying kite of translucent skin over stick bones and sinews. His breast was like the prow of a ship, his muscles twitched and realigned as he shifted from foot to foot, uncomfortable on the earth. A gentle breeze wafted from the nanofans grown out of the web of skin between wrists and ankles. The air smelled of strange sweat. *Whither yourselves?*

The Heaven Tree also, in time, Sol said. *But I must first recover my memories.*

Ah, a father, the Sky man said. *Whose are you?*

Hidden Design, Sol said. *I am father to this woman and her people.*

You are Solomon Gursky, the flying man withsaid. *My progenitor is Nikos Samitreides.*

I remember her well, though I have not seen her in many years. She fought bravely at the battle of St. Judy's Comet.

I am third of her lineage. Eighteen hundred years I have been on this world.

A question, if I may. Lenya's withspeech was a sudden bright interruption in the dialogue of old men. Using an honorific by which a younger adult addresses an experienced senior, she asked, *When the time comes, how will you change?*

An easy question, the Generous Sky man said, *I shall undergo the reconfiguration for life on Urizen. To me, it is little difference whether I wear the outward semblance of a man, or a jetpowered aerial manta: it is flying, and such flying! Canyons of clouds hundreds of kilometers deep; five thousand kilometer per hour winds; thermals great as continents; mad storms as big as planets! And no land, no base; to be able to fly forever free from the tyranny of Earth. The song cycles we shall compose; eddas that will carry half way around the planet on the jet streams of Urizen!* The Generous Sky man's eyes had closed in rapture. They suddenly opened. His nostrils dilated, sensing an atmospheric change intangible to the others.

Another storm is coming, bigger than the last. I advise you to take shelter within rock, for this will pluck the bitter-roots from the soil.

He spread his wings. The membranes rippled. A tiny hop, and the wind caught him and in an instant carried him up into a thermal. Sol and Lenya watched him glide the tops of the lifting air currents until he was lost in the deep blue sky.

For exercise and the conversation of the way, they walked that afternoon. They followed the migration track of the Rough Trading people through the tieve forests of south Coryphee and Emberwilde Cantons. Toward evening, with the gathering wind stirring the needles of the tieves to gossip, they met a man of the Ash species sitting on a chair in a small clearing among the trees. He was long and coiling, and his skin said that he was much impoverished from lack of a host. Lenya offered her arm, and though the Ash man's compatibility was more with the Buried Communication people than the Hidden Design, he gracefully accepted her heat, her morphic energy, and a few drops of blood.

"Where is your host?" Lenya asked him. A parasite, he had the languages of most nations. Hosts were best seduced by words, like lovers.

"He has gone with the herds," the Ash man said. "To the Heaven Tree. It is ended."

"And what will you do when Orc is expelled?" The rasp marks on Lenya's forearm where the parasitic man had sipped her blood were already healing over.

"I cannot live alone," the Ash man said. "I shall ask the earth to open and swallow me and kill me. I shall sleep in the earth until the warmth of a new sun awakens me to life again."

"But that will be two hundred million years," Lenya said. The Ash man looked at her with the look that said, *one year, one million years, one hundred million years, they are nothing to death.* Because she knew that the man thought her a new-hatched fool, Lenya felt compelled to look back at him as she and Sol walked away along the tieve tracks. She saw the parasite pressed belly and balls to the ground, as he would to a host. Dust spiraled up around him. He slowly sank into the earth.

Sol and Lenya did not have sex that night in the pod for the first time since Solomon the Traveler had come to the Old Red Ridge pueblo and taken the eye and heart of the brown girl dancing in the ring. That night there was the greatest earthquake yet as Orc kicked in his orbit, and even a shell of tectodiamond seemed inadequate protection against forces that would throw a planet into interstellar space. They held each other, not speaking, until the earth grew quiet and a wave of heat passed over the carapace, which was the tieve forests of Emberwilde Canton burning.

The next morning, they morphed the pod into an ash-runner and drove through the cindered forest, until at noon they came to the edge of the Inland Sea. The tectonic trauma had sent tidal waves swamping the craggy islet on which Sol had left his memories, but the self-repair systems had used the dregs of their stored power to rebuild the damaged architecture.

As Sol was particular that they must approach his memories by sea, they ordered the ash-runner to reconfigure into a skiff. While the tectors moved molecules, a man of the Blue Mana pulled himself out of the big surf on to the red shingle. He was long and huge and sleek; his shorn turf of fur was beautifully marked. He lay panting from the exertion of heaving himself from his customary element into an alien one. Lenya addressed him familiarly—Hidden Design and the amphibious Blue Mana had been one until a millennium ago—and asked him the same question she had put to the others she had encountered on the journey.

"I am already reconfiguring my body fat into an aircraft to take me to the Heaven Tree," the Blue Mana said. "Climatic shifts permitting."

"Is it bad in the sea?" Sol Gursky asked.

"The seas feel the changes first," the amphiman said. "Bad. Yes, most bad. I cannot bear the thought of Mother Ocean freezing clear to her beds."

"Will you go to Urizen, then?" Lenya asked, thinking that swimming must be much akin to flying.

"Why, bless you, no." The Blue Mana man's skin spelled puzzled surprise. "Why should I share any less fate than Mother Ocean? We shall both end in ice."

"The comet fleet," Sol Gursky said.

"If the Earth ship left any legacy, it is that there are many mansions in this universe where we may live. I have a fancy to visit those other settled systems that the ship told us of, experience those others ways of being human."

A hundred Orc-years had passed since the second comet-ship from Earth had entered the Los system to refuel from Urizen's rings, but the news it had carried of a home system transfigured by the nanotechnology of the ascendant dead, and of the other stars that had been reached by the newer, faster, more powerful descendants of St. Judy's Comet had ended nineteen hundred years of solitude and brought the first, lost colony of Orc into the visionary community of the star-crossing Dead. *Long before your emergence*, Sol thought, looking at the crease of Lenya's groin as she squatted on the pebbles to converse with the Blue Mana man. Emergence. A deeper, older word shadowed that expression; a word obsolete in the universe of the dead. *Birth.* No one had ever been born on Orc. No one had ever known childhood, or grown up. No one aged, no one died. They *emerged.* They stepped from the labia of the gestatory, fully formed, like gods.

Sol knew the word *child*, but realized with a shock that he could not see it any more. It was blank, void. So many things decreated in this world he had engineered!

By sea and by air. A trading of elements. Sol Gursky's skiff was completed as the Blue Mana's tectors transformed his blubber into a flying machine. Sol watched it spin into the air and recede to the south as the boat dipped through the chop toward the island of memory.

We live forever, we transform ourselves, we transform worlds, solar systems, we ship across interstellar space, we defy time and deny death, but the one thing we cannot re-create is memory, he thought. Sea birds dipped in the skiff's wake, hungry, hoping. Things cast up by motion. We cannot rebuild our memories, so we must store them, when our lives grow so full that they slop over the sides and evaporate. We Five Hundred Fathers have deep and much-emptied memories.

Sol's island was a rock slab tilted out of the equatorial sea, a handful of hard hectares. Twisted repro olives and cypresses screened a small Doric temple at the highest point. Good maintenance tectors had held it strong against the Earth storms. The classical theming now embarrassed Sol, but enchanted Lenya. She danced beneath the olive branches, under the porticoes, across the lintels. Sol saw her again as he had that first night in the Small-year-ending ring dance at Old Red Ridge. Old lust. New hurt.

In the sunlit central chamber, Lenya touched the reliefs of the life of Solomon Gursky. They would not yield their memories to her fingers, but they communicated in less sophisticated ways.

"This woman." She had stopped in front of a pale stone carving of Solomon Gursky and a tall, ascetic-faced woman with close-cropped hair standing hand in hand before a tall, ghastly tower.

"I loved her. She died in the battle of St. Judy's Comet. Big dead."

◆

Lost.

"So is it only because I remind you of her?"

He touched the carving. Memory bright and sharp as pain arced along his nerves; mnemotectors downloading into his aura. *Elena.* And a memory of orbit; the Long March ended, the object formerly known as St. Judy's Comet spun out into a web of beams and girders and habitations pods hurtling across the frosted red dustscapes of Orc. A web ripe with hanging fruit; entry pods ready to drop and spray the new world with life seed. Tectoforming. Among the fruit, seeds of the Five Hundred Fathers, founders of all the races of Orc. Among them, the Hidden Design and Solomon Gursky, four-armed, vacuum-proofed, avatar of life and death, clinging to a beam with the storms of Urizen behind him, touching his transforming *sur*-arms to the main memory of the mother seed. Remember her. Remember Elena. And sometime—soon, late—bring her back. Imprint her with an affinity for his scent, so that wherever she is, whoever she is with, she will come to me.

He saw himself scuttling like a guilty spider across the web as the pods dropped Orc-ward.

He saw himself in this place with Urizen's moons at syzygy, touching his hands to the carving, giving to it what it now returned to him, because he knew that as long as it was Lenya who reminded him of Elena, it could pretend to be honest. But the knowledge killed it. Lenya was more than a reminder. Lenya as Elena. Lenya was a simulacrum, empty, fake. Her life, her joy, her sorrow, her love—all deceit.

He had never expected that she would come back to him at the end of the world. They should have had thousands of years. The world gave them days.

He could not look at her as he moved from relief to relief, charging his aura with memory. He could not touch her as they waited on the shingle for the skiff to reconfigure into the flyer that would take them to the Heaven Tree. On the high point of the slab island, the Temple of Memory dissolved like rotting fungus. He did not attempt sex with her as the flyer passed over the shattered landscapes of Thel and the burned forests of Chrysoberyl as they would have, before. She did not understand. She imagined she had hurt him somehow. She had, but the blame was Sol's. He could not tell her why he had suddenly expelled himself from her warmth. He knew that he should, that he must, but he could not. He changed his skin-speech to passive, mute, and reflected that much cowardice could be learned in five hundred long-years.

They came with the evening to the Skyplain plateau from which the Heaven Tree rose, an adamantine black ray aimed at the eye of Urizen. As far as they could see, the plain twinkled with the lights and fires of vehicles and camps. Warmsight showed a million glowings: all the peoples of Orc, save those who had chosen to go into the earth, had gathered in this final redoubt. Seismic stabilizing tectors woven into the moho held steady the quakes that had shattered all other lands, but temblors of increasing violence warned that they could not endure much longer. At the end, Skyplain would crack like an egg, the Heaven Tree snap and recoil spaceward like a severed nerve.

Sol's Five Hundred Father ident pulled his flyer out of the wheel of aircraft, airships, and aerial humans circling the stalk of the Heaven Tree into a priority slot on an ascender. The flyer caught the shuttle at five kilometers: a sudden veer toward the slab sides of the space elevator, guidance matching velocities with the accelerating ascender; then the drop, heart-stopping even for immortals, and the lurch as the flyer seized the docking nipple with its claspers and clung like a tick. Then the long climb heavenward.

Emerging from high altitude cloud, Sol saw the hard white diamond of Ulro rise above the curve of the world. Too small yet to show a disc, but this barren rock searing under heavy CO_2 exerted forced powerful enough to kick a moon into interstellar space. Looking up through the transparent canopy, he saw the Heaven Tree spread its delicate, light-studded branches hundreds of kilometers across the face of Urizen.

Sol Gursky broke his silence.

"Do you know what you'll do yet?"

"Well, since I am here, I am not going into the ground. And the ice fleet scares me. I think of centuries dead, a tector frozen in ice. It seems like death."

"It is death," Sol said. "Then you'll go to Urizen."

"It's a change of outward form, that's all. Another way of being human. And there'll be continuity; that's important to me."

He imagined the arrival: the ever-strengthening tug of gravity spiraling the flocks of vacuum-hardened carapaces inward; the flickers of with-speech between them, anticipation, excitement, fear as they grazed the edge of the atmosphere and felt ion flames lick their diamond skins. Lenya, falling, burning with the fires of entry as she cut a glowing trail across half a planet. The heat-shell breaking away as she unfurled her wings in the eternal shriek of wind and the ram-jets in her sterile womb kindled and roared.

"And you?" she asked. Her skin said *gentle*. Confused as much by his breaking of it as by his silence, but *gentle*.

"I have something planned," was all he said, but because that plan meant they would never meet again, he told her then what he had learned in the Temple of Memory. He tried to be kind and understanding, but it was still a bastard thing to do, and she cried in the nest in the rear of the flyer all the way out of the atmosphere, half-way to heaven. It was a bastard thing and as he watched the stars brighten beyond the canopy, he could not say why he had done it, except that it was necessary to kill some things Big Dead so that they could never come back again. She cried now, and her skin was so dark it would not speak to him, but when she flew, it would be without any lingering love or regret for a man called Solomon Gursky.

It is good to be hated, he thought, as the Heaven Tree took him up into its starlit branches.

☞

The launch laser was off, the reaction mass tanks were dry. Solomon Gursky fell outward from the sun. Urizen and its children were far beneath him. His course lay out of the ecliptic, flying north. His aft eyes made out a new pale ring orbiting the gas world, glowing in the low warmsight: the millions of adapted waiting in orbit for their turns to make the searing descent into a new life.

She would be with them now. He had watched her go into the seed and be taken apart by her own elementals. He had watched the seed split and expel her into space, transformed, and burn her few kilos of reaction mass on the transfer orbit to Urizen.

Only then had he felt free to undergo his own transfiguration.

Life swarm. Mighty. So nearly right, so utterly wrong. She had almost sung when she spoke of the freedom of endless flight in the clouds of Urizen, but she would never fly freer than she did now, naked to space, the galaxy before her. The freedom of Urizen was a lie, the price exacted by its gravity and pressure. She had trapped herself in atmosphere and gravity. Urizen was another world. The parasitic man of the Ash nation had buried himself in a world. The aquatic Blue Mana, after long sleep in ice, would only give rise to another copy of the standard model. Worlds upon worlds.

Infinite ways of being human, Solomon Gursky thought, outbound from the sun. He could feel the gentle stroke of the solar wind over the harsh dermal prickle of Urizen's magnetosphere. Sun arising. Almost time.

Many ways of being Solomon Gursky, he thought, contemplating his new body. His analogy was with a conifer. He was a redwood cone fallen from the Heaven Tree, ripe with seeds. Each seed a Solomon Gursky, a world in embryo.

The touch of the sun, that was what had opened those seed cones on that other world, long ago. Timing was too important to be left to higher cognitions. Subsystems had all the launch vectors programmed; he merely registered the growing strength of the wind from Los on his skin and felt himself begin to open. Solomon Gursky unfolded into a thousand scales. As the seeds exploded onto their preset courses, he burned to the highest orgasm of his memory before his persona downloaded into the final spore and ejected from the empty, dead carrier body.

At five hundred kilometers, the seeds unfurled their solar sails. The breaking wave of particles, with multiple gravity assists from Luvah and Enitharmon, would surf the bright flotilla up to interstellar velocities, as, at the end of the centuries—millennia—long flights, the light-sails would brake the packages at their destinations.

He did not know what his many selves would find there. He had not picked targets for their resemblance to what he was leaving behind. That would be just another trap. He sensed his brothers shutting down their cognitive centers for the big sleep, like stars going out, one by one. A handful of seeds scattered, some to wither, some to grow. Who can say what he will find, except that it will be extraordinary. Surprise me! Solomon Gursky demanded of the universe, as he fell into the darkness between suns.

Saturday

The object was one point three astronomical units on a side, and at its current 10 percent C would arrive in thirty-five hours. On his chaise lounge by the Neptune fountain, Solomon Gursky finally settled on a name for the thing. He had given much thought, over many high-hours and in many languages, most of them nonverbal, to what he should call the looming object. The name that pleased him most was in a language dead (he assumed) for thirty million years. Aea. Acronym: Alien Enigmatic Artifact. Enigmatic Alien Artifact would have been more correct but the long dead language did not handle diphthongs well.

Shadows fell over the gardens of Versailles, huge and soft as clouds. A forest was crossing the sun; a small one, little more than a copse, he thought, still finding delight in the notions that could be expressed in this dead language. He watched the spherical trees pass overhead, each a kilometer across (another archaism), enjoying the pleasurable play of shade and warmth on his skin. Sensual joys of incarnation.

As ever when the forests migrated along the Bauble's jet streams, a frenzy of siphons squabbled in their wake, voraciously feeding off the stew of bacteria and complex fullerenes.

Solomon Gursky darkened his eyes against the hard glare of the dwarf white sun. From Versailles' perspective in the equatorial plane, the Spirit Ring was a barely discernible filigree necklace draped around its primary. Perspective. Am I the emanation of it, or is it the emanation of me?

Perspective: you worry about such things with a skeletal tetrahedron one point three astronomical units on a side fast approaching?

Of course. I am some kind of human.

"Show me," Solomon Gursky said. Sensing his intent, for Versailles was part of his intent, as everything that lived and moved within the Bauble was his intent, the disc of tectofactured baroque France began to tilt away from the sun. The sollilies on which Versailles and its gardens rested generated their own gravity fields; Solomon Gursky saw the tiny, bright sun seem to curve down behind the Petit Trianon, and thought, *I have reinvented sunset*. And, as the dark vault above him lit with stars, *Night is looking out from the shadow of myself.*

The stars slowed and locked over the chimneys of Versailles. Sol had hoped to be able to see the object with the unaided eye, but in low-time he had forgotten the limitations of the primeval human form. A grimace of irritation, and it was the work of moments for the tectors to reconfigure his vision. Successive magnifications clicked up until ghostly, twinkling threads of light resolved out of the star field, like the drawings of gods and myths the ancients had laid on the comfortable heavens around the Alpha Point.

Another click and the thing materialized.

Solomon Gursky's breath caught.

Midway between the micro and the macro, it was humanity's natural condition that a man standing looking out into the dark should feel dwarfed. That need to assert one's individuality to the bigness underlies all humanity's outward endeavors. But the catch in the breath is more than doubled when a *star* seems dwarfed. Through the Spirit Ring, Sol had the dimensions, the masses, the vectors. The whole of the Bauble could be easily contained within Aea's vertices. A cabalistic sign. A cosmic eye in the pyramid.

A chill contraction in the man Solomon Gursky's loins. How many million years since he had last felt his balls tighten with fear?

One point three AU's on a side. Eight sextillion tons of matter. Point one C. The thing should have heralded itself over most of the cluster. Even in low-time, he should have had more time to prepare. But there had been no warning. At once, it *was:* a fading hexagram of gravitometric disturbances on his out-system sensors. Sol had reacted at once, but in those few seconds of stretched low-time that it took to conceive and create this Louis Quattorze conceit, the object had covered two-thirds of the distance from its emergence point. The high-time of created things gave him perspective.

Bear you grapes or poison? Solomon Gursky asked the thing in the sky. It had not spoken, it had remained silent through all attempts to communicate with it, but it surely bore *some* gift. The manner of its arrival had only one explanation: the thing manipulated worm-holes. None of the civilization/citizens of the Reach—most of the western hemisphere of the galaxy—had evolved a nanotechnology that could reconfigure the continuum itself.

None of the civilization/citizens of the Reach, and those federations of world-societies it fringed, had ever encountered a species that could not be sourced to the Alpha Point: that semi-legendary racial big bang from which PanHumanity had exploded into the universe.

Four hundred billion stars in this galaxy alone, Solomon Gursky thought. We have not seeded even half of them. The trick we play with time, slowing our perceptions until our light-speed communications seem instantaneous and the journeys of our C-fractional ships are no longer than the sea-voyages of this era I have reconstructed, seduce us into believing that the universe is as close and companionable as a lover's body, and as familiar. The five million years between the MonoHumanity of the Alpha Point and the PanHumanity of the Great Leap Outward, is a catch of breath, a contemplative pause in our conversation with ourselves. Thirty million years I have evolved the web of life in this unique system: there is abundant time and space for true aliens to have caught us up, to have already surpassed us.

Again, that tightening of the scrotum. Sol Gursky willed Versailles back toward the eye of the sun, but intellectual chill had invaded his soul. The orchestra of Lully made fete *galante* in the Hall of Mirrors for his pleasure, but the sound in his head of the destroying, rushing alien mass shrieked louder. As the solar parasol slipped between Versailles and the sun and he settled in twilight among the soft, powdered breasts of the ladies of the bed-chamber, he knew fear for the first time in thirty million years.

And he dreamed. The dream took the shape of a memory, recontextualized, reconfigured, resurrected. He dreamed that he was a starship wakened from fifty thousand years of death by the warmth of a new sun on his solar sail. He dreamed that in the vast sleep the star toward which he had aimed himself spastically novaed. It kicked off its photosphere in a nebula of radiant gas but the explosion was underpowered; the carbon/ hydrogen/nitrogen/oxygen plasma was drawn by gravity into a bubble of hydrocarbons around the star. An aura. A bright bauble. In Solomon Gursky's dream, an angel floated effortlessly on tectoplastic wings hundreds of kilometers wide, banking and soaring on the chemical thermals, sowing seeds from its long, trailing fingertips. For a hundred years, the angle swam around the sun, sowing, nurturing, tending the strange shoots that grew from its fingers; things half-living, half-machine.

Asleep among the powdered breasts of court women, Sol Gursky turned and murmured the word, "evolution."

Solomon Gursky would only be a God he could believe in: the philosophers' God, creator but not sustainer, ineffable; too street-smart to poke its omnipotence into the smelly stuff of living. He saw his free-fall trees of green, the vast red rafts of the wind-reefs rippling in the solar breezes. He saw the blimps and medusas, the unresting open maws of the air-plankton feeders, the needle-thin jet-powered darts of the harpoon hunters. He saw an ecology spin itself out of gas and energy in thirty million yearless years, he saw intelligence flourish and seed itself to the stars, and fade into senescence; all in the blink of a low-time eye.

"Evolution," he muttered again and the constructed women who did not understand sleep looked at each other.

In the unfolding dream, Sol Gursky saw the Spirit Ring and the ships that came and went between the nearer systems. He heard the subaural babble of interstellar chatter, like conspirators in another room. He beheld this blur of life, evolving, transmuting, and he knew that it was very good. He said to himself, *what a wonderful world*, and feared for it.

He awoke. It was morning, as it always was in Sol's Bauble. He worked off his testosterone high and tipped Versailles's darkside to look at the shadow of his nightmares. Any afterglow of libido was immediately extinguished. At eighteen light-hours distance, the astronomical dimensions assumed emotional force. A ribbon of mottled blue-green ran down the inner surface of each of Aea's six legs. Amplified vision resolved forested continents and oceans beneath fractal cloud curls. Each ribbon-world was the width of two Alpha Points peeled and ironed, stretched one point three astronomical units long. Sol Gursky was glad that this incarnation could not instantly access how many million planets' surfaces that equaled; how many hundreds of thousands of years it would take to walk from one vertex to another, and then to find, dumbfounded like the ancient conquistadors beholding a new ocean, another millennia-deep world in front of him.

Solomon Gursky turned Versailles toward the sun. He squinted through the haze of the Bauble for the delicate strands of the Spirit Ring. A beat of his mind shifted his perceptions back into low-time, the only time frame in which he could withspeak to the Spirit Ring, his originating self. Self-reference, self-confession.

No communication?

None, spoke the Spirit Ring.

Is it alien? Should I be afraid? Should I destroy the Bauble?

In another time, such schizophrenia would have been disease.

Can it annihilate you?

In answer, Sol envisioned the great tetrahedron at the bracelet of information tectors orbiting the sun.

Then that is nothing, the Spirit Ring withsaid. *And nothing is nothing to fear. Can it cause you pain or humiliation, or anguish to body or soul?*

Again, Sol withspoke an image, of cloud-shaded lands raised over each other like the pillars of Yahweh, emotionally shaded to suggest amazement that such an investment of matter and thought should have been created purely to humiliate Solomon Gursky.

Then that too is settled. And whether it is alien, can it be any more alien to you than you yourself are to what you once were? All PanHumanity is alien to itself; therefore, we have nothing to fear. We shall welcome our visitor, we have many questions for it.

Not the least being, *why me?* Solomon Gursky thought privately, silently, in the dome of his own skull. He shifted out of the low-time of the Spirit Ring to find that in those few subjective moments of communication Aea had passed the threshold of the Bauble. The leading edge of the tetrahedron was three hours away. An hour and half beyond that was the hub of Aea.

"Since it seems that we can neither prevent nor hasten the object's arrival, nor guess its purposes until it deigns to communicate with us," Sol Gursky told his women of the bedchamber, "therefore let us party." Which they did, before the Mirror Pond, as Lully's orchestra played and capons roasted over charcoal pits, and torch-lit harlequins capered and fought out the ancient loves and comedies, and women splashed naked in the Triton Fountain, and fantastic lands one hundred million kilometers long slid past them. Aea advanced until Sol's star was at its center, then stopped. Abruptly, instantly. A small gravitational shiver troubled Versailles, the orchestra missed a note, a juggler dropped a club, the water in the fountain wavered, women shrieked, a capon fell from a spit into the fire. That was all. The control of mass, momentum, and gravity was absolute.

The orchestra leader looked at Solomon Gursky, staff raised to resume the beat. Sol Gursky did not raise the handkerchief. The closest section of Aea was fifteen degrees east, two hundred thousand kilometers out. To Sol Gursky, it was two fingers of sun-lit land, tapering infinitesimally at either end to threads of light. He looked up at the apex, two other brilliant threads spun down beneath the horizon, one behind the Petit Trianon, the other below the roof of the Chapel Royal.

The conductor was still waiting. Instruments pressed to faces, the musicians watched for the cue.

Peacocks shrieked on the lawn. Sol Gursky remembered how irritating the voices of peacocks were, and wished he had not re-created them.

Sol Gursky waved the handkerchief.

A column of white light blazed out of the gravel walk at the top of the steps. The air was a seethe of glowing motes.

An attempt is being made to communicate with us, the Spirit Ring said in a flicker of low-time. Sol Gursky felt information from the Ring crammed into his cerebral cortex: the beam originated from a source of the rim section of the closest section of the artifact. The tectors that created and sustained the Bauble were being reprogrammed. At hyper-velocities, they were manufacturing a construct out of the Earth of Versailles.

The pillar of light dissipated. A human figure stood at the top of the steps: a white Alpha Point male, dressed in Louis XIV style. The man descended the steps into the light of the flambeau bearers. Sol Gursky looked on his face.

Sol Gursky burst into laughter.

"You are very welcome," he said to his doppelgänger. "Will you join us? The capons will be ready shortly, we can bring you the finest wines available to humanity, and I'm sure the waters of the fountains would be most refreshing to one who has traveled so long and so far."

"Thank you," Solomon Gursky said in Solomon Gursky's voice. "It's good to find a hospitable reception after a strange journey."

Sol Gursky nodded to the conductor, who raised his staff, and the *petite bande* resumed their interrupted gavotte.

Later, on a stone bench by the lake, Sol Gursky said to his doppel, "Your politeness is appreciated, but it really wasn't necessary for you to don my shape. All this is as much a construction as you are."

"Why do you think it's a politeness?" the construct said.

"Why should you choose to wear the shape of Solomon Gursky?"

"Why should I not, if it is my *own* shape?"

Nereids splashed in the pool, breaking the long reflections of Aea.

"I often wonder how far I reach," Sol said.

"Further than you can imagine," Sol II answered. The playing Nereids dived; ripples spread across the pond. The visitor watched the wavelets lap against the stone rim and interfere with each other. "There are others out there, others we never imagined, moving through the dark, very slowly, very silently. I think they may be older than us. They are different from us, very different, and we have now come to the complex plane where our expansions meet."

"There was a strong probability that they—you—were an alien artifact."

"I am, and I'm not. I am fully Solomon Gursky, and fully Other. That's the purpose behind this artifact; that we have reached a point where we either compete, destructively, or join."

"Seemed a long way to come just for a family reunion," Solomon Gursky joked. He saw that the doppel laughed, and how it laughed, and why it laughed. He got up from the stone rim of the Nereid pool. "Come with me, talk to me, we have thirty million years of catching up."

His brother fell in at his side as they walked away from the still water toward the Aea-lit woods.

His story: he had fallen longer than any other seed cast off by the death of Orc. Eight hundred thousand years between wakings, and as he felt the warmth of a new sun seduce his tector systems to the work of transformation, his sensors reported that his was not the sole presence in the system. The brown dwarf toward which he decelerated was being dismantled and converted into an englobement of space habitats.

"Their technology is similar to ours—I think it must be a universal inevitability—but they broke the ties that still bind us to planets long ago," Sol II said. The woods of Versailles were momentarily darkened as a sky-reef eclipsed Aea. "This is why I think they are older than us: I have never seen their original form—they have no tie to it, we still do; I suspect they no longer remember it. It wasn't until we fully merged that I was certain that they were not another variant of humanity."

A hand-cranked wooden carousel stood in a small clearing. The faces of the painted horses were fierce and pathetic in the sky light. Wooden rings hung from iron gibbets around the rim of the carousel; the wooden lances with which the knights hooked down their favors had been gathered in and locked in a closet in the middle of the merry-go-round.

"We endure forever, we engender races, nations, whole ecologies, but we are sterile," the second Sol said. "We inbreed with ourselves. There is no union of disparities, no coming together, no hybrid energy. With the Others, it was sex. Intercourse. Out of the fusion of ideas and visions and capabilities, we birthed what you see."

The first Sol Gursky laid his hand on the neck of a painted horse. The carousel was well balanced, the slightest pressure set it turning.

"Why are you here, Sol?" he asked.

"We shared technologies, we learned how to engineer on the quantum level so that field effects can be applied on macroscopic scales. Manipulation of gravity and inertia; non-locality; we can engineer and control quantum worm-holes."

"Why have you come, Sol?"

"Engineering of alternative time streams; designing and colonizing multiple worlds, hyperspace and hyperdimensional processors. There are more universes than this one for us to explore."

The wooden horse stopped.

"What do you want, Sol?"

"Join us," said the other Solomon Gursky. "You always had the vision—*we* always had the vision, we Solomon Gurskys. Humanity expanding into every possible ecological niche."

"Absorption," Solomon Gursky said. "Assimilation."

"Unity," said his brother. "Marriage. *Love.* Nothing is lost, everything is gained. All you have created here will be stored; that is what I am, a machine for remembering. It's not annihilation, Sol, don't fear it; it's not your self-hood dissolving into some identityless collective. It *is* you, plus. It is life, cubed. And ultimately, we are one seed, you and I, unnaturally separated. We gain each other."

If nothing is lost, then you remember what I am remembering, Solomon Gursky I thought. I am remembering a face forgotten for over thirty million years: Rabbi Bertelsmann. A fat, fair, pleasant face. He is talking to his Bar Mitzvah class about God and masturbation. He is saying that God condemned Onan not for the pleasure of his vice, but because he spilled his seed on the ground. He was fruitless, sterile. He kept the gift of life to himself. And I am now God in my own world, and Rabbi B is smiling and saying, masturbation, Sol. It is all just one big jerk-off, seed spilled on the ground, engendering nothing. Pure re-creation; re-creating yourself endlessly into the future.

He looked at his twin.

"Rabbi Bertelsmann?" Sol Gursky II said.

"Yes," Sol Gursky I said; then, emphatically, certainly, "Yes!"

Solomon Gursky II's smile dissolved into motes of light.

All at once, the outer edges of the great tetrahedron kindled with ten million points of diamond light. Sol watched the white beams sweep through the Bauble and understood what it meant, that they could manipulate time and space. Even at light-speed, Aea was too huge for each such simultaneity.

Air trees, sky reefs, harpooners, siphons, blimps, zeps, cloud sharks: everything touched by the moving beams was analyzed, comprehended, stored. Recording angels, Sol Gursky thought, as the silver knives dissected his world. He saw the Spirit Ring unravel like coils of DNA as a billion days of Solomon Gursky flooded up the ladder of light into Aea. The center no longer held; the gravitational forces the Spirit Ring had controlled, that had maintained the ecosphere of the Bauble, were failing. Sol's world was dying. He felt pain, no sorrow, no regret, but rather a savage joy, an urgent desire to be up and on and out, to be free of this great weight of life and gravity. It is not dying, he thought. Nothing ever dies.

He looked up. An angel-beam scored a searing arc across the rooftops of Versailles. He opened his arms to it and was taken apart by the light. Everything is held and re-created in the mind of God. Unremembered by the mind of Solomon Gursky, Versailles disintegrated into swarms of free-flying tectors.

The end came quickly. The angels reached into the photosphere of the star and the complex quasi-information machines that worked there. The sun grew restless, woken from its long quietude. The Spirit Ring collapsed. Fragments spun end-over-end through the Bauble, tearing spectacularly through the dying sky-reefs, shattering cloud forests, blazing in brief glory in funeral orbits around the swelling sun.

For the sun was dying. Plagues of sunspots pocked its chromosphere; solar storms raced from pole to pole in million-kilometer tsunamis. Panicked hunter packs kindled and died in the solar protuberances hurled off as the photosphere prominenced to the very edge of the Bauble. The sun bulged and swelled like a painfully infected pregnancy: Aea was manipulating fundamental forces, loosening the bonds of gravity that held the system together. At the end, it would require all the energies of star-death to power the quantum worm-hole processors.

The star was now a screaming saucer of gas. No living thing remained in the Bauble. All was held in the mind of Aea.

The star burst. The energies of the nova should have boiled Aea's oceans, seared its lands from their beds. It should have twisted and snapped the long, thin arms like yarrow stalks, sent the artifact tumbling like a smashed Fabergé egg through space. But Aea had woven its defenses strong: gravity fields warped the electromagnetic radiation around the fragile terrains; the quantum processors devoured the storm of charged particles, and reconfigured space, time, mass.

The four corners of Aea burned brighter than the dying sun for an instant. And it was gone; under space and time, to worlds and adventures and experiences beyond all saying.

Sunday

Toward the end of the universe, Solomon Gursky's thoughts turned increasingly to lost loves.

Had it been entirely physical, Ua would have been the largest object in the universe. Only its fronds, the twenty-light-year-long stalactites that grew into the ylem, tapping the energies of decreation, had any material element. Most of Ua, ninety-nine followed by several volumes of decimal nines percent of its structure, was folded through eleven-space. It was the largest object in the universe in that its fifth and sixth dimensional forms contained the inchoate energy flux known as the universe. Its higher dimensions contained only itself, several times over. It was infundibular. It was vast, it contained multitudes.

PanLife, that amorphous, multi-faceted cosmic infection of human, transhuman, non-human, PanHuman sentiences, had filled the universe long before the continuum reached its elastic limit and began to contract under the weight of dark matter and heavy neutrinos. Femtotech, hand in hand with the worm-hole jump, spread PanLife across the galactic super-clusters in a blink of God's eye.

There was no humanity, no alien. No us, no other. There was only *life*. The dead had become life. Life had become Ua: Pan-spermia. Ua woke to consciousness, and like Alexander the Great, despaired when it had no new worlds to conquer. The universe had grown old in Ua's gestation; it had withered, it contracted, it drew in on itself. The red shift of galaxies had turned blue. And Ua, which owned the attributes, abilities, ambitions, everything except the name and pettinesses of a god, found itself, like an old, long-dead God from a world slagged by its expanding sun millions of years ago, in the business of resurrection.

The galaxies raced together, gravitational forces tearing them into loops and whorls of severed stars. The massive black holes at the galactic centers, fueled by billennia of star-death, coalesced and merged into monstrosities that swallowed globular clusters whole, that shredded galaxies and drew then spiraling inward until, at the edge of the Schwartzchild radii, they radiated super-hard gamma. Long since woven into higher dimensions, Ua fed from the colossal power of the accretion discs, recording in multidimensional matrices the lives of the trillions of sentient organisms fleeing up its fronds from the destruction. All things are held in the mind of God: at the end, when the universal background radiation rose asymptotically to the energy density of the first seconds of the Big Bang, it would deliver enough power for the femtoprocessors woven through the Eleven Heavens to rebuild the universe, entire. A new heaven, and a new Earth.

In the trans-temporal matrices of Ua, PanLife flowed across dimensions, dripping from the tips of the fronds into bodies sculpted to thrive in the plasma flux of ragnarok. Tourists to the end of the world: most wore the shapes of winged creatures of fire, thousands of kilometers across. Starbirds. Firebirds. But the being formerly known as Solomon Gursky had chosen a different form, an archaism from that long-vanished planet. It pleased him to be a thousand-kilometer, diamond-skinned Statue of Liberty, torch out-held, beaming a way through the torrents of star-stuff. Sol Gursky flashed between flocks of glowing soul-birds clustering in the information-rich environment around the frond-tips. He felt their curiosity, their appreciation, their consternation at his nonconformity; none got the joke.

Lost loves. So many lives, so many worlds, so many shapes and bodies, so many loves. They had been wrong, those ones back at the start, who had said that love did not survive death. He had been wrong. It was eternity that killed love. Love was a thing measured by human lifetimes. Immortality gave it time enough, and space, to change, to become things more than love, or dangerously other. None endured. None would endure. Immortality was endless change.

Toward the end of the universe, Solomon Gursky realized that what made love live forever was death.

All things were held in Ua, awaiting resurrection when time, space, and energy fused and ceased to be. Most painful among Sol's stored memories was the remembrance of a red-yellow tiger-striped angel fighter, half-crucified, crippled, tumbling toward the star clouds of Virgo. Sol had searched the trillions of souls roosting in Ua for Elena; failing, he hunted for any that might have touched her, hold some memory of her. He found none. As the universe contracted—as fast and inevitable as a long-forgotten season in the ultra-low time of Ua—Sol Gursky entertained hopes that the universal gathering would draw her in. Cruel truths pecked at his perceptions: calculations of molecular deliquescence, abrasion by interstellar dust clouds, probabilities of stellar impacts, the slow terminal whine of proton decay; any of which denied that Elena could still exist. Sol refused those truths. A thousand-kilometer Statue of Liberty searched the dwindling cosmos for one glimpse of red-yellow tiger-stripes embedded in a feather of fractal plasma flame.

And now a glow of recognition had impinged on his senses laced through the Eleven Heavens.

Her. It had to be her.

Sol Gursky flew to an eye of gravitational stability in the flux and activated the worm-hole nodes seeded throughout his diamond skin. Space opened and folded like an exercise in origami. Sol Gursky went elsewhere.

The starbird grazed the energy-dense borderlands of the central accretion disc. It was immense. Sol's Statue of Liberty was a frond of one of its thousand flight feathers, but it sensed him, welcomed him, folded its wings around him as it drew him to the shifting pattern of sun-spots that was the soul of its being.

He knew these patterns. He remembered these emotional flavors. He recalled this love. He tried to perceive if it were her, her journeys, her trials, her experiences, her agonies, her vastenings.

Would she forgive him?

The soul spots opened. Solomon Gursky was drawn inside. Clouds of tectors interpenetrated, exchanging, sharing, recording. Intellectual intercourse.

He entered her adventures among alien species five times older than PanHumanity, an alliance of wills and powers waking a galaxy to life. In an earlier incarnation, he walked the worlds she had become, passed through the dynasties and races and species she had propagated. He made with her the long crossings between stars and clusters, clusters and galaxies. Earlier still, and he swam with her through the cloud canyons of a gas giant world called Urizen, and when that world was hugged too warmly by its sun, changed mode with her, embarked with her on the search for new places to live.

In the nakedness of their communion, there was no hiding Sol Gursky's despair.

I'm sorry Sol, the starbird once known as Lenya communicated.

You have nothing to sorry be for, Solomon Gursky said.

I'm sorry that I'm not her. I'm sorry I never was her.

I made you to be a lover, Sol withspoke. *But you became something older, something richer, something we have lost.*

A daughter, Lenya said.

Unmeasurable time passed in the blue shift at the end of the universe. Then Lenya asked, *Where will you go?*

Finding her is the only unfinished business I have left, Sol said.

Yes, the starbird communed. *But we will not meet again.*

No, not in this universe.

Nor any other. And that is death, eternal separation.

My unending regret, Sol Gursky withspoke as Lenya opened her heart and the clouds of tectors separated. *Goodbye, daughter.*

The Statue of Liberty disengaged from the body of the starbird. Lenya's quantum processors created a pool of gravitational calm in the maelstrom. Sol Gursky manipulated space and time and disappeared.

He re-entered the continuum as close as he dared to a frond. A pulse of his mind brought him within reach of its dendrites. As they drew him in, another throb of thought dissolved the Statue of Liberty joke into the plasma flux. Solomon Gursky howled up the dendrite, through the frond, into the soul matrix of Ua. There he carved a niche in the eleventh and highest heaven, and from deep under time, watched the universe end.

As he had expected, it ended in fire and light and glory. He saw space and time curve inward beyond the limit of the Planck dimensions; he felt the energy gradients climb toward infinity as the universe approached the zero point from which it had spontaneously emerged. He felt the universal processors sown through eleven dimensions seize that energy before it faded, and put it to work. It was a surge, a spurt of power and passion, like the memory of orgasm buried deep in the chain of memory that was the days of Solomon Gursky. Light to power, power to memory, memory to flesh. Ua's stored memories, the history of every particle in the former universe, were woven into being. Smart superstrings rolled balls of wrapped eleven-space like sacred scarabs wheeling dung. Space, time, mass, energy unraveled; as the universe died in a quantum fluctuation, it was reborn in primal light.

To Solomon Gursky, waiting in low-time where aeons were breaths, it seemed like creation by *fiat*. A brief, bright light, and galaxies, clusters, stars, turned whole-formed and living within his contemplation. Already personas were swarming out of Ua's honeycomb cells into time and incarnation, but what had been reborn was not a universe, but universes. The re-resurrected were not condemned to blindly recapitulate their former lives. Each choice and action that diverged from the original pattern splintered off a separate universe. Sol and Lenya had spoken truly when they had said they would never meet again. Sol's point of entry into the new polyverse was a thousand years before Lenya's; the universe he intended to create would never intersect with hers.

The elder races had already fanned the polyverse into a *mille feuille* of alternatives: Sol carefully tracked his own timeline through the blur of possibilities as the first humans dropped back into their planet's past. Stars moving into remembered constellations warned Sol that his emergence was only a few hundreds of thousands of years off. He moved down through dimensional matrices, at each level drawing closer to the time flow of his particular universe.

Solomon Gursky hung over the spinning planet. Civilizations rose and decayed, empires conquered and crumbled. New technologies, new continents, new nations were discovered. All the time, alternative Earths fluttered away like torn-off calendar pages on the wind as the dead created new universes to colonize. Close now. Mere moments. Sol dropped into meat time, and Ua expelled him like a drop of milk from a swollen breast.

Solomon Gursky fell. Illusions and anticipations accompanied his return to flesh. Imaginings of light; a contrail angel scoring the nightward half of the planet on its flight across a dark ocean to a shore, to a mountain, to a valley, to a glow of campfire among night-blooming cacti. Longing. Desire. Fear. Gain, and loss. God's trade: to attain the heart's desire, you must give up everything you are. Even the memory.

In the quilted bag by the fire in the sheltered valley under the perfume of the cactus flowers, the man called Solomon Gursky woke with a sudden chill start. It was night. It was dark. Desert stars had half-completed their compass above him. The stone-circled fire had burned down to clinking red glow: the night perfume witched him. Moths padded softly through the air, seeking nectar.

Sol Gursky drank five senses full of his world.

I am alive, he thought. I am here. Again.

Ur-light burned in his hind-brain; memories of Ua, a power like omnipotence. Memories of a life that out-lived its native universe. Worlds, suns, shapes. Flashes, moments. Too heavy, too rich for this small knot of brain to hold. Too bright: no one can live with the memory of having been a god. It would fade—it was fading already. All he need hold—all he must hold—was what he needed to prevent this universe from following its predestined course.

The realization that eyes were watching him was a shock. Elena sat on the edge of the fire shadow, knees folded to chin, arms folded over shins, looking at him. Sol had the feeling that she had been looking at him without him knowing for a long time, and the surprise, the uneasiness of knowing you are under the eyes of another, tempered both the still-new lust he felt for her, and his fading memories of aeons-old love.

Déjà vu. But this moment had never happened before. The divergence was beginning.

"Can't sleep?" she asked.

"I had the strangest dream."

"Tell me." The thing between them was at the stage where they searched each other's dreams for allusions to their love.

"I dreamed that the world ended," Sol Gursky said. "It ended in light, and the light was like the light in a movie projector, that carried the image of the world and everything in it, and so the world was created again, as it had been before."

As he spoke, the words became true. It was a dream now. This life, this body, these memories, were the solid and faithful.

"Like a Tipler machine," Elena said. "The idea that the energy released by the Big Crunch could power some kind of holographic re-creation of the entire universe. I suppose with an advanced enough nanotechnology, you could rebuild the universe, an exact copy, atom for atom."

Chill dread struck in Sol's belly. She could not know, surely. She must not know.

"What would be the point of doing it exactly the same all over again?"

"Yeah." Elena rested her cheek on her knee. "But the question is, is *this* our first time in the world, or have we been here many times before, each a little bit different? Is this the first universe, or do we only *think* that it is?"

Sol Gursky looked into the embers, then to the stars.

"The Nez Perce Nation believes that the world ended on the third day and that what we are living in are the dreams of the second night." Memories, fading like summer meteors high overhead, told Sol that he had said this once before, in their future, after his first death. He said it now in the hope that that future would not come to pass. Everything that was different, every tiny detail, pushed this universe away from the one in which he must lose her.

A vee of tiger-striped tectoplastic tumbled end over end forever toward Virgo.

He blinked the ghost away. It faded like all the others. They were going more quickly than he had thought. He would have to make sure of it now, before that memory too dissolved. He struggled out of the terrain bag, went over to the bike lying exhausted on the ground. By the light of a detached bicycle lamp, he checked the gear train.

"What are you doing?" Elena asked from the fireside. The thing between them was still new, but Sol remembered that tone in her voice, that soft inquiry, from another lifetime.

"Looking at the gears. Something didn't feel right about them today. They didn't feel solid."

"You didn't mention it earlier."

No, Sol thought. I didn't know about it. Not then. The gear teeth grinned flashlight back at him.

"We've been giving them a pretty hard riding. I read in one of the biking mags that you can get metal fatigue. Gear train shears right through, just like that."

"On brand-new, two thousand dollar bikes?"

"On brand-new two thousand dollar bikes."

"So what do you think you can *do* about it at one o'clock in the morning in the middle of the Sonora Desert?"

Again, that come-hither tone. Just a moment more, Elena. One last thing, and then it will be safe.

"It just didn't sit right. I don't want to take it up over any more mountains until I've had it checked out. You get a gear-shear up there . . ."

"So, what are you saying, irritating man?"

"I'm not happy about going over Blood of Christ Mountain tomorrow."

"Yeah. Sure. Fine."

"Maybe we should go out west, head for the coast. It's whale season, I always wanted to see whales. And there's real good seafood. There's this cantina where they have fifty ways of serving iguana."

"Whales. Iguanas. Fine. Whatever you want. Now, since you're so wide-awake, you can just get your ass right *over* here, Sol Gursky!"

She was standing up, and Sol saw and felt what she had been concealing by the way she had sat. She wearing only a cut-off MTB shirt. Safe, he thought, as he seized her and took her down laughing and yelling onto the camping mat. Even as he thought it, he forgot it, and all those Elenas who would not now be: conspirator, crop-haired freedom fighter, four-armed space-angel. Gone.

The stars moved in their ordained arcs. The moths and cactus forest bats drifted through the soft dark air, and the eyes of the things that hunted them glittered in the firelight.

Sol and Elena were still sore and laughing when the cactus flowers closed with dawn. They ate their breakfast and packed their small camp, and were in the saddle and on the trail before the sun was full over the shoulder of Blood of Christ Mountain. They took the western trail, away from the hills, and the town called Redención hidden among them with its freight of resurrected grief. They rode the long trail that led down to the ocean, and it was bright, clear endless Monday morning.